1986

Dirt Rich

Clark Howard

===

DIRT RICH

ST. MARTIN'S PRESS

NEW YORK

Design by Laura Hough

Library of Congress Cataloging-in-Publication Data

Howard, Clark.
   Dirt rich.

   I. Title.
PS3558.O877D5   1986   813'.54   85-25150
ISBN 0-312-21225-9

First Edition

10 9 8 7 6 5 4 3 2 1

For Judith,
who was worth waiting for

PART
1

Texas Poor

1

The sounds of the people on the street outside the hotel window woke Georgia Powell from her sound, early morning sleep. She glanced at the young sailor next to her, smiled sympathetically at the memory of his awkward lovemaking, and eased out of bed without disturbing him. Crossing the room, she pulled back a cracked yellow shade an inch and looked at Rivington Street, two stories below, through a window almost opaque with city dirt. A herd of people was heading toward the nearby docks to welcome home "Black Jack" Pershing and his 82nd Infantry Division from crushing the Hun at Saint-Mihiel and the Argonne.

I've got to hurry, Georgia thought. I want Sam to see me the instant he steps off the boat!

As quietly as possible she began collecting her scattered clothes, while trying to remember if the bathroom was to the right or left down the hall. This hotel she and the young sailor had come to was little more than a flophouse, nothing like her room uptown at the new Commodore; but it had been handy and they had been eager. She just hoped to God she hadn't caught anything from the bed linen.

Georgia had come down to this part of Manhattan the previous day to select a good vantage point from which to watch Sam's ship arrive. She thought she would pick out a place a day in advance to make things easier for her in the expected crowd. She found several places along the wharf that looked suitable, but never did get around to deciding on one of them, because she and the sailor had gotten acquainted. Now, she was just going to have to fight the crowd like everyone else.

When she had all her belongings, Georgia cracked the door and peered up and down the hall. It was deserted, and she could see the open bathroom door to the right. Stark naked, clutching her belongings to her bosom, she stepped into the hallway, eased the door shut behind her, and raced for the bathroom. Another door opened as she scooted along. Georgia felt a jolt of panic, ran faster, and managed to get to safety without being seen.

Leaning back against the locked bathroom door, she blew a lock of hair out of her eyes and thought: This is it, kid. Today you *change* your ways.

An hour later, when she got to the docks, Georgia knew at once that she would never spot Sam in this crowd. At least a million people lined the wharves and piers and the streets that led to them, waiting for the troopship to arrive. Everyone was saying it was an even bigger crowd than the one that had overflowed Times Square on the day the armistice was signed.

Georgia was pressed between a fat woman holding a baby and several tough-looking boys wearing slouch caps. When she stood on tiptoe she could see the harbor and the Statute of Liberty, and just beyond that a huge ship being towed, incongruously, by a very small tugboat. The name of the ship was the HMS *Majestic.* It had once been a grand German passenger liner, the *Bismarck,* but belonged to the British now, the spoils of war. They had loaned it to the United States to bring Pershing and his troops home.

The night before, in the seedy hotel room, when she had told the young sailor she was from Kansas City, he had asked her what she was doing in New York. She told him she was there to meet the *Majestic.*

"Got a boyfriend on board?" he had inquired.

"Fiancé," Georgia had replied. It was a lie. Sam had not yet proposed marriage; she was merely assuming—*praying,* more like— that he would.

"Pretty soft, coming home on a liner like that," the sailor had said. "Me, I was on a reg'lar ship, the *Hopewell.* Heavy cruiser. Went down off Gibraltar last March. I was in the water for six hours."

Georgia had given him a dubious look. "You don't look old enough to have been through anything like that," she said skeptically.

The sailor shrugged. "How old do you have to be? I've been in the navy since I was sixteen. I'm twenty-one now."

I'll bet, Georgia thought. Eighteen maybe, nineteen at the most. He still had peach fuzz just under the front of his chin, and his pubic hair was soft as down.

But he was old enough for what Georgia needed.

Wanting to get away from the young toughs next to her, Georgia made her way to the edge of the crowd. The New York City Firemen's Band, set up in a roped-off section dockside, struck up "After You've Gone" march-style, but to Georgia, who had only heard it played in Dixieland tempo, it sounded queer. She began to tap her foot nevertheless.

"Hey, why'd you duck out?" a voice asked. "I been looking for you for an hour."

Georgia looked around. It was the sailor. She smiled. "You were sleeping so soundly, I didn't want to wake you. And you know I'm meeting someone." She winked at him. "Anyway, I figured you got enough last night."

"I couldn't ever get enough of you," he said, slipping a possessive arm around her waist. "I was in love with you before I fell asleep last night. Listen, how serious is it between you and the doughboy on the ship?"

"I told you," Georgia said, "we're engaged."

Behind them, more people were pressing onto the wharves from the direction of Canal Street. If many more arrived, Georgia was afraid the ones in front would be pushed right into the Hudson. A mounted policeman succeeded in clearing a path for some dignitary's car, causing the crowd to press even closer together. The sailor eased up against her, grinning.

"Enjoying yourself?" Georgia asked. He hunched up both shoulders innocently: it wasn't his fault. As soon as the car passed, the crowd spread into the vehicle lane again. The sailor stayed where he was until Georgia put a stiff forefinger against his chest and pushed him back. He pushed out his lip in a pout. A vendor with an ice cooler slung around his neck made his way along the fringe of the crowd, loudly hawking his wares.

"Why don't you get us some Eskimo Pies?" Georgia said. Maybe it would cool him off.

"Okay."

Georgia watched as he snaked his way out to the vendor. His buttocks rolled smoothly in the tight navy bell-bottoms. She made herself stop looking. You're supposed to be changing your ways, she reminded herself.

When the sailor returned with the Eskimo Pies, the *Majestic* was passing Ellis Island and they could see hundreds of brown-uniformed men crowding every inch of the liner's deck, perched upon different parts of her superstructure, all waving hands, caps, handkerchiefs, their voices contributing to a rolling roar that grew steadily louder. The Firemen's Band broke into a lively rendition of "When Johnny Comes Marching Home Again," and the two crowds, on the shore and on the ship, supplied the *Hurrahs!* that punctuated the lyrics.

Georgia finished her Eskimo Pie and wiped her fingers on a dainty handkerchief. She and the sailor were very close again, and he was looking into her eyes with a hunger that was almost pitiful.

"It'll take two hours for that ship to dock," he said. "The room's just ten minutes away. Come on. Please."

Georgia reached down and felt him. He was about to burst out of his bell-bottoms. They *did* have time—

Stop it, she scolded herself. You are changing your ways!

"All right, we'll go back to the room," she said, smiling sweetly. "But first run and get me another Eskimo Pie to eat on the way."

"You bet!" he replied eagerly. At that moment, he would have done *anything* for her. He quickly made his way toward the vendor again.

When he returned, Georgia was gone.

It took Georgia two hours to get from the Battery back uptown to the Commodore Hotel, walking all the way. Traffic was at a standstill as Manhattan prepared for its biggest parade ever. Sometimes it was impossible even to walk, especially along the three avenues—Park, Madison, and Fifth—where the parade would to be held. The crowds there, on both sides of each street, had evolved from a press into a crush; people were simply not moving. Georgia would have taken the subway but she was afraid of getting lost. As long as she could see street signs, she was all right. When she finally reached the Commodore, she couldn't enter through the lobby, mobbed with people waiting for the parade. She had to go in through the delivery door.

In her room on the sixth floor, Georgia kicked off her shoes, took off her garters and stockings, and sat with her feet in a tub of cold water while she reread Sam's letter for at least the twentieth time.

I don't know exactly when I'll be coming home; you'll just have to watch the newspapers. Black Jack has promised no later than June, and he's never been known to break a promise to his men. Besides, the President wants Sergeant York back to give him the Medal of Honor, and York already told the press he doesn't want to come home before the rest of the men even if he is a hero.

If we miss each other at the dock—and it's sure to be crowded—let's meet at the new hotel that just opened in New York a few months ago—the Commodore, I think it's called. Somebody said it has two thousand rooms, but I doubt that. We'll meet in the lobby; whoever gets there first is to page the other every fifteen minutes.

I hope you don't have too much trouble with your mother or brother about making the trip—

Georgia took a Pall Mall from a pack on the bathroom shelf and lighted it. She had not had any trouble at all with her mother or her brother about the trip, because she had not told them where she was going. They thought she was in Lorain, Ohio, visiting Tussy Fowler, whose family had moved there from Kansas City three years earlier. Georgia and Tussy had been best friends for years and had already exchanged one visit each since the Fowlers moved. Georgia had arranged the deception as soon as she knew for certain when Sam Sheridan was coming home, and Tussy, who thrived on deceit, had been only too happy to cooperate. As part of the deception, Tussy had sent Georgia an envelope containing two picture postcards from Lorain, and Georgia had addressed and postdated them, written appropriate messages on each, and returned them in an envelope to Tussy. The day after tomorrow, Tussy would mail them from Lorain to Georgia's mother and brother. Receipt of the cards would be adequate assurance that Georgia was all right and enjoying herself, properly chaperoned by the Fowlers. Thrifty as her mother and brother were, Georgia knew they would never incur the expense of a long-distance telephone call just to check on her. So she was footloose in New York for a whole week. All she needed to complete the adventure was Sam.

After drying her feet, Georgia went into the bedroom and took off her dress and slip. From around her neck she removed a string of eighty pearls and carefully wrapped them in a handkerchief. Everyone thought they were imitation pearls, but they were real. A well-to-do Kansas City businessman, married and older than her father, had given them to her at the end of a three-month affair. He was a regular customer at the Woolworth where she worked, and frequently stopped in to purchase candy or small gifts for his office staff. Georgia had waited on him many times, and he had eventually asked her out. Two other girls in the store occasionally wore similar strands of pearls. The three of them clearly wondered about each other, but had never talked about it. Georgia had taken her own pearls to a jeweler across town and paid two dollars to have them appraised. She was surprised and pleased to find that they were worth five hundred dollars, an enormous sum to a shopgirl who earned only fifteen dollars a week.

Pulling open the drapes in the hotel room, Georgia raised the window and looked down at Park Avenue to see if the parade had started yet. It had not. In the window of an office building directly across the way, she saw three men in business suits looking at her, one of them through field glasses. She stood there in her brassiere and step-ins as the glasses were passed from man to man. When each of them had taken his turn, she moved away from the open window, not bothering to draw the drapes or pull the shade.

Georgia picked up the telephone, waited for the hotel operator, and then said, "Will you page Lieutenant Sam Sheridan, please?"

The operator took her name and room number and promised to send a page boy around at once. Ten minutes later she called Georgia back and said there had been no response to the page.

A while later, Georgia heard the faint sound of a marching band. She leaned as far out the window as she could and saw, down the avenue, the approach of the victory parade. A blizzard of confetti was already filling the air. The three men across the way were still sharing the field glasses. Georgia got a pillow off the bed and made herself a comfortable seat on the windowsill. Lighting a fresh Pall Mall, she settled back to watch.

An honor guard led the parade: three soldiers carrying flags of the United States, the City of New York, and the 82nd Infantry Division. Next, also on foot, came drum and fife players rendering "Yankee Doodle Dandy," followed by a band with a full-instrument rendition of the same tune. Then came several mounted policemen in front of a procession of open limousines. In the first one, riding with the governor of New York and the secretary of state, was General of the Armies John Joseph Pershing, known affectionately to civilian and soldier alike as "Black Jack." At fifty-nine he stood tall, straight, and solemn-faced as he waved to the cheering throng. America had never seen Black Jack smile; not in the newspapers, not in those funny moving pictures they called "newsreels," and not in person. With his piercing dark eyes, thick black mustache, and lantern jaw, he looked like an old gunfighter with a town to clean up. Only when his keen eyes lighted on a particularly pretty woman in the crowd did even a hint of amusement soften his clamped lips. Those young women who caught his passing glance knew instantly that Black Jack was not all steel and leather. But to everyone else he was the ultimate warrior.

Behind Pershing's car, separated by a marching platoon of helmeted, rifle-bearing soldiers, came a second open limo carrying the mayor of New York City and Sergeant Alvin C. York, the Tennessee sharpshooter who had become the Great War's most decorated hero. Tall and whip-thin, wearing the French Croix de Guerre around his neck, York smiled in genuine delight at the people who cheered him. He had never seen so many human beings in all his thirty-one years. He came from a settlement of only a few hundred, and the battlefields of France had seemed crowded to him; but this—this was unbelievable. He reckoned everybody in the country must have come to New York for the victory parade, because God knows, this many people couldn't all *live* there. One thing York was determined to do before he headed for the White House for his Medal of Honor was ride the train everybody told him ran *under* the ground. A *sub-way,* they called it. Getting the Medal of Honor from the President was going to be a great thrill, the Tennessean knew, but riding that *sub-way,* why, that would be something to tell his grandchildren about!

From her window above the street, Georgia could not help

feeling goosebumps as America's two most eminent heroes passed by. She wished she had thought to tear up some paper so she could have something to throw out the window; but it was too late now, so she just clapped her hands and yelled "Yeaaaaa!" along with everyone else. After the lead cars passed, several follow-up cars came along carrying some of Pershing's wounded officers. There were four or five to each car, and Georgia could see that they were wearing head bandages, casts, arm slings, and other hospital dressings. A Red Cross nurse in starched white rode in each car, pinned in the midst of her male patients, being pressed against from all sides. Lucky you, Georgia thought. She briefly remembered the young sailor of several hours earlier, and how hot and firm he had felt in her hands. Glancing across at the office building, she saw that the men were now waving and cheering down at the parade; all except one, who still watched her through the field glasses. Teasingly trying to decide whether to spread her legs a bit, she happened to notice, in the parade below, a soldier with one arm in a sling get out of one of the slow-moving cars and move into the crowd in the front of the hotel. The people parted for him, smiling, touching his back, one woman stretching to kiss his cheek, as they let him through to the hotel entrance. He disappeared from Georgia's view under the sidewalk canopy. Frowning, Georgia wondered if it could possibly be Sam. My God, had he been wounded?

Hurrying to the phone, Georgia called downstairs and asked to have Lieutenant Sam Sheridan paged again. While she waited, she lit another cigarette and paced the room. She was as nervous as a virgin, and she did not know why. Was it because Sam was the man she wanted to marry? Sam, to whom she had given her virginity at the age of seventeen, and never seen since? Or was she worried that he would be able to tell how many others there had been since? Was there a noticeable difference, she wondered, between the experienced woman and the eager virgin?

Georgia sat at the room's vanity and studied herself in the mirror. She did not, she decided, look *used*. Or *hard*. Even with the cigarette between her lips. But Sam still might be able to detect a— a *something* about her. After all, he had been over there with those *parlez-vous* French whores for two years; he probably knew everything there was to know about the things a man and woman could do together. Idly, she interrupted her serious thoughts to wonder if

Sam had ever done it with his tongue. A district manager for Essaness Theaters, where her brother worked in Kansas City, had told her all about tongue love one night in his hotel room, and had actually acted like he was going to do it to her; but at the last instant he had merely kissed the inside of her thigh. She thought perhaps it was because she had a fairly strong odor down there; maybe *too* strong. She washed, God knows, she washed; but as soon as she got the least bit excited, there it came. She *liked* it herself; but someone else, well . . .

Shaking her head, she dismissed those thoughts and, staring into her eyes, asked herself: Why do you want Sam Sheridan to marry you?

Put that way, the answer was simple: because she wanted to get married and nobody else had asked her. Or was likely to. Kansas City was still a small town in many ways. Word had a way of getting around about a girl. Georgia realized that after two years of having her fun, she wasn't exactly a catch anymore. It was either get Sam Sheridan or leave Kansas City.

The telephone rang and she snatched it up. "Hello."

"Georgia? Georgia, is that you?" asked a male voice that she did not even remember.

"Sam? Yes, it's me. Are you—"

"I'm downstairs in the lobby." His voice lowered. "I didn't expect you to have a room."

"Oh? Well, maybe you didn't miss me as much as I missed you."

"I can prove you're wrong about that quickly enough," he replied eagerly. Then he added tentatively, "Listen, Georgia, I've got one arm in a sling—"

"Were you wounded?"

"Sort of. But not really. I have a broken collarbone. A shell concussion threw me up against the side of a truck. So maybe I *can't* prove how much I missed you."

"Can you sit up straight in a chair?"

"Yes."

"Then I'll do enough proving for both of us." Georgia told him the room number. "Hurry up here, soldier."

Hanging up, Georgia swung around on the vanity seat, drew on her stockings, and rolled them at the thigh with garters. In the bathroom, she dusted a little powder into her step-ins. She got halfway into her dress before she decided the hell with it. Stepping back out of it, she hung it up, worked her feet into her shoes, and lighted a fresh cigarette from the butt of the old one. She glanced out the window one last time, watched the parade still going by, glanced over at the men with the field glasses again, then heard Sam's knock.

Georgia started to pull the shade down, but changed her mind. What difference did it make if they watched?

She hurried to open the door for the man to whom she had given her virginity, from whom she now hoped to collect payment in marriage.

2

At three o'clock in the morning, it finally occurred to Sam Sheridan to ask, "Where did you learn that? That chair business?"

"From Tussy Fowler," Georgia lied. "She had a book from Sweden that had all these pictures of people doing it all different ways. When you told me about your collarbone, I remembered that particular way."

"I'm glad you did," Sam said.

You wouldn't be, Georgia thought, if you knew where I *really* learned it. From a policeman who had foot patrol around the movie house her brother managed, and where she sometimes filled in as ticket seller. She had gone to his room with him one night instead of going right home.

"Did you enjoy the Victory Ball?" Sam asked.

"God, did I ever!" she answered. She sat up naked next to him and played with the hair that fell over his forehead. "If anyone had ever told me that I'd meet General Black Jack Pershing someday, why, I'd never have believed it!"

"He's a great man," Sam said in a solemn voice.

Earlier, after the first few hours of their reunion—a long session of chair sex, a rest, a hot bath together—they had dressed, and Sam had taken her to an officer's Victory Ball at the Vanderbilt Hotel. Walking down Park Avenue to the hotel at 34th, they actually had to wade through a river of paper. Both of them had to take off their shoes and empty out the confetti when they arrived at the Vanderbilt.

Pershing, who also had to put in appearances at the Biltmore, McAlpin, and Ritz-Carlton, arrived at the Vanderbilt at ten-thirty, along with Alvin York and members of the official welcoming committee. They formed a reception line, shook hands with everyone present, lifted one glass of champagne in a toast—orange juice for Sergeant York, a teetotaler—then quickly moved on. But while they were there, Georgia had stood before the godlike, unsmiling General of the Armies, heard the rattle of the saber he was never without, felt his great hand engulf her own, and thought she saw in his dark, commanding eyes a sparkle of interest, a hint of simpatico, something that said, *In another time and place, under different circumstances, I'd like to fuck you.*

Georgia had immediately given herself a silent scolding. You have *got* to stop thinking about that all the time; you are going to drive yourself *insane.* For God's sake, you just *had* some!

And would have yet more before the night was through, she purred a promise to herself.

With Sam's one good arm around her, they danced fast to "Swanee" and "Down on the Farm," and slow to "Let the Rest of the World Go By" and "Till We Meet Again." They drank pink champagne, played with balloons and paper streamers, laughed with Sam's fellow officers and their girl friends, joined group sing-alongs of "K-K-K-Katy" and "After You've Gone," and stopped whatever they were doing to kiss whenever they felt like it, just as everyone else was doing. Once, when the lights were low and the music soft, Sam whispered in her ear, "I'm so glad to be home, Georgia. I'm so glad not to have to be scared anymore." Georgia squeezed his hand and kissed his neck, and for the first time since he came back felt a surge of love for him.

They returned to her room at the Commodore and Georgia stripped him, sat him down on the chair again, and mounted him like an animal in season. She rode him in a variety of ways, working around his taped shoulder and slung arm, arching toward him so that he could fondle her breasts with his good hand. She ministered to

---

13

him for an hour and would have continued for another, but he looked like he was swollen to the point of bursting, so she worked him to his release. Afterward, Sam lay back on the bed, exhausted; Georgia, lying beside him, smoking a cigarette, not fully satisfied, felt oddly unsettled. So it caught her a little off-guard when Sam asked her about the chair trick.

"What else did you learn from Tussy Fowler's book?" he wanted to know.

"You'd be surprised," she half teased. Georgia could not tell whether he believed her lie or not. The room was partly dark, the only light coming through the open bathroom door; so she could not see his face that clearly, nor could he see hers. Perhaps, like her, he could not distinguish lies in the dark. She could always tell when a man was lying to her if she could see his face. She had looked into the face of the policeman who had taught her the chair trick, and known he was lying when he said he loved her. Looked into the face of the salesman who had spent a week in Kansas City introducing a new bottled drink called Orange Crush, having her every night of that week in his hotel room, and known he was lying when he promised to come back for her after he had taken the new product to Denver and Oklahoma City. Looked into the face of her American history teacher at Independence High School, who had her on the senior class field trip to St. Louis, and known he was lying when he said he was thinking of divorcing his wife (who was also a teacher at Independence High, English 3 and 4, and who had gone to bed with the captain of the football team on that same trip). Lies became clear to Georgia in people's faces; but in the dark she believed most anything. She only hoped Sam did too.

"What are you going to do now that the war's over?" Georgia asked, trying to keep her tone casual.

"I don't know," Sam replied quietly. "I've been trying not to think about it." She heard him sigh softly. "I don't really have much of anything to go back to, you know."

"What do you mean?" Even as she asked the question, it occurred to Georgia that she really knew very little about this man. She knew he was tall, nice looking, five years older than she (which made him twenty-four), a good dancer, a fair lover, and before the war he had been a clerk at the J. C. Penney Golden Rule store in downtown Kansas City. She knew his mother had died of liver failure four years earlier, his father had long been dead, and he had no brothers or sisters. Probably had no money either.

But none of that mattered to Georgia, because there was also one other thing that Sam Sheridan did not have: he had no knowledge of her somewhat shabby reputation back home.

"What do you mean, Sam?" she asked again.

"Well, just that I don't have any family; I don't own anything; I have a little money saved, but not much; my prospects for the future are limited. I mean, I'll never be a doctor or a lawyer, a professional man. I guess what I'm saying is that I really don't have much to offer a girl."

Georgia felt a tingle of anticipation. "That's not so, Sam. You're a fine, decent man. A person doesn't have to have a lot of family background and all that in order to be somebody. I'm sure you'll do very well in life. Most girls would feel lucky to have someone like you care for them."

"Do you feel lucky?" he asked.

"Are you saying you care for me, Sam?"

"I've cared for you since the night we met. I just didn't think I'd be lucky enough to find you still around when I got back. When you wrote me in France, I thought you were just being nice. A home-front girl keeping up the morale of a doughboy."

"Why, Sam Sheridan, how could you think that?" Georgia asked with a hint of resentment. "After what we did the night we met, I mean, honestly, did you think I just slipped out of my bloomers for every boy that came along?"

"No, I never thought that—"

"You know you were the only one, Sam. You must have been able to tell. It hurt me, Sam. I bled. Couldn't you tell, for God's sake?"

Sam drew her close and held her in his arms. "Of course, I could, dearest. I could tell. I'm sorry I hurt you. But I really wasn't sure about much of anything myself that night. It was the first time for me too."

"What?" She drew back and sat bolt upright. "You mean you were a virgin too!"

"Afraid so."

Jesus! Georgia thought. She had *picked* him because she thought he was experienced. For God's sake, he had been twenty-two, in uniform, an officer! It had been at a farewell dance at the Armory in May 1917. Kansas City was getting ready to send its contingent of state militia to New Jersey as part of the American Expeditionary Force that Black Jack Pershing was leading to Europe the following month. Georgia and her friend Tussy, visiting from Ohio, had told Georgia's mother they were going downtown to the Emerald to see the new D. W. Griffith film *Hearts of the World,* starring the Gish sisters. Georgia's brother Leon, who managed the Essaness Theater, got trade-off passes for them. The girls used the passes, then slipped out the fire exit and went to the Armory. Georgia, who had positively made up her mind to lose her virginity that summer, ended up going with Sam to the deserted troop train sitting on a railway siding. Officers were quartered in sleeping cars with berths, which amazed Georgia because she had never seen one before. She was very excited. She had hoped to be deflowered that night, but never dreamed of it happening in such a romantic setting. They had gotten stark naked in Sam's little cubbyhole, an upper, and, as Georgia later told Tussy, "gone to town." His "thing," she added, was an absolutely marvelous object. Tussy, who had come through the evening hymen intact, fairly oozed envy, and made Georgia promise to help her lose *hers* as soon as possible.

Now, sitting up in bed beside Sam, Georgia was completely incredulous. "I can't believe you were inexperienced that night, Sam! You were so good! You seemed to know exactly what to do."

"I read books too," he said. Georgia frowned, wondering if his remark had a double meaning. As Sam continued talking, she detected no recrimination in his tone. "Maybe we were meant for each other," he said seriously.

"Maybe we were."

Sam pulled her to him again. "What should we do about it?"

"What do you want to do about it?"

"We could get married. Spend the rest of our lives together."

There. He had said it at last. For the second time, Georgia felt love for him. She kissed him softly on the lips and said, "That sounds like a wonderful idea."

Relief coursed through her: relief from the troubling anxiety that Sam would turn out like all the rest, that he would use her and then go on his way.

16

But that had not happened. Not this time. Not with this man. Sam had stayed. Sam wanted her—*to keep*.

Georgia closed her eyes and made herself a silent, solemn promise: she was going to be the best goddamned wife to Sam Sheridan that any man ever had.

3

Sam was surprised to find Leon, Georgia's brother, at the table when he came in for breakfast. Leon worked from noon until midnight at the movie house, and was never up before Sam left for work. Sam rarely saw him except on Sundays.

"You're out of bed early," Sam said, taking his place at the table. Leon already had the morning newspaper that Sam usually read.

"I got up to talk to you about the household expenses," Leon said. "Some kind of adjustment's got to be made."

Sam's expression darkened. Money again. Every month or so, Leon had to remind Sam that he contributed more to the running of the household than Sam did. Sam and Georgia had been living with her brother and mother since their marriage, and not a day passed that Sam did not regret moving in.

Sam did not respond to Leon's overture, but Leon proceeded to talk about household expenses anyway. "Now that Georgia's going to have a baby and won't be bringing home any wages, it would be nice if you could put in a few dollars more."

"Talk to Georgia about it," Sam said. "She handles our money. I don't even open my pay envelope; I just hand it over to her."

"Well and good, but you're the husband. You have to make the decisions; you can't leave that to a woman."

"We have to start saving to pay the doctor," Sam said thoughtfully, almost to himself.

"Having a baby so soon wasn't very smart," Leon pointed out, putting the paper down as his mother came in from the kitchen and set his breakfast in front of him. Georgia, just beginning to show her pregnancy, came in behind her.

"Leon's having German toast this morning," Mrs. Powell said to Sam. "The skillet's still hot if you want some."

"Mother, it's not German toast anymore," Georgia said. "Since the war it's called French toast."

"It'll always be German toast to me, war or no war." Alva Powell was fifty, a big-boned woman who, like Pershing and his saber, was never without her apron. A widow for ten years, she had a small pension as a result of her husband, a stockyards worker, being killed when a defective chain broke and a hooked cow carcass fell on him. She was thankful for two things in life: that she no longer had to subjugate her body and bed to a male presence; and that her daughter, through Sam Sheridan, had saved herself from becoming a tramp. Alva shuddered when she recalled some of the gossip that had reached her about Georgia. "Do you want the toast or don't you?" she asked Sam.

"Sure, if there's enough bread," Sam said. Anything was better than the corn flakes he had day in and day out, every morning except Sunday.

"Speaking of bread," Leon said to his mother, "what does it cost now?"

"Seven cents a loaf," Alva said.

"And milk?"

"Fifteen cents a quart."

"Eggs?"

"Six cents apiece or sixty-five cents a dozen."

Sam said in a clipped tone, "I get your point, Leon."

Leon nodded curtly and asked no more prices. At twenty-six he was six years older than his sister and a year older than Sam. A tall, cadaverous man, he had been deferred from the draft because of fallen arches. He had worked for the Essaness Theaters chain for nine years: first as an usher, then as ticket taker, assistant manager, and eventually manager of his own house. Earning twice the money Sam did, he was decidedly impressed with himself.

Leon finished his breakfast and folded the newspaper. "You and Sis talk about it," he said to Sam. "We'll all sit down together Sunday

---

18

morning and go over the household expenses. Meanwhile, keep in mind that *everything* is going up: electricity, city water, this new property tax—"

"Property tax is your responsibility," Sam said quickly. "The house goes to you someday, not us."

Leon smiled a tight smile. "We'll talk about it on Sunday." Tucking the paper under his arm, he left the room.

The son of a bitch, Sam thought. He couldn't even leave me the paper.

Sam Sheridan had become increasingly disenchanted with things since his first week back in Kansas City. He was not sure just what he expected out of life, but he knew this was not it. Something, some important element, was missing.

Sam's return from the war had begun beautifully: the hero's welcome in New York, the parade, the victory balls, a farewell luncheon Pershing had given for his officers the next day; and, of course, the best thing of all: Georgia being there to meet him. When she opened the door to that hotel room and he saw her standing there in brassiere, step-ins, and gartered stockings, it was like a wet dream come true. The sex sessions that followed—right then, later that night after the ball, again the next morning, again that afternoon following Pershing's luncheon—had been absolutely glorious. Never mind that his cock got so sore and raw that he could barely handle it to go to the bathroom. Georgia had offered several times to "kiss it and make it well," but Sam had not reacted to the offer and Georgia had not pursued it. He *thought* he knew what she was suggesting, but he was not absolutely sure; so he could not bring himself to encourage her. The women in France had done it that way all the time; but with the girl he wanted to marry, it somehow seemed different.

Sam and Georgia had spent three days in New York, "doing the town," as she would later tell her friend Tussy. They saw the newest pictures, *Broken Blossoms* with Lillian Gish, the racy *Male and Female* with Gloria Swanson, and even went to a real *legitimate* Broadway play, *The Rise and Fall of Susan Lenox,* at the 44th Street Theater. They walked in Central Park, stayed up until all hours, made love at the most outrageous times (such as right after breakfast, which was brought right to their *room* on a funny little cart). They did, in fact, have their honeymoon before their wedding, and it was the most glorious time either of them had ever imagined.

When they finally realized how quickly they were spending Sam's mustering-out pay, they left New York and went to Lorain, Ohio, where, with Tussy and her current beau as witnesses, they were married at the Lorain city hall. Tussy's parents, while not wholly approving of the elopement and the absence of Georgia's mother, nevertheless gave them a very nice wedding supper after the ceremony. The newlyweds spent the night in a small hotel near the depot, and the next morning entrained for Kansas City.

Georgia's arrival at her mother's front door with a husband both surprised and relieved Alva Powell. Alva had been expecting her daughter to turn up pregnant for months. How in the world she avoided it, Alva could not imagine, unless she and her men were using those things being illegally advertised by that Sanger woman back East. A piece of rubber. My god.

After talking it over with her reluctant son, who was the main support of the household, Alva invited the young couple to move in. They took the room that had been Georgia's. A weekly sum for room and board had been agreed upon between Alva and Georgia. Leon had complained ever since that it was too low.

"It's all they can afford right now," Alva insisted. "You know what Georgia's job clerking at Woolworth's pays. And Sam's job at J. C. Penney's Golden Rule store isn't much better."

"Why does he have to work for J. C. Penney's?" Leon asked. "Why doesn't he find a better job?"

"Because he's entitled by law to get his job at Penney's back, that's why," Alva replied, putting up a rare defense of Sam. "Lucky for him, too. Jobs aren't that easy to come by with all the soldiers coming home."

"He doesn't make much more than I pay my *ushers,*" Leon said scornfully. He let the matter drop. Temporarily.

Sam and Georgia did not have much money for entertainment after they paid Alva her weekly stipend and put a little away. Leon gave them movie passes, but he did it so grudgingly that after the first few, Sam refused to accept any more. Mostly they sat with Alva in the evening and listened to the new radio Leon had given her the previous Christmas (Jesus, Sam thought, was there *no* way he could get away from Leon's charity?). Sometimes they went to the library and checked out books to read together in bed; they took turns softly reading aloud alternate chapters of *This Side of Paradise* and *The Moon and Sixpence.* Sometimes they would go sit in Bannister Park and listen to the free band concerts. They enjoyed each other and enjoyed their early months of newlywed life, and if each had their own reservations about how everything had turned out, well, that was just part of living, they guessed. Life was not meant to be perfect.

Sam's disenchantments, when they began to surface, were both major and minor. The latter, which nagged at him only at night just before he fell asleep, was that Georgia sometimes seemed remotely unsatisfied after their lovemaking, as if she wanted or needed something more from him. He went as long as he could with her, consciously concentrating on things nonsexual in order to increase his staying power. Some of the time it helped and Georgia seemed as sated as he was; but other times he was left with a nagging suspicion that he should have done more. Thankfully, Georgia's pregnancy seemed to alleviate the situation when her early nausea and fatigue sapped her natural energy. Sam, thinking he had at last satisfied her fully by getting her pregnant, believed the problem was solved, and forgot about it.

Sam's major disenchantment with his new life was a good deal more troubling. He was finding that he could not adjust to being a J. C. Penney salesclerk again.

"Everything I do seems so trivial," he confessed to Georgia one night when they went for a walk. "I sell a man a hat or a box of socks or a pair of suspenders. I stock the new merchandise when it comes in. I try to push the 'P.M.s,' the profit-money items: shoe polish with shoes, neckties with shirts, handkerchiefs with everything. I help keep the display cases neat, the floor swept, the paper-sack bin full. And nothing, none of it, seems important."

"What would you like to be doing?" Georgia asked sympathetically. She knew how disturbing fits of restlessness could be.

"I don't know," Sam said. "There's really no *particular* thing that I want to be doing. Right now I'd settle for any kind of responsibility that mattered. I'd like to be doing something that makes a *difference.* Does that sound silly?"

"Of course not, honey." Georgia squeezed his hand as they walked. "You'll be a daddy in six months. That's quite a responsibility. Do you think that'll help?"

"It might." Sam let go of her hand and put an arm around her shoulder. "I'm looking forward to the baby. I think it'll be fun having a little one around."

That remark made Georgia happy, as Sam had known it would; but he did not really feel that fatherhood was going to make that much difference to him. A baby would probably bring them closer (it was supposed to do that), and undoubtedly would change their personal lives a great deal. But as far as his employment was concerned, Sam could see nothing in the future but the same endless sequence of dull days. He would still be a J. C. Penney Golden Rule salesclerk. Which to him was insignificant almost to the point of being intolerable.

"I feel like a duck in a desert," he told Eddie Miller one day. Eddie was a clerk at the new Walgreen Drug Company down the street from Penney's. Like Sam, he had been in the Great War too: a junior officer in the 40th, the Rainbow Division. He and Sam had taken to eating their bag lunches on Walgreen's receiving dock.

"I know how you feel, buddy," Eddie commiserated. "This ain't much of a life after France."

"In the trenches," Sam recalled, "I used to think that if I got out alive, all I'd want to do was come back home and live a quiet, peaceful life. When I first got back, I remember how good it felt not to be scared anymore. Well, right now I'd *welcome* a little fear."

Eddie grunted. "Me, too. Help keep me awake in there among all the pills and perfumes."

"Do you know," Sam said, "that the two clerks who have seniority over me are both younger than I am. Neither of them would be more than corporals in the army."

"And you were a lieutenant, just like I was. I know what you mean, buddy." Eddie took a bite of apple and looked at the cheap Elgin watch that Walgreen's issued to its clerks so they could time their various duties for the district efficiency expert. "Two minutes to twelve-thirty," he said, getting up. "See you tomorrow, Penney."

"Yeah, see you tomorrow, Walgreen."

For Sam Sheridan, all his days were the same. Week after week. Month after month. Nothing ever changed.

Until the day the letter came.

4

Georgia and her mother could barely contain their anticipation as Sam slit open the envelope. The letter had come in the late-afternoon mail, the second delivery. Its engraved return address was the law firm of Halliburton, Leggett, and Boyd, on Wornall Street. Georgia and Alva had fidgeted over the letter for the rest of the afternoon; Alva had even wanted to telephone Leon about it at the movie house, but Georgia had forbidden it, knowing it would have infuriated Sam. The moment Sam entered the door that evening, Georgia had thrust the letter in to his hands.

"What in the world can it be about?" she asked him. It was the same question she had asked Alva a dozen times already.

"I don't know," Sam said, unfolding the single sheet of stationery. "I don't even know who they are."

His eyes swept the short letter:

Dear Mr. Sheridan:

This office is in receipt of a request from the law firm of Fort & Fort in Dane, Texas, asking that we serve as correspondence counsel in the matter of a bequest concerning you in the Last Will and Testament of the late Mr. Able Chase Patman, of that township.

Will you kindly call at our offices at your earliest convenience to discuss this matter?

> *Respectfully yours,*
> *Angus Halliburton, Esq.*
> *Attorney at Law*

Sam handed the letter to Georgia and she read it with bulging eyes. "My god," she said nervously. "Who is he, Sam? Who is Able Chase Patman?"

"I don't know. I never heard of him."

"But, Sam, you *must* have! The man has left you something in his *will!*"

Sam racked his brain. Able Chase Patman. Able Chase Patman. The name was not familiar at all.

"He must be a relative," Alva offered. "People don't leave things to strangers."

"Think, Sam!" Georgia implored. Then she clutched her swollen stomach and had to sit down. The excitement made her flush and suddenly turn warm. But she was not about to lose her train of thought. "Think, Sam, please," she said in a calmer voice.

"I *am* thinking, Georgia. I tell you I don't recognize the name."

There was no other topic of conversation in the house for the rest of the evening. All possible avenues of explanation were explored. Perhaps Patman was a cousin or other relative of Sam's father, whom Sam had never known. His father had died in a fire when Sam was four. Nell, Sam's mother, had told him about it when Sam was older. His father, whose name was John, had been over in central Kansas working the wheat harvest, Nell had said. A grain silo had caught fire. John had gone into the flames and managed to rescue two of five men who had been overcome by smoke inside; but on his third trip into the burning structure he had been overcome by smoke himself and had perished with the other three.

Sam knew little about his father or his father's family. This fellow Patman down in Texas *might* have been a distant relative, but it would have to have been on his father's side; on Sam's mother's side, he knew there was no one. Nell, like himself, had been an only child, and her own father had died before Sam was born. Sam remembered a maternal grandmother, a gentle, sweet little woman, with whom he and Nell lived until Sam was eight. When she died, there was just his mother and himself. Sam was positive that Able Chase Patman was not a relative on his mother's side of the family.

"Maybe," suggested Alva Powell after supper, "he *wasn't* a relative, after all. Could he have been the father of some soldier you might have helped during the war? Some soldier who might have written home about your kindness?"

That was a new thought. For the next hour, Sam tried to remember the name of every soldier he had befriended in any way. Part of his duty as a junior officer had been to write letters to surviving families. He usually kept them brief and to the point, emphasizing only that the person's son or husband had died like a good soldier in defense of America and democracy. Only on a few occasions, when he had actually been with the dying man, had he tried to include a few genuine last words. As far as "helping" his men, he had pushed through a few emergency furloughs, interceded in several cases of company discipline, and covered up a couple of minor absences-without-leave. It was possible, he supposed, that a man involved in one of those incidents might have written home about it. But the idea seemed so farfetched. And most of his men had been from Kansas and Missouri; he could not recall a single Texan in his outfit.

Thinking of the army made Sam think of his friend Eddie Miller. "If Eddie had a telephone, I'd call him and tell him about this," Sam said. "He's pretty smart; maybe he'd come up with an idea."

"I think we ought to keep it in the family," Georgia had disagreed. "At least until we find out what it's all about."

Georgia had gotten carried away in the backseat of a car with Eddie Miller once, when he was home on furlough. She remembered he had told her she was "one hot toss." Ever since Sam had met and become friends with Eddie, she had lived in fear that Eddie would mention her, or that Sam would invite him over sometime, or *something*. Her skin crawled every time Sam mentioned Eddie Miller, which was frequently.

The unanswered question of who Able Chase Patman was continued to vex them all evening long. Even after Sam and Georgia went to bed, they lay awake in the dark whispering about it. Both were still awake after midnight when Leon got home from the movie house. They heard Alva get out of bed and go into the kitchen, and knew she was telling him about it. That irritated Sam, and he said so to Georgia. This was *his* business, and he did not appreciate everybody knowing about it—"everybody" being Georgia's brother. It felt good for a change to be one up on Leon.

It was nearly two o'clock in the morning when the household finally settled down and went to sleep. Everyone except Sam. For two more hours Sam remained awake in the darkness with his own thoughts, speculating wildly. To know that he was part of something, and not know what the something was, was maddening. Knowing that other people controlled his destiny: he hated that. In the army, there had been a period between the time Pershing issued orders and the time those orders filtered down through staff command and field command and finally got to him. An interim period when all he could do was wait—and wonder.

Finally, at 4:00 A.M., Sam slipped into a restless, fitful sleep. For the first time in a long time, he dreamed about the trenches.

Angus Halliburton, to Sam's surprise, was no older than Sam himself. But he had a gold watch chain draped between his vest pockets, and he handled himself with the assurance of a much older man. Success, Sam thought. It always showed. He kept his own coat closed to conceal the absence of a watch.

"Now then, Mr. Sheridan," Halliburton said when Sam was seated before his desk, "as I indicated in my letter, we are acting as correspondents for the law firm of Fort and Fort in Dane, Texas, and this concerns the matter of a bequest to you by a Mr. Able Chase Patman, lately deceased. The letter from Mr. Clarence Fort, the executor of the late Mr. Patman's estate, did not indicate your relationship to the deceased. Were you his nephew, or—?"

The lawyer let his question hang. Sam wet his lips. Careful now. "Does it make a difference how we were related?"

"It could. From what I gather, this is an outright bequest that appears to be a somewhat insignificant portion of a very large estate. My question as to your relationship to the deceased was to determine whether you might have any rights as an heir. To see if you might possibly be entitled to more than you've been left."

Sam nodded. "I see." He decided to be frank with Angus Halliburton. "To tell you the truth, I don't have any idea who Able Chase Patman *is*. Much less how, or even whether, I might be related to him. I never heard of him before."

Halliburton's eyebrows shot up. "Well, that's interesting." He proceeded to ask Sam a number of questions about his parents and grandparents and any other branches of the family about which Sam might know. A couple of his questions Sam thought curious. "Is it possible that your mother might have been a party to an earlier marriage?" he inquired.

"I don't think so. She certainly never mentioned any such thing."

"Could she have had a—well, a close *friend* after your father died? Someone you might have thought of as an 'uncle' when you were a boy?"

Sam shook his head. Halliburton was talking about a lover. "I don't remember anyone like that."

"Well," the lawyer finally concluded, "maybe you'll never know why Able Chase Patman put you in his will. That's rare, but it does happen. Fortunately, it does not affect your bequest—" he shuffled a few papers in a file folder "—which consists of both cash and real property. Money and land."

Sam's chest turned warm. "Money and land?"

"Yes. Cash in the amount of five hundred dollars. And real property in the amount of one hundred acres located near the township of Dane, in the county of Caddo, state of Texas. The legal description of the land is here, as well as a topographical report. Apparently it's unimproved land: rural raw acreage, they call it."

"What does that mean exactly?"

"Uncultivated. Scrub land."

"Do you know where Dane is?" Sam asked. "What it's close to?"

"No, I never heard of it. You could probably find out at the library. Wherever it is, it couldn't be very large, since it's called a township instead of a city. Probably not even incorporated." The lawyer paused a beat. "There is one other thing. As far as the property is concerned. The firm of Fort and Fort has advised that the principal heir to the estate, a Mrs. Ardelle Patman Spence, has offered to buy the one hundred acres bequested to you for twenty dollars an acre. That is represented as about twice the appraised value of the land. They've sent along a deed of transfer, in case you're interested. And an escrow check for two thousand dollars."

Sam swallowed carefully. *Two thousand dollars.* He sat back in his chair, frowning. Who the hell was this Able Patman anyway? Leaving him five hundred dollars and land worth another two thousand. This was incredible. Twenty-five hundred dollars! His first inclination was to jump in with both feet: sign anything the lawyer put in front of him, and get the money while the getting was good. But something deep inside him made him hold back.

"Does it say why they want to buy the land? What they want it for?"

"No. Possibly it's part of a larger parcel that the principal heir wants to keep intact."

Sam nodded. *Possibly.* Sam wondered who Ardelle Patman Spence was. There was something odd about this.

"I'd like to think about the land for a while," he said.

"All right. But the offer is only good until the close of business on the day that it's tendered. Say until six o'clock."

"And the five hundred?"

"That's yours right now. Just sign this document of receipt and you can have the estate check at once."

Sam signed the paper. He examined the check Halliburton handed him. It was a trust account draft drawn on the Merchants Bank of Dane, Texas. Five hundred dollars. More money than Sam had ever seen before. In a full year of working, he and Georgia had been able to save only forty-five dollars. Now, with a stroke of the pen, he had more than ten times that much. Sam folded the check neatly and zipped it into his billfold.

"I'll let you know about the land sale before six."

It was not quite 10:00 A.M. when Sam left the lawyer's office. He had called the store that morning and said he would not be in until lunchtime. The manager had not liked it, but Sam had said it was personal legal business that had to be taken care of. He knew the manager was bursting with curiosity as to exactly what kind of legal business one of his clerks had, but Sam had deliberately not told him. Sam included the manager in the same category as Leon Powell; both were egotistical pricks, as far as he was concerned.

Pausing at the corner, Sam tried to decide whether to go in to work, or go home and tell Georgia what had happened at the lawyer's office. Unable to make up his mind, he saw an Esso service station across the street and walked over there instead. He got a bottle of Nehi grape soda out of the ice-water cooler and paid the attendant a nickel. Then he saw the shelf of touring maps.

"You got a map of Texas?" he asked.

"Sure." The attendant flipped through the stack and pulled one out. Sam started to reach into his pocket again. "They're free," the attendant said.

Sam spread the map open on the counter and found the coordinates for Dane, population 1,256. Locating it on the map, he saw that it was in northeast Texas, one county over from the Louisiana state line, and about thirty miles south of Oklahoma. Turning to a driving map of the United States, he measured with his fingers and estimated that Dane was about four hundred miles from Kansas City.

Again folding the map to where he had found Dane, Sam leaned back against the cooler and studied it as he drank his soda pop. Dane was about the most civilized name he could find in the area. The other towns seemed to have foreign-sounding names: Nacogdoches, Ponta, Tenaha, Chireno, Magasco. Only as his eyes moved farther away from Dane did he find other American-sounding names: Tyler, Longview, Kilgore. To the southwest was a good-sized forest; to the southeast a large lake that was not named on the map. The Attoyak Bayou stretched north from the unnamed lake.

What was it like down there? Sam wondered. What kind of land was it? It seemed strange to be thinking of faraway land that was actually *his*. Hell, he didn't even know how much one hundred acres was. He realized, with some embarrassment, that he really wasn't very smart. All he had ever done was serve in the army and clerk in the J. C. Penney Golden Rule store. Springfield rifles and Arrow shirts he knew about; the rest of the things in the world were more or less vague.

Suddenly feeling very vulnerable, Sam decided to go home to Georgia. He would feel better about things, talking them over with her. He finished his soda pop, put the empty in a wooden case next to the cooler, and hurried down the street. On his way home, he kept thinking about the five-hundred-dollar check in his pocket—and another one for four times that much waiting for him back in the lawyer's office. All he had to do was sign the deed to the land. Give it back to the people it came from: Able Chase Patman and Ardelle Patman Spence, whoever she was. Take the money and forget about everything else. Why, with twenty-five hundred dollars, he and Georgia and their baby could make a good life for themselves. Buy a little house, so they could move away from Alva and Leon. Maybe even a small business of some kind; not a haberdashery, though: he'd had enough of socks and suspenders.

When he got to the house, Sam heard voices in the kitchen, so he went around to the back door. As he was about to step onto the porch, he heard Leon Powell say, "If he gets any money, Sis, you're going to have to take control of it. For your own sake and the sake of the baby. Sam just isn't smart enough to handle a large sum of money."

Sam stopped at the bottom step and listened.

"How do you know that?" Georgia challenged her brother. "You've got no way of knowing. Sam's never *had* a lot of money."

"That's the point, Sis. Sam's a clerk; he thinks small. He spends his days selling two-dollar shirts. Anything over a hundred dollars would just confuse him."

"Listen to your brother, Georgia," their mother interjected. "After all, he's a success."

"Just look at how foolishly the two of you squandered his mustering-out pay in New York," Leon reminded her, making Georgia instantly regret ever having shared their New York adventure with her mother and brother. "Sam *had* some money then," Leon pointed out, "and all he could think to do with it was spend, spend, spend."

"Well, for God's sake, he was just back from a *war!*" Georgia defended. "He was entitled."

"Entitled or not, that money would make a nice nest egg for you and the baby right now, wouldn't it?"

"You're not being *fair* to Sam, Leon!" Georgia snapped.

"You listen to your brother," Alva interjected again. "After all, he's a success."

"No!" Georgia stormed. "I am sick and tired of hearing what a success Leon is and what a failure Sam is! Leon had *time* to become a success, Mother, while Sam was in the goddamned *trenches!* All Sam needs is a chance!"

Sam stepped onto the porch and entered the kitchen, letting the screen door slam behind him. The three people in the room turned to him in surprise.

"You're right, Georgia," he said evenly. "All I do need is a chance. And I've just been given one."

He walked over to her, untied the apron around her waist, and tossed it onto the table. Taking her arm, he guided her out the back door.

"We've got something to do," he said.

It was three hours later when they returned to the house in a second-hand 1916 Hudson Super-Six. It had cost them eighty dollars. In Sam's pocket was the remaining four hundred twenty dollars from the inheritance check. The other check, the two thousand dollars offered for the land, was still in the lawyer's office. It would be returned to the attorneys in Dane, Texas, along with the unsigned deed. Sam Sheridan was keeping the land.

As Sam and Georgia got out of the car at the curb, Alva and Leon came out on the front porch and stared incredulously at them, and at the car. As the young couple came up the steps and crossed the porch, Georgia said, "I have to pack our things, Mother. We're leaving."

"Leaving? Leaving for where?" Alva asked in surprise.

"Texas," Sam said as they went through the door.

5

The afternoon and evening before the morning they were to depart were spent preparing for the trip. Once everyone got into the spirit, it turned out to be rather pleasant.

"I'll fry up some chicken," Alva said, "so you can take it for a cold lunch tomorrow."

"Maybe I should run down to Kroger's and buy one of those jugs that keeps water cold," Georgia thought aloud. "God, I'd hate to get stuck in the Texas desert without water! What do you think, Sam?"

"Texas isn't a desert," Sam told her. "At least, I don't think it is. They have lots of cattle ranches down there, so it couldn't be." He suddenly remembered the new money in his pocket and pulled out a twenty. "But get a jug if you want one. We can always use it for iced tea. I think people eat outdoors a lot in Texas. Cook outdoors, too." Sam tossed the twenty at Georgia with as much nonchalance as he could muster, knowing that Leon was watching. Then he was immediately sorry he had done it, because he realized it only confirmed Leon's opinion of him as a spendthrift. Amending his move, he said to Georgia, "Be sure to count your change; that's a twenty."

Leon, for once, tried to make up to Sam. Almost as if Sam's decision to move away was the first thing he had done of which Leon approved. He tried to help Sam with the car. "Have you thought about running it down to the Flying Eagle Garage to get it ready for the highway?"

"It's already ready," Sam grudgingly replied. But he was at once uncertain. "I think it is, anyway."

"I just thought you might want to make sure there was enough oil in the engine and water in the radiator. I'm not butting in, mind you, even though my own sister *will* be riding in it. In the condition she's in, too."

"Well, maybe I *had* better have it looked at," Sam conceded. Then, grudgingly again, "Want to come?"

Leon shrugged. "If you want me to."

At the Flying Eagle Garage, a mechanic checked over the engine and pronounced the automobile fit for a highway journey all the way to Texas. Before they left the garage, Leon bought a velvet steering-wheel cover for fifty cents and gave it to Sam. "Might make the driving easier," he said.

"Say, I appreciate that," Sam told him. Maybe, he thought, old Leon wasn't such a prick after all.

After dropping Leon back at the house, Sam drove down to the J. C. Penney store, arriving just before it closed.

"You were supposed to be in at lunchtime, Sheridan," the manager chastised.

"My legal business took longer than I expected," Sam replied, loudly enough for the other clerks to hear. "I just stopped in to collect my pay. I'm quitting."

The manager's mouth dropped open and a couple of the clerks fairly gasped. Nobody *quit* a good job those days.

"I've inherited a ranch in Texas," Sam told them, "and I'm needed down there right away to run it."

The bookkeeper figured what Sam had coming and paid him in cash. Leaving, he hurried down to Walgreen's hoping to be able to say goodbye to his friend Eddie Miller. But Eddie had already gone home.

Back at the house, Sam spent the evening loading the car for an early start. Later, they all went down to Bennie's Confectionery and had dishes of ice cream and mugs of root beer. Sam and Leon argued over the check and finally split it. It was the first time the four of them had ever gone out as a family.

Just after sunup the next morning, Sam and Georgia got ready to leave. Georgia and her mother hugged and cried, while Sam and Leon awkwardly shook hands and tried to conceal their mutual embarrassment at being friendly. Georgia promised to send postcards from wherever they stopped along the way, and to write them all about Texas after they got there.

On their way out of town, they drove past the corner Walgreen's and Georgia thought of Sam's friend, Eddie Miller. Georgia glanced at Sam but said nothing. Then they passed Woolworth's and Georgia thought of the married businessman who had given her the pearls, now wrapped in a handkerchief in her suitcase. She closed her eyes for a moment.

God, but she was *glad* to be getting out of Kansas City.

The first day on the road, they got only as far as Coffeyville, a hundred sixty-three miles. Three flats, three stalls, and a dozen overheatings had made every mile an uncertainty. By four o'clock in the afternoon they were both exhausted by the heat and decidedly on edge from the day's ordeal. They found a boardinghouse and rented a room for the night. Georgia went directly to the bed and lay down, and after Sam unloaded the car he joined her. They rested as best they could, both being nervous about the trip in general and their unfamiliar surroundings in particular, until evening came and it cooled off. Then they bathed and went out for a supper in a little cafe that had a sign in front that said one of the Dalton brothers had died on that very spot during a foiled bank robbery.

"Imagine that!" Georgia said, impressed. "I'm standing right where Grat Dalton *died!*" There was something almost sensual about it. She tried to imagine what Grat Dalton had looked like.

During supper, the day's ordeals, now safely behind them, became an adventure they could talk and even joke about. They recalled the little towns they had driven through—Greeley, Iola, Chanute, among others—and the thriving, swaying golden wheat fields that had lined the narrow Kansas highway. Tomorrow they hoped to get through Oklahoma, if all went well.

Being in the boardinghouse room reminded them of the hotel in New York (not that it was even remotely similar), and that night

33

they enjoyed an hour of extremely satisfying lovemaking, Sam finding Georgia's slightly swollen belly very exciting, and Georgia closing her eyes and pretending that Sam was the outlaw Grat Dalton.

The second day of their journey was better than the first as far as the Hudson's performance: only two flats and two stalls, and not as many overheatings; but the terrain they crossed was considerably less scenic and a good deal hotter. Down through Vinita, Pryor, and Muskogee, they noticed the land becoming less green almost mile by mile. The air, when they rolled the side windows down, had a slightly gritty feel, and milch cows grazing in patchy pastures had ribs that showed through their hides like an old lady's corset. Farther south, outside McAlester, they passed a chain of striped-suited convicts shoveling grainy black soil off the highway. The men looked at Sam and Georgia with desperate, hungry eyes as they rode past.

"Jesus," Sam said to himself. The Hun prisoners they had captured in France were better cared for than those convicts appeared to be.

That afternoon the Hudson overheated quite badly in the little town of Hugo, Oklahoma, and since it had a boardinghouse with eight rooms, all unoccupied, Sam and Georgia decided to spend the night there. It was a disappointing evening: it stayed hotter longer, the water they bathed in smelled of sulphur, and the supper they bought was tasteless. But the thing that depressed them the most was that no one in Hugo smiled. It was a totally cheerless little town.

"It's the heat," Sam concluded. "The heat's got people down."

In their airless little room that night, they found the bed so uncomfortable that if they had not been so tired they would not have slept at all. Georgia had no interest whatever in sex that night; not even if Grat Dalton himself had been there. Turning their backs to each other, they tried to sleep.

Tomorrow they would reach Texas.

The land they encountered on the third day, after crossing into Texas, was ravaged by drought. It was the same drought that had affected southern Oklahoma, through which they had just driven, but somehow, after crossing into Texas, its effect seemed much more severe. In Oklahoma there had at least been occasional patches of woods, green thickets, wild foliage that had resisted the long, dry heat, and their presence seemed to bespeak that all was not lost, that

34

this too would pass. But farther south, on the flatland of northeast Texas, there was nothing. No shrubbery, no grass, no leaves on the trees. The middle of summer and no leaves on the trees.

"They look like they're dead," Sam said when he saw the first stand of them, naked sticks stuck upright in the hard earth.

"I never saw anything like it," Georgia whispered, as if afraid her voice might carry in the vast openness.

The first town they came to, ironically, was Paris, Texas. What a name for it, Sam thought, recalling another Paris. At a Neosha station where they pulled in for gas, Sam got out and stood, hands on hips, looking up and down the main street. It was like a ghost town: a breeze whipping up sand in the gutters, a tumbleweed pitching about, the town's one traffic signal not working, no people.

"Where is everybody?" Sam asked the attendant, a sallow-faced man with yellowish buckteeth.

"Inside. Ever'body's inside." He grunted softly. "Ain't no reason to come outside."

Sam glanced at Georgia. Usually she got out to stretch whenever possible, but in this little town of Paris she remained in the car, window rolled up. Despite the heat, she had a light wrap around her shoulders. There were, Sam thought, different kinds of cold.

"How long's it been this way?" Sam asked.

"All summer. Ain't rained since April. Farmers got no crops, so the stores in town got no customers. You're the first one to buy gas here in a week."

"But don't people go through here?" Sam was incredulous that the town had so little life.

"That's *exactly* what they do, mister; go through. Just like we wasn't here. The truckers and like, why, they go on down to Highway 67 to buy gas. They's a big Commerce station down there, got a cafe next door, pretty girls waitin' tables, magazines. Shit, I cain't buck that. Me, I'm just waitin' for the goddamned bank to foreclose on my station, then I'm headin' for California. Let Texas blow away, far as I'm concerned." He hung up the gas hose. "One buck even."

It was like that from then on. The deeper into Texas they drove, the worse it seemed to become. Little northeast Texas towns were like tombstones in the great northeast Texas cemetery. Bogata, Talco, Mt. Pleasant, Gilmer, Gladewater. Names of the dead and dying.

"Is it much farther?" Georgia asked.

"Not much," Sam said.

With grim determination, Sam kept his foot on the pedal, his hands on the wheel, and his eyes on the forlorn stretch of highway.

There's *got* to be something better up ahead, he thought desperately.

6

They rolled into Dane, Texas, early in the afternoon. The sign at the edge of town read:

TOWNSHIP OF DANE
Pop. 1436

"Guess it's grown a little since our map was printed," Sam said, recalling that the roadmap had shown the population at 1,256.

Dane looked much like every other small town they had seen since leaving Oklahoma. There was a town square with a courthouse set in the middle, and one block of small businesses on each side. Drugstore, five-and-ten, notions, yard goods, Piggly-Wiggly, bank, hardware, dry cleaners, bakery, barber, beauty parlor, Ford car agency, cafe, insurance, Roxy Theater, pool hall, a dozen others.

And one church. Large and white, on the first corner opposite the square on the road in from the north. In front of it, on a patch of hard dirt that had once been lawn, was a white-framed black sign with interchangeable white letters announcing the subject of the next sermon. Above that marquee, permanently lettered in paint, it read:

FIRST BAPTIST CHURCH
Rev. Adolph Jones, Pastor

Land for the Site of this
House of God donated by
Mr. Able Chase Patman
1895

Sam and Georgia exchanged looks. For the first time, both realized that they had finally arrived. The name Dane on the sign outside town had not registered on them that significantly. But the name Able Chase Patman had been etched in their minds for four days. This, at last, was where *he* was. Or had been. Now they would learn why he had named Sam in his will.

Sam drove around the courthouse until he saw Fort & Fort, Attorneys at Law in a window above the Merchants Bank. Parking, he said to Georgia, "You want to wait or come with?"

"I'll come with, Sam. For God's sake."

Sam nodded. Frowning, he looked up at the window and rubbed his palms lightly over the velvet steering-wheel cover Leon had bought for him. He was acutely aware that Georgia was watching him, waiting for him to get out. "I'm not sure just what to say," he confessed.

"Can't you just show him your copy of the letter to the Kansas City lawyer and tell him you've come to find out where your land is located?"

"I guess I could do that. Sure. That sounds all right, doesn't it?"

"It sounds fine."

They got out of the car, crossed the sandy, deserted sidewalk, and climbed a dim narrow flight of stairs between the bank and an insurance office next door. The stairs, wooden and as dry as everything else in northeast Texas, creaked ominously under their weight. Georgia held tightly to Sam's arm. She was relieved when they reached the second floor where there were windows and daylight.

A plain but not unattractive woman in a simple seersucker daydress looked up and smiled from a desk in an outer office. "Good afternoon. Who did you all want to see?"

Sam quickly got out the letter and referred to it. "Mr. Clarence Fort, please."

"All right. And your name?"

"Samuel Sheridan."

There was immediate and obvious surprise in the woman's face. Her mouth dropped open and she looked quickly from Sam to Georgia and back again. "Mr. Samuel Sheridan," she said, composing herself. "Of course. Please sit down. I'll tell Mr. Fort you're here."

Sam and Georgia watched her enter one of two inside doors. "God, did you see that look?" Georgia whispered. "I thought she was going to drop her step-ins."

"You and me both."

The receptionist returned almost immediately. "Come in, please."

Clarence Fort was a heavy-lidded man just beginning to go fat in the middle. He wore a celluloid collar and had a chew of hard tobacco in one cheek. "Have a chair," he say by way of greeting, neither smiling nor offering his hand. A younger man, Sam's age, came in from a connecting office. "My son and partner, Bruce," said the senior Fort.

Bruce Fort and Sam exchanged nods. The younger Fort reminded Sam of Angus Halliburton, the lawyer back in Kansas City. He had the same gold watch chain, the same self-assured attitude, the same cut entirely.

"What can we do for you, Mr. Sheridan?"

Sam, sitting on the edge of a chair, cleared his throat. "I've come to find out where the land is that Mr. Able Chase Patman left me in his will."

"South of town about eight miles, out the Kilgore highway. The county clerk can give you the exact location. His office is in the courthouse." Fort was leaning back in an ancient swivel chair. His son sat on the desk, one leg swung over a corner. "Anything else?"

The lawyer's tone, Sam realized, was bordering on curtness, even rudeness. He pressed on, nevertheless. "I was wondering if you could tell me something about this Able Chase Patman?"

Fort was already shaking his head. "Mr. Sheridan, I really can't discuss the late Mr. Patman or the Patman family with you. I represent the family in a fiduciary relationship, so any knowledge I have of them is strictly privileged. Mr. Halliburton in Kansas City telephoned to tell me you had declined the two-thousand-dollar offer for the land. I had intended writing you a letter, but since you're here, let me say that I'm prepared to double that offer."

"Four thousand dollars?"

"Cash on the barrelhead. We can walk directly downstairs to the bank and you can have the currency in your hands in five minutes." The lawyer's heavy-lidded eyes flicked over Sam's J. C. Penney suit and Georgia's plain maternity dress. "You look like you could use four thousand dollars, Mr. Sheridan."

Sam felt himself blush. *You son of a bitch.* He glanced at young Bruce Fort. *Bet you managed to stay out of the war, too, didn't you, Mr. Success?* "Mr. Fort," Sam turned back to the father and said carefully, "I'm not asking for any private information about anybody. I'd just like to know why this Able Chase Patman named me in his will. I didn't even know the man."

"No, you didn't."

"Then why did he make me one of his heirs?"

"I really can't say, Mr. Sheridan. Now about that land: it's completely worthless, you know. Scrub land. Full of dead trees and mesquite—"

"But you want to give me four thousand dollars for it. Excuse me, Mr. Fort, but you look smarter than that."

Now the lawyer blushed. "*I* do not want to buy the property at all, Mr. Sheridan. I personally wouldn't offer you fifty cents for it. The offer is being made in the interest of the person who owns the property bordering your parcel on three sides. That landowner simply does not care to have a block removed from the main plot."

Sam referred to his letter again. "That person is Mrs. Ardelle Patman Spence?"

"That is correct."

"Just who is she?"

"The late Mr. Patman's primary heir, just as the letter states. That is all I am prepared to tell you."

"I'd like to talk to her," Sam said.

"Not possible," the lawyer told him. "She is away from Dane for the summer. But I am authorized to act for her. *Five* thousand dollars."

Sam felt Georgia nudge his elbow. He shook his head, so emphatically that it surprised her. Standing, Sam took Georgia's hand and guided her to her feet.

"Thanks for your time, Mr. Fort. Come on, honey."

"I'll keep the offer open two or three days," Clarence Fort said as they left. "After you've had a look at the land, you might want to reconsider."

Without responding to Fort's last comment, Sam led Georgia out of the law offices and down the creaky stairs back to the car.

"My god, Sam. Five thousand dollars."

He swallowed, with difficulty. "I know. I know."

"It takes *years* to earn that much money."

"I know."

"Take forever to *save* that much—"

"Georgia, I *know.*" Sam felt physically ill, as if he had *had* the five thousand and then had it taken away from him. Suddenly, there in the thick hot air that was wasting the very earth under him, Sam Sheridan felt a chill and shivered. "Jesus," he said to himself, almost impotently. There were all kinds of cold.

"Sam, maybe we should think about selling," Georgia said. "The land *can't* be any good. The drought has wiped out everything around here."

"Droughts don't last forever."

"I know, but what do we do while it *does* last? We've got the baby to consider." Georgia bit one of her nails. "Five thousand dollars is a *fortune,* Sam."

Sam turned to stare out the side window at a shiny big LaSalle that came around the square and parked in front of the beauty salon. A Mexican in spotless white shirt and trousers slid from behind the wheel and held the back door open for a large white woman. Wearing a flowing dress of pale blue, she crossed the sidewalk and disappeared into the beauty salon.

"Did you hear me, Sam? I said five thousand dollars is a fortune."

"Not to everybody," Sam said. "Not to the successful ones."

He started the engine and drove around the square to the First Baptist Church.

The Reverend Adolph Jones was a strikingly handsome man whose perfect features looked as if they came off an artist's board. A high pompadour crowned his head, and when he smiled his flawless teeth fairly gleamed. It would have been impossible to guess his age: older than thirty, younger than fifty.

"Yes, Mr. Able Chase Patman gave us the land for our church more than twenty years ago. It was presented as a memorial to his son, who I understand met an untimely death. Come, I'll show you the cornerstone plaque."

Pastor Jones led Sam and Georgia to an inside corner at the back of the church and showed them a brass plate attached to the wall. It read: *The land on which this Church stands was donated as a memorial by Able Chase Patman, in memory of his son Lorn Lee Patman. April 12, 1895.*

"A most kind and generous man was Able Patman," the reverend concluded.

"Yes, he was," Sam said. "So kind and generous that he named me in his will, Reverend. And I never heard of the man before."

The minister's tailored eyebrows shot up. "Indeed? Well, our Lord does move in strange ways, doesn't He?"

"Reverend, who is Ardelle Patman Spence?"

"Why, the late Mr. Patman's daughter. She's the sister of this unfortunate young man whose name is on the plaque. Spence is her married name; her husband is Pete Spence, of Spence Cattle Company. Excuse me, what did you say your name was?"

"Samuel Sheridan."

Curious fingers stroked a carefully groomed jaw. "Sheridan, Sheridan, Sheridan." He smiled a tolerant smile. "I'm trying to remember something about that name. Not something I know, but something I heard. You see, I wasn't here when the church was dedicated. I've only been the pastor in Dane for eight years."

"Reverend, can you tell me where I might locate Ardelle Patman Spence? Where she is for the summer?"

"Why, I—no, I don't believe I can." He was obviously not telling the truth. "I do hope it's someplace cooler than Dane, though," he added, to cover his discomfiture. Just as obvious as his lie was the fact that he was not used to lying. "I'm terribly afraid you all will have to excuse me now. I have to make my sick rounds before it gets too late. Enjoy your stay in Dane, won't you."

The Caddo County *Enterprise* was a weekly four-page offset newspaper published every Thursday. A copy was hand-delivered to each merchant on the square that same afternoon; the rest of Caddo County's residents found it in their mailboxes Friday morning. Harley Greb, the editor and publisher, had inherited the paper from his father, who had founded it when Dane was an overnight stop on the cattle trail from Waco to Texarkana. What journalism the younger Greb knew, he had learned at his daddy's knee. He was accustomed to asking questions, not answering them.

"What do you want to know about the Patmans for?" he asked Sam.

"Able Patman left me some money and a piece of land. I'm trying to find out why."

"Your name's Sam Sheridan? And you're from where?"

"Kansas City."

Harley Greb looked from behind a cluttered desk at an older, gray-haired woman who had stopped cutting out long columns of printed type, and was watching and listening to them. "You just go on with your work, Emily," he said, a little sternly. Then, to Sam, "Don't want to start any unnecessary gossip. Well, Mr. Sheridan, Mrs. Sheridan, you two are a long piece from home, aren't you? Don't tell me you came all the way from Kansas City to look a gift horse in the mouth?"

"I'm naturally curious," Sam said. "Wouldn't you be?"

"Maybe, maybe not. You've been to see Clarence Fort, I imagine?"

"Yes."

"What'd he tell you?"

"Practically nothing. Neither did Reverend Jones at the Baptist Church."

Greb smiled a somewhat insincere smile. "Oh, well, Pastor Jones talks mostly with the Almighty. Sometimes us mortals can't get word one out of him." He turned his head. "Emily, will you please bring me a copy of last week's paper?"

The gray-haired woman got up from her work table. When she came over to Greb's desk, Sam and Georgia saw that she was very tiny and had a limp. As she walked away, they could see that one of her high-button shoes had a built-up heel to compensate for a clubfoot. Georgia watched with sad and sympathetic eyes as she limped back to the table.

"Let me show you all something," Greb said, opening the paper. "See this right here? A half-page ad that don't say nothing but "Compliments of Spence Cattle Company." A half-page ad, in case you're poor at arithmetic, is exactly one-eighth of my newspaper's

42

space. All the rest of the ads in the whole paper—all these one-column-by-two-inch ads, two-column-by-one-inch ads—don't even amount to that one Spence Cattle Company ad. These are hard times down here, Mr. Sheridan, and a newspaper is a business too. Do you get my meaning?"

"I'd be pretty stupid if I didn't," Sam replied.

"Yessir, you would be. And I can tell by talking to you that you aren't. So I'll just bid you good afternoon, Mr. Sheridan. Mrs. Sheridan."

Greb looked down at his desk and did not raise his eyes again until Sam and Georgia left.

Outside, Georgia put both hands on her husband's arm almost fearfully. "The people in this town don't like us, Sam."

"No, they don't," Sam said. He looked slowly around the little town square. "I wonder why?"

7

Driving out the highway south of Dane a while later, the Kilgore highway it was called, Sam said, "It's got to be around here somewhere."

Next to him, Georgia scanned the terrain on her side of the road. They were looking for the hundred acres Able Chase Patman had left Sam. The directions they had as to its exact location were barely adequate. The county clerk at the courthouse, where they had gone to obtain specific boundary information, had helped them only reluctantly, giving the impression that it was against his better judgment, that he was only doing so because he was required to by law.

"I never saw such a contrary man in my life," Georgia had said when they left his office.

"Like everybody else in town," Sam told her. He was wearing

his determined look again. "We'll find it anyway," he said, taking her hand. "Come on."

Now Sam was not so sure. Every mile on both sides of the road looked the same as every other mile. There was nothing to distinguish one parcel from another: no fences, no boundary markers, no signs, nothing. They drove ten miles and turned back.

Several miles outside town, they came to a roadhouse. It was a low square wooden building with windows across the front but none on the sides, which were both covered with painted advertisements: Arm and Hammer Baking Soda on one, Murchinson's Bread—Fresh Every Morning, on the other. The place was set back from the highway and had gravel spread on three sides for customers to park. A string of naked light bulbs ran across the front above the single doorway, but it was still too early for them to be on. A sign over the door read: Tully's—Open Pit Bar-B-Q—Dancing Sat. Nite. There were no cars in front of the place. It was late in the afternoon now: too early for supper trade, long past the midday meal Texans called "dinner."

Sam pulled the Hudson onto the gravel and parked. "I'm going to go in and ask directions. You want to wait here or come with?"

"I wish you'd quit asking me that," Georgia said irritably. "I want to come with, wherever you go. Don't you think I'm interested in this too?"

"Well, I didn't know if you were too tired or not. You're always reminding me how hard it is carrying that belly around."

"I'll let you know when I'm too tired to go in someplace."

Sam helped her out of the car and they walked to the front door of Tully's, their shoes crunching on the gravel. Entering, they found a large open room, its floor covered with sawdust. It was furnished entirely with tables for four, all of them wooden and bare of tablecloths, each set with a paper-napkin holder and a Mason jar of barbecue sauce with a wooden spoon in it. Four ceiling fans were valiantly but vainly fighting the oppressive heat. A heavy smell of pork grease permeated the premises. There were no customers.

"Sit anyplace you like, folks," a woman wearing trousers and a man's white shirt told them cheerfully. She was coarse looking, with thick raven-black hair parted in the middle and hanging loose. There was also fine black hair showing on her arms where the sleeves of the shirt were rolled up. The trousers, too large for her, were gathered at the waist and held up by a leather cord knotted where a belt buckle would have been.

"We don't want to eat," Sam told the woman. "I'm looking for directions to a piece of land."

The kitchen door opened and a man emerged, wiping his hands on an already greasy apron. He had receding hair over a craggy, slightly crooked face that could never have been handsome. Wearing Indian moccasins, his footsteps made not a sound as he crossed the sawdust-covered floor to where they stood.

"I'm Tully, the owner. What can I do for you?" he asked.

"I'm looking for a parcel of land," Sam said. "Supposed to be bounded on one side by a dirt road. Choctaw Road, I think it's called. Is it close to here?"

"'Bout two more miles down the highway," Tully said. He studied Sam curiously. "It's just scrub land, you know. Ain't nothing there but an ol' shack."

Sam nodded. "I'd like to look at it. You say it's got a shack on it?"

"Well," Tully disclaimed, "it ain't *much* of a shack. Used to be what they called a line-rider's shack: place for the cowboys on the outer range to fix a meal and get some sleep 'stead of having to camp outdoors. No telling what kind of shape it's in. Might find some Indians living in it, too."

Sam and Georgia exchanged glances. "Indians?" Georgia said.

Tully nodded. "Choctaws. The Spences owns all the land down there, but they's a Choctaw tribe owns the piece bordering that parcel on one side. It ain't a reservation exactly, 'cause the federal government deeded it to the tribe when they was moved over here from Arkansas. But the Choctaws, they *run* it like it was a reservation. They got a council or some such thing that can throw a man off if he ain't following their rules. They're always throwing somebody off for being drunk or stealing eggs from another Indian's henhouse, that kind of thing. When one gets throwed off, why, he sometimes takes up living in a line-rider's shack." Tully cocked his head. "What'd you say your name was?"

"I didn't say. But it's Sheridan. Sam Sheridan."

Tully's expression did not change, but Sam noticed his eyes

brighten for an instant. What was that? Sam wondered. Recognition? Surprise? Whatever it was, Tully controlled it very quickly and the flash of brightness faded.

Frowning, Sam was about to resume asking questions, but Georgia squeezed his arm and said, "Sam, honey, we want to get there before dark, don't we?" She was thinking about the Indians.

Pursing his lips, Sam shifted his eyes from Tully to the woman and back again. Then he nodded and patted Georgia's hand.

"Thanks for the directions," he said to Tully.

"Don't mention it."

Sam and Georgia left the roadhouse, again feeling like outsiders, intruders. But the man named Tully had, Sam was certain, recognized his name.

Sam and Georgia found the land at dusk, and located the shack by the flickering of a kerosene lantern in one of its windows. There was, as Tully had warned, someone living there.

Sam parked in front of the shack. Stepping onto the rickety porch, he knocked on the door. It was opened by a white man, perhaps sixty or so, with an eaglelike face, ropes of white hair combed straight back, and direct, humorless eyes. Behind him stood an Indian: a flat-faced Choctaw with a badly crossed left eye, wearing a greasy buckskin shirt featuring a rawhide lace instead of buttons.

"What do you want?" the white man asked. His tone carried a direct challenge. His right hand rested on the grip of a large pistol stuck in his belt.

Sam parted his lips to speak, but no words came. His eyes flicked from the unsmiling white man to the gun to the Indian. He felt his bowels churn threateningly. Georgia, he knew, was watching him from the car.

"Well?" the eagle-faced white man demanded.

"I'm the—the new owner," Sam said, wiping sweaty palms on his trousers. Bracing himself, he was determined to be firm. "I—my wife and I—we're here to move in."

The eagle-faced man frowned darkly, suspiciously. "The new *owner?*" Speaking over one shoulder, he said, "Tongue, hand me that light." The Indian said something that sounded like "unh," and approached with the kerosene lantern held shoulder high. When the white man saw Sam's face in the light, his eyes widened and his mouth dropped open incredulously. "Who are you?" he asked in a harsh whispery voice.

"My name's Sam Sheridan. I own this land and this house now. I'm sorry, but you'll both have to leave. I need this place for my wife and me."

The white man was still staring at him. "Sam Sheridan." He said the name quietly, as if testing it. Then he shook his head in amazement. "I'll be goddamned. You say you *own* this place?"

"Yes. It was left to me by Able Chase Patman. Do you know the name?"

"Oh, yes. Yes, I certainly do know the name. So he left you something, eh? Well, I'll be goddamned." He turned to the Indian. "Let's get our things together, Tongue. We're leaving."

Sam waited just inside the door while the two men rolled up bedding and packed a few scant belongings into a duffel bag and backpack. Then the white man picked up the lantern and they trooped out of the shack and across the porch. In front of the house, they saw Georgia, who was now standing beside the car. The white man raised the lantern and studied her protruding belly. Georgia put a hand to her lips and cringed slightly in fear. Sam, although still somewhat frightened himself, hurried to her side.

"Well, I'll be goddamned," the white man said still again. Turning to Sam, he asked, "You want to light your lamp before we take ours away?"

"We, uh—we don't have a lantern," Sam admitted.

The white man hesitated a second, then handed Sam his own lantern. "Take this one until you can get one of your own. Me and Tongue can find our way in the dark."

As the two men started to walk off, Sam hollered, "Say, what's your name?"

"Poker," the white man's whispery voice hollered back. "C. J. Poker."

Sam watched the two men disappear into the blackness of the prairie. Poker had recognized his name, he was certain, just like Tully had. Sam's jaw clenched once, briefly.

We'll meet again, old man, he promised silently.

8

Their first twenty-four hours at the line-rider's shack were miserable.

The place was definitely a shack, and not even a good shack. Its floor had several broken planks that dropped down to a highly suspicious crawlspace. Of the three windows, one would not go up, one would not go down, and the glass of the other was shattered. A wooden counter with a broken leg was tied up with a rope. There was a wobbly table filthy with decayed food, and three wooden chairs greasy with grime. Three single bunks lined the walls, and when Georgia examined the bare mattresses, she almost retched. One was so stiff with dried matter it crackled when she moved it.

"My God in Heaven!" she said in disgust. "This place is—is— *ugh!* I can't even find a word for it. I'm sleeping in the car," she declared and walked out the door.

They both slept in the car.

The next morning, they found that in the light of day the shack looked even worse. Apparently it had never been cleaned since the day it was built, which was at least two decades earlier because Sam found someone's initials and "1900" carved next to one window.

"Sam, we can't live in this place," Georgia said, after inspecting it in the daylight.

"We've got to," he told her, "for a while anyhow. Can't we clean it up?"

"God, I don't see how. Can't we just burn it and buy a tent?"

"It's not that bad, Georgia. It just needs attention."

They had no choice, of course, and both knew it. Renting a room and eating in cafes would be too expensive; they had to conserve their money until Sam decided what they were going to do. So they set about doing what had to be done. Georgia made a list of cleaning supplies and sent Sam into Dane for them. While he was gone, she dragged the disgusting mattresses out of the shack and onto the prairie. Then she collected all the loose trash in the place—cans, paper, used stick matches, cigarette butts, Mason jars that had been used as spittoons and contained the most repugnant stuff Georgia had ever seen, and a variety of other repulsive filth—and hauled that outside also. When Sam returned, he found her sitting on the rickety front porch, bawling like a child.

With his arm around her, Sam took her for a short walk on the prairie. Gradually, comforted by his soothing reassurances, she stopped crying and returned with him to face the putrid ordeal ahead. The one redeeming feature of the shack was that it was built, they could tell, on a high water table and there was a well with an inside pump in the kitchen. That, together with the pot-bellied iron stove, persuaded Georgia and Sam that they could make the shack at least barely livable. With hot water, lye salt, brown soap, and scrub brushes, they scoured the wooden floor, walls, and ceiling. Then, while Georgia proceeded to scrub down the few greasy sticks of furniture outside, Sam did his best to repair the place inside: first fixing the broken floor planks, because Georgia was terrified of what might be crawling around underneath; then working on the windows: loosening the two that were stuck, and nailing scrap wood over the broken one. When everything else was reasonably repaired, and Georgia had finished scrubbing down the furniture, they moved things back inside.

The three bunks were merely two-by-fours nailed together and braced at the corners, with canvas stretched between them for a bottom. Georgia had scrubbed the canvasses with a block of brown soap and hung them from the roof overhang to dry, while Sam had taken all three bunks apart, selected the best wood from each, and reassembled them as a double bed. When the three single lengths of canvas were dry, he stretched them widthwise onto the new, wider bed. Then they walked out to inspect the mattresses again.

"No," Georgia said.

"No," Sam agreed. He poured kerosene on them and set them on fire on the prairie.

Returning to the house, they heated water one final time, took off their now filthy clothes and threw them onto the porch, and took turns washing each other in the blue glow of the lantern C. J. Poker had given them and a second one that Sam had bought, along with a can of kerosene, in town. While Sam was washing Georgia's belly, the baby kicked several times. "Must be a boy," Sam said. "Doesn't like to take baths."

"Maybe it's a girl and she's kicking because she's jealous of you rubbing my belly," Georgia said. The thought caused her to frown. "If it is a girl, do you suppose she *will* be jealous when you pay attention to me?"

"If she is," Sam said, kissing Georgia lightly on each nipple, "she'll just have to get used to it. Because I'm always going to pay attention to you."

They kissed then, long and wet and naked, with the baby between them.

After their bath, Georgia took some of their extra clothes and towels and improvised a mattress, while Sam got out the foodstuffs he had bought. They ate sitting up in bed, almost too weary to chew: sliced bologna, cheese, crackers, plum jelly, and two bottles of grape soda that Sam had forgotten to hang down the well so they had to drink them warm. But they were so tired it didn't matter.

As soon as they had enough to eat, Sam put the rest of the food away and turned off the lanterns. Georgia was already asleep by the time he got back to bed. He fell fast asleep the moment he put his head down. It was not yet even eight o'clock, the end of their first full day in Texas. Shortly after they fell asleep, as if drawn to each other for security, they rolled into each other's arms and did not move for the rest of the night.

The next morning, Sam took the borrowed lantern and went driving around his acreage looking for Poker and the Indian. He found them camped on the open prairie, apparently not in any particular hurry to find any place better. Sam pulled up and got out with the lantern.

"Thanks for the use of this," he said. "We'd have been in a fix without it."

"*Nada,*" said Poker, and when Sam frowned, explained, "Spanish. Means 'nothing.' You thanked me, I said it was nothing. *Nada.*"

Sam nodded and looked around their grubby little campsite. "Listen, I'm sorry I had to move you out like I did."

"Your place," Poker said. "Right, Tongue?"

"Unh," said the Indian.

Sam noticed that Poker was again studying him thoughtfully,

curiously. "Last night you said you knew the name Able Chase Patman," Sam said. "Can you tell me anything about him?"

Poker shook his head. "I don't talk about other folks' bin'ess."

"I'm trying to find out why he left me this land. Nobody seems to want to help me."

"Folks hereabouts mostly take care of their own bin'ess," Poker said.

"If I offered to pay you, would you help me?" Sam asked.

Poker shook his head. "If I ever tell you anything, it won't be for money."

"Mind if I ask you again sometime?"

"Why not?" Poker said. "If you're around."

"I'll be around," Sam told him.

Poker squinted at him and half smiled. Sam's statement had sounded almost like a threat.

After a while Poker said, "Hope you don't mind us squatting on your range."

Sam shook his head. "You're welcome as long as you want to stay."

Sam started to get back into his car. Poker nodded to Tongue and the Indian hurried across and handed Sam a large dressed rabbit and a paper sack half full of raw butter beans.

"We got more'n we need," Poker said.

Sam smiled, waved his thanks, and drove off.

That night, as Sam and Georgia ate the tasty fried rabbit and boiled butter beans, Georgia spoke of the future. She wanted to know what they were going to do. Sam could not tell her.

"How long do you think that lawyer, Mr. Fort, will keep open the offer to give us five thousand dollars for the land?" she asked.

Sam shook his head. "I don't know. The Spences are away for the summer, but I imagine the offer will hold at least until they get back and withdraw it." Sam studied her for a moment. "You want to go back to Kansas City, don't you?" he asked after a while.

"I think it would be the wisest thing," Georgia admitted.

"Why?"

"For one thing, Sam, because we *fit* in Kansas City. We don't fit out here. We're different from these people, these Texans. They don't like us, they don't want us here."

"Maybe they're not all that way."

"Oh, Sam. How many people have treated us decently since we got here? That man Tully gave us directions. The old man and the Indian gave us a rabbit and some beans. That's it, Sam. Everyone else has treated us like dirt and you know it."

Sam sighed quietly. Maybe she was right, he thought. Maybe they *should* go back. With five thousand dollars they could buy one of the new touring cars and drive back to Kansas City in style. Maybe start a little business, or buy into one, when they got there. A nice, neat little shop of some kind that he could run by himself, with maybe a part-time clerk to help out on Saturdays.

Sam got up, kissed Georgia on the top of her head, and went out onto the rickety front porch. He stood there for a while, mulling things over.

"What are you thinking about?" Georgia asked, joining him on the porch.

"Those lawyers in town. They want this piece of land in the worst way. Or rather, their client, Ardelle Patman Spence, wants it. Wonder why?"

Georgia shrugged. "The lawyer said it was because she didn't want a block taken out of the main plot."

"Yeah, that's what he said. But I wonder."

Georgia looked at him curiously in the moonlight. "Didn't you believe him?"

"Not entirely," Sam admitted. "I think there's a lot more to this whole thing than we imagine." He looked directly at her. "I want to be very careful here. I don't want anyone putting anything over on us. Understand?"

"Of course, Sam. Whatever you say." Georgia was a little surprised; there seemed to be a new authority in Sam's tone.

After a while, Georgia felt cold and went back inside. Sam remained on the porch, looking up at a huge full moon that bathed the prairie in blue-gray light. A breeze scented with wildflowers wafted now and again. Sam sighed quietly. What in the hell, he wondered, was there about this desolate patch of prairie that prevented him from making a quick decision to sell it? What kept him from just up and leaving it? Was it because the lawyers had made him suspicious? Or was it because the land was *his?* Because for the first time in his life he *owned* something?

Stepping off the porch, Sam walked slowly around the little homesite, picking up a stick, breaking pieces off and idly tossing them away. Something about the thought of this being *his* land had slowly seduced him; something was compelling him to stay when, by all that was logical and reasonable, he should be leaving. It was as if he now had roots in this ground: subtle and invisible roots that had taken hold and grown since his arrival.

But land or no land, there was still Georgia to consider, and their unborn baby. It was not fair to make her an unwilling partner in whatever there was between this land and himself. He had to make a decision, had to find some common ground on which to stand.

Tossing away the last of the stick he had picked up, Sam went back into the house. Georgia was sitting in the light of the lantern, mending one of his shirts.

"Two weeks," Sam said. "If something doesn't come up in two weeks, I'll go back and see the lawyer about selling."

For some reason he did not know, they were the hardest words Sam had ever spoken.

9

Sam parked on the shoulder of the dirt road just outside the Dane cemetery gate. Getting out, he lifted the wooden latch of the gate, entered, and closed it behind him. He walked slowly along the center path, glancing left and right at the headstones.

It took him five minutes to find the grave he was looking for. Its headstone read:

ABLE CHASE PATMAN
BORN 1850—DIED 1921
HONEST and TRUE

Next to that plot was another grave with a stone engraved:

LILLIAN CONWAY PATMAN
BORN 1854—DIED 1889
THE FAIREST OF THE FAIR

On a third grave next to that was a headstone that said simply:

LORN LEE PATMAN
BORN 1873—DIED 1894

There was no sentiment on the third stone. Sam stared at it, wondering why. Lorn Lee Patman, whom he presumed to be the son of Able and Lillian, had lived only twenty-one years.

Stepping over to the resting place of Able Chase Patman, Sam stared long and hard at it, almost as if trying to *will* the dead man to communicate with him, to tell him *why*. What was the motivation for this complete and total stranger leaving Sam one hundred grubby acres of scrub land? Why had this old man reached out from the grave across hundreds of miles to a clerk in a J. C. Penney Golden Rule store in Kansas City and disrupted his normal albeit unsatisfying life with such a strange inheritance? What lay behind it? What was it meant to do to or for Sam, where was it meant to take him?

Many questions but no answers. And the infuriating thing was that the answers were *there,* he was certain of it. Any one of half a dozen people he had encountered since coming to Dane could probably explain the whole thing to him. That lawyer Fort and his son; Tully, who owned the roadhouse; the county clerk; the preacher; that newspaper editor Greb . . .

Suddenly Sam remembered the incident in the newspaper editor's office. When Sam and Georgia had first told him who they were, the editor had looked over at an employee of his, a little woman named Emily, and admonished her to go on about her business. Emily, he recalled, had been staring openly at him and Georgia. Sam was sure she had recognized his name. Maybe, he thought, if he could talk to Emily away from the watchful eye of Greb, she might tell him something.

"I'm going to find out about you, Mr. Able Chase Patman," Sam said aloud. "One way or another."

With a purposeful stride, Sam returned to his car.

* * *

54

As Sam had hoped she would, the slight little woman named Emily came out of the Caddo County *Enterprise* office at one minute past noon and limped down the street. Sam, sitting on one of the benches in front of the courthouse, had forgotten that she had a clubfoot. As he watched her now, moving laboriously along in the heavy midday heat, he felt a pang of sympathy for her. His plan had been only to try and question her; perhaps, he thought, he could also give her a ride. Leaving the bench, he hurried after the woman and caught up with her just as she rounded a corner to leave the square.

"'Afternoon, ma'am," he said.

She stopped and looked up at him, surprised and suspicious.

"Hot day for walking," Sam said. "My car's just over there. I'd be glad to give you a ride wherever you're going."

"I'm going home for dinner," she said. She pointed to a small white cottage not twenty yards away. "I live right there, so a ride's hardly necessary. What is it you want, Mr. Sheridan?"

Her unblinking eyes looked at him almost challengingly. Sam decided at once that she was no one with whom to trifle or be indirect.

"I was wondering, ma'am, if you might spare me a few minutes to tell me a little about Able Chase Patman—"

"Young man," she cut in, "I am a forty-five-year-old crippled woman without a husband or other close relations. My sole support comes from my job at Mr. Greb's newspaper. Even the house I live in there is owned by Mr. Greb. Now I seem to recall that Mr. Greb did not take kindly to you asking questions about the late Mr. Patman. He made that perfectly clear the day you and your wife visited his office. I'm quite certain he would not appreciate me doing something for you that he himself has refused to do." Emily tilted her head and her eyes narrowed slightly. "Times are very hard right now, Mr. Sheridan. A lot of healthy, able-bodied young men are running around looking for work, and not finding any. If it's hard for them, you can imagine how it would be for a forty-five-year-old crippled woman."

Sam felt very chagrined. "I understand, ma'am," he said, embarrassed. "I guess I didn't stop to think what kind of position I'd be putting you in."

"Not only me but anyone else you pester," Emily said tartly. "Nobody in town wants to talk to you, because nobody wants to offend Mr. Pete Spence. He knew through his lawyers that you were coming; I heard him say so to Mr. Greb. Before he left on his trip, he passed the word around about you. 'Give him nothing, tell him nothing while I'm gone,' he said. 'If he's still here when I get back, I'll tend to him.' " Miss Emily's eyes narrowed. "If I was you, I *wouldn't* be here."

Sam stiffened. "Well, I *will* be, ma'am," he declared stubbornly. "I'm not afraid of Pete Spence, I don't care who he is."

"I knew you were hardheaded," the little woman said. "Knew it the minute I laid eyes on you. Knew you were as hardheaded as your mother was."

Sam's mouth dropped open. "My mother? What?"

"That is *all* I have to say to you, young man," Emily announced. "I would appreciate it if you would not annoy me again."

"But you mentioned my mother," Sam said almost desperately as she walked away. "Won't you please just—"

"Good *day,* Mr. Sheridan!" she said over her shoulder.

Tully's roadhouse was not deserted when Sam visited it the second time. It was half past noon and there were a dozen people spread out among the tables eating Texas dinner.

"You want to eat this time around?" the waitress, still wearing a man's shirt, asked when he walked in.

"No. I want to talk to Tully."

"He's busy cooking."

"He can cook and talk at the same time," Sam said, stepping around her and walking toward the kitchen.

"Now just a damn minute," she said, loudly enough to cause the customers closest to them to look up. "You can't just bust in here like you *own* the place—"

Sam pushed through the swinging kitchen door, the woman right behind him. Tully was at the butcher block, slicing pork into very thin strips for barbecuing. The knife he used moved surely and expertly, like an extension of his hand, and each slice that fell was of a perfect thickness.

"I'd like to talk to you for a minute," Sam said.

"He just barged in, Tully," the woman complained, "like he *owned* the place."

Tully glanced up between slices without pausing. His eyes

flicked over Sam, then returned to the pork. "All right," he said. He bobbed his chin at the woman. "Go on back out and see to the customers."

The woman gave Sam a withering look and retreated. She would have slammed it if it hadn't been a swinging door.

"Reba there's my wife," Tully said. "I usually don't let nobody back in the kitchen but her."

"I didn't mean to offend your wife," Sam said. "I'm sorry if it looked like I was barging in."

"That's what you done, though," Tully said flatly. He finished the slab he was slicing and with the top of the knife blade scraped the meat into a pot. From a burlap sack next to the butcher block, he pulled out another slab and began anew. "I'll tell you before you ask," he said, "I ain't doing no talking about Able Patman."

"Will you tell me *why* you won't?"

"Glad to. You see them customers on your way in? Half of them, maybe more, work for a man name of Pete Spence. He's the big man in Caddo County: owns ninety percent of the cattle range outside town, and 'bout sixty percent of ever'thing worth owning *inside* town. All he has to do to put me out of bin'ess is spread the word around that he don't want his friends or range hands eatin' in my place. I'd be closed in a week; that's how tight things is."

"How would he know you talked to me?" Sam tried to reason.

Tully snorted quietly. "Like I told you, half them customers out there that seen you come in here work for him. You find out *anything* in the next couple days that Pete Spence don't want you to know, and I'll be blamed for it."

Sam shook his head. "I don't understand. Why would he object to you or anybody talking to me about Able Patman? The man's *dead.*"

"Look," Tully said patiently. "Spence is married to Able Patman's daughter Ardelle. Ever'body knows that Ardelle don't want you here, that she's offered you an outlandish amount of money for that hunnerd acres her daddy left you. Just you *being* here is going to make Ardelle very unhappy. And what makes Ardelle unhappy, makes Pete Spence unhappy. Savvy?"

"Yeah, I savvy," Sam answered. "What you're saying is that you're scared of Pete Spence."

Tully flushed slightly and Sam saw that the slicing knife missed a beat. "I don't appreciate being told I'm yellow," Tully said. "Especially when it ain't true. I've never been scared of another man in my life. I ain't scared of Pete Spence now. But I am scared of what he can *do.* Me and Reba, we worked a lot of hard years to get this place. We'd be fools to risk it over a stranger."

Sam sighed quietly and leaned back against a drainboard next to the kitchen's big iron sink. It was the same excuse, basically, that he had heard from Emily. Nobody wanted to take a chance of losing what they had, whether it was a menial job and a rent-free cottage, or a small roadhouse on the Kilgore highway. And Sam knew he could not blame them. It was hard to contemplate giving up something one owned. Sam was already feeling that about the one hundred acres that were now his.

"I'm sorry for what I said, Tully," he told the older man. "I'm sure you're not a coward. And I'm not trying to start trouble or to disrupt anybody's life. I'm just trying to straighten out my own. I'll leave you alone."

Pushing away from the drainboard, Sam started to leave. Then he remembered what Emily had said to him an hour earlier. At the swinging door, he turned back.

"Will you answer one question for me? If it's not about Able Patman?"

"Maybe," Tully said without looking at him.

"Did you know my mother?"

Again the slicing knife missed a beat. Tully looked over at Sam.

"I knowed her," he said simply.

Sam nodded his thanks and left.

Outside, after he got in his car, Sam sat with his hands on the steering wheel, staring straight ahead at nothing. His mind was back in another time, another world, remembering his mother.

And he was thinking: Is it possible she *wasn't* my mother?

10

When Sam was ten years old, he got two baths a day: one in the morning when his day began, and another an hour before supper. His mother, Nell, did the bathing. The second bath of the day was the *real* bath, to get him clean after his day's activities. The first bath, which he knew followed his mother's, was, in Nell's words, "just so he could start fresh" each day. While she bathed him, Sam and his mother would talk.

"What are you and Jesse and Enid going to do today?" she frequently asked.

"Play hide-and-seek," he usually answered.

"You children play that nearly every day. You certainly must like it."

Sam shrugged. "It's all right." It was not Sam's idea to play the stupid game; it was Jesse's idea. Jesse was a year older than Sam, and bigger. He liked the game because he liked to hide with Enid.

Jesse and Enid were the children of two women who worked for Sam's grandmother, Mrs. Edna Duvall, as seamstresses. Mrs. Duvall and Sam's mother were in the dressmaking business. Twice a widow, Mrs. Duvall had been left inadequately fixed by both of her late husbands, and had started the business to make ends meet while raising Nell, the daughter of her first husband. Nell's father had died in the eighty-nine influenza epidemic. Mrs. Duvall's second husband, a section foreman for the St. Louis–Midland Railroad, had been a drinker. Since Mrs. Duvall did not permit liquor in the house, he kept his bottle in the railroad toolshed down the hill where the tracks were. In the evening after supper he would take his nightly "constitutional," which meant he would walk down there and have a snort. One night he had more than a snort, lay down on the tracks for a snooze, and the seven-twenty cut him into four pieces.

The two ladies who worked for Mrs. Duvall usually arrived at eight and worked until noon. The dining room had been converted into a fitting and sewing room where Mrs. Duvall, Nell, and the two ladies spent each morning. The children were confined to the front and backyards, and it was there that they played hide-and-seek nearly every day. Because Jesse was bigger, the game always started with Sam being "it." That was so Jesse could take Enid and hide somewhere first thing. Enid was Sam's age, a curly-haired girl whose white dresses looked suspiciously like flour-bag cloth. She wore long stockings and high-button shoes, which she was allowed to take off before they started playing.

The thing Sam hated most about the game was that Jesse insisted Sam count to five hundred before he started looking for them. To Sam that was ridiculous since the hiding places around the house were limited, and any one of them could be reached well within a count of *one* hundred. For a long time, Sam did not understand why he had to count so high; then he found Jesse and Enid under the porch one time, Jesse's flaccid little peter out and Enid's skirt up around her waist, her drawers down, and he understood. After that, he never counted to five hundred again; he only counted long enough for them to hide, then sneaked up and spied on them for a while before starting to "look" for them.

They did not do much, Jesse and Enid. Mostly just giggled and looked and, with one finger, touched. The most exciting thing Sam ever witnessed, without even knowing *why* it was exciting, was when Jesse got Enid to kiss it. After a while, spying on them became as boring as counting to five hundred.

Around ten every morning, the postman delivered the day's first mail to Mrs. Duvall's house. The mail was always for Mrs. Duvall except one letter a week that came regularly for Nell. Once when Sam asked who the letter was from, Nell had patted him on the head and replied vaguely, "Just an old friend I've known since before you were born." Usually when Nell went out to retrieve the mail, it was the signal for Mrs. Duvall to invite the other two ladies into the kitchen for lemonade or tea.

One day when Sam was thoroughly sick of playing hide-and-seek, he decided to repay Jesse for all those times he had made Sam count to five hundred. Working it out so that he "found" Jesse just as the postman arrived, making Jesse "it," Sam watched Enid hide in the shrubbery, then sneaked into the house, which was "out of bounds." With the sewing room temporarily vacated, Sam crawled under the dining room table and hid. The table, covered with a thick pad bristling with needles and laying-out patterns, had a dust cloth that hung to the floor. The dust cloth concealed a perfect hiding place.

No sooner had Sam secured himself in the peaceful dimness under the table, then his mother and grandmother returned and he heard his mother opening the envelope of her regular letter.

"What's the news this week?" Sam's grandmother asked.

"The three companies of Negro soldiers who caused the race riot in Brownsville have been given dishonorable discharges by Teddy Roosevelt," Nell told her.

"Well, that should make those people down there happy," Mrs. Duvall opined.

Nell disagreed. "If President Roosevelt had hanged them, *then* the people down there would be happy."

"My land," said Mrs. Duvall, "I can't imagine people like that."

Under the table, the boy Sam had wondered where Brownsville and "down there" was. There was no way that he could ask, however, not even later, without incurring punishment. He was prohibited from the sewing room. Mrs. Duvall and Nell frequently left material unrolled on the floor, and an energetic young boy, well, it just wouldn't do to let him have the run of the place. So Sam had to sit quietly in his hiding place and listen without any hope of understanding.

After a while he heard his grandmother ask, "Do you suppose you'll ever tell him about them?"

"Never," Nell had replied emphatically. "I never want him to know anything about them."

Sam wondered: tell who? tell what?

And who was "them"?

The two hired seamstresses returned to the room while he was mulling it over, and all of them resumed work. Sam knew that outside Jesse was hunting high and low for him, while ignoring Enid's always obvious hiding places so that Jesse could make Sam "it" again. But Jesse was going to be fooled this time. There was an hour and a half left before their mothers took Jesse and Enid home; Jesse had a lot of looking to do.

Feeling an evil satisfaction at having carried out his scheme, Sam lay down on the floor, put his head on an outstretched arm, and went to sleep.

It was years later, in the shack on a scrub prairie in Texas, that Sam recalled that incident and told Georgia about it.

"It never occurred to me until this afternoon when I was driving home," he said, "that by 'down there' Mother could have meant Texas. But she did. I looked on the roadmap and found the town named Brownsville where the race riot happened. And I think the person she didn't want to tell something to was me."

"What do you think it was she didn't want you to know?" Georgia asked.

Sam took a deep breath. "Maybe that she wasn't my real mother."

"Sam!" Georgia was shocked. "Why would you think that?"

"Because I've had two people down here admit to me that they knew my mother. That little woman Emily who works at the newspaper, and Tully over at the roadhouse. Neither one of them will discuss the matter with me any further, but they did say they knew her. As far as I know, my mother—the woman I always knew as my mother—lived all her life in Kansas City. I don't think she ever traveled anywhere. So Emily and Tully must be talking about somebody else when they refer to my mother."

"Who, for God's sake?"

Sam shook his head. "I have no idea. But I'll bet a new watch whoever she is, she'll be the link to Able Chase Patman. She'll be the reason I was named in his will. You wait, all the pieces will fall into place when I find out who she is."

"*If* you find out, you mean. So far we haven't had much success finding out *anything* from these people." Georgia paused a beat, then added pointedly, "And part of our two-week time limit is already gone."

Sam stared at her. In his excitement he had forgotten about his promise to sell the land and leave in two weeks unless there was some compelling reason to stay. Apparently Georgia did not think the discovery that he might have been adopted was sufficient. Seeing her set lips, the obvious tension in her, he realized for the first time just how badly she *did* want to leave. She did not feel the sense of ownership that he felt, was not drawn to the scrubby land by a feeling of *having* something, did not suspect, as he did, that this bequest from a stranger might be his one and only opportunity to rise above the station of ordinary.

To Georgia, all Texas represented was a succession of hostile people, a filthy shack they had made barely livable, and a diminishing chance to trade the land for a nice nest egg to take back to Kansas City.

Georgia returned his stare without blinking as Sam considered this, and he knew she was waiting to be reassured that his promise still held.

"I'll keep my word about leaving," he said.

Georgia nodded curtly. "I'm glad, Sam."

She turned away, but Sam continued to stare thoughtfully. Her reply had sounded almost like a threat.

11

Sam finally turned to C. J. Poker for help.

He walked across the prairie late one afternoon to a stand of pines from which he had seen smoke, and found the camp of the two men next to a shallow stream. Tongue, the Choctaw, was squatting by a flat rock scaling a fish. Poker was nowhere to be seen.

"Hello," Sam said to the Indian. "Is Mr. Poker around?"

"Unh," said Tongue.

"Does that mean yes or no?" Sam asked.

"Unh," he said again.

"Is that the only sound you can make?"

Tongue turned his flat face up and looked at Sam for a moment with his oddly mismatched eyes. He pursed his lips slightly as if trying to decide something. Finally he said, "Poker downstream. Fish."

"Thanks." Sam glanced at the water to see which way downstream was, and began following the bank in that direction. He found Poker about fifty yards away, tossing a baited, hand-held line into the water. " 'Afternoon, Mr. Poker."

"Howdy."

"Catching many?"

"Just enough to eat. They're your fish, you know, by rights."

"You're welcome to them," Sam said.

"Appreciate it."

"Nada," Sam replied.

Poker grinned. "You learn quick."

"Mr. Poker, may I ask you a question? It's not about the Patmans."

"Ask away."

"This land that's now mine: is it good for anything?"

"All land's good for *something,* " Poker replied. "You own a piece of land, you're dirt rich if nothing else."

Sam waited for Poker to elaborate, but for several minutes the older man remained silent. Maybe, Sam thought, old Poker was going to be as close-mouthed about the land as he was about the Patmans. If so, then Sam was prepared to let the matter drop. He would *ask* for help; he would not beg for it.

But after a moment, Poker said, "Land in this here part of Texas is good for one of two things: growing crops and grazing cattle. That's all. Ain't nobody ever found no other use for it, and ain't likely nobody ever will. Ever' once in a while some fellers from the oil companies come around and do some poking and probing and such, but none of 'em has ever found any oil. And now and again somebody'll suspect that they've got a vein of silver or copper or something else just waiting to be dug up, and there'll be more poking and probing and such; but nobody's ever found any minerals or metals worth digging neither." Poker chuckled. "One feller, believe it or not, some years back, was even convinced that there was *coal* in East Texas. Coal, for Christ's sake! I think he wound up in an asylum somewheres. No, sir, this old ground is good for jus' two things: growing crops and grazing cattle."

"What kind of crops would it grow?"

"Cotton, sweet potatoes, corn, mainly. But in order to grow *anything,* you first have got to have water. Irrigation. The only water you've got on this patch is this here little old pissant stream, and maybe one or two more like it. Not hardly enough to wet a hundred acres."

"How do the other farmers in the area irrigate?"

"Prayer, mostly. They pray for rain. With a good wet spring and early summer, they bring in good crops. Only sometimes the prayers don't work. Like this year. It ain't rained now in thirteen weeks. There ain't a decent crop in the whole county."

"What do the farmers do?" Sam asked. "How do they survive?"

"They go in hock to the banks. Mortgage the last thing they own: their future. Take most of them three years to recover from this one drought."

"Jesus," Sam said softly to himself. But Poker heard him.

"Yeah, Jesus. He's the one didn't send no rain."

"What about the cattle business?" Sam asked. "How does somebody get started in that?"

Poker shrugged, as if it were too simple to explain. "Buy bulls and heifers, produce calves, raise 'em and fatten 'em, then sell at a profit. Ain't much to it. Except nowadays it takes a heap of money to buy that first stock. If you can find anybody to sell it to you, that is."

"What do you mean?"

"Well, the big ranchers know they can sell stock to small landowners like you, and get you started in the cattle bin'ess, and the competition to their operations would be so small they wouldn't even notice it. But they also know that small ranchers have a lot more time to devote to things like breeding techniques and blood lines and experiments with feed and such. In other words, a small rancher is a lot more likely to produce prize cattle than a big rancher. If a feller's got only one kid to raise, he might make that kid a doctor or a lawyer; but if he's got a dozen kids, chances are he's gonna raise a dozen cowboys.

"Now then, if a cattle buyer goes to a few small ranchers and sees a few small herds of really prime beef, he's going to set a nice price on what he sees. Then, when he goes to the *big* rancher and finds a huge herd of cattle that ain't as prime, he'll lower the price accordin'ly. The way a big rancher sees thing, it's a lot easier *not* to sell stock to the small ranchers to start with. Solves a big problem before it even starts."

"So a big rancher wouldn't sell me any stock?"

"Not if you was to offer him ten times what it was worth. Not only that, but woe be unto anybody *else* that he hears of selling starter stock, as they call it, to any newcomer. See, there's a thing called the East Texas Range Association. Ever'body keeps an eye on ever'body else. And they ain't looking for no new members."

"What would it cost," Sam asked, "to stock a small range, provided somebody *could* buy a starter herd?"

Poker rubbed the gray stubble of his unshaven chin and considered the question. "I ain't really kept up much with the beef market lately, so I'm just speculatin' now. But I'd venture it could be done for about two thousand dollars, including supplemental feed. 'Course, on top of that a feller'd have to have money put aside to live on for about three years. Ain't no way a cattle spread's gonna break even until at least the fourth year. Can't count on no real profit until the fifth year, sometimes the sixth." Poker eyed Sam closely. "It ain't a bin'ess for a man without patience."

"Or a man without a lot of money either, sounds like," Sam countered. "What do you figure it's worth an acre? This land, I mean."

Poker pursed his lips, then said, "Six to eight dollars."

Sam nodded. "Man'd be a fool not to take fifty dollars, wouldn't he?"

The figure did not faze Poker. He calmly drew in his fishing line, wrapping it loosely around one fist. "Fifty dollars, eh? Is that what the Spences offered?"

"How'd you know it was the Spences?"

"It just figures. Her nor him neither one would want a hundred-acre chunk taken out of the big spread. Lord, I'll bet she was hot at her daddy when that will was read. Goddamn!"

Sam was now watching Poker as closely as Poker had been watching him a moment earlier. "You know Ardelle too, then?"

"I know her."

"Will you talk to me about *her?*"

"No."

"You figure you owe the Patman family loyalty for some reason?"

"Who I owe loyalty to is my bin'ess," Poker replied coolly. He walked away, heading back upstream where he and Tongue had their camp.

Sam watched him go, then turned and started home himself. He was no better off than when he *came* to C. J. Poker for help. Except that now he knew a number of new things he *couldn't* do.

How long would it be, he wondered, before something came along that he *could* do?

12

At the beginning of the second week after Sam made his promise to Georgia, Ardelle Patman Spence returned to Dane. Sam read of it in the weekly issue of the Caddo County *Enterprise*. He picked up the paper at the grocery store when he drove in to get a few things for Georgia. Back at the house, he told her about it.

"It says she and her two daughters have been touring Europe while Mr. Spence has been back east in Chicago on ranch business, and over in Kentucky and Virginia looking at thoroughbred horse stock. The daughters are Miss Faye Spence and Miss Grace Spence."

"Well," said Georgia, "I hope their return doesn't interfere with Mr. Fort buying the land." He did not reply and she saw that he was thoroughly engrossed in the newspaper story. "Where do you intend to go to buy our new touring car after you sell the land?" she asked, trying to change the subject of the Spences. She had a sudden foreboding that the Spences' return to Dane was somehow going to upset her plans to return to Kansas City. "Didn't you say there was a Willys-Overland car agency somewhere near?"

"Yes. In Longview, about fifteen miles from here." Sam drummed his fingers on the *Enterprise*, which he had spread open on the table. "I wonder what Ardelle Patman Spence would say if I dropped in to introduce myself? The Spences have a house in town, I found out, as well as the ranch."

"It probably wouldn't accomplish a thing," Georgia said, deciding she had better address the topic, since it did not appear that Sam was going to let it drop. "I think it's perfectly obvious that she chose *not* to personally get in touch with you, even though she could have done so very easily. But she chose to have her lawyer do the contacting, for whatever reason. That seems to say she didn't *want* to meet you. For you to force a meeting by going to her home seems kind of tacky."

Sam realized that Georgia was probably right; yet after reading the newspaper article, he could not get Ardelle Spence out of his mind. Over the next few days he felt *drawn* to her. Twice when he had been in Dane on errands, he had gone out of his way to drive past the big house that he had learned was the Spence town home. As if Ardelle Spence might see him from the porch, and for some reason wave him over. After encountering so much hostility nearly everywhere he went in Dane, Sam *yearned* to be welcomed somewhere, by someone. Yet he could not bring himself to simply walk up and knock on her door, unexpected and uninvited. But he could not put the matter out of his mind either.

Sam's promise to Georgia weighed heavily on him. This was the second week, and by its end he was bound to accept the offer for the land, buy a touring car in which she could comfortably travel, and leave. If he had to keep that promise, it would most likely remove him forever from Texas, and end his opportunity *ever* to learn anything more about Able Chase Patman, and whether the mother he had always known *was* his mother. For several days after reading the newspaper article, Sam was in a constant quandary, unable to find a solution.

Finally, just two days before Georgia's deadline, his problem was solved for him. While driving by the Spence home still another time, he saw on the porch a young girl he assumed to be one of the Spence daughters. He did not know which girl it was, Faye or Grace, since he had never seen either of them, but as he was driving past the young lady smiled and waved at him from her chair. It's fate, Sam thought at once, snatching at this sign. He was *meant* to stop. And stop he did.

Pulling the Hudson over to the curb, Sam got out and walked up the sidewalk to the house, wishing desperately that he had worn a necktie that day. But at least his shirt and suit were clean. The house, almost a mansion it was so large, was set back from the street behind an immaculately manicured lawn and flower beds that looked incongruous in the middle of the drought-stricken little community.

When Sam got to the steps of the porch, actually a veranda that belted the house, the Spence girl, wearing cool blue summer seersucker, put a hand to her lips in chagrin.

"Oh, my," she said. "I *am* sorry. I could have sworn you were Edward Apperson, a classmate of mine. He has a car *exactly* like that."

At that moment the screen door opened and an older woman, perfectly coiffed, in an expensive daydress, with a silk fan in her hand, came onto the porch and when she saw Sam, stopped and drew in her breath. Without taking her eyes off Sam, she said to her daughter, "Faye, go into the house, please."

"Mother, what's the matter?"

"Go into the house, I said!" There was no "please" this time; it was a command, to be instantly obeyed, and the girl did so at once. Then the woman came over to the top of the porch steps and looked down at Sam. "I am Ardelle Patman Spence," she said precisely. "Is there something I can do for you?"

"Mrs. Spence, my name is Samuel Sheridan. I'm—"

"I know who you are. What is it you want here?"

"I don't want anything, really," Sam told her. For some reason, he held out both of his hands, almost as if to plead or petition. "I was just driving by and your daughter waved at me—"

"By mistake, I believe I heard her say."

"Yes, ma'am, by mistake," he admitted. Sam cleared his throat nervously. The woman's very direct gaze bore down on him; her firm, unsmiling mouth was silently expectant, her proud chin slightly raised. Sam sensed at once that he was as welcome here as he had been nearly everywhere else in Dane: which was not welcome at all. But he had come this far, and if he was ever going to assert himself he had better do it now. "Mrs. Spence, I'm the Sam Sheridan who was named in your late father's will—"

"My father named a number of people in his will. For example, he named several Mexican house servants who had been with our family for many years. He named some woman in Dallas who had been a paramour of his. He named the surviving families of three men who had suffered fatal accidents while in the employ of the Patman Ranch. He named numerous others. My father was a generous man, Mr. Sheridan. If he named you in his will, you were merely one of many." She tilted her head ever so slightly. "Do you understand?"

Do you understand that you are nothing? Nobody?

"Yes, ma'am, I believe I do," Sam said, his tone quietly even. Ardelle Patman Spence's meaning was clear. Sam felt he should be turning red from anger or embarrassment or humiliation; instead there was the odd sensation that all the blood had drained from his face, that he was turning pale and cold. The woman continued to stand there, a queen on her raised throne, looking down on a peasant to whom she had just explained the difference between royalty and commoners. Obviously she was waiting for the peasant to leave. "Please excuse me for disturbing you, Mrs. Spence," Sam said in a controlled voice. He wanted to add something more, something that would hurt. *Now that I've met you, I'd rather not know anything about your father.* But his resentment was such that he wanted to get out of her sight as quickly as possible—and get her out of his as well. So he merely punctuated his apology with a curt nod and walked away.

All the way to his car, Sam wondered if Ardelle Spence had gone back inside or if she was still standing there watching him.

But he refused to look back and see.

13

White-faced, jaw clenched, Sam drove away from the Spence home and rounded the first corner with tires screeching. On the steering wheel, his knuckles were as white as his face. He drove through Dane and out the Kilgore highway. At the first dirt road, he turned off the highway and parked. For a few minutes he just sat there, still gripping the wheel, willing himself to calm down from the rage Ardelle Spence had ignited in him.

In a little while, he was able to take a deep breath and lean back. Then he started thinking about whether he should tell Georgia or not. As a rule, he was nearly always completely honest with Georgia, rarely deceiving her even by omission. But he was not sure whether he *could* tell her about his meeting with Ardelle Spence. It was so humiliating: the woman had relegated him to the status of Mexican house servants and other nonentities whom old Able Patman had named in his will. Not only that, but she had let him know clearly, by not inviting him into her home, that he was an unwelcome visitor. Sam was not sure he could even talk about the incident, he was so mortified by it.

Nor was he convinced that it mattered. Ardelle Spence's treatment of him today had been the final insult as far as staying in Texas was concerned. He and Georgia would definitely leave now; dispose of their interest in Texas altogether; leave it behind them like the bad dream it was. That being so, it really would not make any difference whether Georgia knew of his last ignominious experience or not.

With his mind made up and their departure from Dane now assured, Sam felt better. The burden of decision was lifted, relieved by what now seemed to be their only choice. Glancing out the side window, Sam saw up the highway a little place he had driven past numerous times but never patronized. Hitchman's, it was called; a roadhouse, much smaller than Tully's and closer to town, that sold bootleg liquor for consumption on or off the premises. Sam had not had a drink of hard liquor since the previous New Year's Eve when he and Georgia had attended an American Legion dance across the river on the Missouri side of Kansas City. Prior to that, he had not had a drink of *any* kind, except bootleg beer, since Prohibition began the previous year. Now he suddenly craved one. Getting out of the car, he left it and walked the short distance to the roadhouse. He would buy a bottle, he decided, and stop by Tully's place and have a farewell drink with him. Tully, after all, had been the only person who had tried, to any extent at all, to make him aware of the Patman-Spence situation.

At Hitchman's, Sam purchased a quart of bootleg rye produced in New Orleans, Louisiana. Maybe, Sam thought on his way back to the car, he and Georgia would take a little vacation to New Orleans before going back to Kansas City. No reason why they shouldn't have a little fun; they'd have money enough, and Sam wanted to make it up to Georgia for all she had been made to endure in this goddamned place called Texas.

Back in the car, Sam opened the bottle, took a hefty swig, and put the brown sack on the seat beside him. On his way to Tully's, he changed his mind about the farewell drink. Tully's wife Reba was sure to be there, and sure to be annoyed by his presence again, as she had been when Sam barged into the roadhouse kitchen over her protests. If they don't like me for one reason, they don't like me for another. Everybody line up and pick out your reason for disliking Sam Sheridan. He reached for the bottle and took another drink. No, he would not stop at Tully's; after Ardelle Spence, he did not need Reba Samuel.

The rye began to warm his insides. He took still another pull. He very much wanted to share it with someone friendly. Not Georgia, however; she was too far along with the baby and it would make her tipsy. Sam had brought home two bottles of bootleg beer one night the previous week, and just part of one had made Georgia practically drunk. Sam could only imagine what hard liquor would do. Still, he wanted to drink with *someone*.

He thought of old Poker and the Indian, camped by the stream on his place. Sam had not considered sharing his bottle with *two* people, but now he thought why not? Tongue, the Choctaw, probably did not drink much anyway. Sam recalled something about there being a law against providing Indians with whiskey, but he was sure it was probably outdated. Especially since, legally, people weren't supposed to have liquor to provide.

Before he came to his own turnoff, Sam drove onto a dirt road that cut from the Kilgore highway on an angle to the creek where Poker and Tongue were camped. The road took him to within fifty yards of their site. Sam left the car there and, bottle in hand, walked the rest of the way. Making his way through the slim pungent pines, he pulled the cork out of the bottle and tossed it away as he downed another swallow. Smiling, he looked at the bottle and thought: they made pretty good mash down there in New Orleans, Louisiana.

Next to the stream, Sam found Poker lying in the shade, dozing lightly. Tongue was sitting nearby with one of his moccasins off, rubbing the bottom with a stick in an attempt to clean what looked like mud off it. Poker awoke at the first sound of Sam's footsteps and sat up as Sam walked into camp. "Celebratin' something?" he asked, glancing at the bottle.

"You bet," Sam replied, smiling. "Celebrating the end of a very unpleasant visit to a very unpleasant place. No offense, you understand."

"None taken," Poker assured him. "So you're packing it in, eh? Quitting."

Sam frowned. "Quitting? Hell, I never got started. This place had me whipped before I got here. Have a drink."

Poker reached up for the bottle and took a drink. Sam noticed that he did not wipe off the mouth of the bottle before drinking. Back in Kansas City, people always wiped a bottle off before drinking after someone else. This, however, was not Kansas City. This was goddamned *Texas*.

"Thanks," Poker said, handing the bottle back. Sam knew Tongue was watching them. If he offered Tongue a drink and he accepted, it would mean that the bottle would then pass back to Sam and he would either have to wipe the bottle off, as Poker had *not* done, or drink after Tongue. Sam could not help wondering if drinking after an Indian was the same as drinking after a Negro. Indians and Negroes were different, but neither was *white;* Sam had never drunk after anyone but a white man, and only then after wiping off the bottle.

Poker was watching him and Sam knew he was waiting to see if Sam offered a drink to Tongue. Stepping over to where the Choctaw was working, Sam extended the bottle. "Drink?"

The cross-eyed Indian studied Sam briefly, glanced at Poker, and took the bottle. He drank, nodded his head, and said, "Unh."

"You're welcome," Sam said, as Tongue handed the bottle back to him. "What's that all over your shoes? I mean, your moccasins."

"Sulphur mud," Tongue said, resuming his cleaning. "Bad shit."

Sam went back to where Poker was and sat down beside him. It was his own turn to drink. Sam knew. He also knew that Poker was still observing him curiously. He's testing my mettle, Sam thought. That takes a lot of goddamned nerve. Living on *my* place, fishing *my* stream, eating *my* fish—and he's got the goddamned nerve to measure *me?* Sam met Poker's eyes for a moment, considered challenging him, decided against it, and—without wiping it off—raised the bottle to his lips, thinking: The Indian's just another man.

73

After Sam drank, Poker reached over and took the bottle without it being offered. "You're all right, Samuel Sheridan," he said.

"I am," Sam agreed. "I am all right. And it's a goddamned shame people around here don't know it." He watched Tongue for a minute and asked, "What's sulphur mud?"

"It's like reg'lar mud," Poker explained, "except that the water mixed in it has a high sulphur content. Seems to make the mud thicker. Hardens faster. And smells funny."

"Smells funny, all right," Sam said, taking the bottle back, "but it's not a sulphur smell."

"What is it then?"

"Not sulphur," Sam repeated. Rising, a bit unsteady now, he went over to Tongue and handed him the bottle again. In return he took the blackened moccasin from the Choctaw's hand and held it to his nose. Nodding his head, he said, "I've smelled this smell before."

"Where at?" Poker asked.

"In France and Germany, during the war. Over there, they don't run their trains on coal like we do; they run them on something like gasoline: they call it diesel fuel. It comes from oil, I think." Sam shook the soiled moccasin at Poker. "And it smells 'zactly like this."

"You sure?" Poker asked, frowning.

"I smelled this smell every time I was in a railroad depot over there," Sam assured him. "This isn't a sulphur smell; this is an oil smell." Now Sam frowned also. "The other day when we talked about what this land was good for, didn't you say it had been explored for oil?"

"It has," Poker declared. "Two or three times Able Patman gave teams of oil surveyors permission to walk all over different parts of his spread. I know for a fact that Sinclair has tested this very section we're sittin' on for oil."

"And they didn't find any trace of it?"

"You don't see no derricks, do you?"

Sam was suddenly becoming sober. Something warned him that this moment was no time to be drunk. His head rapidly clearing, Sam turned to Tongue. "Where did you get this mud on your moccasins?"

"Bog," said Tongue. "Between Patman range and Choctaw land."

"That'd be over yonder," Poker said, "to the west." He glanced

74

irritably at Tongue. "I done told you a dozen times, this ain't Patman range no more. It's Spence land now."

"No, it isn't," Sam corrected Poker. "Not this piece of it. Right now this is *Sheridan* land. How far is the bog from here, Tongue?"

"Half of one mile."

"Will you take me to it?"

"Unh."

Tongue put the moccasin back on his foot, took a drink from the bottle, and started off, Sam right behind him. When they were a few yards from camp, Sam turned back to Poker. "Well, come on," he said impatiently.

"Didn't know if I was invited or not," Poker said, sulking.

"Goddamn it, Poker, come on!"

Poker hurried to catch up. "Call me Draw," he said to Sam. "My friends all calls me Draw."

The three oddly matched men trudged across the prairie, passing the bottle back and forth.

It was after dark by the time Sam got home.

"My god, Sam, I've been worried sick," Georgia said. "Where the hell have you been?"

Sam took her by the shoulders and sat her down on a chair. "Georgia, listen to me. I have to make a trip to a place called Palestine, Texas. It's about a hundred miles from here. Poker and Tongue are going with me. There's a small oil field down there called Boggy Creek. Poker has a friend that's a wildcatter down there—"

"A what?"

"Wildcatter. It's somebody that goes out on his own looking for oil. Anyway, this friend of Poker's has been around oil and oil fields most of his life and knows all about them."

"Sam, I don't understand what you're talking about. Palestine, Boggy Creek, oil fields. What in the world is going on?"

Sam Sheridan swallowed and gripped his wife's hands. "Georgia, I think there may be oil on our land. Think of it, Georgia. *Oil!* On *our* land."

Georgia's excitement was fleeting. "Really, Sam! No, wait a minute. What makes you think so?"

He sat back on his heels in front of her chair and told her about the bog. "It's small, no bigger than that tabletop there. And it's mostly covered with scrub brush, so it's natural to walk around it if anybody's going that way. Tongue just accidentally stepped in the edge of it with one foot on the way back from visiting his people on the Choctaw land. But I've seen it, Georgia. And smelled it. I think it's an oil bog."

"Hmmm. Speaking of smells, Sam Sheridan, do I detect the smell of whiskey somewhere?"

Sam put his hands on her swollen belly and smiled. "I bought a bottle of rye," he admitted.

"I see. Now you've found oil. Pity you didn't buy two bottles; you might have struck gold." Her expression turned serious. "What about your promise, Sam?"

"The two weeks aren't up," he reminded her.

"They will be tomorrow."

Sam let go of her and stood up. "I've got to do this, Georgia. I'd be a damn fool if I didn't. I hope you understand."

"I don't have much choice, do I?"

Sam shook his head. "No." He went to a row of nails on the wall and got a jacket and hat. "Can I have some money for gas? I spent my last dollar on the whiskey."

"What if I say no?"

"Then I'll steal gas. I'll siphon it."

Georgia got her pocketbook and gave him five dollars.

"Will you be all right?" he asked.

"A woman seven months pregnant all alone in a shack on the Texas prairie, completely defenseless, without a friend for a thousand miles—yes, Sam, I'll be just fine."

Sam smiled tentatively. "If I didn't think you'd be all right, I wouldn't leave you." He kissed her lightly on the lips. "You won't be sorry I went, you'll see."

"I'm already sorry."

Georgia watched from the porch as Sam drove off into the night to get Poker and Tongue.

And you'll be sorry too, someday, she thought.

14

The next morning at dawn, Sam's Hudson was parked on the side of the road at the entrance to the Boggy Creek oil field near Palestine. Sam was slumped behind the wheel, Tongue doubled up on the backseat, both asleep. Draw Poker was outside the car, sitting on the fender, collar turned up against the cool morning air, smoking a roll-your-own, watching for his friend. Half a dozen roughnecks, as the oil field laborers were called, had already trudged past on their way to begin their twelve-hour workday that would pay them, in cash, three dollars. Draw had asked the first one that arrived if old Pop Joyner was still drilling for Boggy Creek, and the roughneck said he was.

Presently, when Draw recognized his friend's odd gait far down the road, he smiled to himself, recalling what he had told Sam on the trip down. "Ferdinand Joyner," he had drawled, "is the most bowlegged man you're ever liable to meet. There's those who say he couldn't stop a pig in a three-foot-wide alley; others who say he's the only man in Texas who can get out of both sides of a truck at the same time. He don't really walk, he rolls; like one of them old saltwater sailors on land. But he knows oil, you can bet your bottom dollar on that. He's been around oil and oil fields near 'bout all his life. There ain't a oil field in Texas where they don't tell stories about Pop Joyner."

"I'd like to hear some of them," Sam said. He did not ask outright about Pop Joyner, in case Draw was reluctant to discuss him, as he had been Able Chase Patman. But apparently Draw was not, since he started telling at once the life story of Ferdinand "Pop" Joyner.

At the age of fifteen in Titusville, Pennsylvania, Joyner had been employed as a helper by a railroad conductor named Ed Drake, who had recently been fired by the New Haven and Hartford line. Drake, an avid reader, had studied the history of the petroleum discovery less than four decades earlier in the Russian port of Baku. Because he had found in his backyard a phenomenon similar to the so-called eternal fire of natural gas holes in Baku, Drake was convinced there was oil there. With water-well–drilling equipment, he dug seventy feet into the ground and struck oil. Soon he was bringing it to the surface at the rate of one hundred gallons per day. The following year a young clerk named John D. Rockefeller was sent by a group of businessmen to investigate the potential of Drake's discovery. Rockefeller reported that it had little future; then he borrowed money and bought a small lard refinery to begin marketing the petroleum as an energy source. His first employee had been the young Pop Joyner.

Joyner worked for Rockefeller for four years, throughout the Civil War, which he considered nonsense. In 1864 he quit to return to exploration. He was part of the team that established the four wells in Pithole, Pennsylvania. When his former employer Rockefeller formed Standard Oil, Joyner went back to work for him for a while; but Rockefeller kept trying to make a manager and executive out of him, and soon Joyner left again. In 1871, at the age of twenty-six, he was in Rangoon exploring for Burmah Oil Company. While there he fathered a child by a Burmese girl. Because he did not want the responsibility of a family, he decided to move on; but he would faithfully send money for the child wherever he went.

Five years later, Joyner was back in the United States working a drill in California for Pacific Coast Oil. Then he went to Tidewater Oil, then to Sunoco. For twenty years he worked nearly every field —wet *and* dry—that opened in the United States. He also fathered two more children, leaving both behind as he followed the flow of oil from field to field. To these children, like his Burmese child, he would send money every month.

In 1892, Joyner left America again to work for two brothers who had made enough money in the seashell business to go into oil. Using newly designed tankers, they began shipping oil through the Suez Canal to Singapore for distribution in the Far East. When the brothers had difficulty deciding on a name for their company, Joyner, who was fascinated by some of the large colorful seashells they still had on hand, suggested they call the new firm Shell Oil Company and use a seashell as its symbol.

The following year, Joyner was back home again, working a field in Toledo when oil was struck there. Then he moved to Texas where vast exploration was going on, and was working the Corsicana field when it was brought in. Joyner remained in Texas ten years, eventually working for Gulf Coast Oil as a driller in Beaumont. He was one of the men who fought the Spindletop well when it flowed wild for nine days before being brought under control.

At the turn of the century, more than half the world's oil output was still coming from Russia's Baku field. Joyner, now in his fifties, had never forgotten the stories Drake had told him about Baku, and when, in 1901, Ludwig Nobel, whose brother Alfred had invented dynamite, came to America looking for men to help further expand the Baku field, Joyner volunteered at once. He stayed in Russia two years, fathered another child by a woman thirty years his junior, and like the others supported it when he returned to America.

Back in Texas for the second time, Joyner worked the Sour Lake field, owned by a small group calling itself the Texas Company. Most of the workers referred to it simply as "Tex-Co." Finally the owners decided to officially shorten the name to "Texaco." After Sour Lake came in, Joyner wandered north to the Osage Indian Territory in Oklahoma. He was sixty years old now, but still a vigorous, virile little man, and he fathered his fifth child by a Shawnee woman half his age. Adding her name to his growing list of dependents, Joyner moved on to the site of another Oklahoma strike, a place called Tulsey Town. While he was there, the town fathers decided that the name was too "country sounding," and changed it to Tulsa.

In 1908, Joyner made his last trip abroad as part of a team employed by the shah of Persia to sink a well in Masjid-i-Salaman. In May of that year, they tapped into the world's largest oil reserve. When Joyner finished his job there, instead of returning home he took a contract with Turkish Petroleum to help develop a field discovered in Mesopotamia. He remained abroad until the Great War started in 1914, then at the age of sixty-nine came home for the last time.

"During the war," Draw told Sam, bringing Pop's story up to date, "he worked in Bartlesville, Oklahoma, for two brothers who started a company next to that new highway, Route 66. They added their family name to the highway number and called it the Phillips 66 company. Since the war, why, Pop has wandered back and forth between Oklahoma and Texas, working wherever he feels like working. Hell, he's such a legend in the oil business, he can sign on at any field he wants to, for any job he wants to do. Most companies would put him on the payroll just to have him hang around their field for good luck. But Pop can't be near an oil rig without putting his finger into its operation; wherever he is, he'll be earning his keep."

Draw was proved right the next morning at the Boggy Creek field near Palestine, Texas, when shortly after dawn he saw the bowlegged old man, lunch pail in hand, trooping along to work among men a quarter his age.

Smiling, Draw slid off the fender of Sam's car and walked down the road to meet him.

Sitting in the front seat of the Hudson next to Sam Sheridan, with Poker and the Indian in the backseat, old Pop Joyner, now seventy-six, removed the lid from a Mason jar and sniffed curiously at its contents. Draw and Tongue had collected the sample, scooping it from the soft wet earth in the boggy ground that Tongue had stepped in the previous day. It looked like mud, mostly, with some purplish streaks of mesa clay, a little red gritty sand, and an occasional gaseous bubble of gray sulphurous matter. After Pop Joyner sniffed it a few times, he poured a gob of it onto the inside of the jar lid and commenced touching it in a variety of ways: first poking it cautiously as if it were alive and could bite; then gathering a bit between thumb and forefinger and spreading it into paste; then digging around into its mass like a surgeon exploring for a tumor in a kidney. Finally, to everyone's surprise, he took some on one finger and tasted it, actually smacking his lips in the process. Finally he nodded his head and winked at Draw.

"You've got it, fellers. You've got yourself oil."

Sam gripped the old man's arm. "Are you sure?"

Pop Joyner shook Sam's hand off and grunted, which was as close as he would come to dignifying *that* question with an answer. Was he *sure?* Shit, he had the goddamned stuff in his *veins* by now.

"Pop," said Draw, "can you tell how deep it might be?"

"Where's it at?"

"Caddo County. South of Dane."

Pop frowned. "Pete Spence's land?"

"My land now," Sam said. "A hundred acres, anyway."

80

"Does Pete Spence know you all are looking to drill on that land?"

"I told you," Sam said testily, "where we're thinking of drilling is *my* land. It's none of Pete Spence's business."

Pop rubbed his mouth with the back of his hand. "Ever'thing that happens in Caddo County is Pete Spence's business. Draw can tell you that. Anyhow, the geologists have been all over Caddo. They say there ain't no oil up there."

"We don't care what the geologists say, Pop," Draw told him. "What *you* say is good enough for us. How deep?"

Pop fooled with another gob of the stuff between his thumb and forefinger. "Maybe thirty-five hunnerd feet."

Draw nodded. "What's the price of getting down that far these days?"

"Prob'ly eleven, twelve thousand." Pop glanced at them: an old range boss, an Indian, a city feller. They probably didn't have twelve *hundred,* much less twelve thousand.

"You want a job?" Sam asked him.

"You aiming to buck Pete Spence?"

"If I have to."

"You got the money to operate?"

"I'll get it. You want a job? Yes or no."

Draw leaned forward, put a hand on the old wildcatter's shoulder, and said, "We need you, Pop. The three of us, why, we don't know shit about drilling for oil. But we're willing to work if you'll show us what to do."

"I don't come cheap, Draw, I'll tell you that up front. I get five dollars a day for rigging and field work, ten for drilling."

Draw looked at Sam, who nodded. "You got it," Draw said to Pop.

The men shook hands all around.

"Drive me back into town to the boardinghouse and I'll get my gear," Pop said.

Smiling, Sam started the engine and drove off with a lively toot of his horn.

15

Sam wore his best suit, nicest shirt and tie, and polished his shoes to go uptown to see Claud Maye, the president of the Merchants Bank of Dane. As he was being shown into Maye's office, he dearly wished he had a gold watch chain to string across the front of his vest. Somehow the presence or absence of such a chain always seemed to differentiate the successes from the failures in the world. He would have to remember to keep his coat buttoned during the meeting.

"How do, Mr. Sheridan," said Maye when Sam came in. "Have a chair, if you please. These gentlemen," he indicated three other men, "are Mr. Zack Locklear and Mr. Quinnie Frazier, who along with myself make up the bank's loan committee; and Dewitt Tucker, my junior loan officer." The latter was a younger man, around Sam's age. Sam noticed at once that he had no watch chain either. When Sam shook Tucker's hand, he did so with a grip and an enthusiasm that he did not put into his token handshakes with Claud Maye and the other two. "You telephoned that you were interested in a loan, Mr. Sheridan," Maye said. "Tell us the purpose and the amount, will you, please?"

"Ten thousand dollars," Sam said. "For the purpose of drilling for oil on property I own south of town." Sam was surprised that, though nervous inside, his voice was calm and businesslike. And he was very alert to everything in the office, such as the quick glances exchanged between Claud Maye and the two loan committee members.

"That would be the land you recently inherited from the late Mr. Able Patman?"

"Yes. One hundred acres. I would naturally expect to put the land up as collateral."

Maye smiled a scant, humorless smile. "You're aware, of course, that the land is worth only a fraction of that amount."

"I'm aware that it's *valued* at only a fraction of that," Sam countered. "It could be *worth* many times that if there's oil on it." God, how he wished Georgia could have heard him say that; it was a *perfect* reply. Sam caught a hint of amusement in the expression of Dewitt Tucker. He knew instinctively that Tucker was laughing with him, not at him.

"Mr. Sheridan," said Zack Locklear, "ever' big oil comp'ny in Texas has had experienced men in Caddo County looking to see if there was any oil here. And not a one of them comp'nies has come back to drill. What makes you think you've found oil when they couldn't?" Locklear, like everyone else except Sam, pronounced the subject of their conversation "awl."

"There's a small bog," Sam explained, "on the boundary between my property and the Choctaw land—"

"Hold on," Quinnie Frazier said, "you mean you're going to have to go partners with the *Indians* in this?" There was a definite distaste in his tone.

"Either that, or maybe buy or lease that part of the land that the bog is on," Sam said.

"You can't do that, Mr. Sheridan," Claud Maye pointed out, with an amused glance at the others. Unlike the amusement in Dewitt Tucker's expression, this was amusement *at* Sam, and he knew it at once. "The Choctaw are prohibited by federal law from selling any of their land out there for ninety-nine years from the date it was ceded to them. They've had it since 1879, which is forty-two years. That makes fifty-seven years to go. I don't think you'd care to wait that long, would you?"

"No, I wouldn't." Sam felt himself tightening up; Maye was ridiculing him. "I *am* new to the area, gentlemen," he said quietly, "you all know that, so I am not as knowledgeable as you all about what I can and cannot do. But I *will* find a way to get around the Indian problem. I hope you won't let it influence your decision."

"Go on with your explanation of why you think there's oil under that bog," said Locklear.

"Certainly. I've taken a sample of matter from the bog and shown it to a gentleman who is an expert in petroleum exploration—"

"And who is that?" Maye asked.

"Mr. Ferdinand Joyner."

"With what company?"

"None at the moment. That is, he left the Boggy Creek field to come to work for me. But he's worked for nearly every major oil firm in existence, as well as exploring on his own—"

"Wildcatting," said Frazier. From his tone, he classed it somewhere near stealing or, at best, begging.

Claud Maye sat back in his chair, fingering his watch chain. "Mr. Sheridan, I'm sure you can see the problem your request poses for us. This bank is a local business that must answer to its partners for all aspects of its operations."

"Is Ardelle Spence one of its partners?" Sam asked bluntly.

"No, she isn't, Mr. Sheridan," Maye told him, "but her husband, Mr. Pete Spence, is. That, however, would have no bearing on our decision."

"I doubt that."

"Doubt it all you like, Mr. Sheridan. The fact of the matter is, you have inadequate collateral, and are a poor loan risk besides; I don't believe you even have a job, or *any* source of income. Take your request to a bank in Longview or Kilgore, if you like. I'm sure they'll tell you the same thing."

Sam rose from his chair. "But if I *had* a job, gentlemen; if I *had* adequate collateral; if I *was* a good loan risk: you still wouldn't make a loan to me, would you?"

"We can't project what we would or wouldn't do under speculative circumstances—"

"Say it, goddamn it!" Sam shouted, leaning over the desk and pounding his fist on it. He put his face inches from Claud Maye's face. "I couldn't get a loan from this bank under *any* circumstances. Be a man and admit it!" he demanded.

Maye shook his head very slowly. "All right, Mr. Sheridan. No, you couldn't. Under any circumstances."

Sam straightened. The heel of his hand hurt like hell, but he did not regret hitting the desk. For once, just once, he had made one of the Texas sons of bitches admit that something was rigged against him; that *everything* was rigged against him: not only the bank but the whole goddamned town. As far as he was concerned, there was no such thing as fair treatment on a man-to-man basis. Sam stared at each member of the loan committee: Claud Maye, Zack Locklear, Quinnie Frazier. He memorized their faces, their names, thinking: *Someday, you bastards.*

"Thank you for your time, gentlemen," he said evenly. "I won't forget your consideration."

"Please don't," said Claud Maye, with a smirk that said he knew the words were a veiled threat, and did not care.

Sam felt himself turning red with anger and embarrassment as he left.

Draw, Tongue, and Pop Joyner sat at the table in Sam's little shack of a house and Georgia served them coffee while Sam told them about his visit to the bank. They were not surprised.

"Is there any other way to raise money around here?" Sam asked the three of them. "Could I sell all the land except the acreage the bog is on?"

"Maybe," Draw said, "but that still wouldn't bring what you need."

"You can always look for backers," Pop suggested. "Speculators who'd advance you money against a share of the well if you hit. Damn large share, too, I'll tell you." He paused a beat, then added, "Or, you can take on working partners."

Sam studied the old man. "Like who?"

"Like me," Pop said. "I've got a little money put by. Wouldn't mind investing it in a well like this one."

Sam felt a slight surge of exhilaration. When Joyner first told them he thought they had oil, Sam realized it was just an opinion. And one on which had been based a job offer to Joyner, which, if he suspected it to be pending, could have influenced his judgment.

But this was different. This was the old man offering to back up his opinion with his own money. This, to Sam, was the difference between an IOU and a gold coin. Sam looked at Draw and said, "What do you think?"

Draw shrugged. "Why ask me?"

"Because I need advice. And I trust you."

Draw's hawklike face conveyed obvious delight and he nodded curtly. "Well then, since you ask, I think Pop's got a hell of a good idea. Matter of fact, I've got a few dollars myself if you want two partners."

"I might even be able to use three," Sam said, looking at Tongue.

The Choctaw shook his head. "No money. Tongue go." He rose to leave, but Draw stopped him.

"You don't need money, Tongue. You can give services." Turning to Sam he reasoned, "We got to have somebody to bargain with the Choctaw about the bog being part on their land. It'd be worth a share for him to do it."

"That's fine with me," Sam said.

"You can be a partner with us without money," Draw said to the Indian. "We need you to be our voice to your people. Will you join us?"

Tongue pointed to Sam. "He must ask."

"All right," said Sam. "I ask you, Tongue, to be my partner, along with these two men here. I need your services and will be proud to have you join us."

"Unh," Tongue said and returned to the table.

Later, after they left, Georgia sat down with Sam and poured herself some coffee. "This means we're not going home, doesn't it?" she asked quietly.

"It could mean that," Sam told her. "Nothing is certain yet. We don't know whether we'll have enough money to get started or not. And we aren't a hundred percent sure that the Choctaw will agree to let us use their land. But if those things work out, then, no, we won't be leaving." Sam leaned over the table eagerly. "Honey, this is a chance for us to *be* somebody."

"I'm already somebody, Sam. I'm your wife, and soon I'll be the mother of your child."

"You know what I mean, Georgia," he said wearily, his eagerness evaporating. He sat back in his chair again. "This is an opportunity like we may never get again. An opportunity for us to get rich, to be able to do things for ourselves and our baby that we never imagined we'd be able to." He stared at his hands, curled around the coffee cup. "And it's a chance for me to *do* something, Georgia. To do something that matters; something besides selling shirts and socks in a J. C. Penney store. I'm sorry if you don't understand that. Maybe you've never wanted to be something you weren't."

Georgia thought about that. It was not true, of course. She had frequently wanted to be something she was not. When she was a virgin, she wanted to be an experienced woman. When she was an experienced woman, she wanted to be a *very* experienced woman; she wanted to do everything there was to do, with everyone who came along. After a while, when she *was* very experienced, she wanted to shed her reputation and start clean, so to speak. Regain her virginity, was what Tussy Fowler said she was trying to do. Failing that, she wanted to be married, preferably to someone who was not aware of her soiled reputation. And now that she *was* married, she wanted to live her life safe and protected, far away from any hint of gossip.

But not like this. Not in a shack on the prairie, ostracized from the nearest town, with no girl friends, no movies, no radio, no nothing. This was *too* far away from gossip.

"I'd rather we went home, Sam," she said now, "like we planned to do. I'd rather we sold the land, bought a car, took a vacation in New Orleans like you said we would, then went on back to Kansas City and started a new life there: you, me, and the baby. I don't need to be rich; I just need to be happy. But we'll stay if you want to stay, Sam. Just please stop saying you're doing it for *us.*"

"But I *am,* honey."

"No, you're not. I just got through saying that I don't want it and I don't need it. If we stay, Sam, it's for you, not us."

Sam knew by her tone of voice that Georgia had made up her mind. There would be no convincing her that what he was doing was for the best, for everyone: him, her, the baby. She was different now than when this episode in Texas had begun. Once he had committed himself to come to Texas, she had been behind him one hundred percent; she supported his decision, his plans, and stuck by him all the way. Until recently, when the pressure, loneliness, and uncertainty of the place began to haunt her. Now she was letting him know that she was no longer a partner in the venture, but now a subordinate, her continued participation mandatory instead of voluntary.

If that was the way she wanted it, Sam decided, then so be it. As long as he was able to stay and go after the oil; that's what was important. He was just sorry that Georgia could not see it that way.

"You'll feel differently about it before long," he said, trying for a last bit of reassurance.

But she refused even to address that possibility. Instead, she rose and said, "I'm going to bed now, Sam. I'm tired. Very tired."

Sam nodded and watched her cross to the dark corner where they slept. For the first time in their marriage, he had the feeling that he was beginning to lose her. He wanted to go over and put his arms around her, to tell her that nothing in the world was as important to him as she was. But he could not.

The thought of the oil would not let him.

16

The next afternoon, Sam and the others drove over to the community center on the Choctaw land and Tongue took them to a tribal council meeting that he had requested on their behalf. It was held in one of several ramshackle corrugated storehouses that the federal government had built on the land as part of the tribe's agreement to relocate there from Arkansas. The army corps of engineers had done the construction, and it was obvious from the condition of the structures that the army's main objective had been completion of the project as quickly as possible. The frames of the buildings were crooked, causing doors and windows to slant and not open or close properly, and on one side the entire wall was two inches above the foundation so that prairie dirt constantly blew inside. And, of course, the warehouses were empty because the government had not helped the Choctaw cultivate the land, as agreed, nor provided foodstuffs in lieu of cultivation.

The tribal council, called the Beloved Men, was made up of three members, but it was clear at once that all the important decisions were made by the eldest of that trio, an old Indian named Natchay, who was a descendant of the original Natchez tribe that had been absorbed into the Choctaw after a massacre by the French a hundred years earlier. Tongue had explained on the way over that Natchay was the elder statesman of the small tribe and that, even though a member of the Techantas, the royal family, technically ruled the tribe, it was Natchay who guided them in their day-to-day existence.

When Tongue led Sam and the others into the pathetically constructed warehouse, the Beloved Men were waiting, sitting on upturned empty boxes, smoking roll-your-owns. As Tongue introduced Sam, Draw, and Pop Joyner, the Indians rose and gave each a formal nod of greeting but did not shake hands.

"The older Indians don't touch white men," Draw whispered. "Tongue says it's because of the syphilis the soldiers spread to Choctaw women in the early days back in Mississippi. They're afraid we still might have it."

Following introductions, the white men were invited to join the Beloved Men on upturned boxes, and more cigarettes were rolled. After they had all smoked for a while, Tongue rose to stand in the center of the group and explain why they were there. He spoke in English, with an articulateness that amazed Sam. Gone were the "unh" sounds and other grunts that he used among white men. Sam shook his head in wonder. Was *nothing* in Texas the way it seemed?

Tongue's presentation did not take long; he talked for about ten minutes, occasionally gesturing toward Sam and the others, twice toward himself, frequently toward the Beloved Men. When he was finished, he returned to sit with his friends, more cigarettes were rolled, and another period of smoking ensued.

"What now?" Sam whispered to Draw.

"We wait for old Natchay to consider our proposal," Draw whispered back.

After he had smoked two more cigarettes, Natchay rose to address them. The old man looked to Sam to be easily as old as Pop Joyner, perhaps older: his brown face had deep rolls of wrinkles, like earth plowed in furrows, and his nose was as flat and wide as Tongue's. When he spoke, his voice had a rasp, the kind caused by many years of liquor use.

"As a rule," he said without rancor, "my brothers and I shy away from making pacts with white men. Over the years we have found them to be lacking in honor and possessed of a great variety of untruths that they frequently use to reshape the facts to suit themselves. Our fathers too found this to be so, as did their fathers before them. It is a sad thing when men of mature years cannot face each other without deceit or caution, but that is the way it has become between our races. I do not say this to offend you, but merely to establish the history of our relationships."

Natchay had been gesturing calmly with both hands as he spoke. Now he put his hands behind him and began to pace in a short pattern.

"My brothers and I do not know this man Sheridan whom our nephew Tongue has brought to us. Our nephew tells us that he now owns a small piece of the vast land that once belonged to the old white chief Patman. We remember that Patman was not our friend. He would not hire our young men to work for him when our tribe needed dollars; he would not sell us a few beef from his many when we needed food; he would not even let us cross his land to reach the white man's town of Dane, which would have been a simple gesture of friendship costing him nothing, but instead made us travel around his land, making the journey twice as long. But our nephew Tongue tells us that this Sheridan is not like old Patman. He tells us that Sheridan wishes to be our friend. It would have been easier to believe, of course, if he had come offering his friendship without asking something in return. But Tongue says he is new to our land, from a faraway place where no Indian lives, so he cannot be expected to know about such courtesies.

"Sheridan comes now to ask us for permission to drill for the black water that the white man uses to run his motor cars and flying machines. He says there is black water under the small bog that lies on the boundary between our lands. At least, he thinks there is black water there. If there *is* black water there and he can get it out, it can be exchanged with other whites for many trading dollars. Sheridan asks us to contribute no dollars to the cost of getting the black water out of the ground, which is good because we have so few dollars among us. But if he does raise the black water, he will give our tribe one trading dollar out of every five that he receives."

The old Indian stopped pacing and studied Sam for a moment. He seemed to ponder what he had to say next.

"There is one other fact we have to consider, and that is the white landowner Spence. It is known to our brother Tongue that Spence does not wish this man Sheridan to even remain on the land, let alone drill for the black water. We must consider that if Sheridan fails to find the black water and is driven off by Spence, that Spence then will probably like our people even less than he does already."

Natchay suppressed a wry smile. "But since the man Spence now places us lower than wild prairie dogs anyway, I cannot see where we have anything to lose. It was necessary to mention it, however, lest someone think I have grown old and forgetful."

Now Natchay faced his two colleagues. Neither of them spoke, but waited for him to express his own opinion first, after which they would cast their supporting votes.

"I, for one, believe we should give our permission," Natchay said finally. "This is the only time I can recall in our history when the white man seemed to be giving *to* us more than he is asking from us. While we are not accustomed to such extraordinary treatment, perhaps it is a sign from Him who watches over us. Perhaps He is telling us that at last He has been able to turn the white race into Human Beings like ourselves, and that henceforth we will be dealt with honorably and with dignity. If that is so, we would be fools not to at least taste this new bread being offered us."

The two councillors rose.

"I, too, believe we should give our permission," said one.

"And I," said the other.

Natchay turned to Sam and said, "The tribal council favors the permission you seek. If our decision is approved by the royal line of Techanta, then your request is granted." To Tongue, he said, "Bring the white man Sheridan into the presence of Tunica in one hour."

Natchay and his two councillors left, and Sam said to Tongue, "Tell me more about the royal line of Techanta."

"The royal line of Techanta is the hereditary ruling family of the Choctaw nation," Tongue told him. "Members of that family are descended from the Great Sun who ruled our people before the white ships came. In the beginning the Great Sun put His seed into a chosen woman and she gave birth to our first earthly Sun King. From that time until now, there has always been a descendant of that king among us."

Sam continued to marvel at the preciseness of Tongue's vocabulary. Exchanging quick glances with Draw, he saw in the older man's expression an indication of caution; but it was not necessary. Sam realized that Tongue's solemn, proper speech meant they were listening to the serious business of the tribe, and had to be accepted and treated as such.

"The person you call Tunica is that descendant?" he asked.

91

"Yes. She is but a child, but she is of the royal line and must be accorded the same respect and homage as if she were mature. The Beloved Men do not expect her to decide on matters she is too young to understand. Her only role for the present is to look into the faces of those who are brought before her and say if they are honest or not. This she can do because she has a gift."

"You mean that's what she's going to do to me?" Sam asked. A hint of anxiety crept into his voice. The others noticed it at once.

"You are an honest man, are you not?" Tongue inquired.

"Certainly," said Sam. Perhaps just a bit too quickly.

"You sure don't sound like it," Draw observed.

"He sure as hell don't," Pop agreed.

"Now wait a minute," Sam protested. "I'm as honest as the next man."

"That ain't saying much."

"Sure as hell ain't."

"I just mean," said Sam, "that nobody's *completely* honest."

"Least of all you, it seems," Draw said. To Pop and Tongue he added, " 'Pears we've got a problem here."

Tongue nodded solemnly and put a hand on Sam's shoulder. "Best for you to be alone for a while. Contemplate your acts of dishonesty. You can tell us about them on the way to the presence of Tunica. We will return for you in an hour."

Tongue, Draw, and Pop filed out of the storehouse, Pop saying, "Damned shame, too, 'cause the boy *looked* honest."

"Can't tell a crook by looks," Draw said.

Outside, the three men went around to the back of the storehouse and sat up against it in a row. Pop took a bottle of moonshine out of his inside coat pocket and pulled out its cork with his teeth. Chuckling over Sam Sheridan's discomfiture, they passed the bottle back and forth.

The place where Tunica, the child princess, lived, was a dilapidated frame cabin very much like the line-rider's shack in which Sam and Georgia were staying. On the way there, Tongue, Draw, and Pop listened with mock solemnity as the nervous Sam recited every dishonest act he could recall committing. From stealing an occasional penny from his mother's or grandmother's pocketbook, to taking chalk from his fourth-grade classroom, to cheating on a history exam in his last year at Francis Scott Key High School, to occasionally filching a pair of socks from J. C. Penney, to once keeping as a souvenir an undetermined amount of German money taken off a prisoner of war.

Terrible offenses, Sam's three companions agreed; it *could* cost them their oil well.

Inside the house, in a bare but very clean area partitioned off as a living room, Sam was shown to a straight wooden chair facing a very worn sofa on which the three old Beloved Men sat. Tongue, Draw, and Pop stood by the door. There were no other chairs in the room; Sam wondered where the girl would sit. *Or maybe, since she's supposed to be a princess, we all have to stand. That made more sense.* Now that he was there, and saw that it was just an ordinary house like any other, his nervousness was dissipating. *Those old bastards,* he thought, glancing over at his three friends; *they really had him worrying about that dishonesty stuff. As if any child could look into a man's face and pass accurate judgment on his honesty. That was nonsense. Back in Kansas City, he would never have fallen for a story like that. It was only out here, in this goddamned Texas, where he was trying to do everything right, where he was trying to get a chance, to* make *it, that he would be so gullible. Back home, he—*

His train of thought was interrupted by the appearance at the door of a tall Indian woman dressed in a floor-length white gown. Holding her hand, also wearing a long white gown, was a girl of twelve. She stared straight ahead, eyes fixed, unblinking, and for a terrible instant Sam thought, *My God, she's blind!* But he saw immediately that she was not, for she let go of the tall woman's hand and went over to stand before Natchay. He took both her smooth, young hands into his old wrinkled ones, and the two of them conversed quietly and briefly in what Sam presumed to be Choctaw, but was actually the ancient dialect of the Natchez tribe.

Then, almost before Sam realized it was happening, the girl had touched the hands of the other two Beloved Men, turned, and walked directly over to him. Sam was mesmerized by her face. She had great dark eyes like ripe plums, set in an oblong face, one cheek of which was pockmarked, perhaps, Sam thought, from some poorly treated early disease. Her hair was the blackest Sam had ever seen; blacker even than Tully Samuel's hair, or his wife Reba's, or Tongue's. It was a *thick* black, a black that did not look like a head of hair, but a black that looked solid, as if chiseled from onyx. With her lips parted slightly, Sam could see that she had a narrow gap between her top front teeth, and it was, oddly, the one thing that gave her a little-girl look. Had it not been for that, she would have appeared ageless.

The Beloved Men had not risen in the presence of Tunica, so Sam did not either. Her face was in front of his own, their eyes on the same level, and he not only experienced the incredible urge to kiss this unusual child, but he somehow felt that *she* wanted to kiss *him*. And not—this was the disturbing part—as a man kisses a child, not on the cheek or the forehead; but as a man kisses a woman, on the lips, fully. Her lips were pink and rounded, their corners curved downward slightly, and Sam thought them the most sensuous lips he had ever seen.

Sam's face became warm with tantalizing but irrepressible thoughts, forbidden thoughts, perhaps even unclean thoughts, although God knows they did not *feel* unclean; they felt exhilarating, compelling, demanding. Tunica reached out and put her hands on his face, palms against cheeks, as gentle a touch as Sam had ever felt. He was certain then that he had turned very red: the heat of the moment, her unusual presence, that touch. Then he heard her speak for the first time.

"This person is worthy," she said, her words for everyone and no one, a simple declaration, a pronouncement; and Sam Sheridan, if he had ever had doubts as to his own integrity, had them no longer. He felt the words of the child in front of him as he had never felt anything in his life.

In that moment, that instant, he knew that, everything else aside, he *was* what this Choctaw-Natchez princess ordained him. He was worthy.

With the cooperation of the Choctaw pledged, the four men sat down, inventoried their resources, divided their interests, and made their plans.

"I have three hundred and twenty dollars," Sam announced, writing the figure on a sheet of paper.

"Seven hundred sixty," said Pop. "You can have it all."

"Nine hundred," Draw added. "Likewise."

"Indian got no trading dollars," Tongue said reverting to his vernacular.

"Indian don't need no trading dollars," Sam said, imitating him. "You've done your part." He tallied the figures. "Little less than two thousand. Can we get started with that much?"

"Just," said Pop. "We'll have to cut ever' corner we come to. But I been thinking on it. We can save the thousand-dollar cost of the derrick lumber by chopping down trees on your place and making our own planks. Take longer, but we can do it. Then, 'stead of buying fuel oil at six bits a barrel to run the boiler, we can chop down more trees and fire it with wood. That'll give us blisters on top of calluses, but it'll save us better'n eleven hundred dollars for the fifteen hundred barrels we'd otherwise have to buy. And I think if we avoid buying drilling pipe and cable here in Texas, where it's at a premium right now because of all the exploration, and instead go over in Louzy-anna somewheres' we'll likely save upwards of thirty percent of the cost. If we watch our nickels and dimes, we can get started, all right. Just."

"Okay," said Sam, "I'm ready if the rest of you are." He glanced from face to face. "Anybody against it?"

Nobody was. Sam stood up. Thoughts of the Argonne floated vaguely through his mind. This is where I become a leader of men again, he told himself.

"This is how I propose to divide the interest," he stated, and from his tone it was clear that it was not a matter for discussion. "Fifty percent remains mine. Twenty percent goes to the Choctaw. Ten percent to Draw, ten percent to Pop, ten percent to Tongue."

Again he looked from face to face. No one questioned his division.

"All right. We're in business." He put his right hand, palm down, on the center of the table. "Partners."

Three hands came down on top of his.

As the men made their pact, Sam glanced across the room at Georgia. She should have been happy for him, but she wasn't. Her face was a tightly drawn mask of discontent. There was now no question in Sam's mind where his wife stood.

Clearly, it was no longer with him.

17

Sam walked alongside Pop Joyner in the south Texas Gulf Coast town of Port Arthur, listening to the old man enumerate the various items they had to buy.

"The drill pipe can be bought in sets, but it's too 'spensive that way," Pop said. "We'll buy used pipe in single lengths, wherever we can find it. Cable, now, that there's something else. We want used cable but we don't want *cheap* cable. We don't want it snapping on us ever' few hundred feet." Pop worked his lips a funny way, as if chewing his words before speaking. "Boilers. One big one or two little ones, depending. I'd like to get around three hundred horsepower going if we can. Anything less than that's going to make for slow drilling. Come on, let's try Griff Well and Tool first, see what they've got." He patted Sam on the arm. "Keep the money in your pocket and your mouth shut," he said, leading the way into a big warehouse of a store.

Sam and Pop had left Dane the previous day at dawn, and driven the old Hudson the two hundred ten miles south to the Gulf Coast. That evening they sat on the edge of a pier and ate fried catfish and hush puppies purchased from a waterfront vendor, and watched the gulls wing lazily over the dark oily water. They slept in the car that night and the next morning drove around until they found a dealer who would swap even with Sam, his Hudson for an older model Willys flatbed truck. Then they started shopping for the drilling equipment they needed.

Pop Joyner had a way of trading. He would listen to a price, look astonished, and say, "I ain't a buyer for Sinclair, y'know," or "For Christ's sake, man, you're not talking to Standard Oil here." By emphasizing that he was only an independent driller, he managed to get at least ten percent knocked off, sometimes fifteen; or to get a minor piece of equipment thrown in; or at worst a free tarp to cover the equipment after it was loaded onto the truck.

They spent all day in Port Arthur and by suppertime had everything they needed except one piece. "The drill bit," Pop said. "There ain't a decent used drill bit in town. We're gonna have to drive around to some of the oil fields and see if we can pick one up."

"I hadn't expected to be gone more than two days," Sam said. "Georgia's due to have the baby any time now."

"Poker and the Indian's there," Pop replied. "We got to have a drill bit, son." To him, the securing of a drill bit was infinitely more important than the birth of Sam's baby, which was something God could look after. God sure as hell wouldn't provide them with a drill bit. But Pop saw the concern in Sam's eyes and compromised. "Tell you what: we'll only look for a bit in the fields 'tween here and Dane. If we don't find one, I'll let you out at home and I'll go on looking."

"I appreciate that," Sam said.

The next morning they got up early, ate grits, biscuits, and molasses in a waterfront cafe, and left for the oil field in Jasper.

Georgia felt her first labor pain just after breakfast that same morning. It had not really been a breakfast; just a cup of hot black coffee to take the morning chill off her bones. The old iron stove in the shack—she refused to call it a house—usually went out sometime during the night unless Sam was there to put in more wood; Georgia simply could not force herself from under the covers to do it. She dreaded the thought of facing the cold morning, but there was always the chance that Sam would be home by then, so she waited.

Her labor started at seven. Draw and Tongue had been there at six to check on her, had built a fresh fire for her, then gone off to the pines to cut lumber all day. One or the other of them would be back now and again during the day, and they would come see her at night before they returned to camp. If she had a problem during the night, she was to put a lighted lantern in the west window, where they could see it; they took turns staying awake to watch for the signal, as Draw had promised Sam they would.

Lighting a cigarette and sitting down with her coffee next to the stove, Georgia shook her head in disgust. Wouldn't you know the goddamn pains would start just after Draw and Tongue had left. There was no telling when one of them would return; certainly not for two or three hours. Well, to hell with it; maybe she could last that long.

But it soon became apparent that she could not. With a little lapel watch that Sam had bought her in New York, she timed her pains. They were coming every seven minutes and seemed to be increasing in intensity. Shit, she thought, and put out her cigarette. Going out onto the rickety front porch, she looked first in the direction of the road to see if Sam might be coming. Seeing no sign of him, she stared off in the direction of the bog, near where Draw and Tongue would be chopping down pine trees. They were a mile away, so it would be useless to yell. She really could do only one of two things: stay there and have the baby alone, an option that horrified her; or start walking and try to get to Draw and Tongue before her labor progressed too much further. She felt she had to do the latter.

As she was about to step off the porch, Georgia thought: What if I don't get all the way there? What if I only get *halfway* there? What if I end up having the baby out on the prairie, all alone, among the wolves and the coyotes and the rattlesnakes? My god, how can I protect my baby?

Shuddering, Georgia sat down on the porch step to try to think of some other way, any other way.

In Jasper, Sam and Pop made the rounds of the small drilling supply shops that furnished equipment for the small Curtis field five miles outside of town. But they had no luck finding a used drill bit.

"I doubt you'll find one in East Texas," one of the shop owners told them. "They's more wildcat wells being spudded in than they got drill bits to go around. Why, hellfire, with oil up to three dollars a barrel now, when it used to be a buck-forty, it's worth twice as much to a man if he strikes it. Plus which, they say there'll be near 'bout ten million auto*mo*biles on the highways by the end of the year. Oklahoma ain't gonna be able to furnish it *all*. Why, I bet I could sell a used drill bit ever' day of the week if I could lay my hands on 'em. Say, y'all wouldn't be interested in selling me that load of pipe, would you?"

Sam and Pop drove on, cutting over to Zavalla in Angelina County, having no better luck there, then trying Lufkin, Nacogdoches, and Ponta. By then they were close enough to Dane for Sam to be thinking about giving up for the day and going home to see about Georgia. When he mentioned it again to Pop, the old man said, "All right. It don't look like we're gonna have no luck today anyhow. Tell you what, let's take Highway 110 up through Troupe City. Might's well check the shops there; won't be out of our way none, and won't take but a few minutes. Then we'll head on for Dane."

Sam agreed and they started north out of Ponta.

Georgia had finally decided to try walking the mile across the prairie to where Draw and Tongue were cutting lumber. Her labor pains had increased in frequency to every five minutes and she was becoming very frightened. Goddamn Sam, she thought with every step. She had to move slowly because the ground was rutted, there were tricky rocks and pieces of loose mesquite, and great mushrooms of sagebrush that she had to carefully sidestep. An occasional prairie critter, a jackrabbit or armadillo, would dart across her path and scare the breath out of her. As she walked, Georgia clutched at her collar with one hand and held the other flat on her belly as if to protect the life inside her. Goddamn Sam.

By a wonderful stroke of luck, she only had to walk a quarter of a mile. At that point she saw Tongue trotting toward her. She raised both arms and waved, then sat down on a stump to wait for him.

When Tongue ran up, Georgia said, "Please, I need help."

"Child come?" Tongue asked.

"Yes, child come. Will you help me, please?"

"Unh."

Tongue helped her walk the quarter mile back to the shack and got her into bed.

"I go for white doctor," he told her. "You stay here, lie still."

The Indian left the shack. Georgia raised herself on her elbows and watched out the window as he trotted at a methodical pace toward the Kilgore highway. She watched him grow smaller and smaller. When he was so far away that she could no longer distinguish his form, Georgia lay back down and looked around at the silent, shabby shack. Shivering once, she put both hands on her belly to protect her baby.

Goddamn Sam!

In Troupe City, the local drilling supplies man, who operated from behind a rented counter in the grain-and-feed store, said he had not seen a used drill bit in six months.

"But I might be able to put y'all on to one," he said. "'Course, it wouldn't be right smart of me to do it. If I was to buy the drill bit myself, I could resell it and make a few dollars. Can't do that if I tell y'all where it is, now can I?"

"How much would you make?" Sam asked, violating Pop's instructions to keep quiet. He wanted to be done with this so he could get back to Georgia.

The supplies man shrugged. "Four, maybe five dollars."

Sam fingered five dollars from his pocket and laid it on the counter. "Where is it?"

"'Bout twenty miles north of here. Town called Tyler. There's an old man named Voss been drilling on his place two miles east of there. Finally decided to give up on it and go back to crops. Hear tell he's selling ever'thing but the rig; says he'll use that for firewood." The supplies man picked up the five dollars. "Nice doing bin'ess with y'all."

Outside, Pop asked, "Well, what about it, son. Want to head northeast to Dane or northwest to Tyler?"

It would only take them a few extra hours, Sam thought. Surely Georgia would be all right for a few extra hours.

"Tyler," he said.

Tully and Reba were standing at the cash register when Tongue walked in.

"We don't serve Indians, 'less you want to go around to the back door and buy some food to carry with you."

"Need doctor for white woman who have baby," Tongue said. He pointed to the telephone on the counter. "You call, maybe?"

Tully frowned. "What white woman?"

"Woman of white man named Sam Sheridan."

Tully and his wife looked at each other. "We'd best not mix in this," Tully said.

"The girl's having a baby, Tully," said Reba. "It won't hurt to call for a doctor. It's the Christian thing to do."

Tully thought it over for a moment. Then he nodded curtly. "All right."

Reba jiggled the hook. "Central," an operator answered.

"I need to be connected with a doctor," Reba said.

"Is there an accident somewhere?"

"No, a woman's about to have a kid."

"I'll give you Dr. Goodley."

When the doctor's office answered, Reba explained where she was calling from and where Georgia was. She was told the doctor would go right out there, and to have someone meet him at the dirt road turnoff. Reba hung up and turned to Tongue. "You go on and wait for the doctor where the dirt road meets the highway. Show him where she is."

"Unh," said Tongue, and hurried out the front door.

Five minutes later the telephone rang. Reba answered and listened for a moment, saying only, "All right," before hanging up. Frowning, she pondered a moment, then jiggled the hook again. A voice at the other end answered, "Central."

"Lou Ella, is that you?"

Lou Ella's voice lowered. "I was listening on the line, Reba. Ain't it awful, Dr. Goodley not coming?"

"Who'd the doctor talk to before his nurse called me back?"

"You know as well as I do who he talked to, Reba. Pete Spence. He wanted to find out if the woman having the baby was one of the same Sheridans Pete's trying to run off."

"What did Spence tell him?"

"It was awful, Reba. He told Dr. Goodley to just let her drop the baby by her own self. Said squaw women done it all the time."

"All right, Lou Ella, thank you," Reba said, and hung up. She went into the kitchen. "The doctor ain't coming," she told Tully.

"Why ain't he?" Tully asked, frowning.

"Pete Spence," Reba said simply. No further explanation was necessary.

"Goddamn them Spences anyway!" Tully raged. "Shit!" Then he took a deep breath and shook his head. "Well, hell, it ain't our bin'ess noways."

"Can we try to get her a Mex midwife?" Reba asked.

"I said it weren't our bin'ess."

101

"I know, but she needs help—"

"Help with *what?* Having a kid? Christ, women have babies alone all the time. Having a baby ain't nothing."

Reba's expression darkened. "Tully Samuel, you make me want to puke sometimes," she said angrily.

Stalking into the pantry, she gathered up some towels and a dishpan, and stormed back through the kitchen. Marching outside to the car that she and Tully owned, Reba got in, started the engine, and sprayed gravel all over the back of the roadhouse as she sped away.

In Tyler, Sam and Pop found the farmer named Voss, who had a derrick in an unplowed cotton field.

"Shit, yes, I'm ready to sell!" he declared. "I been punching in this goddamned ground trying to get oil for the better part of a year. Passed up a cotton crop and a watermelon crop for this goddamned foolishness." The farmer grinned in embarrassment, showing black scurvied teeth. "Thought I was gonna get rich, I did. Like a feller over in Edom. Feller had a little old pissant farm just like mine. Little old hard-knock place where you break your back ever' day just to make ends meet. On'y he found oil, by god, right in his own back yard! Shit, he's driving a car today that he had *built* for hisself! Wife wears diamonds just to go uptown to the drugstore!" His voice lowered and he glanced over at his own wife, a gaunt woman sitting nearby on the porch, patching the knee of a worn pair of bib overalls. "That's what I aimed to do. Soon's I hit, why, I was fixing to take the old woman and buy her some sparkly diamonds just like that feller's wife over to Edom. But I was just fooling myself, I know it now. I ain't about to find no oil. So I'm going back to cotton and melons and 'taters, what have you. Least when you got a poor crop, you get *something* for your work. This goddamned drilling the ground for oil, why, don't give you nothing." He glanced at his wife again. "'Cept heartbreak. It gives you that."

The farmer led Sam and Pop over to his rig and Pop examined the drill bit. "Give you fifty dollars for it," Pop said. "Best offer we can make."

"Take it off, it's yours," the farmer said. "Hope it brings you better luck than it did me."

Pop got his toolbox from the flatbed and began dismantling the drill bit attachment.

Reba Samuel held Georgia's upraised knees apart and said, "Push down again. It won't be long now."

Georgia grunted and pushed, and Reba could see a little of the baby's head. Thank the lord, she thought. If this baby had come breech, Reba did not know what she would have done. She had tried helping deliver a breech baby one time; an illegitimate brat her sister was carrying. The baby had been all blue when it was born; had not cried once. Reba had buried it in the backyard and put a washtub of firewood on top of it so the dogs wouldn't dig it up. It had been a messy night.

"Push again," Reba ordered now. Georgia gave another massive effort, and Reba saw a little more of the head: soft and pink, with fine dark hair.

Georgia, sheeted in sweat, caught her breath between contractions and said, "Why are you helping me like this? I thought you didn't like Sam and me."

"Never said I didn't like you," Reba countered.

"You didn't have to say it. It's been obvious. Nobody around here likes us."

"Push down again. Hard as you can this time."

Georgia obeyed, and as she did it flashed through her mind how she had once actively sought out the biggest cocks in Kansas City in her pursuit of ever increasing satisfaction. Now, she thought, it felt like a goddamned Mack truck had been driven up inside her.

"Push harder," Reba ordered. "Harder!"

"Oh, Jesus!" Georgia half shouted, half grunted, as she pushed this time. She was *so* thankful for Reba's strong, reassuring hands on her spread knees. God only knew what she would have done without her.

"That was good," Reba told her. "I can see its little head now. You'll be a mama in just a minute or two."

"The—sooner—the—better—" Georgia reached up and put her hand on Reba's. "Reba, I am so grateful to you—oh—oh—OH! *Jesus!*"

"Push down, honey! Come on, give a good one!"

"Oh, shit! Goddamn Sam! Oh, *shit!*"

"Here it comes, honey! Here comes its little head and face—oh, God, it's beautiful, honey."

Georgia had her head back, teeth clenched, eyes fixed on the gray-weathered, adobe-sealed wooden ceiling of the godawful shack where her baby was being born. Goddamn Sam. Goddamn *all* men.

"Shoulders are coming—arms—elbows—little hands—oh, god, honey, it's a perfect, precious baby boy."

Just what I need, Georgia thought deliriously, another man in my life.

Sam got home at nine that night to find Draw, Tongue, and Tully sitting on his front porch. He knew at once that the baby had come.

"Is Georgia all right?" he asked, getting out of the truck.

Draw nodded. "She's fine. Had a baby boy about three hours ago."

Pop, hopping down, grinned and said, "Just about the time we was buying the drill bit."

Sam hurried inside to find Georgia resting with her eyes closed, Reba sitting next to the bed rocking the baby gently in her arms. "She okay?" Sam asked Reba in a whisper.

"Would have been a lot better if her husband had been here," Reba said curtly. It was not true, of course. If Sam *had* been there, Reba would have just sent him outside until it was over. And she doubted his presence would have made Georgia feel any better. But Reba was not about to pass up an opportunity to make him feel guilty.

"Can I see the baby?" Sam asked.

Deciding that his tone was sufficiently contrite, Reba leaned forward a bit and moved the flannel shawl she was using as a blanket enough for Sam to see his son.

"He looks like Georgia," Sam said.

Reba rolled her eyes in exasperation. "Not a bit! He's you through and through. Peas in a pod."

After Sam looked at the baby, he stepped over to the bed, knelt beside Georgia, and put his palm on her forehead. Georgia opened her eyes.

"I just wanted you to know I was here," he said quietly.

"You're a little late," Georgia said, oddly without rancor, and with a slight, relaxed smile.

"I know. I'm sorry. But you did just fine without me. The baby is a swell little boy."

"Reba was a godsend, Sam. I wouldn't have made it without her. Please don't forget to thank her."

"I won't forget."

"What shall we name him, Sam?"

Sam thought about what Pop had said a few minutes earlier, about the baby being born just about the time they were buying the drill bit. "I want to name him Tyler, after the name of the town where Pop and I found the last piece of drilling equipment we need to get started. I want to name him Tyler Sheridan."

Georgia knew she should have been irked. *He* wanted to name the baby Tyler. Without even consulting her. But she was simply too weary to be upset. It required energy that she did not have. Besides, to be honest, the name was not that important to her.

"It's a nice name, Sam."

Without waiting for Sam to say anything further, Georgia turned her face to the wall and closed her eyes. As she was falling asleep, she made up her mind that Tyler Sheridan was the first, last, and only baby she was going to have.

18

It took the four of them—Sam, Draw, Tongue, and Pop Joyner—a month to cut enough pine timber to build the derrick. After it was cut, the timber had to be split, shaved, and planked. That took another month. Then it had to be sawn into two-by-fours, four-by-eights, and other sizes specified by Pop. When it was properly sized, it was laid out in the sun to cure.

While the wood was curing, the men cleared the area where the platform for the rig would go; the spot where, after considerable walking around, feeling dirt, tasting mud, surveying topography, and other equally odd and unscientific methods, Pop had decided they would sink their hole. The spot was on the north side of the small bog, far enough from it to be on level dry land, but close enough to tap into any oil reserve that might lie directly underneath. The platform, when completed, would stand about sixty-five percent on Sam Sheridan's land, thirty-five on Choctaw land. The hole itself would be on Sam's land, but any reserve pool would be under both properties.

It was the beginning of summer when the men started building the platform and derrick. By the time the derrick was up fifty feet, the days had become long and hot. The East Texas sun burned down on the laborers relentlessly until, after two weeks of working without shirts, the three white men were as brown as Tongue.

"We all Human Beings now," Tongue said, reminding Sam and Draw of the Choctaw-Natchez history they had learned at the meeting with the Beloved Men. Whenever Sam recalled that night, he thought warmly of the girl Tunica, the princess, who had touched his face. Without a doubt, that had been the most memorable moment of his life. More memorable even than the first time he had made love to Georgia in that upper berth, than the first time he had killed a German soldier in France, even more memorable than the surge of independence he had felt when he made the decision, entirely on his own, to come to Texas. The only thing that came close to it was seeing his son the first time. It would not have taken much to convince him that Tunica truly did have a spiritual gift. Except that with everything else on his mind, he did not have time to think about it.

Only three of them could work on the rig after it got off the ground. Draw, the tough, fearless old cowboy, discovered that he could not adjust to height; he became dizzy and almost fell twice. Sam insisted he stay on the platform. This delighted Tongue, who pranced around on narrow beams fifty, sixty, seventy feet in the air as if he had wings and were not cross-eyed. His uncanny sense of balance amazed even Pop.

"I've see'd derricks raised all the way around the world, but I ain't never see'd a man as surefooted as that 'un. Downright spooky is what it is."

For a while Tongue's skill on high afforded him the uncommon luxury of lording it over white men. To Draw down below, he would shout, "You! White man! Send up more timber! Hurry! Work faster!"

"I'll give you fast, you goddamned heathen!" Draw would shout back. "I'll give you a fast draw and a well-placed bullet in your redskin ass!"

Cunning as Tongue was, he invariably ceased his taunting at least two hours before coming down, knowing from experience that Draw, at one time possessed of a temper as hair-trigger quick as his pistol, had now mellowed to the point of carrying a grudge mere minutes instead of months.

After the derrick reached seventy feet, Pop also backed off from further heights. "Gonna be up to you and the Injun from here on," he told Sam. "I'm too goddamned old to top out one of these rigs anymore."

"How much higher does it have to go?" Sam asked.

Pop paced around on the platform, squinting up at the rising structure. "'Bout half again as far, looks like. It ought to top out between a hunnerd ten and a hunnerd twenty. Won't be room but for two to work up there anyways, pretty soon. Can you and the Injun handle it?"

"We'll handle it," Sam assured him. That and anything else that has to be handled, he thought grimly. Sam Sheridan was going to bring oil up out of this ground. He had never been so determined about anything in his life.

At home, Georgia was happier than Sam had seen her in a long time. Little Tyler had changed her, at least for the moment, from a tight-lipped, discontented, silently accusing woman, into a cheerful, humming, pleasant young mother who was obviously delighted with her new baby.

They had ended up naming the baby Tyler Charles Sheridan, taking "Charles" from Draw Poker's given name. Draw, both surprised and touched, had said, "Can't see why you'd want to name no innocent little baby after the likes of me."

"You've been a good friend to us," Sam told him.

"Others have been good friends to you too," the old cowboy pointed out.

"Yes, they have. But you're a cut different, Draw. Don't ask me why I think that; I just *feel* it."

Draw had cleared his throat and looked off at the horizon. It was one of the few times Sam had ever seen the old eagle face soften. Sam decided to see what he could make of the moment.

"You said someday I could ask you again about Able Chase Patman. Are you ready to tell me yet?"

Draw's expression hardened immediately. He looked at Sam with knowing eyes. "No," he said flatly, "I'm not."

The old man had walked away, leaving Sam once again frustrated and discouraged.

But if Sam's past continued to upset and confuse him, his thoughts of the future, because of the baby, certainly did not. Tyler Charles Sheridan was a joy to his father. In the early days after the baby's birth, when Sam would come home at the end of the day, his palms bloody where blisters had formed, broken, reblistered, and split into ugly sores, Georgia would mix boric acid water to soak them in, then rub on Sloan's Ointment. The well was Sam's first exposure to manual labor; clerking at J. C. Penney's had left his hands smooth and soft; even his stint in the army, because he had been an officer, had never raised calluses. So the swinging of an ax and sledge, the handling of chains and rope, the scrapes, cuts, and splinters, wreaked painful results that had to be doctored every night for weeks. Slowly but inevitably, however, his hands became hard and tough.

It was during the period when Sam's hands had to be greased with ointment at night, each one then wrapped loosely in an old dish towel, that he learned how joyful it was to love his son. Georgia would put the baby on the bed and Sam would prop himself up on his elbows and they would take turns amusing each other. Ty was a good baby, happy and cheerful as long as he was fed and clean, and he was easy to entertain and make smile. Sam, whom the infant saw for only an hour or two in the evening, was a special treat for the baby, as was the baby for Sam, and father and son soon cemented a quiet, strong bond.

Sam was also indirectly creating an attachment between Ty and the others working with him on the derrick. Each morning as they all began work, Sam would tell them about the baby's antics of the previous evening: the smiles and laughter, the discovery of his hands and feet, the baby talk, the occasional show of temper. The men listened in fascination to these stories, because for the most part it was their first close exposure to an infant. Draw was a confirmed bachelor. Tongue, a bronco Indian all his life, had never taken a permanent woman, never fathered any children. Pop had left illegitimate offspring all over the world but had never stayed long enough to observe or become attached to any of them. So the day-by-day reports on little Ty were a new experience to which each man, for his own reasons, looked forward.

For everyone, Georgia included, those early months after the birth of Tyler Charles Sheridan were a time of happiness, hard work, and great enthusiasm for each new day.

The derrick topped out at a hundred twelve feet and was pronounced by Pop Joyner fit and ready to be rigged for drilling. From a perch at the sixty-foot level, he instructed and supervised Sam and Tongue in the attachment of the pulleys and cable that would raise and lower the drill bit as it punched its way to subterranean depths. When everything was in place, Pop said, "All right, now we got to find us a cheap boiler to run the rigging. Me and Sam'll go a'hunting one whilst you two"—he indicated Draw and Tongue—"can start laying in a supply of firewood for fuel for when we get back."

Once again Sam and Pop were off scouting in the old Willys flatbed. Pop wanted to find a good used inexpensive oil field boiler that would generate two hundred horsepower. Sam reminded him of the farmer who sold them the drill bit, but Pop shook his head.

"I looked at his boiler when we was there. It was too small, prob'ly no more'n a hunnerd ten horses. Ain't no wonder the feller give up like he did. With that kind of boiler, why, it'd take two years or better to get down far enough to tap into a reserve, if there happened to be one there in the first place."

They headed north and east looking for the boiler, so as not to have to talk to the same suppliers twice. Pop's philosophy was that the fewer people who knew who they were and where they were drilling, the better.

"Word's got a way of getting around to the squatters," he explained to Sam. "Them's the ones who sets up camp within sight of a rig and waits to see if it hits. If it does, the squatters hustles around and buys up oil leases from ever' small farmer in the area, paying them maybe a dollar an acre for the right to drill for oil on their spreads. Them same leases will be thirty, fifty, eighty dollars an acre once the news of the strike spreads, but by then it'll be too late.

The squatters will hold the leases until Sinclair or Herbst or one of the other drilling companies comes around, then sell them for fifty times or more what they paid for them. Bunch of goddamned highbinders is all they are. We don't need 'em setting and watching *our* rig."

They made inquiries in Judson and Jefferson, Karnak, Leigh, Waskom, and all up and down the Bend Reservoir that separated Texas and Louisiana. Finally they drove into Louisiana itself and in Bossier City did the best they decided they were *going* to do, by buying two mismatched boilers: one an old seventy-five-horsepower oil field boiler, the other an even older ninety-horsepower cotton gin boiler. Given the money they could afford, Pop concluded that they were not going to do any better.

"The two of 'em together will give us a hunnerd and sixty-five horses," he reasoned. "It'll be slower drilling, but what the hell. Prices they're asking for bigger better ones, we could go on looking for a month. Meanwhile, we're wasting good drilling days. I say buy these and let's get them back home and hooked up."

"Whatever you think, Pop," Sam agreed.

"You know something, young feller," the old wildcatter told him, "you're going to be a rich important man someday, and I'll tell you why. You *listen.* When somebody knows more'n you do about something, you *listen.* Lots of young fellers don't. They think they know it all, won't pay attention to what *nobody* says. But you, why, you listen to me, to Draw, even to Tongue. Most white men in Texas won't listen to shit from an Indian or a Mex; figure they're too goddamn dumb to be able to learn anything from. But it ain't so. Man can learn from *anybody* that's smarter than he is, don't matter what that person's color is. You seem to know that 'thout being told. That's why I think you'll be rich and important someday." Pop worked his lips, chewing his words, remembering. "Wish to high heaven *I'd* been like you when I was young. Prob'ly be right up there with old John D today."

John D. Rockefeller. Draw had told him about Pop working for Rockefeller in the old days. "What was he like?" Sam asked curiously.

The old man grinned. "Smooth as a whore's silk bloomers. And just as tricky as what was *inside* them bloomers, too. He could *talk.* I mean, he could convince any*body* about any*thing.* 'Cept me. I'd never listen to him. Worked for him twice. He'd of made something of me if I'd let him. But I didn't think I could learn nothing from no fancy-pants smooth talker like him. That's what I mean about listening. A feller's *got* to listen."

Pop gazed out the window, his expression turning melancholy, remembering. Sam left him alone with his thoughts.

They drove home from Bossier with the two pitiful-looking boilers and went to work integrating them with the drill rigging. Draw and Tongue already had a good supply of firewood dried out for fuel, so when the boilers were set up and fired, the men were ready to begin drilling.

"We can spud her in anytime you want to, Sam," said Pop.

"What does that mean, 'spud her in'?" Sam asked.

"That's oil field talk, boy. A long time ago in England they used to dig for water with a funny-looking little tool called a 'spudde.' After a while, that kind of digging got to be called 'spudding.' Now when we punch that first chip out of the ground to start drilling, we call it spudding-in. Oil field talk."

Sam jumped down off the platform and walked over to the truck. From under the seat he pulled out a bottle of bootleg whiskey rolled up in a tote sack. Returning to the platform, he pulled out the cork with his teeth and handed the bottle to Pop.

"First drink's for you, Pop. We wouldn't have been able to do any of this without you."

Pop took a swallow and passed the bottle back to Sam. Sam handed it to Draw. Draw drank and passed it to Tongue. After the Choctaw drank, Sam himself took a long pull. Then he corked the bottle.

"Okay, Pop," he said with an enormous feeling of delight, "spud her in."

Pop Joyner pulled the drill bit down, scored a mark on the ground, threw the drill lever, and guided the drill point as it raised five feet in the air and came thrusting down to chip out the first inch of earth.

The drilling had begun.

The two old mismatched boilers were so faulty that in concert they generated only one hundred twenty-five pounds of steam pressure. That made for very slow drilling. It was just as well, however, since to keep the drilling going everything had to be done by hand. Their water supply for the mud mixture to cool the drill bit had to be hauled from the creek, half a mile away, in two alternating wooden barrels. Fuel for the boilers continued to be wood they chopped manually. If the boilers had allowed the men to drill any faster, they would have had to shut down several times a day anyway, to allow the firewood or water supply to catch up.

Sam tried to organize and distribute the work as fairly and efficiently as possible. Left on their own, Draw, Tongue, and Pop would have addressed particular jobs when necessary: get water when water ran out, chop wood when the pile was depleted. And whichever was handiest would have done it, whether best suited to the task or not. But Sam, with his military experience, knew there was a better way. He logged the lengths of time it took to use a barrel of water and a cord of wood. Anticipating those outages, he scheduled runs to the creek for water an hour ahead of time, and resumed wood chopping when the firewood was down to a quarter of a cord. As for specific assignments, he detailed Draw always to drive the truck, a less taxing job than chopping wood, so that the old man got some occasional relief. Sam himself and Tongue did most of the arduous wood chopping, leaving the shortening of limbs and other lighter work for Draw. Pop, of course, remained on the platform most of the time, guiding the drilling rod, feeding in the mud mixture, sluicing off the diggings.

Sam had other responsibilities as well. He was in charge of their pooled finances, what was left after buying their equipment. This money was to feed them, to fuel their bodies for the long hot days of work ahead. Half the time, Draw, Tongue, and Pop lived off beef jerky and beans that they ate in their creekside camp; but on alternate nights, Georgia would cook for them as she did for Sam—fish or game, greens, sweet potatoes—and they would eat off tin plates while sitting on the front porch. Those nights Georgia would spread a quilt and put the naked little Ty out with them so they could compete for his attention.

Even conserving on food every other day, however, did not prevent their meager capital from gradually being depleted.

"We're running out of canned goods, Sam," he was told by Georgia one night. "Staples, too. I'll need some money by Saturday."

"There is no more money," Sam said quietly. "Except for a few dollars, we're almost broke."

Georgia didn't respond, knowing that with Sam her silence was the loudest disapproval of all. Usually when she remained quiet, Sam would continue talking, either explaining, justifying, or rationalizing what it was that provoked her displeasure. But this time Sam did not pursue the matter; there was nothing else to say: the money was almost gone, that was that.

"You knew when you began," Georgia said at last, "that you didn't have enough to go all the way."

"Yes, I knew. We all knew."

"And you went ahead all the same."

"We went ahead all the same."

"I won't have Ty doing without, Sam." Her words were clearly a warning, and they were like sandpaper on his conscience.

"What in hell makes you think *I* would?" he asked, challenging her.

"I'm not saying you would."

"That's what you meant."

"Don't read my mind, Sam. And don't let's fight over it. Please just tell me what you intend to do to provide for our baby."

Sighing, Sam got up from the table and went out onto the porch. It was early fall, a hot muggy night ending a day thick with humidity. Summer ended slowly in East Texas.

"I don't know what I'm going to do," Sam said from the porch, knowing Georgia could hear.

"Do the others have any money?" she asked.

"No."

"Maybe you could get some money from the Choctaws. After all, they have an interest in the well."

"If you knew how pitifully poor their community is, you wouldn't even suggest that. I went over there last week to get a tire off an old abandoned truck; one of the tires on the flatbed had blown out. It was the first chance I'd had to really look around the place. I've never seen such squalor. Some of them live in huts they've fashioned out of clay and sagebrush twigs; some live in corrugated tin shacks; most of them have dirt floors. Only a few live in regular houses; those were the places already on the property when the government moved them there. They're so poorly clothed, it's unbelievable; I can't imagine what they do in the winter when it's cold. They live mostly on a kind of gruel mush made from the grain the government gives them. Like everyone else in this part of the country, they can't grow decent crops because the ground is so burned up from the drought. And they can't get jobs because no one will hire Indians—"

"Sam, I know all that," Georgia interrupted quietly. "I feel sorry for the Choctaw people too. But I've got to think of Tyler and me first. What are you going to do about us, Sam?"

Sam went back into the house. "I thought I'd try getting a bank loan again. Not in Dane, but somewhere else. Down in Kilgore maybe, or up in Longview. Take Pop with me this time and let him show some of the ground shavings we're bringing up. Pop is sure there's oil down there. The only question is, how *far* down."

"Do you really think a banker is going to listen to an uneducated old man like Pop?"

"I don't know. It's worth a try. *Anything's* worth a try at this stage."

"I suppose," Georgia said quietly, almost absently. "Would the Spences still buy the land, do you think?"

Sam's jaw clenched as he remembered the humiliating incident in front of Ardelle Spence's house. The way she had looked at him, like he was dirt. He had never shared that awful experience with Georgia.

"I don't know if they'd still buy it or not," he said tightly. "But I know this, I'd rather *give* it to the Choctaw than *sell* it to the Spences."

"I see," said Georgia. She did not ask any more questions because she was already contemplating alternatives. She was in touch with her mother and brother by mail, and had kept them advised of the situation in Texas. If this project of Sam's fell through and they became destitute, her brother Leon had already agreed to telegraph enough money for her to take a bus back to Kansas City.

Just her and the baby.

She would be leaving Sam.

19

The Kilgore bank president's name was Cecil Trane. He was an archetypal successful man: immaculately groomed, impeccably dressed, direct and logical. He treated Sam and Pop Joyner very courteously, but made it clear there was no way he could help them.

"I know you've been to both the Merchants Bank of Dane and the Cattlemen's Bank in Longview, Mr. Sheridan," Trane said matter-of-factly. "We all belong to a banking association hereabouts: the East Texas Bankers Group, we call ourselves. It's one of those you-scratch-my-back-and-I'll-scratch-yours organizations. I had a telephone call advising me that you might show up here looking for a loan. So did every other banker in the group." Trane leaned back in his big leather chair, cocking his head inquisitively. "As a matter of curiosity, Mr. Sheridan, just why are you being blackballed?"

"Do you know Pete Spence?" Sam asked.

"The big rancher? No, not personally. Heard of him, of course."

"Well, I have something he wants. Rather, something his wife wants. His wife is the daughter of the late Able Chase Patman; I'm sure you've heard of him too."

"Oh, yes. Had the biggest funeral ever held in these parts, I understand."

"Patman left me one hundred acres of land at the edge of his ranch. I don't know why or for what reason. The rest went to Mrs. Spence. The Spence family wants it back."

"I see." Cecil Trane's eyes flicked to Pop Joyner, and the Mason jar in Pop's lap. "I presume," he said to Sam, "that it's on this inherited land that you're drilling."

"Yes." Sam detected an interest in the banker's voice and felt a glimmer of hope. "We have some ground shavings from the fourteen-hundred-foot level that look very good," he said eagerly. "Mr.

Joyner here has been involved in oil exploration most of his life, and he is convinced that we'll strike a pool under the bog where we're drilling."

"You realize, of course, that this entire area has been gone over by professional geologists? Sinclair Petroleum has had men up there, Humble Oil, West-Tex, a number of others. None of them have seen fit to invest in oil leases and commence drilling. They say unanimously that there are no oil reserves in Rusk, Caddo, or Harrison counties."

"They're mistook," Pop Joyner said flatly. "Leastwise, where Caddo is concerned. Look here, I put ever' dollar I had in the world in this here hole. Think I'd have done that if I weren't *sure?*"

"We can be sincere in our beliefs and still be, uh—'mistook'— Mr. Joyner," the banker replied in his same courteous tone.

"If you'd just have our shavings analyzed, sir," said Sam, "I think you'd find that they show some highly likely trace signs of oil."

"Mr. Sheridan, even if they showed *positive* signs of oil, I couldn't make a loan to you. The association to which I belong would blackball *me.*"

"But this is a bank," Sam reasoned. "Making loans is part of your business. How can you just turn away a legitimate applicant? I'm willing to put up the land and my share of the well as collateral."

"The bankers group was formed for the purpose of each of us protecting the other," Trane said. "Against fraud, against poor investments, against overextending ourselves. Claud Maye, president of the Merchants Bank of Dane, is also president of the East Texas Bankers Group. If I were to make a loan to you after he turned you down, why, it would be like slapping him in the face. By second-guessing his judgment, I'd be putting my entire reputation on the line. Even if you eventually *struck* oil and *justified* my decision, Claud Maye and the other bankers in the group would never forget what I had done, or forgive me for it. You're asking me to jeopardize my position for a stranger whom I don't know and something that only *might* happen. Don't you think that's a rather unreasonable request, Mr. Sheridan?"

Sighing quietly, Sam was forced to agree. "Yes, Mr. Trane, I suppose it is."

"If our positions were reversed, would you do it for me? Be honest, now."

"I guess not." It was a lie, but Sam did not feel like debating the point. He *would* have made the loan, if the ground shavings justified it and the collateral was sufficient. Sam would not have let any *group* dictate how he operated *his* business. But obviously Cecil Trane was a different breed of man; he ran with the pack and liked it: liked the security of numbers, the comfort of support, the assurance that he would never make a mistake alone. Sam realized that arguing the ethics of the banker's position would be futile, fruitless. He suddenly wanted to get out of the perfectly furnished office, to get back into the imperfect outside world. At least out there he could breathe.

"Thank you for seeing us, Mr. Trane," he said, nudging Pop and rising. "I appreciate your frankness."

"I wish I could offer you more."

"Yes, so do I. Goodbye, Mr. Trane."

Out on the sidewalk, Sam and Pop paused for no particular reason and looked up and down Kilgore's lazy little main street.

"What in hell are we gonna do now?" Pop asked.

Sam shook his head. "Don't know, Pop. Just don't know."

When Sam got back to his place, after dropping Pop off at the derrick, there was a brand-new yellow Ford sedan parked outside. Sam somehow knew, even before he got close enough to see the Kansas license plate, whose it was. As he pulled up and parked, his brother-in-law came out onto the porch. Leon Powell was still pale from spending so many hours inside a theater. In the perfect Texas daylight, he was even whiter; next to Sam's deeply tanned skin, he would look ill.

"Hello, Sam." Leon did not come forward to meet him, preferring to have Sam come to him.

"How are you, Leon?"

"I'm fine, Sam, just fine." Leon smiled expansively. "Managing two houses now, more than a thousand seats. Just picked up my new car there; beauty, isn't she?" His smile disappeared. "Sam, I'm a little surprised at your living conditions here. I expected something better."

"Don't worry about it, Leon. We're getting along." The two men faced each other for a moment, but neither offered his hand. "Is Alva with you?" Sam asked, continuing on into the house.

117

Alva Powell was indeed there, sitting on one of their rickety chairs with Ty on her lap. Looking displeased, she had to force a smile for Sam. After greeting him, she immediately said, "Where in the world did you get a name like Tyler for this baby? I've never heard of such a name."

"You're forgetting your history, Alva. There was once a President named Tyler. There's a town in Texas named after his family, and my son is named after the town." Sam was making it up. He had no idea where the town of Tyler got its name.

Georgia, sitting on a pillow at her mother's feet, asked, "Any luck at the bank?"

Sam could have strangled her. "No, not today."

"What will you do now?"

Leon had followed Sam into the house; Sam was acutely aware of his brother-in-law's eyes on him. "Try somewhere else tomorrow," he said. "Some other bank." He would not, of course. It would be a waste of time; the East Texas Bankers Group would see to that. Pete Spence would see to it.

Leon came forward and took Ty off his grandmother's lap. "Hey, big boy. I'm your Uncle Leon. Can you say 'Uncle Leon'?" Ty grinned and drooled.

"Leon wants to take us all out for supper tonight, Sam," Georgia said.

"That's nice," said Sam, "but I'll be at the derrick until late. You all go on without me."

"Oh, Sam. Can't you forget the derrick for one night?"

"We work the derrick until it gets dark, Georgia, you know that. Winter will be here soon and the days will get shorter. We have to use every hour of daylight there is."

Later, when he was able to catch Georgia alone at the sink, with the water-pump handle making enough noise to cover his voice, Sam said, "Please don't mention the money situation in front of them again, Georgia."

"For heaven's sake, Sam, they know all about it. I *do* write home, you know."

Sam stared at her. Of course she wrote home. But for some reason he had never stopped to consider *what* she might be writing. He suddenly realized that he probably had very few secrets from Leon Powell, none at all from Alva, to whom Georgia could relate

118

even the most intimate details of their life. He suddenly felt naked.
"Did you know they were coming?" he asked, looking for something
for which to blame Georgia.

"Not exactly."

"What does that mean?"

"It means I didn't know the *day.*"

"But you knew they were coming?"

"Yes."

"You might have told me."

Georgia looked directly at him. "You've been too busy, Sam."
She walked away.

After Sam changed clothes to go back to work, Leon followed
him out to the truck. "This oil well business, Sam. Sounds pretty
risky to me."

"You catch on quick."

"Have you sunk your entire inheritance into it?"

Sam stopped and faced him. "My *entire* inheritance? You mean
the five hundred dollars? Yes, every dollar is in the well. Plus all the
money my partners could raise. Plus about six months of back-
breaking labor that you—well, let's just say a lot of hard work. Look
at my hands, Leon. Rub your finger across those palms. Go ahead.
Do you have any idea what I went through to get hands like these?
To answer your question: yes, everything I've got is in my well.
Everything and a lot more. Money's the least of it, Leon."

"But you do *need* money, I believe. Isn't that so? I mean, unless
you get money, all the rest is just dreaming, isn't it?"

"I guess so. Why are you so curious, Leon? Thinking of making
an investment?"

Leon shrugged, expansively and self-consciously at the same
time. "Well, I *do* have some capital."

"How much have you got?"

"About twelve hundred dollars. But I—"

"Not enough, Leon." Down to his last few dollars, Sam still
could not resist putting Leon in his place. "We're looking for a bigger
investor. We need about twelve *thousand* to bring in the well. This
is Texas, Leon. We do things big down here."

Hopping into his truck, Sam wrenched the old gearshift into
place and drove off in a trail of prairie dust.

* * *

It was nearly midnight when Sam returned home. Georgia was sitting on the porch in the light of a single lantern, smoking one of the tailor-made cigarettes Leon had left her.

"Have you had any supper?" she asked.

"Yes. I ate over at the camp with Draw and the others." He sat down on the porch step and leaned his head back. "You all go out to eat?"

"Yes. To Tully's. I wanted Mother and Leon to meet Reba."

"Where are they now? Your mother and Leon."

"They went up to the boardinghouse in Dane to spend the night. I couldn't very well ask them to stay in this place."

"It's better than some of the Choctaw have," Sam said, and instantly regretted it.

"I'm sure it's better than some of the poor Negroes in the South have, too. And the coolies in China. But that's not really the point, is it?"

"No, I guess not." He looked away from her and listened to the night sounds of the prairie. There was a small burst of fire as Georgia struck a stick match to light a fresh cigarette.

"I want to go back home with Mother and Leon," she said at last.

Sam was not surprised. He had been expecting it ever since finding his in-laws there.

"Did you hear me?" Georgia asked after a long pause.

"Yes, I heard you."

"Well, aren't you going to say anything?"

"What is there *to* say?" he answered quietly. "I don't want you to go. But I'm not going to try to make you stay. I know how much you hate this place. If you think you can't stand it any longer, then go."

"Will you hate me for it, Sam?" There was a tremor in her voice.

"Of course not." Sam reached up and put a hand on her knee.

"It's just that it'll be so much better for us back there."

"Us?" He pulled his hand away from her knee.

"Tyler Charles and me."

"You're not taking Ty."

"Why, of course I am—"

"No, you're not. Go if you have to, but you go alone. Ty stays here."

"Oh, Sam, really. What would you do with him during the day?"

"I don't know. Leave him with a Choctaw woman if I have to. I'll work it out."

"Sam, I'm going to insist that he go with me."

"Insist all you goddamn want to," Sam said. Rising, he put his face close to hers in the blue glow of the lantern. "You listen to me, Georgia. Ty was born right here on land that his father *owns*. It's not much land, but it's *my* land, and because it's mine, it's his too. And there's oil under this land; I've never been more certain of anything in my life. I made damn sure that I kept a fifty-percent share in that oil, Georgia, not for myself or for you, but for him, for Ty, so nobody could ever take it away from him. Now you want to take him away from *it.*" Sam's eyes were fixed coldly on his wife for the first time ever. "I can't trust you anymore, Georgia. Not when it comes to Texas. You hate the place too much. I can't trust you to bring my son back to me if I let you take him away. And I don't want to have to come to Kansas City and *take* him back. So Ty stays here. That's final."

Sam went inside then, leaving her alone on the porch. She heard the rustle of his clothes through the open window as he undressed. For the first time in a long while she wanted him to make love to her. Maybe it was the aggressiveness he had just shown. She waited until it was quiet and she knew he was in bed. Then she slipped inside and checked on the baby. Ty was breathing softly, deep in sleep. Georgia got out of her dress and step-ins, all that she was wearing. She sat down on the side of the bed.

"You've never spoken to me in that tone before, Sam," she whispered.

"You've never talked about taking my son away from me," he retorted, not bothering to lower his voice.

"Please be quiet, I don't want the baby to wake up." She put one palm on his stomach. He was flat and hard from the work he had been doing. She began to massage him. "You've never really been forceful with me, Sam. Ever."

"There's never been reason to."

"Sometimes a woman likes a man to be forceful." She moved her hand lower and kept massaging. "Sometimes a woman likes to be—well, *made*. Do you know what I mean?"

He did not answer. Georgia kept ministering to him while she waited in the dark for him to rise up from the bed, force her to her knees, and make her do perverted, unnatural things. But, as usual, he did not. Finally, when he was ready, she mounted him, straddling his hips. She wanted to straddle his face, but feared what his reaction would be. Rejection would have devastated her. So she eased him inside of her and rode him the way she always had.

And closed her eyes to imagine what she would rather have been doing.

In the morning, just as dawn was breaking, Sam finished the warmed-over cornbread and molasses that was his breakfast, and drank a second cup of bitter black coffee. While he ate, Georgia changed Ty and nursed him by the stove where they would both be warm. The usual early-morning chill blanketed the prairie; it would last for the hour or so it took the sun to get high enough to burn it off.

As Sam ate, he watched the baby suckle, and remembered how sweet Georgia's milk had tasted on his own lips the night before. It had been very fine last night: very fine and sweet and satisfying. Sam knew he should have felt warm and tender toward Georgia this morning. He *wished* he felt warm and tender toward her. But he did not. He was distrustful and suspicious. And much as he hated to let her know about his distrust, his suspicion, he knew he had to. He waited until the last minute, until he was ready to walk out the door.

"Georgia, I'm going to have the house checked every hour. If you try to take Ty away, you'll only get an hour's head start at most. There's no way you'll be able to get out of Texas before I catch you."

Georgia glared at him, the coldest look she had ever given him. "I thought you understood that last night was my way of saying that I *wouldn't* take him away."

"I didn't understand anything of the sort. All I heard you say was that you wished I was more forceful. At least, that's what I *thought* you said." He glanced outside at the brightening day. "I'm burning daylight, so I don't have time to talk about it right now. If you've really changed your mind, then I'm glad. But if you were just trying to put me off guard, it didn't work. Somebody—me, Draw, Tongue, or Pop—will be by every hour. If you don't want us coming up to the house so you have to explain it to your mother and Leon, put the crib out on the porch where Ty can be seen from a distance. But don't try to take him anywhere."

"Fuck you, Sam."

"You did, Georgia. That's why I'm suspicious."

As he walked out of the house, he heard her yell, "Go to hell, you bastard!"

Sam could not help smiling. Maybe that was an accurate description, he thought. He wouldn't know for sure until he found out who his mother was.

He got in the truck and drove straight across the prairie toward the derrick. No longer did he or any of the others try to preserve the old Willys: they drove it anywhere, road or not. Both axles were bent and the springs were long since broken. It rode like a wheelbarrow over railroad ties, but Sam did not care. All he cared about was the derrick. Keeping it working, every hour there was daylight. Even though he might have to shut it down completely before the week was out. The thought of running out of money, of having to quit, sickened him. So much so that he had almost made up his mind to go back to Leon, to plead with his brother-in-law for the twelve hundred dollars Leon had saved: a loan, an investment, anything. Whatever it took to keep the drill drilling a little longer. The thought of going to Leon sickened him too; but not as much as the thought of shutting down the well.

Halfway across the open prairie between his house and the pines in which the derrick stood, Sam was surprised to see an old Model-T parked, with a man sitting on the running board, smoking. Who in the hell is that? Sam wondered, slowing the bumping, jerking Willys as he approached. He halted next to the car. The man rose from the running board. He was redheaded, heavily freckled, with a face as plain as tap water, wearing an inexpensive business suit. To Sam he was vaguely familiar.

"Remember me?" the man asked, looking up at Sam in the truck cab.

"I can't quite place you," Sam admitted.

"Dewitt Tucker. I work for Claud Maye up to the Merchants Bank. Met you the day you was in for a loan."

Sam nodded. "You were the other one without a chain."

"Beg pardon?"

"A gold watch chain. You and I were the only ones in the room without a gold watch chain."

Dewitt grinned and opened his coat. "Still don't have one. Listen, I'd like to talk to you if you've got a minute."

Something told Sam that what Dewitt Tucker had to say might be worth a few minutes of daylight. "All right." He climbed down out of the truck. The two men sat side by side on the running board of the Model-T, leaning forward with their elbows on their knees.

"Cecil Trane from the bank down to Kilgore called Mr. Maye yesterday," Dewitt said. "Told him you'd been in there asking for a loan."

Sam nodded. "I was turned down. In the best interests of the East Texas Bankers Group."

"That's what old Trane said. But he also told Mr. Maye that he got a look at a jar of shavings from your well hole. Said there was some interesting color in them: some purples and a little red and green. Said he wouldn't be surprised if you was onto something out here."

"How would he know that?"

"Trane, he's from up to Oklahoma where there ain't nothing *but* oil. I reckon he can recognize promising shavings if anybody can."

"I'm glad to hear that's his opinion," Sam said. "It backs up what my own oil expert, Pop Joyner, has been telling me. Pop believes there's oil here too; he's invested every dollar he had in this well."

"Word's around," Dewitt said, "that you and Draw Poker done the same."

"We did," Sam confirmed.

"Word's also around that y'all are right near broke, that you might have to shut down."

"Maybe," Sam hedged, "maybe not. What's it got to do with you?"

"Fact of the matter is, I'd like to invest some money in your well."

Sam's stomach jerked twice, but the excitement passed quickly

124

and he thought, a junior loan officer: how much could he have? Could this possibly be some kind of trick to get him off the land?

"That's interesting," Sam said. "How much did you have in mind?"

"As much as it takes to keep you going."

Careful, Sam told himself. It *is* a trick. "We need a hundred to two hundred dollars a week. And we could need it for another six months. Could run to five thousand dollars. And that's just for operating expenses, to get by. We're feeding five grown-ups and a baby out here. Buying gasoline for this truck. Fuel oil to cook with. Grease for the derrick machinery. Chain and line when they break. Top pipe when we run out. Clothes for outside work in the winter. Parts for the truck when it breaks down. Just everyday expenses. If something major goes out, we'll need even more."

"I'm willing to take a chance," Dewitt Tucker said boldly.

Sam settled his gaze on Tucker. "Just where in hell do you figure to come up with that kind of money? You probably don't make thirty dollars a month."

"Where I get he money is my business."

Sam shook his head. "Not if there's any chance you're getting it from Ardelle Spence and her husband. What'd you have in mind for me to sign?"

"Ardelle Spence!" Dewitt scoffed. "Shit, you must think I'm *way* up the social ladder, boy. The Spences don't even know I'm alive. I'm the one *without* the gold chain, remember?"

"Then where the hell are you going to get the money?" Sam felt he had to challenge him.

Dewitt met Sam's eyes. "I'm going to borrow it from the bank."

There was something about the way he said "borrow." Sam's lips parted in surprise. "You're going to embezzle it."

Dewitt shrugged. "Call it what you like."

"You're crazy."

The young teller turned on him angrily. "I didn't come out here on the prairie at dawn to be tol' I was crazy!"

"What if you get caught? Or the well doesn't come in? I mean, it's fine to have all the confidence in the world that it *will* come in, but we've also got to be realistic and admit that it might *not.* What happens then?"

"I'll tell you what happens, Mr. Sam Sheridan," the redheaded young Texan said fiercely. "I go down to the Huntsville Penitentiary, that's what happens. I do five or ten years, then I get out and I'm a nobody for the rest of my life. *Just like I am now.*"

Sam stared at him. Dewitt got up and began pacing.

"You think you got it bad being a stranger, an outsider? Let me tell you, there's lots worse things. Being poor white trash is one of them. I grew up a sharecropper with my daddy and my three brothers. The five of us used to work from first light to sundown ever' day but Sunday—an' I mean *work* too, mister; work so goddamned hard it'd make that oil drilling you're doing look like *rest.*" He pointed a stiff finger at Sam. "Me and my brothers, the four of us used to strap ourselves in a harness and pull the plow for Daddy 'cause we didn't have no mule. I got scars across my chest from it to this day. Why, I can't stand to eat corn 'cause they was one winter when we didn't have nothing *but* corn—corn mush, corn gruel, fried corn— morning, noon, and night for *five straight months.* Another winter I couldn't go to school 'cause I didn't have no shoes. There wasn't but one pair of shoes in the whole house; my daddy and two oldest brothers had to take turns wearing them. And you think you got it bad being an outsider? Shit, mister, you don't know what bad is."

Dewitt stopped pacing and looked out over the prairie, hurt in his face, eyes momentarily devoid of hope. His hands were shoved in his pockets, shoulders slumped with the weight of what he was.

"I told my daddy and my brothers that if they'd see me through high school so I could get a decent job, I'd help them all get out of debt someday, maybe even get places of their own. I thought that by going to work at the bank, why, I'd be able to get ahead in life someday, move up the ladder, make things better. But I've learned that even though I work in Claud Maye's bank and wear a suit and handle all the bank's money and books, I'm still poor white trash. Hell, I'm not even good enough to court the man's daughter!"

Dewitt's voice broke. Studying him, Sam knew that he had said all he had to say. But it was enough. Sam now understood what was in Dewitt's mind and heart. Perhaps even what was in his soul.

Rising, Sam went and stood next to him.

"I'll take your offer," he said quietly.

20

Sam's arrangement with Dewitt Tucker was a simple one, closed on a handshake out on the prairie. Dewitt would meet Sam once a week and give him a hundred dollars or more in cash. Sam would use whatever it took to keep the drill going, saving any amount that might be left over. Only Sam and Dewitt were to know about their arrangement; Sam was not to tell his partners where the money was coming from, was not to tell even Georgia. If the well failed to come in or if Dewitt was caught embezzling before it did, he agreed to keep Sam out of the subsequent scandal and criminal prosecution, and Sam promised to help him any way he could after Dewitt went to prison. If the well *did* hit, Sam was to return the absconded amount to Dewitt as quickly as possible so that Dewitt could replace it.

"What do *you* want out of all this?" Sam asked, after everything had been agreed on.

"I'll tell you when the time comes," Dewitt hedged.

"I'd like to know now," Sam insisted. "I don't want you thinking you'll get something I can't deliver. For instance, there aren't any more shares open in the well. I can give you part of what I own, and I will if that's what you want, but I can't promise you a share of what the others own. This is a point we'd better settle now."

But Dewitt shook his head. "I don't even want to think about it right now. I'm superstitious; talking about it could jinx us. But I'll tell you this much: it's something that won't give you no problem. You'll be able to do it."

Sam finally took him at his word. But he was curious as to exactly how Dewitt was going to manage his fraud.

"Hell, it won't be hard at all," the young bank employee explained. "It's a private bank so there's not any outsiders involved in audits and the like. Once every year, Mr. Maye, why, he brings in another private banker, like Cecil Trane, and the two of them spend a weekend going over the different accounts, making sure everything balances. That was just done a month ago, so I'm safe for nearly a year. What I'll be doing is taking money out of the larger savings deposits, reducing the balances on the bank's records, but not reducing the balances on the statements I send to each depositor every month. As long as I remember which accounts I've taken from, I'll be all right."

The whole scheme should have made Sam nervous as hell. Back at the J. C. Penney store, on the rare occasion when he slipped a pair of socks into his pocket, he'd felt like a shifty-eyed criminal for several days afterward, half expecting the manager to walk up to him at any moment accompanied by city detectives. Becoming involved in something as serious as this should have destroyed his calm completely. But, to Sam's surprise, it did not. He found that he wanted to keep on drilling so badly that he was frightened only of not continuing. Drilling for oil had changed him in mind as well as in body.

"There's one condition I want to make," he told Dewitt. "No money is to be taken from any account that has anything to do with Ardelle Spence or her family. I won't use their money under any circumstances."

Dewitt agreed to that, and the two men shook hands.

At home, Sam's relationship with Georgia had reached an impasse.

Alva Powell and her son Leon had stayed only two more days after Sam announced that he had secured private, anonymous financing to continue drilling; and Georgia had told her mother and brother that she would not be returning to Kansas City with them. Alva was shocked.

"But I thought you'd made up your mind."

"I had," Georgia admitted, "but my dear husband changed it. He won't let me take Ty."

"Can he do that?"

Georgia thought of the trio that now followed Sam's lead: the old range hand, the bronco Indian, the grizzled wildcatter—all of whom would do whatever Sam asked or ordered. "Yes, he can do it. This is Texas, mother. This land we're on is Sam's land: it's his

128

place. In Texas, a man controls every*thing* and every*body* on his place."

"Certainly seems strange to me."

"It's not strange, Mother, it's just Texas."

After her mother and brother left, Georgia fell into a routine that revolved around two people, little Ty and Reba Samuel, and merely skirted Sam. She saw him for a few minutes at breakfast, which was around dawn, then again late in the evening, after darkness had shut down the drilling, usually after Sam had driven his three men to their creekside camp and had a drink of bootleg with them. For about an hour then it was scrub clean in the water she had heated for him, eat without comment whatever she had cooked for his supper, play with Ty for a few minutes, and collapse into bed.

Between the two short periods with her husband, Georgia had some fifteen hours to herself. Many of those hours were spent with Reba Samuel. Georgia and Tully's wife slowly became close friends, forming a relationship that neither of them consciously initiated but to which both seemed naturally to gravitate. It began the day after Ty's birth, when Reba and Tully drove up to the house with a brand-new baby crib and mattress tied to the top of their car.

"I refuse to have that baby sleeping on a canvas bed," Reba had declared. "If his daddy wants to live like a line-rider, why, that's his business. But this baby is going to sleep on a proper mattress."

After that, Reba started dropping by every day, either in the morning before she and Tully opened the roadhouse, or during the lull between the dinner and supper trade. Usually she brought a little something with her: some leftover pork from the previous night, a gallon can of fresh milk for Georgia to drink to replenish the milk little Ty was suckling, a loaf of bread, some garden vegetables she had bought from a farmer selling at the roadside.

"Reba, you don't have to keep bringing us food," Georgia said eventually, embarrassed. "We have money now. Sam has found some anonymous investor. I thought maybe it was Tully."

"Lord, no!" Reba had declared. "All our money is already tied up—in debts. We're making payments to the bank on our mortgage, payments to the equipment company for our stove and ovens, payments to the car agency for our car. On top of that, Tully went and bought a *pool table* from the pool hall that just closed in Dane. So

we're making payments to the former pool hall owner for *that*.
Sometimes I think the only thing we own outright is the clothes on
our backs—and I ain't too sure about them."

Georgia and Reba speculated as to who Sam's anonymous bene-
factor might be. "I thought at first it might be my brother," Georgia
said, "but he let me know in no uncertain terms that he was too smart
to invest in a longshot like drilling for oil."

"Could be one of the bankers hereabouts, I reckon," Reba
guessed. "Somebody who secretly don't like the Spences and is loan-
ing Sam money under the table."

Whoever it was, they did not let the unknown investor's identity
occupy their minds for long; both were too busy enjoying their new
friendship. For Reba it was the end of a long period of personal
isolation during which she had devoted all her time and energy to
Tully and their business. She had come to Dane a decade earlier as
part of a traveling carnival and sideshow called "Buster's Merry
Games and Freak Show." It had consisted of eight games of chance
—wheels of fortune, coin tosses, and shell-and-pea layouts, inter-
spersed with sideshow attractions that included a bearded lady, a
snake charmer, a hideously ugly, deformed adolescent billed as the
Wolf Boy, a sword swallower and fire eater, a woman with severe
seborrheic neurodermatitis, badly scaly skin, called the Fish Woman,
and, in a special tent behind Buster the owner's trailer, a black
woman named Little Africa who danced naked and accepted coins
with the lips of her vulva.

Reba was the cook for the group and, because she had no beard
or skin disease, was the second-best–looking woman around, next to
Little Africa, and alternated with the black dancer sleeping with
Buster. It was not the worst job in the world, and it had got her off
the little Alabama scrub farm where she and her sister had been
forced into incestuous relationships with their father and two brothers. When she had run off, her father had come after her with a
shotgun, but Buster hid her in a secret compartment in which he
frequently transported underage girls, and denied that she had joined
up with him. A search by the sheriff had failed to turn her up, and
Buster's menagerie was allowed to go on its way.

In Dane, one of Pete Spence's riders, who had formerly traveled
with a show similar to Buster's, pointed out the foot-pedal contrap-
tion that controlled the wheel of fortune, the negative magnets under

the coin-toss board, and other irregularities, and Spence's cowboys hurrahed the show. The bearded lady was forcibly shaved, the black dancer was railroad-raped—a "train" of men lined up and rolled over her one by one—and Buster himself was tarred and feathered. Everybody else connected with the show was given a swift kick in the ass and then they were all run out of town. Except Reba, who had been uptown eating somebody *else's* cooking for a change: having a meal in Tully's Eats, a cafe Tully had owned then.

When Tully saw Spence's riders go through town heading for the carnival camp, he had said to Reba, "That there's a lynch mob. I was you, I'd not go back out there."

"I don't have no place else *to* go."

"I got a room upstairs you can hide out in until it's all over. They wouldn't never think to hunt for you there."

"What's the gimmick?" Reba had asked suspiciously.

"No gimmick. But if there was one, you'd be better off with me than you would with those cowboys. They're gonna fuck ever'thing worth fucking, and what they don't fuck they'll tie up and whip."

"How the hell can they get away with that? Where the hell's the law?"

That was when Tully had explained. "Half the law is the feller those cowboys works for, Pete Spence. The other half is a feller just like him named Patman."

"Don't you have no *real* law?"

"Nope. This here's just a township, ain't even incorporated. We're entitled to Texas Ranger protection, but don't nobody ever ask for it."

Reba shook her head incredulously. "Fuck some and whip the rest, you say?"

"Yep."

"How do I get to that room upstairs?"

She had been with Tully ever since, and became his wife a year after that.

"Oh, I've made a few friends in Dane," she explained to Georgia one day, after telling her the story, "but not many, and certainly nobody with any so-called social standing. See, I was a outsider too, like you and Sam. Most folks figured out that I had been left behind by the traveling show, but nobody was *positive* because Tully, he kept me hid for most a month. After that, nobody could prove nothing.

"Far as friends goes, over the years I've got to know the two gals who own the beauty shop, and the wife of the man who bought Tully's old cafe and turned it into a dry cleaners. But you're the first *new* friend I've made in a long, long time. And," she took Ty out of his mother's arms and nuzzled his neck, making him laugh, "we've got this little feller to thank for that. Hadn't been for him, why, we'd probably still be going on the same silly way we was."

They were soon not only spending part of every day together, but actively *planning* their days ahead so they would have more time with each other. Often Reba would drive over and get Georgia and Ty soon after Sam left in the morning, and keep them at the roadhouse with her and Tully all day. Before long, Georgia began to feel that Tully and Reba were her family, and that Sam was—well, just a *responsibility* to which she had to briefly attend twice a day.

She grew more distant from him with each day that passed.

At the derrick, the long blistering days of summer slowly changed to the short cold days of winter. The vast blue Texas sky, which seemed like the biggest sky Sam had ever seen, bigger even than the sky over the ocean when he sailed to France, now became white with great thick clots of clouds, which made him think of the snow clouds of the Midwest.

"Does it snow here?" he asked Draw.

"Now and again. Flurries, mostly. Blows around on the ground a lot; don't pile up much." Draw scratched several days' growth of beard on his chin. "Listen, speaking of weather, me and the others been talking. That tent over by the creek's getting to be mighty cold of a night. Tongue says there's an old Choctaw woman got an empty room in a 'dobe house over in the Indian community. Said she'll let us sleep in it, all three of us, for a dollar a night. I know we ain't flush with money, even with this mysterious new source of yours—"

"Move into the room," Sam said without hesitation. "You're right, y'all can't camp out all winter." He frowned, realizing it was the first time he had contracted "you all" into "y'all." Pretty soon I'll be chewing plug tobacco, he thought. Draw and Pop had already taken to chewing for the winter, saying it was too cold to roll and hold a cigarette. Tongue had some strange ground-up powder, more yellow than any other color, that he carried in a pouch around his neck, which he occasionally took a pinch of and sniffed up one nostril. It gave him a silly grin for about an hour afterward, but did not affect his work. "Some kind of heathen shit," Draw explained when Sam asked him about it.

Draw used the subject of the Indian woman's room as an opportunity to chastise Sam for not revealing the identity of their new partner. "We can stay there in the tent, of course, if our new money man, whoever he be, thinks a dollar a night's too much to pay for shelter and warmth."

"I already told you to move in," Sam said. He knew Draw was peeved at the anonymity of their partner; knew Draw felt it was all right to exclude Tongue and Pop from the secret, but that he, Draw, should occupy a higher position.

"You *did* name your firstborn after me," he pointed out. "I thought I was like part of your family."

"You are, Draw, and ordinarily you're the first one I would have told. You're my number-one adviser, you know that. But this person set certain conditions and I agreed to them. You wouldn't think I was much of a man if I broke my word, now would you?"

Draw reluctantly backed off and let the matter drop. But he strongly advised Sam to make no more deals that he, Draw, was not privy to. "You don't know these Texans," he warned. "Some of these sons of bitches'll steal the foam off your beer 'lessen you hold your mug right close to your vest."

In November, with the midday temperature hovering just above freezing, they had their first serious accident. A length of drill pipe twisted off the chain and dropped into the well hole, landing at a slight angle and lodging fast.

"Goddamn son of a bitchin' bastard," Pop cursed, a thin line of tobacco juice running down the middle of his chin. But after a minute he became very pragmatic. "Well, shit, something was bound to happen sooner or later. Ain't never seed a well hole go in yet 'thout *something* happening. It could be worse."

"Sure," Draw agreed wryly, "the goddamned derrick could fall in on us."

"Sky could fall," Tongue added cheerfully, joining in.

"Shut the fuck up, you heathen," Draw said.

"What now, Pop?" Sam asked.

"You and me hit the road again. We need a wall hook. That there's a special kind of skinny pipe that we drop down inside the stuck piece. We twist it around until it grips the inside of the stuck pipe; then we pull it out."

"Can we go on drilling in the meantime? Just not put any pipe in?"

Pop shook his head emphatically. "Nope. Too much risk of ruining the drill bit or snapping the chain. We got to shut down."

"Son of a bitch!" Sam said bitterly. He hated losing even an hour.

"Simmer down, boy," Draw said easily. "A couple days idle ain't gonna ruin us. It'll give me and Tongue a chance to get ahead on the firewood."

Sam drove over to Tully's and called Dewitt at the bank. Dewitt had then been in on their drilling scheme for seven weeks and had already given Sam nine hundred dollars. Of that, Sam had managed to save about sixty. He had hoped to save more, but with winter upon them, the timber cutting was severely curtailed by the cold hard wood, so they were buying fuel oil to help keep the boilers burning. Sam was holding back the sixty dollars for something special he had in mind, so now he asked Dewitt for the entire three hundred extra to buy the wall hook. Dewitt whistled softly into the telephone, but immediately assumed a positive attitude.

"You warned me there might be problems," he said quietly. "I bought in for the whole ride. I'll have it for you in the morning."

After Sam got the money, he and Pop left Dane in the old Willys again and began scouring the southern oil towns for a used but serviceable wall-hook. They were gone two days, finally found one in Beaumont, and got home on the morning of the third day. Pop expertly worked the wall hook into place, slowly removed the maverick length of pipe, and they resumed drilling.

Pop Joyner kept a bucket next to the well hole and filled it with ground shavings, "cuttings" he called them, several times a day. Each time the bucket was full, the old man would call Sam or one of the others over to relieve him on the drill, and he would sit down with his bucket of cuttings and examine them for signs of oil. The examination was conducted by sight, touch, smell, taste, and a variety of other means, including rubbing a shaving against wood, dunking it in grain alcohol, and rolling it into a little ball to test its sponginess. Tongue thought the performances were hilarious.

"Old white fool do everything but rub pieces of dirt on privates," he said to Draw.

"He'd do *that* if he thought it would help get to the oil faster."

Finding no discernible signs of oil, Pop would empty the bucket, return to the platform, and stoically start all over.

The bucket, to Pop, was just a vessel in which to collect his cuttings, but to Sam, Draw, and ultimately Tongue, it became something else. They saw Pop fill the bucket and empty it scores of times. Then hundreds of times. By the time they were deep into winter, all three of them hated the bucket. It had become a constant reminder of their failure.

Still, the work went on.

The week before Christmas, Tully and Reba closed the roadhouse early and drove out to see Sam and Georgia.

"Listen, Sam," Tully said awkwardly, "me and Reba is heading up to Oklahoma to see her sister for the holidays. We don't get no business to speak of between now and the end of the year, no how, so we're just shutting the place down. But we hate to go off and leave it with nobody there. So we was wondering if you and Georgia and the baby would mind moving in and keeping an eye on it for us. You can have our living quarters in the back, the icebox is filled with all kinds of food, got some good bootleg hooch in the cabinet, coal oil drums is all full, radio works good, why, I even got a pool table now that y'all can use. What do you say?"

Sam eyed the older man dubiously. "Reba making you do this? So Georgia and Ty will have a decent Christmas?"

"I ain't gonna lie to you, Sam, it *was* Reba's idea, all right. But she ain't *making* me do nothing. I'm still the boss. But I think it's a hell of an idea. And I *will* feel more at ease knowing somebody's in the place."

"Aren't you afraid the Spences might find out and take offense? You once said Pete Spence could put you out of business in a week."

"I can't see no way he'd find out," Tully replied. "I ain't gonna tell him, and I'm sure you won't. Long as you'll stay inside, won't nobody know you're there."

Sam finally agreed and Georgia started packing at once. While she was getting ready, Sam drove over to the Choctaw community to the house where Draw, Tongue, and Pop were living. He had seventy dollars saved by now and he gave the men twenty dollars each.

"Christmas bonus from Sheridan Oil Company," he said wryly.

With the other ten dollars he went into Dane and bought a box of chocolate-covered cherries and a carton of tailor-made cigarettes for Georgia, who despised rolling her own, and a musical top and toy bear for Ty.

They moved down to the roadhouse the morning that Tully and Reba left for Oklahoma. As soon as they got there, Georgia said, "God, Sam, this is going to be heaven!" She handed Ty to his father, ran into the bedroom, and began bouncing up and down on the bed. "Bedsprings! Oh, paradise!"

Following her into the bedroom, Sam could not help feeling glad for her. She was like a happy child in a new playhouse.

"There's a bathtub, too, Sam. In there. And water already heated!" Suddenly she was off the bed and undressing. "Sam, put Ty in his crib and let's take a hot bath together! Come on, hurry."

She stripped to the waist and the sight of her, part naked, all eagerness, stirred Sam. He went back into the restaurant, put Ty on the floor, and quickly unfolded the crib. By the time he returned to the bathroom, Georgia was lying back in a bed of suds, luxuriating in it all. "Get your clothes off and get in here," she ordered.

Sam stripped and stepped into the tub. He stood over her, one foot on each side of her body.

"Just stand there, Mr. Sheridan, and I'll wash your beautiful cock."

Soaping her hands, she then soaped him all over in front, and went far up behind his scrotum as well. He instantly became hard. Georgia sat up a little for better leverage and started sliding her soapy hand up and down his shaft.

"Got to make sure it's good and clean. Top to bottom and all around."

With her free hand, she explored his scrotum and beyond, her wet fingers feeling, tickling, probing. Sam gripped the wall next to the tub, closed his eyes, and let her do whatever she desired. He was hot and throbbing in her hand, and when a finger of the other hand slipped into him from behind, he tensed and felt himself begin to gush. He opened his eyes just in time to see Georgia thrust her breasts out and catch his ejaculate.

Their stay in the roadhouse turned out to be half Christmas holiday, half orgy. Ty became thoroughly confused. One minute his parents were giving him toys that Reba and Tully had bought for him, playing with him, and letting him have the run of the place; the next he was being put in his crib and wheeled into another room, there to remain by himself for an hour while his parents made strange noises in the other room. It was frustrating. But because his mom and dad seemed so happy, Ty was happy too. It was the first time he had spent so many hours with the two of them together, and it delighted him.

For Sam and Georgia it was a renewal of their early passion. It was the troop train in Kansas City, the hotel room in New York, and all the good sex they ever had, rolled into one. They made love in the bed, on the pool table, in the tub again, on the kitchen floor in front of the big oven that they turned up high with the door left open, on two restaurant chairs facing each other, on one restaurant chair, standing up against the wall, and several other locations on the premises where they took a sudden notion to perform.

By the time Reba and Tully returned, Georgia and Sam were exhausted. They drove back to their place almost with relief, for it was only there, they knew, that they would get any rest. When they got home, they found a large basket of fruit and nuts on the porch. There was no note but Sam knew it was from Dewitt Tucker. Georgia became miffed when he would not tell her who had left it.

Two weeks later, Georgia was even more miffed. "Goddamn son of a bitch," she said angrily one day when Reba arrived.

"What is it, honey?"

"No, no, no!" Georgia wailed.

"Honey, what's the matter?" Reba asked, urgently now. "What in the world is wrong with you?"

"Me! *I'm* what's wrong with me! I get too goddamned carried away sometimes. I want it too badly." She looked directly at Reba. "Then when I get it, I have to pay for it."

Reba did not need further explanation. She knew what was wrong.

Georgia was pregnant again.

21

By the middle of January, the hole they were drilling reached twenty-six hundred feet. Then a series of new problems arose. The used equipment they saved money by purchasing began giving out on them. Seldom did a day go by the rest of the month that something did not come loose or snap off or bend or jam or simply break down and quit. And whatever it was had to be taken two or three towns away to a machine shop where they were not known, and fixed. All the while the drilling rig stood idle. And Sam Sheridan cursed a blue streak.

Sam was tired, and his men were tired. They had been working the rig for eight months; the very sight of it sometimes grated on their nerves. Draw was forever muttering darkly to himself. Tongue had grown sullen and withdrawn. Sam himself was tense and edgy most of the time. Only Pop Joyner maintained the same patient pragmatic outlook.

"Jus' keep pushing that hole deeper, boys. That's what gettin' to the oil is all about."

In addition to breakdowns, accidents also began to plague them. One day a mud-ring blew off a boiler and scalded Sam's arm. Draw had to take him home while Pop drove into Dane for a can of burn ointment. After Georgia treated the scald, Sam had to stay home the rest of the day and the day after. For a week he was little or no help on the rig.

A week later, a chain snapped and a length of pipe dropped to the derrick floor so dangerously close to Pop that a plank it displaced skinned one of his ankles bloody. Pop took it in stride, like he did everything, while the rest of them cursed the pipe, which had bent just enough to render it useless. It had to be hoisted, removed, and replaced with a straight piece. Another delay.

Sam now worried constantly about the money he was getting from Dewitt Tucker. The young bank employee had now given him more than two thousand dollars. In the beginning, when the money ran only into the hundreds, the scheme had not seemed all that risky. But now, running into the thousands, with no end in sight, Sam could not help thinking about the enormity of what he and Dewitt were doing. They were stealing: there was no other name for it. And even though Dewitt had agreed to take full responsibility in the event he was caught, Sam now realized there was very little chance that he himself would be left out of it. The thought of being sent to prison made his mouth go dry.

Still, the work went on.

One evening after supper Georgia asked, half seriously, "Am I still a prisoner on this place of yours, Sam, or can I go somewhere?"

"You've never been a prisoner."

"I've felt like one, not being able to take Ty anywhere but over to Reba's."

Sam was not as distrustful of his wife now as he had been during the latter months of the previous year; the departure of her mother and brother, and the short idyll he and Georgia had at Tully's roadhouse over the Christmas holiday, had softened his suspicions somewhat. Nevertheless, he was not incautious. "Where do you want to go?"

"Shreveport. With Reba. She goes over there shopping two or three times a year. It's only seventy miles. I won't spend any money, I promise. Reba said she'd even pay for dinner."

Sam studied her without answering at once. His silence irritated Georgia, who had been edgy herself the past few weeks.

"Listen," she finally challenged, "I've made up my mind to go. I need some relief from this shack and this prairie. If you still don't trust me, I'll just leave Ty with you for the day. You can have one of those squaws in the Choctaw community take care of him. But *I* am going."

Sam continued to maintain his silence, finishing a cup of coffee, glancing over at Ty playing in a corner, looking at Georgia's back as she washed dishes in the sink. Finally he rose and took the empty cup over to her.

"You can take Ty with you," he said quietly. "It'll do him good to get away for the day too."

Sam bent and kissed her lightly on the lips. It made Georgia feel rotten for having deceived him.

Two days later Reba came by for Georgia and the baby, and the three of them headed out the Louisiana highway toward the state line. Reba was nervous for the first time in Georgia's memory.

"Sam Sheridan would kill me if he knowed what I was doing," she said to Georgia, glancing anxiously in the fender mirror to be sure he was not following them.

"Don't be silly, he would not," Georgia assured her. "It's me he'd take it out on. After all, it's me that's doing it."

"Are you sure it's the right thing, honey?"

"I'm positive." The line of Georgia's mouth was set. "And I'd rather not talk about it anymore, Reba."

Reba bit her lip and drove.

They reached Shreveport in three hours. Georgia had Reba pull over at the first pawn shop she saw: Bossier Pawn & Loans. Leaving Ty with Reba, she walked boldly up to the door and entered.

"Yes, ma'am, can I help you?" a lean, balding man without a Southern accent asked from behind a counter. He was frowning; women who entered his front door were few and far between.

"I'd to know how much I can get for these, please." On the counter between them Georgia unfolded a lace handkerchief wrapped around her string of pearls. "They're real."

The pawnbroker took the pearls to a workbench in the corner, stood with his back to Georgia for a moment, then returned and put them back on the handkerchief. "So they are."

"How much can I get for them?" Georgia asked again.

"To sell or to pawn?"

She hesitated just a fraction. "Sell."

"Fifty dollars."

Georgia's mouth dropped open. "Why, they're worth ten times that!"

"Not to me they aren't, lady. If I had any business sense a'tall, I wouldn't even make an offer. There's no way I'll get my money back here in Shreveport. Ladies hereabouts either have heirloom pearls or they wear Woolworth pearls. Order for me to resell these,

I'll have to go all the way to New Orleans. That's an expense right there. Still no guarantee I'll sell 'em, even in New Orleans."

Georgia sighed quietly and folded up the handkerchief. "I'm sorry, I just won't let them go for fifty dollars." She turned to go.

"You're not from around here, are you?" the pawnbroker asked.

"No. I'm from over the line in Texas."

"So if I was maybe to go a little higher," he said, rubbing his chin, "word wouldn't get around Shreveport that I was losing my mind?"

"Not from me. How much higher?"

"Let's say a hundred."

"Look, I'll be honest with you. I need a hundred and fifty to help my sister out of a fix she's in. That's the only reason I'm selling them. They're pearls my grandmother left me because I was her favorite."

"Your sister, huh?" He eyed her with a smirk, considering an off-color remark. Georgia's direct stare stopped him. "One-twenty-five," he said quickly, "and no more sad tales. Final offer."

"Let me have it in small bills," Georgia said, putting the handkerchief back on the counter.

An hour later, Georgia and Reba were sitting in a cool dim parlor, quiet except for the soft buzz of overhead fan blades. Ty, on Reba's lap, was chewing and drooling on the corner of a Big Little book they had bought him.

"Jesus, I'm scared," Reba said. Her hands were trembling.

"You're scared. I'm *terrified."*

"Then let's get out of here while we can."

At that moment a large black woman entered. "Which one of you ladies is it?"

Georgia and Reba looked at each other wide-eyed and open-mouthed. Neither could muster words.

"Well?" the black woman asked after a moment.

"Me," Georgia said. The word caught in her throat.

"Come on with me then."

Georgia quickly squeezed Reba's arm and awkwardly kissed Ty on his drooling lips, then followed the black woman out of the parlor.

In a smaller room at the back of the house, the black woman

---

said, "Take off ever'thing from your waist down and lie down on the table. I be back directly."

Trembling, sweating, Georgia got out of her skirt and underthings, and sat instead of lying on the table. It was a sturdy kitchen table with some kind of pad on it, covered with a sheet. Georgia's lips were quivering and she was sure she would have to go to the bathroom. When the black woman returned, she took Georgia by the shoulders and gently guided her back. Georgia forgot about having to go to the bathroom as she watched the black woman fold a blue bandanna lengthwise.

"I gots to blin'fold you so's you can't see the doctor's face."

Oh, Jesus.

"I thought—I mean, isn't there—don't I get something—"

"'Course you do, sugar. The blin'fold's jus' in case you wake up. But I got somethin' right here's gonna make you rest easy. I'm gonna lay this over your nose now and you breath the vapors. It's gonna feel cold . . ."

It did; it felt very cold. And that was the last thing Georgia remembered.

When she woke up, Reba was sitting beside the table, wiping her face with a damp cloth. There was a sheet over her lower body. Georgia could hear Ty playing on the floor. Her mouth was terribly dry and she felt a little nauseated.

"Where—where's—" she tried to form a question.

"Gone," Reba said. "Both gone. I never even seen the doctor. The nigger mammy said we could stay here until you felt strong enough to walk. She left these cotton pads for you. Are you all right?"

Georgia nodded briefly. "I—think so. What time is it?"

"Just after three. We'll start back soon's you want to."

"Help me sit up, please, Reba."

Shifting her legs over the side of the table, Georgia held onto Reba's arm to balance herself. She was a little unsteady, but considerably more in control than she had been earlier.

"Thank God it's over. I've never been so scared in my life. Reba, they *blindfolded* me! So I couldn't see the doctor."

"I wonder if there really *was* a doctor?" said Reba. "Or if that old mammy did it?"

"Oh, Reba, there must have been a doctor. *Surely* there was."

"Yeah, most prob'ly," Reba amended, for Georgia's benefit, but secretly she doubted it.

"Did she—did she say if it was a boy or a girl?"

"Didn't say." It was a lie. Reba knew the sex of the baby; she just did not want Georgia to have to think about the aborted child as a girl for the rest of her life.

"Was Ty a good boy?"

"Perfect angel. He's always good for his Aunt Reba. Do you think you can walk to the car?" Reba was getting nervous about starting back home.

"Yes, I think so. Get my clothes over there and help me dress."

A few minutes later, they were in the car heading back toward Texas.

As they drove, Georgia tried to deal with a nagging thought. She tried to modify it, rephrase it, justify it, eliminate it, even ignore it. But nothing worked. It remained with her, and it created in her a feeling of dread.

The thought was that she had killed Sam's child.

The dread was that he would find out about it.

22

In the spring they reached thirty-four hundred feet.

Pop Joyner began to get itchy. His buckets of cuttings were making him nervous. First there were some shavings that had the "feel" Pop was looking for. Then a few days later some that had the "smell." Finally, a couple of days after that, he found the "taste."

"We're right at thirty-four hunnerd and fifty feet," he told Sam. "I calcalate it's time to take a core."

"What's that mean?"

"Means another problem. More money. Another piece of equipment. What we got to have now is what they call a core-barrel assembly. What it is, is a hollow bit. We put her on in place of the drill bit and run her down the hole. At the bottom she rotates and packs in a sample of the stratum. Know what stratum is?" Pop grinned and dripped tobacco juice out of one corner of his mouth as Sam shrugged. "I didn't think so. Well, it's a fancy word the geologists use. Means 'layer.' Anyhow, the core barrel packs in this here sample and as we pull her up, a little seat closes and holds it in. That way, we bring up a solid sample of the core to examine; not just cuttings."

Sam called Dewitt and asked if he could meet him out on the prairie.

"I was about to call you for the same thing. I think we got trouble, Sam."

The next morning when they met, Dewitt told him what the trouble was.

"Mr. Maye found one of the accounts I altered. Just accidentally came across it. The balance was off two hundred dollars. I told him I recalled taking the deposit but must have forgotten to post it. I said I included it in the day's figures, which was how we balanced without it. And I told him the bank's debits and credits would balance, if he cared to audit the books."

"What'd he say?" Sam asked.

"He just smiled and said that wouldn't be necessary, ever'body forgot to post something ever' now and then."

"You think he believed you?"

"Prob'ly. Thing of it is, Sam, if he comes across another, he *won't* believe me. He'll have an audit for sure. I don't think I'd better mess with any more accounts."

"You're right, you'd better not." Inside, Sam felt as sick as he imagined Dewitt did. Goddamn, he silently cursed, what had they been *thinking* to begin stealing from a bank like that? They deserved to go to the penitentiary for stupidity.

"What'd you need money for this time?" Dewitt asked.

"Something called a core-barrel assembly. Pop wants to pull a sample up."

"Does it look like we might be close?"

"Pop says this core sample ought to tell us."

"I feel bad about this, Sam. Maybe I could go into just one more account for us."

Sam shook his head emphatically. "No, Dewitt. Definitely not. No more chances in the bank. Just try to cover what you've already done. We'll get the core-barrel assembly some other way."

He had no idea how.

At supper that night, Sam said, "Has Tully ever asked you anything about the drilling we're doing out here?"

"No, why?" Georgia asked.

"He and Reba have any money put aside that you know of?"

Georgia shrugged. "Some, I guess. Not much probably. Why do you want to know?"

"My money source has shut off. I need sixty or seventy dollars for a piece of equipment to bring up a core sample. I thought maybe I'd offer Tully a small share of my interest if he'd put up the money."

"If you give him any of your share, won't that leave you with less than fifty percent?"

"Yes. But this core sample is important."

"You told me once it was important to keep a fifty-percent share so nobody could ever take the oil away from Ty. Isn't that what you said?"

"Yes, it is. Look, I don't *want* to reduce the fifty percent, but I've got to have this piece of equipment. Those men of mine have been breaking their backs for a lot of months on nothing but hope. Pop seems to feel that we're close. A core sample will tell us for *sure.* Not only how close but how good the oil is. Those men *need* to know, Georgia. *I* need to know."

"How much did you say, sixty or seventy dollars?"

"About. What are you doing?"

She pushed two fingers into the toe of an old shoe and worked out a small rubber-banded roll of bills. She tossed it to Sam. "Seventy-five dollars."

Sam was astonished. "Where did you get it?"

Mother and Leon sent me fifty last Christmas. The rest I've had saved for a long time." It was a lie, of course. The money had been left over from the hundred and twenty-five she got for her pearls, after paying the abortionist fifty.

"Why are you doing this now? This money would get you back to Kansas City if the oil's not there."

"Maybe I'm beginning to think it *is* there. Maybe some of your confidence has rubbed off on me."

Sam hefted the roll of bills in his hand as if it were heavy. "This means a lot to me, Georgia," he told her quietly. "Mostly it means that we're on the same side again."

"Don't get gushy on me, Sam. Just go find your core-whatever and get that sample."

After Sam left, Georgia thought about what he had said. It meant a lot to him. And put them on the same side again.

I hope, she thought, that helping him makes me stop thinking that I killed his baby.

With the money from Georgia, Sam and Pop were off again in the old flatbed. After driving most of one day, they found, in the town of Temple, the core-barrel assembly they needed. They bought it and headed home immediately. They got back to Dane at midnight.

At daybreak the next morning, Pop Joyner pulled up their core sample. Opening the hollow bit, he handed Sam a Mason jar and said, "Scrape it into this and take it to a geologist. I ain't even gonna look at it. Don't want to jinx us with no uneducated guesses."

Sam jarred the sample, got back in the truck, and drove off as Pop, Draw, and Tongue watched silently from the platform. Nobody wished him good luck; Pop said it was *bad* luck to wish an oil man *good* luck.

As Sam drove away, the men staring after him, he shared with them a common thought: Their entire futures rested on the contents of that Mason jar.

23

The nearest geologist was a man a half-dozen years older than Sam named Rufus Prine, in Longview. He was soft looking, going fat too early, obviously accustomed to the easy life of the indoor scientist who has left the field sampling to others.

"Got some good mud here?" he asked, smiling, as he took the jar from Sam.

"Hope it's good." There was tight anxiety in Sam's voice.

"How far down did you pull this from?" Prine held the jar up to the light.

"Between thirty-four and thirty-five hundred."

"Well, I'll take it back in the lab and test it out." He smiled again. "Guess you're in a hurry to know?"

Sam could not help grinning nervously. "Kind of."

"All right. Give me about two hours. Go on out and walk around town. Try to relax. Either the sample's good or it's bad; worrying won't change it one way or the other." He gave Sam a pat on the shoulder and sent him out.

Sam did as Rufus Prine suggested. Wearing heavy denim coveralls stuffed into knee-high rubber boots, with roughout boarskin gloves sticking out of his back pocket, a battered old cowboy hat that had once belonged to Draw, a faded red bandanna around his neck, the entire outfit spotted here and there with light brown dried mud, he should have been an object of curiosity as he wandered around Longview. But the town was accustomed to seeing wildcatters waiting out the laboratory results of their hard-earned core samples. Some of them left town whooping and hollering, some skulked out; one even blew his brains out with a pistol on the main street. Every merchant in Longview knew that oil men were odd ducks. So nobody paid much attention to Sam.

He wandered from the nickel-and-dime store to the hardware store to the bakery to the Ford car agency to the Piggly-Wiggly to the picture show, and then started over again. Altogether, he made the town circuit four times. He all but memorized the scene cards outside the movie house: the picture was called *The Round Up,* starring a marble-eyed actor named Roscoe (Fatty) Arbuckle. It looked like a very funny show, but Sam only stared at the cards austerely. He wouldn't have smiled if Buster Keaton had stood in front of him and stared back.

The time passed interminably. Ultimately Sam could not wait the full two hours. After ninety minutes, he returned to the geologist's office. He had to wait fifteen more minutes before Rufus Prine came out of his laboratory. The geologist was not smiling.

"Quick and clean, that's how I give reports." His tone was

neutral. "There's oil in this hole—but it's not easy oil and it's not good oil. When I say it's not easy oil, I mean it's down about seventeen hundred more feet. And when I say it's not good oil, I mean it's heavily tainted with saltwater."

Sam stared mutely at him, his heart feeling as if it were turning thick and soggy, his bowels threatening to evacuate where he stood.

Seventeen hundred more feet.

Tainted with saltwater.

"It's refineable oil, don't get me wrong," Prine continued. "But it's so deep and so tainted that won't nobody make much money off it. You might get back what you put in the derrick and rigging. I say *might.*"

In a sick daze, Sam unbuttoned a coverall pocket and took out his billfold. "What's the, uh—how much do I owe you?"

"Oh, hell, just give me ten dollars for my laboratory supplies. Wish the news was better; I'd charge you two hundred if it was."

Sam paid him and took back the Mason jar into which Prine had put what was left of the core sample.

"Be glad to mail you a written report," the geologist offered.

Sam shook his head. "No. Thanks, anyway. Thanks for your time. Goodbye."

He stood on the sidewalk outside the office in a state of shock, scarcely believing it. All that work: thirteen months of dawn-to-dusk labor in the sweltering heat of summer, the thin cold of winter; suffering injury, breakdown, delay; using embezzled money; risking everything to force a narrow hole thirty-five hundred feet into the crust of the earth—for *nothing.* Sam shook his head in stunned disbelief. The revelation was more bitter than he ever imagined it would be.

The only possible thing worse would be telling the others.

Driving back to Dane, Sam thought about Dewitt Tucker. Over the past seven months, Sam had accepted slightly more than four thousand dollars from the young bank clerk. As he drove, staring straight ahead at the narrow state road, Sam now determined that Dewitt would not go to prison for trying to help him.

In his distressed mind, Sam added everything up. Nine hundred dollars from Draw; seven-sixty from Pop. Tongue didn't put in any cash, but Sam wanted to try to give him a couple of hundred anyway.

And he and Georgia would need bus fare back to Kansas City, and a little extra to tide them over while he looked for a job. And the money for Dewitt to cover himself at the bank. Say sixty-five hundred.

He wouldn't ask for a dollar more. Maybe he had to compromise everything else, but he wanted no goddamned profit. Not from *her.*

When he reached Dane, Sam drove directly to the Spence town home. He parked in the drive, stepped onto the porch, and drew the bell-pull. In a moment the door was opened by a heavyset Mexican woman in a starched white dress.

"*Señor?*"

"Tell Mrs. Spence that Mr. Sheridan is here, please."

"*Sí, señor.* Will you come in, please?"

"No. I'll wait here."

The Mexican maid left the door ajar a few inches. Sam did not move from where he stood: did not pace, did not even shift his weight. He stared straight at the door until Ardelle Spence opened it wider.

She was still the same as the image etched in his memory: a firm, unsmiling mouth, a chin slightly uptilted, eyes devoid of warmth.

"Yes?"

"You win, Mrs. Spence. If you still want the hundred acres, I'll sell them to you."

Ardelle Spence did not even blink. "All right."

"I have to have sixty-five hundred dollars for them. So I can leave Dane without owing anybody."

"Does that price guarantee that you will not return?"

"It does."

She nodded a scant nod. "My husband's office is over the Merchants Bank uptown. I'll telephone. The money and a deed of transfer will be ready by the time you get there."

Sam nodded curtly, and with no further words walked back to his truck.

Fuck it all, he thought as he drove uptown. Fuck Dane and Caddo County. Fuck all the Spences and Patmans, living *and* dead. And fuck this land and these people, neither of which would give a goddamn inch to anyone. And above all, fuck Texas!

Parking on the town square, Sam headed for the enclosed

wooden stairway between the bank and the building next door. He started up the stairs two at a time, but only got halfway to the top. That was where he ran into Rufus Prine, coming down.

Sam stared at him as incredulously now as he had an hour earlier in the geologist's office in Longview. Prine nodded and started past him but Sam put an arm out to block his way.

"What are you doing here?" Sam asked in a deadly quiet voice.

"Why, I'm here on, uh, business, Mr. Sheridan." Prine tried to smile; the effort made him look ill.

"What business? Who with?"

"I don't see where that's, uh, any concern—"

"I'll decide whether it's my concern or not," Sam cut in sharply. He put the palm of one hand squarely on Prine's chest. "Listen carefully to me, Prine. I just got done doing the hardest thing I ever had to do in my life, and it's tearing me up inside. This is not a good time for anyone to make me angry. Now I want to know who you just came from seeing up there."

"Sheridan, I don't have to talk to you. By God, you'd better let me pass!"

"You work for him, don't you? You work for Pete Spence." The cold white fury that had begun in his groin finally reached Sam's mind and took over. He grabbed Prine by the throat with both hands. "You dirty son of a bitch," he said in a terrible whisper, his face close to Prine's. "Admit it. Admit you work for Spence!"

Prine slowly bent back to the stairs above him, as if to escape Sam's grip. But Sam bent with him, not relinquishing or reducing the viselike hold of his labor-strengthened hands.

"You lied about my core sample, didn't you? What did it really show? Answer me, you miserable bastard!"

When he saw Prine's tongue thrust out and his eyes roll back, Sam realized that in his anger he was strangling Prine. Which made no difference to him, except that Prine could not respond. Releasing the geologist's neck, Sam took him by the lapels, jerked him forward, and slammed him painfully against the stairs.

"What did my core sample show?"

"I—never—analyzed it—" Prine managed to gasp.

"Why not?"

"Mr. Spence—he wrote down a—a report that was to be given to you if you ever came in. Gave it to—to me and to the geologists

---

150

over in Kilgore and Nacogdoches. He paid—all three of us five hundred dollars apiece—"

Savagely, violently, Sam dragged Prine back up the stairs. These, he suddenly recalled, were the same stairs he and Georgia had climbed their very first day in Dane, when they had briefly visited the law offices of Fort & Fort. Now Sam pulled Rufus Prine bodily past those same offices and through a door lettered: Spence Land & Cattle Co.

"My goodness!" said a startled receptionist as Sam propelled Prine past her desk. There was a single door marked Private just beyond the reception area. Sam shagged the terrified geologist through that door and found himself in Pete Spence's own office. A man in front of Spence's desk whirled around at the intrusion. It was Claud Maye from the bank downstairs.

Spence rose behind his desk but said nothing. It was the first time Sam and Ardelle Spence's husband had met face to face, although Sam had seen Spence on the streets of Dane. Now, for several tense seconds, they stood silently and studied each other. Pete Spence was a hefty, round-shouldered man, dressed in Western clothes that were inexpensive except for a twelve-thousand-dollar solid-gold belt buckle and a pair of custom-made rhino-hide boots that had cost sixteen hundred dollars. His light thinning hair was parted off-center and he had incongruously delicate lips. As a young man he had been quiet and introspective. Only after taking control of his own father's land and his wife's father's land, and slowly realizing the tremendous responsibility of running both spreads, had he gradually become aggressive. He faced Sam Sheridan now with no fear whatever, even though he knew Sam probably felt he had reason to kill him.

Sam finally broke the silence by flinging Rufus Prine forward, sending him sprawling across Spence's desktop.

"I'm going to break you, Spence," Sam said in tightly controlled fury. "I'm going to break you and I'm going to break this goddamned town of yours. I'm going to beat you both down into the dirt and stomp you into dust. I'm not going to rest a day until I'm where you are—and you're where I am!"

Without waiting for Spence to say a word, Sam stalked out of the office and back down the stairs to the street. People stopped and stared as he strode along the sidewalk, red-faced and talking aloud, pointing at individuals and businesses as he went.

151

"He'll pay!" Sam promised. "You'll pay! They'll pay! This whole goddamned town will pay! *Everybody* will pay for this day for years to come!"

Like a crazy man, he walked all the way around the town square of Dane, delivering his curse.

24

After Sam made a circuit of the square, he went to the public telephone in the corner cafe that doubled as a North Texas Stage Lines bus stop. He paid a nickel to use it and called Tully's place. Reba answered.

"Listen, Reba, I'd like you to do me a favor," he said, putting aside any thought of the dislike she still might harbor for him. Actually, he had not thought about it for quite a while anyway; since Ty's birth and Reba's friendship with Georgia, she had treated Sam at least cordially. "I have to get a message to Georgia, and it's important. Will you help me?"

Reba hesitated just a beat, then said, "All right."

"Tell her that I can't get an honest analysis from the geologists around here: they're all in Spence's pocket. Tell her I'm heading out of town to find somebody I can trust. I'll be back as soon as I can. She's not to worry. And ask her to pass this on to Draw and the others so they won't wonder where I am."

"All right," Reba repeated.

There was a moment of awkward silence on the line. Then Sam said, "Thank you, Reba. I appreciate this."

"All right. Goodbye."

Returning to his flatbed, Sam drove grimly out of town. He headed south first, then west, changing from one state highway to another, going generally in the direction of Austin, the state capitol. The Mason jar with the core sample rode on the seat beside him, wrapped in a piece of burlap in case the springless truck bounced it onto the metal floorboard. As he drove, Sam gripped the steering wheel with white-knuckled hands. His jaw was clenched, his eyes, fixed on the road, dark and dangerous. Never had he hated anyone like he hated Pete Spence.

The first geologist he found was in the town of Alto. "Do you know Pete Spence, up Dane way?" he asked. The geologist did. Without another word, Sam turned around and left.

Next he stopped in Crockett. "Do you know Pete Spence, up Dane way?" Yes. Sam returned to his truck and drove on.

He stopped in Centerville, Marquez, Marlin, Rosebud, each town farther from Dane than the previous one. Each time it was the same question; for a long time it brought the same answer. Yes, they knew Pete Spence. Pete and his father before him, Paddy Spence, were native Texans. The Spence family, on the side of Pete's maternal grandmother, went all the way back to the Alamo. The family was well known in East Texas.

But Sam was gradually leaving East Texas and moving into Central Texas. And he found that the farther he got from Dane, the less known his enemy became. In Navasota, the geologist rubbed his chin and said thoughtfully, "Spence, Pete Spence. I *think* I know him. Or I know *of* him. Not quite sure which."

Finally, after driving most of the day, in the little town of Cameron, less than a hundred miles from Austin, Sam asked, "Have you ever heard of a man named Pete Spence, up Dane way?" and a young geologist replied, "No, can't say as I have."

His name was Owen Milam and he was a tall rangy young man with corn-colored hair, wearing wire-rimmed eyeglasses. He seemed a little embarrassed by Sam's question. "I haven't been in business too long," Owen admitted. "Still don't know many people. Is Mr. Spence an independent?"

"He's not in oil. He's a cattleman."

"Oh. Well, I don't know any cattlemen, except a few small ranchers around here. Sorry."

"Don't be." Unrolling the burlap, Sam put his jar on the counter. "Can you analyze this core sample for me?"

Milam's face lighted up at once. "You bet I can. Take about two hours, if you'd like to walk around town—"

"I'll wait right here."

He sat on a low wooden bench with his back against the wall and watched while Owen, whose laboratory was in the same room, opened the Mason jar and set about separating the core sample into various-size pieces for the respective tests. The young man did not work fast or slowly, merely precisely, the textbook procedures of his profession still fairly fresh in his mind. Although aware that Sam was watching him, he was not bothered by his presence; in fact after a few minutes he seemed to forget Sam altogether. As he worked, Sam noticed that, depending on what he was doing, Owen Milam changed eyeglasses occasionally, seeming to need one pair for very close work, another for more distance.

While Sam waited, his thoughts turned again to Pete Spence and the vile contemptible deceit he had attempted through Rufus Prine. Sam could not recall ever hearing of a lower, more reprehensible scheme than the one engineered by Spence. To know that four men had put everything they had, both financially and physically, into a project like that well, had labored over it for thirteen long grueling months, and then to attempt to deprive those men of the possible rewards of that work by graft and lies; it was almost too despicable to believe. Yet Pete Spence had done it.

But he'll pay for it, Sam vowed silently. The son of a bitch would pay like he had never paid before.

He—would—pay . . .

"Hey."

Sam felt a hand on his shoulder. Opening his eyes, he realized at once that he had dozed off. The long hours of driving while searching for a core assembly the previous day, the long trip back to Dane the previous night, the tension of the morning, then the miles and miles of searching for an honest geologist today: it had all caught up with him. Now the young geologist in Cameron, Owen Milam, had a hand on his shoulder, shaking him.

"I was afraid you were going to fall off this bench. You must really be whipped."

"Sorry," Sam said. "I'll stay awake. Go on back to your work."

"All finished. Step up to the counter and I'll show you what I found."

At the counter, Sam saw that the geologist had each sample section either on a piece of white pasteboard or in a glass beaker filled with some kind of liquid. In front of each was a slip of paper with scribbled notes and figures on it.

"You want me to give you the physical and chemical breakdown on each individual test," Owen asked, "or get right to the conclusion?"

"The conclusion."

"All right." Owen changed glasses and picked up a larger sheet of paper. "Well, sir, you've got oil, all right. And you're close to it. Mighty close. Looks to be no more than, oh, forty or fifty feet down. And it's a very good oil, looks like: light, pretty much free of sulphur, no saltwater traces. Probably be very easily refineable—and that means easy to sell at a good price." He smiled at Sam. "I'd say you've got yourself a strike."

So much relief coursed through Sam that his knees actually became weak. He stepped quickly to the bench and sat down again. In a moment Owen Milam was in front of him, holding out a glass of water. "Here, drink this and take a couple of deep breaths."

When he was composed, Sam looked up and said, "A strike, huh?"

"Yessir, and a right good one too, if that's a true core sample."

"It's as true as they come. Pop Joyner pulled that sample."

Owen's eyes widened behind the glasses. "Really? Pop Joyner? Why, my god, I've been hearing stories about him since I was a little boy. They practically teach a course on him in drilling school. Is he who you work for?"

"Work with. He's one of my partners."

"Well, sir," Owen said, becoming solemn, "you tell him for me that it's been an honor to assay his core sample. Proud to have been a part of one more strike to add to his legend."

"About this sample. Would you say I could get credit on it?"

"No doubt at all."

"Good. Because I don't have the money to pay you." Sam stood up. "Not only that, but I need to borrow five dollars for gas to get back home."

Owen Milam's mouth dropped open; presently he shook his head incredulously. "Mother told me I should have become a dentist," he said, digging into his pocket. He gave Sam the five dollars.

"You'll be hearing from me," Sam promised as he left.

25

Sam and his men now began to drill with a vengeance. They could smell success and it raced their blood. No longer did they even accede to normal drilling hours; Tongue broke their pact with daylight by arriving at the derrick one morning with twelve Choctaw children.

"What's going on?" Sam asked when he drove up. The dozen children were sitting in two rows on the platform, legs crossed, hands folded politely. Next to each was a kerosene lantern.

"Get to black water faster if drill in dark too," Tongue explained. "Before sun come up, I have three young ones stand on each side of platform with lanterns. Give plenty light for work. In early morning and after dark, two hour each time. Four more hour work every day."

Sam stared at the flat-faced, cross-eyed Indian with unconcealed admiration. "That is one hell of an idea, Tongue."

"That mean good or bad?"

"That mean good, very good." Sam cocked an eyebrow. "Tongue, why don't you speak the same way here as you do in the Choctaw community? We're your friends, you know. You don't have to act the uncivilized savage with us."

A hint of a smile crossed Tongue's lips before he quickly controlled it. "Someday, maybe. When time right."

"Okay. Whenever you're ready. Just remember in the meantime, there is no color barrier between us. In fact, there's no barrier at all. I'm as much of an outcast around here as you are. Under our skin, we're both the same."

"Brothers?" asked Tongue.

"Yes, brothers."

Sam looked over at the children. "Let them go home now. They can come back at sundown."

Tongue got the children and their lanterns off the platform and started them in a single-file trot toward the Choctaw community. Their leader was a tall slim girl who glanced back at Sam as they left, and whom Sam recognized at once as Tunica, the young tribal princess. He waved to her. She smiled but did not wave back. "Why is she here?"

"Her choice," Tongue replied. "She volunteer first to encourage others."

Sam was impressed. I'll have to make a point of thanking her, he thought.

From that day on, the twelve Choctaw children arrived at the derrick two hours before sunrise every day, and returned to hold the lanterns two hours after dark each night.

By midsummer, Pop had sunk the drill bit to thirty-eight hundred feet. At that depth, it began cutting into hard sand.

"Drill bit's getting hacksawed," Pop told the others. "It ain't gonna last much longer."

"Will it have to?" Sam asked.

Pop went to his bucket and examined the freshest cuttings. In them he found slight traces of color: a thin string of dark blue, a spot of dull red here and there. "Them's chemical changes in the soil's natural color. Brought on by some foreign element." Pop chewed on his words for several seconds. "Could be our oil. Let's take another core sample."

For the second time the core-barrel assembly was lowered into the hole to capture a sample of the earth from the depth their pipe had reached. When it was brought back up, it contained a grainy soil laced with traces of oil.

Pop grunted. "Oil sand. We're close."

"How good is it, can you tell?" Sam asked.

Pop shook his head. "I ain't no geologist. All I do is find it and bring it up."

Sam remembered Owen Milam's statement that easily refineable oil was easy to sell. "When we go to sell it, it makes a difference what *kind* of oil it is, doesn't it?"

"You bet. The refineries pay by what grade crude they judge it to be."

"Is there any way we can grade it ourselves? Before we strike, and before we start dealing with the refineries? So we'll know ahead of time what we've got?"

"We can bring up a sample of the actual oil and have a geologist test it for grade." Pop laughed wryly and added, "But we'll need another piece of equipment to do it. Thing called a drill stem."

"Shit," said Sam. They were almost flat broke again. Asking Dewitt for more money was out of the question, too risky. Sam was certain that Georgia had no more cash stuck in a shoe. And he had made up his mind not to seek credit on the geologist's report, as Owen Milam had assured him he could successfully do. With a bank involved, there would be no way to keep the strike secret. And he *had* to keep it secret, in order to carry out the plans he had already made.

"Has our piggy bank give out?" Pop asked, seeing the concern in Sam's face.

"For now. But goddamn it, I think it's important that we know what kind of product we're looking at here. I don't have any experience dealing with oil people; I'd like to have as much information on my side as possible."

"That's right good thinking. I agree with you a hunnerd percent." Pop spat a long stream of tobacco juice off the platform. "Tell you what: I heard tell that Sinclair was spudding in some wells over in Van Zandt County. I used to know some fellers at Phillips 66 that's with Sinclair now. What say you and me take a run over there? Maybe I can get somebody to borrow us a drill stem under the table."

"All right, let's try it," Sam agreed.

Once again the two of them were off in the old flatbed.

Van Zandt was sixty miles west, just across the Sabine River. Sinclair was drilling near Grand Saline and it was to that town that Pop directed Sam. They parked on the town square and walked around, checking the bootleg beer joints, pool halls, and boarding houses for someone off-shift that Pop knew. In the beginning when they had gone off on one of their forays, Sam and Pop had been an odd pair: a grizzled old, bandy-legged wildcatter with a hide like a javelina and the corners of his mouth permanently stained with tobacco juice; and a tentative, clean-cut young man still wearing city clothes, still speaking city English. Now, they looked like they belonged together, Sam had changed so much. His tentativeness had been replaced by a confidence born of risk and bred of hazard. The clean-cut looks were gone, leaving in their stead a deeply tanned, tough exterior. City clothes had been discarded in favor of rough oil-field attire, and the city English was giving way more each day to a vernacular common only to one place: Texas.

After a complete circuit of the Grand Saline business establishments without finding anyone reliable enough to trust, Pop said, "Hell, let's drive on out to the field and look the day crew over; maybe there's somebody out there."

At the field they had no better luck. Pop asked around about specific riggers and foremen, but all of them had either moved on to other companies or were at other Sinclair operations. "Goddamn transient bums," Pop cursed. "Never stay in one place long enough to shit."

While they were in the main field shack talking to the field superintendent, the Van Zandt county sheriff walked in with a warrant in his hand. "Y'all got a kid name of Buddy Kyle workin' in this field?" he asked.

The superintendent opened a ledger and ran one finger down the lines on several pages. "Yeah, we got him. Toolshed helper. Been with us four months. Good worker. What'd he do?"

"Run off from the reformatory back in St. Charles, Illinois. I got to pick him up and hold him for a deputy to come take him back."

The superintendent pointed out the window to a nearby shack. "You'll find him right over there."

As the sheriff went toward the toolshed, Sam and Pop got back in the flatbed. There was a tarp in the back of the truck and Sam noticed that it was no longer lying flat but now looked like a sack of grain was under it. Sam said nothing, merely started the truck and drove off.

When they got back to Grand Saline, instead of parking on the town square, Sam parked in an alley behind one of the boarding-houses. Getting out of the cab, he stepped up onto the bed and flipped back one corner of the tarp. A young boy scurried out from under and whirled on Sam with an open pocketknife.

Pop, on the ground next to the truck, growled, "Why, you little bastard," and snatched a shovel from the fender box.

"Easy, Pop," said Sam, jumping down and grabbing the old wildcatter's arm. Sam looked up at the boy. He was a stocky young man with grotesquely crooked teeth, untrained hair, and a scared, trapped-animal look in his eyes. "If I meant to do you any harm," Sam told him quietly, "I'd have done it back at the field when I first saw you." He took the shovel from Pop's hand and eased the old wildcatter toward the back door of the boardinghouse. "Come on in," he said to the boy, "and have some supper. After we eat, if you want a way out of town you can ride with us. We're heading east."

Sam and Pop went inside to the boardinghouse dining room. Several minutes later, the young man on the flatbed closed his pocketknife and followed them.

"They put me in the reform school because I kept running off from the orphan asylum," Buddy Kyle told them over supper. "The judge that done it said I was a incorrigible. I don't even know what that means."

"It's someone who can't be managed," Sam told him. "Can't be trained to do right."

"That's me, I guess," Buddy said with a self-conscious shrug.

"I don't think so," said Sam. "The field super said you'd been a good worker there for four months. That doesn't sound like an incorrigible to me."

"I ain't afraid of work. An' I get along all right when people let me alone."

"Where are your folks?"

"Paw's in Joliet Prison in Illinois. For killing Maw. Caught her in a room with a sailor. Killed him too." Embarrassed, he kept his eyes on his food instead of looking at Sam and Pop. The two men exchanged quick glances. Then Pop leaned forward a little, as if to make sure the boy would hear what he was going to say.

"Listen here, young feller," he said gravely, "don't never waste no shame on who your folks was, or what they done. A man ain't responsible for what he come from. All you ever got to be ashamed of, *or* proud of, is what you do yourself."

160

"Pop's right," Sam concurred. For a moment he wondered how that philosophy applied to himself, now that he was not really sure any longer who *he* was.

Buddy Kyle looked at Sam and Pop with new interest. "But how do you get away from it? How do you keep the past from catching up? No matter where I run to, I can't never seem to get away."

"You stop running," Sam told him. "You make a stand somewhere." Now it was Sam who leaned forward. "How'd you like to come to work for me, Buddy? We'll get you out of this county and take you back home with us. Once you get on my place, I'll *guarantee* that nobody will make you run again."

"We'll goddamn sure see to that," Pop snorted. "Me and Sam's partners with a couple other fellers. We's all got us a well that's about to spurt. After it blows, won't *nobody* mess with any of us, we'll have so goddamn much money. We'll take care of you, son."

"But first," Sam added quietly, "there's something you can do for us." Glancing around the dining room, he lowered his voice even more. "We need to borrow a drill stem from the Sinclair toolshed. Notice I didn't say steal, I said borrow. We want to take it home, use it, and then return it. If we can get it tonight, we can have it back tomorrow night. Pop says there's probably three or four going in and out of that toolshed every day—"

"Six," Buddy corrected.

"—and he says we could probably take one without it even being noticed." Sam paused a beat. "If we can get into the toolshed."

"I got a key to it," Buddy announced.

"We figured."

"What time does the second shift quit?" Pop asked.

"Ten at this field," Buddy said. "It's shut down from ten till six."

"If we can get the drill stem by midnight," Sam calculated, "we can be home and use it first thing in the morning. Put it back around midnight tomorrow. What do you say, Buddy?"

The young runaway swallowed nervously. "You'll let me stay on after I help you? You won't dump me when you're through with me?"

"You help me and you'll have a place with me for as long as

you want it." As with Dewitt Tucker, this was Sam's personal word. And he meant it.

"Okay, then," said Buddy Kyle. "I'll throw in with you."

They were back at their derrick at daybreak, and Pop, using the light of the lanterns held by the Choctaw children, had, in the previous hour of darkness, removed the drill bit and attached the drill stem. At first light they were ready to let it down into the well hole. Pop waited until then because he did not want to examine their first flow sample by artificial light. "Daylight's best," he said around a knot of fresh tobacco in one cheek. "Colors look *natch-rel* in daylight; they don't by man's light."

Getting the drill stem had been remarkably easy. At midnight Sam, Pop, and Buddy had parked the flatbed up close to the barbed-wire fence nearest the Sinclair toolshed. Sam and Buddy hopped the fence from the top of the truck cab. Pop waited at the truck while Buddy opened the padlocked shed, and he and Sam carried the drill stem out and passed it over the fence for Pop to drag onto the flatbed. Buddy went back and locked up the shed again. Their only problem had been getting back over the fence from the ground inside. Sam had torn his pants, Buddy his shirt, and both had sustained several deep scratches from the vicious barbed wire. But it had been worth it. By half past midnight, they were on the road back to Dane.

Now Pop Joyner was ready to extract their first flow sample. Everything else stopped for that moment. Sam and Draw stood on the platform and watched. Tongue was on the ground with the Choctaw children, who had just extinguished their lanterns but not yet left the field. Buddy Kyle was next to the well hole with Pop, helping him with the rigging. No one among the seventeen people there was talking.

As the drill stem was being lowered, Sam looked down at Tunica, who stood with the children. Her great dark eyes seemed even wider than usual as she watched the cable line unroll deeper and deeper into the earth. Her downward curved lips were parted slightly, as if in anticipation. There was an open hunger in her face. My god, Sam realized in surprise, she wants this oil as much as I do. When I look at her, I could be looking at myself. He stared intently at her, confused. She was only a girl. How could she *want* something as desperately as he did?

"She's down," Pop Joyner said to Buddy. In the silence, it was as if he had announced it to everyone.

At the bottom of the well hole, the drill stem opened. A vacuum was created that immediately sucked in a combination of mud, water, gas, and whatever else the stratum held. It drew the mixture up into the hollow drilling pipe and captured it there. From above, Pop began pulling it slowly up to the surface.

Tunica, feeling Sam's eyes on her, looked up at him. Sam smiled and winked at her. She did not respond. Instead, she shifted her gaze back to the well hole and waited, as if mesmerized, while Pop and Buddy got the drill stem out of the pipe and examined its contents.

What the drill stem held was a mess. It was not solid and it was not liquid, but more like an aqueous material with just enough substance to hold loosely together. Gassy fumes exuded from it and diffused in all directions, their unusual but not offensive odor reaching the nostrils of everyone present.

Pop took a handful of the sample and worked it in his hands like a baker kneading dough. Buddy Kyle held a bucket under the old man's hands. After a moment several drops of dark liquid dropped from the mass in Pop's hands into the bucket. Putting the sample aside, Pop quickly washed his hands in the drill-water barrel, wiped them on the seat of his pants, and touched one finger lightly in the drops of liquid. Holding that finger up, he scrutinized it from several angles, held it to his nose and smelled it, and finally touched it to his tongue and tasted it. Then he smiled.

"It's good, partners. Goddamn, it's good! And it's close!"

Only then did Tunica look back at Sam and smile.

Sam had Pop work as much liquid flow as he could out of the first sample, amounting to about three ounces, then had him run the drill stem back down for a second sample. After the second sample had been milked, they had about six ounces of flow in a Mason jar. On the outside of the jar, with a rubber band, Sam attached a note to Owen Milam, the young geologist in Cameron. It read:

Owen:
This is flow from the same core sample you examined. If you think the quality is good, come on up and help us bring her in.
Sam Sheridan

163

When Pop and Buddy had the drill stem removed and back on the truck, Sam and Buddy drove over to the house. Buddy met Georgia, and Sam asked her to fix them something to eat that they could take along on the trip back to Grand Saline. Georgia made some biscuit and sausage sandwiches and put them in a bag with some apples Reba had brought over. While they were at the house, Buddy sat on the floor and played with Ty, who was delighted to have someone new to entertain. Ty was a toddler now and full of energy; Buddy, who had never been around a child that young before, thought Ty was great fun.

Over by the sink, Sam said quietly to Georgia, "If anyone comes around looking for Buddy, don't admit that you know him. He's a reform school runaway."

"Jesus, Sam," Georgia said impatiently. "An old cowboy, an Indian, an oil field wildcatter, and now a reform school runaway. What next, an unwed mother? Or maybe a leper?"

"I'll help anybody that helps me," Sam replied firmly. "I don't care who they are or what they are. When we bring in this well, everybody who stuck by me is going to be glad they did."

Georgia ran her hand inside his shirt. "Does that include me, mister?"

"Especially you," Sam said, kissing her.

Now that Georgia and Sam had resolved their differences about staying in Texas and going for the oil, each had been in a better frame of mind toward the other, and they had begun regular lovemaking again. Georgia did not know whether it was her long period of abstinence after their Christmas idyll, or her feelings of guilt about the abortion, but of late she was throwing herself into their sexual activity with renewed vigor, and Sam was responding in kind.

"You won't be away all night again, will you?" she asked now.

"Afraid so," Sam told her. "We've got a piece of equipment that Buddy helped us borrow from Sinclair Oil without asking them. We have to sneak it back into their toolshed over in Van Zandt county around midnight."

"How far is it?"

"Sixty miles or so."

"You could be back by three or four in the morning, if you wanted to."

"Yeah, I guess I could."

Georgia took her hand out of his shirt, glanced over to make sure Buddy Kyle was not watching them, and lightly squeezed his crotch. "I'll have something nice for you if you do."

"It's a deal." Sam patted her on the fanny and took the sack of food she had fixed. "Come on, Buddy, let's hit the road." On the way out, he bent to kiss Ty, who grabbed his ear. "So long, partner."

In the truck, Buddy said, "You've got a nice family, Mr. Sheridan. Real nice."

"From now on, you call me Sam. And from now on, you're part of my family. You and Draw and Tongue and Pop: we're all family, Buddy."

On the way through Dane, Sam stopped at the butcher shop and bought a long sheet of heavy brown meat-wrapping paper for two cents. After carefully wrapping the Mason jar containing their flow sample, he addressed it to Owen Milam in Cameron and wrote on it: "Please Notify on Arrival." At the Blue Star Cafe, Sam paid fifty cents to have the parcel put on the next Texas Stage Lines bus to Cameron. It would be delivered to the Cameron bus depot, which was probably also a cafe, and the proprietor there would notify Owen of its arrival.

Back in the truck, Sam said, "Okay, let's get this drill stem back where it belongs."

They drove out of town, heading west. On the way, they passed the Spence family town home. As usual when he passed that house, Sam's jaw clenched a little.

Sam and Buddy encountered no more trouble returning the drill stem than they had taking it. By midnight they were on their way back home again and, as Georgia had estimated, they were back in Dane shortly after three. Sam got out at the shack and let Buddy take the truck on to the derrick, where he would sleep on the front seat for what was left of the night.

"I'll hike over soon as it gets light," Sam told him.

Georgia, as she had promised, had awakened when she heard Sam come home.

"Sam, I've got something to tell you," she whispered, sitting up in bed. She felt his hands peel the nightgown from her body.

"Tell me later," he said quietly.

165

Georgia could hear him undressing in the dark. "It's something Reba told me today."

"I'm not interested in Reba right now." He guided her down and slipped a hand between her legs, using his fingers to get her wet.

"Sam, listen. Reba said—"

Her words were interrupted by his mouth closing on hers, bending her head back. His fingertips were moving like little tongues and in seconds she was wet and warm and ready.

Putting out of her mind what Reba had told her, Georgia rolled onto her side, bottom leg straight, top leg bent up to her breasts. Sam straddled the thigh of her straight leg, close against her, and she reached between her legs and guided him neatly into her, cupping his scrotum from the back and urging him forward until he was in her all the way. Then she tightened on him, wet her index finger, and masturbated around him. Only after she had come that first delicious time did she relax enough for him to begin his thrusting. Fuck it, Sam, she thought, but did not say aloud. Fuck it good.

After their lovemaking, they curled up in each other's arms and fell fast asleep for the two hours left of the night. The last thing Georgia thought before drifting off was that she had to be sure to tell him what Reba had said before he left for work. She had to try to wake up when he did.

At the first light of daybreak Sam was up and dressing. Georgia opened her eyes and watched him sleepily. Moving quietly about the shack, he took some cold biscuits and sausage, exactly what she had fixed him for the trip to Van Zandt, and heated up a cup of the previous night's coffee. Turning up his shirt collar against the morning coolness, he eased out the front door and started briskly across the prairie, food in one hand, coffee cup in the other, eating and drinking on the move.

Goddamn it! Georgia thought several minutes later. She had forgotten to tell him! Throwing a blanket around her shoulders, she bolted out of bed and ran onto the porch. Immediately she saw that he was too far away to call.

Sighing, Georgia leaned against a porch column and watched Sam's lean wiry form grow smaller. She remembered their lovemaking of several hours earlier. How different he is now, she thought. He's not the boy he was that night in the troop train berth when she gave him her virginity; or even the boyish young man who had come back from France; and certainly not the slim pale young clerk behind the J. C. Penney counter. Now he was brown and solid and tough. Everything about him had changed: his eyes, the set of his mouth, his hands; he even smelled different. And he *kept* changing, almost daily. He was now more sure of himself than he had ever been. Sexually he was becoming more forceful, more dominant. She liked that.

Georgia watched until Sam's form faded into the gray mist of first light. Then she went back inside.

Tonight, she promised, she *had* to remember to tell him that she might have found his real mother.

26

Sam and Georgia were in the old flatbed, on a narrow bayou highway south of Beaumont, heading for the Bolivar Peninsula on the Texas Gulf Coast, Ty left behind in the care of Reba. They had been driving for six hours, Sam tense and excited at the same time, Georgia patting his hands every few minutes to help him relax his white-knuckled grip on the truck's metal steering wheel.

"I wish you wouldn't get your hopes up so high," she said. "Remember, Reba only told me what she *heard* over the years; she wasn't actually in Dane when it all happened."

"I know." Sam said it again for emphasis. "I know."

Georgia could tell by Sam's squint that his mind was literally *racing*. Whenever he was juggling a variety of thoughts at once, he narrowed his eyes a bit. The more cluttered his mind, the narrower his eyes became. At that moment they were little more than slits. She worried about his driving.

"What did Reba say her name was again?"

"Sarah Spence."

"And she's Pete Spence's sister?"

"Yes. Younger sister. Apparently the elder Spences and the elder Patmans each had two children: a son and a daughter. Able Patman and his wife had Ardelle and Lorn. Their neighbors, the Spences, had Pete and Sarah."

"And the four of them intermarried?"

"Yes. The younger ones married first: Lorn Patman and Sarah Spence. Lorn was the one who committed suicide a month after his wedding."

"I saw his grave when I visited the Dane cemetery to look at Able Patman's. His is the only headstone there that doesn't have any kind of sentiment engraved on it."

"I guess it wouldn't have," Georgia reasoned. "He hanged himself with no clothes on from a rafter in the Baptist Church. Did it late on a Saturday night so the parishioners would find him when they came in for services the next morning."

"Did Reba know *why* he killed himself?"

"No. There was a lot of talk, naturally. One theory is that Lorn found out there was something wrong with him sexually. Another is that he wasn't able to satisfy Sarah in bed and she ridiculed him for it. I don't think anybody really *knows.* Sarah didn't stay around long enough for anybody to find out, before she left Dane and went down to Galveston to live."

"Doesn't she have friends up here that she keeps in touch with?"

"Not according to Reba. Apparently she broke all ties with Dane. She took her clothes, her furniture, her inheritance—which her father gave her in advance, some say to get rid of her—and left. Oh, and she took a young Mexican girl with her: a girl named Conchita, I think Reba said. Conchita had been what Texas families call an *ancilla:* that's a lady's maid, kind of, but in Conchita's case it was almost like she was a sister. She had actually grown up with Sarah. They were the same age, had been playmates together, then schoolmates. When the Spences had tutors come in to teach Sarah, she threw tantrums unless they let Conchita attend class also. When the girls grew up, Conchita became Sarah's personal servant."

"You said a minute ago that Sarah's father gave her an inheritance ahead of time, maybe to get rid of her." Sam glanced at Georgia. "What does that suggest to you?"

"I don't know." Georgia shrugged her shoulders. Then a look of realization spread over her face. "Of course! You think—?"

"Right. She was pregnant. With me. And it wasn't by her husband."

"Who then?" Georgia asked excitedly.

Sam shook his head. "I don't know." He thought for a moment, then asked tentatively, "Draw?"

"Oh, Sam! Really?"

"I get the feeling that he was very close to that family somehow. And he flatly refuses to discuss them with me. Maybe, like you said, there was something wrong with Lorn, and Sarah turned to an older, more experienced man for satisfaction."

It happens, Georgia thought. "You could be absolutely right, Sam. Her own brother, Pete Spence, hasn't had anything to do with her for over twenty years. That could very well be the reason. Why, he won't even permit her name to be mentioned in his presence. Reba says Spence's two daughters don't even know they *have* an aunt."

Sam shook his head incredulously. Remembering how he had loved the two women he had called mother and grandmother, and how he loved his own baby son, it was beyond his understanding how a person could deny his own blood. No matter what they did.

Sam headed the old flatbed out the Bolivar Peninsula, a thin strip of land that separated Galveston Bay from the Gulf of Mexico. On both sides the bayous and scrub swamps gradually gave way to sandy beaches and vistas of blue water. It was a side of Texas they had never seen before.

"God, Sam, it's pretty down here," Georgia marveled. "Are you sure this is still Texas?"

When they reached the southern tip of the peninsula, Sam pulled the flatbed in behind two pickups and an old Ford coupe parked at the dock where a free ferry ran across the narrow strait between the peninsula and Galveston Island, which lay three miles offshore. After they pulled on board, Sam and Georgia got out of the flatbed and stood at the rail, breathing in the sea air.

"Reminds me of the ferry we took to visit the Statue of Liberty when we were in New York," Sam said.

"Yes, it does," Georgia replied quietly. Sam slipped his arm around her waist and she rested her head against him. New York had only been three years earlier, but it seemed like an eternity to Georgia. Things had been comparatively simple then; now *nothing* seemed simple. She wondered if the meeting with Sarah Spence Patman would bring further confusion to their lives.

The ferry docked at the north end of Galveston Island and Sam guided the flatbed ashore and drove the mile or so into town. This Galveston they visited was only slightly more than twenty years old. The original Galveston, at first called Galveztown, had been there since it was surveyed by order of Don Bernardo de Galvez, the Spanish governor of Louisiana, and named after him in 1785. For thirty years it was a transient settlement that failed to attract permanent residents. Jean Lafitte, the privateer, made it his headquarters for a number of years in the 1820s. In 1836, the new Republic of Texas distributed land grants on the island. Within three years it turned into a prosperous little town. During the War Between the States, it was a major Confederate seaport, and following the war, for the rest of that century, it was a thriving commercial city. Then, in 1900, a massive hurricane destroyed most of it, killing five thousand people in the process.

The young town Sam and Georgia saw, was part of the second Galveston, built behind a sea wall seventeen feet high and ten miles long. This Galveston was growing even more rapidly than its predecessor. As Sam and Georgia drove along, they passed in-berthed ships being unloaded of sugar, tea, and bananas; out-berthed vessels being loaded with cotton, grain, and sulphur. And off to the side were smaller craft, from Mexican and Caribbean ports, unloading cargo wrapped in burlap.

"Bootleggers," Sam said, bobbing his chin at them.

"In broad daylight?" Georgia was amazed.

"Texas doesn't go along with Prohibition," Sam said simply.

"Oh." Georgia had been in Texas long enough that no further explanation was necessary.

In town they stopped at the Galveston Island Telephone Cooperative and inquired if a Sarah Patman or a Sarah Spence had a telephone. She did, in the name of Spence, at her home on the South Strand. Sam and Georgia got back in the truck and drove down there.

The South Strand was a residential strip facing the beach on the Gulf of Mexico side. The homes, which had survived the big hurricane and were the oldest on the island, were situated on a grassy bluff rising above the sand, and each had a narrow gravel drive leading off the island highway. When Sam and Georgia arrived at the address they were looking for, they found a two-story green-and-white Victorian house badly in need of exterior refurbishing. Its paint was chipped and peeling onto a lawn that was uneven and weed-ridden. Weather-rot could be seen at the edge of the porch steps. A row of shrubbery and two trees growing in the front yard were unpruned.

"Sam, none of the downstairs drapes are open," Georgia said almost fearfully as they walked toward the porch. "And all of the windows upstairs are shuttered."

"Probably to keep the afternoon heat out," Sam suggested. Nevertheless, his wet lips suddenly went dry. There was an eerie feeling about the place.

Sam drew the bell-pull and they heard a single soft chime inside. They waited a full two minutes but no one responded. But Georgia saw a window drape move. "Someone's watching us," she whispered.

Sam drew the bell-pull again and this time the door opened. A Mexican woman in her forties, with large yellow-spotted eyes and a mature voluptuous figure, stood facing them. "May I help you?" Her full, sensuous lips seemed to squirm when she spoke.

"Mr. and Mrs. Sam Sheridan, to see Mrs. Sarah Patman."

"Mrs. *Patman,* did you say?" the Mexican woman asked. "Miss Spence has not used that name in many years."

"Miss Spence then," Sam corrected.

"Is Miss Spence expecting you?"

"I'm sure you know she isn't," Georgia cut in. "Why do you ask?"

Georgia and the Mexican woman locked eyes for a moment; then the woman smiled the slightest of smiles, and said, "Will you wait here, please?"

She closed the door in their faces, leaving them once again in an eerie silence broken only by the muted sound of the nearby surf. Sam and Georgia waited without speaking, each feeling apprehension, each experiencing an odd sensation of vulnerability that seemed unusual there in the bright daylight of a beach front; it was a feeling better suited to a dark cemetery.

Several moments later, the Mexican woman returned. They almost hoped she would order them away. But she did not.

171

"You may come in." She opened the door wide. "Miss Spence will see you."

Sarah Spence Patman received them in a small sitting room at the back of the house. The room looked out across a wooden deck to the beach and water beyond. Unlike the front of the house, which faced the island highway and was closed off, the back, facing the gulf, was open, undraped and unshuttered.

Wearing a white beach robe, Sarah Spence sat in a large wicker chair, its back high, curved, and thronelike. As Sam and Georgia approached her, they saw that her skin was as dark as the Mexican woman's, but unlike hers was deeply wrinkled and aged. She looked a decade older than the Mexican woman, yet Sam and Georgia instinctively suspected that they were the same age, and that the servant was the one named Conchita, whom Sarah Spence had taken with her when she left Dane.

"So you're Sam Sheridan," Sarah Spence said as Sam and Georgia approached. They stood in silence before her while she studied Sam's face. "Well, you don't look much like your father."

Sam and Georgia exchanged surprised glances. Good God, their looks said, was it true? *Was* this Sam's real mother? Sam scrutinized the woman's face, looking for some resemblance to himself. He found none.

"What is it you want?" Sarah Spence finally asked, in a not very friendly tone.

"Are you my mother?"

Sarah Spence's mouth dropped open. She looked incredulously at the Mexican woman, who waited just inside the door. Then she turned back to Sam, her expression becoming irritated.

"Did somebody *tell* you I was your mother?"

Sam shook his head. "No."

"Then what in the hell makes you think I might be?"

Suddenly Sam felt like a fool. What *had* made him conclude that this total stranger, whom he had never even heard of until the previous night, was his *mother?* He realized in the space of a fleeting moment that the question he had just asked was completely ludicrous. It had been generated by hearsay gossip passed on to him through his wife by someone who herself had learned the story from *other* hearsay gossip passed on to *her.* To the woman sitting before him, it must have sounded at best ridiculous, at worst insulting.

172

"Well?" Sarah Spence insisted.

"I'm not sure exactly what made me think it," Sam admitted. "I was left a piece of property outside Dane in the will of Able Patman. I've been trying for months to find out why. Everybody in Dane is too afraid of your brother and his wife to tell me. And your brother and his wife have been trying to run me off ever since I got there. Two people in town have admitted to me that they knew my mother. As far as I know, the woman who raised me, Nell Sheridan, never left Kansas City, where I was born and raised. I figured that those two people who knew my mother must have been talking about somebody else. I guess maybe I thought some woman from Texas might have come to Kansas City to have a baby, maybe an illegitimate one, and left that baby—me—with Nell Sheridan to raise. I know she used to receive a letter from somewhere every week; I figured out later that they came from Texas, and thought maybe it was support money being sent for me."

Sam paused. Glancing at Georgia, he found her staring at him. Looking over at the Mexican woman, he saw her odd lips curled in a sneer. Returning his gaze to Sarah Spence, he saw that the woman's expression was still one of irritation, her eyes challenging his presence. Sam began to feel his embarrassment give way to a slowly rising anger. *Goddamn* all these people! These smug knowing bastards and bitches who knew everything but would tell him nothing!

This is the end of the fucking road, he decided coldly. From now on, he intended to get *answers.*

"You said when I walked in here that I didn't look much like my father," Sam reminded her evenly. "I want you to tell me how you knew my father."

Sarah Spence now sneered the way the Mexican woman was sneering. Suddenly, except for the wrinkles, they looked a great deal alike. "I only let you in here so I could satisfy *my* curiosity about *you,*" she said smugly. "I don't intend to help you satisfy yours."

Sam's expression darkened. "No," he said softly, but with a menacing edge to his voice. "No, you're not going to do that to me, Miss Spence. I've had enough of that—"

"I don't care to discuss it," Sarah Spence interrupted. "Conchita, show these people out."

The Mexican woman stepped forward. "The *señorita* wishes

you to leave." She took Sam by the arm. Her touching Sam infuriated Georgia.

"Take your goddamn hand off him!" she said angrily. With both hands, she shoved the Mexican woman back several steps. The woman's face contorted in rage. Muttering a curse in Spanish, she started for Georgia with clawlike fingernails raised. Georgia picked up a heavy vase from a nearby table, unceremoniously emptied its flowers and water on the Oriental rug, and held it like a weapon. "I'll smash your goddamned face in!" she threatened.

The Mexican woman stopped and for an instant all four of them were silent and motionless. Then Sam took another step toward Sarah Spence. He closed his right hand into a fist.

"I don't want to hurt you, Miss Spence," he told her in quiet determined anger, "but I'm not leaving here without some answers. I want to know how you knew my father, goddamn it!"

Sarah Spence cringed in her chair, eyes widening apprehensively as she realized that the Mexican woman could not help her. She glanced quickly at the open doors to the deck, as if that might be an escape route. But Sam, following her glance, moved between her and the doors.

"Answer me, goddamn you!" he stormed, leaning forward to shout his words in her face.

"Get away from me!"

"Then answer me! Tell me about my father!" Sam pounded his fist on the arm of her chair. "Tell me, goddamn it!"

"All right!" Sarah Spence finally shouted back. "I'll tell you! Just get away from me!"

Sam straightened and moved back.

"Tell her not to hurt Conchita," Sarah Spence said.

Looking over his shoulder, Sam said, "Put the vase down, honey." Georgia lowered it but kept it in her hand. Sam flicked his eyes back to Sarah Spence. "How did you know my father?"

"I was married to him."

Sam frowned. "Married to him? When?"

"Before you were born." A cruel little smile played on her lips. "Your father was Lorn Patman."

Sam stared incredulously at her.

He was a Patman?

27

A mile from Sarah Spence's house, Sam pulled off on the side of the road, got out of the truck, and walked out onto the grassy knoll edging the beach. He stood there like a zombie, hands shoved in his pockets, staring off at the far horizon of the gulf.

Georgia remained in the truck, knowing that he had to have a little while to himself, a few moments of solitude in which to reconcile what he had just learned about his identity. It was, she imagined, a lot for him to digest at once.

Born in Texas.

Illegitimate.

Grandson of Able Patman.

Son of a suicide.

Nephew of a woman he loathed.

In her mind Georgia relived the last few minutes in Sarah Spence's house. Sam at first had refused to believe that Lorn Patman was his father. But Sarah Spence had been adamant.

"Oh, yes. Lorn Patman. Very definitely. You are Able Patman's grandson. *Illegitimate* grandson, that is." Sarah had smiled maliciously. "Bastard grandson."

"But you're not my mother?" Sam had asked.

"Christ, no!" Sarah Spence had spat the words out, as if the mere thought were vile. "Your mother was Nell Sheridan, as no doubt you've always thought. She got pregnant by Lorn when he was in Kansas City delivering his daddy's cattle to the stockyards one year. She followed him back to Dane and tried to get him to marry her, but he was already engaged to marry *me,* and our wedding was just a month away." Sarah Spence was staring at Sam with a malevolence such as Georgia had never seen before. Each word she spoke could have been dipped in venom. "He *did* marry me, too," the spiteful woman continued, "and left your slut of a mother to deliver you out of wedlock!"

Sam's jaw had clenched at the aspersion upon his mother, but he controlled this new jolt of anger, tempering it, Georgia knew, with a great feeling of relief at knowing that Nell, whom he had loved so dearly, *had* been his mother.

"I'll tell you something else too," Sarah had snapped, "you weren't born in Kansas City either, like you said a minute ago. You were born right there in Dane, in a room upstairs over a cafe where your tramp mother was working!"

A *cafe?* Sam's eyes had narrowed as his mind worked on the word. Georgia could see that he was recalling from his memory a conversation in bed one night with her, in which she told him the story of how Reba had run away from a traveling carnival and hidden in a room upstairs over—

"Whose cafe?" Sam asked Sarah Spence in a barely audible voice.

"A man named Tully. White trash just like herself. Lived with him until her little bastard was born, then run off back up north."

Tully. The son of a bitch knew all the answers, all the time. And wouldn't tell him.

"All right," Sam said, taking a deep breath. Stepping over to Georgia, he removed the vase from her hand and set it down.

"Get out of my house now!" Sarah Spence hissed at them.

"We're fixing to." Sam guided Georgia toward the door. When he got there, he stopped and turned around. His eyes coldly studied the two embracing women for a moment. "Did Lorn Patman hang himself because of you?" he asked Sarah.

Her nostrils flared as if she might be infuriated by the question; but her answer, when it came, was oddly calm. "Partly," she admitted. "But also because of your mother. And you." She smiled her hateful smile again. "Poor Lorn was caught between—"

Conchita said something urgent sounding in Spanish, interrupting Sarah's words. Sarah looked at her thoughtfully for a moment, then nodded. "Of course. All right." She looked back at Sam. "I've told you all I'm going to. Get out."

Sam's frown had turned into a look of disgust. He put his arm around Georgia and they walked out of the old Victorian house, into the sunshine.

Georgia let Sam have half an hour to himself, standing on the sandy bluff, staring out over the water. Then she walked out and put her arm around his shoulders. "Let's take off our shoes and wade in the surf."

Sam stared at her for a moment as if she were crazy, then realized she probably had more presence of mind just then than he did, and shrugged his shoulders. "Why not?"

They left their shoes on the grass, walked across the coarse Texas sand to the surf, and started arm-in-arm up the beach. Sam was silent for a long time, and Georgia let him be; until after a while she decided it might good for him to talk it out.

"Tell me what you're thinking," she said.

"I was thinking about my mother," he replied quietly. "She was such a gentle, caring woman. I can't imagine her being mixed up with people like the Patmans." After a beat, his expression darkened and he added, "Or Tully."

"Are you troubled by the things Sarah Spence said about your mother?"

"A little. It's still another thing I have to find out the truth about: whether my mother was a tramp and a slut, like she said. I imagine Tully can resolve that for me; if she lived with him like Sarah Spence said."

"I hope you won't be too hard on Tully," Georgia said. "He's so afraid of losing his roadhouse."

It was a plea, Sam knew, for her friend Reba. But Sam could not promise leniency or even discretion in dealing with Tully. He intended to have answers from the man, just as he had from Sarah Spence, and Sam was prepared to do whatever it took to get those answers.

"Let's go back now," was all he said to Georgia. A little disappointed, particularly after supporting him the way she had in Sarah Spence's house, Georgia did not put her arm in his on the walk back.

Driving into the town of Galveston, they determined that the next ferry back to the Bolivar Peninsula was not until nine o'clock that night. Parking the flatbed on a side street, they wandered around Broadway Avenue for a while, looking in windows at things they could not afford to buy, but finally splurging fifty cents on a toy horn for Ty that had "Galveston Is." on its flare.

When they got hungry they bought clams and hush puppies from one sidewalk vendor, a jug of lemonade from another, and sat on the grass in a little corner park, listening to a band concert and eating their supper. Georgia thought it was very romantic and started holding Sam's hand again. Sam seemed to have shed the mood that had come over him when they were driving away from Sarah Spence's house; he was his easygoing pleasant self again. But Georgia knew it was only a facade, that what had caused the mood was still inside him, and that he had relaxed only because he had made up his mind what to do next. He only *seemed* easygoing and pleasant; actually, he was *waiting*.

It was dark when they finally drove onto the ferry and left Galveston Island, and nearly ten o'clock when they reached the mainland highway and headed north toward Dane.

"What are you going to do when we get back?" Georgia asked.

"Go see Tully," Sam replied without hesitation.

"Suppose he still won't answer your questions?"

"He will," Sam said confidently. "This time he will."

Sam Sheridan was tired of *asking* people to do things. From now on he was going to *tell* them.

They reached their shack on the prairie an hour before daybreak, to find a young Choctaw boy, with an oil lantern, waiting on the front porch. He ran up to the side of the truck as soon as Sam stopped.

"Elder Tongue want you come quick to well, sir," he blurted.

Georgia started to get out, but Sam stopped her. "Someone may be hurt." Georgia had become the unofficial nurse of the drilling crew; she had doctored not only Sam but Pop, Tongue, and more recently Buddy Kyle. Only Draw had avoided being her patient.

Sam told the Choctaw boy to get into the back and hold on. He gunned the old truck across the rutted prairie, shaking every organ in their bodies. When they reached the derrick and he skidded to a stop in the loose dirt at the edge of the camp, he found that everything looked normal. The Choctaw children with their lanterns were lighting the rig site; Tongue was stirring a pot of pungent-smelling rabbit broth over a fire built well away from the rig; Buddy, who had fallen into the role of Pop's principal helper, was next to the drill hole with him, patiently guiding the cable under his direction, moving the unseen drill bit in its monotonous chipping motion at the bottom of the hole; and nearby, Draw was sizing firewood into lengths that would fit the fuel beds of the mismatched boilers.

"Everything looks all right," Sam said, as much to himself as to Georgia.

Then he saw what the problem was. First he noticed parked at the other edge of the camp an old coupe that he did not recognize. Then, tied in a sitting position to a nearby tree, was a man that he did recognize: a rangy young man with corn-colored hair. It was Owen Milam, the young geologist from Cameron. As Sam got out of the truck, Draw came over to him.

"Feller drove into camp yesterday after you left," he told Sam. "We didn't know him from Adam, so we figured we better hold onto him until you got back."

Sam hurried over to the tree. "Owen, I'm sorry about this," he said as he quickly began untying the ropes.

"Nice bunch you've got working for you," Owen said testily.

"Just aiming to look out for what's ours, mister," said Draw. "No offense intended."

"No *offense!* I've been tied to that goddamned tree all *night!*"

"Owen, we've got kind of a peculiar situation up here," Sam tried to explain. "It's too involved to go into, but believe me when I say we have to resort to unusual methods to protect what we've got here." He helped Owen to his feet and brushed off his clothes a little. Then he tilted his head and said, "I presume we've got something here *worth* protecting, or you wouldn't be here. Am I right?"

"The Mason jar of sample flow is in the rumble seat of my car. I tried to tell those damn fools that. They wouldn't listen."

"They only listen to me, Owen. What about the sample flow? Are we close?"

Now the young geologist smiled a little and nodded. *"Very* close. You'll punch into the roof of that pool any time now. And it's good crude, Sam. Some of the best I've seen, even in college labs. Depending on how much is down there, you could become a very wealthy man today."

Sam felt his blood rushing. "You want to join up with us, Owen?"

"Yes, I do. Very much."

"You're in then."

"Just like that?"

179

"Just like that," Sam confirmed. He bobbed his chin toward where Tongue was cooking. "Go on over and get yourself some of that hot rabbit broth. I want to bring my wife over to meet you."

Owen walked toward Tongue's campfire, Draw returned to his woodpile, and Sam started back for the truck where Georgia waited. On the way he saw Tunica standing next to a group of Choctaw children as they extinguished their lanterns. Daylight had now broken over the camp. Sam walked over to the young Choctaw princess.

"Hello, Tunica."

"Hello."

"I've been meaning to thank you for your help in getting the children here."

Tunica shook her head slightly. "It is not necessary. Our community wanted to help in some way; we did not know how until our brother Tongue suggested the lanterns."

"You refer to Tongue as your 'brother.' Just the other day, he and I spoke of ourselves as being brothers to each other." Sam smiled at her. "Would that make you my sister?"

Tunica dropped her gaze. "I suppose so. If you wanted me to be."

"I do. Very much."

She met his eyes again. "I have thought of you often since we first met." It sounded almost like a confession.

"You have?"

"Yes. Often."

"Well, I have—"

A voice from the platform interrupted him as Pop Joyner yelled, "Sam! I think she's coming!"

Sam forgot that Tunica was even there and rushed over to the rig. Hopping up onto the platform next to Pop and Buddy, he found them staring at several metal tools on the platform floor. Wetting his lips, he started to speak. "What—"

But Pop silenced him with a wave of his hand. "Just watch," he whispered. "And listen."

Presently Sam heard the quietest of rattles, and saw the tools shake slightly. A half grin worked at Pop's tobacco-stained lips. Glancing down off the platform, Sam saw that Draw, Tongue, Tunica, and the Choctaw children had gathered in a group to watch. All of them were frowning expectantly. Standing a little off by himself, Owen Milam, who knew what was happening, had a smile on his face.

On the platform floor, the tools began a slow, quiet, but steady vibration.

"She's coming," Pop said reverently. "By the living Christ, she's on her way!"

No sooner had Pop said it, than the big wooden derrick creaked loudly as its planks and beams shifted slightly. Suddenly, beneath the feet of the group on the ground, there was a faint, barely discernible rumble, a growl, coming from the belly of the earth. Some of the children became frightened and Tongue immediately reassured them. Tunica gathered several of the smaller ones into her arms.

On the platform floor, the derrick machinery and rigging began rocking like a ship caught in a storm. And in fact it *sounded* as if a storm had arrived: a low, rolling din began, a reverberation that sounded like threatening thunder up in the sky—except that it was coming from below instead of above.

"She's ready!" Pop Joyner yelled. "Plug your ears!"

Immediately Owen Milam whipped a handkerchief from his pocket and began tearing it into strips small enough to wad and stick in everyone's ears. Sam hopped off the platform, untying the bandanna from his neck. Following Owen's example, he too began tearing strips.

The sound from the ground increased to a roar that resembled a relentless cannonade, bursting repetitiously. Sam thrust his torn bandanna strips into Draw's hands. "Help get the children's ears plugged! And plug your own!" he yelled. With two strips he still had, he whirled Tunica around to face him and stuffed the material into her ears. She smiled curiously at him as he did it. Then Sam saw Pop waving urgently to him from the platform. He left Tunica and quickly climbed back up.

"I don't think the plug's gonna hold her!" Pop yelled. Late the previous day, when Sam had been into Galveston, Pop had lowered a cement plug to the bottom of the pipe to impede any sudden gush of oil to the surface. But Sam did not know about it.

"What are you talking about?" Sam yelled back.

"Never mind!" Pop said. "Just give me a hand with this capping valve!"

Sam helped Pop and Buddy lift a heavy well cap and valve onto the cemented well casing. With a pair of huge pliers from Pop's toolbox, they began bolting it into place. The derrick floor was rising and falling now, shaking like a frantic animal trying to escape a trap. Several times one or another of the men were thrown to the floor of the platform; once, trying to break his fall, Buddy drove a handful of ugly splinters into his hand. Only after Tongue and Owen Milam also climbed up to help, did they finally get the well cap bolted securely into place. By then the platform was jerking so wildly that none of them could stay on their feet for more than a few seconds. Sam started turning the big valve wheel on the well cap, but Pop pulled him away.

"Leave her open!" he yelled. "Let's see what we got!"

What they got, two minutes later, was a gushing black stream that shot two hundred feet into the air and opened up in all directions like a great liquid umbrella.

At first it was mud. Then it was mud and water. Then, along with vapors of dark gas, it was water and oil. Finally it was just oil.

Oil!

It came pouring down on them, coating them a slick bluish black. Draw Poker was standing on the ground, looking up at the men on the platform. Sam leaped down beside him and the two threw their arms around each other and began laughing. Tongue sat down on the edge of the platform, just above them, his moccasined feet dangling, and grinned down at them. Wiping some of the oil from his face, he tasted it and nodded approvingly. Sam and Draw grabbed his feet and pulled him down, the three of them tumbling to the now oil-wet ground like children at play. When they sat up and looked at the platform again, they saw Pop, Buddy Kyle, and Owen Milam all holding hands, dancing a ring around the well cap from which the stream was shooting. Draw and Tongue quickly climbed up to join them, and Sam was about to also when he felt a tug on his sopping sleeve. He turned and saw Tunica, as oil-wet as the rest of them. Pointing, she directed Sam's attention to the eleven Choctaw children: they were sliding, rolling, and tumbling on the oil-slick ground, just as they had seen the men doing. Laughing, Sam drew the girl to him and kissed her quickly on the cheek. Suddenly Tunica took Sam's face between her palms and pulled him down far enough to kiss him long and hard on the lips. Sam tasted the crude oil on her tongue, but he also detected a sweetness that was from her, not from the earth. When she let him go and they looked at each other, something in her great dark eyes, and the lingering touch of her lips, made her seem far older than her years. Turning, she ran from him and joined the children. Sam stared incredulously after her: a girl, barely in her teens, and she had kissed him more passionately than even Georgia in her most hot-blooded moments.

Georgia!

He had forgotten all about her.

Turning, Sam saw his wife next to the old flatbed at the edge of the camp, looking curiously at him. Standing back from the umbrella of oil, she was still clean. Sam hurried over to her. He held out his black hands as if she could not see the shiny substance all over him.

"Look, Georgia! Oil! We hit it!"

"That's wonderful, Sam. Who was the woman you were kissing?"

"Woman? That was no woman. She's a Choctaw princess named Tunica. She's just a kid."

Georgia's eyebrows shot up. "She seems to kiss awfully well for just a kid. Wasn't her mouth open?"

"Georgia, she's just happy. This means a lot to her and her people." He took his wife's clean hands in his oily ones and grinned. "Come on, take an oil shower with me. Get some of this wonderful stuff on your body!"

Georgia let herself be pulled under the falling gusher and in seconds she was as black as everyone else in the camp. Sam held her close with an arm around her shoulders.

"Our lives just changed, Georgia," he told her solemnly. "We're not poor anymore. We won't have to ask *anybody* for *anything,* ever again. Not the goddamned Texas bankers, not your brother, not anybody. And we won't have to beg to find out things we want to know, either. From now on when I ask a question about my mother or myself, I'll get an answer. From now on—"

A shout from Pop Joyner interrupted Sam. "Hey, you damn fools!" the old man yelled to everyone from the platform. "That there's money spurting out of that hole! Let's get this son of a bitch capped!"

Sam squeezed Georgia's shoulder and hurried back to the platform. He, Draw, Tongue, Buddy, and Owen Milam, following Pop's directions, all gripped the big valve wheel, put their combined backs to the effort, and slowly, slowly, slowly turned it to stem the rushing flow.

A great silence settled over the field when the flow stopped, and everyone stood staring at the black flooded ground and at each other. Even the Choctaw children grew very quiet and looked in awe at the scene around them.

Man, woman, boy, girl, each of them realized that they had witnessed a miracle.

A miracle second only to the drawing of a baby from the womb of a woman.

The drawing of oil from the belly of the earth.

PART
2

Texas Blood

28

Sam waited until the last breakfast customer had left Tully's road-house restaurant and there were no cars parked outside the place except Tully's. Then he pulled off the side of the road where he and Georgia had been parked and drove around to the kitchen door. Reba was just coming onto the back porch with some scraps from the breakfast plates for Tully's dog. Ty was at her heels, carrying a toy pistol, shooting at the dog. When Reba saw Sam and Georgia get out of the truck, her mouth dropped open incredulously. Both of them were still wet with oil.

"Why, my god" Reba said. Instinctively she drew Ty close to her, as if to keep him clean.

"Tully inside?" Sam asked, stepping onto the porch.

" 'Course." Reba ignored him as he passed her and looked inquiringly at Georgia.

"We struck it, Reba," Georgia told her, in a voice oddly unexcited. "Pop Joyner says it's one of the biggest gushers he's ever seen."

"Well, I'll be."

Inside, Tully stopped scraping his griddle and stared at Sam. Unsmiling, Sam pressed some oil onto his hand from his sopping shirt and held it out in front of him. "You know what this is, don't you?"

"I ain't stupid."

"I've hit it, Tully," Sam said fiercely. "Hit it *big*. I'm rich now, Tully, oil rich, not just dirt rich! There's oil under that scrub land of mine! I'm going to be richer than any son of a bitch in East Texas!"

"Good for you." Tully resumed scraping the griddle. Sam watched him for a moment, still unsmiling. Then he said:

"I know where I was born, Tully."

Tully missed a beat but kept on scraping. "Who told you?"

"Sarah Spence. She says I'm Lorn Patman's son and Able Patman's grandson. Bastard son and bastard grandson, that is."

"It's her family," Tully allowed, "she ought to know."

The screen door opened and Reba, now carrying Ty, entered with Georgia right behind her. They stood staring at the two men, feeling the tension of the confrontation.

"Tell me about my mother, Tully."

"Why should I?"

"Because I'm asking you to. And because if you don't, I'll do what you've been afraid for years that Pete Spence would do: I'll break you."

Stopping work again, Tully turned to face Sam. "If I *do* tell you, Spence will break me. What's the difference?"

"Spence won't break you," Sam promised, "because I'm going to break Spence."

"Pete Spence is one of the biggest men in Texas," Tully scoffed. "You ain't about to break him."

"Yes, I will." It sounded like a solemn oath. "I'll break him and I'll break everybody he used against me. Every son of a bitch on that town square who helped Pete Spence is going under, Tully, I swear to God they are—"

"Sam, honey," said Georgia, "please don't talk like that."

"You be quiet," he told her, not unkindly but in a tone not to be argued with either. "I'm not just blowing off steam," he said calmly to Tully. "Those people tried to break me. They were against me from the day I got here. They didn't even give me a *chance.* The lawyers, the newspaper, the Baptist Church, the goddamned doctor who wouldn't deliver my son! They're all going under, Tully." Sam's eyes narrowed. "And you're going with them, unless you tell me what I want to know."

"I don't care to be threatened like that," Tully said stiffly.

"I haven't cared for a lot of things lately," Sam replied flatly. "But I had to take them because I had no way to fight back. Now I do have a way; I've got oil—and oil means money—and money, my friend, means power!" He paused to take a deep breath, feeling the adrenaline rushing. Then, clenching his jaw once, he continued. "I've got a lot to do and not much time to do it in, Tully. I'd like to have my mind clear of the questions that are in it right now, so

I can concentrate on other things. You can answer most of those questions. I'm going to give you one chance to do it. If you turn me down, I'll walk out that door and never give you another chance. And you'll be the first one I break, because you stayed against me when you didn't have to. So make up your mind right now. Will you tell me what you know about my mother?"

In the silence of the kitchen, Sam waited what seemed like an interminable length of time for an answer. He stared at Tully. Georgia and Reba stared at Tully. Even little Ty stared at him. All the while Tully looked down at the dull black surface of his griddle. A bead of sweat ran down his forehead and settled on the tip of his nose.

Finally Sam decided he had waited long enough.

"Suit yourself." He started for the door.

Before Sam's hand touched the screen door, Tully's voice stopped him.

"All right, you win. I'll tell you."

Turning back, Sam suppressed the little smile he felt surfacing. He was going to like being powerful, he decided.

Very much.

29

Tully had been standing in the door of his cafe that day in June of 1894 when Nell Sheridan stepped off the Texas Overland Transport buckboard in the settlement of Dane, Texas. Nell was hot, dirty, and exhausted. She had just traveled from Dallas, one hundred twenty-one miles, on the last leg of a long journey. That last leg had taken her three days.

"Excuse me, is there a hotel in town?" she asked Tully as the buckboard driver pulled her grip satchel from the boot of the wagon.

"No, ma'am, there ain't no hotels nowheres between Dallas and

Longview," Tully had replied. "But there's a boardinghouse over back of the dry goods store. Run by Miz Amelia Meadows. She's usually got empties during the week."

The driver set Nell's satchel at her feet, tipped his range hat, and climbed back aboard the rig. "Best step up on the timbers there, ma'am, so the dust won't choke you when we pull out."

Nell picked up her bag and ascended twelve inches onto Dane's wooden sidewalk. She looked at the small cafe with a painted sign above the door that read: Tully's Eats. A young Mexican boy sat next to the door looking up at her. He had a small rock in one hand. When the transport driver whistled loudly and snapped the reins of his team, the boy threw the rock at the horses, hitting one of them on the shank. The animals did a quick backstep, a substitute for rearing up, and lurched forward. Nell saw the two remaining passengers jerk with the movement and hang on as the buckboard rattled out of town. Thank god that her part of the dreadful trip was over. Now if she could just make it to that boarding house before she collapsed.

"Do you speak English?" she asked the Mexican boy. He smiled but did not answer.

Tully, wearing moccasins and an Apache sweat scarf, said, "He understands English, ma'am; he just don't know you. Did you want him to do something?"

"Yes, I was going to offer him a nickel if he would carry my bag over to the boardinghouse."

"I'll tell him for you." Tully turned to the boy. "*Chico,* take the *señorita*'s bag to Señora Meadows' house. *Pronto!*"

"*Sí, jefe.*" Jumping to his feet, the boy grabbed the grip satchel with both hands and struggled off down the street with it.

"Thank you," Nell said.

"Nothin'," replied Tully. "You gon' be staying with Miz Meadows?"

"For a day or two, yes."

"She serves pretty good grub for a boardinghouse. But if you get tired of town food and want some Mex or range eats, stop in my place here. I'm Tully Samuel. This here's my cafe."

"Thank you, Mr. Samuel. I'll remember that." Nell held out her hand. "I'm Nell Sheridan."

Tully quickly wiped his own hand on his shirt before taking it. "How do, ma'am. Welcome to Dane."

Nell smiled, thanked him, and followed the Mexican boy down the dusty street. She was so glad to be off the buckboard, off and *finished* with it, that she felt like shouting. God, how wonderful a bath and a bed were going to feel.

Nell had ridden the southern spur passenger train from Kansas City to Dallas, which was the closest rail station to Caddo County, Texas, where Dane was located. From Dallas the only way to Dane was by overland transport: a six-passenger buckboard with wooden benches built into its bed and a sailcloth top held up by four poles to help keep the sun off the passengers. But there had been no protection from dust, wind, prairie heat, flies, and the constant jostling of the wooden vehicle as it seemed to locate and bump in and out of every chuckhole on the road.

The first day out of Dallas, the Texas Overland Transport buckboard covered forty miles. The passengers, of whom there were five including Nell and one other woman, spent the night in a barn just outside Elmo, Texas. Coyotes, loud snoring, and other miscellaneous nocturnal noises, some of them downright disgusting, kept Nell awake most of the night. The second day they made thirty-one miles and that night slept on wooden pews in a chapel near Van. Nell was the only female now, and there were five male passengers, two of them quite disreputable looking. Nell forced herself to stay awake in her corner of the chapel lest she be raped under the very eyes of the Virgin Mary, at whose feet she rested. The men she feared might violate her all slept soundly through the night. On the third day, the road was very good between Swan and Kilgore, and with an early start the rig made fifty miles and by midafternoon pulled into Dane. When Nell Sheridan negotiated her sore and aching body from the buckboard, she felt as if she had just been let out of purgatory. If she had known that night two months earlier in Kansas City what she knew about Texas after making the trip to Dane, she probably would have thought twice about shedding her bloomers for Lorn Patman. Or *tried* to think twice. God knows, she had wanted to do it with him so badly that night, she doubted if *anything* could have deterred her. All through her senior year at Francis Scott Key High School, she had felt her secret inner desires becoming more insistent, but had not been able to even *think* of doing anything intimate with any of the boys in her class. After graduation a young man down the block, Denny Murchison, had taken her out a few times, but he was as shy

191

and inexperienced as she was, nothing had happened between them, and gradually they stopped dating.

By the time Lorn Patman arrived on the scene, Nell was seething with the concupiscence of healthy young womanhood. And when the good-looking young Texan walked into the ice cream parlor where she worked, wearing his big Stetson and a perfectly horrid, green flowered neckerchief, she immediately became excited—and stayed that way all evening. Even now as she looked back on it from the dubious perspective of two skipped menstrual cycles, the night had been a romantic girl's dream. Every element was present: young stranger from a remote exotic land; an immediate attraction between them; a passionate encounter in which she had given him her all; and then—

There was the hitch. He had not swept her into his arms and carried her off to his remote exotic land, there to become his wife. In fact, he had not even come back the next day, as he had promised to do.

He had never come back.

After two days of waiting, Nell had mustered the courage to write him a short note and take it to the desk at the Cattlemen's Hotel, where he had told her he was staying. That was when she learned that Lorn Patman had left town and gone back to Texas.

Three weeks later, she missed her period the first time.

A week after her second failure, she left for Texas herself.

Although some of the romance of her liaison with Lorn Patman had lost its initial glow—gold turned to brass—there nevertheless had been an underlying excitement about the trip. Even if her young stranger was not with her, had not sent for her, did not, in fact, even know that she was coming, she was sure it would still be an experience, an *adventure:* traveling to a remote exotic land to be with a lover.

Remote exotic land, my fanny, Nell thought as she walked down the rutted street in Dane, behind the Mexican boy with her bag. Remote, yes. It was that, all right. But exotic? Exotic meaning colorful and exciting? No. Not, as her late father had been wont to say, by a country mile. It was desolate, bleak, and thoroughly uninviting, this great endless wasteland called Texas. Several times over the past three days, bouncing and jerking in the Texas Overland Transport's rig, she had thought to herself: We fought the Mexicans for *this?* The only war she could imagine being fought over this uncultivated prairie was to force some country to take it *back.*

When Nell got to the boardinghouse, she found a rickety, two-story frame structure of unpainted wood that had, like the mesquite blowing down the street, turned a lifeless gray with age. An old picket fence of the same color surrounded the lot. A roofless little porch belted the front of the house, four straight chairs with cane seats lined up in a row across it. A sign nailed to a post next to the porch's three steps read: Rooms. A tall gaunt woman dressed in black sat on one of the chairs, shelling peas from one bowl into another on her lap. The Mexican boy put Nell's bag on the porch and stood waiting.

"Hello," Nell said, stopping at the first step. The woman nodded. "Who may I see about a room, please?"

"That'd be me. I'm Mrs. Amelia Meadows, the landlady." She turned to the Mexican boy. "What are you standing there for? Get!"

"Wait," Nell said, pulling open the drawstrings of her purse. "I promised him a nickel for carrying my bag."

"Penny'll do. Just give him a penny."

Nell saw a flash of disappointment cloud the boy's face. She hesitated, fingers in her change pocket, her glance alternating between the gaunt woman's cold stare and the Mexican boy's drooping expression. Finally she pulled out a silver coin.

"I'm sorry, but I told him a nickel." She handed the coin to the boy. A wide smile split his young brown face.

"Muchas gracias, señorita!" he said happily, and quickly ran away lest the old buzzard in black somehow find a way to deprive him of his reward.

"Don't make no sense to spoil Mexes," Amelia Meadows chided, not looking at Nell as she spoke. She stared out from the porch as if talking to the outdoors. "They're lazy and shiftless enough as it is without getting overpaid for what little work a body does manage to get out of them." She rose from her chair, putting one bowl into the other. "Come inside if you want a room." She pulled open a squeaking screen door and entered the house.

Left alone on the porch, Nell looked back down the street at the fleeing boy. She smiled, pleased with herself. Facing the boardinghouse door again, she impulsively stuck out her tongue at the gaunt woman's back, picked up her bag, and went inside.

Two hours later, after considerable insistence, Nell was half lying in a wooden tub of tepid water, her legs bent at the knees and hanging over the side. The top edge of the tub slats was unfinished and rough against her legs, and she already had a splinter in her bottom from the boards inside; but none of that mattered to her because the feel of the water was heavenly. It soaked her armpits, flowed over and around her privates, loosened her matted pubic hair, and made her nipples stand out firm and hard. It was pure joy. If she had been made to wait another two days for a bath, as Amelia Meadows had suggested, Nell would have died. And it had almost happened.

"Saturday is bath day," Mrs. Meadows said when Nell inquired about a tub. "This is only Thursday."

"Mrs. Meadows, I need a bath now. I don't care what day it is. I've just spent three days in these clothes. And two nights. I'm sure nothing in Dane smells worse than I do. I'd be happy to pay extra."

"Ain't a question of paying," the gaunt woman explained. "Question of getting the water drawed from the well, building a fire under the pot to heat it, and getting it brung up to your room. I don't know as there's anybody around to do all that work. I know I ain't about to do it."

"May I do it myself then?"

"You?"

"Yes. I can draw water from a well, I can heat it, and I can carry it upstairs a bucket at a time."

Mrs. Meadows shrugged. "If you want a bath bad enough to do all that, I ain't going to be the one to tell you no. There's kindling out back for the fire." She pronounced the last word "far." It sounded like "kin'lin fer th' far." Nell was having a great deal of difficulty understanding her.

In back of the boarding house Nell found a well and a wooden tub that had "16 Buckets" painted above a white line on its side. She rolled up her sleeves and went to work. After drawing up the first six buckets of water and pouring them into a big iron pot permanently set on an adobe brick fire-pit, she gave her arms a rest and laid the kindling for her fire. Lighting it, she then returned to the well and pulled up six more buckets of water. Her upper arms and shoulders began to burn from the effort. As she worked, she noticed three

Mexican men sitting nearby in the shade of an adobe fence, watching her.

"Do you want to work for me?" she hollered over to them. They did not reply. Nell walked over to them. "Will you help me, please?" One of them smiled and shrugged. "I will pay you. Pay. Money. Work."

The men all shrugged in unison and one of them said, *"No entiendo, señorita."*

Nell tried gesturing for them to get up and come over to the well, but they merely shrugged some more and talked among themselves. She had an immediate suspicion that they knew exactly what she wanted of them—and had no intention of doing it. Finally she abandoned the idea of trying to employ them and returned to finish the work herself.

After drawing two buckets of water with which to wash out the wooden tub, she dragged it up the back stairs and into her room. Then she managed, barely, to draw four more buckets of water to pour into the iron pot. While she waited for the water to heat, she lay across the bed and rested both hands on her stomach. Somewhere she had heard that hard work and exertion were not good for a woman carrying a baby. She had a fleeting moment of worry about what she was doing. Then she reminded herself that she was strong and healthy, had good arms and shoulders from bending and scooping ice cream all those months, and that if she did not get a bath she would die—it was as simple as that. But she resolved to do the rest of the work nice and slowly, with as little strain as possible.

Nell carried the water upstairs two buckets per trip, taking her time, stopping and resting halfway up. Her bath was not going to be hot, or even very warm, but she did not care. As long as it was *wet*. She could scarcely believe it when the last of the water had been hauled up, when the tub was filled to the white line, when the door was bolted and she was at long last taking off her dusty, grimy, smelly clothes. Sinking slowly into the water gave her the same feeling as getting off the overland buckboard. Pardoned from purgatory.

As she lay there soaking, trying to ignore the alkali smell of the water, Nell wondered how Lorn would react to seeing her again. He had told her that night, their only night together, that she was the most wonderful girl he had ever met. That, after only three total hours together. But it had been so spontaneous, such a sincere statement, so softly and tenderly spoken, that it immediately became etched in Nell's heart and mind. It was primarily because of that declaration that Nell had decided to make the trip to Dane.

"I think it's a mistake to go," her mother had told her. It had not taken Sally Sheridan long to get over the shock and sorrow of her unwed daughter's pregnancy. Sally was a practical woman; she believed in accepting and coping. There was no way to change something that had already happened; all one could do was deal with the result. "If the young man cared anything about you, he would not have run off like he did."

"Maybe he had to leave, Mother," Nell countered. "Maybe something happened to his father, or to the ranch."

"He could have left word for you at the hotel. And he's certainly had time to have written you by now."

"He wasn't very grown-up, Mother. In a lot of ways he was still a boy. Maybe he just didn't think."

Nell's mother had not opposed the trip to the point of forbidding it; she even gave her daughter a little extra money for expenses. But with a disclaimer. "I don't think this will work out at all, but I know you must get it out of your system. When it's over, I want you to come back here, have the baby at home, and we'll raise it together."

Nell had blinked back tears. "I hate bringing any shame on you, Mother. And on Daddy's house and name."

"The shame," her mother said firmly, "would be not doing right by that baby. You come back home where you belong."

You come back home where you belong. Those words were also etched in Nell Sheridan's heart and mind.

When the water in her tub had lost all of its warmth, Nell pulled her legs in, sat up, and scrubbed her body, face, hair, nails, everything down to the soles of her feet, with lilac soap she had brought with her. Then she climbed naked into bed, actually enjoying the scratch of the rough sheets against her clean soft skin. With her wet hair wrapped in one of her extra petticoats, she went immediately to sleep, a smile on her lips, memories of Lorn Patman's handsome young face and oak-hard young body in her head. She slept the deep sound sleep of the exhausted.

That evening, with the day beginning to gray, Nell came downstairs. Mrs. Meadows was in the dining room seeing to two Mexican girls who were clearing off the table. She glanced disapprovingly at Nell's yellow taffeta dress, while smoothing down the skirt of her own black crepe. "You're too late to eat," she said. "Supper's promptly at six."

"Oh." Nell was ravished. "Perhaps I could get something in the kitchen—"

"Guests ain't allowed in the kitchen."

"I see. Well, I guess I'll be good and hungry by breakfast then, won't I? Is there someone who can remove the bathwater from my room?"

"Bath helpers work on Saturdays only. You got it up there yourself, you'll have to get it down yourself. Or wait until Saturday."

"All right." Nell felt the back of her neck burning, as it always did when she became angry. "I wonder, Mrs. Meadows, if you could tell me how to get in touch with Lorn Patman?"

The gaunt woman paused in her supervision of the Mexican girls and looked at Nell with curiosity and suspicion. "What do you want Lorn Patman for?"

"That, Mrs. Meadows, is none of your business."

Amelia Meadows bristled and glared at her guest. "You've got a right smart mouth for somebody that's asking for help, young woman."

"Mrs. Meadows, are you this impolite to all your guests, or is there something about me you don't like?"

"Since you ask, I don't take kindly to strangers who come here and start doing ever'thing different. Paying that little Mex street urchin five times what he should've got, taking a bath on Thursday 'stead of regular bath day, expecting to go into *my* kitchen and eat whenever you want to—"

Nell did not remain to listen to the rest of the woman's tirade. "Good evening, Mrs. Meadows," she said crisply, and abruptly left the room.

On the front porch, three men sat on the cane-bottom chairs and watched the sun go down far across the prairie. Two of them smoked wet-tipped roll-your-own cigarettes, while the third worked on a large chaw of tobacco that made a knob in his cheek. All three wore range clothes and boots.

"Excuse me, I wonder if someone could help me," Nell began. The men looked up at her but none of them rose from his chair. "I'm trying to get in touch with Lorn Patman. His father owns a ranch somewhere near Dane, I'm not sure exactly where."

The men stared almost solemnly at her, without answering. The one chewing tobacco spat a long brown stream off the porch. Jesus, Nell thought, is it possible *they* don't speak English either? They were looking at her the way the Mexicans had that afternoon.

"Excuse me, do you understand what I said?"

One of the men nodded. "You said you was a'trying to locate Lorn Patman."

"Yes." Nell smiled. But the man said nothing further. Nell's smile faded. "Well?"

"Well what, ma'am?"

"Well, can you help me?"

"No, ma'am, 'fraid we can't." He pronounced the last word, "cain't."

"But why not? Don't you know Lorn Patman?"

"Shore, we know him, lady," said one of the other men. "Ever'-body round here knows Lorn Patman. We just can't he'p you get in touch with him, is all."

The back of Nell's neck began to burn again. "Would you mind telling me why not?"

The men grinned at one another. "See that sun a'setting out there, lady?" the tobacco chewer asked. "Well, ever'thing to the north of that there sunset belongs to Mr. Paddy Spence, which is who we ride for. Ever'thing to the south of the sunset is Mr. Able Patman's, Lorn's daddy. Now, Lorn is about eighteen miles out thataway, and we's riding about twenty-two miles over *thataways.* Somebody'd have to ride thirty-six miles there and back to get word to Lorn for you. If it was one of us, that same feller'd have to ride on twenty-two more miles back to Mr. Spence's. That's fifty-eight miles, lady. You ever sit a saddle for fifty-eight miles?" To signify that he was through talking, he let go another thick stream of tobacco juice.

"Thank you for explaining it to me," Nell said, as calmly as she could. "Good evening—*gentlemen.*"

Leaving the porch, Nell walked out to the dirt street and

paused. A soft breeze came in off the mesa, bringing trace scents of prairie grass and wildflowers that grew around the occasional water-hole. From where she stood, Nell heard one of the men on the porch say quietly, " 'Pears to me there'd be somebody here to meet her—if she'd been invited, that is."

You ill-mannered horse's ass, Nell thought, throwing him a withering look in the fading light. The sun was a fiery ball making a valiant last-ditch effort to keep the day alive with great heavenly streaks and splashes of red, yellow, orange. Nell looked down the rutted main street to where the plank sidewalk began. There were a few saddle horses hitched here and there, a couple of parked wagons, a buggy. An occasional man on foot entered or left one of the dozen business establishments. A light flickered on, then another. From somewhere came the sound of soft guitar strumming.

With no particular destination in mind, Nell started walking. Anything was better than standing there being talked about by the three men on the porch, who would probably be joined shortly by that wretched Meadows woman. God, what awful people!

A man on horseback cantered past Nell, kicking up dust in his wake. Thank you kindly, sir, you're a real Texas gentleman, just like the others I've met. Reaching the sidewalk, she lifted her yellow taffeta skirt and stepped up out of the street. At the end store, a dry goods emporium, she paused in the fading light to look at a window display of cutlery, harnesses, and parasols. A sign, looking very new, over a door next to the emporium read: Clarence Fort—Lawyer—Upstairs, with an arrow pointing up a narrow flight of wooden stairs. Next Nell passed a barbershop where a man with garters on his sleeves was sweeping hair into the street. The Caddo County Land Office, next door, was closed. Two Chinese, male and female, sat on boxes outside their hand laundry, eating something awful looking out of wooden bowls. Nell forced herself to keep from shuddering as she passed them.

" 'Evening, Miss Sheridan," a voice said. Nell looked up, star-tled at the sound of her name. It was the man with the Apache sweat scarf on his forehead, who had told the Mexican boy where to carry her grip satchel that afternoon. He was leaning in the doorway of Tully's Eats.

"Oh. Mr. Tully. Hello."

"Samuel, ma'am. Tully Samuel. How you this evening?"

"I wouldn't want to spoil a pretty evening by telling you, Mr. Samuel."

Tully smiled, splitting some of the crags in his rugged face. "After hearing cowboys and drovers and teamsters complain all day, ma'am, it'd be a downright pleasure to listen to a lady like you, no matter what you was talking about."

"That's kind of you, Mr. Samuel."

"I have some cool tea hanging down in my well, Miss Sheridan. Only take me a minute to pull it up if you'd like a glass."

"Why, how nice. Do you know, Mr. Samuel, that you are the only person in this town who has been civil to me since I arrived. I have been ignored by three Mexicans whom I am *positive* understood every word I was saying; ridiculed and made a fool of by three men whom I made the mistake of asking for help; and insulted every time I turned around by that Mrs. Meadows. Is there something *wrong* with me, Mr. Samuel?"

"Sure nothing I can see, ma'am," Tully replied with such earnestness that it surprised them both. "Here, let me get you something to sit on." He reached inside and pulled out a counter stool. "Sorry I don't have no pillow for it, but it's clean; I just washed them down. You make yourself comfortable while I draw up that tea."

He was back in two minutes with a glass of tea in one hand, sugar bowl in the other, holding both while she sweetened the tea to her taste. As she sipped it, she told him about her difficulties with Amelia Meadows, her bath water, the Mexican men, Mrs. Meadows again, and the three men on the porch.

"Don't look like Dane has made you very welcome. I guess Lorn didn't know you was coming."

Nell glanced away. "No."

Tully was quiet for a moment. "Well, I don't think you got much chance of getting word to him, 'less you happen to catch a Patman rider passing through. But tomorrow's Friday anyhow, and Lorn, why, he'll be in town on Saturday. Ever'body comes to town Saturday."

"Yes, I know. It's bath day."

Tully smiled again. "That's one reason, yes, ma'am. Listen, speaking of that, I'll send two Mexes over in the morning to carry out that tub of water for you."

"You're very kind, Mr. Samuel." Tully shrugged and looked away. The ball of fire in the sky was almost completely gone now, only the sliver of a red arc remaining just above the horizon. "It is a wondrous thing watching the sun go down."

Tully said nothing. He glanced at her furtively, drinking in everything about her: the reddish hair and freckled face, the slim neck and deep bosom, the way the yellow taffeta fluttered easily in the breeze, the bare, freckled arms, the tiny waist, her gardenia smell, the nearness of her. Tully would have given a year off his life just to touch her. She thought the sunset was a wondrous thing, but he saw the sunset every day of his life. To him, *she* was the wondrous thing.

"I'd better be going back," Nell said at last.

"I'll walk a piece with you, if it's all right."

"Of course. Thank you."

Tully locked his front door and they started down the sidewalk. The Chinese couple was still out in front of the laundry. The man spoke to Tully in Chinese as they passed, and Tully answered him in Spanish. "We been talking like that for a year," he told Nell, "and never have knowed what the other one was saying."

Nell laughed softly. It was the first time she had laughed since leaving Kansas City. Across the street, loud music came from a saloon called La Cantina. Through its front windows Nell could see men at a bar drinking, and at tables playing cards. In the corral next to it, which had been empty when she walked by earlier, there were now a dozen hitched horses. Three more horsemen rode up as they were walking by. Tully noticed Nell scrutinize them.

"Lorn don't come in during the week," he told her. "The Patman spread's too far out to come in on a workday."

"Oh." She smiled an embarrassed smile. "I guess I shouldn't seem so anxious."

Tully said nothing. When they got to the boardinghouse fence, Nell saw that the porch chairs were now unoccupied.

"Looks like the three gentlemen have gone to bed. What a shame I didn't get to tell them goodnight."

"Guess you'll have to settle for me." Saying the words tugged at Tully's heart. Nell put out her hand and he took it.

"You've been so nice, Mr. Samuel. I can't begin to thank you."

"My pleasure, ma'am."

"Goodnight now."

201

"Yes, ma'am. Goodnight."

As Tully walked back up the road, he silently cursed Lorn Patman. The dirty, no-good son of a bitch. He had just last week announced his engagement to Sarah Spence, the daughter of Paddy Spence, a neighboring rancher. Lorn and Sarah were to be married the following month.

He wondered what Nell Sheridan would do when she found out?

30

As it turned out, Nell did not have to wait until Saturday to see Lorn Patman. Word somehow got to him at the Patman ranch that there was a young woman in Dane looking for him, and he rode in Friday afternoon, a day earlier than usual. Nell was sitting on the front porch with Mrs. Meadows; not exactly *with* her: Nell was on one side of the porch, Amelia Meadows on the other, and there was no conversation between them. Nell was stirring the still hot air around her with a woven straw fan she had found on the chair. Across its face was printed: Ralston Purina Feed Co.—St. Louis, Mo.—Guaranteed No Colic to Horses and Mules. Up until then Nell had thought colic was something only babies got, and she was not even sure exactly what it was. I've got a lot to learn about being a mother, she thought. She was contemplating that subject when Lorn rode up.

At first she was not sure it was him. The rider reined in at a hitching post just outside the fence and swung gracefully to the ground. He wore a battered dusty Stetson, rough twill shirt, denim trousers partly covered by leather chaps, and boots with large spiked spurs. A holstered gun hung on his hip from a cartridge belt. From behind his saddle he removed a large blanketroll with a newer nicer hat and polished black boots hanging by rawhide ties. Then he yelled in harsh Spanish to several Mexicans sitting by the fence and one of them got up and hurried over to take care of his horse.

Only when Lorn was walking up to the porch did Nell recognize him. "Afternoon, Miz Meadows," he said, touching his hat brim as he passed the landlady. Laying his blanketroll on the porch, he walked over to Nell. All she could think of as he approached was how much noise his spurs made.

"Hello, Lorn," she said, smiling.

"Hello."

"You look so different. I almost didn't recognize you."

"These are range clothes. They're not town clothes."

"You wear a gun. My."

"Most ever'body does out here. It's different from Kansas City."

"It certainly is."

"I never expected to see you out here."

"I never expected to be out here."

Aware of the landlady's proximity, Lorn turned his back slightly and lowered his voice. "Did you come here just to see me?"

"Yes, Lorn, I did," Nell replied quietly. "I have to speak to you in private. I have a room upstairs."

"Me too. That is, my daddy keeps a bedroom and parlor upstairs. Rents it by the month so we'll have quarters when we come to town. We can go up there."

Nell rose and walked across the porch with him, and Lorn picked up his blanketroll. "We're going to use the upstairs parlor, Miz Meadows."

"Long as you leave the door open, Lorn," the landlady instructed. "You know the rule."

"Yes, ma'am."

As they pulled open the screen door and started in, Mrs. Meadows added, "Oh, Lorn, congratulations on your engagement. Sarah Spence is such a nice girl. Make you a good wife."

"Thank you, ma'am," Lorn muttered.

Halfway up the stairs, Nell paused and said, "You're engaged to be married?"

Lorn nodded. "We just announced it last Saturday," he said uncomfortably. "Had a big barbecue party at the Spence place.

Ever'body thought it was to announce the engagement of my sister Ardelle to Sarah's brother Pete. Folks sure was surprised."

"I can imagine." Inside, Nell felt as if a claw had dug into her heart. There was movement in her breast that she could actually feel, a kind of palpitating. *I will never make it to the top of these stairs,* she thought. *I am going to be very, very sick—*

She did make it; miraculously, it seemed to her. And after a long journey that seemed to last for hours. Random thoughts coursed through her mind like floodwaters.

He's engaged.

To someone else.

While I'm carrying his child.

I've traveled all the way to Texas for nothing.

This is madness. I don't even know this man.

"In here," said Lorn.

The Patman rooms were at the front of the boardinghouse: a large parlor overlooking the front yard, with a bedroom behind it. Nell entered and sat on the first available piece of furniture she came to, a davenport. Lorn left the hall door open, and took his blanketroll into the bedroom. Nell watched through the door as he unrolled a suit and some other fresh clothes, and hung them in a chifforobe. When he came back into the parlor, he was no longer wearing his range hat, spurs, or gunbelt. Nell wondered if he would sit beside her on the davenport; he did not, instead taking a chair facing her.

"What are you doing here?" he wanted to know.

"Lorn, do you remember my name?" she asked quietly. "You haven't used it once since you got here."

" 'Course I remember your name. It's Nell Sheridan. I'm not simple."

"I just wondered. Maybe people in Texas don't use given names in polite conversation like we do in Kansas City."

"Like I told you earlier: this is different from Kansas City. Are you going to tell me what you're doing here?"

"Certainly. I came to tell you that I'm going to have a baby."

Lorn Patman sighed quietly. Deep down, he had known that was what it was all about; but he kept hoping he was wrong. Now he could stop hoping. Oddly, he found that knowing, even the worst, was a kind of relief.

"Are you saying it's my baby?"

"Yes." Nell looked down at her hands, one of which was busy with an orphan strand of thread in her lap. "You're the only man I've ever been with, Lorn. I told you that the night we were together." She looked up. "Why didn't you come back the next day?"

"Me and my daddy's foreman had to catch the last train out before a railroad strike they was fixin' to have."

"Did you think about writing me? You had my address."

Lorn shrugged and said, "I don't write letters so good. 'Sides, when I got back home, well, there was a lot of work to catch up, there was some problems needed tending to, and, well—"

"And there was Sarah Spence. I don't remember you mentioning her when you were telling me about Texas."

"I might not have. I didn't really pay much attention to her until I got back from this last Kansas City trip." Leaning forward, he put his elbows on his knees. "I sure wish you'd showed up a week sooner."

"If I had, would you not have announced your engagement to Sarah? Would you have announced *our* engagement instead? Is that what you're saying? Because if it is, then the week's difference in time shouldn't matter any. How you feel is what should matter."

Lorn got up and went to the double windows. Pushing aside a lace curtain, he stared out at what he could see of the edge of town. Nell watched him. Incredulously, all she could think of at the moment was that the curtains in *her* room were of the most inexpensive chintz.

When Lorn turned from the window, he walked purposefully into the bedroom, put on his hat, and hung his gunbelt on one shoulder. "I've got to have a little time to think about this," he said. "I'm kind of mixed up about everything right now. So I'm going uptown and get me a drink. I'll be back later and we'll talk some more."

He left the parlor and Nell heard his heavy bootsteps going down the stairs. She rose and walked to the window where he had stood. Looking out, she watched him leave the yard and walk up the dusty street, his heels making puffs of dust with every step. She watched until he was out of sight, then went into her own room.

* * *

Lorn did not return that afternoon. Nor at suppertime. Nor in the quiet twilight time after supper. Nell sat on the front porch until an hour after dark, then went to bed.

It was much later, after she had lain in bed in the darkness for a long time, listening to the others in the house settle down for the night, afterward listening to the sounds of the prairie through her open window that faced the back of the house, that she heard a soft knock on her door. Getting out of bed quickly, she hurried barefoot across the wooden floor and asked, "Yes?"

"It's me. Lorn. Can I talk to you?" He had his mouth at the crack of the door, whispering.

Nell let him in. "There's a settee by the window." It was in gray moonlight, and there was a slight prairie breeze that again brought the fragrance of wildflowers. Lorn sat forward as he had done earlier, forearms on knees, fingers clasped.

"I can't explain what happened with Sarah and me," he told her. "Before you, I hadn't never been with no women except whores and Mex girls. I didn't know what it was like to be with a nice girl, a girl that was clean and smelled good, not like perfume but *good,* like my sister smells, like I remember my mother used to smell. And it was so nice and all with you, not like with whores that's always trying to get it over with quick so's they can take the next one; or Mex girls that's always talking to God and Santa Maria and *Haysoose* while you're doing it to them." He sat up straight. "That night with you was the most wonderful thing that ever happened to me, Nell. And when I got back home, why, I just started seeing Sarah Spence in a whole new light. She's the onliest girl in these parts that's like you and my sister and the way my mother was. I don't know what happened to me: I just started thinking about being with her the way I'd been with you, and the next thing I knew I was courting her."

"Have you done it with her?"

"No. I kind of tried, but she let me know we was to wait."

"Do you think it will be as good with her?"

"I hoped it would," Lorn said, his whisper becoming hoarse. "There hasn't been a night that's passed since I got back that I haven't thought about us on your back porch. I never in my life felt that good before." He leaned close in the darkness and put his arm around Nell's shoulders. "Did you feel the same way?"

"Yes. If I hadn't, I wouldn't have come all the way here from Kansas City." She was wearing a nightdress that left part of her shoulders bare, and she could feel his slightly rough fingers on her skin.

"Do you want to do it again?"

"First tell me what's in store for us, Lorn. What do you intend to do about Sarah?"

"I'll just have to tell her, is all." He played with the elastic that held her nightdress up. "I'll try to explain and just hope she understands. And hope her *daddy* understands."

"Are you saying you want *me,* Lorn?"

"God, yes. More'n anything."

"And your baby? You want your baby?"

"Sure."

Nell turned into his arms, so relieved that she felt weak, limp. She did not resist when Lorn lowered the nightdress to her waist and began to fondle and suck her breasts.

"God, they're even bigger than I remembered."

"The baby does that."

She became aware that he was standing, and she heard the rustle of clothing as he undressed. Then he drew her gently to her feet and pulled the nightdress the rest of the way down so she could step out of it. When he tried to guide her over to the bed, she said, "God, no, Lorn, it makes too much noise. Over here on the floor, there's a hooked rug—"

He found her difficult to enter, just as he had the night in Kansas City, but the more he kissed her, the more he played with her breasts and kissed them, the moister she became, and finally he was getting it up into her, all of it, slow and easy, until it was all in—incredibly; he could scarcely imagine it; all of him was up *inside* this girl!—and then the wet part between her legs felt as if it were sucking him in and pushing him back out, as if it were a mouth over which he, after inserting his cock, had no control. Holding himself above her with stiff arms, Lorn suddenly realized why he felt like that. Looking down at Nell in the gray light, he became aware that he was not doing it to *her;* she was doing it to *him.* He had become perfectly still, like a wooden Indian tilted forward on an angle. It was *she* who was moving. With her knees spread wide, heels dug into his hips, she was thrusting upward with a smoothness and a rhythm like nothing he had ever seen before. Her body seemed almost boneless, without restraint, liquid. The dim sight of her, together with the feel of her, purged his mind of every other concern. He kept his entire body as rigid as the part on which she slid, and watched in absolute fascination as she again brought him to that physical plateau he remembered so well.

As he felt his come get ready to flow, Lorn closed his eyes, opened his mouth, and let that incredible little part of her body suck it all out of him in a stream that seemed to last and last and last.

When it was over, his body and mind were empty of everything except the memory of awesome pleasure.

The next morning, Saturday, Nell heard heavy bootsteps in the hall several times, and hoped each time that it was Lorn coming back to her. She stayed in bed, in her nightdress, in case he wanted to quickly do it again before he went out anywhere. When he had left her the previous night, he had whispered that he would see her in the morning. But he had not said what time.

After being disappointed repeatedly by bootsteps that did not stop at her door, Nell finally got up and put on a wrapper to go get water to wash. With the washbowl in her hand, she had just opened the door when Lorn walked up about to knock. He quickly guided her back into the room. Taking the washbowl from her, Lorn gathered her into his arms.

"I wanted to come earlier," he breathed into her neck, "but my daddy and our foreman rode in a little bit ago."

"Was that all the noise in the hall?" she asked, feeling his hands exploring her back.

"I reckon. Daddy's already had two or three people in to see him, early as it is. Listen, I'm going to be busy with Daddy most of the day, tending to whatever bin'ess he's got. I may not see you until late tonight, when ever'body's sleeping again."

"Oh, Lorn, honest?" she pouted. "What will I do all day?"

"You can find something to keep busy. It can't be helped, honey. Daddy expects me to be there when he's conducting bin'ess. After all, I'll have to do it myself someday. Got to know how it's done."

"Are you going to tell him about me?"

"Just as quick as I get the chance, honey. But the time has to be right. It's kind of a touchy thing, what with the Spences being our boundary neighbors and all. Plus which, Miz Spence, Sarah's mother, spent so much time taking care of my own mother when she was dying, well—"

"All right, Lorn, I understand."

After he left, Nell realized, a little surprised, that she really *did* understand. It was not too difficult once one thought about it. This was a close little world down here in East Texas. In some ways it was still a frontier. There were not all that many people in the community of Dane, and everyone seemed to know everyone else; there was a suggestion of *relationship,* of loyalty, close ties. It was natural, Nell supposed, for people who lived like that to be wary of outsiders.

What had she expected? she asked herself after she had thought the situation over. Here she was, a total stranger, who had just set herself down in the midst of this tight little society, uninvited, unexpected, and probably, to everyone except Lorn, unwanted. For the first time Nell looked at her arrival from the viewpoint of the people in Dane. Was it any wonder that the cowboys on the front porch had denied her their help in locating Lorn; that the Mexicans pretended not to understand her; that Mrs. Meadows was openly hostile toward her? Not at all, she had to admit. Why, her own neighbors back in Kansas City probably would have reacted the same way if Lorn, in rough range clothes, wearing a gunbelt, had suddenly appeared on their street asking questions about her. Wouldn't they have?

No, she answered herself firmly, they certainly would *not* have. People in Kansas City were civilized and hospitable. They would have helped Lorn in any way possible, despite his being an outsider.

Then she began to get angry. It's these people, she decided, these *Texans:* they think they're better than everyone else, with their grubby little town and their once-a-week baths and their lazy Mexicans who slyly fail to understand anything remotely associated with work. They didn't like her because they were *afraid* of her. Afraid she was going to upset their precious status quo. Don't give the Mexican boy more than a penny, Miss Sheridan. Wait until Saturday for your bath, Miss Sheridan. Supper is promptly at six, Miss Sheridan.

Well, to hell with them, Nell thought, in one of her rare uses of an expletive. I am *here.* I am carrying Lorn Patman's baby, so I have a *right* to be here. And I am going to *stay.*

Snatching up the washbowl again, Nell left her room and stalked down the back stairs. In the backyard a young cowboy was sitting on the ground, leaning against the well pump.

"Get out of the way," Nell ordered. "I want to get some water." It was the first time ever that she had failed to include the word "please" in a request.

The cowboy looked her up and down, grinned, and turned his face to spit a stream of dark brown tobacco juice. He made no effort to move. With her outrage already so close to the surface, that was all it took to infuriate Nell. She drew the porcelain washbowl back like a weapon.

"If you don't move, I'm going to smash you in the face!"

"Yes, ma'am!" the insolent cowboy said, and quickly got up. From over by the fence, the ever-present, ever-relaxing Mexicans emitted a chorus of laughter. The cowboy glared at them and stalked away.

Nell, imagining that her hand was around somebody's throat, began pumping the well handle with a vengeance.

Lorn came to her in the middle of the night on Saturday and they made love on the hooked rug again. Afterward, he remained with her for an hour and they sat up against the wall talking in whispers in the darkness.

"I have to go to church with the Spences tomorrow," he told her, "and afterwards Daddy and Ardelle and me are riding out to their place for a big barbecue. I'd hoped to be able to talk to Sarah this weekend but it don't look like I'll be able to."

"I don't understand. Why not?"

"Well, because of the barbecue, honey. There's lots of people invited. The Baptist minister's coming, some of the merchants here in Dane, ranchers from down south of our place and up north of Mr. Spence's spread. Lots of folks'll be riding fifty miles or more to get there. It just wouldn't be right to spoil the day for ever'body."

"No," Nell said in an even quieter whisper, "I guess it wouldn't." They were silent for several minutes, then she asked, "When will I get to see you again?"

"Next Saturday, for sure."

Next Saturday. That was a week away. Nell felt her chest tighten, then flutter, as if her heart had jerked inside her body.

"Lorn, what do you expect me to do all week?" she asked, exerting an effort to keep it from sounding like a whine. "I don't know anybody, I don't have anyplace to go—God, Lorn."

"Listen, maybe I can get in one night during the week. We'll be riding fence all week, mending where the goddamn squatters"—he swore in her presence for the first time—"have tore up our wire to try to homestead. If we end up a day someplace not too far from town for me to ride in, why, I'll slip in and see you. Would you like that?"

"Of course, I would, Lorn." That was not exactly the solution to her problem. But it was better than nothing.

On Sunday Nell put on her prettiest dress and walked uptown. While she was looking in store windows—the ones on the other side of the street, where she had not been before—two fancy buggies went by. In the one in front was an older stern-looking couple and a rather plain young man who was driving. In the second buggy was Lorn Patman and a rather plain young woman who resembled the rather plain young man in the first buggy. Sarah Spence, Nell thought. Lorn did not even glance her way as his team cantered the rig past. Seeing him with Sarah made Nell feel nauseated. She terminated her walk, returned to the boardinghouse, and remained in her room for the rest of the day.

Monday was dreadful. She woke up early with an excruciating headache from not eating all day Sunday. At breakfast she gorged herself, trying to make up for the missed meals, but it only made her sick. She was not used to Texas breakfasts: dollar cakes covered with thick black molasses, slabs of extremely salty fried ham, fried eggs singed around the edges but almost raw in the middle, mounds of tasteless (to Nell) grits, and a bowl of something grayish in color with the texture of lumpy oatmeal that she later learned to be cooked calves' brains. It was the latter discovery that caused her to rush out back and throw up on the prairie, a performance that the lounging Mexicans found immensely interesting.

On Tuesday Nell alternated between lying on the bed in her room, and sitting in a chair on the front porch. She yearned to ask Mrs. Meadows to let her help shell butter beans or dust the parlor or set the table for the next meal, *anything* to do something; but she did not ask for fear the disobliging landlady would reject the request, and perhaps even take personal umbrage as if Nell were implying that Mrs. Meadows *needed* help. So Nell simply remained bored to distraction. She endured Tuesday, then Wednesday, and by the time she went to bed Wednesday night she loathed and hated Dane, Texas.

So oddly physically exhausted was she from the endless hours of doing nothing, so terribly weary of mind from the sense-dulling inactivity, that when Lorn came to her late Wednesday night she welcomed him like a gift from heaven and gave him her body—and *took* his—with such fervor that she surprised both of them. She kissed him all over, licked him, nibbled on him in places that made him want to moan aloud, and pulled his face against her own body to urge him to reciprocate. Both of them were starved for each other, and for hours all through Wednesday night they experienced new tastes and scents and touches that they had not known in their few previous times together.

Lorn went home before dawn. She slept the entire day Thursday, only coming downstairs in the evening for supper, which she ate ravenously. Mrs. Meadows had by now stopped talking to her altogether, which was a mixed blessing. It meant that Nell no longer had to endure the gaunt woman's caustic criticisms, but it also meant that now *nobody* talked to her. The other boarders during the week were mostly transients who stayed for only one night and whom she saw only briefly at supper. During the day there was only Mrs. Meadows and the Mexican help, and of course the latter did not talk to her either. Nell had hoped Lorn would be able to come into town early, on Friday, as he had done the previous week, but he told her he could not.

"Daddy was a little bit sore about me leaving the spread a day early last week. If I tried again this soon he'd be all over my ass."

Nell was a little surprised at how easily Lorn fell into using vulgar language in front of her. During their brief time together in Kansas City, he had seemed such a perfect gentleman, always properly respectful in word and tone. I suppose, she thought resignedly, that's how men talk in Texas. Just one more thing she would somehow have to get used to. But she could not help wondering if Lorn used the same language in front of Sarah Spence.

On Friday the maddening boredom finally drove her from the boarding house to walk uptown again. She wandered into the dry goods emporium and looked around a bit. The proprietor, a male prototype of Mrs. Meadows, apparently knew who she was; he unsmilingly asked if he could help her, and when she politely declined, ignored her the rest of the time she browsed. When she smiled and said goodbye as she left the store, he merely nodded.

Back outside, she passed the sign that read Clarence Fort, Lawyer, Upstairs, and imagined herself walking into his office, sitting down, and saying sweetly, "Mr. Fort, I wish to sue the township of Dane, Texas. Yes, that is correct: the *entire* town, including all of its citizens. Charges? Rudeness, ignorance, arrogance, inelegance, crudeness, incivility, ungraciousness, and general boorishness. On second thought, I want to leave one person out of the suit: that nice Mr. Tully—I mean, Mr. Samuel—who owns the cafe. He is the only gentleman I have encountered since I said goodbye to the conductor when I left the Kansas City–Dallas train—

"'Afternoon, Miss Sheridan," a voice interrupted her daydream. She snapped back to the present to see Tully Samuel in the doorway of his cafe, smiling at her.

"I was just thinking about you, Mr. Samuel," she admitted.

"I'm right flattered, ma'am," he replied, slightly taken aback, a little embarrassed.

"Yes, I was just thinking that you are the only gentleman I've met in this—this outpost."

Tully looked down at his denims, greasy apron, and scuffed Indian moccasins. " 'Fraid I don't look much like a gentleman," he said, blushing, fully discomposed now.

"Clothes have nothing to do with being a gentleman, Mr. Samuel," Nell lectured. "It's how a man *acts*. How he conducts himself. It's what's inside a man that is the measure of his worth. You are very definitely a gentleman."

Two cowboys walking by heard Nell's words and glanced curiously at her and Tully.

"I appreciate your kind words, Miss Sheridan," Tully said awkwardly, "but if it's all the same to you, let's keep it our secret. There's some around here might find that right funny."

"Of course. I—understand—I—"

Suddenly Nell was flushed and dizzy. Her eyes went out of focus. She had to reach out and put a hand on the doorjamb to maintain her balance. Then everything around her went black and she saw a million bursting spots before her eyes.

Before she realized it, Tully had taken her by the arm and

guided her inside. His voice sounded very far away. "Just sit down right here, Miss Sheridan. Are you all right? Let me get you some nice cool water."

He hurried out back and drew a bucket of fresh water, cool and clear, from the well. He gave her some in a coffee cup, helping her hold it steadily to her lips.

"It must be the sun. You're not used to it."

"I'm going to have a baby, Mr. Samuel," she told him quietly.

When she was feeling a little stronger, Nell let Tully take her out behind the cafe where he had a homemade wooden swing suspended from an A-frame. It was set up in a lean-to, in the shade. "If you just swing to and fro a little," he suggested, "you'll get a mite of breeze." He brought her a cool cloth soaked in the well water; it felt marvelous on her face and neck.

"Thank goodness it happened while I was with you. Anyplace else and I'm sure I'd have been left right where I fell. I can just see Mrs. Meadows grumbling because she and the Mexican girls had to step over me." She looked at Tully and smiled. "Don't you have any questions?"

Tully shrugged. "What gives me call to ask questions?"

"Because you're my friend. My *only* friend in Dane. That gives you the right. If you want to ask."

"All right then. Is the baby Lorn Patman's?"

"Yes."

"Does he know about it?"

"Yes."

"Is he intending to do anything about it? Do right by you, I mean."

"He says he is."

"What's he intend to do about his engagement to Sarah Spence?"

"He says he's going to break it. He's waiting for the right time to talk to her about it."

Tully grunted quietly. "He better not wait too long. The wedding's in three weeks."

Nell looked at him incredulously. "Three weeks? That can't be right. You must be mistaken."

Tully went inside and came back with a two-page weekly newspaper called the Caddo County *Enterprise:* a single sheet printed on both sides. Handing it to Nell, he pointed to an item on the front page. Nell read it twice, unable to believe it the first time. It was a short item, reporting that the previously announced engagement of Miss Sarah Beth Spence to Mr. Lorn Lee Patman would culminate in Sunday afternoon nuptials at the First Baptist Church of Dane three weeks hence.

"I—had no idea—things were this far along," Nell said, as much to herself as to Tully Samuel. "Lorn has been talking as if the wedding day was some time off in the future. He said—he said the engagement had just been announced two weeks ago."

"That's right, it was," Tully confirmed. "But people here in Texas don't have long formal engagements like folks has back east. They like to get it over with and get on with the bin'ess of having kids. That's important out here: having kids. Families has got to have kids to help with the land; kids to pass the land on to. Old Able Patman and Paddy Spence have been trying for a couple years now to get Patman's daughter Ardelle and Spence's son Pete hitched, but they ain't had much luck. Now with Lorn and Sarah deciding to do it, why, I guess neither side wants to waste any time."

Nell looked up and stared out at the raw prairie behind the row of stores. "I never should have come here," she said, again as much to herself as to Tully.

"Prob'ly not," the cafe owner agreed. "This here part of the country ain't for no nice girl like you. Ardelle Patman and Sarah Spence, now, they're both nice girls in their own way, but they was borned here. They got some rough edges, of course: both ride like ranch hands, both of 'em can brand heifers and castrate bulls, and neither one of 'em's got nice ways and talks nice like you do; but as far as being ladies is concerned, why, they're just as proper as those society gals over in Dallas or down in Galveston. Point is, they *fit* this here country; they was raised in it. You, well, you're something else. Dane must seem like a foreign country to you."

"Yes," Nell admitted. "Quite foreign." She rose and extended her hand. "Mr. Samuel, I want to thank you again for being so kind. And for letting me share my troubles with you. I'm sorry if I've been an imposition on you, or caused you any embarrassment."

"You haven't." Tully blushed a little again as he briefly shook her hand. "Do you know yet what you're going to do?"

"Yes, I think so. Do you own a gun, Mr. Samuel?"

"Sure."

"Will you let me borrow it?"

Tully shook his head. "No, ma'am. Lorn Patman ain't worth you going to the penitentiary over."

"I don't intend to go to the penitentiary. I don't even intend to shoot him."

"Then what—?" Tully asked, and suddenly his eyes got very large. "You ain't thinking about yourself, for God's sake!"

"No, I'm not. I don't intend to even fire the gun, Tully, please believe that."

It was the first time she had ever addressed him by his given name, and Tully was instantly affected by it. Hearing his first name spoken in her voice moved him. He yearned to reciprocate by calling her Nell, but he could not muster the courage to do so. "Why, uh, why do you want a gun if you don't plan to use it?"

"I want it to make sure Lorn Patman never puts his hands on me again. I thought having a gun would help. He *would* be afraid of a gun, wouldn't he?"

"Oh, yes, he'd be afraid of a gun, all right," Tully allowed. "Lorn may be a lot of things, but he ain't simple. You point a gun at him and he'll back off."

"That's all I want to make him do," Nell assured Tully. "Just back off."

Tully thought it over for a minute, then went inside and got a .32-caliber revolver with a bone handle. "I'm trusting you," he said as he handed it to her.

On her way back to the boardinghouse, the revolver heavy in her pocketbook, Nell could not help regretting having lied to Tully Samuel.

The truth was, she had not definitely decided just *how* she would use the gun.

31

On Saturday morning there was the usual noise up and down the hall outside Nell's door. Nell guessed that it was people coming and going to see Lorn's father, as it had been a week ago. Nell stayed close to her room most of the morning, leaving only to get water to wash, and once to quickly use the outhouse (watched, as always, as she entered and left, by the omnipresent loitering Mexicans). She thought she might encounter Lorn on one of her trips, but each time she ventured out the hall was empty, the back stairs deserted. She skipped the noon meal, which she had learned the Texans called "dinner," as well as the evening meal, supper. By now she was used to going a full day without eating, then making up for it the next day. Fleetingly, she wondered if such a schedule would have any adverse affects on the baby she was carrying. Worrying that it might, she purchased a few staples—hardtack, cheese, a twist of beef jerky (which she tried and liked very much), and a small jar of plum preserves—and slipped it up to her room when Mrs. Meadows was out in the kitchen (Mrs. Meadows allowed no eating of food anywhere in her house except the dining room). Thereafter, when Nell did not feel like going down for a meal, such as breakfast served at the crack of dawn, she could remain in her room and not feel guilty about depriving her baby of nourishment.

Lorn did not visit her all day on Saturday. Nell had not really expected him to. She had resigned herself to the cruel fact that he came to see her for one reason, and one reason only. She waited for him on Saturday night with mixed feelings of anger and anticipation. Anger because it was now clear to her that he was not about to change the course of his life to accommodate her, baby or no baby. And anticipation because she was still enormously attracted to Lorn, still coveted their illicit lovemaking, because it made her body and being feel so thoroughly and completely marvelous. She hated Lorn Patman for what he was *doing* to her, but she loved him for what he *did* to her. It was a most curious and disconcerting feeling.

As soon as it was dark enough inside and out, Nell undressed and stood at the washbowl to wash herself all over with some still cool water she had drawn while everyone was down at supper. This nightly ritual of hers was the one personal pleasure to which she looked forward each evening. Alone, in the darkness, naked, slowly, gently drawing the cool, wet, slightly rough cloth over her face, neck, arms, breasts that had always been ample but now seemed to be *huge,* slightly swollen belly, hips, legs, feet, and finally, because it felt so good she saved it for last, up between her legs, back and forth for longer than she should, until she felt a tingling, a trickle of the sensation that came when Lorn was inside her.

When she finished her sponge bath, Nell stretched out on the bed, arms and legs akimbo, and let the soft evening breeze from her open window caress the bottoms of her feet, the insides of her thighs, her armpits and neck. Some nights, those when she knew Lorn would not be coming, she would eventually move one hand down to the softness between her legs, play with the mound of thick hair, and presently, when she was wet, work a finger, then two, then three into herself and pretend it was Lorn. When she was through, she put the fingers in her mouth and sucked off the sweet taste of her own self.

On this Saturday night, even though she knew Lorn would be there later, Nell did not refrain from her solo pleasure, did not save all her passion and desire for him. Instead, raising and bracing her heels on the footboard of the bed, she experimented enthusiastically and enjoyed herself *with* herself a number of times before she heard the slight noise of the doorknob that told her Lorn had arrived. From the bed she saw a flash of yellow light from the kerosene lantern hanging in the hall, as Lorn quickly opened the door, entered, and shut it soundlessly behind him.

"Nell, honey—" he whispered.

"On the bed," she commanded quietly.

Nell left her heels up on the footboard. When Lorn sat on the edge of the bed, reached out and felt her nakedness, followed her body with his hand and formed an image of her position, he said, "God almighty—"

"Undress, Lorn." She listened as he shed his clothes, waited until he returned as naked as she was. "Stand here, up close to the bed—" She took his right hand and guided it between her legs, his left she put on her breast; then she turned her head and encircled him with her lips.

"Oh, goddamn—oh, goddamn—" Lorn gasped, struggling to keep his voice down.

Presently Nell got off the bed, which had begun to squeak, lighted a candle, and drew him to the now familiar hooked rug. This time, however, instead of lying down under him, she guided him onto his back and straddled his hips. Easing him up inside her, she reached back and pulled his knees up, braced her arms against them, and began to ride him. Once again, watching in the candlelight as her flawlessly rhythmic body pumped back and forth, Lorn was fascinated by the combined sight and feel of her. Those enormous titties rolling in great perfect circles while the deep wet inside of her slipped up and down his shaft so smoothly, so hotly. All the while he kept thinking of how it had felt in her mouth, how exciting that had been for him, and he conceived a plan to do it that way again with the candle burning so he could see her mouth around it.

So engrossed was Lorn in his present and projected ecstasy that he paid no attention to Nell as she reached over to get something from under her pillow. He was unaware of what she was doing until he felt her slide off of him, felt her fingers close around his throbbing shaft, and felt something cold pressed against the head of it. Then he heard the unmistakable *click* of a pistol hammer being cocked.

"What are you doing, honey?"

"Getting ready to shoot it off."

"Honey, be careful! Are you crazy?"

"Maybe." She moved the barrel down to his balls. "Are you going to marry me, Lorn?"

"Why, 'course I am, honey." Fear colored his normally confident tone.

"Before or after you marry Sarah Spence in three weeks?"

"Now, Nell, I can explain that. Please, honey, be careful with that gun—"

"Have you told Sarah about me yet? And don't you lie!"

"Honey, I have to wait for the right time. I explained all that to you."

"Have you told your father?"

"Well, no, but—"

"You no-good son of a bitch," she said, pushing the gun barrel hard against his scrotum. "You were just going to keep coming over here putting it to me right until the day you got married, weren't you? I ought to blow it off of you, balls and all, right now!"

"Nell, please, for God's sake—"

"You don't care anything about me, and you don't care anything about my baby. You don't care if this baby is born a bastard, do you?"

"I do, Nell, I do! Oh, Jesus—" His member was flaccid now but she still held onto it, still kept the cold gun barrel pressed none too gently against the bottom of his scrotum. He had been warm and slick with sweat from their lovemaking moments earlier, but now he felt chilled and began to shiver. He was sure she was going to shoot him.

Nell stood and said, "Get up. Pick up your goddamned clothes. Hurry up."

With his clothes, hat, boots all bundled in his arms, Lorn felt her prodding his lower spine with the gun barrel, pushing him toward the door. Once there, she forced his face against the wall and held him there while she spoke.

"This baby isn't yours anymore, you son of a bitch. *I'm* not yours anymore. You just go on and marry your horse of a Texas woman in three weeks. But don't you ever come around me and my baby again. If you do, I swear to God I'll shoot you." She opened the door wide. "Now get out."

As Lorn stepped through the door, Nell shoved him as viciously as she could, then slammed and bolted the door behind him.

Still holding the cocked pistol, she sat down naked on the floor and cried.

32

Very early Sunday morning, while all the Saturday night boarders were still asleep, Nell packed her grip satchel and went downstairs. Mrs. Meadows was already dressed in her church clothes, sitting on the front porch, reading her Bible.

"I'm leaving, Mrs. Meadows," Nell announced. "I'd like to settle my bill, please."

The landlady looked up with her usual dour expression and said, "Leaving? Leaving for where? There's no transport through here on Sunday."

"Will you kindly just tell me how much I owe?"

"Your bill has been settled," Mrs. Meadows answered contemptuously. "As if you didn't know."

"No, I did *not* know," Nell snapped, the back of her neck burning. She quickly controlled herself, thinking: Do not give this woman the satisfaction of seeing you angry. "May I ask when he settled the bill?"

"Yesterday. You're paid up for another week, so you might's well stay. No transport today anyways."

"I am not staying for another week, so you can just refund Mr. Patman's money. And I wish to pay my own bill through last night. Will you tell me how much that comes to, please?"

Mrs. Meadows told her and Nell opened her pocketbook and counted out the sum. The landlady saw that there was only two dollars left in the pocketbook. "How far along are you with that baby?" she asked impulsively.

Although surprised by the sudden question, Nell managed not to show it. "Three months." She looked directly into the older woman's eyes, refusing to lie, evade, or back down.

"Is it Lorn Patman's baby?"

"It was. Now it's all mine."

The landlady sighed quietly and gazed off across the prairie. Nell frowned. Had that been a hint of sadness she had seen flicker across the old crow's face? A glimmer of sympathy? Nell shook her head briefly. Not likely.

"Goodbye, Mrs. Meadows." With satchel in hand, Nell left the porch and walked across the yard. Surprisingly, Mrs. Meadows rose and followed along behind her, the Bible pressed to her bosom.

"Is two dollars all the money you've got, girl?"

"That is none of your business, Mrs. Meadows," Nell replied crisply.

"If you'd go see Able Patman, Lorn's daddy, why, he'd see to it that you was properly cared for. He'd do right by you; probably settle some money on you and see that you got back where you came from. St. Louis, was it?"

"Kansas City. And no, thank you. I want nothing further to do with any member of the Patman family." She opened the gate and started off down the road, toward town.

Amelia Meadows stopped at the gate, but her voice followed Nell. "It ain't Christian what men are allowed to get away with. You can punish them if you'll just muster your strength and do it. Why, the Patmans own half of Caddo County. Able Patman's got more money than—"

"I don't care!" Nell shouted at the woman, and kept walking. The nagging voice continued, and only when Nell got well up the road did she escape it.

Dane was deserted that early on Sunday morning; none of the businesses were open, and it was still nearly two hours before people would be riding and walking through town on their way to church. Shifting her satchel from one hand to the other, Nell went directly to Tully's Cafe and knocked on the window. There was no response, and when she shielded her eyes and peered inside, she saw no one. Lugging the bag, which had suddenly become very heavy, she walked to the end of the block, cut over to the rutted alley at the edge of the prairie, and made her way back along the rear of the businesses. Behind the cafe she found Tully, shirtless, sitting with his moccasined feet propped up on a barrel, sipping coffee from a metal cup, reading a well-worn book.

222

"Good morning," Nell said, dropping her bag and collapsing into a chair next to him. "What are you reading?"

"Why, hello. Uh, it's a book called *Life on the Mississippi*. I used to ride the riverboats with the man that wrote it." Suddenly remembering that he was shirtless, Tully turned red and immediately sat up, reaching for his shirt.

"You don't have to do that on my account." She opened her pocketbook again and handed him his gun. Tully sniffed at the muzzle. "It hasn't been fired," Nell said shyly, a little embarrassed herself, remembering how she had used it. Folding her hands in her lap, Nell braced her shoulders and said, "Mr. Samuel, will you give me a job?"

"A job? What for?"

"Because I need one. I have exactly two dollars, no place to live, and I'm expecting a baby."

Tully shook his head and said, "I won't give you no job, but I'll loan you the money to go back to Kansas City."

"I don't want to go back to Kansas City. Not until after my baby is born."

"Why not?"

"Because I want to hurt Lorn Patman. I want this baby to be born right here, and I want everybody to know it's Lorn Patman's child. *Then* I want to leave."

"Miss Sheridan, have—"

"Please call me Nell. I already call you Tully."

"All right. Nell. Have you ever heard the term 'Saturday night bastard?' "

"I don't think so."

"A Saturday night bastard is a kid that's made on a Saturday night by a cowboy who's in town for a little fun. Mostly it's a half-breed kid; the mother's a Mex or a squaw. Once in a while one of the white, uh—women over at La Cantina—"

"A whore, you mean?"

"Yeah." Tully blushed again. "One of them will have one. Do you want your baby called a Saturday night bastard?"

"I don't care what it's called," Nell said obstinately. "Not by people in Dane, anyway. After it's born, I'll take it away from here. It'll grow up someplace civilized and I'll never tell it about this place or its father. But I am going to *have* it here. If I left now, Lorn

Patman wouldn't be losing anything except a pregnant woman that he used and abandoned. But if I leave after my baby comes, then he'll be losing a son. Or a daughter." Nell's expression turned sinister. "And I intend for him to see the baby. Just once before I leave. I'm going to carry it into that church he goes to some Sunday, and let him get a good close look at his firstborn. Then I'm going to take the baby away from Dane and never return."

"That's some plan," Tully said quietly.

"You don't approve, I suppose."

"I reckon Lorn's got it coming, all right. It just don't seem like the kind of thing a person like you would do."

"Do you think it's beneath me? Is that it?"

"Yes, I do, since you ask."

"So you won't help me?"

"I didn't say I wouldn't help you." Tully had a sudden fear that she would get up and walk away, that he would never see her again. "I didn't say that at all."

"Then give me a job. You won't be sorry. I'll work hard for you, right up until the baby comes. I can cook and clean and wait on customers, I'll do your laundry, I can do any mending you need done and—"

"I've got Mex women to do my mending and laundry, and I do all the cooking. But I could use some help waitin' tables. You know you'd cause a lot of talk by staying, don't you?"

"I know."

"A lot of the cowboys are going to make remarks, maybe right to your face."

"I know."

Tully shook his head, partly in surprise, partly in admiration. "You're a tough one."

To his great surprise and relief, Tully found out the very next day that Nell was going to make his job not only much easier but much more enjoyable. Nell had moved into a spare room above the cafe. She came downstairs that first morning wearing a simple white daydress under an apron she had fashioned out of a cotton skirt. Her hair was pulled back severely into a bun, and she had a piece of cloth that matched the apron tied around her head. To Tully she looked as pretty as anything he had ever seen in his life. Pitching right in, she helped him mix pancake batter, boil grits, cut great thick slices of cured bacon and ham, keep an eye on bread and *tortillas* in the oven, and wash the pots and pans as they were used so that they did not pile up in the tub.

When Tully opened the door at five, half a dozen customers, all cowboys, were waiting outside. They exchanged glances after eyeing Nell suspiciously, and attempted to ignore her by hollering their breakfast orders directly to Tully in the kitchen. But Tully backed Nell all the way. "I'm jus' the cook now, boys," he hollered back. "Y'all want to eat, you best tell my new waitress what you want." The men grumbled but decided that food was more important than protocol, so they complied. But they would not look at Nell as they ordered.

Nell served twenty-one for breakfast that morning, and Tully discovered at once how much the arrangement suited him. Not having to hurry from the kitchen to the front to take orders and serve food, instead being able to concentrate on the cooking, he was able to prepare the food with more care and attention, and his customers noticed it at once. The fried eggs were not singed around the edges, the grits not lumpy, the meat not underdone or overcooked. Tully had tried once before to use help in the front of the cafe, but had only been able to hire Mexican women, and they had mixed up the orders so badly that Tully finally let them go. But Nell was keeping everything straight, ordering the food and then serving it efficiently and promptly.

None of the cowboys, who made up the bulk of the breakfast trade, commented on the improvement in the food, not immediately, and not to Tully, but they did talk about it among themselves. Finally, on Friday, after five days, the reserve was broken by a crusty older cowboy who, when paying for his meal, said almost grudgingly, "Food's improving, Tully. This here little lady teachin' you how to cook? If she is, it's about time somebody did." After which comment he left a nickel tip—Nell's first. Following that, she was pretty much accepted, except by a few of the diehards on the range who had nothing to do with *any* woman unless she worked in a saloon or a whorehouse.

With the townspeople, however, it was another story. All of them were supported to some degree by the Patman ranch and Patman riders. When the Dane merchants found out that Nell was carrying Lorn Patman's Saturday night bastard, and that Lorn did not intend doing anything about it, they at once categorized Nell as a "fallen woman," no better than the La Cantina girls or the several working whores who each month included Dane in their East Texas circuit. Consequently, although they allowed Nell to wait on them, none of them so much as smiled or gave her a kind word in the process. "I told you it'd happen," Tully said. "The kind of bin'ess these folks gets from Patman, and Patman hands, they ain't about to risk losing over you."

Nell had shrugged. So be it. She would survive. Tully had shaken his head. "You're tough," he told her.

The one exception among the town folk was a young clubfooted woman named Emily. About the same age as Nell, she was very plain and wore a terribly ugly mismatched shoe with a built-up heel. Her father, a widower, was a typesetter-printer for the Caddo County *Enterprise,* and Emily was a general office clerk and bookkeeper at the same place. Because her father was a stern, severe man who had notions that no self-respecting male would ever claim Emily for a wife, she was not permitted to have anything to do with either the cowboys or the eligible young town bachelors in Dane. That made her existence extremely narrow. She went to work with her father in the morning, went home with him at night; went to church with him on Sundays, prayer meetings on Wednesday nights; cooked, mended, and kept house for him; turned over all of her meager salary to him and was given a small allowance in return; associated only with the people in town that he associated with, and had no friends of her own. It was, therefore, a distinctly pleasant surprise for Emily to find Nell working at Tully's Eats. Part of Emily's job was to go to Tully's three times every working day—at nine, noon, and three—and fetch a bucket of coffee for Mr. Greb, the *Enterprise* owner, and her father. It was during these frequent visits that Emily and Nell became good friends. After word spread who Nell was, thanks to Amelia Meadows, Emily had to be very discreet about the friendship, but she maintained it nevertheless. It was a wonderful experience for her, knowing Nell Sheridan, for through Nell she was given a glimpse of life outside Texas: what it had been like to live in the great metropolis of Kansas City, where they had trolley cars, gramophones, inside plumbing, and all manner of other wonderful things. And for Nell Sheridan it was a valuable friendship also, for in Emily the lonely young pregnant woman found another female with whom she could talk about things that she could not discuss with Tully, her only other friend. Emily was to help Nell Sheridan over some extremely traumatic times while she remained in Dane.

Not the least of those times would be the birth of her child.

The Patman-Spence nuptials, as the *Enterprise* referred to it, was easily Caddo County's preeminent social event of the year. To East Texans it was like the merging of two royal families. It meant that no outsider would ever have access to the combined land interests of the two ranches, because if one family line became extinct, the other was sure to take over the range left behind. It also meant continued economic prosperity for Dane. It meant a tranquility of sorts, too; while cowboys from both spreads might continue to raise hell in Dane, at least no ruffians from *other* areas would be tolerated. The union promised, above all, to maintain the status quo—and that seemed to be what most of Dane and Caddo County wanted.

The day of the wedding was marvelous: clear, sunny, pleasantly warm. Nell watched from the cafe window as, twenty minutes before the announced time of the ceremony, an expensive, brass-fitted carriage of gray and gold, waxed and polished to a gleaming shine, came down the street behind a smartly harnassed, matched pair of blooded Mexican parade horses. The rig was driven by Able Patman, who looked like an old Lorn with gray-streaked hair and a drooping mustache. He was dressed in a new black suit, his spotless white shirt collar closed with a gray four-in-hand. His daughter Ardelle, a pretty, healthy-looking young woman who also resembled Lorn, wore a green satin dress that everyone in Dane knew her father had dispatched two riders and four horses all the way to Dallas to fetch for her. Lorn, in a striking gray cutaway coat and black-and-gray striped cravat, rode next to his father and sister, looking mature and dignified, and extremely handsome.

As the carriage moved down the street, Nell stepped outside and continued watching it. She kept her eyes on it all the way to the far end of the street where it drew up in front of the Baptist Church. Although the figures were very small that far away, Nell continued to watch as they alighted from the carriage and began shaking hands with the people gathered outside. She could not be certain, but she thought she saw Lorn pause and glance back at where she stood. Maybe it was just her imagination; wishful thinking. But because she wanted to, she decided to believe it. She continued to watch. Only when the crowd absorbed the three Patmans did she finally relent and go back inside the cafe.

Upstairs in her little room Nell sat on her cot and used a dainty handkerchief to dab at her eyes. Why? she wondered. Why can't it be me in that church today? Me and my baby? Why?

She had no answer.

Pressing her face into the pillow, she sobbed as quietly as she could so that Tully, downstairs in the kitchen, would not hear her.

33

In the month that followed, Nell tried as best she could to put Lorn Patman out of her mind. It's over and done with, she told herself. The only thing remaining is to have the baby, make sure Lorn sees it at least one time, and then go back home to Kansas City. She had written to her mother and explained her circumstances, emphasizing that she was well in health, outlook, and employment. Because she did not want her mother to worry, or feel she had to make the long wearying trip to Dane, Nell said that she had been taken in by Mr. and *Mrs.* Tully Samuel, who were taking very good care of her in exchange for a few hours' light work in their cafe each day. She assured her mother that she would return home as soon after the baby was born as she could travel.

At the cafe Nell plunged into her job with a vengeance, finding that the harder and longer she worked, the less time she had to brood about her circumstances, and the quicker she was able to fall asleep at night. Often she was up and in the kitchen when Tully got out of bed in the morning, and just as often she returned at night, after the cafe had closed, to do something she did not want to let go until the next day. Tully overlooked it for a while, because he guessed what she was doing, and with his growing feeling for her he wanted her to forget Lorn as much as she herself wanted to. But soon he began to worry about her working so hard, and after Emily said to him one day, "Tully, she doesn't look well to me," he decided to slow her down.

"You're doing too much around here, Nell," he told her. "I want you to stop coming down so early; you've been in this kitchen at three o'clock every morning this week. And I want you to stop working after we close at night."

"I will not," Nell replied testily. "You're giving me room, board, and a salary. I intend to earn it."

"Well, you're *more* than earning it," he insisted. "Slow down."

"I will not."

Tully had stopped what he was doing, cutting up green peppers, and stared at her. "This is *my* cafe. I'm the *boss*. You'll do what I tell you."

"I will not," she repeated.

"All right, goddamn it then, you're fired!" he shouted. He threw the cutting board and green peppers on the floor and stalked out back, slamming the screen door so hard that one hinge broke.

Emily, who had witnessed the scene, said, "He cares for you, Nell. He's concerned about you." She lowered her eyes. "You don't give him anything else; least you could allow him that."

Nell had turned red. She and Emily had talked once about Tully's feelings for Nell. Emily was certain Tully was in love with Nell, and told her so. "He's always looking at your bosom, every chance he gets. Don't be surprised if he comes up those back stairs some night."

Nell had thought Emily was exaggerating; she dismissed the observation as silly. Later, she was to catch Tully several times surreptitiously glancing at her breasts; and noticed that he found reasons to walk past the sink when she was bending over it; and became aware of an occasional creaking board when she was naked in the lean-to bath house built onto the back wall of the cafe. Upon closer inspection, sure enough she discovered a tiny peephole from the other side of the back wall—Tully's bedroom.

"Why don't you treat him friendlier?" Emily had asked. "You could do lots worse. He'd take good care of you and the baby. He's not as handsome as Lorn, but he's not ugly either. Least you could do is give him a chance. You know, let him. You sure wouldn't have to worry about getting pregnant."

Nell had rejected the suggestion. But when Tully had stormed

out of the cafe the way he had, Nell realized that she had under-
estimated the extent of his feelings for her. When he shouted at her
and fired her that day, she was shocked. Asking Emily to watch the
cafe for a minute, she went out back and found Tully sitting in his
rocker, smoking a roll-your-own, staring moodily at the prairie. Nell
went up behind him and put her hands on his shoulders.

"I'm sorry, Tully. I'll slow down if you want me to. I appreciate
your concern for me."

"I ain't trying to be bossy," he said quietly without looking up.
"It's just that I don't want nothing to happen to you."

"I know. Thank you for caring." She decided at that moment
to leave the peephole alone. There was no harm in it, and she concluded that she probably owed him that much.

On the fourth Friday after his marriage, Lorn Patman rode into town
and hitched his horse outside the cafe. It was midafternoon and there
were no customers. Tully, as was his habit, was in the back room
having his *siesta*. Nell was at the counter writing out the next day's
menu when Lorn came in.

It took a great deal of self-control, but Nell managed to look up
and say simply, "Hello, Lorn. What would you like? There's fresh
coffee and pecan pie."

Lorn sat on the stool nearest the door. "Coffee, I guess."

Nell saw him glance at her belly as she got up. She was showing
nicely now, her belly swollen high so that she had to tie her apron
in an arc above it. Emily told her she looked cute, and Tully winked
at her now and then when she sat down and folded her hands over
the natural shelf she now had. As for herself, Nell felt mispropor-
tioned and dumpy, and she knew she waddled when she walked.
Sometimes she tried to control it in front of the cowboys, who teased
her by making duck noises. But now, in front of Lorn, she let herself
be completely natural: dumpy and all. Because, after all, he was the
one who had made her like that.

"Five cents, Lorn," she said, putting his coffee in front of him.
She noticed that he looked very tired, with the beginning of dark
circles under his eyes. Unable to resist, she asked, "Well, how's
married life treating you?"

"Fine." Raising the cup to his lips, he blew gently on it to cool
the steaming coffee. Nell tilted her head and studied him. There was
something about the way he had said "fine" that rang false.

"You don't sound fine, Lorn," she observed. "Don't look it, either."

"Well, I guess I'm not, really." He tried to grin but it turned into a self-conscious grimace. "Sarah and me, well, we ain't, uh— man and wife yet, you know."

"Oh?" Nell's eyebrows shot up. It had been almost a month.

"You must have heard talk about us." It was not quite a question.

"No, Lorn, I haven't. But I'm sorry you're having problems." She realized that, surprisingly, she *was* sorry.

"Sarah's got this *ancilla,*" Lorn said, avoiding Nell's eyes. "Mex gal named Conchita. The two of them growed up together. Conchita found out about you and told Sarah. Before the wedding. Sarah said she never wanted to marry me in the first place. She only agreed because her daddy said he'd whip her if she didn't. But she won't have nothing to do with me in bed." He grunted softly. "Her and Conchita have rooms of their own, with a door between them."

Sarah stared at him for a moment as the significance of what he'd said settled in. Then, shaking her head, she abruptly decided that she did not want to discuss the matter any further, did not want to get involved in any new problems. Suddenly her own circumstances seemed very comfortable to her. "I have to finish the menu." She returned to the other end of the counter.

Lorn sat blowing on his coffee until it was cool enough to sip. Several times he glanced down at Nell, seemed about to speak, but did not. Nell was aware of his discomfiture. But there's nothing I can do to help him, she told herself. After all, *he* came *here.* If he's got something to say and can't work up the nerve to say it, then he might as well leave.

But finally Lorn did say it. "Uh, you're sleeping here now, I hear."

"Yes. Upstairs."

"With him?" Lorn asked, bobbing his chin toward Tully's kitchen.

"That's none of your business, Lorn. But no, not with him. I have my own room. I just work for Tully, nothing else."

"Would you move back to the boardinghouse? If I asked you to?"

"What for?"

Shrugging self-consciously, Lorn said, "Well, I been thinking a lot about you, and about the baby. I just been wondering if maybe I made a mistake with Sarah. I thought maybe if you was to move back to the boardinghouse, where I could come see you and we could talk—"

Nell felt the back of her neck begin to burn. "Will you move into the boardinghouse with me, Lorn?"

"Now you know I can't do that. I have to be on the ranch to he'p Daddy during the week."

"Will you take me out to the ranch with you then?"

"Well, see, Daddy still don't know about you yet. Ever'body's scared to death to tell him. 'Cept me, of course, but I hadn't found the right time yet." He was becoming nervous; his hand shook slightly and he set the coffee down. Nell could see agony in his eyes. "I don't know what to do, Nell." He addressed her by name for the first time since coming in. Wasn't it odd, she thought, that he found it so difficult to say her name? And he always averted his eyes whenever he did say it. "I'm not happy," he admitted now. "Not happy at all. Being married to Sarah's not how I imagined it would be. I thought it was going to be like it was with you and me. I keep wishing you were with me instead of her, but—" He shrugged helplessly.

"But you can't bring yourself to accept me openly, can you." It was more of a statement than a question. "Because I'm carrying your Saturday night bastard."

"Where'n hell did you hear that?" Lorn asked irritably.

"It's true, isn't it? Don't some of the cowboys talk about me like that?"

Lorn blushed deeply. He stared at his cup of coffee, refusing to look at her.

"But that's not what really bothers you, is it, Lorn? You don't mind the cowboys talking about *me*. What's tearing you up is that they're talking about *you*. They know about Sarah and her Mexican girl, don't they? And they know I left the boardinghouse and came over here. You started out with two of us and now you don't have either. You're not the cock of the walk anymore, are you? Do the cowboys think that's funny, Lorn? Frankly, I do."

Nell managed to curb her rising anger. He's not worth it, she told herself firmly. Don't upset yourself over it. She took a deep breath and found that it helped immediately; her anger began subsiding. She looked at Lorn Patman with scornful pity but not hatred.

"I'm sorry for you, Lorn. But there's nothing I can do for you. I'm afraid you've made your own bed. It's too bad there's no one in it with you."

Nell left him and went into the kitchen. A moment later she heard Lorn leave.

It was the last time she would ever see him.

34

On Sunday morning Nell and Tully were sitting in the front of the cafe eating a late breakfast and watching with only casual interest as the good people of Dane paraded past the window on their way to church. A few minutes earlier they had seen Emily limping along beside her Spartan-faced father who never looked either to the right or to the left, always dead-straight ahead. Emily had sneaked a quick look at them and wiggled the fingers of her free hand in a surreptitious wave as she passed. Nell and Tully exchanged brief smiles. They both liked poor little Emily, as they invariably referred to her when she was not around. They hated the bad fortune that had caused her to be born with a clubfoot, and the even worse luck that dictated who her father would be. But of course there was nothing they could do about either. Clubfeet, as everyone knew, were permanent; and *just* as permanent was a father's absolute control over an unmarried daughter in East Texas. All Nell and Tully could do for Emily was be her friends in the moments of freedom she dared steal for herself. Nell secretly hoped that once she went back to Kansas City, Tully and Emily might somehow come to need each other enough to become lovers. Except for the deformed foot, Emily was not at all unattractive. She did not have the bosom Nell had—few women did—nor the overall aura of womanliness; but in her own way she was completely feminine and nicely put together. Except for the foot.

They were not sure which was Emily's greater burden: her handicap or her father. After she and her father walked by on their way to church, Tully, rolling a cigarette to smoke with his coffee, said, "If that old buzzard ever smiled, his face would crack like a clay pot. Emily'll be better off when the old fool cashes in."

"What a terrible thing to say!" Nell scolded. "I'm sure Emily has a genuine love for her father, however narrowly he treats her. And don't forget, when he dies, she'll be all alone. Poor little thing." Nell watched carefully to see if those last words had any effect on Tully; if they made him stop and think, or frown, or anything. But apparently they did not, for he simply shrugged and dug his thumbnail into the head of a stick match to light his cigarette.

It was a few minutes later when they heard the unmistakable clump-clop of Emily's gait on the wooden sidewalk, only much faster, more urgent, than usual—clump-clop! clump-clop!—and they knew she was running toward the cafe. Running, something Emily *never* did. Anxiously, they rose together and went to the door to meet her.

Emily's eyes were wide and she was white with fright. "Lorn Patman committed suicide!" she blurted. "He hanged himself from a rafter in the front of the church!"

Nell stared incredulously at Emily and slowly began to feel faint. Covering her eyes with one hand, she became limp; her knees seemed to be melting. If I fall, I'll kill my baby, she thought. Nevertheless, she was sure she was going to fall.

Then Tully's strong arms were supporting her, one around her waist, one holding her hand, and she heard him say to Emily, "He'p me get her out back and up the stairs."

Between the two of them, they managed to get her up to the cool comfortable darkness of her room and onto the bed.

"Get her some cool water from the well," Emily said, "while I loosen her skirt here where it binds her stomach."

Tully left and Nell began to cry, and presently Emily began to cry with her. Together they wept for so many losses: the young man himself, the people he left behind who would die a little bit with him, the wife he could not love, the lover he could not wed, the child he would never see, all the years that were to come and now would not. "God," Nell said through her tears, "the waste, the waste!"

"They just found him there when the minister unlocked the door," Emily blubbered. "He had broken a window to get in. His clothes were all in a pile on the floor. He was just hanging there naked, his face all swollen and black, and his—his *thing*—it was standing straight up, hard as could be—"

Tully made her shut up when he got back with the water, and sent her over to the wardrobe to find something to pour a little of it on so he could wipe Nell's face. He sat on the side of the bed and ministered to Nell, giving her sips of water, laying the damp cloth on her forehead, holding her hand and talking softly to her: "All right now, Nell—there, there—everything's all right—calm down now—'member you've got your baby to think of . . ."

In a little while, partly from the shock of the news, partly from her pregnant condition, Nell fell into a deep exhausted sleep. Emily removed her shoes and put a coverlet over her, and she and Tully tiptoed out. Nell slept for fourteen hours, only waking up once, at six o'clock that evening when the church bell began ringing. Nell did not know it was six o'clock, or that the bell was sounding to announce that although the morning service had been canceled, life did go on, and the evening service would be held as usual.

When the bell woke her, Nell stared straight up at the ceiling and remembered that she had planned to tell people back in Kansas City that the father of her baby was dead.

Now, she thought, it would be the truth.

35

Nell's labor pains started at two o'clock in the morning. Twice during the previous week she had experienced false labor, and when the real one began, she was not sure whether it *was* real or not. She sat up on the side of the bed, and suddenly was wet all the way down the inside of both thighs; then she knew it was real.

Tully had rigged a string that ran from a nail next to her bed, across the ceiling and out the window, down the back wall, and through the window of his room. There it was connected to an old iron dinner bell that he had bought from the blacksmith. Nell had thought the idea of the thing sweet but ridiculous when he first suggested it. She had only let him rig it up because she did not want to hurt his feelings. Now, sitting in a circle of liquid and feeling slightly off-kilter, she was thankful he had thought of it. Reaching for the string, she gave it three hardy tugs.

Tully came bounding up the stairs so quickly that she was sure he must have been lying awake just waiting for the bell to sound. He hurried into the room, wearing only his pants, and Nell smiled weakly at him in the glow of a lantern she had just lighted.

"Send the boy for Rosa," she said. "I'm sure this time. Tell him to tell her my water bag broke."

Without a word, Tully was gone, running down the back stairs to the lean-to, where for a week a young Mexican boy, the same one who had carried Nell's satchel the day she arrived in Dane, had been sleeping every night. Tully shook him awake, saying urgently in Spanish, "Go get Rosa, hurry! Tell her the *señorita*'s water bag broke! Go on, hurry! Run!"

Rosa was a Mexican midwife who served the Mexican and Indian women, the La Cantina girls, and anyone else the town doctor in Dane considered beneath his social level. Tully had spoken to the doctor about Nell early on. "I'm afraid not," the doctor had said. "I'm not going to risk offending either the Patmans or the Spences. I don't know how the two families see this young woman, but I do know that most of my practice comes from one ranch or the other. You'll have to use the Mexican woman. She's a good midwife. You shouldn't have any trouble."

You better hope we don't, doc, Tully had thought darkly when he left. He had gone directly to the Mexican quarter and made arrangements with Rosa.

By the time Rosa arrived, with two young Mexican girls and the boy to assist her, the baby's head could already be seen. Rosa began issuing sharp orders in Spanish and her helpers were off to build a fire, draw water, secure towels, and do whatever else she bade them. Tully stood in the midst of all the activity feeling like an idiot, not knowing what, if anything, he was supposed to do; until finally he was unceremoniously ushered out of the room and the door closed

236

in his face. Tully went downstairs, and because he could think of nothing else to do, he started baking a cherry pie.

A while later, Rosa came down and said, "The *señorita* asks if you can get Señorita Emily. She says she would like Señorita Emily to be with her."

Tully put on his moccasins and a shirt, and hurried over to the little house behind the *Enterprise* office where Emily and her father lived. Knocking on the door, he realized that he was probably starting trouble for Emily as well as himself with her father; but he did not care. If Nell wanted Emily with her during the birth of her baby, then she was going to *have* Emily there—father or no father.

It was Emily, not her father, who came to the door, carrying a candle. "It's Nell," Tully said urgently. "It's her real time this time, and she's asking for you."

"I'll have to lace on my boot," Emily replied, embarrassed. "Then I'll come right over."

Before Tully left the porch he heard Emily's father come out of his bedroom and say, "What in the name of blue blazes is going on?"

"It's Nell Sheridan, Daddy. She needs help having her baby."

"Well, by blazes, *you're* not going to help her! She's nothing but a whore! Go back to bed."

"I *am* going to help her, Daddy."

"Don't you dispute me, girl! It's been a while since I gave you a good strapping—"

"Yes, it has, Daddy. It's been so long that I can barely see the marks on my back in the mirror anymore. So if you want to get your razor strap, go ahead. I'm still going to help my friend, even if I have to do it with a bloody back."

Tully waited on the dark porch, listening, thinking he might have to help Emily. If the old son of a bitch started strapping her, Tully was prepared to give him a whipping he would never forget. But it did not become necessary. After a minute or two, he heard Emily's father say, "All right, girl. Go ahead. I reckon it's the Christian thing to do, no matter who she is." Tully hurried away then, surprised, but thinking that the old son of a bitch really wasn't a *bad* old son of a bitch after all.

Emily barely got to the cafe and up to Nell's room before Tully and the Mexican boy, who had now been relegated to the kitchen with him, heard the unmistakable sound of a baby crying. Tully and the boy exchanged wide smiles, sharing a moment of satisfaction that they personally had participated in something very special. To celebrate, Tully cut the hot cherry pie in half and they ate it.

Rosa came down and got Tully a little while later and took him upstairs. Emily was sitting on the bed next to Nell, stroking her pale forehead; the baby was wrapped in a bundle between them. Nell smiled weakly and said, "It's a baby boy, Tully." She took Tully's hand. "If you'll let me, I'd like to name him after you. I'd like to call him Samuel. Samuel Sheridan."

Tully swallowed and nodded self-consciously. "Sounds like a right nice name for a boy. If you're sure that's what you want."

"I'm sure. Next to my father, you're the finest and kindest man I've ever known. I'm proud to name my son after you." Nell turned to Emily. "If it had been a baby girl, I was going to name her Emily."

Emily cried for a while, Tully stood there holding Nell's hand, Rosa and the two Mexican girls giggled and whispered, the Mexican boy came in with cherry pie on his chin, and Nell continued to smile wanly.

Through it all, newborn Sam Sheridan slept as peacefully in his blanket as he had in the womb.

Nell waited until little Sam was six weeks old, then began making plans to return to Kansas City. She wrote to her mother shortly after Sam's birth, advising her that she was now a grandmother and that both mother and child were in excellent health. Nell promised her mother that she would start home sometime after Sam was a month old and before he reached two months.

As soon as Nell began to talk of leaving, Tully became sullen and grouchy. "It ain't good for a little baby to make long trips like that," he declared, basing his statement on Nell knew not what. "Them stage transports bounces too much and shakes up a baby's insides. And trains is even worse; smoke from engines has been known to strangle a baby's lungs." Nell knew he was just trying to frighten her into staying, so she paid no attention to his horror stories.

Emily became almost spiteful when Nell began her final plans. "I never saw anyone just up and abandon their friends like you're doing," she accused. "You have no gratitude at all."

"Em, you know that's not *so,*" Nell defended herself. "You and

Tully have known all along that I intended leaving just as soon as I could after the baby came. The only reason I stayed in the first place was so I could flaunt the baby at Lorn. Why, I would have left right after Lorn's death if I hadn't been so far along with Sam."

"Speaking of Sam, I think it's downright cruel of you to let Tully and me become so fond of the baby and then take him away from us like you're doing." Emily began to cry. "It just tears my heart in two to think that I'll never see that precious little baby again."

Nell consoled them both as much as she could, but no amount of dramatics on either part was about to dissuade her from leaving. She loathed, hated, and despised Dane, Texas, and most of the people in it, and would have died before she allowed her son to grow up in such a place. Nothing in the world could have made her stay.

On the night before she left, Nell took her last bath in the wooden tub in the lean-to behind the cafe. The curtain was drawn so that no one could see her from the outside. Nell had no idea whether Tully still watched her through the peephole; she had rarely given it a thought since making up her mind to do nothing about it. But on this last night, taking this last bath, she could not help wondering if he was there, standing behind the wall, looking at her nakedness, perhaps doing what men did to themselves when they were alone and excited.

On the premise that he *was* watching, Nell took a little extra time with each step of the bath. After drawing the curtain and lighting the kerosene lantern, she undressed more slowly and deliberately than usual, removing each article as if it were special, hanging it carefully on one of the wooden pegs in the wall behind which she suspected Tully stood. When she was naked, she feigned a long leisurely yawn and stretch, concentrating on moving every part of herself from the ground up.

She stepped into the tub of still hot water that Tully paid two Mexicans to heat and carry to the lean-to every night. After getting wet all over, and being sure to face the peephole wall, she sat on the edge of the tub, spread her legs, and slowly and luxuriously began soaping herself. The soap was homemade by a widow lady in town; it was neither solid nor liquid, but a combination of the two, and came in a round glass jar from which one had to scoop it out as needed. The soap always seemed warm, even on the coolest nights, and Nell found that it felt unusually pleasant as she applied it. Perhaps it was because she had remembered she was being watched; or perhaps because all day she had been thinking about what she was going to do tonight.

Soaping herself, Nell left her breasts for last, covering her whole body, even her face, with the smooth yellow soap, but deliberately going around and over her breasts so that they stuck out full and white and red-tipped from the yellow figure to which they belonged. When at last she did them, it was with slow, caressing, tantalizing movements that rolled, lifted, cupped, and squeezed them into half a dozen different shapes, teasing them until their nipples swelled up as hard as unshelled pecans.

When she began to get very hot, she slipped down into the water, rolled around a bit, and rinsed. Then she stepped out and took her time drying, performing directly for the peephole but never looking at it or letting on that she was aware of it. Slipping into a duster, she gathered her clothes and hurried upstairs to her room.

The lanterns were already lighted, three of them, and placed strategically with their backshields up so that all light was reflected into one corner of the room. In that corner she had affixed on several pegs a colorful Indian blanket that covered two feet of each wall from the corner where the walls met. On the floor of the corner were several other blankets, folded into squares to form a stack nine inches high. Which, she thought, should be just about right.

The string was still in place that ran across her ceiling, out the window, and down to Tully's room. Nell pulled it several times, hearing the faint ring of the old dinner bell at the other end. While she waited for Tully to come up the stairs, she removed the duster and stepped up onto the blankets. When Tully knocked and she told him to come in, he entered the room and found her like that: standing naked, ankles and knees apart, nine inches off the floor, bathed in lantern light.

"I wanted to do it with you just once before I left," she told him. "And I wanted to do it with you in a way that I had never done it with Lorn."

It had taken her days to perfect her idea. There was so little that she had not done with Lorn; but it was important to her to find some way, *something,* that would make it unique with Tully. She felt she owed him more than she could ever repay; and giving herself to him

240

was little enough on her part; but if she made it somehow special, in some way memorable . . .

"Take off your clothes and come over here."

While he undressed, she leaned back against the hanging blanket, protected by it from the splinters in the wall, and using both hands slowly massaged herself wet. When Tully came over to her, erect and throbbing, she was able to pull him close and slip it right into her; no working, no easing, no heavy breathing; just in and up, like a greased wagon hitch.

Nine inches, she found, was exactly the right height.

Nell left aboard the same Texas Overland Transport buckboard in which she had arrived. The same driver put her same grip satchel in the same wagon boot. Tully Samuel was standing in the doorway of Tully's Eats just as he had been the day she arrived. A different Tully Samuel, to be sure, just as she was a different Nell Sheridan. Each of their lives having been changed in some way by the other.

Emily was there also, weeping into a handkerchief, slobbering all over Sam, swearing aloud for everyone to hear that Nell was absolutely, positively breaking her heart by taking the baby away. Nell consoled her as best she could, but that was really very little. She realized without exaggeration just how much her leaving was hurting both Emily and Tully. It was hurting her also. Perhaps they were not as important to her as she was to them; perhaps she did not love them quite as much as they loved her; still there *were* feelings on her part, and it was all she could do to control them. Later she would wonder why she *had* controlled them, even regret it a little; but in the hour of departure she had felt she was doing what was best.

"I'll miss you both terribly," she had said in a tightly restrained voice just before boarding, "and I'll never, ever forget you for being so good to me."

"Promise you'll write," Emily implored.

"Of course I will," Nell said, squeezing the clubfooted young woman's hand.

When she kissed Tully lightly on the lips, a warm waterfall of the previous night's sweet wet memories deluged them both. "You'll always be in my heart, Tully."

"I'll always love you, Nell." It was the first and only time the word love had been spoken between them.

Nell climbed aboard, took the baby from Emily, and when the

241

transport pulled away, did not allow herself a backward glance. Instead, she buried her face next to Sam's and whispered, "My precious baby boy, I'm taking you away from this terrible place, this Texas."

36

"I never saw your mother again after she left," Tully told Sam.

Tully was leaning his elbows on a table in his roadhouse, a cup of cold coffee untouched in front of him. Sam sat across from him. Georgia and Reba were at the next table, listening with rapt attention.

"Emily exchanged letters with her for a long time. While I still had the cafe uptown, she'd always stop in and read Nell's letters to me. But as the years went by, well, things just kind of changed: Reba came along, we sold the place uptown and started this one, and Emily and me, we just didn't see each other very much to talk about Nell. By and by, I reckon she just slipped out of our minds like she'd slipped out of our lives." Tully sat back in his chair. "That's all I can tell you."

Tully watched Sam's face as the younger man digested the story he had just heard. Tully had not, of course, told him *everything:* he had not told him about that last night with Nell, about the peephole in the bathhouse, about the attraction of Nell's incredible freckled breasts. Those things were Tully's, and his alone. Aside from the private things, however, he had told Sam all he knew about Sam's mother, and how Sam had come to be born in Texas.

"Do you know why Able Patman decided to include me in his will?" Sam asked.

Tully shook his head. "Anything you want to know about the Patmans, you can ask your friend Draw. Him and Able was like brothers for more'n forty years. Until Draw shot him one time."

Sam stared incredulously at the craggy roadhouse owner. He had been aware all along that Draw had *known* Able, and Lorn as well; Draw had said as much when he and Sam first met; but *like brothers? For forty years?* Sam shook his head. "I had no idea they were that close," he said, as much to himself as to Tully.

"They come from same part of south Texas. Hunted Comanches together back in the old days, I've heard tell. Draw was with Able ever' step of the way, from the day he staked out his first acre."

"And you say Draw *shot* him?"

Tully nodded. "They had a bad falling out over something; don't nobody know for sure what it was. That was five years ago. Draw left the ranch and throwed in with that cross-eyed Indian; they been drifting around, living off the land ever since."

Sam studied Tully for a long moment, a slight frown pinching the top of his nose. "There's one thing I don't understand, Tully. You were a good friend to my mother, despite the fact that everybody else in Dane shunned her because of the Patmans. Yet you wouldn't give me the time of day when I showed up, because you were afraid of how Pete Spence would take it. Why?"

Tully sighed quietly and shrugged. "Couple of reasons, I reckon. When Nell was here I was younger, didn't have much that was mine. I ain't as brave now as I used to be, and I got more to lose. Plus which, when Nell was here, it was Able Patman I would have had to answer to. Whatever else he was, old Able was fair. Pete Spence don't know what fair is. All he knows is that he's got the power, an' he uses it however it suits him." Tully paused a beat. "Like you done when you said you'd break me if I didn't do what *you* wanted me to do."

Sam glanced at Georgia and Reba, and saw that they were looking at him. He looked back at Tully and found the older man's eyes riveted on him. The words, Sam suspected, were designed to make him feel ashamed for what he had done; they classified him with Pete Spence, the man they knew he hated, and he guessed they expected him to feel contrite because of it.

They were wrong.

"I appreciate what you've told me." Sam stood up. "And I'll keep my end of the bargain. Anything Spence tries to do to you, just get word to me. Any money you need is yours for the asking. You don't have to deal directly with me, either, if you'd rather not; just have Reba let Georgia know." Turning to his wife, he said, "Take Ty and let's go. There's things to do."

As they were all filing back through the kitchen, Tully said, "I'd like to ask you a question, Sam."

"All right."

"Would you really have broken me?"

Sam paused, looked him directly in the eyes, and said, "Like a dry stick."

When Sam and Georgia got back to the shack, Pop Joyner and Owen Milam, still covered with dried oil as well, were sitting on the porch waiting for them. They stood up as Sam approached. Owen was smiling widely, Pop grinning like a kid.

"You ready to become an oil magnate?" Owen asked.

"Past ready," Sam replied. "Where are the others?"

"Buddy's standing guard at the well," Pop said. "Tongue's out in the Choctaw community making sure his people understand not to tell anybody about the strike."

"And Draw?"

Pop glanced off at the prairie. "Gone, I reckon."

"Gone where?" Sam asked, frowning.

"Durned if I know. Jus' said to tell you he was hitting the trail now that the job was done. Said to give his share to the boy there," Pop bobbed his chin at Ty, whom Georgia was holding.

Sam turned and stalked back toward the truck.

"Where you off to?" Pop yelled.

"To find Draw."

"Sam, wait." Owen Milam hurried after him. He caught Sam by the arm. "There's things you ought to be doing, Sam. You can't keep this strike a secret indefinitely."

"I'm finding Draw first," Sam said, shaking off the geologist's hand.

"Suit yourself. But you're going to end up a one-well oil man, not a magnate. Other people are going to come in here and skim the cream right off the top."

Sam stopped and stared into space for a moment. Then he returned to the porch and sat down on the edge. "All right, what do we do first?"

"Get capital," Owen said, sitting down beside him. "We need

money to buy up drilling options on as many of the small farms around here as we can. It has to be done as quickly as possible, before Shell and Sinclair and the other big boys can get representatives up here. To get capital we have to make a deal with a refiner and get an advance. We have to pick that refiner *very* carefully. Now Pop here knows most of the companies and the men behind them; and I know the value of the oil we're going to be selling them; but we need two more people on our side before we begin negotiations: we need a lawyer, and we need a financial man, a banker."

"I've got a banker." Sam was thinking of Dewitt Tucker. "Do you know any lawyers?"

"A couple."

"I want a Texan," Sam specified, "but I don't want anybody with ties to East Texas cattle interests or East Texas banking. I want someone who will give me one hundred percent loyalty without any reservations."

"I'll go around and talk to the ones I know," Owen offered. "Then I'll report back to you."

"Fine." Sam turned to Pop. "I want you to sit down and make a list of every independent refiner you know. Only independents; no giants, no chains. After each name, I want you to write down everything you know about them, good and bad. Will you do that?"

"Nope."

"What? Why not?"

Pop looked off at the prairie again. "'Cause I can't write."

Sam smiled and nodded his head. "Georgia will sit down with you and do the writing." He turned back to Owen. "Anything else right now?"

"Yes, can I take a bath here?"

"Take a bath. Georgia, see that Owen gets a bath, will you?"

"My pleasure," Georgia said, and Owen Milam turned bright red.

"I'm going to look for Draw," Sam told them all then. "I'll be back as soon as I can."

At the Choctaw community, Sam found Tongue at the shanty home of Natchay, the Beloved One. Tunica was with them. Tongue and the girl had bathed and changed.

"Where'd Draw go?" Sam asked Tongue.

245

"I don't know, Sam." Tongue once again spoke the precise English he used when among his own people. "He didn't even tell me he was leaving; I found out from Pop Joyner after he was gone."

"I want him back with us. I want to find him. Will you help me look for him?"

"Of course. Pop said he got cleaned up and set off walking toward the Kilgore highway with everything he owned rolled up in a blanket. I don't think he would have gone into Dane, so he's most likely heading south. Probably hitchhiking."

"That's where we'll look then," Sam decided. "But first I've got to get this oil off of me. Have you got some spare clothes?"

"A few."

"Let's get them and stop by the creek." Sam nodded toward Natchay. "You told him about the strike?"

"He told me," the old Indian answered for himself. "We are very pleased, for you as well as for our people."

"As soon as we arrange to sell the oil," Sam told him, "I will see that you begin receiving your share of the money. You'll be able to buy many things for yourself then."

"The most important thing I shall receive," Natchay said solemnly, "is the peace of mind in knowing that no Choctaw child of this community shall ever go to sleep hungry again."

"Of course," Sam said, a little embarrassed. He had to remember that money meant different things to different people. Not everyone wanted, or needed, power.

As Sam and Tongue were leaving, Sam realized that he had not spoken a word to Tunica, or she to him, while he was there. He was already climbing into the truck when the thought occurred to him. Looking back at the house, he saw that she had followed them out and was standing at the front door. Perhaps, he thought, the same thing had occurred to her. He smiled and waved. Her young brown face broke into a wide smile of her own and she waved back.

"'Bye, Sam," she yelled.

"'Bye, Tunica."

It was the first time she had ever called him Sam.

The two men drove south on the Kilgore highway, watching the shoulders for Draw. They drove all the way to the city limits of Kilgore itself without finding him. At a Globe filling station just inside town, Sam pulled in and asked the attendant if he had seen a man Draw's age, with a blanketroll, hitchhiking alone. The attendant said no.

"Maybe we were wrong," Sam speculated. "Maybe he *did* go into Dane. Let's check there."

They doubled back, driving north, all the way past Sam's place and into Dane. Circling the square several times, they scanned the sidewalk and storefronts, the courthouse steps and benches, down the side streets. There was no sign of him. In desperation they parked and Sam went into several stores, inquiring of the proprietors if they might have seen the old cowboy on the square earlier. As usual, Sam got no cooperation from the Dane merchants. He did not know if they actually had not seen Draw, or if they simply would not tell him. The line of enmity between Sam Sheridan and the people of Dane was drawn on both sides now.

Back in the flatbed, Sam drove randomly around the side streets and back roads of the town. He kept up the search for another hour without success. Finally Tongue, again using his pidgin vocabulary, said, "Old man gone. We not find now."

Sam knew that Tongue was right. Draw had obviously known what he was doing and when to do it. He had given himself enough head start on them to disappear completely.

The one man who had been closest to Able Patman and could tell Sam things he wanted to know about the Texas blood that flowed in his veins. The one man who might be able to tell him why the elder Patman had left him just enough in his will to lure him back to Dane.

The one man who might be able to fit the final pieces of the puzzle together.

Now he was gone.

37

The lawyer Owen Milam found for Sam was a young Texan named Tom Prater.

"Comes from Porter," Owen explained, "a little town down towards Houston. His daddy's got a barbershop there. Tom worked his way through law school at the University of Texas over at Austin."

"Doing what?" Sam asked.

"Worked in an ice house one summer. A pig farm one summer. Hardware store. Whatever he could find, I reckon."

"No ranches or banks?"

"Nope."

"Get him."

From the list of independent refineries that Pop made with Georgia's help, Sam, Pop, Owen Milam, and Dewitt Tucker sat down and reduced to nine the number of companies to which they would offer the Sheridan oil. With Owen Milam's expertise in grading the product, Pop Joyner's in-depth knowledge of the independents' backgrounds and personnel, and Dewitt Tucker's understanding of Texas banking, Sam felt he had enough support to deal with any of them. After he met Tom Prater and the young lawyer joined his team, he was even more confident. Prater was one of those lanky easygoing Texans with an air of beguiling innocence about him. But his new associates soon learned that he had a steel trap for a mind and absolutely no mercy when negotiating for his client.

Sam and his men, all except Dewitt Tucker, who had not publicly joined them yet, met with representatives of all nine interested companies, one at a time, in a private corner of Tully's roadhouse. Four tables had been pushed together so that Sam's men could all sit with him. Sam and Tom Prater did all the negotiating, and questioning; the others made notes; when the meeting was over, they had a brief conference concerning the offer, then asked the next representative in.

Most firms had sent a vice-president or other officer, with a chemist in tow to check Owen Milam's grading. But a company called King Refineries had been represented by Rutland "Rut" King himself, the firm's sole owner. And he had not brought a geologist with him. "I'll take your man's word for the grading," he said. "One chemist is pretty much the same as another, if they're honest."

Sam liked Rut King at once. He was an informal, white-haired man of sixty; he wore expensive clothes, but there were calluses on his hands to show that he had worked for them. But even though he liked King, Sam was still cautious. "Are you related to the King ranching family?" he had asked the refiner. Rut had smiled.

"Wish I was; be a lot easier to raise capital. No, Sam, I'm a different King. We're not even cousins."

In the end, Sam decided to sign with Rut King. The offer was a dollar fifty-five per barrel, which was four cents less than two others had offered, but it was a price guaranteed for three years. "Take it," Owen Milam advised. "The price is bound to drop next year. I think you'll come out ahead."

Sam and Rut closed the deal. Within a week the first of four huge storage tanks were being constructed near the well head. And soon after, Rut King began surveying for construction of a four-inch pipeline to reach from his refinery at Galveston to the railroad station nearest Sam's land, which happened to be a flag stop called Tipton. The pipeline would follow the railroad right-of-way, which was usually the most direct route and over terrain most easily excavated. A delivery pipe would run from Sam's well to the larger line at Tipton. Completion of the line would take a year. Until then, a steady stream of King Refinery oil-tank trucks carried the crude all the way to Galveston by highway.

"How much advance on royalties can I get?" Sam asked Rut King the day they closed the deal.

"Much as you want. Hundred thousand do?"

"Ah, yes, that'll do fine," Sam said, glancing at his friends and partners. Their smiles looked a yard wide. Rut King wrote the check on the spot.

The check for one hundred thousand dollars was given to Owen

Milam to be deposited in the First City Bank in his home town of Cameron, which was out of the sphere of influence of the East Texas Bankers Association that had blackballed Sam. Owen was instructed to turn over fifteen thousand in cash to Dewitt Tucker as soon as the King check was certified. Owen did not know for certain what the money was for, but he did not have much trouble guessing. He got the cash for Dewitt as quickly as possible. Sam also had Owen withdraw five thousand each for Tongue and Pop Joyner, put five thousand in a separate account in Draw's name, and bring him thirty thousand in cash. Twenty of the thirty thousand, Sam and Tongue delivered to Natchay at the Choctaw community.

"This is the first of much money to come for your people," Sam promised. "Your wish is coming true: no Choctaw child will ever go to sleep hungry again."

The old Indian embraced him. To explain why his eyes suddenly became watery, he complained of having a "draft in the head."

"I understand. I myself had the same symptoms one night last week, out on the prairie by myself." Sam's admission brought a smile to Natchay's wrinkled old face.

Sam left Tongue there to more fully explain what had now happened and what was going to happen in the future, and to tell Natchay that Sam had a friend who had studied the white man's law books and could be trusted to represent the Choctaw council if it so desired. Natchay accepted the offer, and Tom Prater subsequently became legal counsel not only to Sheridan Oil but to the Choctaw community as well.

The only thing that dampened Sam's enjoyment of it all was that Draw was not there. At first Sam thought he resented Draw's leaving because he wanted Draw to tell him about Able Patman, to fill in the gaps that still existed in *who* Sam was; but gradually he came to realize that he really *missed* Draw. Sam had come to rely on the old man as his chief adviser. The others around him were good men— Owen with his geology expertise, Tom with his legal, Dewitt his financial—but it was Draw who had the common sense, the *instinct*, that Sam needed to complement his own ability. He wanted—*needed* —Draw back. Badly.

"Tom," he told his young lawyer, "I want to hire some detectives to locate an old man who used to work for me. He left just before Owen brought you down. Name's Charles Poker. Can you handle it for me?"

"Sure thing," Prater said easily. He had already decided to make himself as valuable to Sam Sheridan as possible, because he knew, as the others knew, that Sam was going to become a force in Texas one day: a rich, powerful, influential man. And Tom Prater wanted to be around to share in it.

Sam gave Tom all the information he had and referred the young lawyer to Tongue for more. Then he felt better. Maybe, he hoped, he would have Draw back soon.

Everything except Draw seemed to fall into place for Sam Sheridan after the storage tanks were in and the well began pumping. The well produced four thousand barrels every twenty-four hours, bringing in slightly more than six thousand dollars a day. Of that, Sam got three thousand, the Choctaw community got twelve hundred, Pop and Tongue each got six hundred, and six hundred was put aside for Draw. The surplus, some two hundred twenty dollars a day, went into a payroll account in the Cameron bank, from which were disbursed salaries of four hundred dollars a week each to Owen Milam and Tom Prater, and two hundred to Buddy Kyle. This in a time when men were working fourteen hours a day for fifteen dollars a week. If they were lucky enough to *be* working.

Tongue decided to take his share and start a general store in the Choctaw community. "My people have had to trade in the white stores in Dane for too long," he explained to Sam. "It's time they had a place of their own to trade. I will not take advantage of them as the Dane merchants have. I don't need to make a profit at all, in fact."

"I think that's a fine idea," said Sam. "And I notice you're not speaking pidgin English any longer."

Tongue smiled and shrugged. "Why should I? I'm a man of substance now." Suddenly his face became serious, and slightly embarrassed. "Listen, Sam, will you help me with something?"

"Of course. Anything."

"I'd like to get this crossed eye of mine fixed. The doctors around here won't have me for a patient, and the hospital up in Longview doesn't admit Indians. Do you suppose you could find out where I could go?"

"I'll have Tom Prater look into it right away," Sam promised. "You want him to help you set up the store too?"

"I didn't want to ask too much, Sam."

251

"Heathen. You *couldn't* ask too much. I'll arrange everything with Tom."

Pop Joyner decided to stay on the job, "in order to pertect my innerests," he told Sam; but the truth was he had no place else to go except to another oil field, and at long last he was tired of always moving on. Sam made him operations manager of Sheridan number one and assigned Buddy Kyle as his assistant.

Tom Prater was at work fifteen hours a day, buying oil leases on every small ranch and farm in the area. It took less than a day for word of Tom's activities to reach Pete Spence, and the news effectively told Spence that Sam Sheridan had probably struck oil. By the morning of the second day, Tom Prater began encountering the father-son lawyer team of Clarence and Bruce Fort, who on Spence's orders had begun contacting the same small farmers and ranchers in an attempt to prevent them from leasing drilling rights to their land. Tom Prater learned how they were doing it when he arrived at one rancher's home in time to hear Bruce Fort's offer.

"Mr. Spence is leasing additional grazing land for his cattle," young Fort told the rancher. "He'll pay you twenty-five cents a day per acre for grazing rights. The money is payable whether he actually puts any stock on your land or not."

"Fine idea," Tom Prater allowed. "Grazing rights won't interfere with drilling rights. All we need is a little patch to put up a derrick."

"I'm afraid that wouldn't do," Fort countered. "Mr. Spence would require that no drilling rights be let. He personally doubts that there's any oil under this part of the county, but he's afraid that drilling will bring up saltwater and taint the pastures."

"I see. So it has to be one way or the other then. Grazing rights or drilling rights. Looks like it'll be up to each farmer or rancher to choose individually."

Prater went back to Sam with the news. Sam had been wondering how Pete Spence would try to stop him. Now he knew.

"Double our offer if you have to," he told Prater. "Triple it, I don't care. You can use as much of my share of the income as you have to. Just get those leases. They're important, for more reasons than one."

Prater went back to work. Very quickly he learned that he would not *have* to double or triple Sam's original offer. The small farmers and ranchers were almost unanimous in their excitement about the possibility of finding oil on their land. Pete Spence's offer for grazing rights did not excite them at all. For years they had lived in close proximity to the Patman-Spence ranches, and this was the first time any of them, Patmans *or* Spences, had shown any interest in doing any*thing* for any*one* except each other. But this newcomer, this Sam Sheridan, appeared to be of a different cut. He was a small landowner like themselves, with only a hundred acres; and it was no secret that the Spences didn't like him. That put him more on *their* side than on the side of the Spences. Plus which old Draw Poker had helped Sheridan bring in the well, and Draw was a man who could be counted on—so Sheridan *must* be all right. Ultimately, most of the small ranchers and farmers shunned Pete Spence and went with Sam Sheridan.

While Tom Prater was busy with the oil leases, Owen Milam had obtained plat maps of Caddo and Rusk counties, and was plotting likely places for Sheridan's second well, and third. Every day he analyzed the grade of crude sent to him the previous afternoon, and to his and everyone else's delight, the oil remained light and fine: an exceptionally good product. It kept pouring out, and the money kept pouring in.

Dewitt Tucker quietly replaced all the money he had embezzled from the Merchants Bank of Dane. "I don't think Claud Maye even suspected what I was doing," he told Sam. "I thought for a while he might, but I think I was just scared. I probably would have got caught in a couple of months, though; the next time they audited."

"It's all over now, Dewitt."

"Yeah, it is. I quit today. I'm ready for you to pay me back, Sam."

"What do you want?"

"I want to open my own bank."

Sam smiled broadly. "So that's what it was."

Dewitt nodded. "Will you help me?"

"Just tell me how."

"Put up your half of the well as a guaranty against a million-dollar performance bond. And advance me twenty-five thousand dollars so when I find the right location I can lease a building, furnish it, and hire a staff."

Sam pursed his lips in a silent whistle. Dewitt was asking for everything Sam now had. But then, he had *risked* everything—including his freedom—to help bring in the well. There was really nothing to decide; Sam owed him whatever he asked for.

"Make the arrangements you have to for the bond. I'll get the other money from Rutland King whenever you say. Maybe I'll even have it myself by then. Listen, will you do me a favor? Consider putting your bank right here."

Dewitt frowned. "Right where?"

"Right here on my land. Where the town of Sheridan is going to be."

"The *town* of Sheridan? Are you serious?"

"Very. I've got a plan, Dewitt. I've been working on it with Tom Prater ever since he joined us. Across the highway from my hundred acres is a three-mile stretch of undedicated state land. It's land that can be homesteaded simply by filing on it in Austin. After filing, the homesteader has one year to make acceptable improvements on the land. If those improvements are made, the state deeds the land to the homesteader. Improvements can be the building of a home or business structure, the putting in of a water well, any cultivation of the land in crops, and so on.

"My plan is to homestead the entire three-mile stretch and then let it out in small parcels to people who want to open businesses near where the oil wells are going to be. I'll pay all the homesteading fees, the land tax for the first three years, and run water and electricity up to each parcel. The individual businessmen can make construction improvements by putting up their stores. After three years, they can start paying their own taxes; every year after that I'll deed to each one of them a ten-percent interest in the property. After a total of thirteen years, they'll all own their places outright."

Sam's eyes were burning with excitement, but Dewitt remained skeptical. "Where do you intend to get all these people to open businesses? There's not exactly a real healthy economy in East Texas right now."

Sam smiled. "The merchants in Dane don't own their property, do they, Dewitt?"

"No. Pete Spence owns most of the property in Dane."

"He ever offer to let the businessmen eventually become owners?"

"Why, hell, no. He—" Dewitt suddenly stopped talking as he

realized what Sam was planning. His eyes became as excited as Sam's. "I'll be a—! You're going to get the merchants in Dane to move over *here!* You're going to close down Dane to start *your* town!"

"Exactly. And after we get the businesses here, Tom Prater says we can petition to extend the town limits to include all the small farmers and ranchers who are leasing us the drilling rights on their land. He thinks we can eventually even get the Caddo County seat moved here too."

Again Dewitt frowned. "I thought you hated those people in Dane?"

"The only thing wrong with the people in Dane is that they're under the heel of Pete Spence. Take Spence out of the picture and I'm sure you'll find some decent people."

Dewitt studied Sam in fascination and admiration. Dewitt's own plan to start a bank had been daring, but nothing on the scope of *this.* Sam was talking like a goddamned *pioneer.*

"If you'll agree to construct a building instead of leasing one," Sam said, "I'll give you the first lot that's surveyed. A prime corner location."

"Sheridan," Dewitt said, as if testing the name. "Sheridan, Texas. The First Bank of Sheridan. By god, I like that, Sam! I like the sound of it."

"Sheridan Oil will be your first account. I'll see if I can get King Refineries to give you some business too."

Dewitt Tucker put out his hand. "Sam Sheridan, you've got yourself a bank."

And the beginning of a town, Sam thought, as he shook on the deal.

That night, lying in the dark with Georgia in his arms, Sam told her things about his plan that he had not been able to tell Dewitt Tucker.

"I want to build something good, Georgia." His voice was soft, solemn. "I want to build the kind of town that would have *helped* my mother, with the kind of people who would not have turned their backs on her. I've seen quite a few Texas towns in the past year, traveling around with Pop trying to locate equipment; the one thing I noticed about them is that they're not like Dane. None of them. They were all friendly towns, with friendly people in them."

Sam raised up on one elbow in the dimly lighted line-rider's shack, so that he was looking down at his wife. Georgia was staring at him in much the same fascinated way Dewitt had earlier.

"I've given this a lot of thought," he continued, "and I've come to the conclusion that what's wrong with Dane is Pete Spence. Ever since the town started, it's been under the heel of a Patman or a Spence. One or the other owned the land, controlled the economy, virtually ruled everybody who did business there. That's been going on for years, and it's no different today. Pete Spence owns the people of Dane just like he owns his cattle." Sam shook his head in the dark. "That's no way for people to live. People who live that way are like prisoners; they can't draw free breath. It's not right."

"So you're going to change it," Georgia said quietly. It was not a question; she *knew* Sam would do it.

"Yes. I'm going to offer the people of Dane a new town: Sheridan. I'm giving it the name of my mother's family, just like she gave *me* that name. With the help of the people I get to move here, I'm going to make it the best town in Texas; a place my mother would have been proud of. And a place *we* can be proud of, Georgia: you and me and little Ty."

"Sam, Sam," Georgia whispered in the dark. She drew him back down to her and held him close to her, drawing warmth and strength from his firm body. They were naked but there was nothing sexual in Georgia's feelings at that moment. All she was aware of was an enormous sense of pride that she was part of the man beside her.

And would be part of the adventure that lay ahead.

38

The day Sam had Owen Milam bring him thirty thousand dollars, twenty thousand of which he gave to Natchay, Sam took the rest of the money home and tossed half of it on the sink ledge where Georgia was peeling potatoes.

"Here you are, Mrs. Sheridan. Buy yourself a car tomorrow. And find us a better place to live until I can get an architect to draw up plans for a house. Buy whatever else you want, too; when this money runs out, let me know and I'll give you more."

Georgia stopped working and looked at him. "Oh, Sam, really? Are you sure?" Her voice was reluctant, even a little disbelieving.

"I'm sure," Sam said, laughing.

"Maybe we should wait and make sure the well doesn't peter out in a few days. Reba says oil wells do that sometimes."

"Not this one," Sam replied confidently. "Owen Milam predicts that this one will flow for a year. And by the time it stops, Sheridan Oil will have more derricks up and be bringing in oil from *them*." He pushed a curly lock of hair off Georgia's forehead. "We've made it, honey. The struggle's over."

Georgia's eyes moistened and she put down the half-peeled potato and paring knife. Wiping her hands on the worn apron around her waist, she looked around at the line-rider's shack. "Are we really going to get out of here at last?"

"Yes. And the sooner the better. I'm going to need this place for a temporary office."

"You can *have* it," Georgia said fervently.

Sam smiled. "Soon as you get a car, start looking for a house to rent. But stay away from Dane; I don't want to live there. Try Kilgore, that's a nice town. Or one of the smaller communities south of here: Mount Enterprise or New Salem. But stay clear of Dane."

"All right, Sam." She looked curiously at him. His expression became very set when he talked about Dane.

"I think you should hire a woman to help you, too," Sam added. "Hire a couple if you want to; one to take care of Ty." His mind was in high gear now, his eyes narrowing to slits. "Try to get everything done as quickly as possible, because I'm going to have a business for you to run pretty soon."

"What do you mean?"

That had been the first time Sam told her about his plans for a town. When he finished, he draped an arm around her neck. "Soon as I can set it up, Mrs. Sheridan, you're going to become president of Sheridan Realty. I'm going to put you in charge of leasing lots for the new town."

"Sam, how wonderful!" Georgia beamed. She shook her head in slight amazement. "I can't get over it: you want *me* to work for you!"

"I want you to work for *us.*" He bent and scooped up Ty, who had run in and grabbed his leg. "From now on, we're all going to work for each other. You, me, Pop, Buddy, everybody. We're all part of the Sheridan family." He looked intently at her. "I'm going to make that name mean something in Texas."

"I believe you, Sam," Georgia told him.

For the first time, she really did.

Sam hired an architectural firm in Marshall to design and supervise the building of a twelve-room mansion directly in front of the line-rider's shack. After Georgia found a house to rent in New Salem and moved their things, Sam had the shack cleared out and put in some desks. Then he went into Dane to order several telephones. Afterward he walked over to the offices of the Caddo County *Enterprise*. Harley Greb, the publisher who had declined to help Sam when he first arrived in Dane, looked up from his desk.

"Well, well. The big oil man. What can I do for you?"

"You can't do anything for me. It's not you I came to see." He stepped over to the table where Emily, the little clubfooted lady, worked. "Miss Emily, you were kind to my mother once when she needed a friend. I'd like to repay you for that. Sheridan Oil Company is opening an office out on my place and I need someone to be in charge of it. I need some ledgers set up, a payroll system started, things like that. I'd like you to come work for me. I'll pay you twice what Greb here gives you."

"Now, see here," Harley Greb blustered, "you can't come in here and do that! Emily, tell this *outsider* that you're perfectly happy where you're at."

Emily looked from one to the other, perplexed.

"Make that three times what Greb's paying you, Miss Emily."

"Get off my premises!" Greb ordered.

"I—I live in a house Mr. Greb owns," Emily said.

"That doesn't matter," Sam assured her. "I'm having some houses built out on my place; when they're ready, I'll *give* you one. Until then, you can live with my family in a big house we're renting over in New Salem."

"Emily, don't you be foolish now. This man is not one of us. He is an *outsider,* a troublemaker, a Saturday night—"

"Don't say it, Greb!" Sam warned. "If you call me a bastard, I'll shove the words right down your throat!"

Greb swallowed and shut up. Emily looked from one to the other several times again, and finally made up her mind. Rising, she took her pocketbook and limped toward the door.

"Emily, what about my week's accounts?" Greb almost whined.

"Do them yourself," said Emily, walking out. And she muttered to herself, "If you know how."

Sam's eyes fixed coldly on the newspaper publisher. "This is only the beginning, Harley," he said quietly.

Then he followed Emily out the door.

Because the oil strike on Sam Sheridan's land had been accomplished by a tightly knit group of men, in all of whose best interest it was to keep quiet about it, and because Sam quickly developed a plan of action and immediately set Tom Prater out buying oil leases without announcing the strike, the usual big rush to corner the land, which normally would have begun the same day the well was brought in, was much slower to start; it did not really mushroom until four days after Sam had concluded his deal with Rutland King.

Prior to that no outsiders except Tully and Reba actually *knew* that Sam and his men had struck oil. Pete Spence *surmised* that he had, because of Sam's bid to buy drilling leases; the attorneys Ford came to the same conclusion; but as far as concrete knowledge, even the small ranchers and farmers were not told that a well had already been brought in. Tully and Reba had been sworn to secrecy, as had the Choctaw elders, Tunica, and the children.

The news of the Sheridan strike first began to filter out after Owen Milam deposited the King Refinery check in the Cameron bank. Because Cameron was not in close proximity to the actual strike, it took a little longer than usual for the news to build and start people thinking about possibly getting in on the venture while it was still brand new. By the time anyone's interest had been piqued enough to investigate the location of the strike, Tom Prater had completed his round of the small farms and ranches in the area and obtained drilling leases from all but three, who decided to go with Pete Spence on a grazing-rights lease.

Oil drilling leases were selling for one dollar an acre and eight percent royalty all over Texas in places where no oil was known to exist. Although Sam knew that there was oil under *his* hundred acres, there was no guarantee, as emphasized daily by Owen Milam, that there would be reserves under *any* of the property on which Tom Prater was securing leases. Nevertheless, Sam had a confidence born of success, and offered *five* dollars an acre, fifty dollars cash bonus for signing with Sheridan Oil, and a ten percent royalty. Because of the continuing drought, as well as the general economic recession in Texas, his offer was like the answer to a prayer for some families. And not only did his representative, Tom Prater, pay cash within seven days of signing the lease, but Sheridan Oil promised to commence drilling within ninety days on most properties.

It was after construction of Rut King's oil tanks began on Sam's land that actual news of the strike broke. When the townspeople of Dane learned of it, word spread rapidly not only of the strike's existence but also of its exact location. *Then* the rush was on. People began to flock into Caddo County: wildcatters, lease buyers, speculators, geologists, roustabouts, roughnecks, and anybody else who, as Pop Joyner put it, "sucked oil for a living." The newcomers headed first for Dane, because that was the nearest town of any size; but it soon became obvious that, unlike most strikes, the nearest town was not going to be the one to boom. No sooner did people arrive in Dane than they somehow heard that a closer community, on the very edge of the strike, was opening up. It was down on the Kilgore highway, south of town, at a crossroads leading onto the Spence ranch in one direction, Choctaw Indian land in another. Because it was closer to where the oil actually *was,* everyone promptly moved there. Dane got a sprinkling of business, but that was all.

At the crossroads, new arrivals found that a settlement was indeed springing up. In a tent just inside the Sheridan land, a young woman—this was Georgia—assisted by an older woman with a clubfoot, was leasing quarter-acre homesites at the edge of the road that led to the Sheridan strike, and leasing business lots on a stretch of homesteaded land directly across the highway. Enterprising carpenters were standing by to build one-room structures in a single day for seventy-five dollars. Some merchants, those who had been first to move from Dane, had already begun operating out of large tents, as Georgia Sheridan was doing. Within a fortnight, the settlement boasted four restaurants (of sorts), two barbershops, a hardware merchant, a bakery (using a portable wood-burning stove), a butcher shop (selling dressed prairie game that it bought from Indian boys), and two hotels (one a large tent, the other a triple-size house on which three carpenters had collaborated).

On one of the sites Sam set up an employment tent and had Pop Joyner hiring men who could build and rig derricks. At the same time, Buddy Kyle, in the flatbed, was scouring every lumberyard in the nearby counties ordering all the planed two-by-fours and four-by-fours on hand, to be delivered to the headquarters of Sheridan Oil Company—the old line-rider's shack. Owen Milam by now had moved away from his plat maps and was in the field, surveying the property of each oil lease Sam now owned, selecting the site for a derrick on each farm or ranch. As Pop Joyner continued hiring eight men for each derrick Sam was preparing to erect, word of the strike began to filter out to even more distant points, spread by bus drivers, railroad conductors, truck drivers, and other transients, that a place in Caddo County called Sheridan was really booming; and more and more roustabouts and roughnecks rolled their packs or slung their duffels and "lit out" for the big boom town. Before the first month was out, five more "hotels" had opened on Sheridan leases, and a field of smaller individual homesites, for tents and cabins, had opened up when Sheridan Realty began letting one-sixteenth acre plots. And still the people came, by the hundreds more.

Other wildcatters like old Pop Joyner, as well as leasing representatives from the organized oil companies, began to appear, scouting for unleased land. Geologists, both company men and freelance, prowled the ground, tasted the soil, and sniffed the air for signs of oil. Every small company operating in the Southwest had men in Caddo County: Brandt Oil, Danciger Oil, Herbert Oil, Humble, Jasper Oil, Marland, Mid-Kansas, McAfee, Parade, United, Uncle Dan, Virginia Oil, Zeppelin. No one was taking a chance on missing this one. Even the ones who had sworn on a stack of geology manuals that there were no oil reserves in Caddo, Rusk, or Harrison counties, sent men back to see if it was for real. Only the giants—Gulf, Shell, Sinclair, Texaco—ignored the strike.

What the lease buyers discovered when they checked around was that there was a great square of land that they could not explore. That was the Spence Ranch: fenced in with barbed wire, patrolled by armed boundary riders. Some of the buyers approached Pete Spence at his land-and-cattle office in Dane. They were told firmly and not too politely that there would be no exploring for oil on Spence property.

The story of Spence's refusal to open his land to exploration eventually reached Tom Prater, who told Sam and Pop Joyner. "Spence has been approached by half a dozen people," Prater reported, "and he's turned down every one of them." The young lawyer shook his head incredulously. "He conceivably has something *under* his land worth maybe a hundred times its surface value, and he doesn't even seem to care. He told one lease buyer he didn't give a damn if there was a *billion* dollars' worth of oil under his place, he wasn't interested in it. Said his place was *cattle* land, not oil land, and he wasn't going to dirty his pastures with black slime."

Sam shook his own head along with Tom Prater. Only Pop Joyner seemed to understand.

"Cattle men's like that," the old wildcatter explained. "I've seed it before, in Oklahoma. To them the land is something special; it nourishes their herds year after year, keeps their cattle bin'ess going, gives 'em a sense of belonging somewheres. To oil men like us, why, the land is just something we have to get *through* to get what we're after. We don't have no feeling for the earth like cattlemen do; we on'y have a feeling for what the earth's hiding." Pop looked at Sam. "You don't have to worry none about Spence getting any oil from this here strike. He'd probably die before he'd let a driller on his place."

Lease buyers had no better luck along the Choctaw side of the Spence Ranch. The Indians refused to even talk to them; Sam Sheridan was the only white man with whom they would discuss oil business. The buyers did find a tiny patch of one hundred acres, extending into the Spence Ranch and bordering on the Choctaw land, and for a brief moment thought maybe they had stumbled onto something; but then they learned it was owned by Sam Sheridan, and that the strike well was in fact partly on one of its boundaries. The other three sides of the Spence Ranch were bounded by a series of small individually owned farms and ranches, and Sheridan Oil had drilling rights to nearly all of those *too*. The lease buyers were determined to buy leases, however; if they could not get as close to the strike as they wanted, they would get as close as they *could*. They began buying leases to farms that *bordered* the farms that bordered the ranch. They bought leases on property that was three miles, five miles, eight, ten, twelve miles from the Sheridan strike.

"Goddamn fools," Pop Joyner said, shaking his head in disgust. "Why, they must think we're standing on top of a goddamn *ocean* of oil!"

Then, incredibly, it began to happen.

Six months after the Sheridan well hit, near the town of Henderson, five miles to the east, a wildcatter named Bradford tapped a reserve not even *half* as deep as the one Sam and the others had hit.

Two months after that, south of Kilgore—which was even farther away from Sheridan number one—a hole gushered on the farm of a widow named Lou Crimmins, this one at three thousand feet, eight hundred higher than the Sheridan strike.

With better equipment and auxiliary lighting for around-the-clock drilling, aided by reserves higher than the Sheridan well hit, the latecomers began bringing in strikes much more quickly than Sam and his crew had done. They began to hit all around Caddo County, and to turn up in Rusk County, and then Harrison County.

The strike that almost did Pop Joyner in, was one that came nine months after Sheridan number one. It was in Lathrop, more than *twenty-three miles* north. And it was the same grade crude that was being pumped out of Sheridan number one. Pop simply could not believe it. "That *can't* be one pool," he told everyone who would listen. "It just damn well *can't.*"

By now even the giants had sat up and were paying attention. Gulf, Shell, Sinclair, and Texaco all sent their best geologists with the most advanced geophysical tools: the new diamond-core drill that could cut through *anything* to provide information on the nature of *any* underground formation; and the torsion balance, recently developed by a physicist in Budapest, which could measure even the scantest fluctuation in gravity; and of course the new miracle instrument, the seismograph. This latter tool was the most extraordinary yet developed for determining subsurface formations. Simply by setting off a charge of dynamite on the surface, then recording the speed of energy waves reaching the instrument several miles away, the entire formation *below* the two points could be classified. If the energy waves were slow to reach the seismograph, it meant they were traveling over soft beds, such as sand or shale; if they were fast, it indicated solid beds of rock.

When the giant oil companies came in and surveyed the land between the various strikes that had been made, and then surveyed beyond those points as far as they could obtain positive readings, they found that they were, indeed, standing over an ocean of oil. The field was charted to be forty-five miles in length from north to south, and from five to twelve miles wide from east to west. It lay under more than one hundred forty *thousand* land acres.

Officially it was named the East Texas Field. Everyone who had anything to do with it, however, called it the "Black Giant."

It was the richest oil field ever found on the North American continent.

In the months following the first strike, Sheridan Oil brought in nine more wells: three on Choctaw land, five on leased acreage, and one on Sam's own property. From the Indian wells, Sam took drilling costs and thirty percent, paying an unusually generous seventy percent royalty to the Choctaw people. On the leased land, he paid the landowner ten percent, Tom Prater five percent for having obtained the lease, and kept eighty-five percent for himself. The second well on his own property, of course, he owned outright. As the newly found oil flowed, Sam found himself quickly on his way to becoming a millionaire.

As Sheridan Oil grew, so too did the community of Sheridan. The three miles of undedicated land across the highway from Sam's acreage had been filed on in Austin, and as soon as Tom Prater had secured all the drilling leases Sam wanted, the young lawyer was assigned the task of soliciting the merchants of Dane to relocate their businesses in Sheridan. At first they were suspicious and hesitant; then one moved, then another. There was no mass exodus out of Dane, but week by week several more left and moved down the highway to pick out lots in Sheridan. It was happening slowly—but it *was* happening. Dane began dying to give life to Sheridan.

People from Dane were not the only settlers. As the new wells started coming in, Sheridan became a legitimate boom town. Scores of *new* business people arrived to open up shops to compete with the

Dane merchants; their stores lined the newly surveyed main street, which Sam named Pop Joyner Road, and which stretched the length of the three-mile town. Soon there were half a dozen restaurants and cafes, two drugstores, several laundry and dry cleaning shops, bakeries, barbershops and bathhouses, beauty parlors, hardware stores, even a furniture store; a few dry goods and general merchandise stores, several auto and truck repair garages, six gasoline stations, five welding shops, five boiler plants, five machine shops, ten drilling equipment supply stores, an ice plant, thirteen makeshift hotels, sixteen makeshift boardinghouses, and nine general building contractors who were kept busy day and night constructing more and more stores.

And there was one bank: First Bank of Sheridan. Dewitt Tucker, president.

And one real estate agency: Sheridan Realty, managed by Georgia and run by Miss Emily, who had four people working for *her* now.

Once the awesome size of the field had been determined, Caddo, Rusk, and Harrison counties experienced the biggest rush ever: bigger even than the California gold strike or the Oklahoma land rush. New wells were going in daily; the hammering on new derricks under construction was constant. In what became known as the "Second Belt"—the circle of farms surrounding the circle on which Sam owned the leases, some farmers were actually tearing down their homes to make room for derricks.

With the influx of hundreds of new people, there also came the element of lawlessness. Sheridan Realty, Georgia had decided with Sam's approval, would not lease its lots for certain types of businesses: saloons, gambling houses, whorehouses. But that did not stop the bootleggers, gamblers, and whores from coming. On one of the small farms on which Tom Prater had been unable to obtain an oil drilling lease because the farmer had leased grazing rights to Pete Spence, the owner, not wanting to miss out on the sudden prosperity, went to Spence and asked to cancel the contract; not to drill for oil, but to divide his land into one-tenth-acre parcels and lease it to *anybody* with money, for any *kind* of business. Spence readily acceded to the request; he knew what kind of people would move onto the farmer's land—and he was right.

The converted farm quickly became a vice-ridden area of gambling, whoring, and illegal drinking establishments that attracted crooked gamblers, whores, pimps, con men, bootleggers, thieves, and every other kind of hustler imaginable. Honky-tonks remained open around the clock; fiddle and guitar music were as constant as the monotonous churning of the drilling rigs that now dotted the countryside. Drinking and dancing were continuous, one shift taking over when another was ready to go back to the fields. Surrounding these businesses was soon a shanty village of tents and clapboard shacks. Seldom did a day go by that a dozen new drifters did not show up, looking for easy money. From Dallas, Fort Worth, Houston, Galveston, Amarillo, even as far away as El Paso, the scum of Texas migrated to the great new oil field. And wound up on a ten-acre slice of Sodom and Gomorrah that lay halfway between Sheridan and Dane.

Its name was Pistol Hill.

When the boom was at its peak, Tom Prater came to Sam with some news.

"I just had a call from the Pinkerton Detective Agency in Houston. Their men have found Draw Poker. He's working in a pool hall down in McAllen."

"Where's that at?" Sam asked.

"Down near the bottom tip of the state, just a couple miles this side of Mexico. Tough little border town."

"Figures," Sam said, smiling. "He's a tough old bird."

"Want me to send somebody down to get him?"

Sam shook his head. "He wouldn't come."

"I could have the Pinkertons *bring* him back; they're ex officio lawmen."

Sam's smile widened. "I wouldn't want us being responsible for any Pinkerton men getting killed. No, I'll go down there myself and try to *talk* him into coming back."

Even as he spoke the words, Sam realized that his chances of talking Draw into returning were only about fifty-fifty at best.

But he had to try.

39

McAllen was four hundred fifty miles downstate; it took Sam twelve hours to drive there in his new yellow Packard sedan. He arrived at six o'clock in the evening, with two hours of daylight still in the sky, and drove down Laredo Street, a three-block stretch of inferior asphalt lined on both sides by illegal saloons operating as "private clubs," whorehouses operating as hotels, flophouses, pool halls, guns and ammo shops, saddleries, cafes, fortune tellers, and storefront gambling houses. As Tom Prater had said, it was a tough border town.

The Pinkertons had reported that Draw was working in a place called Felson's Billiard Parlor. Sam found it in the middle of the second block. Draw was out in front, sweeping the wooded sidewalk. Sam felt a tug in his chest at the sight of the old cowboy with a broom in his hand. Nosing the Packard up to the curb, he parked and got out. Draw stopped sweeping and scrutinized the shiny new car. "You're looking prosperous," he drawled by way of greeting.

"I am prosperous." Sam handed Draw a bankbook. "You are too."

Draw thumbed open the little book. It showed several pages of daily deposits of six hundred dollars each. The balance, as of the previous day, was nearly fifty thousand. "I left definite instructions that this money was to go to the boy. Didn't Pop tell you?"

"He told me," Sam acknowledged.

"Well?" Draw demanded.

Sam shrugged. "I figured if you wanted Ty to have it, you ought to give it to him yourself. When he's older and can appreciate it."

Draw glared at his visitor for a moment, then stuffed the bankbook into his shirt pocket and said, "Have it your way." He resumed sweeping the planks on which they stood.

"Is this what you're doing now? Sweeping sidewalks?" He could see Draw glower.

"I do other things too," the old cowboy said defensively.

"Such as?"

"I rack balls. Fill the talc cans. Brush down felt on the tables. Lots of things."

Sam nodded. "Flunky work."

A glimmer of a smile flickered on Draw's face. "If you're aiming to insult me and make me mad, you made a hell of a long drive for nothing. Might's well get back into your pretty yeller rich man's car and head on back."

Sam stepped in front of him so that he had to stop sweeping. "Why'd you run out on me?"

"That's my business. Besides, I didn't *run out* on nobody; I stayed until the job was done."

"The *job,* Draw, is just *beginning,* and you know it. I've needed you a hell of a lot more *since* we brought the oil in than I did before we hit."

"You've got plenty of good hands without me," Draw insisted. "I agreed to help bring in the well, that was all."

"You ran out because you didn't want to have to tell me that I was Able Patman's bastard grandson, didn't you?" Sam challenged.

Draw stared at him in surprise. "You found out," he said after a moment.

"I found out. I also found out that you and he were like brothers all your lives."

"We was," Draw admitted, nodding slowly. "Most all our lives, anyhow."

"Why didn't you tell me who I was, Draw?" Sam asked evenly. "You knew how hard I was trying to find out what it was all about."

"I ain't real sure you'd understand if I *did* tell you."

"I want to know anyway, whether I understand or not."

The old man studied Sam for a moment, finally sighed, and said, "Well, let's get in out of the sun then."

Draw led Sam into the poolroom, where he put his broom in a small closet and said to the man at the cash register, "Grady, I'm gonna sit down for a little bit with this here feller. Holler if you need me."

Grady nodded and Draw led Sam to a bank of six booths against the wall. Each of them had an opening into the cafe next door where food could be ordered and passed through. Draw and Sam sat down in the back booth and Draw asked through the window for two mugs of coffee. When they came, he sat back and stirred his with a spoon while he talked.

"At first," he told Sam, "I decided not to tell you nothing about your relationship to Able because I wanted to let you see what *you* could do with those hundred acres he left you. What Sam Sheridan *himself* could do; not Sam Sheridan, the grandson of Able Patman. I figured it would make a difference to you in the long run; figured you'd be prouder of yourself if *you* brought in the oil; just you, just Sam Sheridan, without knowing nothing about your Texas blood. I'd made up my mind to tell you about Able only if you gave up and started to leave, which you didn't. You stayed; you done it your own self, without knowing, just like I figured you could and would."

Although the coffee was still steaming, Draw raised the mug to his lips, blew on it a few seconds, and took a quick sip. Sam continued stirring his.

"I figured all along to tell you the whole story once you made it on your own. But the closer we got to the oil, the more doubts I begun to have about whether it was *my* place to tell you anything. You see, I was on the Patman side for a long, long time; most of my life, in fact. It weren't only Able I was close to; I knowed your Grandmother Lillian just as well. I was there when Ardelle and Lorn came along; hell, I helped raise them kids, taught 'em both to ride and how to take care of their mounts. I watched 'em grow up. I was with your daddy in Kansas City on the trip where he met your mother, though I didn't know about it until months later. And I was the one cut your daddy down after he hanged hisself."

Sam leaned forward and clasped his hands together tensely. "Why *did* he hang himself, Draw?" It was as close to a plea as Sam Sheridan could make.

Draw sighed a deep, hollow sigh that almost sounded like a death rattle. The memory of Lorn hurt him more deeply than anyone had ever known. "Your daddy was a poor, tormented soul. He was a boy beset by things that would have drove a *man* crazy. You see, Sarah Spence, the girl he married, was—well, she wasn't the kind of woman who liked men. She liked other women."

Draw paused and cleared his throat. For a moment he gazed

away from the booth. It was obvious that he had cared for Lorn and grieved over the young man's long-ago hurt.

"Sarah's daddy suspected it. He whipped her until she agreed to marry Lorn. As if that would solve the whole problem. 'Course, it didn't solve nothing. What it did was kill Lorn. He ended up caught between a wife who kept a Mexican girl in her bed, and your mother, who was carrying you at the time. And it came down to neither one of 'em wanting him. And folks *knew,* you see. The Mexican help knew about it, so the cowboys did too, before long. Lorn was being talked about and laughed at all over the East Texas range. It was something he just couldn't stand."

"My god," Sam said quietly. "The poor bastard." He realized at once how odd that sounded. It was, after all, *he* who was the bastard.

Draw blew on his coffee again and sipped a little of it from the thick white mug. He stared at the table for a moment, then said, "Getting back to why I never told you nothing, the more I thought about it, the more I begun to see that it was a blood feud, between you and your Aunt Ardelle. It didn't have nothing to do with me on either side. So I made up my mind to stay out of it. I made up my mind to help Sam Sheridan bring in an oil gusher, *as long as he didn't know he had Patman blood.* When the well come in, or if you learned about the connection between you and Able in the meantime, I'd pull out, because then I figured it'd be between two people with Patman blood. Turned out I got to help bring your well in. I was glad of that. But soon's it was in, I kept my promise to myself and hit the trail." Draw sat back, both hands around his coffee mug. "That's about the size of it. I don't know if it makes sense to you or not. I stayed as long as I felt I *could* stay. I didn't run out on you, like you think."

"No," Sam agreed quietly, "you didn't run out on me. I apologize for saying that."

Draw shrugged. *"Nada."*

The two men sat in silence for several minutes, sipping their coffee, Draw rolling a cigarette, each with his own thoughts. In front of them, the pool hall was beginning to get busy as cowboys drifted in with toothpicks in their mouths, and paper-bagged bottles sticking out of their hip pockets. Draw left the booth a couple of times to set a rack of balls on a table, but then the night man came on duty and he sat back down again.

"There are two things I want now," Sam told him at last. "I want you to come back and work for me again. I'm starting a town, Draw: the town of Sheridan, Texas. We're already leasing lots for every kind of business you can imagine: drugstore, notions, grocery, baker, barber, you name it. Every kind of business they've got in Dane. I'm going to close Dane down, Draw. I'm going to turn it into a ghost town—for what it did to my mother and what it *tried* to do to me."

"You get back hard, don't you?" It was not a question at all, but Sam answered it anyway.

"When I've been walked on hard, I do."

"After you finish with Dane, when you're so rich can't nobody stop you, then you're going to start in on Pete Spence, I reckon."

"Exactly. I'm going to cut him off just like he tried to cut me off: right at the knees. Anything I can do to him, I will. I'll buy his employees, I'll close down every access to his ranch that I can legally get hold of, I'll siphon off as much of his water as I can legally siphon off, I'll—"

"I get the general idea." Draw sucked in on the skinny cigarette he had rolled. "'Course, ever'thing you do to Pete, you'll be doing to Ardelle, your own blood."

"My own blood! That's a joke, Draw."

"No, it ain't no joke, boy," Draw said firmly. "It's a fact, is what it is. Don't matter that neither one of you honors it. It's still there." He stared into space for a moment. "I recollect the day your Grandmother Lillian gave birth to Ardelle. Pretty sunshiny day, it was. When Ardelle was little I used to rock her on my knee. Used to wash her scrapes and cuts before her mother seen 'em. When she was older, I once had to pistol-whip a young roughneck rider we had that tried to drag her behind the barn." Draw smiled a melancholy smile at Sam. "Done lots of other things I can't even remember right now." Sighing quietly but heavily, as only an old man can, he finally said, "I'll come back to work for you, Sam, but only on the condition that I don't have to do anything directly to hurt the Spences. I can't turn on Ardelle this late in life."

"I wouldn't have asked you to."

Draw nodded. "You said you wanted two things. What's the other'n?"

"I want to know everything there is to know about my grandfather. You kept your bargain with yourself by not telling me who I was. I found that out on my own. I'll find out everything else sooner or later too, from other sources; like you said, I'm going to be so rich that nobody will be able to stop me from doing anything. But I'd like to hear about my grandfather from you, because I trust you. I'd like to hear it the way it really was. Texas in the old days. My grandfather, my grandmother, my father, even Ardelle. Will you tell me about it, Draw? Will you tell me about *them?*"

Draw did not even have to think it over. He had already made up his mind.

"Yes, I will."

40

The original Patman ranch, owned by Able's father, Luke Patman, lay far to the south and west of where Able would eventually locate his empire. Luke Patman had staked out land near the settlement of San Marcos, some forty miles north of San Antonio, where the Alamo stood. With a dozen longhorn steers and heifers he and his brother had bought and driven up from Mexico, they started the first cattle ranch at the Canyon Lake end of the Guadalupe River. When the brother died of cholera, Luke became sole owner. He married a pretty preacher's daughter named Clementine Chase, from nearby Bulverde, and over the years they had six children: two boys first, William and Earl; then three girls, Maria, Elena, and Rosa; then a third son, whom they named Able Chase Patman.

For a long time there was no schoolhouse in San Marcos, so the two older Patman boys never learned to read or write. After a school was finally started, there was so much work to do on the growing ranch that the three daughters, who could work almost as well as their brothers, were also deprived of an education. But when Able came along, the family had prospered to the point where it was decided that at least one Patman was going to get some book learning. Able was furious at this blatant discrimination against him simply because he was the youngest. Headstrong, he flatly refused to go to school. Luke took him out to the barn and whipped him with a harness strap until he changed his mind. Thus it was that from the age of twelve on, Able Patman rode his horse into San Marcos every weekday for five hours of school.

And thus it was that he escaped the fate of the rest of his family —a fate he learned when he rode home one afternoon, found his father and two brothers lying in the sun slit open from throat to crotch, and his mother hanging naked by her spread wrists from a rafter, so much dried semen on the inside of her thighs that it looked like it had been poured on. She had died with her eyes wide open in horror, her face contorted in excruciating pain. The last thing to be shoved up her vagina was a tomahawk.

The three Patman girls, Able's sisters, were nowhere to be found.

That was in the spring of 1868.

A posse of ranchers and hands from the surrounding spreads went in search of the savages who had made the raid. A trail of unshod horse tracks was followed west to Spring Branch, where it was discovered that a second ranch, belonging to the Herman Poker family, had also been sacked. One daughter, Effie, had been taken, and the rest of the family slaughtered, except for the youngest son, Charles Jonas, age ten, who like Able Patman had been off the place attending school.

The posse continued on to Comfort and Camp Verde and Mountain Home before they gave up. The fugitive band, with many stolen horses and therefore able to change mounts frequently, managed to stay well ahead of its pursuers, and the men of the posse realized that, given such a handicap, they might trail the band all the way to Oklahoma or New Mexico without *ever* catching them.

Young Able Patman, however, did not see it that way. When the posse returned, he ran out of the Baptist preacher's house where he had been taken, screaming, "What are you doing back here without them! Why didn't you keep after them! You've let them get away, you bunch of yellow cowards!"

Even after he calmed down later that day, Able refused to

accept any excuse for the posse giving up. To him, their returning was nothing short of treachery. His mother, father, and two brothers had been butchered, his three sisters kidnapped—and this posse turned *back?* Unforgivable. At the funeral of his family the next day, Able tearfully vowed that as soon as he was old enough, and knew enough, he would strike out on his own and find his sisters.

It was later decided from evidence gathered at the sites of the two slaughters that the savages responsible for the raids were Nokoni Indians, members of the widely ranging Comanche tribe. The band, some thirty strong, was led by a chief named Tochoway. Until several months earlier he had lived quietly on an Oklahoma reservation. When General Philip Sheridan had come through on his inspection tour of the Western frontier, Tochoway had been introduced to him as "one of our good Indians." It was on that occasion that Sheridan, unaware that Tochoway understood English, had made his now infamous remark, "The only good Indian is a dead Indian."

Gravely insulted, Tochoway had taken a few young men and left the reservation the following day. Within a week he had arms, ammunition, horses, and more followers, and was leading raids on wagon trains and small settlements. Both white and Mexican settlers would pay with their blood for Sheridan's stupid remark for the next fifteen years.

Young Able Patman remained a ward in the preacher's home for four years. During that time he quietly learned everything he could about Tochoway and his Nokonis. From every cavalryman, scout, or frontiersman who stopped even briefly in San Marcos, he solicited what scraps of information he could get. He read every newspaper account of Indian activities that he could get his hands on, studied every treatise published up until then on the Comanche nation, its history, and the ways of its people. He learned, for instance, that the very name "Nokoni" meant "wanderer," and had been applied to that segment of the tribe because of its penchant for camping all over the Southwest. He learned that the group was descended from a band that years earlier had raided Elder John Parker's stockaded religious community near Waco, during which they stole their first white girl, little Cynthia Parker, age nine. Subsequently taken in marriage by the chief of the band, she had eventually given birth to a son who grew up to be Quannah Parker, the feared Comanche leader. Since that time, the Nokoni had been widely known and feared for their record of kidnapping white females to either keep for their own use or sell to other tribes as slaves.

While he was gleaning all the information he could about the Nokoni, Able was also learning other things. With his late father's pistol, he would slip out onto the prairie and for hours practice a fast draw. When he could secure ammunition, either by purchase or theft of a bullet or two at a time, he would also target-shoot. Over the years he became quite proficient at both drawing and firing the gun. He also taught himself to throw a knife, use a bullwhip, box, wrestle, ride, and rope. By the time he was eighteen, where most lads his age knew the detailed scope of farming or ranching or clerking in some business, Able was ready to enter the outside world as a hunter and tracker of men, and ultimately, he hoped, as a shootist. For he fully intended to kill as many Nokonis as he could find.

Taking his leave of San Marcos on his eighteenth birthday, with nearly a thousand dollars that the sale of his father's farm had brought, Able rode first to Spring Branch. He wanted to meet Charles Jonas Poker, the other survivor of the Nokoni raid, and get a description of Poker's sister Effie, who had also been taken captive. During the four years since the massacres, the two boys had heard of one another, but there had never been an occasion for them to meet. Able found Charles at the home of an uncle and aunt who were raising him. The boys sat on the front porch swing and talked. Charles described his lost sister as "jus' an ordinary girl. She looked like every other girl; they all look 'bout the same." He did remember that Effie had a mole at the corner of her left eye, and said she was two years older than himself: twelve when taken, sixteen now. Able's own sisters had been fifteen, sixteen, and eighteen, and like Effie were now four years older. Able tried not to think of what they had probably been through during those years. He only hoped they were still alive.

When Able got ready to leave that day, Charles Poker wanted to go with him. "How old are you?" Able asked.

"Fourteen."

"That's too young. I was fourteen when it happened, and I had to wait four years until I was ready. If I find out anything, I'll write you a letter at your uncle's."

Charles followed him out to his horse, arguing all the way, pleading to be taken along, swearing he would be a big help and never get in the way. He held onto Able's arm and would not let him go.

"Look," Able said patiently, "I'd like to take you, honest I would. Be nice to have a trail partner on a hunt like this here. But you're jus' too young. You can't take care of yourself yet. Watch this." He stepped into the road and pointed to a whiskey bottle lying fifty feet or so away. "When you can do this, I'll let you ride with me." In the blink of an eye, Able drew the pistol that had once been his father's and disintegrated the bottle with a single shot.

"You really mean it?" Charles asked eagerly. "If I learn to shoot like that, you'll let me be your trail partner?"

"Sure do. I'll write you from time to time to let you know where I am; you can write back and tell me how you're doing."

"Where are you going from here?"

"Mountain Home. That's where the chicken-shit posse turned back."

"And where from there?"

"Somewhere north, I don't know where. Wherever the trail leads to. They got to be somewheres." Able swung into the saddle. "Goodbye, Charles."

" 'Bye, Able."

Able rode off that day and never came back. And never wrote to Charles as he promised to.

The trail of the Nokoni led Able over a good part of West Texas. From Mountain Home he rode north to San Angelo, then to Sweetwater, to China Grove, to Seagraves. In each place, he found something that pointed him somewhere else. Because the large majority of Comanche were then living under a peace treaty, it was not unusual for small bands of them to ride into towns to trade. If they were outlaw bands, like the Nokoni, they left their kidnapped women and stolen horses under guard well out of town, while only a few of them rode in for supplies. Word of the massacres at San Marcos and Spring Branch had spread from town to town, usually a few days after the band was seen; it had caused a great deal of excitement at the time, and even generated a few small hunting parties to see if they were still around; thus they were remembered even after four years.

Able rode all the way to Pampa, in the Panhandle, before he finally lost track of the band entirely. He stayed around town for a few days, resting his horse and himself, before deciding to go over into Oklahoma to Kiowa territory and make inquiries there. There were four tribes that the Nokoni were known to be friendly with, and to whom they often sold or traded white women. The Kiowa were one of those tribes.

It had taken Able six months to get as far as Pampa, and now he spent another six months roaming the Kiowa camps in Oklahoma, trying to make friends with Indians that might help him, but not moving too fast or being too persistent; never insisting, never demanding. He knew from his studies that the more interested and anxious a white man appeared, the more withdrawn and reticent an Indian became. During his long months in Oklahoma, Able learned to take several hours or even half a day to accomplish what should have taken only minutes. Indians simply could not be hurried.

During his second winter on the trail, Able was caught on the Oklahoma flatland in a flash blizzard. He managed to make it into Strong City but caught pneumonia in the process. By the time he got to a livery stable and found a boardinghouse that was not full, he was burning up with fever and shivering with chills at the same time. Only the good fortune of being taken in and nursed by Mrs. Odelia Conway at Conway's Lodgings saved him from dying. He was bedridden at Mrs. Conway's for two full months, and took another two months to properly convalesce.

One of the reasons that Able's recovery took so long was the fact that Odelia Conway had a sixteen-year-old daughter named Lillian. She was, to Able, a dream. The first time he saw her, during the rigors of his fever, he actually *thought* he was dreaming. When he finally regained his senses, he was pleasantly surprised to find that Lillian was real. Because her mother liked Able and considered him a suitable marriage prospect for her daughter, and because she was there to keep a close watch on them, Mrs. Conway allowed Lillian to do most of Able's nursing. She had seen the way the two young people looked at each other, and had shrewdly reckoned that keeping them in close proximity during the long winter would result in some serious planning in the spring. She was correct. Before the thaw even came, Able and Lillian had professed their mutual love and were making plans to be married.

Able told both women about his search for his sisters and made it plain that even if he were to marry and settle down, there might come a time when news of one or more of his sisters would call him away for a while. For the present, however, he was willing to declare a moratorium on his pursuit of the Nokoni raiders. By April, when the first warm days came to Strong City, Able was up and about, feeling stronger and ready to resume living.

Then, out of the past, there arrived in town an angry young man bent on killing him.

Lillian Conway answered the knock at the door to find a sharp-featured young man with thick hair combed straight back and dark direct eyes that looked like bullet holes.

"I'm looking for Able Patman, miss," he said quietly. "Is he here?"

"Yes, he is. Please come in."

"No, thank you. I'd appreciate it if you'd ask him to step out on the porch."

"All right," Lillian said hesitantly. With a glance she had taken in the young man's gunbelt and tied-down holster, and the fact that he did not smile and that his eyes were cold. Anxiously, she hurried to warn Able. Her fiancé did not feel threatened, however; Able did not have an enemy in the world, not that he knew of. He calmed Lillian down and went out onto the porch, unarmed. The young man waiting there looked vaguely familiar.

"Get your gun, Patman. I'm calling you out."

"Me? What for?"

"Because you're a liar."

Able stiffened a little. Calling a man a liar was not quite as bad as calling him a horse thief or a cattle rustler, but it was close. As soon as Able began to anger, however, he suddenly recognized his challenger. Charles Jonas Poker.

"I remember you now. Charles Poker."

"You promised to let me know where you were," Charles accused. "You said if I learned to handle a gun so I could take care of myself, that you'd let me ride with you to hunt the Nokonis. You let me slave over my gun work for a year, but you never kept your word. I kept on with the gun work: another three months, another six months, another year; always thinking any day you'd keep your word and let me know where you was. Finally I woke up and figured out you'd made a fool of me; you never *meant* to let me know. It was a lie from the very beginning. So I'm calling you out." A little self-consciously, Charles hitched up his gunbelt. "So go put on your gun."

"Can we talk it over for just a minute?" Able asked. "Are you sure you know what you're doing? I'm awfully fast."

"You'll have to be."

"Think you're that good, do you?" Able looked around for a suitable target. There were no whiskey bottles in the road—not in the vicinity of Mrs. Odelia Conway's home, there weren't—but there was, across the road, an old post remaining from a long-ago fence, leaning forlornly, a few strands of cut barbed wire hanging from it. Able pointed to it. "Take out that old post yonder, if you're so good."

Charles looked at it, glanced back at Able with a smirk, and turned quickly. The pistol seemed to leap into his hand, aimed, hammer cocked. Charles fired from the hip, five times. He cut two strands of wire off the post clean, then removed the post itself with three bullets in a horizontal row across its base. Able Patman's mouth fell open.

"Jesus, Charles, who learned you to shoot that good?"

"I learned myself." Automatically he began reloading. "Think I can take care of myself now?" he asked caustically.

"I reckon so," Able allowed.

Just then, Lillian burst onto the porch, pale as a ghost. "My god, what's happening! Able—?"

Able put his arm around her at once. "It's all right, honey. Charles here was just showing me how good he's got with a gun since I seen him last. Charles, this here's my betrothed, Miss Lillian Conway. Honey, this is Charles Poker. You remember, I told you about him; his was the other family."

"How do, ma'am," Charles said, removing his hat. He looked irritably at Able. "You didn't tell me you was fixin' to get hitched."

"You never gave me a chance."

Smiling nervously, Lillian said, "Would you like to come in for some coffee and cookies, Mr. Poker?"

"Well, uh—I don't reckon so, ma'am—uh—"

"Oh, hell, come on inside," Able insisted, taking him by the arm. Leaning close, he whispered, "You can shoot me later."

Within a few minutes, Charles was completely smitten by Lillian and found that he still liked Able Patman as much as when they had met the first time. Able never did outright admit that he never had any intention of getting in touch with Charles, but by talking around it, telling Able how ill he had been, having it confirmed by Lillian, and reciting the history of his long months on the trail and wandering the Kiowa lands, Able subtly constructed an excuse for failing to keep his word that Charles could accept and still save face. Charles was, after all, despite his proficiency with a gun, only sixteen years old, and an orphan in a strange place. It did not take much effort for Able to get back in his good graces. When he did, he immediately changed the subject to something they had in common: the Nokonis.

"You pick up any word of the band at all?"

"Not a lick. Are you, uh—" Charles started to ask, then glanced at Lillian and did not finish his question. But Able knew what he meant.

"Am I giving up the search, is that what you want to know? In a way I am, but in a way I'm not. I ain't going to wander around every waterhole town on the frontier hoping I'll run across them. Me and Lillian's getting married next month and I'm taking what money I got left and her dowry, and we're going to get us a place down in Texas and raise cattle. Now then, if I ever get word about where the Nokonis actually *is,* or hear anything at all about my sisters, or your sister, why, I'm going to light out and look into it. I think that's a fair way to do it. What do you think?"

"I guess so," Charles said, shrugging. "Pretty hard to look for somebody with no place to start. You going back to San Marcos?"

Able shook his head. "Too many bad memories. Every time I saw a member of that posse, I'd want to shoot him. Besides, there's plenty of open range over in northeast Texas. I'm gonna get me a piece of that." He paused, then added, "I could use a good hand. You want to work for me, you can come right along with us."

Charles had been hoping that Able would take him on. He had thought it would be as a trail partner looking for the Nokoni, but this was all right too. He never really meant to shoot Able; just wanted to prove that he was grown up now. As for finding Effie, well, after six years with the Nokoni, or whomever they might have sold her to, if he found her she wouldn't be the same anyway. She'd be a wild-eyed savage just like they were. So he was grateful for the chance to go with Able.

"How about it?" Able asked.

"Yes, I'd like that."

Charles looked at Lillian Conway, and she saw him smile for the first time.

41

In 1870 there were two written laws and one unwritten law regarding land in Texas. The two written laws were: one, if a white citizen desired to occupy land currently occupied by an Indian, the Indian must "withdraw"; and two, a white man could file on as much land as he wanted, but for every two acres he claimed, he either had to put one acre in crops within six months, or he had to run two head of breeding cattle on it. The *un*written law was that once a man had claimed land, it was up to him to keep it—however he could, by whatever means it took.

To Able Chase Patman, the only law that meant anything was the second one. As a cattleman, he needed one cow for every acre. The quicker he built up his herd, the more land he could claim. There was plenty of it out there, and Able meant to have as much of it as he could get.

The first law, about Indians being on the land, was, to Able, needless. It went without saying that white men were better than Indians and therefore entitled to take what they wanted from them. That Indians were inferior was an unspoken tenet of his upbringing, and since the Nokoni raid, he now looked on them as savages: not only inferior but undesirable, dangerous, and in need of extermination. Able Patman would as soon shoot an Indian as he would a coyote. During the early years he proved it three times, when he caught Indians stealing and slaughtering beef on his land. It made no difference to Able that they were starving; he summarily executed them on the spot.

As far as the unwritten law was concerned, that one too was just plain common sense to Able. No one was going to take what was his. Most particularly when he had Charles Poker to back him up. Aside from his own, Able had never seen a gun hand as fast as young Charles. Secretly, he wondered if Charles was even faster than he, but Able never let on about it; he always *acted* as if he, the older and more experienced, were naturally the faster. He observed that, oddly, it did not seem to make any difference to Charles.

After his marriage to Lillian, Able had taken his new bride and Charles and headed south, back into Texas. He looked at land around Electra, kept going and checked out Bowie and Buffalo Springs, followed the Red River west to Bonham and Blossom, and then, deciding there was no suitable range that far north, turned straight south. He looked around Sulphur, Birthright, and Bonanza, then bore east again to Rosewood and Big Sandy. Finally he came to a vast range that had soil that pleased him, prairie grass with blades sharp enough to keep cattle well cleaned out, enough tree growth for shade, and a good quantity of natural water without unusual danger of flooding. "This seems like it," Able said quietly, carrying around a handful of soil, chewing blades of grass, kneeling on one knee and squinting off at the horizon. "Seems like it."

The nearest settlement was a crossroads known simply as Dane's Store, for the name of a general store operated there by a man named Peter Dane. In addition to Dane's store, there was a saloon next door, a blacksmith across the strip of mud that served as a street, and a combination doctor's office, dentist, and barbershop a few yards up from that. Nothing else—for fifty miles in any direction.

Able bought twenty head of Hereford stock from a rancher in Nacogdoches, to the south, and afterward filed on twenty acres of open range. He and Charles cut timber and put up a two-room log-and-adobe house, into which he and Lillian moved. Charles lived in a prairie tent. Able sold the wagon and team horses for enough money to buy six more head and file on six more acres. Before the year was out, he and Charles had scoured the range for forty miles in every direction but north, where a man named Sean Spence had a spread, for unbranded strays. They found nine and put the newly designed Patman brand on them. And Able filed on nine more acres. Able finished the year with thirty-five acres. Sean Spence, his ranching neighbor to the north, gave him a hearty pat on the back. "That's three more'n I had the end of my first year, lad. You're on your way, you are!"

Early in their second year there, Lillian bore Able his first child, a girl. Able was disappointed that it was not a boy, and said so to Charles, who immediately took umbrage.

"Don't you dare let on to Lillian how you feel," Charles warned him angrily.

"What the hell's eating at you?"

"Nothing. Not a damned thing." Charles had suffered along with Lillian every day of her pregnancy. He seethed at the thought that anyone would even suggest that she had not done a perfect job of childbearing. For Able to complain about the baby's gender— well, shit.

"I wasn't *going* to say anything to her, Charles," Able told him coldly. "I don't need you to tell me how to deal with my own wife. Or do you think different?"

"I don't think different," Charles said, not very convincingly. The words between them, Charles realized, were getting out of hand.

"Sure as hell sounded like that's what you thought," Able accused.

"I didn't mean nothing by it," Charles told him, backing down. He did not want a fight between them. It would be too upsetting to Lillian, who was still weak from delivering. And he did not want to risk losing his place there. "I just kind of think of Lillian as the sister I lost," he lied. "I have a natural urge to protect her."

Able believed him. But he was still peeved. "That's well and good, Charles. That's fine. But don't try to protect her from her husband, hear?" For a long moment Able remained sullen. But he wanted to end the quarrel also. So finally he grinned and said, "Trying to protect her from me could get awful embarrassing at times!" And he laughed out loud. Charles laughed along with him, but only on the outside.

The baby girl was named Ardelle, after Sean Spence's wife, who had become like a second mother to Lillian. Able and Lillian frequently visited the Spence ranchhouse on Sundays, and Able and Paddy Spence, Sean's son, became good friends. They were all like one big happy family, except for Charles, who was considered hired help by the Spences and not included in any invitations.

During the third year, Able's herd, by sale, profit, repurchase, and the rounding up of strays from the south, increased to eighty-eight head, and his land grew to the same number of acres. The year following that each more than doubled to a hundred seventy-eight.

One Saturday afternoon when Able, Sean Spence, and Paddy were drinking in the saloon, and Charles was playing cards with some cowboys nearby, two riders on their way to Arkansas stopped to rest and eat. Because strangers passing through were their only source of news from the outside world, the men were the center of attention for the hour or so they stayed.

"There's a bunch of fellers up in the middle west somewheres," one of the riders reported, "that calls theyselves the Greenback party. They're trying to get the gub'ment to put out green paper money 'stead of gold coin."

"Damn fools," Sean Spence snapped. "There's only one kind of money: good old gold."

"Silver was struck in the Panamint Mountains a few months ago," the other rider announced.

"Where's that at?" a listener asked.

"Nevady."

"Feller up in Victoria, Kansas," said the first rider, "has brung in four head of some new breed of cattle from someplace on t'other side of the ocean. Place called Scotland. The stock is called Angle or Angus, somethin' like that."

"And they done built a bridge up in St. Louie that goes clean across the ol' muddy Mississip."

"Oh, and the cavalry's done found that savage Tochoway and his Nokonis over in New Mexico but ain't been able to corner 'em yet. They's supposed to have about twenty white women that they carry around as slaves."

Both Able and Charles got to their feet at the same time and went over to the table where the riders were eating. "Where 'bouts in New Mexico, do you know?" Able asked.

"Tucumcari, last word we had."

"How long ago was that?"

"Not more'n a fortnight. The news was fresh when we come through Amarillo."

"Much obliged," said Able. Charles was already leaving. Able caught up with him outside the saloon where their mounts were hitched to the shade pole.

"Ain't no reason for you to go," Charles told him.

"What the hell do you mean by that?" Able's ire rose at once.

"You got a wife, a baby, a place to look after, stock to tend, and—"

"Horseshit. I'm going."

Able made arrangements with Sean and Paddy Spence to take care of his spread while he was gone, and Mrs. Spence insisted that Lillian and little Ardelle move in with them until he returned, for which Able, and Charles, were very grateful. Lillian cried when they left, but understood, as did the Spences, why they had to go. It was a point of family honor; no one questioned whether it was smart or not.

Riding two of their best mounts and leading two spares carrying supplies, the men set out across Texas: west to Fort Worth, to Abilene, then north into the Panhandle to Lubbock, on to Amarillo. From there they crossed Ute land into New Mexico territory and began their search. From friendly Utes they learned that Tochoway and his band had indeed been living in the Conchas region of New Mexico for several years, and that they traded horses, arms, and slaves with both the Zuni and Pueblo tribes.

Able and Charles rode southwest to Montoya and inquired about slave women of the Zunis living there. For a price, they were shown two slaves, but they were both Negro women. The men rode on. In Puerto De Luna, north of Fort Sumner, they saw others, some black, some white, but none of them familiar.

"I don't know as we'd recognize them even if we was to find them now," Able brooded. "Some of these women look like wild animals."

"We got to keep on anyhow," Charles insisted.

"I know," Able quietly acknowledged. "We got to try. But God knows, I'm almost afraid to find them."

"Me too," Charles admitted.

Up into the Capitan Mountains they rode, to Carrinazo to search the Pueblo lands. They went through Fort Stanton, Lincoln, Hondo, finding the same story wherever they went. Yes, the Nokoni had traded there; yes, they had traded slaves; yes, the white riders could look at the slaves, for a price: a pouch of tobacco, a bottle of whiskey, a few bullets. Then the slaves would be brought out from some secret place deep in the camp. Dirty naked women, bruised and welted from abuse by the Indian women and torment by the children, their eyes glazed, spirits destroyed. No, they were not the women for whom the white riders searched. Yes, the Nokonis rode south.

Able and Charles followed them as far as Tularosa and lost the trail there because the Mescalero tribe of the Apache nation, while producing their slaves in exchange for rifle bullets, flatly refused to tell them where the Nokonis had gone from there. Able and Charles tried to pick up the trail by inquiring in several small settlements south, east, and west of Tularosa, knowing that the Nokoni never doubled back over their own trail; but they found no clue. By now the two young men had been gone six months. Worried about Lillian, both were ready to call it quits.

"We're licked, Charles," Able said morosely as they sat in their camp at the edge of the White Sands desert.

"I reckon," Charles agreed.

"I'd give anything I own to be able to find them, but it just don't seem like it's in the cards."

"You're right. And I know you been away from Lillian and Ardelle for a long spell; I know you're worried about them." Charles sighed quietly, wearily. "I say we head on back."

"Me too." Able studied the ground for a moment, then looked across the fire at his friend. "Thank you, Charles."

"What for?"

"For not making me be the one to say it."

The next morning they rode south, and two days later they made El Paso and were back in Texas.

42

When Able and Charles got back to the ranch south of Dane's Store, Able drove the buggy up to the Spence place to get Lillian. He was surprised to find her swollen with child, seven months pregnant.

"Did you know before I left?" he asked, taking her in his arms.

"Not for certain. I thought so, but I didn't want to discourage you from doing something that I knew was very important to you. Did you find them?" Lillian asked, meaning his sisters.

Able shook his head. "We lost them in southern New Mexico territory," he answered, meaning the Nokoni.

When Lillian and Able got home, after Ardelle was in bed, Lillian said, "Do you mind if I go out and say hello to C.J.?"

" 'Course not. Why would I mind?" He glanced at her ballooned belly. "Don't tell him you're expecting; let's surprise him when the baby comes."

"Very amusing, Mr. Patman."

Lillian put a shawl around her shoulders and with a lantern made her way a hundred yards back of their house to a little cabin Charles had built for himself in his spare time. At her knock Charles, shirtless, opened the door.

"Oh. Lillian. Hello. I thought it was Able." He noticed her belly at once. "When'd that happen?"

"A month after y'all left," she replied dryly.

Charles turned red. "Sorry," he muttered, reaching for a shirt.

"Don't get dressed on my account." Lillian came in and set down the lantern. "I just wanted to say hello. And tell you I'm sorry you didn't find your sister. And that I'm glad you came back."

Charles looked directly at her, something he rarely did. "You knew I'd come back."

"Yes," she admitted after a moment, "I guess I did."

He got a chair for her but she did not sit down. Instead, she wandered around the little cabin, touching things that were his.

"Have you been as sick this time as you were with Ardelle?" Charles finally asked.

"No. This time has been much easier."

"Probably because Able and me ain't been around to worry you about nothing."

"Perhaps." Lillian's vocabulary was improving since she had been around Mrs. Spence, who had once taught school. She frequently used words like "perhaps" instead of maybe, "certainly" instead of sure. Charles loved to listen to her talk; he thought the sound of her voice was the most beautiful thing he had ever heard.

Lillian picked up the lantern. "Well, I must be getting back." She put her free hand palm-down on the middle of his bare chest and stretched up to kiss him lightly on the lips. "I *am* glad you're back, C.J."

She left very quickly. After Charles closed the door, he stood and stared at it for a very long time, the taste of her still on his lips.

A month later Paddy Spence and the daughter of another rancher, Elouise Brunt, were married and there was a wedding celebration to which even the cowhands were invited. Two weeks later Lillian delivered her second baby, a boy, and Able summoned the Spences and all of their hands to the saloon for drinks on him. He named the boy Lorn Lee Patman, the first being an old Patman family name, and the middle in honor of Sean Spence, whose own middle name was Lee.

To celebrate Paddy's wedding and the birth of a baby named in part after him, Sean Spence, in a burst of generosity, ordered from the great King Ranch in the Rio Grande Valley two prime Brahman bulls, one for Paddy and one for Able. In the year that followed receipt of the animals both young ranchers successfully crossbred the bulls with Longhorn heifers and produced the first of the North Texas breed of Santa Gertrudis cattle. It was a breed that sweat through its skin like horses, making it highly resistant to pasture heat and tick fever, therefore much healthier than other cattle. Both Able and Paddy were justifiably proud of their new breed.

Able's herd and ranch continued to grow. From two hundred acres he went to four hundred, to seven hundred, then past one thousand, then two. Within several years he owned more than five thousand acres and was rapidly catching up to the Spence spread, which by then had expanded to seven thousand. Sean Spence, seeing that Paddy had as good a head as his own for running their place, and observing that Paddy and Able worked very well together as unofficial partners controlling the area, stepped back a bit and gave the young men free rein. It was one of the smartest things he ever did. The two became so close that one habitually included the other in any cattle deals that were made, consequently profiting from each other instead of competing, and their respective holdings increased much more rapidly than they ordinarily would have.

When Paddy and Elouise had a son, nine months to the day after their wedding, the boy was named Peter Sean Spence, after Sean and Sean's own father, whom Paddy had never known. Though by then little Ardelle Patman was going on three, the two couples nevertheless speculated on a marriage between them someday. When the young Spences had a daughter the following year, naming her Sarah, the four parents continued their matchmaking by assigning this newest infant to marry Lorn Patman. A lot of this fanciful planning was done for the benefit of Sean Spence, who absolutely delighted in it and swore to all who would listen that he damn well intended to live to see those two weddings, by God!

Sean did not live that long, however. The following year a pork chop bone lodged in his throat at supper and before anything could be done for him, he choked to death on his dining room floor.

Following the death of Sean Spence both Paddy and Able seemed to change. The women, noticing it, said it was the burden of realizing that they were totally on their own now, that neither of them had the crafty old Irishman to fall back on when they needed advice about something. True, they had been running the ranches by themselves for several years, but both had known that Sean was *there,* and that had given them a good measure of security. With Sean gone, their young faces seemed to become a little more solemn, a little less smiling; their eyes narrowed a bit, as if now looking at things a little more carefully.

As the two ranches grew, so too did the little community that separated them. Peter Dane eventually passed away and his store was inherited by an Eastern cousin who came out to run it. Other stores and businesses opened, a few professional men settled in the area, and a man named Greb started a little weekly newspaper. A town council was formed and voted to officially name the town Dane, after the man who had opened the first store there.

With prosperity inevitably came trouble. Instead of just transient preachers and other travelers with news of the outside world, there now came an occasional gunman, a gang of rowdies, a few gamblers, and women who showed more calf than they should. A second saloon opened, this one with a side room for gambling. Soon there was a whorehouse behind it. The local women, including Lillian and Elouise, complained to Able and Paddy about it. The two ranchers could easily have squeezed both businesses out simply by asking other merchants, who were almost totally dependent on Able and Paddy for their livelihood, not to trade with them. But Able and Paddy declined to take action. After talking it over, they decided that a limited amount of local gambling and available whores was necessary to keep in their employ the ever increasing number of riders they needed to help run their growing ranches. To help alleviate the fear that Dane was going to turn into another Fort Griffin or Pasco, wide open and lawless, the two ranchers agreed to subsidize both a permanent preacher and a schoolteacher for the community, and contributed the material and labor to construct a small Baptist church and a one-room schoolhouse.

It was the arrival of the schoolteacher in town that earned Charles the nickname of "Draw." The teacher, a spinster past thirty from Ohio, was arriving on a regular run of the East Texas Stage Lines, which now had a route that included Dane as a stop. Lillian Patman, Elouise Spence, and two other respectable ladies of the town, wives of two of the newer merchants, were delegated to meet her. Charles was assigned by Able to drive Lillian and Elouise to town in the buggy, where they would meet the other two ladies and wait for the coach. After Charles did so, he parked the buggy next to the stage lines office and went across the street to the saloon for a cup of coffee.

There was a trio at a table that Charles did not recognize: men slightly older than himself, a little grimy in appearance, all wearing gunbelts. Such riders, usually transient, were not a rarity in Dane anymore, and Charles, drinking his coffee at the bar, at first paid little attention to them. Presently, however, he noticed that they were

290

looking out the saloon window and laughing low nasty laughs. Momentarily, they finished their drinks, got up, and left. Charles walked to the window to see what they were going to do. They crossed the street to where Lillian and the other ladies were waiting. Charles immediately set down his cup and followed them.

By the time Charles got to the middle of the street, one of the men was already annoying Lillian, another was bothering one of the other ladies, and the third was encouraging his friends.

"You fellers move away from them ladies," Charles commanded, walking toward them.

The one annoying Lillian, so close he was breathing his whiskey breath on her, asked, "Why should we? They yours?"

"Mine to look after. Start moving."

"You figure to make us move?" another asked.

"You bet." Charles was still walking toward them.

"Start trying it then!" the third man challenged, reaching for his gun.

Charles outdrew him easily and shot him down before his pistol was even leveled. The other two men were pulling their weapons at the same time. Charles shot the second one just as he was aiming his gun. The third man managed to get off one shot, but it went wild as Charles drilled him also. All three men pitched to the wooden sidewalk as Lillian and the other ladies cringed in terror.

For a moment Charles just stood there, smoking pistol in his hand. He was twenty-two years old, and it was the first time he had ever actually shot anyone. He had felt all along that he was fast enough to outdraw most men, but had sometimes wondered how it would feel to actually gun someone down. Now he knew. It was a sick feeling: it made his stomach churn and his mouth go dry with a bitter taste.

Lillian, quickly composing herself, hurried out into the street. "C.J., are you all right?"

"I think so. The bullet missed me."

"I know the bullet missed you. It hit that horse over there."

Turning, Charles was surprised to see a wounded saddle horse lying in front of the saloon, its head pulled up grotesquely by reins still tied to the hitching post. Blood was spurting from a hole in its side, and it's hind legs were kicking spastically. "Here." Lillian took the gun from his hand. "I'll do it."

The gun barrel and cylinder were hot and Lillian winced as she got the grip in her hands. Then she walked resolutely over to the wounded animal and shot it once in the head. Returning to Charles, she put the gun in his holster, took his arm, and led him toward the buggy.

"You'll have to meet Miss Davenport without me, ladies," she said to the others. "I'll send another buggy for you." Then, to several merchants who had hurried out, "Please get those men off the sidewalk before the coach arrives. I don't want our new schoolteacher frightened away before she even gets started."

Lillian guided Charles onto the buggy seat, climbed up beside him, and drove out of town.

Before the day was over word had spread to everyone in town what a lightning-fast draw and deadly shot Charles Jonas Poker was. The following Saturday, when most of the cowboys were in town, word reached them also. The gunfight between Charles and the three drifters was told and retold dozens of times by everyone who had witnessed it. Forgotten, or simply ignored, was how stunned young Charles had been by what he had done; so stunned that he had to be led away by Lillian. Elaborated upon, however, and even exaggerated by some of the witnesses, was the speed with which Charles had dispatched his opponents. Some said that all four parties had drawn at once, and that Charles had been the fastest and had cut them down in a sweep of bullets. Others said the three men facing him already had their guns drawn, but that Charles was so fast that he had shot them all before they could fire. Somewhere along the line they started calling him "Fast Draw" Poker. Eventually someone shortened it simply to "Draw" Poker.

Able was fascinated by what his friend had done. A fast draw and expert shot, Able had never been in a shoot-out, had never faced another man in a test of skill. He was a little envious of Charles. "How did it feel to drop a man?" he asked Charles curiously that night.

"Not real good. I hope I never have to do it again."

"They had it coming, if you're bothered about that. Lillian said one of them put his hand on her arm."

"Them having it coming don't make it no easier," Charles said quietly. He stared intently at Able. "You don't realize how final it is until you've done it."

"Final or not, I'm glad you was there. So's Paddy Spence. He'll be telling you so hisself. We appreciate what you done to protect our womenfolk."

Only Lillian and Charles himself knew that he had not done it to protect the *womenfolk.* He had done it to protect Lillian. If she had not been involved, he doubted he would even have interfered. Paddy Spence's wife meant nothing to him, nor the other two. Only Lillian's presence in town had made him leave the bar and look out the saloon window to see what the men were up to; only her vulnerability had caused him to spark a confrontation with three armed men.

"My god," Lillian said the next day, "what have I done to you, C.J.?" She had seen him ride in from the range and had gone over to the corral where he was unsaddling his mount. "You came back here because of me. You stay on because of me. And now you've killed three men because of me. Where will it all end? When will you start living your own life?"

Charles looked at her over the saddle-wet back of his horse. "Being around you *is* my life, Lillian."

"But it's *wrong,* C.J.," she insisted. "I have nothing to offer you."

"I ain't asked for anything."

"You should have a wife of your own, children of your own, you—"

"I don't want that."

"What *do* you want?" If he said he wanted *her,* Lillian made up her mind to go with him to his cabin that moment, the consequences be damned. But Charles thought too much of Able to ask that.

"I just want to stay here. I want to be around you, and Able, and the children. I want to be part of everything y'all are part of."

That brought tears to Lillian's eyes and, shaking her head, she turned and hurried back to the house.

After the gunfight nothing changed for a number of years in Dane, except that after a while everyone started calling Charles "Draw."

Everyone except Lillian, who still referred to him as "C.J." The children, Ardelle and Lorn, grew up calling him Draw. Even Able took to calling him that. Soon it was almost forgotten that his name was Charles.

Able's ranch, after nearly ten years, had grown from its original thirty-five acres to now more than twelve thousand, with an equal number of cattle, half of them the new strong disease-resistant Santa Gertrudis. The Spence ranch likewise had grown, to twenty thousand acres, but its rate of growth had slowed as farmers homesteaded land along one of its boundaries and stopped it from spreading in that direction. Able had no doubt that his would one day surpass the Spence spread in size. Much as he liked Paddy Spence, he yearned for the day when he could say that he, Able Chase Patman, was the biggest cattleman in East Texas. He knew he would never be the biggest in *all* of Texas: the King and Kennedy ranches, down in the Rio Grande Valley, had already spread from the south Gulf Coast inland practically all the way to Laguna Salado, and north past Grullo Bayou, and south practically to San Perlita. There was nothing to stop them from exceeding a million acres each. They would always be the giants. But next to them, Able expected someday to be near the top. He could expand farther south than Paddy Spence could expand north. If the farmers just stayed away from his boundaries for another two or three years, he hoped to round out at a quarter of a million acres.

The outstanding feature of Able's empire was the new combination ranch headquarters and home that he had designed and had built. A three-story, fifteen-room Victorian structure, it housed Able's office on one side of the first floor, and the family living quarters in the remainder. So impressive was it that on completion the Dallas *Herald* had sent a photographer all the way to Dane to take a picture of it.

The town of Dane had, like the ranches, enjoyed a steady growth for several years; then it reached a plateau and stopped. It had one of everything: doctor, dentist, newspaper, lawyer, bank, hardware, notions store, blacksmith, cafe, and Chinese laundry. Off and on, it had one, two, three, or four saloons, and one or two whorehouses, depending on the time of year. The East Texas Stage Line terminated its route through Dane due to lack of passengers, but a smaller line, Texas Overland Transport, which ran buckboard coaches, began stopping there twice a week; once eastbound, once westbound. That was frequent enough for Dane. Strangers only seemed to bring trouble anyway. And since the newspaper was on the telegraph line, the town no longer had to count on travelers for its news.

In 1880, a decade after arriving at Dane's Store, Able Patman turned thirty, and Charles "Draw" Poker turned twenty-six. Both had almost forgotten what had drawn them together in the first place. But in the spring of that year a story came over the newspaper's telegraph that Tochoway, the Comanche chief, had surrendered his band of Nokoni raiders to the cavalry in Show Low, Arizona Territory.

"I can't go this time, Draw," said Able. "There's just too much looking-after that has to be done around here. We got fourteen thousand head or more to round up for the cattle buyer. Got more'n sixty riders to boss. There just ain't no way I can go this time."

"I didn't expect you to. If I was in your place, I wouldn't go neither." That was a lie, but Draw knew it would make Able feel better. Draw did not *want* Able to go; he wanted Able to stay on the place and look after Lillian and the children. Draw knew he would feel much easier on the trail knowing Lillian was all right.

"I doubt that there's much chance of you finding them, anyway," Able rationalized. "Christ, it's been *sixteen* years." They were in Draw's cabin, where he was packing his gear. The impact of Able's words settled on him and he paused and stared into space as Able said, "Jesus, my oldest sister Maria would be thirty-four now."

"Effie would be twenty-eight," Draw said, and sighed. "You're right: I prob'ly don't have a chance in hell of finding her. But I got to try anyway."

Lorn, who was seven now, burst into Draw's cabin. "Draw! Can I go with?" he demanded loudly, before he saw his father.

"Get over here, boy!" Able ordered. Lorn edged over to him and Able smacked him hard across the britches. "Don't never let me see you bust into nobody's house like that again!"

"It's all right, Able. He's in and out of here all the time."

"It's not all right! I won't have him growing up wild. His mother wants him to have manners."

Draw hunched down in front of the boy. "I can't take you with me this trip, partner. But I'll bring you something real special when I come back."

"A scalp!" Lorn said eagerly. "Bring me a Comanch scalp! Nate says you're going hunting Comanches."

Nate was Able's trail cook. "Guess I'll have to kick that big mouth's ass," Able said.

"The boy'd just hear it somewheres else," Draw reasoned. "And Nate's a good cook."

Now it was Able who sighed. "I reckon."

Lillian came to the door, Ardelle right behind her. "I just heard from one of the Mexican girls in the kitchen." She looked at Able, sitting while Draw packed. "You're not going?"

"Me? Can't. There's just too much—"

"I know." Lillian turned to Draw. "C.J., were you going to leave without telling me goodbye?"

"Or me, Draw?" Ardelle said. At nine, she was a miniature of her mother.

" 'Course I wasn't." It was another lie. Much as he cared for Lillian, Draw had hoped to get away without having to say goodbye. He did not want to leave hurting any worse than necessary.

When he had his duffel and saddlebags on the horse, Draw swung Lorn into the saddle and led the rest of them to the big house where Lillian had instructed the Mexican kitchen women to prepare some cold food for him to take on the trail. One of the Mexican girls, Vida, who occasionally visited Draw's cabin at night, had the packet ready, and when she handed it to him, she leaned forward and whispered, "*Vaya con Dios,* Draw."

"Thanks," Draw said, embarrassed.

"That will be all, Vida, thank you." Lillian's tone was cool.

Back outside, with Ardelle and Lorn now both pouting because they could not accompany him on the grand adventure, Draw kissed them goodbye, and Lillian said, boldly, "I'm going to have a kiss too, in case I never see you again." Draw took off his hat and she kissed him lightly on the cheek and gave the muscle of his arm an extra squeeze. Then Draw and Able shook hands.

"Good hunting, Draw. Look after yourself. And remember we're your family. Come back to us."

"*Adios,*" said Draw, and rode off at a canter.

43

By the time Draw rode into Show Low, Arizona Territory, the surrendering Nokoni had been processed by an agent of the Bureau of Indian Affairs and had left in the custody of the 18th Cavalry Regiment to be escorted south to an unspecified location where a reservation had been prepared for them. The location of the new reserve was not revealed on orders from Washington; because of much heated public sentiment against the band, the government feared that some organized retribution might ensue if its whereabouts were made public. All anyone knew was that the band had been taken south. That was all Draw could learn about its destination. As far as white slaves were concerned, he found out little more.

"The Indian agent picked out four women he was certain was white," the Show Low sheriff told him. "They'd been with the band so long they couldn't even 'member how to talk English at first. After a while, it come back to 'em and the agent was finally able to find out who they was. I've got their names in my logbook here."

The names were Warren, Bradley, Vick, and Milb. No Poker and no Patman.

"Wonder if there might have been some that the agent missed?" Draw asked.

"Wouldn't surprise me none," the sheriff admitted. "Them agents is all political 'pointees, you know. Ain't none of 'em all that bright."

Draw rode south. At Fort Apache he learned that the band had camped there one night before being moved on. He continued south, across the Natanes Plateau, through the San Carlos reservation where the Apaches were then contained, and down the Gila River to Kearney. There, he learned, the army had let the band rest two days and three nights. Draw asked around the saloon about white slaves.

"There was some talk," a bartender told him, "that some of the women in the band had been white once. But they sure as hell weren't anymore. Ain't no white woman gonna run around buck-ass nekkid, eating dog meat. And that's what them Nokoni women was doing."

Draw resumed his trek south. He cut around Black Mountain and rode into Oracle. From there he went to Wildhorse, to Benson, to St. David. In each town he confirmed that Tochoway's band had passed through under cavalry escort. Still heading south. Draw felt that he *had* to be catching up to them; there were only fifty more miles between St. David and the Mexican border.

By two o'clock the next day, Draw had found the Nokoni. They were living in army tents at the northern edge of Naco, on a treeless plateau, with a few soldiers standing loose guard around them. A large headquarters tent had been erected between them and the settlement. Draw started to ride past it, but a sentry stopped him.

"Who are you and what's your business?"

"Name's C. J. Poker. I'm looking for a white woman that was took by this band some time back. My sister. I'll pay the chief to let me look at his slaves."

Draw was taken into the tent to a Captain Crossman. He was a stout man with a handlebar mustache. "How in hell did you find this camp?"

"I tracked you," Draw said. "All the way from Show Low."

The captain slapped his uniform gloves against the field desk. "Shit. Nobody's supposed to know about this camp."

"I won't tell nobody. All I want to do is look at the slaves to see if my sister's there."

"No one's allowed to fraternize with these people," the officer said. "Besides, they're not supposed to have slaves now. The Indian agent picked them out in Show Low."

"What they're supposed to have and what they *do* have might not be the same thing. The Indian agent could have missed some."

"Well, you can't see them anyway. It's against my orders. That's final. And I'd appreciate it if you'd keep this location to your-self."

"Like hell I will. You got a lot of crust, Captain. Won't do me no favor, but you want me to do you one. Horseshit, mister. I'm a civilian; I'll do as I goddamn please once I leave here. I'm gonna spread the location of this camp all over the goddamn Southwest." Draw started for the door of the big tent.

"Now, just a minute," the captain said anxiously. "Perhaps we can compromise here. You, ah, you say all you want to do is look for your sister?"

"That's all." Draw came back to the desk. "You don't even have to be involved. Just let me into the camp and tell me where Tochoway is. I'll pay him to let me see any slaves he's got left; there's tobacco and whiskey in my saddlebags for that. If I find my sister, I'll bargain with him to turn her loose. There won't be no trouble."

"If I let you in, will you give me your word not to tell anyone else where we are?"

"You got my solemn promise on that, Captain."

The officer relented and allowed Draw to enter the camp. Draw got his saddlebags, and the captain had a sergeant of the guard take him to a tent in the center of the camp. There, Tochoway was pointed out to him. The feared Comanche was now past sixty but appeared still physically fit and healthy. He was sitting on a deerskin in front of the tent, drinking *pulque* from a gourd. Several young Indian women hovered around, attending him. The guard sergeant said to one of them, "Tell the *jefe* that this man wishes to sit and talk and bargain with him."

The young squaw translated the words; Tochoway nodded and pointed to the ground. Draw sat. With the young squaw interpreting, Tochoway asked, "What does the white cowboy have to bargain with?"

"Whiskey and tobacco," Draw replied, unstrapping the flap of one saddlebag. He set a pint of Eagle Brand whiskey and two cakes of Mercy Plug tobacco on the ground.

"What does the white cowboy seek in return?"

"I want to see the Nokonis' white slave women."

Tochoway shrugged. "The Nokoni have no such women any longer. It is not permitted." He looked directly at the sergeant as he spoke.

"He's not going to bargain with me while you're here," Draw told the sergeant. "How about waiting for me back where we left my horse?" Draw saw the sergeant hesitate, so he fingered a five-dollar gold piece out of his shirt pocket and tossed it to him. "Just between us," he said, winking. The sergeant took the coin and left. Draw turned to the interpreter. "Tell the *jefe* that these gifts," he pointed to the whiskey and tobacco, "would just be for *looking* at the slave women, if he had any. There would be other gifts if I wanted to *buy* a slave woman. But if the Nokoni do not have slave women, then I will go."

Draw started to reach for the whiskey and tobacco, but Tochoway raised a hand to stop him. A sly smile on his face, the old warrior spoke and his young woman translated. *"Jefe* says he suddenly remembers two slave women who are still with his people, by their own choice. He will allow you to see them."

Two squaws helped Tochoway to his feet and followed him as he led Draw away from his own tent, deeper into the camp. Toward the rear of the encampment they approached a larger tent, bigger even than the headquarters tent. Three slits had been made in its top, through which lodge poles had been crossed to provide ventilation. Wisps of gray smoke were drifting out of two of the slits. This, Draw knew, was the cooking and eating tent, where the male members of the band took their meals together. It was also where the band's slaves lived and worked.

Tochoway led Draw into the tent. Draw's nostrils were immediately assailed by the stench of burning dog meat. He saw in a pit in the center of the ground a bed of hot coals upon which pieces of dog were being singed. Kneeling at the pit, fanning the coals as they prepared their own food, were two filthy naked women, their hair—on their heads and between their legs—matted and dirty; their faces bearing several crude tattoos; buttocks and backs scarred with welts; a long cactus needle through the nipple of each breast, and from the needles a rawhide thong with which to pull the woman if she were too slow. They were not as young as the women around Tochoway; Draw judged them to be at least thirty. One of them, he saw, swallowing hard, had a mole at the corner of her right eye.

"I want to talk to them," Draw said, and waited for his request to be translated. Then one of the young squaws nodded. *"Jefe* says you may speak to the dog eaters."

Draw knelt on the ground and faced the two women across the pit. They both stared at him, frowning. He removed his hat and said to the one with the mole, "Effie, do you remember me? I'm your brother, Charles Jonas. We used to live together in Spring Branch, Texas. We were children together."

The woman's lips parted and she made an incomprehensible sound, guttural, from deep in her throat. The other immediately began to make a similar noise, and both started groveling on the dirt floor. One of Tochoway's squaws hurried over and kicked each one in the face, then grabbed the nipple thongs and pulled them to their feet. "*See-tah! See-tah!*" she shouted, which meant "silence" in the Nokoni dialect. She lashed them with a braided leather crop until they became quiet. Then she said to Draw, "These dog eaters cannot speak. *Jefe* has had their tongues cut out."

Draw suddenly felt as ill as he had the day he killed the three drifters in Dane. If he had been alone somewhere, he would have let his body go and puked his insides out. But he dared not show signs of weakness before Tochoway or the Indian might refuse to bargain with him because he was less than a man. Steeling himself, he turned to the squaw.

"I would have offered much for one of these women if their tongues had not been taken out and their breasts mutilated and their faces tattooed. As they are, I am not sure I want either of them."

When Draw's words were repeated in dialect, the old Comanche shrugged. "It is of no matter to me. I will keep the whiskey and tobacco for letting you see the slave women, and you and I owe one another nothing."

Draw nodded when he heard this. "That is fair. I am sorry that these women are in such pitiful shape, because I have a rich gift in my pony bag that I know the *jefe* would have wanted. But, some other day, maybe."

The squaw and Tochoway spoke back and forth, and then she said, "*Jefe* asks what the rich gift is? Not that he wants it, but he grows curious in his late years and cannot sleep if his mind wonders about things."

From his other saddlebag, Draw brought forth a small wooden music box with a thirty-eight-star American flag on top. Draw turned the box over and wound the key, then set it upright and opened the lid. It began to play a six-note version of "Oh, Dem Golden Slippers." Tochoway's mouth fell open and he stared in wonder at the little box. Draw let it play a full minute, then snapped the lid shut and returned the box to his saddlebag. The old Indian looked as if his heart had broken. He began to speak rapidly to his squaw.

"*Jefe* says he regrets the women are so poorly. If he could put their tongues back, he would do so. He will have the tattoos sliced off, if you like, and their tits untethered. Since you have come to him in friendship when most whites come to him in anger, he begs you to take both women as a gift, and owe him nothing."

It was, Draw knew, the Indian's way of reopening negotiations for the slaves without losing face. "Tell *jefe* that I am grateful for his generosity. Tell him, however, that I cannot take a woman unless I know something about her. I know about the one with the brown spot by her eye: she was taken from the Texas country many legends ago. But I know nothing of the other woman."

"She too came from the big land called Texas," said Tochoway. "She was the middle of three white sisters. The other two are long dead: one from the prairie fever, the other whipped to death for disobedience."

So this was Elena Patman, Draw thought. Only she and his sister, Effie Poker, had survived. If this could be called survival.

"I accept *jefe*'s gift," said Draw. "Ask him if he will trade two blankets to cover them with, for the box that makes music."

When Tochoway heard that offer, he fairly beamed. Not only would he now obtain the music box, but he could legitimately boast that he got it for two worthless blankets. No mention need be made of the dog-eating women; they had been a gift and that was another matter. Ah, he was indeed a master trader!

Draw put Effie in his saddle, Elena just behind her, and covered them both with blankets. He left the camp walking, leaving the horse. Soldiers lined up to watch him go, shaking their heads, pitying him, thinking him a fool for trying to take two savages back to a life they could not even remember. Draw ignored them one and all.

Late that afternoon he made camp by a desert hot springs and with his razor cut the rawhide thongs from the women's nipples. He did not tamper with the cactus needles; the breasts had grown proud flesh around them and they were firmly imbedded. He gave the women soap and tried to coax them into the springs to bathe, but they threw the soap aside and pulled away from the water. Draw tried to talk to them, tried to get them to nod if they understood anything he was saying. They only stared dumbly at him and occasionally made throat noises. Later he cooked some beans and jerky together and offered them some. They sniffed the food and quickly rejected it. A prairie dog came near their camp an hour later and both women looked hungrily at it. Draw got his rifle and shot it. The women ran to where it had fallen and tore it apart with their bare hands. Squatting on their haunches with the carcass between them, they ate their fill: raw meat, blood, gristle, hide, and hair. As they ate, they made more animal sounds with their tongueless mouths. When their fingers became too sticky to use, they wiped them on the matted bush between their legs.

Draw watched for as long as he could stand it. When it got to be too much for him, he took his rifle out again and shot them each in the head one time.

Very late that night Draw made his way back to the camp at Naco, slipped past the sentries to Tochoway's tent, and while the old Indian slept, cut his throat.

Escaping undetected, he returned to his own camp, rode away from the two fresh graves there, and headed for home.

For Texas.

44

Draw never told Able that he had located two of their four missing sisters. He did not want to have to describe to Able the wild subhuman condition in which he had found Elena and his own sister Effie; nor did he want to admit murdering the two women on the prairie. There was no telling how Able would have taken that. So he told Able that through an interpreter he had talked to several old Nokoni women who had told him that all four of the girls had died of "prairie fever" just two years after they had been kidnapped.

"That probably would have been in the big cholera epidemic of sixty-four," Lillian reasoned.

"My god," Able said incredulously, "that means they were all dead before I even started tracking the band."

"Appears that way," Draw cemented the lie.

"Well, bless their poor hearts," Lillian said, "at least their suffering at the hands of those savages didn't go on for years, like I've heard it has with some white women. Dying young is sometimes a blessing. Our Lord moves in strange ways, just like the Scriptures say."

Draw later told Able how he had slipped into the Nokoni camp at night and cut Tochoway's throat. He asked Able to please not tell Lillian about it; he did not want her to know he could kill with a knife like a savage. "Bad enough that she's seen me kill with a gun." Able promised that he would never mention it, and he never did.

Able Patman's ranch flourished. By 1885 his acreage and the size of his herd reached one hundred thousand, and at some point that year his ranch and the ranch of his friend Paddy Spence became equal in size. Able, however, had room to continue growing.

"Well, ol' friend, looks like the Patman spread is going to come out on top," Paddy said one Sunday after their families had dinner together. "My spread's completely hemmed in now by dirt farmers." He gazed off across one of his pastures. "Daddy used to wonder which one'd be biggest."

"Hadn't been for your daddy," Able said, recalling old Sean Spence, "wouldn't neither of us have near as much, I don't think. He was a good man." Able draped an arm around his friend's shoulders. "And it don't matter none how much bigger my place grows: you and me'll always be partners. Someday the whole of the two spreads'll be one big ranch, half owned by Pete and Ardelle, half by Lorn and Sarah."

"I hope so. Lord, I truly hope so." He looked intently at Able. "Nothing makes me sicker than to think of some outsider, some *foreigner,* getting part of this land."

"Me too," Able agreed. He knew that "foreigner" meant any-one not from Dane in particular or Caddo County in general.

Able's ranch, not yet completely hemmed in as Paddy's was, would continue to grow until it *was* hemmed in, and by that time it would have increased to half again as large as the Spence spread: it would reach and just barely exceed one hundred and fifty thousand acres. Then the last parcel of open land bordering it would be home-steaded and the Patman empire would be complete. It would take almost thirty years.

In 1889 the worst influenza plague in history struck. It was so widespread that medical people said it passed the epidemic stage and became pandemic: it affected an exceptionally high proportion of the population. By the time it had run its terrible course more than twenty months later, it had touched forty percent of the earth's people, and been fatal to thousands. One of the persons it killed was Lillian Conway Patman.

Ardelle was eighteen when her mother died; Lorn was sixteen, the same age as Pete Spence; and Sarah Spence, Pete's sister, was fourteen. They all gathered at Lillian's bedside after the doctor from Dane said there was absolutely nothing he could do for her. Along with the children were Paddy Spence and his wife Elouise, and his mother, old Sean's widow. They all stood around and whispered and sobbed quietly and tried to comfort Able, who sat in a big chair next to the deathbed and stared straight ahead as if trying to will himself to join Lillian.

When it became obvious that Lillian's last hour was upon her, Able rose and said, to no one in particular, "Somebody fetch Draw. He ought to be here too."

Paddy Spence nodded to Pete, who went to do it. But his grandmother caught him in the hall. "Never mind," she instructed. "It's not fitting to have a hired hand present at a time like this. Able's so grief-stricken that he's not thinking right. Just come back in a few minutes and say you couldn't find him."

"Yes, Grandmother."

Sean's widow returned to the deathwatch, convinced that she had done right. She knew that Sean, up in heaven, would approve. He had always drawn a definite line between who was family and who was not. A time like this, she thought, a time for dying, was for family.

When Lillian began to fade, everyone in the room took a turn touching her delicate cold hand, or kissing her soft cold cheek.

"Where's Draw?" Able asked, when everyone had filed past the bed.

Young Pete Spence's grandmother fixed her eyes rigidly on him, and Pete said, "I couldn't find him, Mr. Patman."

"All right," Able said wearily. "Will everyone leave now, please."

When they were gone, Able locked the bedroom door, undressed, and got into bed with his dying wife. She smiled faintly at him as he gathered her in his arms. He held her close to him, stroking her fine soft hair, as she died.

The widow of Sean, the last of her generation, far exceeded the life expectancy of her era, which was forty-seven years, and lived until 1893, when, at age sixty-three, she died of a myriad of ailments that had kept her confined to bed for most of a year. After her passing, her son Paddy and his friend Able began to contemplate the fact that neither of them was a young man any longer, and that definite steps had to be taken to preserve their respective domains. Each in his own way began to apply subtle pressures on their offspring to think about marriage.

Pete Spence was twenty, Ardelle Patman twenty-two; Lorn Patman was twenty, Sarah Spence eighteen. Time was wasting. To the surprise of the two fathers, however, they found that their children were in no hurry to accommodate them. Ardelle, now the woman of the Patman home, was convinced that her widowed father and younger brother could not get along without her. On top of that, she felt a little odd about marrying a man that much younger than herself. Pete was in no hurry to get married either. A somewhat reserved young man in most situations, he was, unknown to his parents or sister, or to Able Patman and his daughter, a veritable stallion when it came to the many young Mexican girls now employed on the two ranches. Lorn Patman knew about him, and most of the riders, both Spence and Patman, knew. The general consensus was that if Pete had not fucked a Mexican girl, she could probably outrun a deer. His prowess was known far and wide; it was only by extraordinary luck that he had not fathered at least one half-Mex Saturday night bastard. Pete liked Ardelle Patman all right, but he too felt a little uneasy about the age difference, particularly since he would be marrying a woman more than two years his senior.

There was no age problem between Lorn Patman and Sarah Spence: with Lorn the older by two years, they were perfect for each other. But Lorn was simply too preoccupied to court Sarah. At twenty he was at once cocksure and insecure, confident and faltering. He was reticent around his father, who spent almost no real time with him; open and outgoing with Draw, to whose shirttails he still clung. He was smilingly confident with a pistol in his hand, because Draw had taught him how to use it; faltering when it came to book learning or social graces; bold with the occasional Mexican girl he bedded, or the whores he found at the end of the cattle drive; shy around nice girls like Sarah Spence, who always seemed to be waiting for him to *do* something. Life to Lorn was a series of good times alternating with distressing dilemmas.

It was not until his twenty-first year, on a trip to Kansas City, that Lorn Patman realized for the first time that his diverse traits could meld into a single acceptable personality.

That realization was brought on by a girl named Nell Sheridan.

It was by no means amazing that a select inner circle of those closest to him were not immediately aware of the reasons for Lorn Patman's suicide in 1894. Very simply, nobody around Dane dared tell them. Very few people ever spoke to Able Patman or Paddy Spence on a personal level. The two men had absolutely no peers in East Texas save each other. The same could be said for Spence's wife, Elouise: the death of Lillian Patman had left Elouise the reigning matriarch of Caddo County. Around the Spences and Able Patman people knew their place and kept it.

One generation further along, Ardelle Patman should, as Lorn's sister, have had an inkling of what was going on; at least have become aware of Nell Sheridan's pregnant presence in Dane; but, concerned as she was with assuming her late mother's responsibilities as mistress of Patman Ranch, she missed out on most of the good gossip, except what she got from Elouise and Sarah Spence.

Sarah, of course, *had* found out all about Nell Sheridan, but only because she had a close, *very* close relationship with the Mexican house girl who was her personal servant. Conchita Conega, called "Chita" by the Spence family, was the same age as Sarah. The two had grown up together, Chita being first a playmate for Sarah, then a schoolmate when Sarah had a tutor for several years, and finally an *ancilla,* or lady's maid, after Sarah became a young lady. While there was not exactly a lesbian relationship between them, because it was not reciprocal, Sarah nevertheless made use of her *ancilla* in a sexual way. While she languished in a great oaken tub of perfumed bathwater, reading aloud from *Romance Stories* or *Popular Love,* she had Chita wash her with a soft cloth. When she came to a particular passage in a story that excited her, Sarah would say, "Now, Chita, honey," and the Mexican girl would wash between Sarah's legs. Sarah would close her eyes, press her face into the magazine, and tremble through a moment of ecstasy. Sarah had bathed that way every day since she and Chita were seventeen.

It was Chita who told Sarah Spence about the pregnant woman living above Tully's Eats in Dane, working in the cafe, carrying Lorn Patman's Saturday night bastard. By that time Sarah was already engaged to Lorn. He had returned from a cattle-selling trip to Kansas City and begun courting her almost at once. Sarah had tried, as subtly as she could, to discourage him; she was perfectly happy with her *ancilla.* But her father, whom she suspected knew what was going on with Conchita, threatened to whip her with his razor strap if she did not accept Lorn Patman's marriage proposal. So she did, and they announced their engagement.

After they were married, they moved into a new house near where Sarah's parents lived. Sarah had taken Chita with them, keeping her just as close to her as when she was single. Chita still dressed her, did her hair, went on errands with her, and, every night, bathed her in the big oaken tub. Sexually sated by the time she was ready for bed, Sarah went to sleep in her own room, having let Lorn know on the night of their wedding *why* she had married him; advising him that she knew about Nell Sheridan; and putting him on notice that they were going to be husband and wife in name and appearance only.

Night after night Sarah left Lorn frustrated, insecure, ashamed of himself for some vague reason, and ultimately extremely bitter. After two weeks he thought he might be going crazy; after a month he was certain of it. He convinced himself that only one person could save him: Nell Sheridan. He went to see Nell at Tully's cafe, but Nell, swollen with their baby, rejected him. Lorn then decided on death before insanity. Very late the following Saturday night he got a rope and looked for a secluded place to use it. He finally decided on the First Baptist Church.

After Lorn's suicide, the Patman and Spence families retreated unto themselves and had little to do with the rest of Dane and Caddo County. Sarah Spence remained in seclusion in the house, with Chita, for a year, then moved to Galveston. Chita, of course, accompanied her mistress. Just prior to Sarah's departure for Galveston,

Pete Spence and Ardelle Patman were quietly married in a small private ceremony in the Spence home. Despite their difference in age, Ardelle had realized that it was now up to her and Pete to assure the perpetuity of the Patman-Spence ranches. She proposed marriage to Pete and he accepted. It seemed to Pete the easiest way to assure that his lifestyle would never have to change. For the first few months of their marriage he cooperated fully with Ardelle in her efforts to become pregnant. When she did not, he lost interest in her and resumed fucking the Mexican girls. After that there was little chance for Ardelle unless she caught Pete before he got out of bed in the morning; he had nothing left for her by the time he got back home for supper.

It took Ardelle Patman Spence nine years to become pregnant, at age thirty-four, with her first child. Praying desperately for a grandson for Able, and someone to perpetuate at least the Spence name, in 1905 she gave birth to a daughter. Ardelle named her Faye. Three years later she managed to catch Pete again and in 1908 at the age of thirty-seven she had a second child, still not a boy, whom she named Grace. Her delivery of Grace was excruciatingly painful and damaged her uterus horribly. She was told not to have any more children. The order devastated her. She stayed in bed for six months and rarely, if ever, smiled after that.

In 1910 Paddy Spence, whose own father had met an accidental death, was also killed in an accident: a stallion he was riding bolted at a harmless grass snake and threw Paddy into an iron gate, breaking his neck. He was sixty. Two years later, Paddy's wife Elouise, also sixty, expired of melancholia complicated by the vapors and general inactivity of her muscles and blood.

Once the two proud ranches had been teeming with family: Able and his wife Lillian, their daughter Ardelle and son Lorn; old Sean Spence and his wife Ardelle, their son Paddy and his wife Elouise, and *their* son Pete and daughter Sarah. The future had seemed blessed and bright. But life is a series of debits and credits, and must ultimately be paid for. The enormous success of the two cattle empires, totaling a quarter of a million acres and more than that number of cattle, had to be balanced by something, and it turned out to be accidental death, suicide, and the failure to produce a male heir that would propagate at least one of the family names.

Into the twentieth century the ranches continued to prosper.

309

But they were no longer places blessed and bright. They had become dark and moody.

In 1916 due to an accidental slip of the tongue, Able Patman learned that he had an illegitimate grandson.

It was on one of those gray bleak East Texas mornings in early winter, with no threat of rain, too early for snow, only the promise of long, cheerless hours until night fell. Able was having problems with gout in his left foot and had it propped on a stool in front of the hearth where a good fire danced on seasoned oak, making it crackle and pop. Ardelle had come over after getting Pete off to work and the girls, who were eight and eleven, off to school. She baked Able a devil's food cake and cut him a slice while it was still hot. Father and daughter were in a reminiscing mood as they sat with their coffee before the fire.

"Mother's birthday is coming up," Ardelle said. "She would have been sixty-two this year."

Able nodded, pursing his lips at the thought that Lillian had been gone more than twenty-seven years. Over a quarter of a century he had lived without her. And almost as long without his son. "Lorn, he would have been forty-three," Able sighed.

"Yes. His son is a grown man now."

The statement had been made wistfully, foggily, and to Ardelle it seemed as if *she* had not made it at all, but some other being, some *spirit,* speaking from a haze very close to her. *Oh, Jesus God, don't let him have heard that,* she prayed. Sometimes Able missed words or sentences and they had to be repeated. *Let this be one of those times,* Ardelle silently begged.

But she knew from the look on her father's face that it was not.

"What son?" Able asked quietly.

Ardelle forced a smile. "I don't know what made me say that, Daddy. I meant, if he'd *had* a son."

Able took his eyes from her and looked back into the fire. "I'll wait until you're ready to tell me." His voice was as even as a knife edge. Ardelle knew he would not speak to her again until she told him the truth. If need be, he would go to his grave not speaking to her, because he could not tolerate being lied to. Ardelle began to cry.

"Oh, Daddy—"

310

Able looked at her then and opened his arms, and she dropped to her knees beside his chair so that he could embrace her. Sobbing her tears into his shirt, she told him about Nell Sheridan and the baby boy Nell had delivered in the room above Tully's Eats.

"My god almighty," Able said when the story was finished. He could hardly believe it. "Lorn had a son."

"An *illegitimate* son, Daddy," Ardelle emphasized, suddenly afraid of the past that now seemed to threaten her. Not only her but her husband, her daughters, what was theirs. "A Saturday night bastard, Daddy. Just like the trashy Mexican girls have."

Able shook his head in wonder. "Lorn's son. My god." He took Ardelle by the shoulders and held her at arm's length. "Why did you never tell me?"

Sniffing, wiping her eyes with her palms, Ardelle said, "I didn't know about it for a long time, Daddy. Sarah told me after Lorn— well, after he was gone. You were so sick with grief that I just couldn't bear to hurt you any more. Then after the Sheridan girl took the baby away, why, there just didn't seem to be any point in telling you. Draw agreed with me—"

"Draw?" Able's face clouded. "Draw *knew?*"

"Yes, Daddy. I had to talk to somebody about it, and he was as close to family as there was."

"Draw knew about it all along?"

"Yes, Daddy."

"And never told me," Able whispered. He shook his head again at this new disclosure. Able could understand Ardelle not telling him about the baby. She was a woman, and women could always find reasons for everything: she didn't want to hurt him, there was no point, it wouldn't have made any difference. Women's reasons.

But *Draw?* Draw was a man, just as Able was a man. There was no excuse for Draw not telling him.

No excuse at all.

Draw lived in a three-room foreman's house that Able had ordered built for him ten years earlier. It was set back behind the big Patman mansion some one hundred yards. Draw had never liked the place; it was cheerless and empty of memories, not like his old cabin through which Lorn and Ardelle had romped as children, where they had hidden from their parents when they had a licking coming; which Lillian had visited now and again to bring him something she had baked especially for him, or to ask his advice about something, or just to sit on the tiny front porch and talk. Draw lived in the new place only because Able had it built for him, because Able wanted him to be more comfortable. And because Able had the old cabin torn down, saying it was an eyesore. Lillian had never called it an eyesore.

Draw had been sitting alone in that old cabin the night Lillian died. He had wanted desperately to go up to the big house and see her one last time, say goodbye to her, but the Spences had been there and he knew it would not be proper for him to intrude. He had to wait for Able to send for him, to invite him. But when the hours passed and no one came to fetch him, and he saw the lights in her room go out, to be replaced with flickering candles at the four corners of her bed, he had known it was too late. All alone he had walked out onto the prairie and sat down on the hard ground and cried.

Draw had not gone to see Lillian in her casket the next day because he did not want his last memory of her to be that way. He had seen her three days earlier when she sent one of the Mexican women to fetch him. In her room he had sat holding her terribly weak hand and she had asked him to promise that he would stay on and help Able with the children because she knew that he loved the children and understood them more than their father did. Of course he promised her anything she asked, as he had always done. That last hour with her in the bedroom was how he chose to remember her, not lying stiff and waxen in a coffin.

Nowadays mostly all Draw did was ride around and check the near ranges once a day. The ranch was run by younger men and Draw had three section foremen: one for grazing, one for feed, and one for fences. On overcast, damp days, like the day Able found out about Lorn's son, Draw mostly stayed around the house, in case Able wanted company and sent for him to play checkers or look at photo albums, or just sit by the fire and sip rye whiskey. He was just passing time, doing nothing in particular, that day when Able knocked on his door. Draw, expecting a Mexican woman, was surprised to see him.

"My god, what's the occasion? You ain't been down here in a

year. You oughtn't be out in the damp, you know." Then he noticed that Able was wearing his old gunbelt, something he had not done in fifteen years. "You expecting trouble?" Draw cracked.

"Why didn't you never tell me Lorn had a son?"

Draw was not shocked by the question; a little surprised was all. He had thought that Able would probably find out about Nell Sheridan and her baby someday, some way, and now and again he wondered just how Able would take it. Seeing the gunbelt around his hips, Draw knew at once that it had angered more than hurt him.

"Answer me," Able said harshly. "Why didn't you never tell me?"

"I considered telling you," Draw admitted. "But then I looked into the matter and decided against it. I found out that the baby's mother had made up her mind to take the boy back to her home in Kansas City and raise him there. She wanted him to grow up as a Sheridan; didn't want no part of the Patman name or the Patman family. It was her choice."

"And you let her do it?" It was an accusation more than a question.

Able's eyes were as cold as Draw had ever seen them. *This is bad*, his old instincts told him. *This is the worst that's ever been between us.*

"It's what the girl wanted."

"What the *girl* wanted? You owed your loyalty to *me!*"

"Weren't a question of loyalty," Draw said stiffly. "It was a question of what was right. That girl, she had a *right* to decide."

Able shook his head vehemently. At the moment he did not give a goddamn about "right." What mattered was loyalty. Draw had betrayed him.

"You're fired. There's no place for you here anymore."

"It's your place," Draw said coldly.

"What's more, I'm calling you out." Able hitched up his gunbelt.

"Oh, for Christ's sake, Able. This is 1916."

"I don't give a shit. I calling you out!"

"Able, you're sixty-six years old. I'm sixty-two. I ain't *touched* a pistol in ten years."

"You're gonna touch one today, by god, or get a hole blowed in you for *not* touching one." A slight cheerless smile flickered over

Able Patman's lips. "I've always wondered which one of us was fastest. Now I'm fixing to find out. You ain't scared of me, are you? Big bad gunfighter like you?"

"No," Draw replied quietly, "I ain't afraid of you, Able."

"Disloyal all these years!" Able ranted. "Not a trace of trustworthiness in your whole body! I thank God that my Lillian didn't live to see you found out."

"I'd as soon you didn't bring Lillian's name into this." The words were clearly a warning.

"Why not?" Able demanded. "Afraid to admit what she would have thought of you?"

"I *know* what Lillian thought of me," Draw retorted, putting a finger close to Able's face. "Weren't for my promise to her, I'd probably have left this place years ago. You know, Able, you never was good enough for her. Never. And you always resented how much she thought of me. Why, you wasn't even man enough to send for me the night she died."

"That's a goddamn lie! And you're a goddamn liar! I did so send for you. You wasn't around."

"Horseshit! I was right there in my cabin until the candles was lit around her. You're the one who's the goddamned liar!"

"Get your pistol, you son of a bitch!"

"All right, I will, you old bastard!"

It took Draw a minute to remember where his gunbelt was, and another minute to put cartridges in the cylinder and buckle on the belt and tie down the holster. All the time Able was pacing up and down in front of the house, shouting, "Hurry up, goddamn you! And don't try sneaking out the back door either!"

Presently Draw stomped out and faced him with thirty feet of air between them, and said, "All right, do it! Pull it!"

And Able did.

It was no match. Draw was twice as fast. He shot Able in the upper right arm and Able was knocked to the ground as if a mule had kicked him. His pistol fell beside him without ever being aimed.

"You can thank Lillian for that slug not being in your chest," Draw told him quietly. Holstering his gun, he stalked away.

Ten minutes later Draw emerged with his blanketroll and duffel bag. He started lacing them onto Peso, his mount, saddled and hitched outside the house. Able had got to his feet now. "That there's a Patman horse." Draw stopped and stared at him. Able managed a tight smile. "Got a Patman brand on him. You ride out of here on that horse, I'll see you swing for it."

Draw took his gear back off the stallion, shouldered it, and walked off the ranch. He never sat a horse again, never fired a pistol again, and never saw Able Chase Patman again.

45

"I still don't know why Able included me in his will," Sam said as he glanced over at Draw, in the passenger seat of the new Packard. "Even after all you've told me about him, that's the one thing that doesn't make any sense."

They had just driven through Cat Springs, about halfway back to Dane from McAllen. Draw's blanketroll with his few personal belongings was in the backseat.

"I'm afraid I don't have the answer to that one," Draw said, "except to tell you that there *was* a reason. Able never done nothing less'n he had a damn good reason. Or what he *thought* was a damn good reason."

"You told me once that he didn't know about the oil reserves on the land, right?"

"Right. Hell, *nobody* knew about 'em. At least three times whilst I was still with Able, why, he gave different fellers permission to survey parts of his spread for signs of oil. I think I told you, that day Tongue showed you the bog, that the Sinclair people had been all over the section Able left to you, without finding nothing. No, Able didn't know about the oil, I'm sure of that."

Sam shook his head in quiet frustration. "Do you think he might have put me in the will just to spite his daughter? To let Ardelle know that he still held it against her for not telling him about me all those years?"

"I reckon that's possible," Draw allowed. "But, tell the truth, it don't *sound* like Able. Not the Able I remember. The Able I knowed would have *said* so right in the will if that'd been his reason."

"He might not have *been* the Able you knew. Don't forget, it had been five years since you and he had your falling out. He was past seventy. Maybe his mind was, well, slowing down. What do you think?"

Draw sighed quietly and stared out at the plush green countryside of south central Texas. "It's hard for me to imagine that. But I got to admit you could be right."

"Of course, there's an even simpler explanation, too. I've talked to Tom Prater about it; he's the lawyer that's with us now, the one who hired the Pinkertons to find you for me. Tom says Able might have been *advised* to put me in his will. Even though Texas law doesn't recognize illegitimate members of a family as legal heirs, Tom says that including them in a will for some token inheritance prevents them from contesting the will in court. It's when they don't get *anything* that they can tie up a will and cause trouble. Maybe the hundred acres and the five hundred dollars was insurance against me causing trouble."

Draw was shaking his head even as Sam spoke. "That don't figure. If he hadn't put you in the will, you wouldn't even have known about your Texas blood. Seems to me that includin' you was the first step toward surefire trouble."

"But, Draw," Sam argued, "Able and the Spences had no way of knowing whether I knew about them or not. They couldn't be sure but what my mother had told me everything. For all they knew, I could have been back in Kansas City just *waiting* for Able to die so I could show up in Dane and contest his will. They might have figured that by giving me a tiny piece of Able's estate, they would get the jump on me and prevent that."

"All right," Draw nodded in agreement now, "it makes sense put that way."

They rode in silence for a while, each with his own thoughts. Just north of Cochran, they crossed the Brazos on a rickety old wooden bridge that creaked indignantly under the strain of the heavy new Packard. All around them were broad vistas of horse ranches, their whitewashed fences stark against the deep green of pasture clover. The blooded stallions out to stud pranced defiantly at the sight of the bright yellow car, while their mares and colts shied away from the highway fence. There were pretty sights at every turn of the road in that part of Texas, but Sam and Draw were too concerned with the puzzle of Able's will to enjoy them.

"I suppose," Sam said at last, "that I may *never* find out the whole truth."

"Possible." The old cowboy studied Sam from the seat beside him. If you *don't,* he wondered, how will you take it?

"Well, I can live with it," Sam said firmly, as if in answer to Draw's silent inquiry. "There's enough to do in the future without worrying about the past. I've got a town and people to think about. And more oil wells to drill. A company to run. Not only that, but—"

As Draw watched, Sam continued naming things he had to do. The younger man's eyes narrowed to a squint as each plan, each responsibility, rolled off his tongue. At that moment, Sam Sheridan reminded Draw of Able Patman reborn.

I wonder, he thought, where it will all end for *him?*

Outside of Esperanza Sam noticed that Draw's head had slumped forward; the old cowboy was dozing. Glancing fondly at the grizzled, worn, eaglelike face, Sam realized that he was probably experiencing for the first time the feeling a son had for his father. The only father Sam had ever known was the myth created for him by his mother. That had now been replaced by the story of his actual father, Lorn Patman. A myth, a story; never a person. This old cowboy, this gunfighter, Indian hunter, killer of men in another time, was the only *man* to whom Sam had ever felt a real attachment. In a way Sam was a little bit sorry that one of his speculations about his roots had *not* been true; he would not have minded being Draw Poker's illegitimate son—though certainly not by Sarah Spence. The one constant in all the confusion, one for which Sam was deeply grateful, was that Nell Sheridan had, indeed, been his real mother. That was something he *never* wanted to be different.

Thinking of his mother as he drove, Sam pieced together all he now knew about her. A young girl raised in Kansas City. Her father, the other grandfather Sam never knew, dying in the influenza epidemic of 1889. Nell's mother, Edna Sheridan, remarrying and

---

317

becoming Edna Duvall. Nell's stepfather later being killed while lying drunk on the tracks of the railroad for which he worked. Edna being able to maintain a decent lifestyle for her and Nell by supplementing her two small pensions with seamstress work done in her home. Then her eighteen-year-old daughter becoming pregnant out of wedlock by a visitor from Texas. Edna agreeing to help Nell go to Texas to see him. Nell's yearlong ordeal in Dane, and Sam's own birth there. Then back to Kansas City to live with Edna. Mother and daughter expanding Edna's seamstress business to the point where they took on two other ladies to work half days helping them.

Sam had only fond memories of his youth. Mother and grandmother had never doted on him but had loved him in a caring, more secure way. He was not spoiled, did not have some of the more elaborate things of which other children boasted, but he never went without nourishing food, decent clothing, and a modest allowance from the fourth grade on.

After his grandmother died when Sam was twelve, Nell had continued the seamstress business and things had changed very little, except for the loneliness of life without Edna. Thinking about it in retrospect, Sam wondered why his mother had never married. She certainly had never seemed bitter toward men, or about her own circumstances. As the years passed, Sam supposed she had more or less adopted the attitude that Edna had. His grandmother, after being twice widowed by less than successful husbands, had simply concluded that men really were not necessary at all if a woman had a source of *income.* Yet Sam could not help being curious about his mother's sex life. She had been a healthy, active woman; surely there had to have been desires. Or had all such normal feelings been decimated and ultimately destroyed by her year in Dane, Texas? His mother had survived the ill will and harsh treatment tendered her by the people of Dane—most of the people—but, Sam asked himself, at what price?

Shaking his head as he drove, Sam realized that he would never know the extent of his mother's trauma. He only wished, with all his being, that Nell could have lived to see him return to Texas. She had never wanted him to know about his Texas blood; but if she were alive, he felt that she would have been glad. Because she would see how he was going to use that Texas blood, and the wealth it had brought him; she would see him build the new town called Sheridan. In her own way Nell had fought against the *kind* of town Dane was;

she had taken a stand against the unfriendliness and unwelcome of that cold closed little community. With his ambition to build Sheridan, Sam felt as if he would be continuing a battle his mother had begun years earlier.

A battle Nell never really won, but which Sam was determined he *would* win.

A while later when Draw woke up, Sam asked, "What about the Spences, Draw? Why do they hate me the way they do?"

Draw grunted softly. "You can blame Pete for that, I reckon. You see, for years and years the Patmans and the Spences was like royalty in East Texas. Their families was *perfect;* ever'thing they did was *right.* Then out of the blue each side of the clan had a scandal. Lorn fathers an illegitimate child by an outsider, then hangs hisself; Sarah's carrying on with that *ancilla* of hers was found out, then her and the *ancilla* went off together. Them two things kind of drove Pete into a shell. He drawed up inside hisself and backed off from ever'body; like he was waiting for somebody to say something bad about his or Ardelle's family. Not jus' waiting, either; more like *daring.* For years after he took over the ranches, if he even *suspected* that anyone was talking about the families behind his back, why, he'd run 'em clean out of the county. He laid the law down for ever'body to see: Caddo County was *his.* As far as he was concerned, with Lorn and Sarah gone, the family was pure again." Draw looked over at him. "Then you come along and open up the wounds. I reckon Pete felt he didn't have no choice but to reject you. To him, it must have been like having Lorn come back to life. I reckon Pete *had* to hate you, son."

"Ardelle too?" Draw detected a trace of bitterness in Sam's voice. "Ardelle is my blood. Doesn't that mean anything to her?"

"Ardelle took her husband's side," Draw replied matter-of-factly. "For her, it was the right thing to do. After all, Pete had turned away Sarah, *his* blood, to protect the family name. He wasn't expecting Ardelle to do nothing he hadn't done. They had their two girls to think of, don't forget."

Sighing wearily, Sam shook his head. "What a goddamned mess," he said, as much to himself as to Draw.

The older man studied Sam for a mile or so, then asked, "You still aim to pay Spence back for all the wrong he's done you?"

Sam took a while to answer, his eyes narrowing as he pondered the question. "Getting even with him isn't as important to me as it once was," he admitted finally. "There are lots of things taking priority right now; things much more important than Pete Spence. I'm not forgiving him, not by a long shot, and I'm not forgetting anything he's done. I'll deal with him when and where I have to. In the meantime, like I said earlier, I've got a town and people to look after. That comes first."

Draw turned his face to the window, a slight smile on his weathered lips. He'll do just fine, the old gunfighter decided. Like it or not, he had a lot of his grandfather in him.

Able, this boy of ours is all right, Draw said silently.

PART
3

Texas Rich

46

Sam and Draw were in Sam's office going over plans for the town's first real hotel, which Sam was building and which would be called the Sheridan House, when Buddy Kyle burst in unannounced. The youth was white-faced.

"Pop's had a stroke of some kind," he said nervously. Sam and Draw looked up incredulously. "It happened about two hours ago. We was checking the drill over on the Simmons lease when all of a sudden he just grabbed his armpit with one hand and passed out. Mr. Simmons helped me get him into the truck and we quick carried him down to the hospital in New Salem. The doc down there said it was a stroke."

Sam and Draw were both visibly shaken. "Is he dead?" Sam asked fearfully.

"No, but he's paralyzed and all drawed up on one side. His face is twisted something terrible." Buddy, who had grown very close to the old wildcatter, had to fight back tears. With a mouthful of wire braces to straighten his grotesque teeth—something Georgia had made him do—he looked like a schoolboy.

As Sam stood there stunned by the news, Miss Emily limped in from the Sheridan Realty office next door. "Samuel, there's a delegation from the town of Dane to see you," she announced. "Mayor Rozelle Rice, Chief of Police Verle Noble, Reverend Adolph Jones, Clarence Fort and his son Bruce, the lawyers, Claud Maye of the Merchants Bank, and my former employer, Mr. Greb, of the newspaper. They're waiting in the realty office."

Sam and Draw exchanged glances. "They carrying a lynch rope?" Draw asked.

"They might as well be, from the looks on their faces."

"Where's Georgia?" Sam asked.

"She may be at home," Miss Emily said. "She was going to stop there when she finished looking at the farms over east of the field."

Now that Sheridan had grown sufficiently, plans were being made to incorporate it as a bona-fide city. To that end, a survey was being conducted that included the surrounding farms that would become part of the new community. Georgia, deciding that there would be no poverty in Sheridan, was personally inspecting every farm and its family, with an eye toward somehow upgrading the economic status of each.

"Bring the delegation over here to the conference room," Sam told Miss Emily. His offices were in an unfinished two-story building next to Georgia's realty operation; they had been designed along the same lines as Rutland King's headquarters in Galveston, by which Sam had been very impressed. King had sent his own assistants to help Sam plan and lay out the building, to be called upon completion the Sheridan Oil Building.

"You want me to go see to Pop?" Draw asked. "So you won't have to worry about him?"

"No, I need you here. Pop's in good hands in the hospital." Sam turned to Buddy. "Does Pop have a drilling schedule for all sites?"

Buddy nodded. "It's on a clipboard out in the truck."

Sam picked up a phone and pressed Owen Milam's intercom button. When the geologist answered in his office upstairs, Sam said, "Owen, Pop Joyner's had a stroke of some kind. He's in the hospital. Can you take over field operations for a while?"

"Sure I can. How bad is Pop?"

"Don't know yet. But he's seventy-eight years old, so his field days might be over. Why don't you start looking over the crews to see if we've got anyone to replace him. Buddy's in my office now; I'll have him get Pop's drilling schedule and come upstairs."

When Sam hung up, Buddy Kyle said, "I'd sure like to have a crack at that job myself, Sam."

"If you were a little older, I'd give it to you," Sam told him. "But you're only seventeen. We've got sixty drilling crews out there. I don't think you could control them, Buddy."

"I been working right alongside Pop for fifteen months. I know his job front and back."

"I don't doubt it. But you're still only seventeen years old.

324

You're probably younger than every field worker we've got. They just wouldn't take you seriously."

"I'd *make* them," Buddy insisted, turning red.

Sam shook his head. "I'm sorry, Buddy. The time's just not right." He bobbed his chin toward the door. "Get that schedule and take it up to Owen. I'm depending on you to give him all the help you can."

Still red-faced, Buddy spun around and stalked from the room. Sam and Draw exchanged resigned looks and Sam picked up another phone and jiggled the hook for Central. "Sheridan one hundred," he said, giving the operator his home number. A Mexican maid answered and he asked if Mrs. Sheridan was there yet. Georgia had just arrived and got on the phone.

"Pop's in the hospital down in New Salem," Sam told her. "A stroke of some kind."

"Oh, Sam. That's terrible. How bad is it?"

"Don't know yet. I want you to go down there and stay with him until I or somebody else can get there."

"Isn't there somebody else who can go now, Sam? I've still got half the farms on the east side to look at and—"

"I don't care what you've got to do, Georgia." His voice had a decided edge. "We're the only family that old man's got right now. I won't have him waking up with nobody but strangers around him. You get down there. Right now."

"Yes, your lordship!" Georgia snapped. She slammed the receiver down without saying goodbye.

Shaking his head, wishing he had not spoken so dictatorially, Sam picked up his intercom phone again and pressed the button for Tom Prater's office.

"Tom, Pop's in the hospital with a stroke."

"I'm sorry to hear that," Prater said. "When did it happen?"

"This morning. We don't even know yet how bad it is. I'll keep you posted. Listen, Tom, there's a delegation of some kind from Dane waiting in the conference room to see me. Come on down, will you?"

"Be right there."

Sam hung up and turned to Draw. "Okay, let's see what the good people of Dane want."

Leaving his office, Sam led the way across the building's lobby to a large, comfortably appointed meeting room dominated by a fourteen-chair conference table. The seven men had not sat down, but remained standing in a tight little cluster, not far from the door. There was subdued conversation, but it ceased the instant Sam and Draw entered. Sam pulled out his chair at the head of the table and sat down. Draw shoved both hands in his pockets and leaned against the wall behind him; still the gunfighter providing backup. "What can I do for you, gentlemen?" Sam asked.

Mayor Rozelle Rice stepped forward and said, "Mr. Sheridan, we're here on a very grave matter—" He paused as Tom Prater entered and sat in the chair nearest Sam. Then he continued: "Late yesterday afternoon a fourteen-year-old girl from our town missed the school bus and was walking the four miles out to her daddy's farm when she was dragged into the bushes at the side of the road and raped by three of your oil field workers—"

"What are the men's names?" Tom Prater asked, opening a legal tablet and uncapping his fountain pen.

Rice looked around at Chief Noble, who said, "They haven't been identified as yet."

"Then what makes you say they're Mr. Sheridan's oil field workers? There are fifteen companies drilling in this county."

"It happened near Pistol Hill," the chief said. "The Sheridan field is the one closest to there."

"Even if they *were* Sheridan Oil employees," Prater stated, "their unlawful conduct doesn't impute any legal liability to Mr. Sheridan."

Reverend Adolph Jones stepped forward and said, "We're here to discuss *moral* liability, sir."

Sam remembered the reverend. He was one of the people who had refused to help Georgia and him the day they arrived in Dane. It seemed like a decade ago.

"What exactly do you want, gentlemen?" Sam asked.

The mayor said, "To be perfectly honest, Mr. Sheridan, we don't know *who* raped that young girl. All we know is that it happened when she was walking innocently past the area known as Pistol Hill. And it isn't the first incident of one of our citizens being harassed or molested in some way by people from there."

"That place is Satan's playground," Reverend Jones proclaimed. "It ought to be razed to the very ground on which it stands!"

"Raze it, then," Sam told him. He glanced at Chief Noble. "You've got a lawman. Send him in there and clean the place out."

"Frankly, Mr. Sheridan, we feel that *you* should clean up Pistol Hill." This was Harley Greb speaking. The newspaper publisher. Another who had turned Sam and Georgia away.

"Why?" Sam asked. "I've got nothing to do with Pistol Hill."

"It was your strike that opened up the field," Greb pointed out. "You started all this."

"By that theory I'd be responsible for *everything* that's happened since then. That's stretching the principle of responsibility a bit thin, Mr. Greb."

"Let's stop beating around the bush," Clarence Fort said, speaking for the first time. "This is getting us nowhere. Mr. Sheridan, I am legal counsel for the Township of Dane—"

"And for Spence Land and Cattle," Sam interjected.

"That has nothing to do with the problem at hand, sir." From his inside coat pocket, Fort removed a folded legal document and tossed it on the table in front of Sam. "You are hereby served this class action affidavit bearing the signatures of the mayor and other duly elected officers of the township, advising you that the citizens of Dane consider the area known as Pistol Hill to be a public nuisance in that it presents a clear and continuing threat to the safety and peace of mind of those citizens. The shocking rape of that young girl is sufficient evidence of the claim. This affidavit also advises you that Pistol Hill lies *outside* the township limits of Dane, and therefore is not legally within our jurisdiction. Being outside our boundaries, and since the settlement of Sheridan, still unincorporated, *has* no boundaries, it follows that Pistol Hill is legally a part of Sheridan. We are hereby serving you four weeks' notice, as required by state statute, that unless Pistol Hill is brought under control by you, it is our intention to request that the Texas Rangers be sent in to close it down." Fort glanced around at everyone in the room. "That is all we have to say. Good day, sir."

The lawyer stalked abruptly out of the room, followed quickly by the other six delegates from Dane.

"This is Spence's doing," Sam said, after the delegation left.

"The son of a bitch just won't let up. How's it look?" he asked Prater, who was studying the affidavit.

"I think they've taken a good position."

"What can we do to counter it?"

"We could quickly establish the boundaries of Sheridan somewhere this side of the Hill, and file papers incorporating it as a township, the same as Dane. The two communities would then be on equal footing, with Pistol Hill no more our responsibility than theirs."

"That wouldn't solve the problem of Pistol Hill itself," Sam said, shaking his head. "I don't want the Texas Rangers coming in. Their presence would imply exactly what Spence wants: that Sheridan is some kind of hellhole. We've got good people settling here, and more coming in all the time. A lot of them are moving here from Dane. I don't want them frightened away."

"You could try to shut Pistol Hill down," Prater suggested. "Cut off the profits up there by making the area off limits for all Sheridan Oil employees, and ask the other companies to do the same. Might be kind of hard to enforce, of course."

"No 'might' about it." Draw pushed away from the wall as he spoke for the first time. "It *would* be hard to enforce. Fact, it'd be damned near impossible. Only about half the men working these fields have got families here; the rest are on their own. When they're off shift, they've got to have someplace to go, something to do, some way to let off steam. You *need* Pistol Hill, Sam."

"What's the answer, then?"

"Bring in your own law," Draw advised. "That's what they did in the old days. Brought in a professional shootist to lay down some rules and back 'em all the way. Let them people on Pistol Hill know that they can keep on operating only so long as they stay in their own pasture and don't bring no trouble to either Dane or Sheridan. Make it damn hard for 'em anytime they get out of line."

"What do you think, Tom?" Sam asked.

The lawyer raised his eyebrows. "Might work. Anyone you bring in won't have legal status as a peace officer, of course, but we could remedy that at the next election by having him run for county sheriff. In the meantime, you could call him an oil field security officer or something. You and the other drilling companies can give him authority by acceptance." Prater emphasized his words with a nod. "Yeah. Might just work."

"Let's do it then," Sam decided.

Two nights later Sam and Draw were making their way through the teeming waterfront streets of Galveston. They moved slowly, going from ship berth to ship berth along the great main dock, stopping in bootleg saloons, brothels, gambling houses, seamen's hotels, cafes, tattoo parlors, dance halls, and a variety of other businesses that sought a share of the sailors' shore pay. Sam and Draw had been walking around since sundown, observing. Finally they found the man they were looking for. Sam saw him first. He touched Draw's arm and said, "Take a look at this one."

Draw saw a tall, husky, square-headed young man dressed in the blue uniform of a city policeman. Around his waist he wore a Sam Browne belt with a holstered .44 pistol. In one hand he carried a fourteen-inch nightstick.

"Folks get out of his way when he moves," Draw observed. "That's a good sign. Let's follow him a spell."

They watched the young officer for two hours. During that time he broke up three minor street fights, disarmed a drunk with a loaded Derringer, subdued two thugs who came at him with sheath knives, dispersed several illegally gathered prostitutes, and talked a small group of college boys into leaving the area before harm could befall them.

"He's cool as a brook," Draw concluded. "He's tough. He won't bluff. And there ain't a lick of fear in his eyes. I think he'd do us just fine."

Sam and Draw approached the policeman, introduced themselves, and asked if he would meet with them after his tour of duty to discuss an offer of employment. He agreed, and at one o'clock in the morning, at a fish house called Finnegan's Reef, the three of them had a meal together and talked. The policeman's name was Bill Pete Masters. Now thirty, he had given up the sea three years earlier to join the Galveston Police Department. His superiors, he admitted to Sam and Draw, had told him he was a natural-born police officer.

"That's exactly what we're looking for." Sam explained the situation at Pistol Hill, including the recent attack of the young girl. When Bill Pete Masters heard the story, he shook his head sadly.

"Rape's a terrible crime," he said. "I've a younger sister; I can imagine how I'd feel if it was her who'd been attacked. Sure, I'll come back with you and take the job. I hope I can help you."

The three men shook hands on the deal.

Pop Joyner never left the hospital bed to which he had been confined following his collapse. He was awake and alert for a month after it happened, but could not speak above a whisper or feed himself. Despite the doctors' best efforts, the old wildcatter's condition gradually deteriorated. Everything seemed to be giving out at once.

"A feller can't expect to go on forever," he whispered philosophically to Sam, who stopped in to see him every day. "So I reckon it's time to make some arrangements for my kids." Sam saw what passed for a grin on the unparalyzed side of his face. "I sent money to raise my first four kids until each of 'em was twenty years old, and I'm still sending money to my youngest, my Shawnee daughter up in Tulsey Town; but I ain't seen any of 'em since they was babies. Ever' once in a while one or another of 'em would talk about getting together with me, but I always had some excuse not to. Tell you the truth, Sam, I've always been a little scared of meeting any of 'em. But now that I'm dying, why, hell, I ain't scared of nothin' now except that. So I'd kind of like to meet 'em now, Sam: *all* of 'em." He squinted his good eye. "You don't think I'm an old fool, do you?"

"You know better than that, Pop," Sam told him. "Tell me how to reach them and I'll take care of it for you."

Pop only knew how to get in touch with four of his five offspring. His oldest son, who was forty-eight, lived in Pennsylvania. Another son, in neighboring Ohio, was the same age. They had never met. Two daughters were a generation younger: the eldest, in Baku, Russia, was twenty-three; the half-Shawnee girl from Tulsa was only nineteen. Pop had years earlier lost track of his first child, the half-Burmese daughter born in Rangoon, who was now fifty-three years old.

Sam had Tom Prater contact the Soviet Embassy in Washington to forward a message to the Russian daughter, while he himself got in touch with Pop's two sons. The eldest was a typesetter in Erie, Pennsylvania, who was married and had grown children. The other son was a pharmacist with his own drugstore in Canton, Ohio, also married but childless. Sam talked to them long distance; neither of them was interested in traveling to Texas for the death of a father they had never known. So surprised was Sam at their refusal that he did not even have time to try and persuade them; the calls were over that quickly. Neither would be coming.

The outcome was the same two days later regarding the Russian daughter. She was still in Baku, employed in a government oil laboratory, the only one of Pop's children who had pursued a career in the petroleum industry. "The embassy says she is unable to make such a long journey at this time," Tom reported. "Whether that means she doesn't want to, or they won't let her, I don't know. They might not even have contacted her. You know the Bolsheviks."

"Jesus," said Sam. "I don't suppose there's any way of finding that daughter in Rangoon?"

"We could start looking, but chances are pretty slim. Frankly, I don't think anyone from Rangoon *or* Russia would make it in time anyway. He won't last that long."

"Jesus," Sam repeated.

"There's still the youngest girl. She's a waitress in some cafe up in Tulsa. I'll call her."

"No." Sam shook his head resolutely. "Don't call her. I'm going to go *get* her. That old man's not going to die without at least *one* of his kids here."

Sam had Georgia come with him. They made the nearly three-hundred-mile trip in one day, talked to Rose, the young half-Shawnee girl, that night and drove her back the next day. Pop was delighted when she walked into his hospital room, hugged and kissed him, and called him "Daddy." He had not seen her since she was twelve.

Sam did not lie to the old man about the others. "They just weren't interested, Pop."

The old wildcatter shrugged. "Can't blame 'em none. Little late in the game for me to ask my kids to start treating me like a father." He patted Rose's hand. "This pretty little thing's here; that's plenty for me."

That evening Pop did a lot of reminiscing, telling Rose, Sam, Georgia, and Buddy about some of his adventures in the "old days." As the hours passed, he seemed to grow melancholy.

"I've put up a lot of derricks in my time, spudded in a lot of wells, tapped a lot of oil pools. All the places I been, things I seen and done, somehow it jus' don't seem worth it now. If I had it to do over again, why, I'd of stayed put in one place and watched this little gal of mine grow up. That's what I *wish* I'd done. Having a daughter like this, why, hell, that's worth more than all the oil I ever found."

Rose cried at her father's words; even Georgia had to hold back tears.

Later, when everyone but Sam had gone, Pop said, "You didn't believe that shit I said earlier, did you? That was for the girl. I wouldn't change a goddamned thing, Sam." The old man winked. "It's been a hell of a life."

Ferdinand Joyner left his oil royalties and everything else he owned to Rose. He passed away very late one night, alone in death as he had been in life. He was seventy-eight years old and had devoted a remarkable sixty-three years to the business of "sucking oil."

Shortly after Pop was stricken, Sam emerged from his hospital room one night to find Owen Milam waiting for him.

"I think I've found the man to supervise our field operations," he said, gesturing toward the end of the corridor. Sam looked and saw a tall bony whip-thin man with the pale brown coloring, black eyes, and black hair of a half-breed Indian, but the smooth even facial features of an Anglo. His posture was pole-straight but his arms were loose and relaxed. Long-legged, he looked as if he might be able to run great distances; only the strong set of his mouth indicated that he never would.

"His name is Kee O'Hara," Owen said. "The first name is short for 'Cherokee,' the tribe his mother came from. The other half of him is Irish. He grew up on a reservation in Oklahoma; been working the oil fields for fifteen years, since he was a kid. Right now he's a rigger on Sheridan number six."

Sam was dubious. "I'm not sure how our crews would react to being bossed by a half-Cherokee."

"I thought about that too," Owen admitted. "But O'Hara's got a reputation as a fighter, both with his fists and with a knife. Most of the men I asked about him said they'd never challenge him. And he knows the fields, Sam, probably as well as anyone except Pop and Buddy.

332

Sam was depressed at Pop Joyner's passing. He did not want to spend a lot of time discussing the old wildcatter's successor. And he knew he could trust Owen Milam's judgment.

"All right, if you think he'll do, go ahead and promote him."

"I don't think you'll regret it, Sam." Owen waved his hand and Cherokee O'Hara walked down the corridor toward them. "Kee, this is Mr. Sheridan, owner of Sheridan Oil. He's just approved your promotion to field supervisor. Sam, meet Cherokee O'Hara."

Sam Sheridan and Cherokee O'Hara shook hands.

There was nothing about the meeting to warn either man that he was shaking hands with someone who would drastically alter his life.

47

When the right front tire of her Chrysler blew and Georgia lost control of the car, the first frantic thought that flashed through her mind was: *Oh my god, if we crash Ty will be killed!*

"Hang on to the seat, Ty!" Georgia shouted as she wrestled with the steering wheel.

She held the wheel and managed by some miracle to keep the Chrysler out of a ditch. After the wild, twisting car finally ground to a screeching sideways halt, she looked over and saw Ty with both arms around the back of the passenger seat, holding on for dear life. How determined his young face looked, she thought fleetingly; like Sam's those long months he had worked to bring in the first well.

Getting out of the car, Georgia walked around and looked at the tire. "Son of a bitch," she said, and kicked the miserable tire with the toe of her shoe. The shoe was white and came away with an ugly smudge on it, making her even angrier. "God*damn!*" The car door opened and Ty started to get out. "No, no, no! Stay in the car! I don't want you getting all dirty!"

Pushing some hair out of her eyes, Georgia looked up and down the road. There was not a car in sight, and might not be for an hour; it was a dirt road she had taken, one that ran parallel to the Kilgore highway, about a mile from town. If she had taken the main road that led through Sheridan, someone would already have come along. But not on this road. Shit, she thought. Looking at her watch, she decided she would wait fifteen minutes; if no one happened along by then, she would take Ty and walk the hot dusty mile to town. Sitting down on the running board, she lighted a cigarette and ignored the little face peering down at her from the side window.

They had been there ten minutes, Georgia was about to light her second cigarette, when off in the distance she saw the familiar blue-and-gray colors of a Sheridan Oil pickup truck. It was out on the prairie, going very fast, leaving a swirling cone of dust in its wake. Georgia threw the fresh cigarette down and got quickly onto the front fender. She began waving her arms and yelling. The truck kept going. On impulse, Georgia stripped off her blouse and started waving *it* in the air. Presently the truck slowed down and turned toward them. Relieved, Georgia climbed down, got out another fresh cigarette, and lighted it as she stood waiting for her rescuer. Only when the truck was almost there did she remember that she still had her blouse off. "Oh, Jesus!" She had on no slip, only a brassiere that was sheer, and her nipples, which had darkened considerably since Ty was born, showed through prominently. She managed to get the blouse on and buttoned just as the truck pulled to a stop on the other side of the drainage ditch that ran alongside the road. A tall lean brown man got out and came toward her. Georgia could not tell whether he was a half-breed Indian or just deeply tanned. He wore denims faded almost white, close fitting, she noticed, at the crotch.

"Thank goodness you saw me!" Georgia said as he stepped lightly across the ditch. "I'm Mrs. Sam Sheridan. You must work for my husband."

"Cherokee O'Hara, Mrs. Sheridan," he said easily. "I'm Sheridan Oil's field supervisor. I saw you through my binoculars."

"Oh." Then Georgia remembered her sheer brassiere and dark nipples. "Oh!" she repeated, feeling herself blush.

O'Hara smiled a slight, amused smile. "I'll take care of that tire for you. Maybe you'd better get in the car out of the sun."

Georgia sat in the car with Ty and watched O'Hara change the tire. Before he started he took off his shirt and she saw that he was the same even golden brown all over; but she decided it had to be a suntan, he simply could not be a half-breed, his features were too clean and fine.

"Did you say you were the field supervisor?" she asked through the window.

"That's right, Mrs. Sheridan."

"You took Pop Joyner's place then."

"Took his job, yeah."

What did he mean by that? Georgia wondered. Took his *job,* not his *place?* She watched O'Hara's upper arms ripple as he lifted the flat off and set it aside, then lifted the spare into its place on the wheel.

"I'm surprised we haven't met before now. Sam usually has his new managers out to the house for supper to get acquainted." Oh, god! She regretted it the instant she said it.

"That so?" Kee O'Hara replied. He did not look at her. "Guess I must be an exception, Mrs. Sheridan."

Georgia sensed that her blunder did not bother him in the least. Nevertheless, she tried to undo it.

"Of course, he *has* been very busy lately. Anyway, I'm surprised we haven't run into each other someplace else. Sheridan's not *that* large."

O'Hara stopped working and looked directly at her. "We don't exactly run in the same circles, Mrs. Sheridan." The way he said it sounded almost insulting, as if her circle was beneath his.

"Exactly which circle do you run in, Mr. O'Hara?" she could not resist asking.

"The Pistol Hill circle. I only work in the oil fields to get money to gamble, Mrs. Sheridan." He continued to stare directly into her eyes. "That's what I really am: a gambler." A hint of a smile played at his lips. "Do you gamble, Mrs. Sheridan?"

"Why, no—no, I, ah, don't gamble."

"I didn't think so."

O'Hara resumed changing the tire. When he was finished, he tossed the flat across the ditch by his truck and said, "I'll have the field garage bring a new one out to you." Snatching up a tuft of prairie grass, he started wiping the dirt off his hands.

"Here," Georgia said, opening the glove box, "try these. They're something new, called 'Kleenex.' "

O'Hara took a few sheets and used them. As he put his shirt back on, she realized she was glad that it was short sleeved and would not cover up those gorgeous arms. She watched every move he made.

"Why are you staring at me, Mrs. Sheridan?" he finally asked quietly.

"I'm sorry. You suddenly reminded me a great deal of General Pershing. Except that he had a mustache and was older. My husband served under him in France and I met him once. Were you in the war, Mr. O'Hara?"

"No, I wasn't. I'm half-Indian and half-Irish, Mrs. Sheridan. It's not likely I'd fight in a war for America and England." To himself he added, "The other side, maybe," and Georgia heard him.

So, Georgia thought, he *was* a half-breed, and a smart one, at that. She was impressed. "It sounds like you know your world politics."

"I know what I am, that's all," O'Hara simplified.

They faced each other in silence for a long moment, with nothing else to say, but seeming not to want their meeting to end. But it got to be terribly awkward, facing each other like that, not talking, so finally Georgia said, "Well. Thanks so much for your help."

"A pleasure, Mrs. Sheridan."

Cherokee O'Hara was still standing there as she started the engine, smiled self-consciously at him, and drove off.

After returning from Galveston, Sam had Tom Prater call a meeting with the men in charge of drilling operations for the other independent oil companies in the Black Giant field. Sam told them of the visit by the delegation from Dane, and advised them of the prospect of the Texas Rangers being called in unless Pistol Hill was brought under control. He then introduced Bill Pete Masters and explained the plan Draw had come up with to address the problem. The oil men did not even have to discuss the matter; they voted unanimously to appoint Bill Pete Masters security marshal of the East Texas field. Legally, he had jurisdiction only within the confines of the oil field, but it was made clear to him that he was expected to extend that authority to Pistol Hill. Sam and the other oil men promised him all the legal and financial support he needed.

Bill Pete bought a Forbes Recovery twelve-gauge double-barrel shotgun. With it cradled in one arm, and the young rape victim, in the company of her father and older brother, at his side, he paid his first visit to Pistol Hill. He took the young girl to the door of each saloon and gambling hall along the dirt street and let her look at the myriad of faces inside. At the seventh establishment they came to, a bootleg saloon called Greek George's, the girl tensed at Bill Pete's side. Clutching his arm, she pointed to two men at the bar. "Those are two of them," she said nervously.

Bill Pete let the girl's father and brother take her home. He entered Greek George's alone and walked up to the two men.

"I'm arresting you two for rape," he said calmly. "There was a third man, too: who is he and where is he?"

The two men sized up Bill Pete at once. "We heard about you," one of them said with a smirk.

"You ain't no real lawman," the other challenged. "You can't arrest nobody 'cept in the oil field."

"That so?" Bill Pete smiled a cold smile. "Put your hands on that bar, both of you."

"Go fuck yourself, mister."

Still smiling, Bill Pete swung the stock of the shotgun into the speaker's face, smashing his nose, lips, and teeth in a quick bloody blow. From the corner of his eye, Bill Pete caught a slight motion at one of the tables off to his right, away from the bar. A third man, rising from a chair, was pulling a revolver from the pocket of his oil field coveralls. Bill Pete was already retracting the shotgun, but he knew instinctively that he would not be quick enough; he was going to take a slug.

To Bill Pete's surprise, he was wrong. As he got the shotgun in position to fire, he saw that a tall dark gambler had risen from a nearby card table, drawn a revolver of his own, and put its barrel against the third man's ear.

"Drop it or I'll spill your brains," the gambler ordered.

Bill Pete watched as the gun was tossed onto the floor. Then he realized that the other man at the bar had taken advantage of the opportunity to also pull a pistol. Bill Pete calmly arced the shotgun's barrels back again and fired one of them. The Forbes Recovery had a full choke on it and Bill Pete's blast tore out the man's stomach before he could trigger his pistol.

After the noise of the shotgun blast reverberated into silence, and the blood and guts stopped flying, Bill Pete walked over to the man with the gambler. He held the shotgun muzzle very close to the man's face, his finger on the trigger of the second barrel.

"You rape that young girl?" he asked quietly.

"Y—yes—"

"That one do it too?" Bill Pete bobbed his chin at the man bleeding on the floor.

"Y—yes—"

"And him over there?" he asked, indicating the man he had just killed.

"Y—yes—"

"All right. Throw your friend over your shoulder and head for the door." Bill Pete raised his voice for everyone in the saloon to hear. "If you've got any more friends in here and they try to stop us, I'm going to blow your back off with the load I've got left."

"Nobody's going to try to stop you," the tall gambler said, sticking his own gun back in his belt. "The people up here on Pistol Hill don't like child rapers no better than the people in town do."

Bill Pete nodded curtly. Then he put out his hand. "Bill Pete Masters. Thanks for the help."

"Cherokee O'Hara," the gambler said, shaking hands. "Don't mention it."

Bill Pete delivered the two surviving rapists to Chief Verle Noble at the Dane jail. The next day Bill Pete had a thousand leaflets run off by a printer in New Salem and personally passed them out to every business on Pistol Hill. The leaflets read:

NOTICE

THE AREA BETWEEN THE DANE TOWNSHIP LIMITS AND THE SETTLEMENT KNOWN AS SHERIDAN WILL HENCE-FORTH BE PATROLLED BY MARSHAL BILL PETE MASTERS.

338

ANY AND ALL VIOLATIONS OF THE LAW IN THAT
AREA WILL RESULT IN IMMEDIATE ARREST. ANYONE
RESISTING SUCH ARREST WILL BE SHOT.

BILL PETE MASTERS
MARSHAL

From that day on, Bill Pete Masters never had to kill another lawbreaker. The mere sight of Bill Pete, along with the knowledge that he could and would kill, was enough to dissuade most of the criminally inclined. He took men to jail in Dane once or twice a week, but usually for nonviolent offenses such as larceny or bunco or car theft. The most violent violation he normally had to contend with was brawling, and that rarely ended in arrest; most often Bill Pete just kicked both participants in the rump and sent them their separate ways. He came to be known as a tough but fair lawman; even the bootleggers, gamblers, whores, and pimps eventually developed a grudging admiration for him.

Pistol Hill remained where it was, its drinking, gambling, and whoring totally contained and no longer a bother to the citizens of either Dane or Sheridan.

The Texas Rangers never had to be called to keep the peace.

Once again, Sam Sheridan had won and Pete Spence had lost.

48

Georgia Sheridan had to exert extreme self-control to keep from letting the people she interviewed know how depressing their dirt-poor existence was to her.

"How many children do you have, Mrs. Durkee?" she asked the worn-looking woman across from her. Not much older than Georgia herself, the woman looked forty.

"Five," replied Pearl Durkee. "I got five kids." One was at that moment suckling at her mother's breast. Another, barely able to stand, held onto her mother's chair, a dirty thumb in her mouth.

"Is water your problem, Pearl?"

"Yes'm. We ain't got enough water to wash with, let alone put on crops. We barely got enough to drink. Sometimes Horace slips over to the Conoco filling station when they's busy and gets us a bucketful from their hydrant. We try to keep some on hand for the children; they get so thirsty sometimes at night when it's so hot, they can't hardly sleep."

Georgia and Pearl Durkee were sitting at a bare kitchen table in the dilapidated farmhouse. While Pearl answered her questions, Georgia took notes, although by now she found the practice redundant; the problem was the same on all the small farms: water. Three consecutive years of drought had all but sealed the coffin on the small farmers of East Texas. Sealed it in spite of the fact that each of the farms around Sam Sheridan's land and the Choctaw land now had an oil derrick somewhere on its acreage, and drilling crews sinking a bit into the hard ground around the clock.

"We thought when Mr. Sheridan bought the drilling lease and put up the derrick, that we'd get enough money out of it to get crops going again. But it ain't worked out that way." Pearl shrugged her shoulders, momentarily pulling her nipple from the baby's lips; she quickly replaced it before the infant could protest. "Horace"—she pronounced it "Horse"—"don't understand it. He says we're a'setting smack on top of a ocean of oil. He don't understand why the drillers ain't found it."

Georgia forced a weak smile. "It's not a question of finding it, Pearl," she explained. "We know it's there. It's a question of getting to it. I couldn't understand it either until Mr. Milam, my husband's geologist, explained it to me. It has to do with the formation of the earth, the ground, far under the surface. There may be solid rock under your farm that the drillers will never be able to get through; while the farm right next to yours might be on sand or saltwater or something else that they can drill right through to the oil deposit."

"You mean even if the oil's under both of us, the folks next door could get rich and we could stay poor?" Pearl asked incredulously. "That don't hardly seem fair."

"No, it doesn't." Georgia reached over and brushed dirty blond hair out of the eyes of the toddler sucking her thumb. "That's why Sheridan Oil is trying to find some way of helping the farmers who won't benefit from the oil strike. We don't want you to lose your farms to the bank."

"I reckon we wouldn't exactly lose the place," Pearl said. "Mr. Maye at the bank in Dane, he said if we couldn't meet the mortgage note again this year, that Mr. Pete Spence would take it over, pay us two hundred dollars to boot, and let us stay on as sharecroppers."

Georgia nodded. She had heard the same story at other farms she had visited. Pete Spence, she thought, was like a goddamn vulture sitting up on a telephone pole, waiting for some farm family to suffer financial death so he could swoop down and feast off the carcass. "Has your husband accepted Mr. Spence's offer?"

"No, ma'am. He's thinking on it."

"Well, please tell him not to make a decision until after he sees what Sheridan Oil plans to do. As soon as we finish talking with all the farmers who have nonproducing wells, we'll work out a plan for everyone. In the meantime I'm going to have a Sheridan Oil tank truck stop by here every other day to give you enough water to drink, to cook with, and to bathe. You've got to keep your children clean, Pearl; if you don't, they're going to get sick."

"Yes, ma'am," the worn young woman replied, her eyes shifting downward in humiliation and defeat. And perhaps some fear also, Georgia thought, for she drew the suckling baby a little closer to her.

"That dirty son of a bitch!" Georgia ranted to Sam about Pete Spence that night. They were in Sam's study. "These are *his* people, Sam! These are East Texans, born and bred, some of them second and third generation on the same land. If they were outsiders like us, I could understand his attitude toward them. But they're *his* people, for Christ's sake!"

From behind his desk Sam shook his head. "No, Georgia, they're not. His people are named Spence and Patman. He doesn't feel any more obligation to help the farmers in Caddo County than he feels toward the Dane merchants. That's why so many Dane people are moving to Sheridan. In Sheridan they're treated like people; in Dane, if you're not a Patman or a Spence, you're cattle."

Georgia took a sip of some bootleg Canadian whiskey Sam had

poured for her, shaking her head in frustration as she swallowed it. "What are we going to do for them, Sam?"

"There's only one thing we *can* do for them: irrigate the land. And advance them funds to pay the bank and to live on until they can start producing crops again."

"When, Sam? How soon can we do it?"

Raising a placating hand, Sam said, "Not right away. It takes a lot of planning, a lot of money, a lot of time—"

"These people don't *have* time, Sam!" his wife insisted angrily. "Jesus! If you had *seen* them like I did, you'd know that! Filthy children, a whole family making a meal out of a head of cabbage, drinking water stolen from a filling station in a bucket! Oh, Sam, it's awful."

He came around the desk to where she was sitting and knelt to put his arms around her. Georgia had not cried in a long time; it touched him. "All right," he comforted her quietly, stroking her hair, "all right."

"How *soon,* Sam?" she asked tearfully.

"I've already got Owen surveying to see where a main line can be run in from Chickoree, the nearest water table. Tom is contacting pipeliners for prices and availability. And Dewitt is looking into the possibility of a Dallas or Fort Worth bank cofinancing the project." Sam took a handkerchief from his pocket and dabbed away the wetness on her cheeks. "It's not something that can be done overnight," he said gently.

Georgia shook her head in frustration again. "I just don't see how they'll survive if it takes too long."

"They'll survive," he assured her, "because you'll *help* them survive. That idea of yours to have a tank truck take water around was wonderful. You can come up with other ideas just as good. Get together with Tongue and have him order canned goods and staples wholesale through his store, and distribute them where they're needed. Sheridan Oil will pay for it. Find someone in town who can help you get clothing wholesale too. You can keep them going, honey; I know you can. If you need help, let me know; I'll send Buddy Kyle around to give you a hand."

After she stopped crying and took another sip of her drink, Georgia asked, "What's Buddy been doing since Pop died?"

"Just odds and ends," said Sam, returning to his chair. "The new field super, fellow named Cherokee O'Hara, didn't want him; said he didn't need an assistant."

Cherokee O'Hara. Georgia had thought of him often since their encounter on the back road. "Why didn't we have Mr. O'Hara out to the house for supper when he was hired?"

"I don't know," Sam replied idly.

"Well, there must be a reason," Georgia insisted.

Sam shrugged. "He's not really one of us."

"One of us? I'm not sure I know what you mean."

"Part of the Sheridan Oil family. I don't think he'll be that permanent. I hear he likes to gamble; spends a lot of time up on Pistol Hill. Besides, he's a breed: half-Cherokee."

"Does that make some kind of difference?" Georgia asked, feigning innocence. "I mean, do we treat him differently? Say, than the Choctaws?"

"No, I guess not." A slight frown pinched Sam's forehead. "I don't really know *why* I never had him out. It was right when Pop was dying and everything. Anyway, it's too late now."

"Yes, I suppose it is," Georgia said quietly. "It's good you remembered to invite Bill Pete Masters when he came up from Galveston later. At least we didn't overlook everyone." Before Sam could comment, she asked, "How often may I count on Buddy Kyle's help?"

"Full time if you want him."

"I'll take him. The sooner we're able to give those people some relief from this savage poverty, the sooner I'll be able to sleep nights again."

Sam forgot about Cherokee O'Hara and smiled fondly across the desk at his wife. "I'm very proud of what you're doing, Georgia. I want you to know that."

"Thank you, Sam. That means a lot to me."

Another goal Georgia Sheridan had, one that took root almost as soon as the first well was brought in, was to move her mother to Texas. To accomplish it, she worked on Sam whenever she felt the opportunity was right.

"We should share what we have now, Sam," she said one night. "After all, Mother did let us move in with her when we were first married."

Sam persistently resisted the idea, because he was certain such a move would include his brother-in-law Leon as well. "You can share what we have without moving Alva down here."

"Oh? How?"

"Any way you like. Have her house painted and redecorated. Buy new furniture for her. Send her to Palm Beach for a month."

"That's not the kind of sharing I meant, Sam. I'm talking about sharing our *life:* sharing Ty, sharing our home—"

"You want Alva to move *in* with us?" Sam asked, appalled. He still had memories of Kansas City.

"No, of course not. But she could live near enough to see Ty every day, and have dinner with us on Sundays, and share birthdays and holidays with us."

In all their discussions, neither of them had ever alluded to Leon or whether he would be included in any potential arrangements. Sam decided to bring the matter of his brother-in-law out into the open. If he caught Georgia at a weak moment, maybe he could get a compromise: Alva, no Leon.

"What about Leon?" he asked abruptly. "Would he move out here too?"

Georgia was caught slightly by surprise, but not enough to discompose her. "Well, of course, Sam," she said, as if taking it for granted. "You don't want Mother living with *us,* and I can't have her living alone; especially in the beginning, in unfamiliar surroundings."

Her self-assured reply irritated Sam a touch. He tried at once to put Georgia on the defensive. "Just what do you think Leon would do when he got here? Work for Sheridan Oil?"

Georgia had an answer for that too. "Not at all. He could do what he's best at: running a movie house. Don't you think it's time Sheridan, Texas, had a movie house?"

Sam tried to quickly think of some compelling reason why the town should *not* have a movie house, but Georgia did not allow him time to conjure one up.

"Well, don't you?" she insisted.

"Yes, I suppose," he conceded with a sigh.

Leon. The very name irked him. In all the time he had known Georgia's brother, they had spent only one—*one*—decent evening together: the night before Sam and Georgia left Kansas City. And that occasion had since been overshadowed by Leon's visit to Texas while Sam and Georgia were still living in the line-rider's shack. At that time Sam found Leon to be the same self-impressed prick he had always been. Now Georgia wanted to move him here where Sam would be exposed to him on Sundays and birthdays and holidays. Jesus Christ.

"If you won't do it for me, Sam," Georgia said in a much quieter voice, "then do it for Ty. After all, he *is* entitled to have *one* grandparent. Don't you agree?"

Sam was not prepared for that line of attack either. He remained silent until Georgia insisted again.

"Well, *don't* you?"

"All right, yes, I agree. I'm just not ready to have them move out here yet."

Later, in his study, the matter still bothering him, Sam took a single slip of paper from under his desk blotter and studied it. There was a list of names on it, printed neatly in Sam's own hand. They included Zack Locklear, Quinnie Frazier, Claud Maye, Dr. Alfred Goodley, Rufus Prine, Reverend Adolph Jones, Clarence Fort, Bruce Fort, and Harley Greb. They were the people in and around Dane who Sam felt had wronged him in some way; the people with whom he had felt for so long that he had to get even.

The main name, of course, had not even been written down. Pete Spence. The loathing Sam had felt for Spence was so total, so consummate, that to have included him with the others would have been ludicrous. Pete Spence's name had long ago been etched in a separate place—in Sam's mind. But it was not Spence he was thinking about now; it was Leon.

Sam pondered the problem of his brother-in-law. Leon had made Sam's life miserable from time to time, but he certainly could not be classed with those men of Dane who had treated Sam like some kind of pariah. Toward the men whose names were on his list, Sam still had an intense dislike; toward Pete Spence, he still harbored an abiding hatred; but toward Leon Powell he now felt only a vague resentment. Much of his hostility toward Leon had disappeared when he himself had struck oil and subsequently became wealthy. Leon, for all his boorishness, had suddenly become quite insignificant. If it had not been for Georgia mentioning her mother so often, Sam would rarely have thought of Leon at all.

Sam had been sincere when he told Georgia he was proud of her efforts on behalf of the poor farmers around the Black Giant. Just as he was proud of her for the way she had set up and run Sheridan Realty for him. It had been mainly her planning and foresight that were making Sheridan the attractive little town it was becoming. Things like keeping certain businesses—grocery, butcher, baker, laundry, dry cleaners, tailor—clustered close together to make patronizing them easier. The new medical center was next to the new pharmacy; a library was planned near the post office; dry goods, notions, five-and-ten, were all nearby. Georgia had spent hours on the layout of the town, loving every minute of it. "It's our town, Sam," she said. "I want it to be as perfect as it can be." Which was the same reasoning she applied to her efforts to abolish local poverty. "It's got to be a good town for *everybody,* Sam. Not like Dane."

Not once since the first well came in, Sam realized, had Georgia let him down. And really only one time before then: when she wanted to take Ty and return to Kansas City with Alva and Leon. That, he had long since decided, had been brought on by their own hard times in the line-rider's shack. And she had more than made up for it by giving him the seventy-five dollars she had hoarded for him to buy the core-barrel assembly they had so desperately needed.

She's given a hundred percent, he told himself. Now it was time for him to give a little.

Sam found Georgia at the kitchen table, checking off on a plat map the farms she would visit the next day. Stepping behind her chair, he put his hands on her shoulders.

"Move your mother out whenever you want to. Leon too."

As he said it, he hoped he would not regret it. Georgia rose, turned, and pressed herself against him. Sam had to smile. One thing was for sure—he would not regret it tonight.

49

Georgia worked hard to complete her survey of the farms while Alva and Leon were making arrangements to relocate from Kansas City. She wanted to have the job finished so that she could take some time to help her mother settle in.

"I think you've done them all, dear," Miss Emily said to her late one afternoon in the Sheridan Realty office. "The Lawson place was the last one."

"Isn't there one more?" Georgia asked, unrolling a plat map on her desk. "There's a small place over here in section four, about half a mile up from the creek, I think. I'm sure I saw a house over there."

"That's the Lewt family. No need to bother with them."

"Why not?"

"We don't have a drilling lease there, for one thing; it's state land, never been homesteaded. The Lewts are squatters." Miss Emily paused a beat, her lips tightening slightly. "On top of everything else, Billy Lewt is a squaw man."

"A what? A squaw man?"

Miss Emily nodded darkly, as if some terrible scandal had been exposed. "Got a Choctaw woman and three half-Choctaw brats."

"I see." Georgia sighed inwardly. Texans, she mused. She wondered if *any* society *anywhere* had as many class levels as Texans and Texas had? From the ultrarich like the Spences and the Patmans; the fairly rich like the lawyers Fort; the near-rich like banker Claud Maye; the well-to-do like the businessmen around the town square in Dane; the middle-class townsfolk who worked for those businessmen; the lower middle-class who worked for *them;* the lower class who sharecropped or tried to make a living on their own patch of scrub land; the white trash who loitered around the Dane pool hall and *never* worked; the occasional Negro hired hand; the Choctaw or other Indian; the lazy Mexicans; and at the bottom of the heap, any white man who lived with any woman who was *not* white.

Sheridan, Georgia grimly determined, was not going to have such distinctions—not if she could help it.

"Tell me about this Billy Lewt," she asked Miss Emily.

The little lame woman shrugged. "Not much to tell. He came from a decent family down Crowder way. Came up here to ride for Pete Spence some years back. Took up with a girl from the Choctaw village; got her pregnant. The Choctaws, why, they would've let her stay and have her kid in the village, but they wouldn't allow Billy there; so she ran off to be with him. Pete Spence, when he found out about it, he fired Billy and told him to get off the place. Billy, he took the squaw and went back to Crowder; his daddy took one look at the girl and *he* ran them off too. Finally they came back up here and squatted on that piece of scrub the other side of the creek. Lived in a tent while they built a shack. She had her kid and they've been there ever since. Had two more kids somewhere along the way."

"How do they get by?"

"Scratching as much as they can get from the land. Billy hunts small game, sells the skins when he can; the squaw, I reckon she cans wild berries and such, and she knows how to make food from roots, things like that."

Georgia shook her head incredulously. "How some of these people manage to stay alive amazes me." She rolled the plat map up. "I'm going out to see them."

Georgia knew Miss Emily would not approve, but it would not be the first time they had disagreed. There were several merchants from Dane who, if Emily had had her way, would never have been allowed to relocate in Sheridan. Over the years the little lame woman had developed some strong prejudices and dislikes. Georgia would not have kept her on, but Sam refused to hear of letting her go; he felt adamantly that he owed Emily a permanent debt for being the only woman to befriend his mother when she was in Dane.

"Don't see what you expect to accomplish," Miss Emily said after Georgia announced her intention. "They probably won't even talk to you; they keep strictly to themselves, don't have nothing to do with anybody, Indian *or* white."

"It won't hurt to try. At least I can assure myself that their children aren't being deprived of any necessities. I'll run by the place on my way home."

"Suit yourself," Miss Emily muttered.

"I usually do," Georgia muttered back.

Keys in hand, Georgia walked out onto Pop Joyner Road to her car, a bright yellow Maxwell she had bought a month earlier. Several passersby smiled and spoke to her. Georgia was easily the most recognizable person in Sheridan, including Sam. Flamboyantly familiar in her habitual garb of jodhpurs, riding boots, and colorful Mexican blouses, there was not a person over the age of five who did not know who she was. Some of the newcomers and some of the Mexicans occasionally confused the identities of Sam, Dewitt Tucker, Tom Prater, and Owen Milam, but there was never any question who *Georgia* was. She was the *Señora* Sheridan, and not since Sam's grandmother, Lillian Conway Patman, had a woman occupied a position of such loftiness in Caddo County. Even Ardelle Patman Spence, herself no insignificant power, now stood in Georgia's shadow.

As she drove her shiny new car out of town, Georgia was not even remotely aware of the awe in which most people held her. She simply knew that because of who she was, she could get things done for the people in Sheridan who needed help. That was enough for her.

When she arrived at the Lewt place, Georgia was surprised to find a Sheridan Oil pickup truck parked outside. A tall dark man was lifting a wooden carton out of the truck bed. When she got closer, Georgia recognized him at once as Cherokee O'Hara. She pulled up behind his truck. When he saw it was her, he waited, the carton in his hands, until she got out.

"Hello, Mr. O'Hara," she said, walking over.

"Mrs. Sheridan," he acknowledged with a slight nod.

Glancing at the carton, Georgia saw that it was packed with groceries. "Are you a friend of the Lewts?"

"Kind of."

"I'm not sure I understand that answer," she said, smiling.

"I'm more a friend of the eight-year-old boy, Johnny, than the rest of the family. Johnny shines boots on Pistol Hill on Saturday nights. He gave me a shine one night and we got to be friends. He's got two little sisters, six and four. I bring them a few things once in a while."

"I see. You've sort of adopted the family."

"Not really. Billy Lewt, the daddy, told me to get off the place the first time I showed up. Said he didn't want any charity. The two little girls, why, they don't like me at all because their daddy doesn't like me. And the mother, well, she'd like to be friendly but she knows her husband wouldn't approve; like a good Indian wife, she won't show any disrespect for him. So I guess it's just Johnny I've adopted. But I bring enough for everybody anyway."

"So I see." The carton, Georgia noted, contained cans of condensed milk, stewed tomatoes, spinach, green peas, carrots, and other foods. There were also some twine sacks of okra, potatoes, and corn. And a bag of mixed jelly beans. "Are you going to take it in to them?"

"I usually just leave it on the porch. They aren't at home anyway."

"Oh? How do you know?"

"Johnny told me they were going to Mount Pleasant to visit Billy's brother. I guess he's the only one in Billy's family who hasn't disowned him for taking an Indian woman."

"Becoming a squaw man, isn't that what they call it?" Georgia asked, testing her recently acquired knowledge.

O'Hara nodded. "That's what the whites call it. 'Squaw' is a white man's term; there's no such word in any Indian tongue."

"Oh. I didn't know that."

"Most white people don't."

O'Hara started toward the house and Georgia walked beside him. On the rickety porch he set the carton next to the door. Georgia looked around; the place reminded her of the line-rider's shack. O'Hara fished a partial pack of Avalons from his shirt pocket.

"You smoke, don't you, Mrs. Sheridan?" He offered her the pack.

"Yes," she said, taking one.

"I thought I remembered you having a cigarette in your lips when I saw you through my binoculars the day you had that flat." Digging his thumbnail into a stick match, he lighted both their cigarettes with the same flame.

"I'm afraid that's not all you saw. I had no idea you were looking at me through field glasses."

"We both got fooled. I had no idea you'd turn out to be Sheridan's wife."

Georgia noticed he did not say "Mr." Sheridan. "Would you have come to my rescue if you'd known?"

"Sure." O'Hara smiled. "But maybe not as fast."

Georgia returned his smile. "Let's sit down, shall we?"

They sat on the edge of the porch and smoked. By now it was twilight, the only soft part of the East Texas day; the cool, moisture-filled morning hours past, the harsh, sun-scorched day dead, and cold black night not yet arrived. A pleasant breeze came in off the prairie, wafting wildflower fragrance. Complete silence surrounded them.

"It's really quite nice, what you do for Johnny Lewt," Georgia remarked after a while.

"He's a good boy." O'Hara stared at the ground between his feet. "I know what he'll go through later on, being a half-breed."

"Tell me what he'll go through," Georgia said quietly.

"Mostly he won't belong. He won't be white and he won't be Indian, and neither side will ever accept him. He'll be an outcast. Without choice, he'll have to become a loner. All his life he'll have to take chances, just to break even."

"Is that why you're a gambler, Mr. O'Hara?"

"I suppose. I started taking chances early in life." His eyes caught hers. "I feel like taking one right now."

Georgia swallowed. Jesus Christ. Here? On the front porch of a shanty farmhouse?

But she could not help herself.

"Why don't you?"

O'Hara threw his cigarette into the dirt. Reaching over, he began unbuttoning the fly of her jodhpurs.

50

Georgia hated herself for doing it.

Later that night she had stared at her reflection in a mirror. She felt she had completely nullified all the effort she had put into being completely faithful to Sam. Even when she attempted to qualify the act, tried to salve her conscience with the disclaimer that it was only *one* time, she could not do it. A woman was either faithful or she wasn't.

Georgia wasn't.

Why, why, *why?* she demanded of herself. How could she have been so goddamned stupid?

But it was not stupidity. It had not even been promiscuity, as in her younger days. What she had done with Cherokee O'Hara had been caused by something else: something deeper, stronger, more compelling. It frightened her. Even lying with her back up against Sam's hard body that night, where normally she felt safest of all, she was frightened. This feeling was something unlike anything she had ever experienced, something she did not completely understand, something she was not at all sure she could handle.

It disturbed Georgia to think that this might be love. Because if it *was,* then she had been missing it all her life. She had mistaken and accepted other, much weaker feelings for it. She had only been sipping at a spring in which she had now bathed.

But Georgia was not certain. The desire for O'Hara had been overwhelming; she wondered if she was trying in her mind to *make* it love, and in that way perhaps justify it. After all, a woman in *love* could not be held totally accountable for her conduct. But those thoughts made her even angrier at herself. Goddamn it, she thought, why should she *have* to justify something that felt so marvelous, something that made her feel for the first time ever that all the *parts* of her were connected; that she wasn't just cunt here, tits there, ass behind; that they were instead part of a *whole* being, a complete woman.

A great terrible fear crept into Georgia's thoughts. Had it been so good simply because she had been such a long time with no one but Sam? Or had it been that way because of *him,* O'Hara, because of *her,* because of *them,* together?

Georgia could only shake her head in confusion. God help her, she did not know. She did not know *any* of the answers. There was only one thing that she *knew.*

Cherokee O'Hara was constantly in her thoughts.

Georgia fervently hoped that the arrival of her mother and brother from Kansas City would help her put O'Hara out of her mind. She threw herself totally into making preparations.

"I wonder if we should have made it larger?" she asked Sam of the house that was being constructed for them. It was within walking distance of the mansion in which Sam, Georgia, and Ty now lived. The mansion stood near the old line-rider's shack. Georgia had assumed that the shack would be torn down when the mansion was built, but Sam decided to let it stay standing.

"It'll be a good reminder of everything we once didn't have," he explained. "Keep us from becoming like the Spences."

"Sam, really." Georgia herself would have had the place razed.

"Besides, it's where Ty was born. If he ever becomes President of the United States, it'll become a national monument. Like Lincoln's log cabin."

As regarded Alva and Leon's house, Sam let Georgia do whatever she wished. "If you think it's too small, stop construction and call the architect back."

"What do *you* think, Sam?"

"It has ten rooms, Georgia. That's four more than they had in Kansas City." Sam silently prayed that Georgia would not interrupt the construction. Alva and Leon would be living with them until the house was completed; the briefer that period was, the better.

"I suppose it's large enough," Georgia said at last, to his great relief. "What about the movie house?"

"I've already spoken to Dewitt about financing it for Leon. As far as where to build it, I thought we'd let him have the lot next to the ice cream parlor that fellow from Dallas opened."

Georgia's eyebrows shot up. "That's very generous of you, Sam; that's a prime location."

Sam shrugged and Georgia immediately felt a new wave of guilt. Here Sam was extending himself for her brother, someone he never liked, while his supposedly devoted wife was fresh from spreading her legs for one of his employees. She did not even attempt to suppress the guilt, hoping it would make her feel detestable. It did not. Every thought of O'Hara, even accusatory ones, sparked new desire for him. It frightened her, the intensity with which she wanted him again.

It seemed to Georgia that it took an eternity, but finally Alva Powell completed the sale of her modest home in Kansas City, and Leon quit his job with Essaness Theaters after fourteen years, and they drove to Texas. On the day they arrived, Georgia got them settled temporarily in the mansion, then hustled them into her yellow Maxwell for a tour of Sheridan. She was overflowing with pride about the growing little town she and Sam had created, but even as she gave Alva and Leon a brief history of each business along Pop Joyner Road, she still kept a covert eye out for O'Hara. When she did not see him, she abruptly decided to extend the tour to the oil field itself. For most of the afternoon, she took the newcomers up and down dirt roads, from the pump that replaced the derrick where Sheridan number one came in, through the complete sequence of pumps and derricks on Sheridan wells two through thirty-two, the majority of which were on small farms or Choctaw land. At the end of the hot dusty drive, Alva and Leon were exhausted. And Georgia had failed to catch even a glimpse of Cherokee O'Hara.

The presence of Leon Powell in Sam's home reawakened some of the old resentment he had felt toward him for so long. Not to the extent that he wanted to hurt Leon or get even with him in any way, but merely to *show* Leon that if he wanted to, he could. After supper their first night there, Sam had taken Leon into his richly furnished study and poured him a drink of the finest Canadian whiskey that money could illegally import. Then Sam opened his safe and removed a sheaf of hundred-dollar bills.

"How much do you figure I owe you, Leon?" he asked, sitting at his desk. "From when Georgia and I lived with you and Alva?"

Leon blushed. "I don't know, Sam. It's been so long—"

"It hasn't been *that* long, Leon." Sam broke the paper band on the bills and spread them out. "How much?"

Leon shrugged self-consciously. "Sam, really, I never kept track of it."

"You used to keep track of every *penny,* Leon." Sam's unblinking eyes were fixed on his brother-in-law. "You used to have your mother recite to Georgia and me on a regular basis the price of a quart of milk and a loaf of bread and a dozen eggs."

Leon swallowed dryly. His spine felt suddenly cold. And he had a sudden urge to go to the bathroom.

"How much, Leon?"

"A hundred dollars?" Leon replied weakly. "Is that all right, Sam? I want to be fair."

Sam pushed one of the hundred-dollar bills across the desk. He continued to stare at Leon until his brother-in-law picked it up. His eyes seemed to say: This isn't Kansas City, this is Texas. Things are different in Texas. Remember that.

When Sam was satisfied, he let Leon save face. "I'll take you up to the bank in the morning and you can arrange for the loan to build your movie house. From then on, it will be up to you. I hope you do well as a member of the Sheridan business community."

"I will, Sam, I promise," Leon said quickly. "I won't let you down. You can count on me."

Leon kept that promise. Sam had rarely seen a man work with such dedication and enthusiasm. Leon personally designed the new theater, supervised the construction of it from the ground up, and oversaw the installation of its seats, screen, and projection equipment. When it was completed, he named it the Georgian, after his sister, and held a gala grand opening one Saturday that included free movies for the entire town from 8:00 A.M. until midnight, along with all the free popcorn anyone wanted.

While Leon had been planning his all-day open house, Georgia suggested that he also hold an invitation-only dedication the previous evening, for the Sheridan business people and other select individuals. On the guest list that Georgia herself prepared for the occasion, she included the name of Cherokee O'Hara.

The dedication party turned out to be a rousing success. When Georgia checked the invitations the following morning, she found that all but one had been turned in at the door.

That one belonged to Cherokee O'Hara.

Georgia gradually grew desperate to see him again. She went into town at times when she thought he might be there: during the noon hour; shortly after the day shift ended; on Saturday afternoon when, it seemed, *everyone* was in town. She even took to making random runs along the back road where she had the flat, in the hope of seeing him out there again. If she kept circulating, she told herself, she *had* to run into him sooner or later.

Each time before she went out, Georgia primped for twenty minutes, just in case that would be the time she encountered O'Hara. Abandoning her jodhpurs, Mexican blouses, and boots, she started dressing decidedly more femininely. Before a full-length mirror she made sure her flapper dress hung just right, that her stockings were pulled up tightly and rolled securely so they wouldn't bag, that her makeup was applied flawlessly, her combed-out hairdo just so. Several times she got a feeling of déjà vu, realizing that she had done the same things years earlier in Kansas City when she had been going out with the expectation of being picked up, of ending up in bed with a new man. That brought on still a new wave of guilty feelings, which took a concerted effort to control. By now she had stopped letting the guilt consume her; there was nothing she could do about how she felt, so she refused to continue punishing herself. She became quite good at excising guilt. The ability to do so, she sometimes felt, was all that kept her sane.

After a month of pretending to be on important errands, of furtive glances up and down Pop Joyner Road to see if he was around, of ridiculous drives to nowhere on back roads, she grew angry and resentful of the whole affair. She began to imagine that O'Hara was secretly watching her from concealed places so that he could purposely avoid her. Times like those she cursed him for the half-breed son of a bitch she was sure he was. But she was immediately contrite. I didn't mean that; please, I'm sorry I thought that; just let me see him one time to find out if he feels the same way I do. Just one time. Georgia was not sure to whom she was silently praying; but she *was* praying.

On a rare day when she was not consciously looking for him, she finally ran into him. She was leaving Evelyn's French Wave Beauty Parlor and O'Hara was coming out of Tru-Valu Drugs with a carton of Avalons in one hand. They stopped on the sidewalk, close enough to touch.

"Hello," he said quietly.

"Hello." Just as quietly.

Something about him was different; it took Georgia a moment to realize what. She half smiled. "You've grown a mustache."

"I wanted to look more like General Pershing."

"You do." Georgia took a deep breath, steeling herself. "I have to ask you something. Have you been avoiding me? I've been trying for weeks to run into you. I've prowled this street morning, noon, and night; I've driven back roads; I've—"

"So have I," he interjected.

"—even gone into the oil field." Georgia frowned. "What did you say?"

"I said, so have I. Prowled this street, driven the back roads. I've driven past your house a couple dozen times, hoping to catch you leaving so I could follow you. I even bought a new suit to go to that movie theater opening. Then I saw you there with your husband and brother and mother and all the bigwigs from town; I knew I wouldn't be able to get a minute with you, so I didn't even go in."

Georgia closed her eyes and lowered her head, shaking it briefly at the absurdity of it all. Then, remembering that she was on a public street, she quickly composed herself.

"How do you feel about this?"

"About what?"

"*This.* Me."

"It's pretty plain how I feel about you, isn't it? I'm in love with you. If I wasn't, do you think I'd be driving myself crazy trying to find you?"

"I suppose not," Georgia replied quietly.

"I want you again." His pitch-black eyes moved down to her lips, where they paused; down to her throat, where they paused; down to her breasts, where they paused. Georgia felt her nipples become hard. She glanced around to see if anyone was watching them; no one appeared to be. O'Hara's eyes kept moving. Down to her belly and hips, and paused. Down to the slight fold in the front of her dress where her legs came together. And paused. Paused there longer than anyplace else. Georgia's whole being grew warm with excitement. His eyes moved back up to her face. "I want you now."

"Where?" Her throat constricted on the word.

"Head out Route Thirty-one," he told her. "Couple miles south of town, you'll come to a roadhouse called the Cactus Club. Park around at the side. I'll pick you up."

"All right."

O'Hara picked her up in a car she had never seen before and drove her to a little house he rented at the edge of Pistol Hill. She did not speak a word to him, nor he to her, on the way. He parked behind the house and led her through the back door and into a bedroom. After pulling the shades, he took her in his arms.

"We're crazy," she whispered. "It's broad daylight."

He kissed her neck and her throat, while he undid the buttons down the back of her dress. Pulling it off her shoulders, he let it drop around her waist.

"I'd never cheated on Sam before you," she said, starting to cry. "I'd thought about it, but never done it."

O'Hara slid the straps of her slip and brassiere off her shoulders, pulled the slip to her waist, and took the brassiere off completely. Bending, he kissed and sucked her nipples.

"I love you, I love you," Georgia whispered.

In seconds he had her dress and slip the rest of the way off, had her shoes off, her step-ins, everything but her hose, which were rolled and gartered at her thighs. He sat her on the side of the bed and while she watched removed his own clothes. She stared in fascination at his erection, inches from her face. Kneeling, he gently parted her knees.

"Oh my god—" she gasped, when she saw what he was going to do.

O'Hara put his lips on her, looked up over her belly and saw the nipples of her breasts standing up rigidly from the dark, dark areolas that he remembered seeing through his field glasses. His tongue made a swath through her hair and he pressed his lips to her lips and drew in the taste of her.

Georgia began a soft, steady moan.

358

51

After their second time together Georgia was totally consumed by, totally committed to, her love for Cherokee O'Hara. The hours of her existence began to run together in a new series of time segments that began and ended when she was with him. No longer were there days or weeks or months. No longer was she aware of the clock or the calendar. Only her inner senses recorded the passage of time. For her it was now divided into two parts: heaven, when she was with Kee; hell when she was not.

When she could manage to be out of the house after dark—if Sam stayed late at the office or took Ty somewhere—she would drive to a meeting place and Kee would pick her up. She traded her bright yellow Maxwell for a smaller, less striking car, a dark blue Vauxhall, that was not as conspicuous. Most of the time she parked it behind Tully's roadhouse, so that if anyone saw it she could say she had been visiting Reba. She told Reba about the affair, in case her friend had to cover for her. Reba was surprised by Georgia's infidelity but did not try to talk her out of it.

"I ain't never seen you this happy," she told Georgia, "so I reckon it must be good for you. I just hope you get it out of your system before you get caught. Sam could kill you both, you know, and walk away scot-free. That's how it is in Texas when a married woman cheats."

Reba's warning fell on deaf ears. Georgia kept meeting Kee, as often as she could. After Kee would pick her up and take her to his house, they would revel in an hour or two of naked enjoyment of each other, doing everything that Georgia had dreamed and fantasized and longed to do for so many years. Kee was totally uninhibited, unashamed, unrestrained; he touched her, kissed her, licked her, bit her, tasted her, sucked her, put his fingers in every part of her, put *himself* in every part of her, *used* every part of her, and each time made her feel complete and whole and absolutely female all over again. She took the come from his body in a dozen different ways and places, and at night dreamed that she was in a bathtub with Kee O'Hara standing next to it, filling it and covering her with an endless stream of his semen.

When nights were impossible, as so often they were, Georgia drove into the woods and met him during the daytime in a place he found not far from Draw and Tongue's old camp: a clearing just large enough for her car and his pickup truck, concealed from all but immediate view by an overgrown thicket and tangled vines. They were almost as abandoned out there under the open sky as they were in Kee's bed. He spread a quilt in the back of the pickup, or on the ground, or over the hood of her Vauxhall, and they performed for each other's body like two perfectly synchronized machines, Georgia's pale white, Kee's golden brown, both warmed by the East Texas sun, or wet with the East Texas summer rain. In winter when it was cold, they undressed in the cab of the pickup or on the backseat of the Vauxhall, leaving the motor running, the heater on, and contorted their bodies to whatever space restrictions the vehicles imposed on them. Nothing stopped them: not inclement weather, too little time, husband, child, employer, job, threat of discovery, conscience, menstruation, not even illness. They needed one another with an urgency beyond desperation. It simply *had* to be.

In her growing familiarity with Kee's lean, brown, lithe body, by far the most beautiful male body she had ever seen, Georgia became acutely aware of her own not-so-perfect self. True, she had regained her slimness in comparison to her condition during pregnancy, but on critical, naked examination before her full-length mirror at home, she realized that she was no longer the Georgia Powell of 1915, or even the Georgia Sheridan of 1920. Two pregnancies, one childbirth, and an abortion had added a pound here, an inch there, a sag where there was once only firmness, a stretch mark where there was once only smoothness. She was not yet thirty, but she was far from eighteen. Her body, still attractive, still desirable, was nevertheless soft and spreading. While Kee's was like a rock. The difference disturbed her.

"You're crazy," Kee told her when she mentioned it to him. "There's nothing wrong with your body. I love your body."

"You love my body? Or you love me?"

"What's the difference? You. Your body. I love everything about you."

"Honest?"

Kee frowned. "Sure, honest. You think I could fuck you the way I do if I didn't love you?"

"Oh, Kee. That's no way to measure love. You've probably fucked more women than you can remember."

"I have. But not the way I fuck you. You almost become a part of me when we're doing it. No matter how we're connected—by hand, mouth, cunt, cock—we seem to change from two people to just one. It's never been like that for me before, Georgia."

"Honest, Kee?" She sounded like a schoolgirl, she knew, but it did not matter. Not if it was true. Not if he felt about her as she did about him. And she was certain he did.

Georgia tried more than once to analyze her love for Kee. It was a feeling that enthralled her and she wanted to know as much as possible about it and about him. In their afterglow, lying in the dark smoking, she pestered him with questions about everything: his parents, the reservation, growing up, running away, being on the road, learning to gamble, developing the silent inner strength that he seemed to exude even in his quietest moments. In some ways he was the most *alone* person she had ever met; not *lonely:* he was too individualistic, too autonomous, to be lonely; his self-reliance precluded loneliness. But he was so totally by himself; clearly the outcast from both races that were part of him, just as he said young Johnny Lewt would be someday. Yet he could be so childlike sometimes in his need for her. Where Georgia was concerned, he no longer wanted to *be* alone. That was what she was more grateful for than anything. Even the physical gratification, which was enormous, fell second to the knowledge that Kee *needed* her.

They had only one disagreement during their affair: when Georgia offered Kee money. He had casually mentioned that as soon as he had a little more money saved he would be quitting his Sheridan Oil job and buying a partnership in a small gambling club on Pistol Hill.

"Why wait?" Georgia had asked. "Tell me how much more you need and I'll give it to you. I have my own bank account, you know."

Kee's expression had darkened. "No, thanks. I'll have it on my own before long."

"But, Kee, that's silly. Honey, I've got plenty of money. You're welcome to—"

"I *know* you've got plenty of money, Georgia. I know your husband is the richest man in East Texas! And I know I'm just a half-breed Indian that works in his oil field! But I *am* a man, Georgia! I *can* do things on my own!"

"All right, Kee, all right." She had never seen him angry before. "I'm sorry. I didn't mean to offend you."

"Well, you *did* offend me!" he snapped. "All my life I've seen bigwig whites lording it over the Indians and the breeds with their goddamned money. Thinking they could *buy* anything. Buy the land, buy the labor, buy the women! The white man always gets what he wants with his money, even if he makes the Indians and the breeds feel like they're *less* than men. Well, this is one half-breed that's his *own* man. I don't *want* any white man's money—except what I work for or win!"

"All right, Kee, all right," Georgia said again, trying to soothe him. "I'm sorry. I didn't know how you felt."

She finally got him calmed down. He never mentioned the incident after that night. Not that it was necessary, because Georgia never *forgot* it.

And she never offered him money again.

One uncommonly cold day in mid-September Georgia had been without Kee for six days and nights, and was drawn to a nervous edge. Three wells had come in, one after another, all in separate fields on the other side of the Spence ranch, and all requiring Kee's presence. Sam had mentioned that they were all capped, so she knew Kee would be back in his field office now. She was desperate for him.

Sam was getting ready to drive up to Longview for an all-day business meeting with the other Black Giant drillers. Ty had already been sent off to his morning kindergarten class. While Sam was in the shower, Georgia called Miss Emily at the realty office.

"Em, I won't be in until later. I have a raging migraine that I've got to get rid of before I leave the house. I'll probably see you around noon."

That settled, Georgia quickly figured how she could get rid of the household help. The cook she would send uptown to do the week's shopping a day early. The houseboy would go with her, as usual. The two Mexican girls she would invent errands for. Thank God, she thought, it was the housekeeper Mrs. Pilcher's regular day off.

With Sam's shower still running, she called Kee. "I'll have this house empty in about an hour, if you're interested."

"Your house?" Kee hesitated. He had never set foot in the Sheridan mansion. Fucking Sam Sheridan's wife was one thing; but fucking her in Sam Sheridan's *home?*

"What's the matter?"

"I don't know. His *house.* I mean—"

"It's also *my* house," Georgia said urgently. "Kee, *please.*"

There was something initially distasteful to Kee about the idea. As if by doing it, he would lose some of his pride. "I don't know," he said again, his voice reflecting his uncertainty.

"Kee, I *need* you," Georgia pleaded. "I've been going crazy without you."

"Can't we meet out in the brush?"

"It's too cold this morning and I can't wait until this afternoon. Besides, I want you stretched out straight, not bent over double in a car. *Please,* Kee."

She sounded so desperate. "All right," he agreed at last. "How?"

"Park in the trees behind our back fence. Wait until the only car left is mine. Then come to the back door. I'll be waiting."

The next hour seemed interminably long. Sam did everything but leave: trimmed his toenails, pulled a button off his shirt and had to change, decided to have an extra cup of coffee, fooled around with a Labrador puppy Draw had given Ty. Behind his back Georgia glared at him; she was infuriated by *anything* that kept her from Kee, and her husband was no exception. Finally, to keep from screaming at him, she went to the kitchen and proceeded to assign errands to the household help, working it so they would each have to go to several places looking for unusual items: purple thread, beeswax, a bottle of green ink, a star-shaped cookie cutter. She also organized their transportation. There were four cars parked behind the mansion. Sam would take one; the cook and the houseboy one; and the two Mexican girls she was sending on errands one. That would leave just her car. Now if she could just get everybody the goddamn hell *going!*

She finally got the procession started: the cook and the houseboy first; then Sam kissed her on the cheek and left; and as soon as he was off, she was shouting at the two Mexican girls to *please hurry!* In the course of five minutes, there were cars heading off in all directions.

Suddenly Georgia was in the house alone. In the silence, she froze. What in the name of God was she *doing?* Bringing Kee into her own home, into *Sam*'s home? This was insane.

But she could not help herself. She had to do it.

Hurrying upstairs, Georgia began undressing in the hall while watching out a back window for Kee. She was down to her underwear when she saw him step from the concealment of the trees, vault their back fence with one hand, and hurry toward the house. Leaving her clothes where they fell, she ran down the stairs and opened the kitchen door just as Kee ran onto the porch.

"I'm about to *burst* for you." She pulled open his Levi's jacket and began to unbutton his shirt.

"Me too, for you." He ran his hands over her bare shoulders, glancing around apprehensively. "Are you sure this is all right?"

"Come *on,* Kee!" Still unbuttoning his shirt, she pulled him up the stairs and into the master bedroom suite. "I want your mouth all over me. Hurry!"

In seconds they were both naked and at each other's hungry body on a thirty-thousand-dollar Oriental rug that Georgia had bought for the bedroom. With Kee lying on his back, Georgia lowered herself above him and rode his face like a saddle.

"I'd have *died* this morning without you." Her words were punctuated by the throw of her hips. "Jesus God, this is—so—goddamned good—"

When her legs got too tired to maintain the position, she straightened, pulled him to his feet, and sat on the corner of the bed with him in front of her.

"Fuck my mouth, Kee."

Georgia had no idea how much time had passed. For her, when she was with Kee, time was measured not in minutes but in positions. Kee was in her mouth, then her legs were being pushed apart and he was leaning over to enter her, then he was on his knees using his mouth, then standing again, in her mouth again . . .

Then Sam was there in the doorway looking at them, and it was all over.

Everything that had been was over.

52

Georgia and Kee stared at Sam, both of them stricken, shocked, frozen in position like obscene statues. Then Georgia became aware that Sam was coming into the room, walking around the bed. Terror tore at her heart.

"Kee, he's got a gun over there!"

Cherokee O'Hara made a desperate dive across the bed. But he was not nearly quick enough. Sam jerked open the drawer of his bedtable and snatched out a silver-plated, pearl-handled .38 revolver with his name etched in gold on the barrel. The weapon had been a gift from Draw on Sam's last birthday. Now he pointed it at Kee O'Hara's face and cocked the hammer.

"Sam, for God's sake, don't!" Georgia shrieked.

O'Hara crouched motionlessly on the bed, his black eyes fixed not on the gun but on Sam, his lips parted tentatively as he tensed himself to be shot.

"I ran into a ditch," Sam said dully, as if required to explain his presence. "I swerved to miss a jackrabbit and I ran into a ditch. So I walked back to call the field garage—" Blinking several times, then shaking his head clear, he seemed to refocus on Cherokee O'Hara. "Get the hell off my bed." His voice seemed almost totally foreign to Georgia, and it was the most broken voice she had ever heard. Sam's normally clear precise tones came out raspy, strained.

"Sam, for God's sake, don't shoot!" Georgia begged.

"You shut up! Move ahead of me, O'Hara," Sam ordered, nodding toward the door. "Downstairs." Kee reached for his trousers. "No!" Sam snapped. "No clothes! Just move!"

"Sam, what are you going to do?" Georgia bawled, tears streaking her cheeks. "Tell me, Sam—"

"Shut up!"

Sam marched the naked Kee to the bottom of the stairs and halted him in the foyer. At a table there Sam picked up a telephone receiver and signaled the operator. "Central, this is Sam Sheridan. First I want you to ring the field shack at Sheridan number three for me; then I want you to call Sheriff Masters and tell him I said come out to my place as quickly as he can."

"Yes, sir, Mr. Sheridan."

Halfway down the stairs, pulling on a chenille bathrobe, Georgia felt a surge of relief. If Sam was sending for Bill Pete Masters, it meant he did not intend to kill Kee. Thank you, God. She began to sob loudly.

Sam listened to the phone ring a dozen times, then a gruff voice answered, "Yeah, Sheridan number three."

"Sam Sheridan speaking. Who's this?"

"Scotty Welch, Mr. Sheridan. Crew boss."

"Bring your whole crew across the field to my house, Scotty. Quickly, please." Sam hung up. "Outside," he told Kee. He walked him out the front door, across the drive, and over to the fence. Georgia, barefoot, in her robe, followed them.

"What now?" Kee asked, his back to the fence.

"I'm going to whip you," Sam said evenly.

Georgia stared at her husband with wide, frightened eyes. "Sam, no! You can't!"

"I can," Sam assured her. "And I will. Either that, or I'll shoot him. It's his choice."

"And her?" Kee asked. "You going to whip her too?"

Sam looked hatefully from one to the other, then shook his head. "I wouldn't waste leather on her. But I intend to see you bleed."

Beyond the fence the four-man crew from Sheridan number three was hurrying toward them.

"Sam, please!" Georgia pleaded. "Just let him go! Put down the gun, Sam, please!"

"Don't beg for me," Kee O'Hara told Georgia sharply. He raised his chin an inch. "I've been whipped before."

"Not like I'm going to do it, you haven't," Sam promised. His four men trotted up and Sam said to the first two, "Take off your belts and strap his arms to the fence."

"Sam, Jesus Christ, no!" Georgia screamed.

"Do it!" Sam ordered.

"Stop begging him, Georgia." Hearing his wife's name on Kee O'Hara's lips made Sam turn white with fury. Kee smirked and calmly turned to face the fence, arms straight out. In seconds the derrick workers had him strapped in place.

"Let me have your belt," Sam said to a third man. When Georgia rushed forward, screaming again, arms flailing at Sam, he said, "Hold her!" and his men grabbed Georgia by the arms and restrained her. With the heavy leather belt loose in his hand, Sam planted himself firmly behind Cherokee O'Hara. "Say goodbye to your back, half-breed."

"Fuck you," Kee said.

Sam started lashing. The belt landed on its flat side first, then on its edge, flat side, edge, in rhythm with Sam's swing. At first it turned Kee's golden flesh an angry red, then a deep brown. With Georgia's relentless screams filling his ears, Sam whipped Kee's shoulders, upper back, lower back, buttocks, and the back of his thighs. It took no more than four lashes in each area to snap the skin open; then the belt began to draw droplets of blood. Every time Sam drew it back, a few drops of fresh blood would fly through the air, like red raindrops. It hit Sam, Georgia, the men: spotting their faces, arms, clothes. Still Sam continued to lash. Kee never screamed, never cried out, but after a while terrible gruntlike moans began to escape his clenched teeth.

Ruthlessly, Sam whipped Kee's skin to shreds, the entire back of his body from shoulders to knee joint turning to pulpy gore. The other men there were sure Sam would have beaten him completely to death if the sheriff had not arrived.

Bill Pete Masters, once the East Texas Oil Field security marshal, was now, by official election, sheriff of Caddo County, with an office, jail, and four deputies in Sheridan, the newly selected county seat. As soon as Bill Pete received Sam's urgent message, he got in his patrol car and drove directly to the mansion. When he saw what was happening, he leaped from the car and rushed over to grab Sam's arm and stop him. "What in the hell's going on, Sam!" he demanded, shocked by the sight of Kee O'Hara's back. "Take him down from that fence!"

Sam, laced with sweat from his effort, still pale with anger, stood breathing heavily as Kee was unstrapped and lowered gently, face down, to the ground. Georgia rushed over and dropped to her knees beside him, crying hysterically.

"Jesus Christ, Sam," said Bill Pete Masters, "you can't do a man like that."

"I did it." His voice was a clear challenge. He pointed to Kee and Georgia. "I want them both out of this town, this county"—he stopped and shook his head— "no, out of this *state*. I want them out of Texas. Today."

"I can't force people to leave the state, Sam—"

"I want them *out,* goddamn it! *Today,* goddamn it! You get hold of Tom Prater; he'll find a way for you to do it."

"Sam, Georgia's your wife," Bill Pete tried to reason with him. But Sam shook his head emphatically.

"She stopped being my wife," he said hoarsely, "when she took that half-breed's cock in her mouth." Sam's eyes fixed unblinkingly on Bill Pete. "I want this done." There was no equivocacy in his tone. Bill Pete Masters knew that Sam would accept no alternative.

"All right, Sam," he said quietly.

Two hours later at the jail, a Sheridan doctor finished dressing Kee's back and gave him a bottle of morphine tablets. "Take one of these with some whiskey when the pain is severe," he instructed. "They won't *stop* the pain, but they'll ease it some. The dressing will have to be changed every three days. There's no telling how long it'll take you to heal: six months, maybe a year. You'll never be the same again, so don't expect to be. Your days of doing hard work are over."

They were in an open jail cell, Kee facedown on the bunk, still naked, Georgia kneeling next to his head gently washing his face with a damp cloth. The doctor closed his medical bag, glanced distastefully at Georgia but did not speak to her, and left the cell. Bill Pete Masters and Tom Prater came in. The sheriff handed a bundle of clothes to Georgia.

"Here are some things of mine that'll probably fit him," he said, bobbing his chin at Kee. "The women's things I got at the dress shop up the street and charged to the county. They're not fancy but they'll do you."

"Why can't I have my own clothes, from the house?" Georgia asked angrily.

Tom Prater answered her. "You know why as well as we do, Georgia. Sam won't let us take a thing for you."

"For Christ's sake, Tom. Sam Sheridan isn't *God!*"

"He's the next thing to it in Caddo County. Now you and your friend here put on those clothes and Bill Pete is going to drive you to the Oklahoma line."

"Bullshit!" Georgia stormed. "You can't do that to us! God-damn it, Tom, that's illegal and you know it!"

"You listen to me, Georgia," Tom said harshly, "and I'll tell you what's *illegal*. What Sam caught you and O'Hara doing is *illegal*. We've got a miscegenation law here in Texas. It is *illegal* for a Caucasian female and a non-Caucasian male to engage in any form of sexual intercourse. We also have sex perversion laws in Texas. It is *illegal* for one person to copulate the sex organs of another with his or her mouth. Now then, if you want to insist on your right to remain in Texas, the sheriff here is going to charge both of you with violation of those two statutes. You're going to be tried, you're going to be convicted, and you're going to be sent to prison, probably for about ten years apiece. O'Hara will go up to Huntsville and probably wind up on a road gang. You, Georgia, will go to the women's prison and probably serve your time working in the burlap factory. If that's what you want, it can sure as hell be arranged." Tom Prater's glare was as mean as his voice. "Y'all make up your minds what you want to do. I'll give you five minutes."

The young lawyer walked out of the cell.

Thirty minutes later Kee O'Hara was lying sideways in the backseat of a patrol car with his head in Georgia's lap, and Bill Pete Masters was driving the couple north out of Texas.

When they got outside Harris, the first town across the Oklahoma line, Bill Pete pulled to the side of the highway and stopped. Turning in his seat, he said, "Georgia, you want me to find a hospital for him?"

"No hospital," O'Hara answered before Georgia could speak. "They wouldn't let me in anyway, Masters; you know that." Painfully, he raised his head from Georgia's lap. "Where are we?"

"Town limits of Harris," Bill Pete said.

"Can you take us a little farther?" Kee asked.

"I'll take you wherever you want to go, O'Hara. I owe you one, remember?"

Kee nodded slightly. "Northeast of here about twenty miles is a town called Moon. There's some Ouachitas living there. They'll take us in." O'Hara's eyes rolled up as he got the last word out and he dropped his head back into Georgia's lap, unconscious.

As Bill Pete pulled back onto the road, Georgia asked, "What are Ouachitas? Indians?"

Bill Pete nodded.

"But he said he was an outcast," Georgia told Bill Pete. "What makes him think they'll help us?" She had to blink back tears again.

"Just because they won't let him marry their daughters, doesn't mean they'll refuse to help him when he's hurt," Bill Pete said. " 'Specially when he's been whipped by a white man."

"How will they know it was a white man?"

"Indian wouldn't do a man like that."

Georgia shook her head angrily. "Goddamn Sam!"

"I wouldn't be goddamning Sam Sheridan if I was you, Georgia," Bill Pete said flatly. "Seems to me you're the one caused all the trouble. And he *could* have shot him, don't forget. You too, for that matter."

Georgia said nothing further for the rest of the trip, concentrating instead on stroking Kee's face and head as he lay unconscious. When they got to Moon, Bill Pete asked a little boy walking home from school where he could find the Ouachita settlement. The boy directed him to a cluster of shanty houses behind the town cemetery. At one of the houses Bill Pete made arrangements for O'Hara and Georgia to be taken in. After Bill Pete had carried the unconscious man inside, Georgia walked back out to his car with him.

"Here," Bill Pete said, handing her some currency. "It's all I've got on me."

"Thanks."

He nodded, a little sadly. "I'd best get on back," he said after a moment. "Take care of yourself, Georgia." He got into the patrol car. Georgia stepped forward.

"Tell Sam—"

Bill Pete hesitated starting the engine. He waited a full minute, staring at her. But Georgia never finished the sentence. Finally Bill Pete drove off, leaving her standing there, the words forever unspoken.

As he headed back to Texas, Bill Pete watched Georgia Sheridan grow smaller and smaller in his rearview mirror until she disappeared altogether.

53

Alva Powell was smart enough to know who had the most influence with Sam. She went to see Draw late one afternoon at his office in the Sheridan Oil Building.

"Sam has banned me from the mansion," she complained. "Leon and me both. He's ordered the help not to let us in." Her lips pursed spitefully. "He is cutting me off from my own grandson."

"Sam's got problems right now, Alva," said Draw. "That thing with Georgia has whipped him pretty bad."

"That's not the only problem he's got. Everybody in town knows he's on the bottle. Two ladies were talking about it at the church social night before last. The *church social!*"

"Sure, Sam's drinking a little," Draw admitted. "But it ain't out of control. Nowhere near." Draw only wished that were so.

"I will not be kept away from Tyler," Alva announced. "I don't care what Georgia's done, Sam Sheridan cannot keep my only grandchild from me!"

"In this county, Alva, Sam can do just about anything he wants to do," Draw reminded her as inoffensively as possible. He did not want any conflict with Georgia's mother or brother, if he could avoid it. His main concern just then was Sam; he hoped he would not have to deal with anything else. "I think maybe if you and Leon just back off a bit," he suggested quietly, "don't try to push Sam or go around what he wants, why, this whole thing will probably blow over." It was an easy lie.

"In the meantime, am I just supposed to stop seeing Tyler?"

Draw shrugged. "I don't see that you've got much choice. It's Sam's house and Ty is Sam's son."

"Well, I think it's outrageous! Tyler's just a little boy. Why, I haven't even had a chance to talk to him about his mother going away."

Which, Draw thought, was probably one of the reasons Sam was keeping her away. When Draw had asked Sam what he was going to tell the boy about his mother, Sam had replied, "As little as possible. Just that she went away to live with somebody else. Something like that. I don't want him hurt any more than necessary."

Draw came around his desk and gently guided the distraught Alva toward the door. "Just be patient, Alva. This is going to take a little time. But it'll work out, you'll see."

After Alva left, Draw walked up to the second floor to Sam's office.

"Mr. Sheridan hasn't been in today, Mr. Poker," the secretary told him.

"He call?"

"No, sir."

"I'll see him tomorrow then. Nothing important." Draw kept his tone as casual as possible; he knew Sam's secretary found it awkward when she did not hear from him, sometimes for two and three days at a time.

On his way back downstairs, Draw decided it was time to talk to someone about Sam. Up until then he had kept his own counsel, never discussing with anyone Sam's growing dependency on the bottle. But Alva Powell's comment about the church social had touched a nerve. Apparently the knowledge of Sam's drinking problem was filtering down to the community. That was not good. Most of the town knew about Georgia and Kee O'Hara; too many people had been involved in the episode to keep it quiet; besides which, the absence of Georgia Sheridan left a noticeable void in the town itself. Draw was not bothered by the townspeople knowing about Georgia, however. If anything, it reinforced Sam's reputation: he had coped with the situation in a manner that was heartily approved of, as a good *Texan* would: whipping the offending male and running off the offending female. For days afterward, whenever Sam went into town he was the recipient of gentle pats on the back from the men, light touches on his arm from the women. We're all with you, Sam, they were saying.

But this drinking was something else. It was wholly different from being cheated on by one's wife. Instead of strength, it was weakness. Men were expected to drink, even to get drunk at times; they were *not* expected to become drunkards. Certainly not over someone who clearly was unworthy.

Draw's problem was to *whom* he should talk. Owen Milam and Tom Prater were close to Sam, but they were latecomers in his life, joining him at the very end of his long struggle to bring in Sheridan number one. Buddy Kyle had not been around much longer; anyway, Buddy was too young to offer advice, on drinking and women anyway. Tongue, of course, was an obvious consideration, but his philosophy and values were Choctaw, and while they might make sense to Draw, could not be expected to apply with any success to the white community of Sheridan. Draw even thought vaguely of Rutland King, the refiner of whom Sam thought so highly, and who had been of such great help in advising Sam on how to structure his growing young company. But King was an outsider, really; his perspective would focus too much on Sam the oil tycoon rather than Sam Sheridan the man. Draw needed to find someone who *knew* Sam: not only what was in his heart, but how it got there.

When he reached the lobby, it suddenly came to Draw who his confidant should be. A person so close as to be easily overlooked. The person who knew one half of Sam as well as Draw knew the other: who had known his mother as Draw knew his father.

Draw walked next door to Sheridan Realty. "Could a tired old cowboy get a cup of coffee in here?" he asked, standing in the doorway of Miss Emily's private office.

"There might be one cup left," the little lame woman said, "but it's not fresh. It's been made since morning."

"Long as it's hot."

He watched Miss Emily turn on the electric hot plate under the coffeepot she kept next to her desk. She had, he thought, aged considerably in the time that Georgia had been gone. For all her disagreements with Georgia Sheridan, Draw knew that Emily cared for her as Sam's wife. Though she never spoke of it, Emily admired the good that Georgia had done in Sheridan, and was proud to have been a part of it. After so many drab years of being nothing but a clerk for Harley Greb at the *Enterprise,* it had given Emily fresh life to feel the sense of accomplishment that came as a natural consequence of working for someone as dynamic as Georgia Sheridan. Much of Emily's current weariness was the result, Draw knew, of trying to keep Sheridan Realty moving at the high energy level at which Georgia had operated. Emily was trying desperately to perpetuate the projects Georgia had begun, but little by little, day by day, she was losing ground.

"I saw Alva Powell go in a while ago," Emily commented. "Did she go to see Samuel?"

Draw shook his head. "Sam's not in today." Keeping his voice casual, he watched closely for her reaction.

"Oh." Emily averted her eyes. She was not about to match stares with an old gunfighter like Draw Poker.

While the coffee was heating, Draw and Emily chatted about the latest Dane merchants who had, after months of observation and procrastination, finally seen the obvious benefits and moved to Sheridan. "More than half of Dane has moved out," Emily observed.

"Must be driving Pete Spence crazy."

Emily nodded. "Cal Trask said that when he was loading his hardware store stock to move, Pete came uptown and stood on the sidewalk glaring at him the whole time. Never spoke a word; just glared."

"We'll have to deal with Pete one of these days," Draw said. "There'll be a final showdown, mark my words."

"Well, I hope Samuel will be up to it." Now it was Emily who made an attempt to keep her tone casual. Draw read her words easily, however.

"What have you heard, Em?" he asked, dropping all pretense.

"That Samuel is drinking heavily. *Very* heavily."

"How far's the word spread?"

"All over town." Her expression softened. "Is it true, Charles?" She never called him Draw.

"It's true."

Shaking her head, she asked, "*Why,* Charles? For God's sake, why?"

"Same reason you're working yourself to death, Em," he replied quietly. "Something's gone out of your life and you're trying to fill the hole it left."

Miss Emily blinked back tears. "Charles, why in *hell* did she go and do a thing like she did?"

"No telling. But *why* she done it ain't really what we ought to be worrying about. It's the damage she left behind that we got to deal with."

Emily poured a cup of coffee and handed it across the desk. "Have you talked to him at all about it?"

Draw nodded. "I stayed with him all night long that first night after he run 'em off. We spent the night in his study; he drank and cried all night. Then the next day he seemed to come out of it. We talked about Tyler and what Sam would tell him. He seemed to get hold of the situation right quick, like you'd expect Sam to. I didn't think nothing at all about him getting drunk that first night; seemed like the natural thing to do. I didn't find out about the steady, everyday drinking for a long time; Sam done it quietly, at home, at night mostly. First time I suspected anything was one morning when I smelled liquor on his breath at the office. I called him on it, but he just smiled and said, 'Don't worry about it, Draw. I can handle it. I just need a shot ever' now and again to help wipe out the images.' "

Miss Emily frowned. "Images?"

"I reckon he meant the picture of Georgia and O'Hara together. Damn shame he had to catch them that way."

"God*damn* her!" Emily surprised Draw with the sudden expletive. "How could she *do* such a thing to him?"

"No telling." Draw blew on his coffee and took a sip. He thought of Mrs. Pilcher, the housekeeper at the Sheridan mansion. "You go to church with Wynona Pilcher, don't you? Has she said anything about Sam's drinking?"

Emily looked surprised. "Why, Wynona's not there any longer, Charles. I assumed you knew. Sam let her go last month. Claimed she wouldn't do things the way he wanted them done; said she kept saying 'Mrs. Sheridan did this' and 'Mrs. Sheridan did that,' until he got tired of it and fired her."

The news disturbed Draw markedly. "Who's running the place? Who's looking after Ty?"

Emily just stared at him. So busy had she been with Sheridan Realty problems, that she had not given any thought at all to the ramifications of the housekeeper's departure. "Have you been out there recently?" she finally asked, almost fearfully.

"No. Sam asked everybody not to drop in for a while, until Ty got used to Georgia not being there. We've all shied away since then. But with nobody running the place, I think it's time I went out for a look-see."

"Do you want me to go with you?"

"No, Sam might think we're ganging up on him. I'll find something in the office that I don't think Tom Prater should sign for him, and use that as an excuse to stop by. May or may not fool him, depending on how much he's had to drink. But at least I'll get a chance to look around."

"Please call me, Charles, and let me know," Emily said. "I'm very concerned now."

"I'll do it," Draw promised.

By the time Draw drove out to the mansion, the sky had clouded and a sudden, driving rain was pelting down. Draw pulled around behind the big house and parked as close to the kitchen door as he could get. Hurrying from the car, he was thankful to find the screen door unlatched. In the kitchen one of the Mexican housegirls was sitting at the table, smoking and reading a magazine. Immediately Draw saw a sink filled with dirty dishes, a stovetop coated with grease, and the refrigerator door open to reveal some of the food moldy and rotting.

"Where's Adelita at?" Draw asked the girl. Adelita was the Mexican woman who oversaw the kitchen help.

"Adelita, she go home. I am in charge." She continued reading, not bothered at all by Draw's presence. He was not, after all, a member of the household.

"Shouldn't there be some supper cooking?" Draw asked.

The girl shrugged. "*Señor* Sheridan and the boy, they tell me when they get hungry."

Draw walked through the house, the Mexican girl making no attempt to stop him. In the living room he stopped and looked around again. It was a scandal. Newspapers scattered about, ashtrays full, empty glasses on every table, empty Nehi and Pure-Grape soda pop bottles on the floor, Baby Ruth and Butterfinger wrappers lying about. Shaking his head, Draw walked through the rest of the house. It was the same in every room he entered: a mess.

In the master bedroom Sam was sprawled across the bed, fully dressed, snoring loudly in a drunken sleep.

"Don't Daddy sound funny?" Tyler asked. The six-year-old was sitting on the floor next to the bed, twirling Sam's pistol on one finger. Draw's heart jerked at the sight. Even from where Draw stood, he could see there were cartridges in the cylinder.

"Does your Daddy know you've got his pistol?" Draw asked quietly.

Ty shook his head. "He was already asleep when I decided to play with it."

Careful now. "He sure is snoring away, ain't he?" Smiling, Draw moved forward very carefully. Ty grinned.

"Sure is."

"Sounds like an old truck your daddy had when we was drilling number one. Made all kind of noise on cold mornings." He kept advancing, his eyes on the gun as Tyler twirled it. "Sometimes, why, it just needed a full tank of gas to make it shut up. Wonder if your daddy needs his gas tank filled?"

Ty started laughing, and when he did he stopped twirling the pistol. Draw stepped quickly to him and snatched the weapon out of his hand. Taking the boy by his shirt collar, he jerked him to his feet.

"You listen to me, boy," he said harshly, "I ever hear of you touching a gun again without a grown-up's permission, I'll strap your ass from here to Kilgore and back, you understand me?"

"Y-yes, Draw," Tyler said, startled.

"You remember where your bed's at?"

"Y-yes, sir—"

"Then go get in it!" He gave the boy a rough shove out of the room.

Draw put the pistol in his coat pocket and went around the bed to the telephone. He called Tongue at his house behind the Choctaw store. "Can you come over to Sam's place? There's a problem over here I need some help with."

"Sure as shooting," Tongue said. "Be there in fifteen minutes."

While he waited for Tongue, Draw returned to the kitchen. The Mexican girl was still smoking and reading her magazine. "Get out," Draw told her. "You're fired."

She curled her upper lip at him. "You cannot fire me. Only Adelita can fire me."

Without another word, Draw walked over, took her by the arm, and escorted her through the back door and out into the rain. She ran off into the night, screaming for Adelita.

Tongue arrived a few minutes later. There was not much about him to indicate that he was now a well-to-do man; despite continued income from Sheridan number one, he still wore work clothes and lived as simply as the rest of the Choctaws. He operated his large general store on a nonprofit basis, and lived in a modest house behind it. His one concession to wealth was automobiles; he usually had at least three cars, and traded them in for different ones every few months. At the present time he had a Studebaker, a Chevrolet, and one of the new boxlike, wooden-sided Fords called a "station wagon." He never seemed to get any older; on this night he looked much as he had years earlier when he and Draw, both camping illegally on Able Patman's range, had met. The only change in the Indian's flat, broad-nosed face was that his left eye, once crossed, was now normal. Sam had arranged for Tongue to have eye surgery in St. Louis. Because Tongue had been extremely nervous about making the trip alone to a strange white city, Sam had accompanied him. Since then, there was nothing Tongue would not do for Sam Sheridan.

"I found Tyler upstairs twirling this on one finger." Draw showed him the pistol. Tongue saw immediately that it was loaded, and rolled his eyes toward the ceiling. "Place looks like a pig sty," Draw continued. "Sam's dead drunk in the bedroom. Something's got to be done."

"You got a plan?"

"Yes, I have. If you'll stay here and keep an eye on things, I'll go get someone to help us attend to this problem. If any of the Mex help comes back, keep 'em out."

"Sure thing."

"Be back in a little bit," Draw said, and left.

* * *

A while later Draw arrived back at the mansion with Miss Emily. They found Tongue in the kitchen engaged in a vociferous argument with Adelita, three Mexican housegirls, and one Mexican houseboy. Tyler had wandered in and was observing the fight with interest. Into their midst limped Miss Emily, her face set in a scowl. She slammed her folded umbrella down on the table with a mighty blow, knocking an empty bottle and a saucer to the floor, and shouted, "Si-*lence!* I will have si-*lence!*"

Immediate silence. All eyes fixed on Miss Emily uncertainly.

"Who is in charge of these people?" she asked in flawless, authoritative Spanish, acquired over a lifetime.

"I am, *señora.* " Adelita pointed an accusing finger at Tongue. "This man—"

"I did not ask you anything about that man!" Emily interrupted indignantly. "You will respond *only* to what I ask."

There was silence again, until Draw said quietly, "Excuse us, Em. We'll go see to Sam."

"All right, go along," Emily said, waving her hand impatiently. As Draw and Tongue left the kitchen, Emily turned to Adelita again. "Do you wish to continue working here?"

"*Si, señora,* if—"

"No conditions. Yes or no?"

Adelita lowered her eyes. "*Si, señora.* "

"Very well." She waved a hand around the room. "I want this filthy kitchen cleaned up, *now.* Walls and floors scrubbed. Table and counters scrubbed. Grill and oven scrubbed. All dishes and utensils scrubbed. Refrigerator emptied and scrubbed. Get to work."

Amid a flurry of immediate activity, Emily turned to Tyler, who was studying her curiously. "Do you remember me, Tyler Charles?" He had seen her a few times uptown.

"No," the boy said, shaking his head.

"No, ma'am," she corrected.

"No, ma'am."

"I am your Aunt Emily. Not your real aunt, you understand, but you will address me as 'Aunt' anyway. You will say 'Yes, ma'am' and 'No, ma'am' when answering me, and you will always keep your tone respectful. I was a very close friend of your grandmother on your father's side, and I was there when your father was born, so I am entitled to the same respect as if I were blood kin. Is that clear?"

"Yes, uh, ma'am."

"Good." Emily nodded curtly. An offensive odor made her nose crinkle. "When did you last bathe?"

Ty shrugged. "I don't remember. Uh, ma'am."

"Memories do fade with time," Emily muttered. "Go upstairs and run a tub of hot water," she instructed. "Scrub yourself good all over. I will check you; if you are still dirty, *I* will bathe you. Do you understand?"

"Yes, ma'am."

Ty hurried out of the kitchen, Emily limping along behind him as far as the stairs. There she met Draw and Tongue carrying a limp Sam Sheridan down from the bedroom. The little woman and the boy both stopped to stare.

"We're taking him out to the Choctaw community for a while, Em," Draw said. "Prob'ly take him ten days or so to dry out. Will you see to Ty?"

"Certainly." A melancholy expression settled on her face as she watched Sam being carried out. Nell Sheridan's child, she thought. How strange life was. There had been a time when she was heart-broken at him being taken away; another time when he had returned a grown man and she had rejected him. Now here she was, taking care of *his* child.

Taking Ty by the hand, Emily limped up the stairs.

54

Sam awoke to find himself in his underwear, tied to a bed. He saw Draw sitting across the room, reading a newspaper.

"Where the hell am I?" Sam asked thickly.

Draw put down the paper and came over. "How you feeling, partner?"

"Like a Mack truck ran over me. Who tied me up?"

"Me and Tongue. Took both of us, too; you was sure set against it."

"Where are we?"

"Tongue's house."

"How long have I been here?"

"This here's the fourth day."

"All right, untie me."

"Sure thing, partner." Draw began undoing the smooth hitching rope with which Sam's wrists and ankles were anchored to the bedposts. "Think you could use a little something to eat?" he asked as Sam sat up.

"I think I could use a drink." Seeing his clothes on the back of a chair, Sam walked unsteadily over and started dressing.

"Now, wait a minute," Draw said. "The whole idea of bringing you here was to dry you out."

"I'm as dry as I intend to get." His tone had a hint of surliness. "I want a drink."

Draw reached up and gave several jerks on a length of twine that ran over the top of the door and out of the room. He heard the faint sound of a cow bell ringing up front in the Choctaw general store. A moment later Tongue came in.

"Sam wants to go out and get a drink," Draw told him.

"Why'd you untie him?"

"See if he had any sense yet."

"Does he?"

"Not a lick." Draw tossed two of the hitching ropes to the Indian. Both men advanced on Sam.

"You two wait just a goddamned minute!" Sam protested. He had a boot in his hand, which Draw snatched away from him; then Tongue leaped behind him and pinned his arms to his sides. "Stop it, Draw! Goddamn it, Tongue, let me go!"

Dragging him back to the bed, Draw and the Choctaw managed to get first one, then the other, wrist tied to the headboard again. Sam struggled, twisted, yelled, and kicked, but they got his ankles secured again too.

"You're staying here until you're dried out, partner," Draw told him. "I don't care if it takes six months."

"You're fired, Draw!" Sam bellowed.

"Good. Now I don't have to take no orders from you."

Sam directed his attention to Tongue. "Holding a white man prisoner on Indian land is bad business. You can get in a lot of trouble for this."

"I've been in trouble with white men before," Tongue replied matter-of-factly.

"Goddamn you both! Turn me loose!"

"Later, partner," Draw said, patting him on the arm.

Tongue went back to his store and Draw resumed reading the newspaper, while Sam yelled himself hoarse.

Sam fought and cursed for two more days, roundly condemning Draw and Tongue as the lowest, most despicable sons of bitches ever born, swearing that when he got free he was going to take great pleasure in seeing them both run out of Caddo County permanently.

Then he got sick.

As the first effects of withdrawal set in, Sam became too weak to struggle, felt too bad to curse. He suffered terrible stomach cramps; his mouth became so dry he couldn't speak; and his head throbbed painfully and unremittingly every moment that he was awake. His body shook with chills so bad that the bed shook with him; then he sweated so profusely that he soaked the sheets. Draw and Tongue took turns sitting with him around the clock. One or the other of them was there to put extra blankets on him when the chills began, to take them off again when the sweating started.

"Jesus," he would whisper over and over again. "Jesus, Jesus, I'm sick—"

In his agony he would forget his threats and plead with them to help him. Always one of them was there, the cynical Choctaw or the leathery old gunman, always within reach so that when Sam sought reassurance that he was not alone in the black pit of his withdrawal, he felt one of their hands touch his face or his arm or his chest, and drew strength from them.

"Sick, Draw," he gasped. "So—sick—so—sick—"

"I know, partner, I know," Draw comforted. "It'll be over soon. Ride it out, son. You can do it."

"Head hurts, Tongue," he told the Indian. "So bad—hurts—so bad—"

Then he would feel Tongue's strong fingers massaging his scalp and neck, relieving the throbbing tension.

After ten days Sam still wanted a drink.

"Draw, just get me one shot, please—"

"I won't get you one *drop,*" the old man told him one day, "but I'll untie you and let you get it yourself."

"You will, Draw? You will?" Sam was elated.

"Sure will." With Tongue watching, Draw again undid the ropes from Sam's chafed wrists and ankles.

"Thanks, Draw. I won't forget this."

"Don't reckon you will."

Sam stood up for a split second, then fell flat on his face. Mouth open incredulously, he found that he could not maneuver at all. The least bodily movement started his brain spinning inside his head; his equilibrium had vanished. After a great deal of effort he was finally able to stand, barely, but walking was out of the question. If there had been a full bottle of whiskey on the dresser across the room, Sam could not have reached it. He might have tried; he tried several times to get to the door; but all he did was get sick and puke all over himself. Every time he stood, he puked. Every time he tried to take a step, he puked. When he sat back on the bed, he puked. It went on until he dry-puked, choking and gagging as nausea swept over him and tried vainly to dredge something up from his insides. Finally Sam just fell back onto the bed, wishing he had a gun so he could blow his brains out.

When the nausea was its most severe, it brought on waves of blackness that seized his frantic mind. Sometimes, coming out of that blackness, the room and the faces in it would be in such soft focus as to appear cloudy and undefined. He could only determine who was with him by sound or touch. Several times the presence was a mystery to him; the touch was gentle, the sound feathery. He struggled to identify it, but never was able to clear his mind before it was gone.

He finally decided it was a dream.

By the third week Sam began to feel human again. Tongue's woman, a Choctaw widow who lived in the house, made him some kind of thick, dark broth that he managed not only to get down, but *keep* down.

"What is this stuff?" he asked Tongue, who watched him gulping the murky liquid.

"You don't want to know."

"Why not?"

"It's got things in it that white men don't usually eat."

Sam did not care. The concoction was delicious, whatever it was made of. He had almost finished it when Draw came in and saw what he was drinking.

"Giving him some snake-and-buzzard soup, I see," Draw commented.

Sam looked with instinctive disgust at the little bit left in the bowl. Then he simply shrugged and drank the rest of it.

"Where is Ty?" he asked Draw when he finished.

"At the house. Miss Emily's looking after him."

"Get me my clothes. I'm going home."

Draw shook his head. "Couple more days, Sam."

Sam's eyes narrowed a fraction. "I'm sober now, Draw." His words were clearly a warning. He turned to Tongue. "Get me my clothes, Tongue."

"Unh," replied Tongue.

Sam's eyes flicked from one to the other and he began to get angry. "To hell with you both. I'll go home without clothes."

He got up, naked, and started unsteadily for the door. Before he got to it, the door opened and a tall, very thin Indian girl came in, carrying a Mason jar of something blue in her hands. She had an oblong face with great dark eyes, and a pockmarked right cheek. Her hair, black as pitch, hung straight down her back. Her lips curved downward and when she parted them Sam could see a slight gap between her top front teeth.

"Hello, Sam. I'm Tunica, remember me?" She did not seem embarrassed by his nakedness.

Sam nevertheless put his hands in front of himself. "Yes—sure I do. Tunica, yes—"

"I brought you some fresh blueberry juice," she said, holding out the Mason jar. "It will soothe your stomach."

"Ah, thank you—" Keeping one hand modestly in front, Sam accepted the gift and edged sideways back to bed. He got quickly under the sheet.

"Come on, Tongue," said Draw, "let the princess visit our patient for a while. We'll be back in a bit, Sam."

As the two men left, Tunica pulled up a straight chair to the bed, sat down, and smiled. "You look terrible."

"You should have seen me last week."

"I did. I helped Tongue and Mr. Poker clean you up after you'd been sick a few times. You probably don't remember."

So it was her, Sam thought. Not a dream after all.

"Liquor can be very bad," Tunica said gravely.

Was this skinny slip of an Indian girl going to lecture him? "Did Tongue tell you to say that? Or Mr. Poker?"

"Oh no," she replied in the same solemn tone, "I speak from my own experience. As a very young child, I watched my father slowly drink himself to death. That was long ago before you came here. My father was a prince of our people, but he was not a strong-willed man. He was forever confused by the ways of the white men with whom he had to conduct the business of our tribe. The only thing that gave him peace was the liquor. In the end it gave him a final peace. My mother, who loved him very deeply, ate the roots of a black nightshade plant and killed herself so that she could join him. In a way, the liquor killed them both."

Sam studied her for a moment, thinking again what an unusual young girl she was. She did not look different than any other Choctaw adolescent that could be seen around the Indian community. Dressed in old jeans and a plain cotton shirt, homemade moccasins, and a single narrow band around her head, there was nothing about her appearance that set her apart as a princess. Yet when she looked at you and spoke to you, there was a feeling that she *was,* somehow, different. Sam remembered sensing it the very first time he saw her, when she was only twelve. He sensed it again now. There was an almost mystic quality about her.

"How old are you now, Tunica?" he asked, opening the Mason jar and taking a swallow of the blueberry juice. It was pure, sweet, and delicious.

"Eighteen last month."

"You go to school here in the community?"

"Yes. For a long time we had only our elders to teach the young people as they grew. But now that there are royalties from the oil, we have built a small schoolhouse. And we have a real teacher: Mr. Abraham White Deer, from Oklahoma. He is of the Cherokee tribe." Tunica noticed Sam's face darken. She was at once contrite. "Please forgive me. It was thoughtless to mention the Cherokee. I had forgotten about your trouble."

"That's all right. I guess I can't be upset at the whole Cherokee nation for what one man did. Anyway, he was only half-Cherokee."

There was a knock at the door and Sam was surprised to see Buddy Kyle stick his head in. "Excuse the interruption, Mr. Sheridan. I just wanted to let Tunica know I was here." He glanced at Tunica. "I'll wait outside for you."

"Come on in here, Buddy. I haven't seen you in weeks. Where've you been keeping yourself?"

"Just busy," Buddy said, shrugging. "School, the movie house." He came in and closed the door behind him.

A handsome young man of twenty now, with straight teeth and wavy hair, he had lost the animal tenseness that he had once emanated. Sam had taken him out of the oil fields and made him go to school; he was now only weeks away from a high school diploma. After school he worked for Leon Powell in the theater. Sam's long-term plan was to give Buddy experience in several businesses around town, including Dewitt Tucker's bank and Sheridan Realty, then send him to college in the fall.

"How're you doing at the theater?" he asked Buddy now.

"Real good. Mr. Powell, he's teaching me everything there is to know. I can make popcorn, run the projector. He's showing me how to book films now."

"Sounds good," said Sam. "I'll have to drop in some night. I haven't been to a picture show in a couple of years."

"Lots of good pictures coming. Next week we've got *Seventh Heaven* with Janet Gaynor. She's pretty popular. Week after that we'll have *What Price Glory* with Victor McLaglen and Dolores Del Rio. All the men in town will like that one. We've got *Camille* coming this summer. Norma Talmadge and Gilbert Roland."

"Buddy's taking me uptown to see *Wings* at the matinee," Tunica said. "It has Buddy Rogers and Clara Bow in it."

Sam smiled. "Do you two go together?"

"Kind of," Buddy replied, at the same time Tunica was saying, "Not really." Both of them were embarrassed then, and avoided Sam's eyes. Sam tried to put them at their ease.

"Well, if you do, I think it's very nice. And if you don't, maybe you should." Winking at Buddy, he said, "I want you to keep up the good work in school and at the theater. I've got plans for you, Buddy." He took Tunica's hand. "Thank you for coming to see me.

And for the blueberry juice. You two go on now and have a good time today."

After they left, Sam set the jar of juice aside and rested his head back against the pillow. He could not help remembering how wonderful it had been to be in love. Those early feelings for Georgia, feelings that he had carried with him into the trenches in France, brought back with him, taken into their marriage, were feelings that had been warmer, fuller, more uplifting and satisfying than any he had ever known. There had never been anything to equal them. Before he had begun working on Sheridan number one, his love for Georgia had comprised the only really *good* feelings he had. His later feelings about the land and the oil had competed with, perhaps even modified, those feelings of love. But they had never replaced them.

Sam knew he had not completely lost his love for Georgia. Even now, with the image of her and O'Hara together so deeply etched in his mind, he still loved her. Every night without her was a miserable stretch of hours made shorter only by whiskey. He was off the whiskey now, but he wondered how long he would stay off once he returned to the mansion, to the memories, to the long night hours alone.

Georgia, Georgia, Georgia, his tortured mind cried.

He put his face down into the pillow and kept it there, even after he had cried the pillow wet.

55

Draw walked into the room to find Sam in a bathrobe, sitting with his feet propped up on a table, looking through one of a stack of old magazines Tongue's woman had given him.

"How come you're not chomping at the bit to get out of here, like you was a couple days ago?"

Shrugging, Sam kept idly turning pages. "I guess I realized

there's really no rush to get back. Long as Ty's being cared for and the business is being run all right, there's nothing for me to hurry back to." He paused a beat. "And nobody."

"You been sulking ever since Tunica and Buddy was here," Draw said. "How come?"

"I'm not sulking," Sam replied, looking away.

"Seeing them two together reminded you of you and Georgia, didn't it? Now you're feeling sorry for yourself."

"I'm not feeling sorry for myself," Sam told him, with a slight edge now.

"Look, partner," Draw said firmly, "there's gonna be a dozen things a day that'll remind you of Georgia. You're gonna have to face up to that; if you don't, it's gonna drive you plumb out of your mind."

Sam fixed his friend in a steady gaze. "I appreciate what you're trying to do, Draw. You know I'll always take your advice on matters you know something about. But you can't help me on this one. You can't possibly understand what I'm feeling right now."

"Can't, eh?" Draw said, snorting loudly. "Why in the hell is it that young people always think they *invented* their problems? Always think *their* problems is *original?* Lemme tell you something, son: I *lived* with the kind of ache you've got for twenty years. Years that I was in love with your Grandmother Lillian."

Sam's expression was suddenly infused with interest. He took his feet off the table and sat up. "You were in love with Able Patman's wife?"

"From the first minute I laid eyes on her. She was already pledged to marry Able and they was fixing to head for Texas together. When Able asked me to ride along, why, the only reason I went was to be near her." Draw's rough old face softened. "I wish you could have knowed her, Sam. She was the gentlest, delicatest lady that ever lived."

Nodding, Sam said quietly, "So you do know how I feel. And you must know there's no way for me to get Georgia out of my mind."

"I didn't say there was. I said you had to *deal* with it. You've got to whip it before it whips you."

"How, Draw?" The simple question was more than a plea; it was the admission of terrible hurt.

"By being a man, son," Draw replied, just as quietly. "By being strong. By taking care of your responsibilities to your son, yourself, and your town."

Sam leaned forward, elbows on knees, and looked down at the bare wooden floor. "I don't know if I *can* be that strong," he admitted, both to Draw and to himself.

"Well, there's one sure way to find out. There's a visitor waiting outside to see you. She's got something important to tell you."

For an instant there was anxiety in Sam's eyes. *She?* Was it possible that—

Then Draw opened the door and little Miss Emily limped in. "Hello, Samuel," she said, half smiling. She came over to the table and Draw held a chair for her.

"Hello, Miss Em. I want to thank you for taking care of Ty for me."

"Thanks aren't necessary, Samuel. I've had a wonderful time with him. He calls me 'Aunt Emily,' you know. It was his own idea. I hope you don't mind."

"Of course not. He can keep on calling you that if you want him to."

"Thank you, Samuel. That's very nice."

Draw put a hand on Emily's shoulder. "Tell Sam what you told me a little while ago."

Emily's expression turned serious. "Pete Spence is uptown, Samuel."

"Uptown in Sheridan?" Sam was surprised. Pete Spence had never been to Sam's town before, not even with the delegation that came to threaten Sam with Texas Ranger intervention on Pistol Hill.

"He's visiting all the businessmen who moved from Dane, making them the same offer you did: a chance to own the property they had their stores on in Dane if they'll move back. He's telling them that Sheridan isn't going to last." Emily shifted her eyes from Sam. "He's telling them that Sheridan is nothing but a temporary boom town named after a drunk whose wife ran off with a half-breed."

Draw watched Sam very closely. At first Sam was amazed; it had never occurred to him that anyone would be *talking* about his drinking, much less trying to use it against him. Then Draw saw Sam's eyes narrow and turn hard; he recognized the set that came to Sam's lips: a tight line of determination that Draw remembered from their drilling days. The old cowboy kept a straight face, but inside he smiled.

Sam stood up.

"Would you excuse me while I get dressed, Miss Emily? Then I'll go uptown with you."

Pete Spence's car was not difficult to find. It was a brand-new silver Packard with the Spence Ranch brand on a gold disk on each door. The car was parked in the middle of a block on Pop Joyner Road. Sam pulled up behind it.

"Don't try fighting him, Sam," Draw cautioned as they got out. "You ain't in no condition to fistfight right now."

"Charles is right, Samuel," Emily agreed as Sam helped her out of the car.

"I'm not looking to fight him. He's twenty years too old and fifty pounds too heavy. But if he starts something, I won't back off."

"Let's hope he don't," Draw said. "But if he does, don't let his weight fool you. Pete may be fat, but he's strong as a stud bull. He gets his arms around you, he'll break your back."

The trio walked along the sidewalk looking through store windows until they found Pete Spence in Barger's Meat Market. He was talking to Lem Barger, who owned one of the two butcher shops in Sheridan. As Sam walked in, he heard Spence saying, "You come back to Dane, Lem, and I promise you'll have the only butcher shop in town. I won't let nobody else open one. You won't have no competition at all."

"You won't have any customers either, Lem," Sam interjected as he entered. He stopped six feet from the counter where Pete Spence stood. Putting his hands on his hips, he looked directly at Spence although continuing to speak to the butcher. "Dane's a dying town, Lem. If you move back, your business will die with it."

Silence fell over the shop. Pete Spence stared back at Sam. It was only the second time they had come face to face, the first since Sam had dragged the bribed geologist Rufus Prine into Spence's office and flung him across the cattleman's desk. Now, with Spence standing up, Sam was surprised that he was so tall. Because of Spence's girth, Sam had expected him to be shorter. But Spence was as tall as Sam himself, and half again as broad. Round-shouldered even in a tailored split-suede coat, and pot-bellied above his solid silver belt buckle, Spence nevertheless made it easy for Sam to understand Draw's warning. His hands were like hamhocks, his biceps bulged through his upper coat sleeves; he probably *could* break a man's back, Sam thought.

After locking eyes with Sam for a tense minute, Spence turned back to Lem Barger. "You've heard my offer, Lem," he said quietly, his incongruously delicate lips shaping each word. "You and the others can move back home anytime you've a mind to, with no hard feelings on anybody's part. That's all I have to say."

Spence turned to leave. Before he reached the door, Sam said, "Just a minute, Spence." The cattleman stopped, not turning around. "I understand you're telling people that this town is named after a drunk. I'm here to tell you that's a lie. This town is named after my mother and her family." Spence kept his back to Sam. "I also hear that you've been making remarks about my wife running off with a half-breed. If we're going to bring families into this, I'll have to start talking about your sister and who *she* ran off with—"

Spence whirled around and glared at Sam with more anger and hatred than Sam had ever seen in a man's face. Draw tensed, expecting Spence to pounce. It was probably the first time in a quarter century, Draw suspected, that anyone had dared mention Sarah Spence to her brother. The audacity of it turned Pete Spence livid.

But the cattleman did not attack. He did not even deign to address Sam directly. Turning to the butcher again, he said in a tightly controlled voice, "Don't worry none about Dane dying, Lem. Towns don't die, not really." For a split second his eyes shifted to Sam. "People die."

Then he strode out of the shop.

Sam, Draw, and Miss Emily followed Spence outside and watched as he got into his silver car, made a U-turn, and drove away.

"He didn't look at me once," Draw said quietly. "It was as if to him I wasn't even there."

"Same with me," said Emily. "What an eerie feeling."

"Why didn't he fight me? I gave him plenty of reason. Was he afraid of me?"

"Not of you and me put together," Draw assured him. "He didn't fight because it wasn't his choice of time and place."

Sam looked at Draw. "He'll be back, then?"

"Sure as shooting," Draw said ominously.

Following the confrontation with Spence, Sam's reputation was restored to its previous eminence. Word spread quickly that Sam, admittedly looking a little pale and drawn but certainly far from being a falling-down drunk, had faced up to Pete Spence and backed the big cattleman right out of town. Spence, the story went, had been given two reasons to fight Sam, for Sam had first called him a liar, then spoken openly of a subject long prohibited by Spence: his lesbian sister. But Spence had chosen not to fight; he had done nothing more than make a vague threat and backed off. The encounter proved two things: Sam Sheridan was back, as powerful as ever despite the loss of Georgia; and he was without question *the* strong man of Caddo County. Not a single merchant moved back to Dane.

There was, as Draw saw it, one remaining problem to clear up in order to help Sam recover as completely as possible. That problem was Alva Powell and her son Leon. Draw went to see them at home one morning a couple of weeks after Sam's confrontation with Pete Spence.

"I'm sure you've already heard that Sam's back in control now," he said. "He's quit drinking entirely and he's hard at work again. Right now he's talking to some young doctors about getting the medical center. I'd say he's pretty much his old self again."

"Does that mean I can begin seeing Tyler?" Alva's tone was decidedly rigid, giving the impression that she did not much care whether Sam was well or not; she was concerned only with seeing her grandson.

"I wish I could say yes, Alva," Draw told her frankly. "But I'm afraid not. I figure it's going to be a long spell before Sam can get through a day without thinking about Georgia—and until he can, he's going to be walking a pretty thin line. Me and Miss Emily and the others, we've decided we got to get Georgia pushed as far into the past as we can—and as fast as we can."

"What's this got to do with my mother seeing Tyler?" Leon asked.

"It ain't really a question of her seeing Tyler. It's a question of you two *being* here. You're both constant reminders of Georgia."

Leon looked incredulously at Draw. "What are you saying?" he asked, although he already knew. "Did Sam send you here to run us out of town?"

"Sam don't even know I'm here. And I'm not trying to *run* you anywhere. But I do think it would be best for everybody concerned if you and your mother was to voluntarily move away."

"I won't do it!" Alva snapped. "You've got no *right* to ask such a thing! Just because you work for Sam Sheridan doesn't mean you can control people's lives! Leon, tell him we will not leave!"

"Before you do that, Leon," Draw said, "let me point out a couple of things. First, this house you're living in is owned by Sam; if you do decide to stay, why, you'll have to find other quarters. Second, Alva, you've been drawing an allowance from the bank that Georgia arranged; that will now be cut off. Third, you'll both have to start living solely on Leon's profits from the movie house. That's all right, long as those profits keep coming in. But supposing a *new* theater was to open right across the street from you? A bigger, better theater. One that outbids you for the best new pictures. One that has a lower admission than you. One that gives a free bag of popcorn with every ticket. How much profit would you make then?"

"Sam wouldn't do that to me."

"Sam wouldn't have to," Draw told him. "He's got enough friends to do it for him."

Leon dropped limply into a chair. "I've put so *much* into the Georgian," he said, almost to himself.

"I know you have, Leon," said Draw, "and I want you to understand that you'll be well paid for that work. Sheridan Realty is ready to give you a more than generous price for the theater."

Leon's expression became curious. "How, ah, how much?"

Alva was shocked. "Leon! You can't be serious!"

"Mother, please! Can't you see the position we're in? We could end up broke!" He looked back at Draw. "How much do you think I'd get?"

"You and Miss Emily and Tom Prater will have to work out the exact figure."

"Leon, I will not go!"

"You certainly will, Mother. Unless you want to end up homeless and starving in Sheridan, Texas."

"I'll get a job and support myself," Alva threatened.

Leon and Draw exchanged knowing glances. "Who would hire you, Mother? Once word got out that Sam didn't want us here any longer, who in *hell* do you think would give either of us a job?"

393

Alva's expression became dark and pinched. "The high and mighty Sam Sheridan!" she spat. "Always talking about how terrible it was that Dane was controlled by Pete Spence the way it was. Now he's controlling Sheridan the same way!"

"You're wrong, Alva," Draw told her quietly. "The people in Dane always danced to Pete Spence's tune because they was afraid of him. People in Sheridan ain't afraid of Sam; they're behind him because they care for him. He gave them their first chance to be independent, and he treats ever'one of them like an equal. People in this town *love* Sam Sheridan. That's the difference." Draw rose and picked up his hat. "Leon, I'll have Miss Emily and Tom Prater keep tomorrow morning free for you. Let's get this done as quick as we can."

As he drove away from the Powell house, Draw Poker felt no pride in what he had just done.

But, for Sam's sake, he felt no regret either.

56

On a late summer day more than a year after he had quit drinking, Sam Sheridan, driving a new Chrysler Airflow, guided the car slowly around the town square of Dane. The Airflow was the first car ever produced with a curved, one-piece windshield, and it afforded Sam an unobstructed view of the fading little town. At one time there had been sixty-four retail businesses along the four blocks that formed a square around the old Caddo County courthouse, and at least that many more professional offices above them. Now there were less than a dozen of each. The courthouse was closed, its offices having moved to the new Caddo County Civic Center in Sheridan, which was now the county seat. Sam had donated the land on which the new center had been constructed.

To see a vehicle parked on the Dane town square these days was an oddity. The hundred or so people who still worked in Dane either lived close enough to walk to work, or if they drove parked their cars or trucks behind their places of employment, a practice begun in better times to save space in front for customers. As Sam circumnavigated the square on this day in late August, there were only two other vehicles in sight. One was an old stake truck parked near the Blue Star Cafe, which was still in business because it received a subsidy for doubling as a bus station. The truck reminded Sam of the Willys flatbed for which he and Pop Joyner had traded Sam's Hudson Super-Six in Port Arthur the time they went looking for used drilling equipment to get Sheridan number one started. It seemed like a lifetime ago.

When he had made one full circuit around the square, Sam drove partway around again in order to park near the newspaper office. He pulled up to the curb next to a large van that had Riley Salvage—Houston on its cab door. Two men were loading furniture from the newspaper office onto the back of the truck. Sam got out and stood on the sidewalk watching them. Presently, Harley Greb came out with a newspaper in his hand and walked over to him. He handed Sam the paper.

"Yesterday's Caddo County *Enterprise,*" he said. "Our last edition. Thought you might like a copy as a souvenir."

Sam accepted the paper without comment. Opening it, he looked at a photo on the front page of a man named Alonzo Jennings. At one hundred three, Alonzo had been the oldest person in Caddo County.

"Died yesterday." Greb sighed quietly. "I had hoped to be able to end the paper with a lead story that was happy, but I guess it wasn't meant to be."

Still Sam said nothing. Greb stepped past him and stood at the curb, his gaze moving slowly around the square.

"Town'll be completely dead in a few months." He looked over his shoulder at Sam. "You did a good job, Mr. Sheridan." His lips pursed in thought for a moment. "Let's see, it was Dr. Goodley who wouldn't come tend your wife when she was delivering, and you ruinned his practice by subsidizing your new Sheridan Medical Clinic that provides health care at about half what he had to charge. You got even with Rufus Prine, from up Longview way, and those other two geologists Pete Spence bribed by having your man Owen

395

Milam establish the Sheridan Geology Center, which furnishes chemical reports on well samples at no cost to the driller. Zack Locklear, of Locklear Meats and Produce, and Quinnie Frazier, who had a Piggly-Wiggly franchise grocery, were members of the loan committee that blackballed you at the Merchants Bank, so they both went under after you helped open a big meat and grocery co-op warehouse in Sheridan that sold way under their prices. And the president of the bank, Claud Maye, not only lost his depositors to his former teller's new high-interest bank in Sheridan, but his only daughter Maxine ran off and *married* the teller. Then Reverend Adolph Jones was forced to look for another parish after he lost ninety percent of his parishioners to the new air-cooled First Baptist Church of Sheridan. The Forts, father and son, being unable to survive with just Pete Spence for a client, have uprooted their families and moved their law practice to Dallas." Greb paused dramatically. "Have I left anyone out?"

"Just yourself," Sam replied quietly.

"Oh, yes. The Caddo County *Enterprise*. Well, as you can see," he gestured toward the movers, "I'm going too." He sighed quietly again. "You know, Dane might have survived right alongside Sheridan if it hadn't been for you. With all the oil strikes in every direction around here, why, there was enough for everybody's economy. Look how Kilgore's grown, look at Longview, at New Salem; they're all coexisting with Sheridan. Dane could have too, if you hadn't made the kind of offers you did to our business people."

"They had a choice."

Greb grunted derisively. "Not with the kind of offer you made, they didn't. It was like asking a ten-year-old boy to choose between fishing and Sunday school." Greb's expression sobered. "No, you killed Dane, Texas, Mr. Sheridan. You killed the whole town." His eyes turned sad. "Including its newspaper."

"You know, Greb, we don't have a newspaper in Sheridan yet."

Greb's eyebrows shot up. "Well, well. A crack in the granite?"

"I want a newspaper in Sheridan. I'm willing to subsidize one for as long as it takes to begin making a profit."

"That's mighty tempting," Greb admitted. "I won't lie to you: it hurt me to close the *Enterprise*. My own daddy started that paper in the back of a wagon. Now it's all finished. Me, I've taken a job as a rewrite man on a daily over in Waco. Lucky to get that, I suppose."

"A new paper in Sheridan could still be called the Caddo County *Enterprise,*" Sam suggested. But Harley Greb shook his head.

"No, I don't think so." He squinted at Sam. "Tell you the truth, Mr. Sheridan, I don't think I'd ever feel real *comfortable* working for you. I think I'd always be afraid of doing something that would make you angry. I'd best go on over to Waco and be a rewrite man. I'll sleep better at night over there."

Sam smiled a slight understanding smile and nodded. "Good luck, Greb," he said, then got back in his car and drove away.

That's it, he thought on his way out of town. My fight with Dane is finished.

One morning a week later Sam was in his office discussing a trip to Washington that Tom Prater was urging him to make.

"I don't think there is any doubt," Prater said, "that if a Democrat gets into the White House in the next election, we're going to see a tax on gasoline. It won't be much: probably a penny a gallon; but it *will* be a tax. In my judgment, you and the other independent drillers should be doing everything you can to help the other side."

Sam was unconvinced. "What makes you think the Democrats have that much of a chance? They're running a *Catholic,* Tom," he reminded the lawyer, referring to the New York governor Alfred E. Smith. "The American public would never put a Catholic in the White House."

Prater shook his head. "When you talk about the American public, *never* say never. What I'm saying is, let's not take any chances. Ever since Coolidge made it clear that he would not run again, Herbert Hoover has been the favorite candidate in the Republican party. His record as secretary of commerce under Coolidge hasn't shown how he feels about the petroleum industry one way or another. I believe it's essential that we go to him, personally, and let him know that we'll support him financially in the coming election. If we can get four more years for our lobbyists to work on subsidy and parity and depletion bills, it won't *matter* how much tax is eventually put on gasoline; the consumer will be paying it, not us—"

Prater was interrupted by the office door bursting open and Buddy Kyle barging in unannounced. Sam and Tom looked at him, startled.

"What is it, Buddy, what's wrong?" Sam asked anxiously.

"I want to talk to you." Buddy's tone and expression were angry. Sam's own expression darkened at the unwarranted intrusion.

"I presume it's something that can't wait," he told the young man evenly. "I hope it is, anyway." Sam looked over at Tom Prater. "Go ahead and talk to the others. Tell them I'm in favor of a courtesy visit to Hoover to show industry support for his campaign. If a majority of the drillers agree with us, go ahead and arrange the trip."

"Right." Tom glanced at Buddy, then asked quietly, "Do you, ah, want me to stay?"

Sam shook his head. "Thanks anyway."

There was silence in the office as the lawyer gathered his papers and put them in his briefcase. Sam sat drumming his fingers soundlessly on the leather chair arm, and Buddy Kyle stood just inside the door, hands on hips, feet apart, as if preparing to enter an arena. Presently, Tom Prater departed, pulling the door closed behind him.

"All right, Buddy, what's on your mind?"

"I came to tell you I'm through!" Buddy snapped. "I quit! You can take your job and your movie house and your Sheridan Oil and Sheridan Enterprises and Sheridan Realty and ever'thing else Sheridan and stick 'em right up your ass!"

Sam's jaw clenched and he felt his stomach churn. He forced himself to remember that Buddy Kyle was young, impetuous, hotheaded, and came from a reform school environment that bred confrontations of this sort into a person's nature.

"Why don't you sit down, Buddy," he said in a controlled voice, "and tell me what you're angry about."

"I can tell you standing up!" Buddy moved to the middle of the office and pointed an accusing finger at Sam. "When I first throwed in with you, why, you handed me a lot of talk about becoming part of the Sheridan 'family' and having a home here as long as I wanted one. You was the big shot that was gonna take care of me if I stuck with you. Only thing is, it turns out that all your talk was just a lot of bullshit!"

"Buddy," Sam leaned forward and entwined his fingers on the desktop, "if you expect me to sit here and take that kind of talk, you'd better start being specific. What *exactly* is bothering you?"

"Lots of goddamned things!" Buddy shouted his reply.

"Ever'body else who was in on Sheridan number one has got lots of money today—except me! I'm still just a goddamn employee—and not a very important one, either! I wanted Pop Joyner's job when he died, but you wouldn't give it to me. You put Cherokee O'Hara in it instead. Then when he started fucking your wife and you run him off—"

Sam got to his feet, livid. "You just stepped onto very thin ice, kid," he warned. But Buddy Kyle, oblivious of the gravity of his words, kept right on talking.

"—had a second chance to make me the Sheridan Oil field supervisor, but you passed me over again and gave it to somebody else. Then you took me out of Sheridan Oil and put me in Sheridan Enterprises to work for Leon in the movie house. You told me, 'I've got big plans for you, Buddy.' Said it right in front of Tunica! Then when Leon got run off, you made me the manager. Was that your 'big plans'? Having me run a movie house for you?" The anger on Buddy's face changed into a look of satisfied cunning. "Never dawned on me *why* you never kept your word. Not until last night, that is, when Tunica told me that *you* were the reason she could never get serious about *me*. It all made sense then—"

"Wait a minute," Sam said, frowning. "What was that again?"

"—whole thing was to make me look like a fool to her!"

"What in the *hell* are you talking about?" Sam demanded. "Tunica told you *what?*"

"That you and her was the reason she wouldn't marry me. I asked her to marry me last night. She said she couldn't. Because of you."

"Buddy, you must have misunderstood her." *Jesus Christ, was this whole mess over a mistake?*

"I didn't misunderstand a goddamn thing," Buddy Kyle told him unequivocally. "I'm jus' sorry it took me so long to find out about you and her. Jesus, I must have looked like the biggest fool in Texas these past two years. I guess y'all had some good laughs over it."

"Now wait a minute, Buddy," Sam began. But Buddy was already heading for the door.

"Save it." With his hand on the doorknob, Buddy paused and looked back. "You know, it was a pretty dirty trick, running your wife and Cherokee O'Hara off for doing the same thing you was prob'ly doing with Tunica at the time. You're a real prick, Sheridan."

Before Sam could come around the desk, Buddy Kyle was through the door and gone.

Sam went immediately out to the Choctaw community to see Tunica.

The young Indian princess now occupied her own small house not far from Tongue's store. It was much less elaborate than she could have had now that the tribe was thriving on its oil royalties. Like every other community in America during the Depression, the Choctaw were making do on a greatly reduced income; the fortunate thing for them was that the reduced income was *greater* than the community had enjoyed before the oil strike. That plus the fact that they had had five years of substantial earnings before the price of crude oil plummeted, which along with their natural thriftiness, made the Choctaw much better prepared for hard times than most.

Tunica's house was an example of their thriftiness. As princess of the tribe, she was entitled to the best, most expensive dwelling in the community, and had only to ask it of the Beloved Ones and it would be hers. Instead, she requested only what her needs required. The result was a modest five-room house with two bedrooms: one for Tunica, one for the "grandmother" who stayed with her. As a princess without a family, three older women, called "grandmothers," alternated staying in the house with Tunica: cooking her meals, doing her laundry, cleaning, acting as chaperone for her when she was younger. Now that she was grown Tunica did many of the chores herself, and mostly the old women were there just to keep her company; and to satisfy the Beloved Ones, who did not think it was proper or healthy for a young woman to live alone. Tunica would have preferred being alone, but she did not want to be disrespectful to the Beloved Ones, who had seen to her care since her father's death and her mother's suicide, and to whom she was very grateful. Besides, it was only for three months of the year; the rest of the time she was away from the community at college.

Tunica and one of her grandmothers were quilting in the living room when they saw Sam drive up. Spread over the floor was a large, elaborately patterned quilt of many shapes and colors that Tunica, with all three of her grandmothers, had worked on most of the summer. Tunica got up off the floor to open the door for Sam. "Hello, Sam," she practiced saying as she crossed the room. "Why, Sam! How *are* you!" Perhaps she should be dignified—or at least *try* to be. "Sam, what a pleasant surprise." She wished she could tell him she wanted go to bed with him. "May I offer you my nubile young body, Mr. Sheridan?" she whispered to herself. "I've saved it just for you all these years."

Suddenly he was there, at the door, and with great effort she controlled herself.

"Hello, Sam," she said simply as she opened the door.

"Hello, Tunica." He smiled. "You've grown even taller."

"It's been a year and a half since you've seen me. A person can't stay the same forever."

Her sarcasm went right past him. "Tunica, I'd like to talk to you about Buddy Kyle."

"Oh." Jesus, Buddy *had* gone to Sam. God, I'd like to *strangle* him! She smiled at Sam. "All right. Come in, please, Sam."

In the living room Tunica asked the grandmother to leave them alone for a while. The grandmother objected and went on with her quilting. Tunica was used to such a response. The grandmothers constantly attempted to run the house *and* her, as if she were still a girl, instead of running the house *for* her, as they were now supposed to do. Bending over, Tunica snatched the quilt from the grandmother's hands and told her sharply to leave. "At once!" she emphasized in the Natchez dialect. "And do not return until you are summoned!" Tunica always used the Natchez dialect when she wanted to remind the grandmothers of her royal position within the tribe. As the old woman left, Tunica made a mental note to do something nice for her to make up for being so stern.

"Come into the kitchen, Sam, and have some coffee," Tunica said when they were alone. "You've never seen my house, have you?"

"Not the inside, no. But I really came to talk about Buddy."

"Oh, let me show off a little, please," she begged. "Let me show you my house."

"All right, sure." Sam let her lead him around to every room and nodded politely at all the little features and decorating ideas she had incorporated. She was trying to impress upon him that she was a good homemaker; actually, the house was very plain, showed only limited imagination, and accurately reflected the previously austere lifestyle of the Choctaw rather than their more recent prosperity. "It's really quite nice, Tunica," Sam lied. "You've done a good job with it." Even Draw's house, Sam realized, which Georgia had once said was done in Early Junk, seemed warmer and more lived-in than this lifeless little place. The only splash of color in it was the quilt they were making on the living room floor. Everything else was perfectly clean, tidy, and dull.

"May we talk about Buddy now?" Sam asked when they finally got to the kitchen and she poured him a cup of coffee. She poured one for herself and they sat down at the table. "Buddy came to see me this afternoon. He was very angry and quit his job. He said you had told him that you couldn't marry him or be serious about him because you and I were involved in a relationship. I said I was sure he had misunderstood you. But he was positive that's what you'd said."

Tunica blew gently on her coffee and took a slight sip. Sam was looking at her across the table, waiting for an answer, an explanation. She nodded and said, "Yes, Sam, I'm afraid he did misunderstand me."

"I was certain that's what had happened. You know, Buddy's such a hothead; half the time he only hears what he wants to hear. What did you say to him, exactly?"

Tunica put down her cup and looked directly at him. "I told him that I could not be serious about him and could not consider marrying him because I was in love with you. I did not say we were involved, however."

Sam stared at her, dumbfounded. "Why in the name of God did you tell him you were in love with me?"

"For just one reason, Sam: because it's true."

Sam shook his head condescendingly. "Tunica, honey, I've known you since you were a little girl—"

"Yes?" she asked aggressively. "Does that mean something? Does that mean I can't love you?"

"Well, no, I suppose not. But you've been like a little sister to me."

"We're not discussing what I am to you, Sam, but what *you* are to *me*. There's a difference."

Sam fell silent and stared at her. She was not twelve nor fifteen, or even eighteen. She was no longer a girl. This was a young woman sitting across the table from him: how old, twenty? He was not sure, and some instinct told him he dare not ask. There was clearly anger in her dark eyes. Sam suspected he had better be careful what he said.

"Yes," he agreed, "there is a difference. "Well, ah—you're all grown up, it seems."

"How nice of you to finally notice." Her voice was as cool as her eyes were hot.

"All right," Sam said, spreading his hands in surrender. "I'm sorry. You *are* grown up now. You're a young woman. I should have been paying attention, but somehow I missed it. I guess I kept thinking of you as a girl, going to the picture show with Buddy."

"You're a bit behind times. I'm in college now."

"I knew *that,*" he tried to defend himself. "Tongue told me when you first went away. You go to school in Massachusetts, don't you?"

"Pennsylvania."

"I knew it was back there somewhere." Sam smiled his best smile. "How do you like college?"

Tunica looked at him knowingly. "That's a little off the subject, isn't it?"

Sam sat back and sighed. "Tunica, I'm sorry. I don't seem to know what to say."

Tunica herself felt contrite then. "I'm sorry too," she apologized. "I didn't mean to make you so uncomfortable. For that matter, I didn't mean to hurt Buddy, either, or to upset him. I have simply begun being honest with myself and everyone else. I've started *telling* the truth instead of evading it or diluting it to fit the person I'm talking to. I'm afraid it isn't working out too well."

"It's probably my fault." Sam felt very ill at ease. This was the first woman to whom he had spoken privately or about personal matters since Georgia left. Clearly he was not doing very well. In addition to saying the wrong things, he apparently was causing Tunica to do the same. "Let's start over and try again, want to?"

"I'm for that." Tunica got the coffeepot and filled their cups.

After a long moment Sam asked, "How long have you, ah—felt the way you do?" Had she loved him before Georgia left?

"How long have I been in love with you, you mean? I don't really know, Sam. It seems like a long, long time."

"Are you sure you're not getting that kind of love confused with another kind?" he asked gently. "You did lose your father at an early age, and I *am* quite a bit older than you."

Tunica gave him a tolerant smile. "I don't have a father complex, Sam. Believe me, what I feel for you has absolutely nothing to do with a parent-child relationship. Not unless it's incestuous." She leaned forward inquiringly. "Do you find it so difficult to believe that any woman besides Georgia would fall in love with you, Sam? Or is it just that you can't believe that *I* would love you?"

Sam stiffened a little at the mention of Georgia's name. Although he himself had just thought of her a moment earlier, he resented having her name brought into the conversation. "I hadn't really given it any thought. And I don't think we need to discuss my wife."

"Your *wife,* Sam?" Tunica asked in astonishment. "Do you really still consider her your *wife?* How long has she been gone now?"

"Just a minute. That has nothing to do with what we were talking about—"

"Oh, but it does," Tunica insisted. "We're talking about me being in love with you. How you feel about Georgia is going to have a definite effect on any relationship you and I have."

"Just what makes you think we're going to *have* a relationship?"

Tunica sat back in her chair, both surprised and hurt by the tone of his question. Looking down at her coffee cup, she worked desperately to keep control. "You're absolutely right," she admitted. "I was being very presumptuous."

Sam sensed that he had hurt her feelings and immediately felt badly about it. Now it was he who leaned forward over the table. "Tunica, listen. Please. I'm not expressing myself very well today. This whole thing has caught me so much by surprise. You know I've always cared for you, like a—"

"Little sister," she said without rancor, and then looked up at him. They both smiled faintly.

"I thought you *liked* being my little Indian sister," he chided.

"I *never* liked it." Mischief flashed in her eyes. "It was just the best I could do." Suddenly Tunica could not restrain herself; she left her chair and came around the table, dropping to her knees next to him. "Sam, listen," she said, taking his hands, "I *know* this is all sudden and new for you, but it isn't for me. I've lived with it for such a long time, because I've loved you for such a long time. I think I probably started falling in love with you when I was twelve; I remember thinking then that you were the most beautiful man I had ever seen: so clean featured, so serious looking, your skin so light, eyes so very blue. You were the first white man I was ever close to, the first I ever touched. I know I loved you that day the well came in; you must have realized it by the way I kissed you."

"I do remember that kiss," Sam admitted.

Tunica stood and pulled him to his feet. "There's no reason why you shouldn't let me love you, Sam," she insisted. "If you don't love me yet, you *will* love me soon, after you have me, Sam, after I belong to you."

Drawing him forward, Tunica backed out of the kitchen, into the hallway, on into the bedroom.

"This isn't right, Tunica, for either of us."

"We can *make* it right, Sam, please believe me. I feel it so strongly inside of me, so powerfully."

In the bedroom Tunica let go of his hands and quickly unbelted her skirt, letting it drop to the floor. Just as quickly she was out of her shirt, and then she was before him in only her cotton drawers. She put her arms around his neck and tried to kiss him.

"No." It was a firm, unequivocal no, a final no. He pulled her arms from around his neck. "Tunica, I'm sorry. I simply do not feel right about this. I—feel as if—well, as if I'm taking advantage of, well, of—"

"Of a child?" She stepped back and stripped off her drawers. "Do I look like a child, Sam?" Hurt was filtering into her expression. "Oh, I realize I don't have the kind of body that Georgia had, God, but I'm no child either. Look at me, Sam! Look at my breasts: they're swollen for you, the nipples are hard for you. Look between my legs: that's a woman's hair you see there. And if you touched me, you'd find I was wet. Jesus Christ, Sam, I *want* you! I want you to be the first. Please, Sam, love me—"

"No," Sam said again, shaking his head, walking out of the bedroom. "I can't, Tunica. I won't take that from you."

He had a fleeting thought of an upper Pullman berth on a siding in Kansas City, and Georgia telling him the same thing: *I want you to be the first.*

"I'm sorry, Tunica. I'm sorry."

Leaving her standing there naked and humiliated, Sam hurried out of the house.

When Sam pulled up in front of the mansion, Tyler came hurrying out to the car. He looked as if he had been crying.

"We've been calling all over, Daddy, trying to find you," he said anxiously.

"I've been out at the Choctaw community. What's the matter?"

"We called there, Daddy. Tongue said he hadn't seen you."

"I wasn't at Tongue's; I was at Tunica's house. Now will you please tell me what's the matter?"

Ty looked curiously at his father for a fleeting second. Then he said, "It's Draw, Daddy. He's dead."

57

Sam and Tongue discussed where to bury Draw: in the old cemetery near what was left of Dane, or the newer one outside Sheridan.

"I thought about Dane because the Patman family is buried there," Sam said. "Draw came to this part of the country with Able and Lillian. He told me not long ago that he had been in love with my grandmother for years. I thought maybe he'd like to rest with them in death."

But Tongue shook his head. "That was too long ago, Sam. Too many years. I think Draw would want to be here, where you and Ty will be someday. You are the ones he loved when he died. Let him rest here."

Sam did not argue with the Indian's logic. Plans were made to have the funeral and burial in Sheridan.

Draw had died of a heart attack while teaching Tyler to saddle a horse. He had taught the same thing to Lorn Patman, to Ardelle

Patman Spence, and more recently to Sam himself. Despite age and a bad back, he was bound and determined to teach Tyler also. Sam objected, but Draw, more obstinate the older he became, insisted on doing it.

"He'll be the third generation to learn from me," the old man declared. Because it seemed so important to him, Sam relented and told him to go ahead. Draw suffered his massive heart attack as he was swinging a saddle onto the back of a bay mare. Sam did not feel guilty about having given the old cowboy permission. If he had *not* given permission, Draw would have done it anyway, out on the range somewhere instead of at the corral.

Draw's death was a terrible shock to Sam. Over the years Draw had come to represent to him everything in life that was decent and honest and manly. Even during Sam's dark period, when it seemed that Dane and everyone in it was against him, when he regularly and vociferously cursed and damned this foreign land called Texas, Sam seemed to know that deep down he was condemning his own situation and not Texas. Because Texas was not the petty, frightened people with whom Sam had clashed; Texas was Charles Jonas Poker.

Draw had been the spirit of Texas, Sam thought in retrospect. He had been the strength, the determination, the grit, and the guts. He, more than anyone Sam had met since coming there, *was* Texas. The *real* Texas. For eighty years he had been part of its life and progress, its dying and setbacks, part of its massacres, revenges, and gunfights, part of its cattle, its oil, the progression of trails to roads to highways, hamlets to towns to cities, horses to coaches to trains, through the bad and the good, hard times and easy, the terrible and the wonderful.

Draw was Texas to Sam Sheridan and always would be.

For Draw's final resting place, Sam selected a plot next to Pop Joyner's grave. On impulse he purchased two plots on each side of those, and six more in a row directly above them. Sam had no notion *why* he had bought that many plots, enough for ten more people; he would someday occupy only *one* of them. He guessed Tyler could figure out someday what to do with the rest. But it made Sam feel better to have them.

Sam had decided to keep Draw's funeral simple, as he knew Draw would have wanted it. But when he first stated his intent to

Tongue, Tyler, who was in Sam's study with them, ran from the room, crying hysterically. Sam, baffled, started to get up from his desk.

"Let me talk to him," Tongue said, and went after the youngster.

Sam made some calls about the funeral plans and a few minutes later Tongue returned with Tyler in hand. "You remember how Draw used to say, 'When I cash in, boys, don't make no fuss over me. Just throw me out on the prairie somewheres and let the coyotes have a good feed.' That's what the boy thought you meant when you said you were going to keep the funeral simple."

To reassure his son that nothing of the sort was going to happen, Sam let Ty look through the coffin catalog with him and Tongue, and help them select one for Draw.

They got a solid oak coffin, and when the old gunfighter was laid out in it, his face looked like it should have been on a Texas coin. The eaglelike features were still sharp, the white hair still thick and tough as a horse's mane. Viewers at the funeral home knew that though closed, his eyes were no colder or less direct in death than they had been in life.

There were quite a few people at the funeral. Tully and Reba Samuel closed their roadhouse for the day, sent a large wreath, and attended. Natchay and the other two Beloved Ones served as escort for Princess Tunica. Wearing traditional tribal dress, the Indians stood off to the side and did not mingle with the white mourners. The Tom Praters were there, and the Dewitt Tuckers, the Owen Milams, and Sheriff and Mrs. Bill Pete Masters. Many of the small farmers and ranchers attended. A few of the older hangers-on from the now closed Dane pool hall came out of hibernation and showed up. A couple of old cowboys who lived at the Caddo County old folks home, who had known Draw during what they called the "old days, when a man, by Jesus, was a man," managed to get someone to drive them over. Some oil field hands took off work and showed up. And there were three older Mexican women who cried openly when they saw the old man laid out in death. Sam, Tyler, Tongue, Bill Pete Masters, Owen Milam, and Dewitt Tucker were Draw's pallbearers. There was some speculation at the funeral home about the propriety of Tongue being included, since he was not white, but Sam never considered *ex*cluding him. An icy glare from Sam was all that was needed to squelch such talk.

Sam had hoped that perhaps Buddy Kyle would come back for the funeral, and maybe give him and Buddy an opportunity to talk; but there was no sign of the young man, who had been gone four days. Someone who *did* show up was Ardelle Spence. Like the Indians, she remained well off to the side and spoke to no one. Sam was aware of her presence but made no attempt to speak to her, even as a courtesy.

Only one song was played at the service: a slow version of Draw's favorite, "Buffalo Gal." It was rendered first on an organ at the funeral home, then by an oldtimer with a harmonica at the gravesite. Several people in the gathering could be heard softly singing:

> *"Buffalo gal, won't you come out tonight,*
> *Come out tonight, come out tonight?*
> *Buffalo gal, won't you come out tonight,*
> *And dance by the light of the moon?"*

The music wafted mournfully over the open prairie as the old gunfighter was lowered into the ground.

Watching, Sam Sheridan cried unashamedly.

When it was all over, the mourners were invited back to the Sheridan mansion for refreshments. Tom Prater called Sam, Tyler, and Tongue into the study to read Draw's will. Draw left his savings of six hundred thousand dollars in trust for Tyler Charles, his namesake. All of his personal property and his house went to Sam. His share of the income from all Sheridan wells in which he was a partner was to be divided equally between Tyler and Tongue.

Later that evening Tom Prater spoke to Sam about the Washington trip they had been discussing the day Buddy Kyle burst into Sam's office. "I hate to bring it up at a time like this," Tom apologized, "but it *was* initiated by us. We have a legitimate excuse to cancel, of course; all the others know how close you and Draw were. The thing is, arranging a second trip is going to be very difficult; Hoover is going to begin extensive campaigning next month and his schedule will be extremely tight. He might not be able to fit us in. If you could see your way clear to go ahead with it now, why—"

"I don't know why not," Sam decided. "Maybe getting away for a few days will do me good. When do you have it scheduled?"

"Right after the geologists' convention in Baltimore. The other drillers are at that right now; you can meet the group when it goes down to Washington."

"All right," Sam agreed. "Go ahead and confirm it."

Tom Prater drove Sam to Dallas the next day and he caught the *Liberty Flyer* to Washington via Little Rock, Nashville, and Richmond.

It was a two-day overnight trip. Sam had his usual bedroom near the club car. Once aboard he stretched out on the compartment's recliner; he dozed off shortly after the train pulled out of Dallas. The next thing Sam knew, Carter, the bedroom car porter, was gently shaking him.

"Mis' Sheridan, suh. It's the last call for dinner, suh."

Coming out of a deep sleep, Sam asked, "Where are we, Carter?"

" 'Most to Texarkana, suh. Was you planning on dinner tonight, Mis' Sheridan?"

"I reckon I better, Carter. Too long to breakfast."

Sam washed his face and put on his coat. The dining car was toward the rear of the train. When he got there, he found himself behind a tall, dark-haired woman waiting to be seated. She glanced back at him and he saw that it was Tunica.

"Damn," she said quietly.

"What are you doing here?" Sam asked, surprised.

"Going back to school. Pennsylvania, remember?" Tunica sighed. "I saw you get on in Dallas. I was already aboard. I waited until the last call for dinner, thinking you'd have eaten by then."

"Normally I would have. I fell asleep. But you didn't have to try to avoid me, Tunica."

"I thought it would be easier on both of us, after the other day."

The dining car captain came up. "Excuse me, folks, are you dining together?"

"Yes," said Sam, before Tunica could answer. He took her arm and they followed the captain to a table. He gave them menus and order blanks to fill out.

"I haven't had a chance to tell you how sorry I was about Draw," Tunica said. "I guess he was about the best friend you had."

"Easily," Sam admitted. "I feel almost as bad losing Draw as I did when my mother died, years ago."

Tunica reached across the table and touched his hand, briefly. Their waiter came then and they quickly looked at the menus and wrote down their orders. Beyond the window the countryside began to darken as the speeding train crossed into Arkansas.

"Buddy has been on my mind a lot since the funeral," Sam said. "I can't help thinking that this whole misunderstanding could be straightened out very easily if we could all sit down together."

"I'm not so sure," Tunica replied skeptically. "He was *awfully* upset when he left me. I can imagine how upset he was by the time he got to you."

"Yes, but that's the point. Everything that caused his anger is so easy to explain. Not only the fact that I didn't know how you felt about me, that we weren't having a love affair behind his back, but my keeping him employed at the movie house. I planned to *give* him that theater eventually. I'd been waiting because it was losing money during the past two years. I had to subsidize it through Sheridan Realty to keep it open. If I had gone ahead and given it to him, he would have been bankrupt in three months. I suppose I should have set him down and explained everything; I just assumed he understood and trusted me to do right by him."

"You've had a lot on your mind, Sam," Tunica gently reminded him. "Everybody knows how much you've done for the people in Sheridan this past year, and even before that. There are people who never would have made it without your help. And everybody knows you've had personal problems." She looked down at the table, almost tearful. "I know you lost Buddy at a time when you needed his support. That was my fault and I'm sorry. I wouldn't deliberately cause you grief for anything in the world." Tunica bit her lower lip.

"I know you wouldn't." Now it was Sam who reached over to touch her hand. As he did, he took a close look at her for the first time since sitting down. Her long hair was rolled in a Spanish bun at the back of her head; she had a bit of lipstick on, and enough rouge to almost conceal the pockmarks on her right cheek. She was dressed in a fashionable two-piece dark suit and a plain but smart white blouse. She looked older and more grown up than Sam ever remembered seeing her. For a fleeting moment he felt a pang of sadness that he did *not* love her. He was surprised, nevertheless, to find that it unsettled him a little that she was going off to college where she would no doubt be very popular with men more than a decade younger than himself.

411

"I'm very glad we ran into each other," he said, because he felt he had to say *something*.

"Oh, Sam. So am I. Even if you don't care for me the way I do for you, I couldn't stand us not at least being friends."

"I do care for you, Tunica." Their eyes met and held across the table. "If I were completely free of my feelings for Georgia, I would probably fall in love with you."

Sam was as surprised at his words as he imagined Tunica must be. He had never verbalized his continuing painful yearning for Georgia, not even to Draw, his closest friend. Part of him was ashamed for still *having* such feelings, after the betrayal he felt Georgia had dealt him. Now to speak of them, to *admit* them, to Tunica, was totally unplanned, unexpected. But he was not sorry he had.

Their dinner was served and they began eating. Dark night fell and blackened the countryside, and soon all they could see in the window next to the table was their own reflection. They ate quickly, with a minimum of conversation, as if having silently agreed to get out of the public dining car as soon as possible. When they finished the main course, instead of lingering over coffee and dessert, Sam paid the waiter and they left.

"Where is your compartment?" he asked as they passed between cars.

"The next car. I have a roomette."

"Come sit with me for a while. I have a bedroom; it's larger."

His bedroom had been turned down for the night, the two seats by the window made into a lower berth. There was still the recliner to sit on; Sam tried to give it to Tunica, but she insisted he take it. Removing her coat and shoes, she made herself comfortable on the berth, sitting with her legs curled under her.

"I usually have a drink of whiskey before I turn in." Sam took a silver flask from his Gladstone. "Do you drink yet?"

"Now and then," she admitted. "And, yes, I will have one, with a little water, please."

He gave her more than a little water, in case she was only trying to impress him. They sat and sipped whiskey and talked: about people—Tongue, Natchay, Pop, Draw; about the past—the long hard months of work to bring in Sheridan number one, and the many setbacks they had had; about Sheridan, the town—how well Sam expected it do now that President Roosevelt was systematically ending the Depression.

The train kept speeding through the night, its clatter becoming rhythmic after a time, soothing. As the whiskey warmed and relaxed them, they refilled their glasses, laughed a little, and eventually Sam took off his own coat and shoes, joined Tunica in the berth with the whiskey flask, and they turned off the compartment lights, raised the shade, and looked out at a now silvery, moonlit night, the dark countryside interrupted by occasional bright dots from far-flung farmhouses as the *Flyer* sped through Arkansas toward Tennessee.

Hours passed and they continued to talk, their voices growing softer and softer, their shoulders touching, their closeness no longer awkward but now comfortable and secure. Soon the whiskey and the hour and the rails made them sleepy, and they slipped down into the berth with their clothes on, drew the warm Pullman blanket over them, and Sam put his arm around Tunica and they began to drift off.

"We'll be lovers someday, Sam," she whispered as her heavy lids finally shut all the way.

"I know we will."

But Sam went to sleep, as usual thinking of Georgia.

58

On a soft spring day the following April, Tunica was trying to make up her mind whether to cut her last morning class and go back to her room in the dormitory. John White Feather, sitting beside her in Indian Civics, could have predicted what her decision was going to be.

"You're getting bored again, Tunny," he whispered. "I can tell by your scribblings."

Tunica glanced down at the marks she was making on her

notepaper: lots of arrows, lots of squares with geometric Indian patterns on them, like war shields; lots of signs and symbols that in ancient Natchez drawings would have represented horses, warriors, weapons, and battle. John White Feather was right; those were her restless scribbles: quick, nervous little marks indicating a desperation to be someplace else. When Tunica was content, or at least not *dis-*content, she scribbled in a flowing, feminine script with many swirls and circles. Sometimes she even wrote Sam Sheridan's name over and over again in a delicate, cursive flow of ink. Occasionally she wrote "Sam and Tunica" just to see how it looked. It was only when she absolutely hated what she was doing that she resorted to drawing arrows and such. For Tunica, it was like putting on warpaint.

When the bell ending the Indian Civics class sounded, Tunica gathered up her course materials and with John White Feather and the other students filed out of the room.

"Going to skip Indian History, I'll bet," said White Feather.

"You'd win that one," Tunica told him. "If I have to sit through another class this morning I will go *crazy.*"

"You've just got the spring semester drags. What you need is a little relaxation."

"Such as?" she asked dubiously.

"Such as a drive into Lancaster this weekend in my brand-new Lincoln coupe with disappearing headlights. Such as a visit to a cozy little nightclub, of which I am a regular customer. Such as sitting in a dimly lit corner, listening to Carmen Lombardo records, and drinking until we're ready to go somewhere for an orgy."

"You goddamned Indians," Tunica shook her head in mock disgust, "always thinking about your firewater first."

"We think about sex too."

"Yes, but *after* you think about firewater," Tunica insisted. "Have you heard the latest Chickasaw joke? It goes like this: Chickasaw men like their firewater so much, they'll crawl over twelve naked maidens to get to a bottle."

John White Feather chuckled. "With Chickasaws, I can believe it. But I'm an Osage, honey. We're very virile." They came to an intersecting hall where they were to part. "Seriously, how about this weekend, Tunny?"

"Maybe," Tunica told him. "If I haven't died of boredom by then."

They parted and went their different ways. Tunica walked to the end of the intersecting hall and pushed through double doors that let her out of the building. Outside, it was a clear sunshiny day, everything around her seeming to be turning green with new life. It was beautiful and Tunica wished she could muster the proper frame of mind to enjoy it. But she could not. This was the last semester of her third year of college, and the oppression of school was draining her very soul.

Tunica did not care for college and never had. Her freshman year had been exciting for all of three months. Her sophomore year, the newness had worn off in two months. This year she had gone just six weeks before utter despair set in. She had barely made it to Christmas vacation, and had to force herself to come back. As she walked across campus, mindful of the stately, dignified buildings of Woodhull University, she shook her head again, in real disgust this time. You silly goddamn little fool, she thought. There were a thousand Indian girls who would have given *anything* to go to this fine Indian university. And all she was doing was hating it. Sometimes she actually despised herself. This was one of those times.

In her three years at Woodhull, Tunica had to study very little. What the school taught about Indian history, Indian languages, Indian government, and other Indian-steeped subjects, she had already learned from the Beloved Ones while growing up. As for the non-Indian courses such as home economics, physical education, public speaking, debating, and the like, she found them decidely unexciting, to the point where she had developed a way of appearing to be an attentive, interested student, when in fact her mind was usually miles away.

In class Tunica daydreamed: either about her community and her people, for whom she was constantly homesick; or about Sam Sheridan, whom she continued to love so much it was painful. Tunica longed for the days following the strike at Sheridan number one, when her tribe had begun receiving regular amounts of income from its oil royalties. That had been a glorious time for Tunica. Under the guidance of the Beloved Ones, she had, with Tongue's help, first seen to the immediate needs of her savagely poor people: distributing great baskets of canned goods and other foodstuffs, fitting everyone—men, women, children—with new underwear, new shoes and socks, new dresses and overalls, and seeing that every family in the community built up a basic wardrobe. Next came the urgent matter of medical and dental services to combat the malnutrition, scurvy, rickets, and other deplorable conditions that were rife throughout the community. It took months of diagnosis and treatment by two Indian doctors, one a Northern Cheyenne, the other a Mohawk from New York, whom the community hired to move there and begin a clinic; months of injections and inoculations, medical routines, therapeutic treatment, and close hygienic supervision; in all of which Tunica helped as a doctor's assistant, going on house calls to reassure patients facing the unfamiliar doctors from strange far-away tribes. And when the community's health problems were under control, there were other projects: a new sewage and waste disposal system, a new water treatment plant, a school, the location and selection of a teacher, a playground for the children, recreation facilities for the young people, a lodge where the older people without families could live and be cared for, and, it seemed, a hundred other less involved but nevertheless important matters to complete.

It was in that work that Tunica had thrived and matured: work that had *meant* something, that she could see *culminate,* that she could watch *benefit* her people. She grew from a girl to a young woman in such work, and took much personal satisfaction from it. There came a time, however, after a period of years, that much of the work was done, and her community was healthy, well fed, well clothed, being well educated, prospering. There was still work to do here and there, but nothing urgent, nothing critical. That was when the Beloved Ones came to her and asked her to honor them and the community by becoming the first of their tribe to attend college. It would, they foresaw, bring them much respect in the white community; but more importantly, it would set an example and encourage the young of their tribe to also covet higher education. Tunica loathed the idea, but only from a personal perspective; in her role as the Natchez-Choctaw royal princess, she had to concede that it was an excellent plan. She had no choice, she knew, but to accept; so she did, though with great trepidation.

The Beloved Ones had given her a surname: Chahta, which was the Indian spelling for Choctaw. So she became Tunica Chahta, freshman, at Woodhull University. And began her miserable exile nine months of each year. Now she was in her third awful year of that purgatory, and even though it would be over in just a few short weeks, she was nevertheless having serious difficulty staying there. A lot of it, of course, had to do with Sam Sheridan. Now that she had made her love for him known, and especially after their night, albeit sexless, on the *Liberty Flyer,* Tunica felt she should be back where Sam was, working on breaking down his resistance, dissipating any ridiculous feelings he still had for that slut Georgia—God, sometimes Tunica hated her!—and somehow convincing Sam that it was now time for them to become one in body, mind, and spirit, as lovers.

She thought about Sam all the way back to her dorm after cutting third class, thought about how his body had felt next to hers in that berth, even with their clothes on, remembered how Sam had got an erection despite himself, but would do nothing about it, and the more she thought about him the warmer she could feel herself becoming. She would have the room all to herself when she got to the dorm; her roommate, a Blackfoot from Idaho, would be in class. How fun it would be, to take off all her clothes and lie down on the bed with her picture of Sam in one hand . . .

Excitement made her hurry a little faster. When she finally got there, she was flushed with desire from her own unbridled imagination. Locking the door to the room, she pulled down the shades, turned on the little Du Mont radio next to her bed, and got undressed. The picture she had of Sam was a newspaper photograph in a small frame, showing him smiling after being elected to a two-year term as president of the East Texas Drillers Association. Lying down, naked, with the picture propped up on the pillow by her face, Tunica smiled at the music being played on the radio: it was Dorothy Fields' new song, "I'm in the Mood for Love."

God, am I *ever,* she thought, discovering how moist she already was, just from thinking about it. She began moving the tip of her forefinger in rhythm to the music.

"Oh, Sam, honey . . ."

An hour later Tunica went downstairs to the pay phone and called Sam long distance. After her solo session in bed, she had another uncontrollable urge: to hear the sound of his voice.

"If I order a barrel of oil from you," she said when her call was put through, "will you personally deliver it?"

"I'd be tempted," Sam replied, laughing. "How are you, Tunica? How's school?"

"Unbearable. I mean, really, Sam, it is *dreadful* this semester."

"You sound like Tyler. He was complaining last night that the fourth grade was 'twice as worse' as third."

"He sounds like my kind of kid. Is he old enough to run away with me?"

"Not quite, I'm afraid. Anyway, he doesn't like girls."

"Hell, I might have known. I don't have *any* luck with Sheridan males."

"I wouldn't say that."

Tunica's heart fluttered a little. "What do you mean?"

"I mean that I miss you," Sam said quietly. "I've missed you ever since you went back after Christmas. I suppose I shouldn't be telling you that; it probably won't make staying at school any easier."

"Oh, Sam, it *will!*" she assured him, delighted. "My god, you just changed my entire *outlook!* You gave me something to look forward to!"

"I did?"

"Oh, yes! Easter, Sam! The Easter vacation! Oh, Sam, can we be together then? Can we have a night for ourselves, just us? *Please.* "

Before he could really consider the implications of such a plan, Sam, inspired by the sheer excitement in her voice, said, "Yes, by god, we can. Why not? We deserve to be happy, just like anybody else. Easter vacation, it is. You and me, Princess Tunica."

"Oh, *god!* I can't believe it! Sam, listen to me," she lowered her voice to a throaty whisper, "I was upstairs a minute ago lying on my bed completely naked, with a picture of you on my pillow. Shall I tell you what I was doing?"

"Absolutely not. Say, what kind of a school are you going to, anyway?"

"You'd be surprised. An Osage named White Feather invited me to a drunken orgy a little while ago. Would you mind if I went?"

"Yes, I would mind."

"I'm so *glad.* " Then she said in an emotional voice, "Oh, Sam. Sam."

"Hold on, Tunica." Sam was suddenly all business. "What's the matter?" She heard another voice, but could not make out the words. Then Sam came back on the line. "Tunica, I have to go. There's a fire in one of the fields."

"All right, Sam—"

There was a click as he quickly hung up.

Sam notified Owen Milam at the Sheridan Oil laboratory, then rushed to the site. It took him fifteen minutes to reach the fire, which was on a farm lease next to the Spence ranch. Skidding his pickup to a dusty stop, he jumped out and hurried over to the field foreman in charge of fire control.

"How'd it start, Sherman?"

"No telling, Mr. Sheridan. Could have been a spark from the pump, a cigarette somebody threw away, sun reflecting on something shiny. No telling."

Sam quickly surveyed the scene. The fire was burning around the base of the pump that was Sheridan number thirteen. It had spread along the ground, following natural gas and crude oil seepage in a circle about thirty feet wide; its flames were five feet high. Sherman, the fire-control foreman, had a dozen men digging a slit-trench around the perimeter of the flames to contain the spread. Fifty yards away stood the farmer's house on whose land the well had been sunk. Moses Garrity, the farmer, and his wife and four children were standing on the front porch, watching anxiously.

"Think you can control it?" Sam asked Sherman.

"We've got generators and steam hoses on the way," the foreman said. "When they get here, we can smother it. We can control it on the ground until then. Thing is, we can't control it *above* the ground." Wetting a forefinger in his mouth, he held it up to the early afternoon air. "There's a little bit of breeze. When that pump platform gets burned down far enough for the wood to crumble, why, there's a chance the breeze'll pick up hot cinders and blow 'em about. If that happens, we'll have a bad problem." He glanced up the road. "Can't figure why the steam hoses ain't here by now."

"If they're not here in five minutes, I'll go after them. Meantime, I'll have a word with the Garritys." Hurrying over to the house, Sam stood next to the porch and reached up to shake hands with Garrity. "We'll have it whipped in a few minutes, Moses," he said, trying to sound confident.

"Afternoon breeze is coming in," Garrity warned ominously.

"We'll put it out, don't worry. Any idea how it started?"

Garrity shook his head. "No smokers on the place but me, and I ain't been near it. Ain't been no spring lightning today. None of the stock's been out. Nobody at all around that pump except one feller about an hour ago."

"What fellow?"

"Feller in a black pickup. Stopped to take a leak. But the fire didn't start until long after he was gone."

"Look out!" a voice shouted from across the yard. All heads at the house snapped around and saw that it was Sherman yelling and waving his arms. At the same time they saw that a gust of wind was carrying a stream of live ash toward the farmhouse.

"Lord God!" Mrs. Garrity screamed. Two of her children started to cry.

The ash settled on the roof of the house and began to smolder.

"Get your children out in the cornfield, Mrs. Garrity!" Sam ordered. "Moses, let's get some water on that roof!"

As they were preparing to fight the threat on Garrity's roof, another Sheridan Oil pickup raced up to the farmyard and Owen Milam leaped out. His normally calm features were terribly strained.

"Sam! Number nine is on fire too!" he yelled.

"What?"

"Nine! The platform and about sixty feet of ground seepage! I had to divert the steam hoses over there to keep it from spreading to the number three storage tank!"

Sam and the geologist stared at each other. *Two* wells? Catching fire at the *same* time?

"Help Garrity try to save his house," Sam said after a moment. "I'll go over to nine and get a steam hose over to you as quickly as possible. If you get things under control in the meantime, I want you to find Bill Pete and have him meet me over at nine. We may have a problem that needs a lawman."

As Sam hurried toward his truck, the Garrity roof broke into flame.

Tunica slept most of the afternoon, not waking up until nearly five o'clock, then coming out of her long nap ravaged by hunger. She had skipped breakfast, being too depressed to eat; then she had completely forgotten about lunch, being so excited after making plans on the telephone with Sam for Easter; so she actually had not eaten for nearly twenty-four hours.

Hurrying out of the dorm, Tunica crossed the campus to the dining hall. At the first table just inside the dining hall door, John White Feather and some other students were listening to a radio they had connected to an extension cord.

"Tunny," White Feather called as Tunica entered, "come here."

"I'm going to eat, John. I'm starved."

"No, come here first." The Osage's uncharacteristic seriousness made Tunica stop and look at him. His expression was as grave as his voice. Frowning, Tunica went over to the table.

"Radio says there's a big oil field fire outside Sheridan, Texas. Isn't your village near there?"

The shocked expression on her face, as she suddenly remembered the end of her conversation with Sam, told them that her village was indeed there. "How bad is it?"

"Out of control," White Feather said quietly.

Tunica hurried back to the telephone in her dorm. She tried first to call Sam at his office and home, then Tongue at the store in Choctaw Village. Telephone service to both places was restricted to official use only. She tried to call the sheriffs in Dane, New Salem, and other communities near Sheridan. None of her calls could be put through.

Tunica went up to her room and packed a small bag. She got John White Feather to drive her to Lancaster, the nearest small airport. There she got on the next Allegheny air ferry hop to Trenton. In Trenton she explained her plight to the operations manager, but there was nothing he could do for her; there were no westbound flights until the next day. A mail pilot down for refueling overheard the conversation.

"If I was you," he told her, "I'd get up to Newark quick as I could. American Airlines has one of them new Douglas DC-3s that flies Newark to Memphis to Oklahoma City to Phoenix to Glendale. A sixteen-hour run. Leaves at nine o'clock if you can make it."

Tunica hired a taxi for the fifty-mile drive to Newark. She got to the Newark airport with an hour to spare, but found the American flight fully booked: all twenty-one seats filled. A Catholic priest,

421

hearing of her emergency, gave up his seat, and a grateful Tunica bought a ticket.

Before the flight boarded, she listened to more news of the fire on the radio in the waiting room. It had been raging for eight hours and had spread over an estimated seven square miles. Burning between the towns of Dane and Sheridan, it had thus far done only minor damage to the outskirts of each. But unusually dry weather the past few weeks, coupled with gusting spring winds, were spreading the blaze to the raw prairie where it was being fueled by brittle sagebrush and dead scrub grass. Prairie winds were whipping up loose piles of fiery brush and blowing them haphazardly in all directions. Firefighting equipment from communities as far as fifty miles away had responded to the emergency, but at least nine farmhouses had been destroyed and four persons were known injured.

There was no mention of Choctaw Village.

Tunica tried to sleep on the flight west, but worry about her people kept her wide awake. She sat staring at the darkness, fearing the death she would find waiting for her. That was the way she remained until the plane landed in Memphis at 3:00 A.M.

Tunica was the only passenger to debark in Memphis. At the operations desk there, two layover flight engineers tried to figure out how she could get closest to her home.

"That feller Paul Braniff," one of them asked, "where's he flying now?"

"Tulsa to Wichita Falls," the other answered. "Way too far west for her. What about that Hudson terraplane that flies down to Little Rock? Varney Air Transport, ain't that what it's called?"

"Not no more. Changed the name to Continental Airlines. Fancy, huh? Got a couple of Ford trimotors now. Where would she go after she got to Little Rock?"

"I heard of a feller down there name of Clyde Cessna, designed hisself a ship he calls the Travel Air. Gives demonstration flights to people inners'ed in buying. If she could get him to fly her down to Shreveport, Louisiana, why, she'd on'y be about fifty miles from home." He turned to Tunica. "You willing to try that, little lady?"

"Yes, of course. Anything."

With a route and schedule they drew up for her and confirmed by radio, Tunica left Memphis at 5:00 A.M.

Radio reports said the fire was still burning.

59

As Tunica was traveling her circuitous route home, another person was also making an effort to get to the site of the fire as quickly as possible. He was a man named Reb Jackson, a thirty-year-old Texan who was already becoming a legend for controlling and extinguishing oil field fires. Jackson had left his operational base in Houston at midnight on the day the fire started, leading a convoy of twelve trucks and fifty men. Eight of the trucks were mounted with high-pressure steam generators connected to quad-hoses capable of quickly producing and spreading enormous bursts of fire-smothering steam. The convoy reached Sheridan shortly after daylight. Reb Jackson found Sam Sheridan in a field shack that was being used as a fire control center. With Sam were Owen Milam and fire chiefs from five surrounding communities. The seven men were slick with soot and sweat. Owen, who knew Reb Jackson, introduced him to Sam and the others.

"I hope to God you can help us, Reb." Sam's eyes, like everyone else's, were dull with fatigue from eighteen hours of futile attempts to control the blaze.

"Fire ain't been started that I can't put out," Reb Jackson replied simply. He was a small man with thinning sandy hair and a heavily freckled face; his eyes were a very light green. Jackson's parents had been killed when their small Texas farmhouse burned down a decade earlier. Fire was his natural enemy.

After the introductions Jackson said to Owen, "Got it mapped?"

"Over here."

They all gathered around a table on which was spread open a plat map of the south half of Caddo County. Reb Jackson took a box of children's Crayola crayons from his shirt pocket and selected a red one.

"Where'd it start and what time?" he asked.

Sam told him and Reb marked the information on the map.

"Which way did it spread?"

"North and west, toward this point," said Sam, putting a finger on the map. Then he moved his finger and added. "Another one started over here at roughly the same time."

Jackson exchanged a quick glance with Owen Milam. The look said: *That doesn't happen. At least not accidentally.*

"Which way'd the second one spread?"

Sam told him, then said in a cold, ominous voice, "There were three others too."

Reb Jackson pursed his lips in a silent whistle. After he had marked each of the five points of the fire's origin and drawn red arrows indicating directional spread, he asked the fire chiefs, each of whom had men and equipment in one of five sectors of the burning field, to brief him on how far the fire had spread, what the human habitation and condition of the terrain were in each area, and the approximate height of the flames. The chiefs, not overjoyed at an "outside specialist" being called in, grudgingly answered Jackson's questions. Jackson then asked Owen Milam to give him an estimate of the amount of natural gas leakage and crude oil seepage in each place. As the various men fed him information, Jackson made red crayon signs and symbols on the plat map: numbers, arrows, arcs, circles, heavy double lines. When he had all the information he wanted, he strode to the door and stuck his head out.

"Wilbur! What's the wind doing?"

From the bed of a truck equipped with air velocity instruments, a lanky man with a toothpick in his mouth shouted back, " 'Tween four and five, gusting to seven, from the southeast, steady!"

"Humidity?"

"Forty-two and climbing, boss!"

Jackson turned to four men waiting in a group near the door. "All right," he said. The men hurried into the shack behind Jackson and gathered around the map table with him. Jackson put the red

424

crayon back in the box and took out a green one. With it he began making new marks, talking as he did so. "The fire in these two sections ain't going nowhere right now 'cause the wind's against it. Buster, take charge of both areas; put a steamer in each one and back up the blaze as far as you can. Cecil, you move over here to this area with two steamers; hold the spread as best you can for now. Bubba, you do the same over here in this other area. Big Jim," he tapped a forefinger on one of the sectors, "this is the main problem right here. This sucker here can spread ever' which way but down. I want four steamers over there pronto: one here, one here, two here. Deploy them in a number six pattern and give 'em full pressure all the way." Jackson's light green eyes swept the faces of his four men. "Get cutting."

As his men hurried out, Reb Jackson turned to the five community fire chiefs.

"From what I can see, chiefs, you and your men have done an outstanding job of keeping this fire under control until special equipment could get here. There's no doubt in my mind that if y'all had equipment like mine, I wouldn't even have to be here; you men would have put the fire out already. That's what I intend to tell the newspaper boys when this is all over. I'm gonna make sure each of you and your department gets full credit for the fine job you've done."

As Jackson walked out to join his men, he threw Owen Milam a wink. The five fire chiefs, pouting up to then, grinned and nodded at each other.

"Why don't y'all each get back to your sectors," Owen suggested, "and make sure your men cooperate with Jackson's men. Let's get this son of a bitch put out."

"Damn straight," one of the chiefs said, and they all hurried out. As the chiefs were leaving, a uniformed sheriff's deputy shouldered his way in.

" 'Scuse me, Mr. Sheridan. Sheriff Masters said to tell you the feller in the black pickup's been caught. Sheriff's holding him down at the jail."

Under the soot and sweat that had already darkened his face, Sam's eyes turned even darker.

"Take over here, Owen," he said. "I'll be down at the jail."

* * *

425

The black pickup was parked outside the Sheridan jail when Sam got to town. Sheriff Bill Pete Masters, almost as grimy as Sam from helping fight the fire himself, met Sam as he walked in.

"Where is he?" Sam asked.

"Back here." Bill Pete led the way down a corridor to the lockup section. There was a row of six cells, only one of which was occupied. The solitary prisoner was a chunky man with a flat bulldog face and tightly coiled black hair. He was wearing oil field denims. Sam stared at him through the bars.

"His name's Joe Bob Thurmond," Bill Pete said. "From down Del Rio way."

"Long piece from home, aren't you?" Sam asked quietly.

"Free country," the prisoner replied.

"Sheriff Delby of Freestone County stopped him the other side of Cayuga," Bill Pete said. "He was heading west. We brought him back a little while ago. Searched his truck but didn't find anything except tools and a roadmap. Nothing in his pockets but a plug of tobacco, a jackknife, and his billfold." Bill Pete paused a beat, then added, "And two thousand dollars in hundred-dollar bills."

"Lot of money," Sam said to the prisoner. "Where'd you get it?"

"That comes under the heading of my business," Thurmond replied cockily. His eyes shifted to the sheriff. "You better turn me loose. You ain't got nothing on me and you know it."

Sam took a sudden step toward the cell, causing the prisoner to retreat quickly from the bars. "You set fire to my wells, didn't you?" It was a statement more than a question.

"I ain't set far' to nothing."

"A black pickup was seen at three of my five wells that started burning."

"Mine ain't the only black pickup in Texas." From the safety of his cell Thurmond smirked. "Anyway, what's five little ol' wells to a big oil man like you? You won't even miss 'em."

"If you'd stayed around awhile after doing your dirty work," Sam told him, "you'd know we aren't just talking about five wells. That fire spread to *twenty* wells. It burned down at least a dozen farmhouses and ruined hundreds of acres of cotton crops." Sam paused thoughtfully for a moment, then added, "And it's killed some people, too. You're not just an arsonist, Thurmond; you're a murderer."

The prisoner turned pale. Swallowing, he said in a shaky voice, "I ain't no such thing. You ain't got nothing on me."

"Is he right, Sheriff?"

"Afraid so, Sam," Bill Pete confirmed. "There's no real evidence against him."

"All right then, I want two things from you," Sam said in a measured voice. "I want the key to his cell, and I want you to stay away from the jail for two hours."

Bill Pete Masters stared silently at Sam for a long moment. But finally he nodded and said, "I reckon I can do that." He handed Sam a ring of cell keys. "It's number four."

"Now just a goddamned minute here!" Joe Bob Thurmond protested indignantly. "What the hell is this? Why, you can't do that!"

Bill Pete walked out of the lockup without responding. Sam stepped over to a turnkey's desk in an anteroom to the row of cells and picked up a telephone. "Give me Sheridan six-five-two." A moment passed, then he said, "Owen, this is Sam. Pick out four good men and send them over to the jail right away. Have them bring a rope."

Replacing the receiver, Sam turned to see Joe Bob Thurmond staring at him in wild-eyed incredulity. "What—what are—? Why, you can't—"

"Yes, I can," Sam told him coldly. "I can—and I *will.* You're going to hang, you murdering son of a bitch." He started for the door. "I'll be back as soon as my men get here with the rope."

"Jesus God, wait a minute!" Thurmond pleaded. "Please, just a minute! Give me a chance!"

"A *chance!* What kind of chance? The kind you gave those poor farmers and their families that watched their homes and crops go up in flames? The kind you gave the people who *died?* Why, you scum bastard, you're lucky I don't *burn* you to death!"

"I didn't mean to kill nobody," Thurmond said, beginning to cry. "I didn't know the far' would spread. He said he jus' wanted to burn some of your wells to teach you a lesson. He said—"

"Who said?" Sam demanded. "The man that paid you the two thousand?"

"Yeah."

"Who was it?"

Thurmond wiped his mouth with the back of one hand, trembling now, trying to muster the courage to complete his confession.

"Name him, goddamn you!" Sam stormed.

"M-M-Mr. Spence," Thurmond stammered. "P-P-Pete Spence."

Sheriff Masters walked back in from the corridor and Sam returned the ring of keys to him.

"Hear enough?" Sam asked.

"Enough."

"Then let's go."

On their way out Bill Pete said, "Should we tell Thurmond that nobody really died in the fire?"

Sam shook his head. "Let the son of a bitch suffer. God knows, he's made enough other people suffer for his goddamned two thousand dollars."

Sam and Bill Pete sped to Dane in the sheriff's police car, with red light flashing. They parked on the deserted town square in front of the boarded-up Merchants Bank. The only other vehicle in sight was Pete Spence's silver Packard. Together they climbed the stairs to the offices of Spence Land and Cattle Company. Pete Spence was alone in his private office, at his desk, reading the Dallas *Times*.

"What can I do for you, Sheriff?" he asked Bill Pete, ignoring Sam's presence entirely.

"You're under arrest, Mr. Spence."

Spence chuckled and laid the paper aside. "Is that a fact? On what charge, Sheriff?"

"Conspiracy to commit arson."

"My, my. That's a serious charge. How'd you come up with it?"

"You paid Joe Bob Thurmond to set fire to the oil field."

"Shit. You got about as much chance of making that stick as a bull has giving milk."

"We'll make it stick," Bill Pete told him confidently. "We've already got a confession out of Thurmond."

"His word against mine," Spence said, shrugging his round shoulders. "Ain't a trial judge in Texas would take the word of some white trash against mine."

"Sounds like you know the man, all right," Sam said, speaking for the first time. The sound of Sam's voice seemed to infuriate Spence. He leaped to his feet and pointed an accusing finger at Sam.

"You want to arrest somebody, Sheriff, why don't you arrest that illegitimate bastard right there! He's the one that turned Caddo County into a goddamned oil field in the first place! This used to be decent cattle country before he came along! Arrest him! He's the one to blame!"

Bill Pete pulled a set of handcuffs from his belt. "You want to come quietly, Mr. Spence, or you want me to put these bracelets on you and haul you out?"

Spence's fleshy face turned crimson. "You'll be sorry you're treating me like this."

"Coming quietly or not?"

Spence glared hatefully at the lawman, but said, "Put your goddamned handcuffs away, I'll come quietly." He walked around the desk and took his hat from a coatrack. "Let's get it over with. I'd like to be charged and taken in front of a judge as quick as possible so I can be home in time for dinner."

Spence walked past Sam without a glance. Bill Pete followed him and the three of them went down the stairs. As they reached the sidewalk, a Spence Land and Cattle feed truck screeched to a stop next to Bill Pete's police car. A young cowboy got out and hurried toward Spence, his expression urgent and frightened. Spence stopped and frowned.

"What is it?" he asked. "What's the matter?"

"It's your ranch house, Mr. Spence!" the cowboy blurted. "It's burning up! Wind blowed some burning mesquite across the range a little while ago and set the place on fire! Some of the boys is trying to put it out but they ain't having much luck. They sent me in to see if there was a fire engine in town—"

Pete Spence's ruddy face drained sheet white. "Lord God Almighty . . ." he muttered. "My girls went out there yesterday. They said they might stay the night—"

"Your *daughters?*" Sam asked, appalled.

"What about Mrs. Spence?" the sheriff asked.

"She . . . stayed at the house . . . in town," Spence replied haltingly. "Did anybody see my girls out there?" he asked the cowboy.

429

"No, sir. We didn't see nobody about."

Spence shook his head. "I don't know . . . whether the girls came back or not. I was up and out early this morning—"

Spence suddenly whirled and ran upstairs to his office. Bill Pete hurried after him. Sam turned to the young cowboy. "You know where the field shack's at between Sheridan wells number eight and nine?"

"Yessir, Mr. Sheridan."

"Get out there quick and ask for Mr. Milam. Tell him I said to let you have some men to help put out the fire at the ranch house. Tell him—" Sam had to swallow around the words, "—tell him there may be people trapped inside. Hurry!"

"Yessir!"

The cowboy rushed back to the truck and sped out of town. Sam remained on the sidewalk for several moments, moving a few steps here, a few steps there, trying to think of further action to take, something positive to do. In the back of his mind lurked fleeting images of the two young cousins whose pictures he had seen in the society pages so often, but whom he had never known. In desperation, he finally started up the stairs but was met halfway by Pete Spence and Sheriff Masters hurrying down.

"He just called Mrs. Spence," Bill Pete said. "The girls didn't come home last night."

"Good god—"

The three men ran out to the police car. Because neither Sam nor Pete Spence thought to do otherwise, both crowded into the front seat with the sheriff; Bill Pete gunned the engine and the car shot out of town, red light flashing again. Spence was in the middle, his burly frame squeezed between the other two, leaner men. Staring straight ahead, his eyes wide with terror, he was oblivious to the fact that he was shoulder-to-shoulder with the nephew he loathed. The stink of dread rose from his body, both Sam and the sheriff smelling it, recognizing it. Neither of them looked at Spence.

When they turned into the country road leading to the ranch house, the men could see billows of smoke rising from beyond a stand of trees. Unlike the thick, black petroleum smoke, this was a thin-nish, gray matter that came from the burning of wood, cloth, paper; perhaps people. No sooner had they seen it than from behind them came the incessant blowing of a horn on another automobile. Sam and Spence both twisted in their seats to look back. Dividing the cloud of dust being created by the speeding police car was another big Packard like Spence's, driven by Ardelle Spence. Her own eyes panic-wide, she gripped the steering wheel with one hand and with the other kept the horn depressed.

"I can't pull over!" Bill Pete yelled. "There's no room for her to pass!"

"Keep on going," Sam told him. "We're almost there."

In five minutes the two cars skidded simultaneously to a halt in front of the big three-story house that was engulfed in out-of-control flames. A dozen men had formed a line from a well and were passing buckets to the fire as fast as possible; three others had garden hoses hooked to faucets outside the nearby stable. It was immediately apparent that all their efforts were futile; the collective water being applied to the leaping flames was too insignificant to even delay, much less contain, the fiery menace.

"My babies!" Ardelle Spence screamed, rushing past the men, going headlong toward the flames. Bill Pete Masters managed to grab her mere feet from disaster. Pete Spence, stumbling back and forth in front of the burning house, features contorted in anguish, held both hands out as if pleading with someone, *any*one, for help. Thinking that Spence, like his wife, was getting too close to the licking flames, Sam ran over to one of the men spraying with a garden hose.

"I'll take this!" he shouted. "You see to Spence over there! Keep him back!"

The ranch hand hurried toward Spence. Sam moved a few steps closer with the hose nozzle; his face and arms quickly became hot. Glancing over his shoulder, he saw the sheriff wrestle Ardelle Spence to the police car and handcuff one of her wrists to the steering wheel; all the while she was screaming, "My babies! My babies! My baby girls—!"

Sam had moved closer to the inferno than the ranch hand he had relieved on the hose, but after less than a minute the heat became too intense and he had to step back. It was useless anyway; by then everyone there knew it: so much of the house had burned that its walls were getting ready to collapse. The men on the bucket line gave up and stopped. A few of them gravitated over to Pete Spence, who immediately stopped stumbling around and went to each of them in turn, asking, "Did you see my girls? Were my girls in there?"

Most of the men looked away, unable to cope with the question. A couple of them managed a shrug. Only the ranch foreman was able to muster words.

"They didn't get out, boss," he said. "Them nor the Mes'can help neither. It just spread too quick. Too quick for ever'body."

As he spoke, the front wall of the house fell inward, dropping the two upper floors into a pile of rubble and sending a great puff of ash and smoke dust mushrooming out from the flames. The sudden shifting of matter displaced enough oxygen to create a momentary vacuum that extinguished the inferno's center; after everything settled, only the outer edges of the structure were still ignited. Harsh, choking smoke began to drift up from where flames had died, silent mourners of the lost house. At the police car, Ardelle Spence, like the wall of the house, also collapsed. When her screams ceased, the prairie was left eerily quiet. Only Pete Spence's voice could be heard, barely, as he shook his head and said softly to himself, "Oh my Lord . . . oh my Jesus." Over and over he repeated the same phrase, "Oh my Lord, oh my Jesus," until the words became a whimper; then he began asking, "What have I done? Lord God Almighty, what—have —I—done?"

Sheriff Bill Pete Masters spoke quietly to Sam, who nodded agreement to what he said. The sheriff stepped over to Pete Spence and put a hand on his arm. "Mr. Spence, let me take you and your wife back to town—"

Without warning, Pete Spence reached down and snatched the sheriff's revolver from its holster. Shoving Masters away with one hand, Spence put the pistol to his own head with the other and blew his brains out.

60

Tunica got as far as Little Rock, Arkansas, on the flight that left Memphis at 5:00 A.M. By nine-thirty that morning she was on still another plane, her fourth since leaving college in Pennsylvania sixteen hours earlier. At one o'clock that afternoon she was on an Ark-Tex bus, traveling from Shreveport, Louisiana, to Longview, Texas. When she reached Longview, she was within thirty miles of home. She hired a taxi to drive her the rest of the way.

Between Sheridan and Choctaw Village, Tunica saw Owen Milam with a group of men at the side of the road. She had the driver stop and got out. Owen, still black with soot, saw her and hurried over.

"Tunica," he said, surprised, "I thought you were away at school."

"I was. Is Sam all right?"

"Yes, he's okay. He and Bill Pete are driving around to survey the damage. The fire's completely out now. Are you on your way to the village?"

"Yes. Is it very bad out there?"

"I don't know, Tunica. The fire got that far, but I haven't heard how much damage it did. We'll get some help there as soon as we can."

"Thank you. Please tell Sam I'm here."

Tunica returned to the taxi. The drive the rest of the way to the village was a nightmare. Everywhere there was devastation. Oil derricks lay burned into sticks, their drilling rigs twisted and snapped off. Farmhouses, barns, and silos had been reduced to piles of ashes and charred wood. Crops in the fields had been blackened as if sprayed with coal dust. Trees were smoldering; telephone and power poles burned down, their wires melted. Farm animals and livestock were lying dead, crows and blackbirds already beginning to pick at their cooked carcasses.

As the taxi approached the Choctaw community, Tunica's eyes filled with tears. Even from a distance, she could tell that much had been burned. Alighting from the taxi next to a pile of rubble that had been Tongue's general store, she paid the driver and stood looking around as he drove off. Down the road she saw several people sitting in front of a burned house. She walked briskly over to them.

"Where is everyone?" she asked in Choctaw. "Where are the rest of the people?"

"Dead," an old woman answered. "Burned up by the evil fire."

Looking around, Tunica saw no bodies anywhere. "Did some of the people hide from the evil fire?"

"Yes. In the place where the young ones gather."

Of course, Tunica thought. The recreation center. It was constructed of brick. She hurried off down the road.

As she neared the recreation center, Tunica saw four young children outside, looking off in different directions. "What are you doing?"

"Watching for the evil fire to start again," one of them answered.

"Who told you to do this?"

"The older ones."

Tunica went inside. Several dozen village children were sitting on the floor with their backs to the wall. The older girls, of high school age, were humming and chanting, some of them moving to and fro in the death rock. The young men were together in another group, some with their faces buried in their hands, others staring blankly at nothing. They looked retarded. The older people were off in corners, huddled together, staring like zombies.

"What is going on here?" Tunica demanded. "Why are you all in here when there is work to be done?"

"The evil fire will return," one of the young men said.

"Who says this thing?"

The young man shrugged. "It is so. One of the elders was overheard to say it."

"It is not true," Tunica announced for all to hear. "There is no more fire; it has been put out. Come, all of you, follow me outside. There is much work to do."

Many of them looked up and stared at her, but none moved.

"Come *on!*" Tunica shouted. "Outside! Now!"

Still none of them moved.

Tunica went to the young man who had answered her questions. Kneeling in front of him, she said firmly, "I am the Royal Princess Tunica. In my body flows the blood of Techanta, the great Sun King. You will obey my commands. I order you to rise and go outside. Do it now."

The young man stared at her but remained immobile. Tunica slapped him hard across the face.

"I order you to rise and go outside. Do it now."

Still he did not move. Tunica slapped him twice more.

"I order you to rise and go outside. Do it now."

Slowly the young man got to his feet and started for the door.

"You," Tunica said to another young man, "follow him."

The second young man followed the first. Tunica got another started, and another. Then she turned to the girls.

"Follow the boys outside."

The girls obeyed at once. Soon all the young people in the building were lining up to file out the door. Tunica did not bother with the older people; they would come to their senses when they saw for themselves that it was safe. She went among them only briefly to ask if any of them knew where the elders, the Beloved Ones, were. None of them did. When all the young people were outside, Tunica joined them, standing in their midst and putting her arm around the young man she had slapped.

"Listen to me," she said. "Our tribe and our village have suffered a great tragedy. The oil field that has given us so much in the past few years has now taken some of it away. The fire burned part of our village and destroyed many of our homes. Many white homes have been destroyed also, and as usual whites will help whites. We of the Choctaw must do for ourselves. Listen carefully to me and I will tell you what to do.

"First, each of you go to your homes. Look and see how much damage has been done, and determine who in your family has been injured. Bring back here to the recreation center everyone whose home was burned, along with any food you can salvage and any bedding you can find. It will be dark in a few hours and all who are without homes must be back here to spend the night. If any of you find any undamaged cars or trucks and can get them started, use them to pick up the food and bedding of others. Go now, and hurry!"

After the young people had gone off in all directions, Tunica walked down the road to look at her own house. She found it burned to the ground. Tihasta, one of the old grandmothers who had helped raise her, was lying on her stomach in the ashes with a charred ceiling beam across her back. Tunica was able to identify her only by a bone bracelet she wore; although burned black, its design still showed. Tunica dropped to her knees beside the burned house, crying and chanting a little. She tried to remember if she had ever told Tihasta that she loved her. She did not think she had.

For a few minutes, she prayed to the Choctaw gods for the old woman's spirit.

When Tunica returned to the recreation building, she found that several vehicles had been located, and that there was a good supply of food and enough bedding for at least half the people there. Setting everyone to work—the girls cleaning up the soot inside and making pallets, the boys sorting and checking the food and setting up cooking stoves, the adults, now mobilized, out searching for usable cookware and utensils—Tunica then got into one of the pickups and drove off to search for other survivors. She first circled the outside perimeter of the village to see if anyone injured or in shock might be wandering around disoriented. Making one complete revolution of the village, she found no one. Driving up and down the outlying streets next, she came to a dozen survivors who were huddled together near their burned homes. Stopping to speak with them, she explained what was being done at the recreation center, and sent them there. Continuing on to the next street, she was surprised to find, miraculously, a row of small frame houses virtually undamaged. The occupants of each house were sitting out on the prairie nearby with a few of their possessions, all watching their respective houses with much the same vacant expression that the people in the recreation center had had earlier. Parking the pickup, Tunica went over to the closest family and knelt in front of them.

"Do you know me?" she asked.

The eldest male of the family spoke for them. "You are Tunica, the royal princess."

"That is correct. Why do you and the other families sit on the prairie instead of in your homes?"

"We wait for the evil fire to return and take our houses. It took all those," he pointed to the burned houses across from them, "but it missed mine and these others. It is a very hungry fire; it will return."

"It will *not* return," Tunica told him authoritatively. "Go tell the others that Princess Tunica has spoken to you and told you that the evil fire has been put out. The fire is now in the past, and our tribe is free to continue living in the present. I want everyone to return to their homes and prepare them to be shared with some of your people who were not so fortunate."

Before she left, Tunica asked if anyone knew where the Beloved Ones were. Another man stepped forward. "I saw them try to stop the fire," he said solemnly. "They stood in a row with their holy blankets held before them, and asked the gods to stop the flames. The fire overcame them."

Tunica clenched her jaw to hold back tears. It would not do for her to cry in front of her people when they needed her strength so much. "Go," she said, "and do as I have instructed."

As Tunica drove off, she saw that the other members of the family to which she had spoken were already returning to their home, while the eldest male had begun spreading her word to the rest of those out on the prairie.

Once more driving up and down the side streets, nearer now to the center of the village, Tunica found a few more stragglers and sent them to the recreation center. Finally she reached the middle of the village, where the taxi had brought her earlier. Looking around at the blackened remains of the few modest Indian businesses—the barbershop, the bakery that made only corn-meal products, the small repair garage, the dressmaker's shop—she again felt her eyes water. So much work, she thought. So terribly much work, to make a village we could be proud of and our children could be proud of. And then in a few hours to have it all gone. God, what awful inequity. What gross, senseless wrong.

But I cannot come apart, she told herself. This isn't Woodhull University, a study assignment I've not prepared, a lecture I can't force myself to attend. This is the real world. The world of my people. *My* world. I must maintain control.

Walking around the rubble of the demolished general store, Tunica began to scavenge for anything from its stock that might be salvageable. There were blackened canned goods everywhere, their labels burned off, making them unidentifiable without being opened. Scattered in smoldering ashes, they were still too hot to touch. Tomorrow, she decided, she would bring a group of the older boys to the site and they would—

Suddenly Tunica stopped thinking, stopped moving, almost stopped breathing. There in the rubble was a burned body, its face turned up. Oh god, no, she thought, and looked away. Swallowing with difficulty, after a moment she made herself look back. Steeling her nerves, she moved closer and studied the corpse. At once she recognized the design of a large silver belt buckle.

It was Tongue.

"No!" Tunica screamed aloud. "No! No! No!" She shook her head with an hysterical fury. With her bare hands, she began to dig and claw at the smoldering waste to uncover her old friend, her Indian "uncle," to get his body free of the charred wood and ash and soot. There was broken glass in the rubble, protruding nails, and in seconds Tunica's fingers and palms were scratched and cut as well as singed by the heat. Her hands turned black and red. Ash rose and clung to her sweaty, teary face; her eyes burned from it, and from her sweat. Her stunned mind rebelled.

"Why? Goddamn it! Why?" She looked up at the late afternoon sky turning pink. "What did we do?" she asked whatever god might be listening. "How have we angered you?" Again her head swung from side to side in utter frustration and defeat. "We're only human," she said in a less angry voice, seeking understanding. "We can only try—"

Suddenly there were two strong hands on her arms, drawing her to her feet; then two arms encircling her and holding her close; and Sam's deep, kind voice saying, "All right, Tunica. It's going to be all right."

She became vaguely aware that some other white men were with him, and that he was giving them instructions. "Some of you finish digging Tongue out of there, and search the village for any other dead. Start a large grave back over there on the prairie somewhere. Get as much done as you can before dark. We're going to have to get the dead buried as quickly as possible to prevent the spread of disease."

Then Tunica was aware of being carried in Sam's arms to his truck, laid on the big seat, her head resting against his leg as he started the engine and drove away.

Sam drove to the bank of a stream that was far enough away not to be covered with soot. From under the seat he took a thick lap rug and spread it on the ground beneath an umbrella of overhanging willow branches. There were two kerosene lanterns in the toolbox, which he lighted and set at two corners of the blanket. Then he lifted Tunica gently from the truck seat and carried her to the edge of the stream. He lay her on a bank of grass and dipping his handkerchief into the cool water of the stream, washed the caked dirt from her tear-streaked face, and the blood from her injured hands. Rinsing the handkerchief clean again, he used it to wet her thick hair and rub it back from her forehead. For a little while she seemed to relax and grow calm; then her lower lip began to tremble, and Sam knew that the last few terrible hours were crowding into her mind again. She put both hands over her face and began to sob, her body jerking and shaking with her grief.

Sam removed his boots, socks, and trousers, and stepped thigh-deep into the stream. Standing next to the bank, he carefully undressed Tunica, down to her underwear. Then he took off his shirt and, wearing only his shorts, lifted her into his arms and walked out into the cool water. She clung to him, buried her face in his neck, turned her breasts against his chest. He walked out until only their heads and shoulders were above water.

"Is it too cold for you?" he asked.

"No," she murmured into his neck.

The stream water was still tepid after two days of raised air temperatures due to the intense heat of the fire. With dusk becoming darkness, the water around them was like a pool of oil, only the blue light of the lanterns on shore reaching out to illuminate them.

"Does the water make you feel better?"

"Yes. But, Sam, all that destruction, the homes burned, the dead—"

"Let me go under with you," he said, holding off her mounting hysteria. "Close your mouth and breathe out through your nose."

Sam went down with her still in his arms and the dark stream enveloped them both in its freshness. When he stood up again, they both felt cleaner, purged of the day, the still-warm night air caressing their skin. Her face turned up to his and she kissed him with open lips as she had dreamed so many times of doing; and his own lips opened with hers and their tongues explored each other as if they, too, had dreamed. Tunica's right hand went down under the water and he felt it slip under the front of his shorts, her fingers circling where he was already hard.

"This is mine, Sam," she whispered like a hurt child.

He carried her back to the bank and let her down onto the lap rug, while she held onto him. Standing over her, he unbuttoned his wet shorts and peeled them off. Then he pried her fingers off his erection.

"If that's yours, there are some things that are mine." Dropping to his knees, he stripped her cotton underpants off, spread her thighs, and buried his face in her soft wetness. His lips parted her and his tongue entered her and she threw back her head and responded to his mouth with the same abandon that she would to the rest of him.

Mine, mine, mine, her thoughts raced. She was full and whole at last. This was what she had prayed for, to both white and Indian gods. She did not know which had answered her prayers. And at the moment she did not care.

61

Sam was grateful that the sanitarium was on the eastern outskirts of Dallas, so that he did not have to drive through the city to get to it. At one time, in his younger days in Kansas City, he thought there was nothing to compare with city life: the rush, the hustle, the energy; but after more than a decade in rural Texas, he had become thoroughly acclimated to country pace and country quiet. It was a rare thing in Sheridan to hear anyone honk an automobile horn. Only on Saturdays when the small farmers and ranchers made their weekly trip to town were the streets even crowded. That was the way

Sam liked it. He was making this drive to Dallas only because he had to.

It had been nearly six months since the terrible oil field fire. Sam looked drawn and tired from the work he had done during that period. He and all his people had put in extremely long hours for weeks on end helping rebuild homes, restore land for new crops and for grazing, secure new livestock and poultry, obtain farm equipment, put up silos and barns, find clothing for the homeless, find furniture, bedding, dishes—everything from the ground up. The money to do most of it came from Dewitt Tucker's bank, secured by Sam's personal notes and, in cases involving larger amounts, mortgages on his wells and liens against his production royalties. Sam never hesitated to put up whatever collateral bank regulations required. He still considered the town of Sheridan *his* personal responsibility—and that obligation extended to the people *around* the town as well as in it.

In addition to rehabilitating the small farms and ranches, Sam also had his wells and the fields to consider. The spreading fire had burned down many derricks on new wells being drilled, and had also effectively ruined the pumps of wells in production. That, along with Sheridan Oil Company trucks that had been destroyed, toolsheds and their contents virtually wiped out, telephone and power poles and lines burned up, and the explosion of two storage tanks, had brought Sam's company and its revenues almost to a complete halt for sixty days. Afterward, business had begun its slow but steady recovery until now, four months later, it was approaching full production again.

Only after the community had been well on its way toward regaining its previous prosperity had Sam found the time to devote to the endeavor that was taking him to Dallas. This was his eighth and, he hoped, last visit to Sunnymeade Sanitarium. If all went well on this day, he would not have to come there again.

Parking his car in the visitors lot, Sam walked along a flower-lined brick path to the main building where he signed in and sat down to wait for Dr. Lake. The doctor, who came out several minutes later, was a pale, thin man some twenty years older than Sam.

"Hello, Mr. Sheridan. Ready for the big day?"

"I'm ready," Sam replied quietly, almost solemnly.

"Nervous?"

"Some." He rose and walked with the doctor down a hall.

Dr. Lake glanced at Sam and smiled. "Frankly, I'm nervous too, a little. This has been a most unusual case. Single subconscious rejections are quite common; even cases of double subconscious rejection aren't all that rare. But *multiple* subconscious rejections, those are something else. This is only the second one I've ever seen." He led Sam around a corner into a second hallway. "In addition to everything else, of course, in this case we've had to deal with the problem of trying to prompt reacceptance of *some* but not *all* of the subconscious rejections that were causing the mental distress."

"How much will she remember, Doctor?" Sam asked, as they stopped at a door.

"I'm not sure. Let's see, shall we?"

Sam followed Dr. Lake into a small private room nicely decorated in pale pastels with pretty curtains, soft lighting, and fresh flowers on a small table. Sitting next to the window was Ardelle Patman Spence.

"Mrs. Spence, you have a visitor," Dr. Lake said cheerfully. Ardelle looked around. When she saw who was with the doctor, her expression brightened.

"Why, Samuel! What a nice surprise! And it isn't even Sunday."

"Hello, Aunt Ardelle." Sam went over and kissed her on the cheek, something he had been doing, at Dr. Lake's suggestion, since his third visit.

"You nephew has made a special trip today," Dr. Lake said. "There's something he wants to ask you."

"My goodness." Ardelle put a hand to her cheek. There was the slightest hint of anxiety in her eyes. "Is it terribly important, Samuel? It's such a pretty day, I'd simply despise having to spoil it with anything serious."

Dr. Lake drew up a chair and motioned for Sam to sit down. "Go ahead."

"Aunt Ardelle, I want to ask if you would like to leave here and come live with me, in my home."

"Oh, my." Flustered, Ardelle quickly looked around at the doctor. "This is such a nice place."

"We're glad you like it here, Mrs. Spence," Dr. Lake told her. "Of course, you're most welcome to stay, if you wish."

"Everyone here has been so kind to me." She looked back at

Sam. "I had such a terrible time after the girls were killed in that awful fire, and then Pete shooting himself over it. Such a terrible, terrible time. There for a while, why, I wouldn't even admit to myself that it had really happened. Dr. Lake and the others, they helped me to finally accept it. It just doesn't seem right to go off and leave them after all they're done for me."

"I wouldn't ask you to do it, Aunt Ardelle, except for the fact that I need you. I've been trying to raise my son Tyler alone ever since his mother left. I've got household help, of course, but no one who's family."

"That's right, you *do* have a youngster, Samuel!" Ardelle exclaimed. "Why haven't I ever met him?"

"If you'll recall before the fire, Aunt Ardelle," Sam said gently, "I never came around much. Pete and I didn't get along too well, remember?"

"Oh, yes." Ardelle smiled sadly. "The girls used to argue with him about that. They thought he should invite you and your family over. Of course, I had to take Pete's side. Lord, he was a hardheaded man!" She sighed quietly. "Well, I just don't know, Samuel. I don't want to seem like an ingrate to Dr. Lake and all the other nice people here."

"Don't you worry about that," Lake said, coming over and patting her hand. "We'd miss you, of course, but we'd certainly understand. After all, family obligations come first. I know how strongly you feel about such things; you've told me so much about your parents and your brother Lorn, and the way you grew up. We all know it wouldn't be like you to refuse to help Lorn's only son when he needs you."

Ardelle frowned slightly and her eyes narrowed a little as she studied Sam for a moment. "Lorn's only son," she repeated to herself, as if remembering. Then she blinked rapidly several times and said, "I didn't help raise you, did I, Samuel?"

"No, Aunt Ardelle. I was raised by my mother in Kansas City."

"Oh, yes. But you want me to help you raise your son? Tyler, is that his name?"

"Yes, Tyler. And yes, I want you to help me raise him. I *need* your help, Aunt Ardelle."

Ardelle smiled. "Well, of course, it's settled, then. Dr. Lake, I *do* hope everyone understands. It isn't that I'm not happy here, but if my nephew needs me, why, I must help him. Our family has always been *very* close; it's a matter of strong blood ties, you see."

"I understand perfectly, Mrs. Spence," Dr. Lake assured her. "Would you like to go home with your nephew today?"

"Yes, I think I'd better."

"I'll have someone get your things packed." Dr. Lake and Sam exchanged quick glances of relief, and Lake left the room.

"Now, Samuel," Ardelle said sternly, "there are certain responsibilities with Tyler that I must insist be left strictly to me. One of them is his diet. It is essential that growing youngsters eat certain foods whether they like them or not. Don't you agree?"

"Yes, Aunt Ardelle."

Ardelle continued talking, enumerating other areas of concern over young Tyler's upbringing. As he listened, Sam experienced a quiet inner hope. He had been expecting it, wanting it to be there.

It was the hope that with Ardelle, he and Tyler would feel like they were part of a family again.

62

On a sunny July day in 1933 a group of people from Sheridan, Texas, stood staring up at a huge sign that stretched across the entrance to a great world's fairground in Chicago. The sign, so large that it could be read from two miles away, said:

A CENTURY OF PROGRESS

"Come on, Daddy, come on!" twelve-year-old Tyler Sheridan pleaded with his father, tugging at his hand to pull him toward the entrance. "If we don't hurry, we'll *miss* something!"

The women in the group, holding back their own children, smiled, and the men chuckled, while Sam Sheridan assured his son that he would not miss anything. "We're going to be here for a week, Ty. There's plenty of time. You're not going to be able to see it all today, so you might just as well calm down."

They had arrived in Chicago the previous day, traveling in two private railroad cars that Sam had leased from Southern Pacific: one a sleeper containing eight bedroom compartments, the other a club car with a small kitchen and rear observation deck. Sam had hired two porters, two cooks, and two waiters to man the cars for the duration of the trip from Dallas to Chicago and back.

The people in the group consisted of Ty and his Aunt Ardelle; the Dewitt Tuckers and their son, the Owen Milams and their son, the Bill Pete Masters and their two daughters, and the Tom Praters and their son; Sam and Tunica; and four Mexican girls to help the ladies. Sam was paying for the entire trip.

When Sam told Ardelle he was planning the trip, she had exclaimed, "Why, Samuel, that will cost a fortune!"

"I don't care, Aunt Ardelle," Sam had replied. "Nineteen thirty-two was a miserable year for everybody. In fact, the last *few* years have been generally rotten. But we've got a new President now and he's enthusiastic about the future. The city of Chicago is showing its support by putting on a World's Fair despite the worst depression the country's ever had. I think that people have got to start feeling good again. A trip to the World's Fair is just the thing to do it."

"I swear, Samuel, you sound just like a politician," Ardelle said. "You speak so *well.* Lord, I hope your Grandmother Lillian is listening up in heaven. She did *so* admire proper speech."

To finance the trip, Sam sold outright to Standard Oil one of his producing wells, which brought to a total of twenty the number he had been forced to dispose of during the Great Depression in order to assure that no one in the town of Sheridan and its environs did without the basic necessities: food, fuel, clothing. By the time the Depression ended, more than half the people in the community owed money to Sam Sheridan. Much to the chagrin of Dewitt Tucker and Tom Prater, Sam did not even have a written record of most of the loans.

"The ones who *can* pay me back someday, will," Sam told his banker and lawyer. "The ones who can't pay me in money will pay me in other ways. They'll work even harder to help Sheridan grow and prosper. They'll be the ones who repay me with their *time.* You two stop worrying. Money was meant to be *used;* that's all I'm doing with it."

The World's Fair trip was planned for July, after Ty and the other children got out of school for summer vacation. The group traveled in a convoy of four automobiles from Sheridan to Dallas, left the vehicles in a public garage, and boarded the leased railroad cars. The cars were hooked onto the *World's Fair Special* that night when the streamliner stopped in Dallas. Two days later the group arrived in Chicago. They checked into the world's largest hotel, the Stevens, which stood like a jewel on Michigan Avenue, facing Grant Park and the lake. It boasted three thousand rooms.

"Me and Bubba Milam are gonna count ever' one of them," Ty announced, "to make sure they ain't lying."

"Aren't lying," Ardelle corrected. "Bubba Milam and *I.* And you won't have to count them. The rooms all have numbers on the doors."

"Oh," Ty said, disappointed. It would have been keen to catch a big hotel *lying* about the number of rooms it had. But he soon forgot his detective work as they prepared for their first visit to the fairgrounds.

Ardelle, who had somehow taken charge of *all* the children, made a list of the attractions she considered suitable for them. "There's the Fairy Princess," she told them the first morning, "the Miniature Zoo, the Little Red School House—"

The two little Masters girls smiled in delight, but the boys began to moan at once. "Aunt Ardelle," Ty said, "we don't want to see *that* stuff! We want to see things like the Bagdad Giant that's eight feet tall! We want to see the Cutthroat Pirates Den! And go on the Sky Ride!"

"I'm sorry," Ardelle replied firmly, "but none of those attractions is on my list."

The boys immediately rushed to their parents. "Dad-*dy!*" Ty complained. "Aunt Ardelle's made a dumb ol' list and left all the good stuff off!"

After some arbitration by Sam and the parents of the other boys, a compromise was reached. For every attraction on the list that the boys visited with Ardelle and the girls, they would be allowed to select one *not* on the list to visit with their parents or the Mexican help when Ardelle was taking her afternoon nap.

Both Ardelle and the boys reluctantly agreed to the arrangement.

On their third afternoon at the fairgrounds the children were with Sam and the Owen Milams. Ardelle had returned to the hotel for a nap; Tunica and Bill Pete Masters' wife, who was half-Chickasaw, were off at the Northern Plains Indians pavillion; and the others were visiting the General Motors exhibit, where they were going to see an entire automobile assembled from the first bolt.

Sam and the Milams were taking the children to the giant double Ferris wheel, which everyone except Ardelle had ridden the first day, and which the children wanted to ride again for the spectacular view it offered not only of the fairgrounds but the surrounding city. On the way there they stopped at a Libby, McNeil, and Libby booth where pineapple juice was being introduced to the American fairgoing public for five cents a cup.

"This stuff is pretty good," Sam said, and the Milams agreed. But Ty and a couple of the boys made sour faces.

"You can have mine, Daddy, I don't like it," Ty declared. "Can I have a nickel for a Pure-Grape?"

Sam gave nickels to Ty and the other boys and watched them run over to a nearby Pure-Grape stand. Then he happened to glance over at the entrance to Mike Todd's Streets of Paris and saw a woman staring at him. For a second he could not believe his eyes. His hands began to tremble and he almost spilled the two cups of pineapple juice he was holding. Setting the cups down, he stared incredulously at the woman. She smiled slightly, but it was not a pleasant smile at all.

It was Georgia, there was no doubt about it.

Sam saw her look over at the Pure-Grape stand where Ty and the others had just run. She took a tentative step in that direction. *No!* Sam thought, panic rising. He stepped away from the pineapple booth and walked briskly over to the boys. Georgia, seeing him hurry to them, stopped and waited.

When Sam had the boys back with the Milams, he said to Owen,

"You and Sharon take them on the Ferris wheel without me, will you? I'll wait here for you."

"Sure," Owen said. He too had noticed Georgia when Sam was staring at her.

Ty registered a minor complaint that his father was not going with them, but after a moment joined the others and ran the short distance up the midway to the Ferris wheel entrance. As soon as Sam saw that Ty was safely aboard one of the cagelike enclosed seats of the big double wheel, he left the pineapple juice stand and walked over to Georgia.

They stood facing each other, alone in a crowded fairground, after more than seven years. It was Georgia who finally spoke.

"Well, Sam. Hello."

"Hello, Georgia."

"Ty looks like a little man, he's grown so."

"Yes, he's getting pretty big."

"Who all's here?"

"The Milams, the Tuckers, the Praters, the Masters, all their children." He did not mention Tunica but he did add, "And my Aunt Ardelle."

Georgia smiled knowingly. "You're not surprising me, Sam. I'd heard that you and your aunt mended your fences. I also heard about your drinking after I left."

"It's nice you can keep up with the local news." Sam stiffened a little. He had always suspected that Georgia was keeping in touch through Reba Samuel. He wondered if Reba had heard and passed along any rumors about himself and Tunica. If she had, Sam was sure Georgia would mention it.

"How long are you in town for?" she asked.

"Until Saturday."

Georgia fixed him with a stare. "I want to see Tyler, Sam. I want to spend some time with him."

Sam shook his head. "No."

"Why not?"

"I don't think it would be good for him. There's no point in it."

"What did you tell him when I left?"

"That you had gone someplace else to live and that we would both have to learn to get along without you. We have."

"That's *all?* No explanation, no reason, nothing?"

448

"Nothing."

Georgia was incredulous. "Doesn't he *ask,* Sam? I'm his *mother*. Doesn't he have questions?"

"Now and then. He asks where you are; I tell him I don't know. He asks why you left; I tell him because you thought you'd be happier somewhere else."

"But you don't tell him that you *ran* me off?"

"No."

"Why not?" she demanded.

"Because," Sam told her, "I don't want to have to tell him why."

Georgia took a cigarette from her dress pocket and lighted it. "I want to see him, Sam. Please."

"No."

She reached out and touched his arm. "Listen, I'll agree to any story you want me to tell him. All I want to do is sit down and be with him for a little while."

It was not easy to do, but Sam removed her hand from his arm. "You're not going to see him, Georgia."

Her face turned ugly. "You fucking bastard! Who do you think you are? This isn't Texas, Sam, it's Chicago! I'll see my son if I want to!"

"I told you Bill Pete Masters was in the party traveling with me, Georgia," Sam told her quietly and evenly. "He's a Texas lawman, remember? I always thought there might be a chance that you'd try to come back to Sheridan someday, so after you and your, ah, *boyfriend* were out of the state, I had Bill Pete file fugitive warrants on both of you for violation of the Texas miscegenation and sex perversion statutes—"

"You son of a bitch." Georgia was incredulous.

"You and O'Hara are wanted criminals in Texas," Sam said coldly, "and will be until those warrants are canceled. You go near my son, I'll have Bill Pete make arrangements with the Chicago police to arrest you. O'Hara too, if he's around."

Georgia stared at him as she exerted effort to bring the rage she felt under control. Then she smiled a cold, deliberately hurtful smile. "Oh, he's around, Sam. He'll never be far from me. Know why, Sam? Because there's not another woman alive can suck his cock the way I do. I suck it all the way down into my throat, Sam, until I can feel his hairy balls touch my lips."

449

Sam turned and walked away from her. His hands were shaking and his jaw was clenched so tightly it hurt.

The next afternoon Ty and the other children were with Sam, Tunica, and the Dewitt Tuckers at the entrance to a sideshow tent featuring a variety of bizarre and unusual people: a sword swallower, tattooed woman, human skeleton, a fat lady weighing five hundred pounds, strong man, snake charmer, and several others. Sam started to buy tickets for everyone.

"Daddy, I don't want to see no freaks," Ty said. "Can I wait out here and play Penny-Pitch?" He pointed to a Penny-Pitch game across the way.

Sam gave him fifty cents to exchange for pennies. "You stay right there now," he cautioned. "Don't go wandering."

"Okay, Daddy."

Ty hurried over to the concession and got his half-dollar changed. He had already begun to pitch his pennies as Sam waved to him and went with the others into the freak show. As soon as they were inside, Ty pocketed the rest of his pennies and ran over to freak show ticket seller. "Hey, mister, how long's this show last?"

"Twenty minutes, boy."

Ty turned and dashed back down the midway. From the high double Ferris wheel the previous day, he had seen his father talking with a vaguely familiar woman. They both seemed to be mad about something. His father had stalked away. The woman had walked down the narrower midway called the Streets of Paris. Ty had watched her enter one of the concessions there.

When he found the Streets of Paris entrance, Ty walked slowly along the line of concession booths until he came to the one the woman had entered. It was a Wheel of Fortune layout, being run by a tall dark man with a thick black mustache. Several people were standing at the counter, putting pennies and nickels on numbered squares. When all the coins were down, the tall man spun the colorful upright wheel and it whirled around with a melodious clickety-click-click sound. If a customer had a coin on the same number where the wheel stopped, a prize was awarded: small prizes like cap pistols and spinning tops for a penny bet; stuffed animals and music boxes for nickel bets; shiny radios and gleaming zircon jewelry for the occasional dime bet.

Standing just back of the wheel, Ty saw the woman he was looking for. She was unpacking some stuffed animals from a box and putting them on a shelf facing the front of the booth. Ty ran back a few booths, found a space between two, and went around behind the row of concessions. He walked up to the back of the Wheel of Fortune booth and stood watching the woman. Presently she noticed him. She stopped working and smiled.

"Why, hello."

"H'lo." Ty studied her for a moment, then said, "You're my ma, aren't you?"

"Yes." Georgia thought her heart would split wide open, so badly did she want to reach out and hug him to her body. Instead, she steeled herself and kept smiling. "How did you know I was here?"

"I seen you talking to Daddy from the Ferris wheel."

"Oh. Well, I'm glad you did." She looked him up and down. "You certainly are tall."

"I'm fourteen," Ty lied.

Georgia smiled. "Not quite, I don't think. Going on thirteen, maybe?"

"Where do you live now?" Ty asked, changing the subject.

"Here, in Chicago."

"With him?" Ty bobbed his chin toward the front of the booth where Cherokee O'Hara was busy running the wheel.

"Yes." Georgia changed the subject. "We'll be moving when the fair closes. Out west to Nevada. A place called Reno."

Ty nodded. "You prob'ly won't never come back to live with me and Daddy no more, I guess." It was a statement, but only because the boy could not make himself frame it as a question. Nevertheless, it cut deeply into Georgia's heart. Only with great effort was she able to keep the tears back and the smile on her face.

"Maybe we could write to each other," Georgia suggested. "Do you think that would be fun?"

"I don't know," Ty replied dubiously. "Daddy prob'ly wouldn't let me."

"Your daddy doesn't have to know. The post office has a General Delivery window; I could send your letters there and you could pick them up. I could use a different name on the return address so nobody at the Sheridan post office would know who they were from."

Ty shrugged. "What name would you use?"

"Well, let's see." Georgia glanced up at a large banner strung across the Streets of Paris midway. It read: See Sally Rand and Her Dance of the Fans. "How about Sally for a first name?" Georgia suggested. Ty's face lit up.

"Okay. And how 'bout Fair for the last name? After the World's Fair!"

"Marvelous!" said Georgia, delighted. "Sally Fair! Ty, it'll be such fun! And it'll be our secret, just yours and mine!"

"You gonna tell *him?*" Ty asked, indicating O'Hara again.

"No," Georgia swore, raising her right hand in an oath. "No one will know except you and me." She lowered her hand and held it out to him. "Shake on it?"

Ty shrugged again and said, "Sure."

She almost cried when she felt his hand in hers, but she was terribly afraid that crying would spoil everything. Again she stifled her feelings and forced a smile.

"I gotta go," Ty said suddenly, remembering the time.

"All right. I understand. There'll be a letter waiting for you when you get home."

"Okay." He backed away, smiling a little, breaking her heart. "'Bye."

"'Bye, Tyler."

When he was a few feet away, he cut and ran, not looking back.

If he had he would have seen his mother with her hands over her face, sobbing in anguish.

63

Sam found out about Ty's correspondence with Georgia several months later.

In attempting to deceive Sam, Georgia apparently had forgotten how much the town of Sheridan belonged to him; how much the people there cared for and respected him. It was an even stronger affection than when Georgia had been there, because during the years since her departure the Great Depression had plagued the country. It was during those lean, spare years, when crude oil was reduced to only six cents a barrel, that Sam had begun *selling* his producing wells, one after another, in order to have money to lend to the people of the community who needed it. There were men in Sheridan who would have taken a beating to save Sam Sheridan one, men who would have taken a *bullet* for him, because Sam had loaned them money to keep their wives and children from going hungry. That was not something a man, *or* his wife and children, ever forgot. Anyone trying to put *anything* over on Sam Sheridan, had to avoid a lot of eyes to get away with it. One such pair of eyes belonged to Elzie Thomas, postmaster of the Sheridan post office.

Sam had personally selected Elzie for the job of postmaster after Elzie, a drugstore clerk, had waited on him several times. Sam was impressed by the young man; he reminded Sam a little of his old friend Eddie Miller, back in Kansas City. When a post office was finally built in the growing town of Sheridan, Sam asked Elzie if he would like to go to Houston for a three-month training course, then return to become Sheridan's postmaster. Elzie was overwhelmed. He had a wife and four children, and had barely been getting by on his clerk's wages. After he told Sam he would be honored to take the job, Sam arranged through U.S. Senator Amos Rischer first for the training course, then for Elzie's appointment to the job. It had cost Sam a hefty campaign contribution to the senator, but Sam felt it had been well worth it; Elzie Thomas had been an exemplary postmaster.

Several months after the trip to the World's Fair, Elzie came to Sam's office one day particularly embarrassed. "Mr. Sheridan, I don't quite know how to say this, sir," he told Sam nervously. "I sure hope I'm not about to make a fool of myself."

"Don't see how you could do that, Elzie," Sam replied easily. "Nobody in the office but the two of us. I consider us friends. I'd never think a friend of mine was a fool, no matter what he did. What's on your mind?"

"Well, sir, it's your boy Tyler. For some time now he's been getting mail at our General Delivery window. They're letters from somebody by the name of Sally Fair. At first they came from

Chicago, but the last couple have been from out in Reno, Nevada."

Georgia, Sam thought. He took care to see that his expression did not change.

"I didn't pay it much mind at first," Elzie continued. "Be honest about it, Mr. Sheridan, boys his age sometimes send for things out of magazines that they don't want their folks to know about: how to build muscles, how to kiss girls, things like that. But I got to thinking that maybe this was something a little out of the ordinary. I thought you ought to know about it." Elzie took a small white envelope from his pocket and handed it to Sam. "This here's the latest one; come this morning."

The envelope had been typed and bore the return address of Sally Fair, Box 309, Reno, Nev. Sam studied it for a moment, then handed it back unopened.

"I'll look into it, Elzie," he told the young postmaster. "Meanwhile, just let Ty go ahead and use General Delivery if he wants to. I appreciate your coming to me."

Sam stopped in at the sheriff's office on his way home that evening. "Bill Pete, can you check with someone out in Reno, Nevada, and find out if Georgia is living there?"

"Glad to, Sam. Is there a problem?"

"I'm not sure," Sam replied, but did not elaborate.

A week later Bill Pete came to see Sam. "Georgia's out in Reno, all right. Still with Cherokee O'Hara. He's managing a small gambling house called the Lucky Dollar. She's working as a shill for him."

Sam concluded that somehow Georgia and Ty had run into one another at the World's Fair and started corresponding. He had no idea how or when they had met, but that made no difference, really. He was reasonably certain that their meeting had not been intentional on Georgia's part; he doubted that she would have risked Cherokee O'Hara's freedom after the threat Sam had made. Most likely it had been a chance encounter, and Georgia had simply made the most of it.

Sam hated the thought that Ty was deceiving him, but as he saw it, there was very little he could do, at least right then. He could, of course, exercise his parental prerogative and *order* Ty to discontinue the correspondence, but that, he knew instinctively, would not work to his advantage, not in the long run. Ty was strong willed and would resent it. It might, probably *would,* shift his loyalties more toward Georgia. By the same token, Sam could restrict Ty's receipt of her letters exclusively to the house, prohibiting the use of General Delivery, and see how that worked. Maybe Ty would not be so eager to continue the correspondence if it were not secret. Again, however, such an action might incur deep resentment, perhaps even open defiance.

Ultimately, Sam decided to do nothing. Although it grated on him, he let Ty continue corresponding with Georgia through General Delivery, and did not say anything about it. Not until more than three years later, when he confronted Georgia herself with it.

After Tunica told him she was pregnant.

Tunica was convinced that her child was preordained.

"Everything points to it," she told Sam after breaking the news to him. "You were the first white man I ever touched. I began loving you the very first time I saw you, the night you came to ask permission from the Beloved Ones to drill for oil on Choctaw land. I've never told you before, but that was the night I had my first monthly flow and began becoming a woman. I have never loved or made love with any other man but you; I have never *thought* or *dreamed* or *wanted* to love any other man; always only you."

They were in bed in the modest little house that had been built for Tunica after the fire. She was raised up on one elbow, her right breast and one hand resting lightly on Sam's chest.

"The child in my body was conceived when we had our picnic two months ago. On the bank of the stream where we spread our blanket, under the willow trees. It is the same stream to which you took me after the big fire; the same bank where we made love the first time." She smiled happily. "My spirit tells me that the child will be a daughter. Since she was conceived under the willows, that is what I will name her: Willow."

"Willow." Sam tried it for the first time. "Willow Sheridan."

Tunica's smile vanished. "Her name will not be Sheridan," she said quietly.

Sam frowned. "What do you mean?"

"I am not your wife. The mother of your son is still your wife."

Sam stared at her. He suddenly realized that the child he had just learned about had been conceived illegitimately. As he himself had been.

Fool, he silently chastised himself. You should have known this might happen. You should have been prepared for it. One bastard in the family was enough. It was time he put his life in order again.

He decided he had to go see Georgia.

Sam told everyone that he was going to Los Angeles on business. He booked a bedroom on the *Sunrise Limited,* which ran from New Orleans to Dallas to Albuquerque to Las Vegas to Los Angeles.

Nearly four years had passed since Tyler had begun the correspondence with his mother. At one point Elzie Thomas had let Sam know that Ty's letters had started coming from Las Vegas, Nevada, instead of Reno. Sam had Bill Pete check on Georgia again. The sheriff learned this time that she and O'Hara had moved down to Las Vegas a few weeks earlier, and that O'Hara was now manager and part-owner of a casino called the Cherokee Club, on Fremont Street.

It was nighttime when Sam got off the train in Las Vegas and stood with his Gladstone bag on the passenger platform. The *Limited* pulled out behind him and sped on its way. A few other passengers had also debarked; they left the platform quickly, all seeming to know where they were going. Sam looked across the tracks where Fremont Street began. On a corner was the Hotel Apache. Picking up his bag, he walked over to it. A white neon sign in the entrance read Dry Air Cooled. In the lobby Sam checked in, got a key, picked up a newspaper, and carried his own bag up to a front room on the second floor.

Feeling stale from being on the train so long, he unpacked, hung up his clothes, and ran a cool tub for himself. As he sat in the tub, he read the little four-page newspaper. An item on the second page caught his eye. Under Social Notes it said:

> *Mrs. Georgia O'Hara, wife of the part-owner of our town's popular and prosperous Cherokee Club, has formed a committee to start a home for wayward girls. Along with Mrs. Alvin Hubbard and Mrs. Roger Eaton, whose husbands are partners, respectively, in the Nuggett Club and the Desert Casino, Mrs. O'Hara has rented a small house on South Third Street and the ladies are*

presently in the process of refurbishing it to resemble a college dormitory.

The reason for the effort, according to Mrs. O'Hara, is the number of young runaway girls who arrive in our desert oasis throughout the year seeking thrills and excitement. "Most of them end up on the streets, broke and hungry," Mrs. O'Hara told our reporter. "At least now they will have a decent place to stay until arrangements can be made to send them home." This columnist says, "Three cheers for Mrs. O'Hara and company!"

Well, well, Sam thought. Mrs. Georgia *O'Hara.* He might have an easier time with Georgia than he expected. As he got out of the tub and dried himself, he thought about the article. It reminded him of all the good programs Georgia had started when the town of Sheridan was just beginning. For some reason, he was pleased to know that at least that part of her apparently had not changed.

Later that night, after the heat of the desert day finally dissipated, Sam came out of the Apache feeling fresh and rested. As he walked down Fremont Street, he wondered what Georgia's reaction would be at seeing him again. She would probably think that he was there because he had realized that the day was quickly approaching when he would no longer be able to control whether Ty had anything to do with her or not. Tyler was a sophomore in high school now; it would soon be his own decision as to how much a part of his life his mother would become. Georgia had managed to establish a relationship of sorts through their correspondence; they exchanged small gifts by mail at Christmas and on their birthdays. Sam continued to hate the fact that Ty was deceiving him, but he had done nothing to interfere with the letters. He hoped his discretion would count for something with Georgia when he talked to her.

Crossing Fremont, Sam entered the Cherokee Club and looked around. It was a medium-size casino for its day: a roulette wheel on each side of the front entrance; four craps tables in a neat square; eight small twenty-one tables spread along the side walls; and, for the serious gambler, two high-stakes poker tables, both stud, in the rear. Slot machines were scattered throughout the room; a change girl with a tray of chips and silver coins circulated among the tables.

In a rear corner Sam saw a bar-and-grill arrangement with

several tables for eating. Behind the bar was Tully Samuel; at the cash register was his wife Reba. Sam suppressed a smile. After the World's Fair trip, when he had confirmation that Georgia was monitoring his life through Reba, he had suggested to Tully that it might be best all the way around if he and Reba sold out and left. Tully, knowing that Sam could *run* him out, acquiesced. Sheridan Realty paid them a good price for the roadhouse and the couple departed. Now they were with Georgia and O'Hara.

Continuing to scrutinize the room, Sam's eyes came to a side wall against which there was a money cage for cashing in chips. A woman in a low-cut strapless dress, with creamy shoulders and a deep crevice of cleavage, sat in the cage, idly smoking a cigarette.

It was Georgia.

Sam made his way through the tables and players, and walked up to the cage.

"Jesus Christ," said Georgia when she recognized him.

"Hello, Georgia."

"What in the hell are you doing here?" It was not a challenging question, not angry, merely curious. "You haven't taken up gambling, have you?"

Sam shook his head. "I only gamble with drilling rigs," he replied lightly. "I came to talk to you, Georgia. Maybe this isn't a convenient time or place—"

"It's convenient, I suppose. Just a sec." Georgia caught the change girl's eye and beckoned to her. When the girl came over, Georgia said, "Take over the cage for a while, Alice. I'll be back in the office."

"Sure." Alice glanced curiously at Sam.

Georgia came out of the cage and led Sam toward the rear of the club. As he followed her, Sam could not help admiring her figure. At thirty-six Georgia had put on a little weight, mainly in the hips and bust. She had the frame to carry it, however, and Sam thought she looked extremely good.

As they made their way past the high-stakes poker tables, Sam noticed that Cherokee O'Hara, looking very dapper in a white silk shirt and black tie, was dealing cards at one of them. He did not appear to notice Sam and Georgia as they passed.

In a small private office, with the door closed behind them, Georgia went to a sidetable and opened a bottle of Scotch. "I don't know whether to offer you a drink or not. After your problem with the stuff."

"You can pour me one," Sam told her. "There's no problem anymore. I was drinking to forget. I've forgotten."

"Have you." Pouring two short ones, straight with no ice, Georgia handed him his. As Sam accepted it, she noticed that he glanced down the front of her dress. Have you, indeed, she thought. Smiling, she turned away and walked behind the desk. "Take a chair, Sam." Lighting a cigarette, she sat down herself. Sam sat facing the desk as Georgia, exhaling her first drag, leaned back in her chair and studied him.

"I see a little gray, Sam."

"More than a little, I'm afraid."

"It's becoming. You're getting better looking as you get older."

"I was just thinking the same thing about you. I've never seen you looking this good. You weren't this beautiful when you were twenty."

"Oh, my. Thank you." Georgia took a sip of whiskey. A moment of awkward silence followed. Finally Sam spoke.

"How's Alva?"

"My mother is dead. Five years ago. Kidney failure."

"I'm sorry. Leon?"

She shrugged. "Last I heard, he was head usher at the Oriental Theater in Chicago. We don't keep in touch too often." She took another drink. "Things about the same back in Sheridan?"

"Pretty much. Miss Emily passed away last year. Had a stroke at her desk in the realty office."

"That sounds like Emily," Georgia remarked. Nevertheless, Sam saw that she took a tissue and dabbed at the corner of one eye.

"I noticed Tully and Reba as I came in," he said.

"Yes. They moved here after you bought them out. I suppose I should thank you for that, even if it did cut off my source of gossip. But I'm glad to have Reba around; she's been a good friend."

Sam sipped at his whiskey. "I see by the paper that you call yourself Georgia O'Hara."

"Does that bother you, Sam?" she asked, arching one eyebrow.

"A little."

She shrugged. "It's just simpler that way."

"How's the home for wayward girls coming along?"

"Just getting started, really. What did you come here to talk about, Sam? Let's get to the point, shall we?"

"All right." Sam drew in a deep breath before beginning. "I guess the first thing I'd like to do is ask whether you're happy. Whether you have any regrets. Whether this thing with you and O'Hara is—well, still there."

Georgia's expression hardened a touch. "Regrets, Sam? Yes, I have regrets. Doesn't everyone? I regret that I haven't been able to watch Tyler grow up, and I blame you for that. I don't think I'll ever forgive you for that, any more than you'll forgive me for what happened with Kee. As for my being happy, and this 'thing,' as you call it, with O'Hara, well, all I can tell you is this, Sam: I would *die* for Cherokee, if he asked me to."

Choking back his hurt, Sam nodded very slowly. "I guess you can't be much plainer than that."

"I guess not."

"How would you feel about a divorce?"

Georgia smiled knowingly. "Found somebody else, Sam? Did it finally happen to you, too?" Sam did not reply, and after a moment Georgia merely shrugged her bare shoulders. "It doesn't matter to me one way or another. If I give you a divorce, will you let Tyler visit me?"

"If he wants to, yes. Incidentally, I know about you and Ty writing to each other."

Georgia tried not to act surprised, but two tiny wrinkles pinched her forehead just above her nose. "Oh?"

"Yes, Sally Fair, I do. I've known about it almost since it started. I know about the Christmas presents too, and the birthday gifts."

"Did Ty tell you?"

"No. He doesn't even know that I know. The post office brought it to my attention."

Georgia nodded resignedly. "That's right, the town *is* named Sheridan, isn't it? Well," she challenged, "why haven't you done anything about it?"

"There wasn't any way *to* do anything about it," he admitted, "without turning Ty against me. I wasn't about to do that. I just wanted you to know that I knew."

"I don't understand this visit, Sam." Her voice became edgy now. "Is it just the divorce, is that all you want?"

Sam set his glass on the desk. "I guess what I really came for was to see if we could resolve things between us. To see if we could reach some kind of understanding. To see if we could be, well—"

"Friends? Is that what you're trying to say?" Georgia looked at him in amazement. "You want us to be *friends*, Sam?"

"I don't know if we can go quite that far," Sam said frankly. "But I don't think we have to be bitter enemies, either. There must be something in between." He leaned forward, a searching look in his eyes. "Our son is growing up very quickly, Georgia. I'm sure he wants to know more about you, wants to know *you* yourself. I'd like for him to feel that he can do it openly, without recriminations from either of us. I don't want him to ever again feel that he has to go behind my back to do anything. I'd like you to tell him in your next letter that I was here, that we talked, that he can write to you without hiding it from now on. I'd like him to see that you and I can at least be civil, maybe even cordial, to each other. Do you think we can do that?"

Georgia stared at him for a long moment after he stopped speaking. Then she shook her head almost wearily. "God, I don't know, Sam. So many things have happened. There are some pretty awful memories, on both sides." She mashed out her cigarette in an ashtray shaped like the sign outside the club. "I just don't know."

"We can't do anything about the memories," Sam reasoned, "except try not to dwell on them. And the things that happened can't be undone; most of them, anyway. There's one that can, however, and I'd like to undo it right now." From his inside coat pocket he removed two folded documents held together by a rubber band. He put them on the desk in front of her. "These are the outstanding warrants that Bill Pete Masters has been holding against you and O'Hara. They've been withdrawn. You're both free to come and go in Texas as you please."

Georgia lighted another cigarette and Sam noticed her hands trembling slightly as she did. Giving her the warrants had taken her by surprise. She had become nervous, not knowing what to say next. Confrontations she could handle with ease; reconciliation and compromise she had difficulty with. It took several drags on her fresh cigarette and a final swallow of whiskey before she appeared to be in control again.

"So," she said after a moment, "you think we should get a divorce?"

"Seems like the logical thing to do."

Georgia smiled. "You're a wealthy man, Sam. Are you going to offer me a settlement of some kind?"

"I'd consider that, yes."

"Well, don't," she said, laughing. "Kee would kill me if I even *thought* about taking your money. But I agree with you about the divorce. If you'll arrange to have papers sent to me, I'll sign them."

"All right, I will."

The office door opened and Kee O'Hara came in. With him were two of his employees, one dressed as O'Hara was, the other in Western garb. Both were large, unsmiling men. The door closed behind them, and O'Hara stood looking across the room at Sam. "Well, well, well," he said quietly.

Sam rose and stood where he was. O'Hara's men remained at the door, while O'Hara walked slowly around Sam to the desk. He put a hand on Georgia's shoulder. "Are you all right?"

"Yes, Kee. We've just been talking, that's all."

"Do you need more time?"

Glancing at Sam, Georgia shook her head. "No, I think we've finished."

"Good."

O'Hara turned his eyes to Sam, to find that Sam's were already on him. The tension, the obvious hatred, when their eyes met, was almost electric. Sam, who was trying to neutralize all the deep animosity he had harbored for so many years, for so many people, could not begin to control his feelings for this man who had taken his wife from him. And O'Hara, his persona that of the cool, calm professional gambler, his veneer always smooth and unruffled, met and matched Sam's hostility with his own malevolence, born of the lash scars he carried on his back.

"I wondered," O'Hara said in the same quiet voice, "when the day would come that I could prove I'm a better man than you are, Sheridan."

Sam glanced at the two men at the door, who were obviously

waiting to be told by O'Hara what to do. "You sure you've got enough help?"

Kee O'Hara's eyes turned very cold. "Less help than you had," he reminded Sam, "the day you had me tied to your fence."

Sam said nothing. There was nothing *to* say. O'Hara was right. But Sam had no regrets about what he had done, not even now, with retribution staring him in the face. If O'Hara wanted revenge, let him take it. Sam was willing to fight him *and* his men, with whatever strength he could muster. He expected a thorough beating, but was determined to get in a few good licks himself while he did. No half-breed Indian would make him crawl, that was certain.

Suddenly, totally out of context, a new and startling thought surfaced in Sam's mind. He was the father of an unborn child who would be a *half-breed*. The realization, coming at such an inopportune moment, both surprised and offended him. He struggled to suppress the thought, aware that Kee O'Hara was speaking to him again.

"What did you say?" he asked O'Hara.

"I said if you're finished here, you can leave. There's the door."

Glancing over, Sam saw that the two unsmiling men had moved out of his way. Frowning, he walked to the door and opened it. He paused and looked back, perplexed, at Georgia. She was prepared for him.

"Like he said, Sam, he's a better man than you."

As he walked back through the noisy club to the street, Sam might as well have been in an empty room. Georgia's voice blocked out everything else in his mind, leaving only her words to reverberate like an echo.

He's a better man than you.

64

Tunica refused to marry Sam.

Even after Sam was given an uncontested divorce from Georgia, when the way was open for Tunica and him to wed and begin living together as husband and wife, she refused. Even after her stomach began to swell with their child, she refused.

"I don't understand." Sam was incredulous. "I thought you *wanted* to marry me. I thought that was why you made an issue out of the fact that the baby wouldn't have my name."

"I'm sorry if you misunderstood. I did not intend it that way. I only meant to emphasize that *my* child couldn't have *your* name."

"This is ridiculous," Sam said impatiently. "Why *won't* you marry me?"

"I cannot violate tribal custom by marrying a white. If I were an ordinary person, it would not matter so much. But I am of royal Choctaw blood; that makes a difference."

"But you've never *believed* that stuff, Tunica," Sam argued. "You've never taken it seriously before. Why start now?"

"Never believed it, Sam? Perhaps not. But never taken it *seriously?* I'm afraid you're mistaken. I've *always* taken it seriously. Even if I myself did not wholeheartedly agree with all the mysticism the elders attributed to me, all the symbolism they said I stood for, all the history they said I represented, never once did I ever intimate to them that I was anything *less* than they believed I was. You must remember, Sam, that before the oil, *I* was literally all that my people had. *I* was their hope, *I* was their pride. Whether I liked it or not, their feelings toward me imputed some serious obligations *to* me. And still do."

"But what about the baby? Do you realize what having it born illegitimate will mean? It's a terrible stigma to put on an innocent child."

Tunica smiled faintly. "Yes, I can see how it's ruined your life, made you the failure you are today."

"You're not being reasonable," Sam accused.

"From your point of view, I'm sure that's so. But from mine, with the responsibilities I feel toward my people, I am. Really, Sam, I thought you of all people would understand that."

"Me? Why should I understand heathen nonsense like that?"

"I wasn't referring to 'heathen nonsense,' as you call it. I meant that I thought you would understand my obligations to my people. You are in practically the same position as regards the people who live in Sheridan. You take it upon yourself to watch over them, to protect them, to see that they get and give fair treatment among themselves. Face it, Sam, you're as much a king to your people as I am a princess to mine."

"These people of yours whose welfare you value so highly, what are they going to think of you when you have an illegitimate baby?" Sam challenged.

"Illegitimacy is the creation of the whites, Sam," she replied. "To the Choctaw, there is no such thing as an illegitimate child. Newborns come to us in complete innocence and with a great capacity to give and receive love. My people will not question why this child is born, or who its father is. They will merely accept it as another infant Human Being to love and be loved by."

Tunica absolutely refused to be swayed. No matter what Sam's approach, no matter what his argument, his logic, his reasoning, Tunica remained firm in her position. She would *not* marry him; further, she intended to have her baby in the village with Choctaw midwives, instead of in a hospital with white doctors; further, it would definitely be a girl child; further, she would name it Willow, and it would live with her in the Choctaw village, in her modest house, the spare room of which Tunica was already converting to a nursery.

Sam wanted to build her a modern ranch home on his land, but that she refused to consider. "The child must live among her own people," Tunica decided.

Her attitude infuriated Sam. For the first time in many years, he was not in complete charge of something that affected him, his life, and his "place." He was not the master of all around him, the great and wise benevolent ruler, the *patrón,* the tallest man in the room. Time and time again he attempted to change Tunica's mind;

465

by common sense, guile, bribery, trickery, threats, and any other ploy he could conjure up. But nothing worked. Finally he gave up trying to be lord of the manor, and assumed the role of the downtrodden. He got much more being the victim than he had achieved being the boss.

"I've decided that you're right," he told her one day midway through her term. "It will probably be better for the child if she doesn't know me at all. I haven't done too well as a father."

"That's not true, Sam," Tunica argued. "You've been a very devoted father."

"Devoted doesn't always mean successful. Just look at the facts. I tried with Tyler to be the best father I knew how to be, and he still went behind my back to write letters to his mother. He knew I wouldn't approve, but he did it anyway. If that's not failure on my part, I don't know what is."

"Oh, Sam. You're talking about *one* instance."

"One instance that lasted four years. And would still be going on if I hadn't worked things out with Georgia."

"That's still no criterion."

"I think it is," Sam insisted stubbornly. "Anyway, it's not just that. I haven't been able to give Ty any sense of *values*. He's not interested in the oil business, doesn't give a damn how I had to work and sacrifice to get where I am today. The only thing he thinks about is airplanes. Not even sixteen and he wants to learn to fly. A week doesn't go by that we don't argue about it. And it's a losing battle for me: I can't stop him from taking lessons; all I can do is postpone it until he's old enough to fly without my permission." They were sitting in Tunica's kitchen. Sam gazed up at the ceiling and tried to look sad. "I'm a failure as a parent, Tunica," he concluded. "This new baby, well, it'll be better off without me trying to help raise it."

"Sam, I don't want you talking like that," Tunica said firmly, seemingly unaware that their roles had just reversed. "I want the child to know you as a person while she is growing up. When she reaches a level of maturity where I believe she is ready to understand, I expect to tell her that you are her father."

Sam shook his head. "Won't work. With you keeping her out in the Choctaw village, she'll grow up knowing only one world: the Choctaw world. She'll never accept me, a white man, as her father. If she grew up in a house *I* built, on *my* place, seeing me a little every day, why, we'd probably love one another like father and daughter whether she knew we were or not. She could accept it then; she'd be used to it." He paused and looked away. "But I can see your reasoning in not wanting it that way. Too much exposure to me might make her too much *like* me."

"That's not true!" Tunica protested.

Sam controlled the urge to smile. He had, finally, successfully, planted in Tunica's tough little mind the seed of doubt that perhaps she was not being completely fair, not only to the father of her child, but to the child itself.

Perhaps, Tunica found herself thinking, she *had* been putting too much emphasis on her own culture. Perhaps it was not her right to force this child to lean too far in one direction, from white to Indian, or Indian to white. Something that important probably would best be left up to fate.

She decided to compromise. While still refusing to marry Sam, she decided to meet him halfway on the matter of a house. "Suppose I let you build a house for the child and me. Would it be possible to put it on the boundary between your land and Choctaw land? Like where Sheridan number one was drilled."

"Certainly," Sam assured her. "That's no problem." He began thinking at once how he would situate such a house so that the child's bedroom would be on *his* land.

After further contemplation, Tunica finally said, "All right, I agree then."

Sam had an architect draw up plans for a sprawling nine-room ranch home incorporating the latest and most modern innovations and conveniences. Tunica studied and approved the plans, and Sam initiated construction.

"I will have my daughter on the day the house is ready," Tunica told Sam mysteriously one day as they watched it being built.

Sam humored her. "That will be very convenient for everyone," he said as seriously as possible.

Tunica realized he was being condescending, but chose to ignore it. Men, most particularly white men, simply did not understand the spirits.

On the day the house was completed Tunica gave birth to her baby girl.

She named her Willow.

65

One pleasant spring night in 1940, on the back porch of the big ranch house, Tunica lay in her swing with one bare foot on the porch floor, the other up against the chain that held the swing to the ceiling. It was not a very ladylike position, but it was comfortable, and there was no one around but Sam to see her. With her legs spread like that, her peasant skirt hiked well above her knees, an occasional light breeze caressed the insides of her thighs and gently ruffled her naked pubic mound. It felt cool and nice.

"We had a little ceremony at the village cemetery today," she said quietly. "Did you remember that it was the anniversary of the fire?"

"No." Sam was in a nearby rocker, holding the sleeping Willow in his arms after having rocked her to sleep.

"Your Aunt Ardelle probably remembered. I'll bet she went to the cemetery in Dane."

Sam made no comment. Willow was not yet deeply enough asleep for him to say more than an occasional yes or no. The child felt good against his chest and shoulder; he was always deeply content when he held her.

"That man who has the Western wear store next to Walgreen's is a crook, I think," Tunica said after a while. "He's selling felt hats to some of my people and telling them it's beaver. The hats shrink when they get wet. Real beaver wouldn't do that, would it?"

Never heard of a beaver shrinking yet, Sam thought. He did not answer aloud, nor did Tunica expect him to. She knew Sam heard her, would remember, and in a day or two would have Sheriff Masters drop in on the dishonest merchant. The store owner would either change his ways or be pressured out of town. Sheridan had a mayor and a city council now, but it was still Sam's town, just as it had always been, and he kept it as honest as the Sunday collection.

In the moonlight Tunica could see Willow's face lying against Sam's shoulder. The child looked, Tunica thought, like she herself would have looked if she had been prettier. If she had not had the gap between her teeth, which she could have had fixed anytime she wanted but never had; if she had not had the "pox pits," as she called them, on her right cheek; if she had not had a few other flaws, which taken together kept her from being very pretty. Which certainly did *not* mean she wasn't attractive. She was: she had a very definite *something*, and she knew it. Buddy Kyle had wanted her, and his desire had driven him away and he'd never come back; two Indian boys at college had wanted her; several young men in the village had shown definite interest in her; and—her deep secret from Sam—Tom Prater had once asked if she would be interested in meeting him somewhere, Dallas or Houston, for a weekend. She had demurely thanked him for his interest and declined.

So she was, Tunica knew, possessed of something that attracted an occasional man, though it clearly was not beauty, not in the conventional sense anyway. But if she *had* been beautiful, then Willow would have looked exactly like her. At three, Willow had an oblong little face exactly the shape of Tunica's; her teeth, though only baby teeth, were perfect pearls; her complexion was as flawless as egg yolk; her lips bowed downward like Tunica's, her hair was long and shiny black like Tunica's, her eyes great ripe plums like Tunica's. She was her mother's child, right down to how secure and comfortable she felt in the protective arms of Sam Sheridan. This last thought was accompanied by a twinge of jealousy. Shame on you, Tunica silently scolded herself.

"Would you like to take her in now?" she asked Sam.

He listened with an expert ear and decided the little girl's steady, effortless breathing meant she was sound asleep enough to be put to bed. "All right," Sam said quietly. He stood and Tunica held the screen door open for him to carry Willow into the house. In Willow's room he lowered her onto her bed and raised the guardrail so she would not roll out. Tunica adjusted a light cover over her, brushed some hair out of her face, and gave her a goodnight pat. Then Tunica and Sam went back onto the porch and both sat in the swing.

"Did you hear from Tyler today?" Tunica asked, leaning her head back.

"No." After a pause, Sam added, "The paper said Roosevelt

sent a hundred more Army attack planes to Canada. From there, of course, they'll go to England."

Tyler Sheridan, his father knew, would be flying one of them. Ty had learned to fly in spite of his father's disapproval. When the war in Europe started, the young man had left college without permission, gone to Canada, and enlisted in the Royal Canadian Air Force. He was a lieutenant, ferrying planes across the North Atlantic to English air bases. The danger he was in never left Sam's mind.

"Do you think we'll eventually get into the war?" Tunica pivoted around and put her head in Sam's lap.

"Hard to tell. If Wilkie gets elected, he might keep us out."

"Wasn't he at that Republican dinner in Austin last month?"

"Yes."

"What do you think of him?"

"Haven't decided," Sam said thoughtfully. "He's a *big* man, which I didn't realize; tops out well over six feet. Way he talks sometimes, he sounds more like a Democrat than a Republican. All he says about the war is that if he's elected, he'll 'outdistance Mr. Hitler in any contest he chooses.' I'm not sure exactly what that means. I do know one thing: there'll be a peacetime draft before the end of the year, no matter who wins in November. Congress will see to that."

Tunica sighed quietly. "I'm glad Willow's a girl. At least she won't *ever* have to go to war." A sudden, terrible thought occurred to Tunica. "You wouldn't have to go, would you, Sam?" she asked anxiously.

Sam grunted derisively. "What would they want with an old man like me? I'll soon be forty-five, Tunica."

"That doesn't matter. You're a better man than most men half your age. If I was in a war, I'd want you in *my* army."

Tunica giggled and Sam replied, "Yes, and I know in what capacity, too. But I won't be going, so don't worry about it. Crude oil production will be an essential industry. The government couldn't spare men like me for anything as ordinary as shooting at the enemy. My job will be to keep the gas tanks filled."

"Good. I'm glad."

A cool wind began to blow across the porch, coming without warning, whipping the pages of a magazine Tunica had left on the steps, rocking the chair Sam had occupied earlier. It suddenly started raining and some of it carried onto the porch. Lightning cracked.

"Let's get inside," Tunica said quickly. Angry weather was a sign of angry gods.

When they got into the kitchen, they paused without turning on the lights and listened to hear whether the lightning had awakened Willow. Apparently it had not. They were standing very close. Muted light filtered in from a lamp in another room. Tunica's blouse was already half open. Sam began to undo the rest of the buttons.

"Here to join my army?" she teased. "An old man like you?"

Sam undressed her all the way, then himself. Guiding her to the kitchen table, he helped her sit up on it. She was already moist when he tasted her, but she was so sweet that he went ahead anyway for several minutes while she braced herself on her palms and threw her head back.

Then Sam stood up, and entered her.

66

America's entry into World War II did not come as a shock to Sam or any other independent oil producer in northeast Texas. By the time it happened, they had been expecting it for six months. They had already discussed at length on numerous occasions how important each of them and their oil fields would be to their country's war effort. None of them, however, came close to realizing the magnitude of that importance. They would not know for another month.

A few minutes after the radio announcement that Pearl Harbor had been bombed, Sam called Tom Prater. "I think the independent drillers had better get ready to see President Roosevelt. Our oil is going to be extremely high on his wartime priority list. He'll call in the steel men first, of course; then probably the auto makers. After that, I think it'll be oil's turn. Ask Owen to pull all our pertinent production figures and we can all go over them at the office in the morning. I don't know how the other independents will feel, but I think it's essential that the President be given realistic rather than patriotic figures at this stage."

That done, Sam allowed himself to be occupied with thoughts of Tyler. For the rest of the afternoon he did not wander far from the telephone. Tyler finally called early in the evening, from the RCAF base at Sudbury, Ontario.

"Daddy? Listen, I'll be home on Tuesday. Just for a few days. All the Americans are being discharged to come home and join their own services. Find out where the nearest Army Air Corps recruiting office is for me, will you?"

"Ty, can't you wait a little bit?" Sam was almost desperate. "War hasn't even been *declared* yet."

"Come on, Daddy," Ty chided. "That's paperwork and you know it. We're at war right now."

Ardelle was already beside herself. When Sam told her about the call, she broke down crying and went off to her parlor. She had been terribly disturbed when Tyler Charles left college and joined a flying corps in Canada. But at least he had just become a ferry pilot there. Now he was *really* going to war, and she did not think she could bear it.

The whole thing made Sam feel very old. As soon as he could, he hurried over to the ranch house to be with Tunica and Willow.

Somehow, holding his little daughter in his arms, he always felt a little bit younger.

It was early in January that the oil men were summoned to the White House. FDR had them ushered right into the Oval Office.

"Come in, come in, come in!" he greeted them jovially. "From the looks of all those Western boots, these must be the oil men of Texas. Did I say it correctly, gentlemen?"

The oil men laughed. FDR, he of the grandly precise diction, had pronounced it "awl."

"Men," FDR gestured toward a bulldog-faced little man with round eyeglasses and a firmly clamped jaw, "I want you to meet my friend Harold Ickes, who has served in my cabinet as secretary of the interior. I have just appointed him chief of a new department that we have decided to call the PAW. That stands for Petroleum Administration for War. For the duration of our conflict with Japan, Germany, and Italy, Mr. Ickes is going to be responsible for all petroleum fuels needed for our armed forces. He is not a particularly easy man to get along with, and God knows he's nothing to look at, on top of which he is a *Republican;* but I am personally asking each of you to give him your utmost cooperation in the great war effort that lies ahead." Clamping an ivory cigarette holder between his perfect teeth, FDR said, "Harold, why don't you tell them what we're going to do."

"Certainly, Mr. President." Ickes rose, buttoned his double-breasted suitcoat, and strode to a covered easel at the side of the room. Flipping back the black cloth cover, he revealed a large map of Texas.

"No applause, gentlemen, please." FDR got another laugh. Then he lighted a cigarette in his holder. "Go on, Harold."

"It has been determined by a survey of our petroleum reserves that the state of Texas has the capability of providing eighty percent of *all* the oil that we have projected will be required by *all* the Allied forces while they are winning this war.

"This field here," he fingered the Eastex Field, "is going to be responsible for seventy percent of the Texas quota. Our studies have firmly convinced us that this is a figure that *can* be met. I don't have to tell you Texas wildcatters what a 'big' oil field is. You already know. A 'big' oil field is one that produces a million barrels of crude during its lifetime. The Eastex Field—the 'Black Giant,' I think you fellows call it—has already produced one and three-quarter *billion* barrels of oil. It has gone beyond big. The Eastex Field is colossal. It's going to win the war for us. I'll show you how."

Ickes flipped the page to a map of the United States. On it the states were outlined and named, but otherwise it was blank except for a black line that ran from East Texas on an angle up to roughly where Illinois, Missouri, and Kentucky all met, then continued across the top of Kentucky and West Virginia, up into Pennsylvania and across into New Jersey. Beside the map was a list of printed block letters that made no sense at all to the men: LV—LR—NC—PV—LN. Ickes interpreted them for the group, and with his finger followed the path of the black line as he spoke.

"LV is Longview, Texas. LR is Little Rock, Arkansas. NC is Norris City, Illinois. PV is Phoenixville, Pennsylvania. And LN is

Linden, New Jersey. We're going to build a pipeline, men, from *here,*" he pointed to Longview, "to *here,*" and swept across the country to Linden. "It's going to be twenty-four inches in diameter, fourteen hundred miles long, and capable of moving three hundred thousand barrels of crude to the eastern refineries *every day.* It's going to cost eight hundred thousand dollars to build, take fifteen thousand men to do it, and we're going to get the job done in *one year.* Any questions?"

There were none. The oil men from Texas sat before the little bulldog like awed children. At his desk FDR beamed. Nobody, he was convinced, could pick people like *he* could.

Ickes reached into his inside coat pocket and drew out a little dime-store spiral notebook, the cover of which he thumbed open.

"It is my intention," he said, "on behalf of the President of the United States, to ask for the following volunteers:

"J. R. Parten, of Woodley Petroleum, to be director of transportation for PAW.

"W. Alton Jones, president of Cities Service, to be chairman of the War Emergency Pipelines Department.

"Burt Hull, of Texaco, who I'm sure you'll agree is the best goddamned pipeliner in the business, to be superintendent of construction.

"Sam Sheridan, president of Sheridan Oil, to be coordinator of independent production—"

It was the proudest moment of Sam Sheridan's career. In his mind he shared it with Ty.

Now we're in it together, son.

67

Ardelle's eyesight was failing, so Sam did all the reading, aloud, of letters from Ty. The morning mail arrived around eleven; if there was a letter, Ardelle would call Sam at the office and within the next thirty minutes or so he would drive home and they would sit together somewhere—the veranda in the summertime, the living room in winter, Ardelle's parlor next to her bedroom if she was feeling poorly —and Sam would open the letter and read it to her. In the evenings, if there had been a letter in the afternoon delivery, they would repeat the routine.

Tyler was a first lieutenant, training as a heavy bomber pilot at Elgin Field, Florida. His letters from Elgin were clever and chatty, full of news about other pilots, friends of his with nicknames like "Buzz" and "Looper" and "Crash." He reported a seemingly endless succession of house parties, beach parties, beer parties, and just plain party parties. In one letter Tyler confessed to having started smoking, and hoped no one at home, meaning Ardelle, would mind. Occasionally he mentioned a girl, usually someone with a "back East" name like Olivia or Marcia or Angela. Very little was ever said about his training, except that it was in heavy bombers and was "intense," which meant they were up twice a day, morning and afternoon, practicing medium-range bombing runs.

In May, Tyler came home for five days. "Can't tell y'all where they're sending me next," he told Sam and Ardelle as he unpacked his B-4 bag. "I *am* brushing up on a foreign language, though," he added in his best Texas drawl. "It's called English." He was hardly giving away a military secret; at that time all bomber crews from Elgin were being sent to England to participate in the daily air raids of occupied countries in continental Europe.

Ty had been awarded captain's bars just before his leave and cut a splendid figure in his brown-and-tan uniform with its dark shirt, khaki necktie, and crushed, jaunty-angled garrison cap. The young ladies in Sheridan did everything to get his attention except put their hands in his fly. Ardelle gave a lawn party for him, inviting all his former high school classmates, including as many of the boys as were left who had played on the Sheridan Oilers football team with him. She even invited several of his old teachers. It was a delightful afternoon and Ardelle saw to it that the society editor of the Sheridan *Journal* was there, with a photographer.

Sam invited Tunica and Willow to the party too, but Tunica declined. "It wouldn't do, Sam. People would spend all afternoon looking from Ty to Willow, Willow to Ty, trying to decide whether they resembled each other. It's Ty's party; don't let's detract from it."

As usual, Sam had to agree with her sensible logic. Ty did get to meet his little half-sister another time, however. When he was in Sam's office the last day of his furlough, Sam said, "Come on down to the Roxy and say hello to Tunica. She runs the theater for me now."

They walked down the street to the movie house that Leon Powell had originally built and named the Georgian, but had since been enlarged and renamed. Tunica, who had not seen Tyler since before he went to Canada, raved about him.

"My god, how tall you are, Ty, and how handsome! Sam, doesn't he look splendid in his uniform! And a captain too!"

It was while they were there that Ty met for the first time a beautiful, wide-eyed little four-year-old named Willow, who went to Sam without reservation and whom Sam held in his arms as if it were the most natural thing in the world.

After he and Sam left, Tyler remarked, "Pretty little girl, that Willow. Lot lighter than her mother, isn't she?"

But he never asked who Willow's father was.

A few days later Tyler was on his way to England and the air war.

When the man who had replaced Buddy Kyle as manager of the movie theater was drafted, Tunica had offered to take his job.

"You've got enough to do in the village," Sam objected at first. "Not to mention taking care of Willow."

"What I do in the village is organizational work," Tunica insisted. "I make up assignment sheets for the women responsible for collecting newspapers and tin cans, and the ones who are knitting socks and mufflers for our men overseas, things like that; I could take care of all of it in my spare time at the theater. The manager is really only busy for a little while before the show starts, again at the intermission, and then when the show ends. In between, there's not all that much to do. Anyway, I don't know where you're going to get anybody else. There's a manpower shortage, you know."

As usual, Tunica had done her homework and was right on all points. Manpower, along with a lot of other things, *was* in short supply. Despite enormous oil production, civilian use of gasoline was strictly curtailed. Gas stickers lettered A, B, and C were issued to all car owners, and most people restricted to four gallons per week.

Sam, because of his work with PAW, had a special T sticker that permitted him unlimited gas, but he was a rare exception. Sugar rationing went into effect: eight ounces per week per person. Cheese was rationed: four pounds per week, but it required a red ration stamp that could also be used for meat, so many people stopped buying cheese altogether. Butter could be had, four ounces per week, but *it* took red stamps also. Flour was rationed, fish was rationed, canned goods were rationed. Even shoes: three pairs per year, per man, woman, and child over two. Everywhere Americans went, they heard a singsong jingle:

> *"Use it up,*
> *Wear it out,*
> *Make it do,*
> *Or do without!"*

Tunica took over the Roxy and ran it in a remarkably efficient manner. For the first year, Willow was still a preschooler and spent almost as much time in the theater as her mother. She quickly became an avid movie fan, sitting through the same feature over and over again—*Meet Me in St. Louis* twelve times, *Going My Way* ten times, *National Velvet* eleven times—often memorizing some of the lines or songs and performing them later for Sam and her mother. Many times, however, Sam would protest the long hours she sat in the dark auditorium: "The child's going to go blind," he told Tunica; and he would take Willow someplace with him: to his office, out to the oil fields, around town on business.

Of course, there was endless speculation about who Willow's father was. Half of Sheridan believed that it was Sam; the other half wasn't so sure. The child was definitely a shade or two lighter, but that did not always guarantee a half-breed. "Some injuns, like some niggers, is jus' lighter, is all," the good ol' boys reminded each other. A few of the more calculating citizens even figured Willow to be Cherokee O'Hara's child, and thought Sam was being so adoptive of her just to deprive Cherokee of his daughter and get back at him for stealing Sam's wife so long ago. If Sam had ever heard *that* theory, he would have detonated like a dynamite cap. But like his grandfather Able Patman before him, Sam rarely heard *any* gossip unless it was directly related to "awl." Actually, not too many people really *cared* who had fathered Willow. If it *was* Sam, well, fine; there wasn't much Sam Sheridan could do that people in his town would disapprove of.

When Willow was six and it was time for her to enter first grade, Tunica registered her at Pop Joyner Elementary as Willow Chahta, using the Choctaw tribal name she herself had used at college. On the school registration form, Tunica simply left blank the line that called for the child's father's name. No one questioned her about it. She was, after all, a Choctaw princess, and worked for Sheridan Enterprises managing its movie house. And it was Sheridan Enterprises that not only sponsored the local "Teacher of the Year" award that included a one-thousand-dollar prize, but also provided permanent movie passes for every teacher in town, in recognition of their important community service, and encouraged all retail merchants in town to give them a ten-percent discount on purchases. So Tunica was allowed to register Willow however she wanted to, and every teacher throughout Willow's kindergarten and elementary years paid a little extra attention to her, just in *case* Sam was her father.

The Sheridan School District rolls by 1942 showed approximately ten percent Choctaw Indian attendance, for which federal educational subsidy funds were received. Indian students were no longer the oddity they had once been. When Willow began first grade, she was just another little girl as far as the rest of the class was concerned; darker than some, lighter than some. She was easily one of the prettiest little girls in her class, and would retain that status every year as she got older. Tunica could not have been prouder of her; and the only way Sam could have, would have been if she had Sheridan for a last name. But that, he had resigned himself, would never be.

Although Tunica continued to love Sam, and continued to sleep with him, she also steadfastly continued to refuse to marry him. For years Sam had proposed to her on a more or less regular basis, but as time went by, as he got caught up in PAW and the war effort, working harder than ever, approaching his late forties, he finally slacked off and only restated his request on rare occasions, at odd moments. Once when he was using his mouth on her, and had brought her to the very edge of climax, he suddenly stopped, looked up over her stomach, and said, "Say you'll marry me or I'm going to break off our relationship right now." Tunica had forced his head back down, come, and then told him that what he had done was "not one goddamned bit funny." She reminded him that she had ways of getting even. For weeks thereafter, every time she used *her* mouth on *him,* Sam expected some sort of retaliation. But nothing ever happened. It did not occur to him that his own anxiety had been Tunica's revenge.

Letters began arriving from Ty again. A lot of the contents of the little photostated V-Mail letters had been blocked out by the censors. Ty liked (BLANK) and was eating a lot of (BLANK) that was grown nearby in (BLANK). He had met a very nice (BLANK) girl named (BLANK) from (BLANK), and went to her house for dinner on Sundays. Her father was a (BLANK). After dinner, they sometimes went for a walk in the woods around (BLANK). The weather had been unusually (BLANK) lately. He had spent a day in (BLANK) recently and bought a few souvenir (BLANK). Rumor had it that they were getting ready to (BLANK-BLANK-BLANK). So long from (BLANK).

However frustrating the censored letters were to read, they nevertheless were to Sam an important link to his son. He did not care what they *said;* what mattered was that Ty was still alive and well enough to write. Sam prayed to God every night that he would remain so.

Ardelle, no less than Sam, *lived* for her great-nephew's letters. She could not have loved Tyler more deeply if he had been her own son. In the privacy of her parlor, she frequently compared his photograph to a fading old tintype she had of her long-dead, tragic brother Lorn. The two strongly resembled one another, except that Tyler's face had a strength Lorn's had lacked. Tyler, even more than Sam, became Ardelle's link with those she remembered from so long ago: Able, Lillian, Lorn, old Draw (and how she *wished* she had made her peace with *him* before he died).

So the content of Tyler's letters was of little concern to either his father or his aging great-aunt. The *fact* of the letters was what bolstered them. All the letters had to do was arrive, telling them that on some particular date usually four or five weeks earlier Tyler had been alive and well.

That was all the news they needed.

* * *

Sam's job as independent production coordinator for PAW was a nightmare during the long months it took to construct the pipeline from Longview, Texas, to Linden, New Jersey. Until the pipeline was ready, crude from the Black Giant had to be pumped into tank trucks, driven to railheads, transferred into railroad tanker cars, then moved by rail to the eastern refineries. Such logistics required enormous manpower, unlimited fleets of tank trucks and tanker cars, and constant good luck—all at the same time.

It seemed to Tunica that Sam was perpetually on the move. He had to make sure every well owned by every driller in every field in the Black Giant was pumping at absolutely maximum efficiency; that the requisite number of tank trucks was always there to take the flow without interruption; that the trucks all had drivers; that priority highway routes were open to all railheads in use; that the proper number of tanker cars was waiting at each railhead; that those tanker cars had been manifested to proper trains bound for correct refinery locations; and that the trains had route clearance and priority all the way there.

To accomplish all that was required of him, Sam often had to work days that stretched into nights, sixteen and eighteen hours long. He had to cover hundreds of miles in a single day, and still have time to work when he arrived at his destination. Many times he ate in his car while driving; many times his rest consisted of a few hours' sleep in the backseat while parked at the edge of some oil field. His weight dropped one to two pounds each month and his face began to look gaunt. Always tired, he never seemed to get enough rest. Tunica worried about him constantly. Nothing she said or did made any difference, of course; he had a job to do, he intended to do it. If it had taken another month or two to complete the pipeline, Tunica secretly doubted that he would have lasted.

Harold Ickes had said the pipeline would be built in a year. It was completed in eleven months and sixteen days. An awesome undertaking, it became a monumental accomplishment. The men of Burt Hull's pipeline construction division of PAW moved that pipeline across eight mountains, under thirty-one rivers, and through one hundred sixty-three streams. They worked twelve hours a day for three hundred and fifty-one consecutive days; each man took off an average of only eleven days during that period.

When Harold Ickes reported that the line was completed, FDR

dictated a note to be mimeographed and sent to every man who had worked on the project. It said:

> *An Allied invasion of enemy territory could not at this time be planned or hope to succeed without the aid of the gigantic pipeline that you men, under wartime conditions, have constructed in record time.*
>
> *Your country and your President are grateful and proud.*
>
> *Franklin D. Roosevelt*

To the men like Sam who had served without salary in executive positions during the arduous period, FDR added a personal sentiment. Sam's read:

> *Sam, my friend—you are the one who kept the oil moving until the pipeline was ready. You did a magnificent job!*
>
> *FDR*

Tunica was thrilled when Sam showed it to her. "Sam, how marvelous! Look, his very own *handwriting!* Oh, Sam, we *must* find just the right frame for it and hang it in your office!"

Before they could accomplish that, however, Sam received another piece of correspondence: one that made Tunica as sad as the President's letter had made her happy.

68

The telegram was delivered to the Sheridan mansion early on a Saturday afternoon. A star on the envelope identified it as an official notification that a member of the armed forces had been killed, wounded, captured, or was missing in action. Adelita, who was now the mansion's housekeeper, accepted the telegram at the front door.

She knew what it was; by that time few Americans were unaware of what the star on a telegram signified. Her tears had already begun as Adelita took the telegram to Sam in his study. At the sight of it Sam went white. His hands began to tremble as he opened the envelope.

THE WAR DEPARTMENT REGRETS TO INFORM YOU THAT CAPT. TYLER C. SHERIDAN, USAAC, WAS KILLED IN ACTION ON 2 APR 1943. THE GOVERNMENT OF THE UNITED STATES EXTENDS ITS DEEP SYMPATHY TO THE FAMILY AND FRIENDS OF CAPT. SHERIDAN, WHO TO THE END PERFORMED HIS DUTY IN KEEPING WITH THE HIGHEST TRADITIONS OF THE U.S. ARMY AIR CORPS. SINCERELY,

> GEN. ARTHUR C. MOONEY
> CHIEF OF STAFF
> U.S. ARMY AIR CORPS
> WASHINGTON, D.C.

Sam's head slumped forward and he began to cry.

"Is he dead, *señor?*" Adelita asked, her tears increasing. Sam could only nod. Adelita turned to leave. "I will wake the *señora.*"

Sam, through his own tears, said, "No. Let her sleep, Adelita. We won't tell her until after she's taken her afternoon medicine."

Adelita nodded and went off to tell the other members of the household staff. Sam called Tom Prater and told him.

"Jesus, Sam, I'm so sorry," Tom said, stunned. "Listen, Estelle and I will come right over."

"No, please don't, Tom. I appreciate your concern, but the more quietly this is handled, the better it will be for Ardelle. Her health is already so delicate, I don't want to take any chances with it. You *can* do two things for me, though. Call Owen and Dewitt and Bill Pete and everybody. Pass the news on to them but tell them not to come over or telephone, not until we've seen how badly it's going to affect Ardelle. I'm going to have the doctor here when she wakes up, just in case. The other thing I want you to do is get hold of someone in Washington; I'd like to have some details about exactly what happened, and where. I know it's not customary, but—"

"I'll take care of it," Prater assured him. "God, Sam, I am so sorry. So terribly sorry. Ty was—"

"Yes, he was," Sam interrupted, not wanting to hear the words. "Thanks, Tom."

While Ardelle was still sleeping, Sam drove over to see Tunica. The moment he entered the house, she knew from his face that something was terribly wrong. He could not speak; he could only hand her the telegram and sit down at her kitchen table, sobbing.

Tunica read the brief terrible message and whispered, "Oh, God." Dropping to her knees beside Sam's chair, she clung to him. "My poor darling."

Willow came into the kitchen from outside. She had a stunted tomato in one hand. Seeing her mother and Sam crying, the kindergartner asked fearfully, "What's the matter?"

"I will tell you later," Tunica said. "Go back out and play."

"This grew in our bict'ry garden." She showed Sam the tomato.

"That's—very—nice," Sam managed.

"Please play outside until I call you in." Tunica's tone was gentle but firm.

A worried frown on her little face, Willow went back out to the yard.

Tunica steeled herself, hugged and kissed Sam several times, then forced herself to put coffee on to heat. "Sam, have you called Georgia?"

Sam shook his head.

"You must." Sam made no effort to move. Tunica waited a few moments, then said, "I'll see if I can find out the number for you." She went into her bedroom where the telephone was. Presently she returned and put a slip of paper on the table in front of him. "This is the number that Information has." Sam still remained seated.

When the coffee was ready, Tunica poured him a cup and put a shot of brandy in it. Pulling a chair close to his, she sat and helped him sip it, steadying his hand as he raised the cup.

"The flying," Sam said bitterly. "The goddamned flying—"

"The war, Sam," she corrected gently. "The war."

Sam shook his head miserably. "So young. His life hadn't even *begun*. Just a boy—"

"No, Sam, Tyler was a man. A very good man." She spoke as

soothingly as possible, but she was determined that Sam was not going to lose his objectivity entirely. It was the war that had killed a man, not flying that had killed a boy.

When Sam finished the coffee, Tunica took his arm and urged him up. "Come on, my darling." She got the slip of paper and walked Sam into the bedroom. The phone was next to the bed, as was Sam's private line over at the mansion, because he and Tunica always talked late at night before they went to sleep. Even if Sam had just left her bed, he called to talk for a few minutes.

Tunica sat him down on the bed. "I'll get the number for you." Contacting the long-distance operator, she put the call through. When a woman's voice answered, she handed the receiver to Sam.

"Georgia?"

"Yes. Who's this?" Then instantly she seemed to know. "Sam?"

"It's Tyler, Georgia—"

A swift terrible realization came over Georgia. "Oh, Jesus. Is he dead, Sam?"

Sam could not reply. He found himself unable to confirm the horrible fact.

"He is dead, isn't he?" It was more a statement than a question. Then she lost control entirely. "Oh, God! Oh, no! No, no, no—"

Sam heard a click and knew that Georgia had hung up. He sat staring at the receiver, as if not knowing what to do next. Tunica took it from his hand, checked to make sure no one was on the line, and hung up. Gently, she pushed Sam back onto the bed and put a pillow under his head.

From outside they could hear Willow calling to her dog, Snow, a white Belgian shepherd Sam had given her on her last birthday. "Snow, come here! No, no, Snow, don't dig the ground there, those are our *carrots!*"

Listening to her voice, Sam began to cry again. "My god, Tunica, that child didn't even *know* her own brother. And now she never will—"

"Sam, please. Don't torture yourself."

"Ty died not even knowing he *had* a baby sister—"

"Sam, sweetheart—"

"I took him away from his mother and I kept him away from his baby sister. God forgive me," Sam Sheridan pleaded.

Covering his face with both hands, he sobbed in uncontrollable anguish.

Tom Prater came to see Sam two days later.

"Ty was flying a B-25 that was shot down over Germany," he reported in the quiet of Sam's study. "He'd been part of a large-scale Eighth Air Force bombing raid on the Nazi U-boat works near Bremen. His plane was seen going down in flames over the town of Delmenhorst after suffering extensive flak damage. None of the crew got out."

Tom paused and took a sip of the whiskey Sam had poured for him a few minutes earlier. Sam himself had already been drinking when Tom arrived.

"The War Department said the raid was the biggest daylight attack ever on Germany. Winston Churchill even mentioned it in the House of Commons the next day."

Sam nodded, but said nothing for several long moments, merely sat and stared and sipped. Tom began to feel terribly uncomfortable. He did not want to stay, but he did not know how to leave.

Finally Sam looked over at him and said, "Thanks for your help, Tom. I appreciate it."

Prater seized the opportunity and rose, tossing down what remained of his whiskey. "Anything I can do, Sam, you know that." Sam got up and walked to the front door with him. Before he left Tom asked, "How is Ardelle taking it?"

Sam shook his head. "Not well."

As if to underscore his words, Adelita rushed down the stairs just then. "*Señor* Sam, please come quickly! I cannot control the *señora*—"

Sam closed the door in Tom Prater's face and hurried up to his aunt's bedroom. She was sitting up in bed, her eyes wide with fright.

"Fire, Samuel!" she exclaimed when she saw him. "Fire killed my girls! Fire caused Pete to kill himself! And now fire has taken Tyler Charles from me! I saw it in a dream a few minutes ago. Tyler Charles went to his death in a flaming plane crash, didn't he? It's true, isn't it, Samuel?"

Sam sat on the side of the bed and took Ardelle in his arms. "No such thing, Aunt Ardelle." His voice had the same soothing tone

Tunica had used with him. "There was no fire, darling. Ty's plane crashed in the sea. The English Channel."

"He didn't burn?" Ardelle asked with relief.

"No, he didn't burn."

"Thank God, Samuel! Thank almighty God!"

Sam held the old lady and rocked her gently as he unwillingly saw in his own mind an image of Ty going down in flames.

Ardelle's health failed rapidly following the news of Tyler's death. Nearly seventy-two, she already had a myriad of ailments: gallbladder problems, varicose veins, diminishing eyesight and hearing, heart palpitations, and some other vague symptoms that she absolutely refused to discuss with anyone but Adelita. To all that was added cancer of the uterus, detected later that summer of 1943. Her doctor called in a cancer specialist from the Houston Medical Center, whose prognosis was that she had less than sixty days to live. His only advice was to keep her as comfortable as possible.

One night as Sam sat alone in his study, Adelita knocked softly and came in.

"The *señora* has passed," she said quietly.

Sam went upstairs with the housekeeper. Ardelle looked more peaceful in death than Sam had ever seen her in life.

"She has found heaven." Adelita was half crying, half smiling.

Sam patted the Mexican woman's arm. "Better call the doctor so we can begin making arrangements."

After Adelita left the room, Sam sat in a chair near the bed, realizing that he was without family in the big mansion for the first time in his life. He had a daughter, but she would never live with him. He had Tunica, but she would never marry him or live with him either. And Georgia—well, he had long since abandoned his secret hope that Georgia might someday come back to him. Slowly, over the years, Sam had come to realize that much of the blame for what Georgia had done rested with him. His long affair with Tunica had taught him that. The physical passion he and Tunica had together, he should have realized with Georgia years earlier. Too late he recognized that Georgia must have had the same demanding sexual needs that Tunica had; needs that he had failed to satisfy. Sam lamented the realization a thousand times, in a hundred ways: he blamed it on his consuming quest for oil; his bitter hatred for Pete Spence and many of the people of Dane; his search to find out who he was; his doubts, at times, of Georgia's loyalty; and any other reason that fit at any given moment of remorse.

In the end he forced himself to face the truth. He had not made the effort to learn his wife's robust nature, and she had, willingly or unwillingly, taken her needs to another man.

So, he thought as he stared at the corpse of his aunt, he had come all this way only to end up alone. Shaking his head, he contemplated the future with absolute dread.

After a while he left the dead woman's room and returned to his study where he kept the whiskey.

69

Sam Sheridan walked into the dining room of the Statler Hotel and paused. The maitre d' hurried over to him. "Good afternoon, Mr. Sheridan. Are you lunching alone, sir?"

"Good afternoon. No, I'm meeting Mr. Garner and some other gentlemen."

"Oh, yes. Mr. Garner hasn't come in yet, sir, but Mr. Stallings is at his table. This way, please."

Crossing the large elegant dining room, Sam smiled and nodded to several people he knew who were in Los Angeles for the same reason he was, to attend the National Petroleum Trade Show. At a round table in the corner another independent Texas oil producer, Fred Stallings, already sat, a glass of whiskey in one hand, long Cuban cigar in the other. There were three nearly full bottles of premium whiskey on the table, along with a bucket of ice. As Sam approached, Stallings set a glass and one of the bottles in front of an empty chair. Sitting down, Sam put ice in the glass and poured himself a drink.

"What do you think of the show so far, Sam?" Stallings asked without preliminary greeting.

"I think the industry's engineers have been reading too many comic books," Sam said wryly, "from the looks of some of the gadgets they've come up with."

"Gadgets is right," Stallings snorted. "Play toys is what I call most of 'em. You see that *colored* cable they coming out with? Yellow cable, blue cable, *pink* cable. Jesus Christ, you'd think we was drilling for perfume 'stead of oil.

"Who else John got eatin' with us today, Sam?" Stallings was referring to their host, John L. Garner, a cousin of the former Vice-President of the United States, John Nance Garner, and like themselves an independent driller.

"Billy Love and P. L. Hunter, I think." Sam took his first long swallow of whiskey. Crossing the lobby a moment earlier, he had seen a young Air Force officer who reminded him of Ty. Sam thought about Ty a lot; he had never gotten over that Ty's body was never found, that his only son was dead and he could not bury him. Thinking of Ty made Sam remember that Fred Stallings had three sons in the war also. "Are all your boys back home now, Fred?"

"All but just my youngest. He's with the occupation forces in Japan. I tol' him I could pull some strings and get him home any time he wanted it, now the war's over; but he said he'd just take his turn like ever'body else." Fred winked at Sam. "Personally, I think I *know* why he's staying: he likes that Jap nooky."

John L. Garner walked up, accompanied by Billy Love and P. L. Hunter, two refinery owners. The men sat down and immediately began pouring themselves drinks.

"John, you in fast comp'ny with them refinery boys," Stallings kidded.

"I know it," Garner allowed, "but these fellers are handing out all kinds of good stuff. Lookit here." Garner produced a black plastic cylinder and began drawing circles on the tablecloth. "It's called a 'ball-point.' Never have to fill it. When it quits working, you th'ow it away."

"Shit, tha's how I do my *cars,*" Stallings said, and they all laughed. The newly developed ball-point pen was passed around the table and tried by each of the men.

"And lookit here." Garner produced a silver coin. "This here's an advance sample of the new FDR dime, straight from the U.S. mint."

Everyone examined the new dime also, and agreed, since they had all met the late President, that it was a good likeness.

They drank for a while, then ordered lunch: steak sandwiches all around, and French fried potatoes. "Not that I *need* the French fries," said P. L. Hunter, patting his thickening middle. "My wife's done told me that if I come back one pound heavier, she's gonna cut me off for a month."

"Hell, you wouldn't even *notice* that," Garner quipped.

"Sam, when you gonna start selling me some Sheridan crude?" Billy Love asked.

Sam, who had never sold his crude to anyone except Rutland King, his original buyer, smiled and said, "Maybe next year, Billy."

"Don't you believe him, Billy," said Hunter. "Tha's what he told me *last* year. Sam's softhearted; he likes to he'p them little refiners like Rut King stay in bin'ess."

"Got to keep you tycoons from forcing everybody out of the industry," Sam retorted. "Little companies have to help other little companies. And I'm just a little company myself."

"Shit!" John Garner scoffed. "Sheridan Oil ain't *never* been little."

"I had your money," Stallings joked, "I'd th'ow mine away."

There was general laughter around the table again, and more drinking, and then someone asked, "Any of you fellers seen that new Crosley car they coming out with?"

"I have," said Billy Love. No one was surprised. Billy Love was one of the most flamboyant of the Texas oil millionaires. He put ten thousand dollars worth of clothes on every day: sharkskin boots, gold belt buckles, pearl shirt buttons, tailor-made silk suits (even during the war), diamond-studded hatbands. He always carried several thousand dollars in cash on him, owned at least one model of every car made, and had been married three times, twice to show girls.

"What's the Crosley like?" he was asked.

"Like ever'thing we ever dreaded in a car," Billy announced. "Goddamned thing ain't but twelve feet long. Got a *two*-cylinder engine that gets *thirty-five* goddamn miles to the gallon. It's the absolute worse car ever produced."

"What we going to do about it?" one of the men asked.

"I think we ought to engineer some kind of strike at their plant," said Fred Stallings. "Ain't nothing like a good strike to screw ever'thing up. Shit, lookit what's happened just this year 'cause of strikes. Electrical workers closed down GM. Meat packers closed down Swift. Steel workers closed down US Steel. Truman's already had to seize the goddamned railroads and the goddamned coal mines, and the year ain't half over yet! Yessirree, a strike'll do it ever' time."

They talked some more about the Crosley, speculating whether such a small car would capture the postwar American public's fancy. Finally they decided it would not.

Their lunch was served and while they ate, the conversation went from the new gasoline-saving Crosley to the new Kaiser automobile that literally *sucked* gas, and of which they all heartily approved. Then they discussed the fifty percent share that Gulf Oil managed to negotiate in its deal to drill for oil in someplace called Kuwait, wherever the hell that was; then to the major oil expansion being started by the Russians to get at the vast oil deposits allegedly lying between the Volga River and the Ural Mountains; then to the new Douglas commercial airliner, the DC-7, that carried seventy people and cruised at three hundred miles an hour.

"That many people in the same airplane scares the shit out of me," John Garner admitted. "That's just too heavy a load. They can't keep making them airplanes bigger and bigger; they got to draw the line somewheres."

The conversation was casual but always oil related in some way; these men never got too far from what was closest to their hearts and billfolds. Sam, for the most part, sat and listened to the others, only making an occasional comment to agree or disagree, or when one of them asked him a direct question. Throughout the meal he continued to sip whiskey.

When they finished lunch, the group returned to the trade show and began strolling through the exhibits again. At the American Petroleum Institute exhibit, Sam wandered off by himself and paused to look at a working model of the early refraction seismograph introduced by Marland Oil. As he stood there, an executive of the institute walked up to him.

"Mr. Sheridan? I'm Richard Dunn, the executive secretary of

API. I've been hoping to run into you. We've got something in common, you and me."

"We have?" Sam said, shaking hands. "What's that?"

"I did the very first geological survey on your field."

Sam frowned. "I'm afraid you're mistaken, Mr. Dunn. My own geologist, Owen Milam, is the only person who's ever surveyed my field."

"I did it *before* it was your field," Dunn explained, smiling. "When it was a cattle ranch owned by an old fellow named Able Patman."

Sam was astonished. "You did a survey for Able Patman? When?"

"Well, let's see. Must have been around 1920, maybe 1921. I was working for Marland Oil then, just a kid right out of college." Dunn's smile turned sly. "I was using Marland's new seismograph to do surveys on my own, on weekends, for the extra cash, you know. Mr. Patman was one of the people who gave me a job." He chuckled. "I still remember when I gave him my report. It didn't excite or even impress him. I told him there was a *lake* of oil under his ranch, but he apparently didn't care. You know how some of those cattlemen were; if something didn't have horns or udders on it, they couldn't be bothered. Of course, I tried my *damnedest* to get him to lease me drilling rights, but he said he wasn't interested. Paid me in cash for my work and saw me to the door. I always aimed to go back and make another pitch someday; but I went down to Venezuela for a few years, and by the time I'd come back, why, you had the land and had already struck it. Funny how things work out sometimes. Anyhow, I thought the story might interest you."

Sam thanked him, and as an afterthought complimented him on the operation of the American Petroleum Institute and promised to continue supporting it.

After Dunn walked away, Sam stood for a long time staring at the exhibit in front of him without really seeing it. His mind was racing.

So old Draw was wrong; Able *had* known about the oil. Sam could hardly believe it. His grandfather had left him the hundred acres fully aware of its vast potential; fully aware that it could make Sam richer and more powerful than Able's daughter Ardelle and her husband, Pete Spence. But the old man had not left a single *clue* to go along with it. Suppose I had not, somehow, recognized the potential of the land myself? Suppose I had let Georgia prod me into selling the land to the Spences and going back to Kansas City, as she had tried so hard to do? Sam could only shake his head in wonder. That vast ocean of oil, the richest strike ever made on the North American continent, might still be lying there untapped. God knows, every oil company in Texas had already written off the area as dry. And even though Richard Dunn had known about the oil under Able's place, he had no way of realizing the enormity of the overall field. Besides, if Dunn *had* gone back, he would have had no better luck leasing drilling rights from Pete Spence than he had with Able Patman. Chances are, he would have simply given up.

What in the hell could have been the old man's motive? Sam wondered. Was it just to test me? To see if I had the backbone to make something, anything, out of those hundred acres of scrub? If that was so, what an incredible outside chance Able Patman had taken. The odds had to have been heavily in favor of Sam *not* realizing there was oil on the land; *not* being able to start a small cattle spread or farm; *not,* in fact, being able to do anything with it. Except sell it back to Ardelle. In which case, the *legitimate* side of the family would have retained everything, and the *il*legitimate side would have faded quietly away. Maybe that was what his grandfather had decided was fair. Ardelle was the only legitimate heir, so he made the odds about ninety-nine percent in her favor. But he still recognized that Sam *did* have Patman blood, and was entitled to at least a chance, however remote. So he gave Sam a tiny piece of that huge ranch, did not let on that it had the potential to far exceed the value of the rest of the property, and left it up to fate whether the Saturday night bastard from Kansas City, a total stranger to Texas, could *do* something with it.

Ten years earlier the knowledge that Able Patman had concocted such a scheme would have infuriated Sam. He would have loathed his grandfather with the same passion with which he hated Pete Spence. But Sam was fifty now; he had mellowed considerably. He had learned that to hate so intensely took too much out of a man; too much that he needed for other things. Like spending more time with his wife and perhaps saving his marriage.

So instead of being furious with the long-dead Able Patman, Sam merely nodded his head wryly. I don't know why you did it,

Able, he thought of the grandfather he had never known, but whatever your reasons, I thank you.

Sam's thoughts were interrupted by a hand on his arm.

"Sam," said John Garner, "you're a thousand miles away. What you standing there plotting?"

Sam looked around and smiled. "Just trying to figure some underhanded way to get the wells you boys own without having to pay you anything for them."

"That's what I call constructive thinking."

As the others in their group ambled over, a man none of them knew went running past them shouting, "Any of you boys from East Texas? Somebody said there's a big twister heading there!"

Sam and the others all hurried after him. He led them to the convention office where there was a radio broadcasting news. They crowded in to catch what they could of the latest bulletin.

"—massive tornado that has already caused widespread destruction across the states of Kansas, Missouri, and Oklahoma, and is heading now toward Arkansas and northeast Texas," the newscaster said tersely. "Already described as possibly the worst tornado in our country's history, it has left entire towns destroyed in its wake and has killed hundreds of men, women, and children. Motorists driving toward Arkansas and northeast Texas from surrounding states are being turned back by state police—"

Sam edged out of the group, went to a phone, and called the airport to locate the pilot of his private plane. He wanted to get back to Sheridan at once.

70

They called it the "Devil Twister." It was the most unusual, most destructive tornado ever to strike the south central states.

Tunica was one of the first in Caddo County to hear of the

monster wind. At eleven o'clock that morning she walked into her kitchen where the radio was playing and instead of music heard one of the emergency bulletins the Mutual network had begun to broadcast.

"—most surprising thing about the tornado," the announcer was saying, "is that it is moving in a south*easterly* direction. The overwhelming majority of destructive tornados in the United States move from south*west* to *north*east. In addition, while most tornados travel at a speed of ten to fifty miles per hour, this one has blown at no less than seventy miles per hour, and at some points has approached the awesome velocity of one hundred miles an hour.

"To recap for our Mutual radio audience, a massive killer tornado began several hours ago on the tabletop plains near the town of Jetmore, Kansas. It completely destroyed that small farming community in less than four minutes. The tornado then headed east, missing several other small towns, but struck St. John, Kansas, and again leveled the entire town. It has also hit Darlow, Elmer, and Yoder, Kansas, causing minor damage in those towns. The tornado blew south of the city of Wichita before going on to destroy another small farming community, the hamlet of Sedan.

"At this time, the tornado is known to have traveled about two hundred ten miles. It has struck six towns, three of which it destroyed entirely. More than one hundred persons are feared dead. The tornado is reported to be heading south toward Oklahoma and East Texas, but predictions are that it will dissipate before reaching the city of Tulsa, some sixty miles away—"

Those poor, poor people, Tunica thought when the bulletin ended. She paused to whisper an Indian prayer for those in the six towns already hit. Then, on impulse, she went to the phone and called the village council office. Ranthia, a young member of the tribal council that Tunica had created to replace the Beloved Ones, answered.

"Ranty, have you been listening to news of the tornado?"

"Yes, I have. Sounds pretty bad."

"I want you to keep listening," Tunica instructed, "and write down the names of all the towns it mentions. I just heard some of them: Jetmore and Elmer, I think, and St. John; I don't remember the others. Anyway, there's a reservations map around there somewhere; I brought it back from college for Natchay when he was still alive. Look on it and see if there are any Indian communities that might have been hit. If there are, we'll send a couple truckloads of food and clothes and some of our young people to help them."

"Good idea. I'll do it right away."

Ranthia, Tunica thought as she hung up, was a solid, dependable man. He was in his early thirties and had been elected, as had all the council members, by tribal vote. Ranthia had a degree in education from Woodhull; he taught at the village school attended by those Choctaw children whose parents had decided against sending them to the Sheridan schools.

Tunica had been proposed to several times by Ranthia; she was seriously considering marrying him. It would be good for the tribe, good for Willow to have an Indian stepfather, and, Tunica had to admit, probably good for her also. Things had not gone too well between Sam and her since the deaths of his son and his aunt. He stayed alone in the mansion a lot, brooded a lot, drank a lot. Sometimes she caught him looking at her in an odd way, as if blaming her that he now had no family. She was unsure whether he was trying to use guilt to coerce her into bringing Willow and living with him, or whether the look simply meant that it was over between them. Her own ardor, she knew, diminished a little every time he drank too much. A normal life with Ranthia looked better all the time.

Glancing at the kitchen clock, Tunica saw that it was half past eleven. Willow's second-grade class at Sheridan Elementary would be having its lunch period now.

The path of the Devil Twister was a nightmare, even for weathermen experienced in tornado tracking. While Oklahoma waited anxiously, the deadly funnel cloud did an odd little dance on the Kansas plains and headed due east again, skittering along the Kansas-Oklahoma border. It terrified the little towns of Valeda, Chetopa, and Treece, but only did token damage to each. Then it flattened Baxter Springs, in the far southeast corner of Kansas and, as Oklahomans breathed a sigh of relief, blew into Missouri.

The twister had blown for four hours in Kansas, along an erratic two hundred ninety-mile path, hitting nine towns, destroying four, killing a hundred seventy-four persons.

Sheridan Oil Company's twin-engine Beechcraft Bonanza made its first stop in Tucson, Arizona, which was the farthest point east to which it could get clearance from Los Angeles. In the operations room Sam and his pilot, waiting for further eastbound clearance, listened to the National Weather Service's uninterrupted report on the tornado.

"—blown south of Joplin, Missouri, still on a due east course until it hit the hamlet of Wentworth, where it did only minimal damage. Its course then changed fifty-one degrees to the southeast. It has passed the towns of Pierce City, Purdy, and Butterfield, again causing only very minor damage. At the present time it is headed directly into the Mark Twain National Forest, where experts believe the rolling hills and close stands of trees will break it up—"

Sam, as many Oklahomans had done, breathed a sigh of relief. "Sounds like it's going to miss East Texas, after all," he said to his pilot. Just then, an airport operations man motioned to the pilot from the clearance desk. Sam waited while he went over. It was almost a physical relief to know that Tunica and Willow were safe. Walking idly over to a window, he could see the maintenance men finish refueling his plane. When I get back, he promised himself, I'm going to try to make things a little better between Tunica and me. I'm going to cut down on the drinking and not upset her so much. He turned from the window just as his pilot came back with a slip of paper in his hand.

"They've cleared us on to Carlsbad, New Mexico, Mr. Sheridan. That's as close to Texas as they're permitting air traffic right now. Planes are grounded in five states; Texas is one of them."

"Carlsbad's closer than Tucson," Sam said. "Let's go."

Tunica was waiting at the side of the road half a mile from her house when she saw the school bus coming. The bus had been purchased by the village to take Choctaw children to both the elementary and high school in Sheridan; Caddo County school buses would not stop at the village because the Choctaw paid no county or state taxes.

The bus slowed to a stop where Tunica stood and Willow came bounding out the moment the door opened. A lot of the children waved and shouted to Tunica, their tribal princess, and she smiled and waved back. As the bus pulled away, mother and daughter walked hand in hand down the gravel lane toward home.

"What did you learn today?" Tunica asked.

"More numbers," Willow said disinterestedly. "Adding and taking away. Taylor Tucker pulled my hair at recess."

"Oh? Why did he do that?"

" 'Cause he's mean."

"Did you do anything to him?"

"Pinched his arm."

"Before or after he pulled your hair?"

"After. If he does it again, I'm going to knock his teeth out."

"Little ladies don't knock people's teeth out, or even say they're going to," Tunica told her gently.

"I don't care," the child said determinedly. "I don't like having my hair pulled."

Tunica parted her lips to emphasize what was proper conduct for little ladies, but checked herself. What the hell, she thought, I wouldn't like my hair being pulled either. Let her knock his teeth out.

When they got home the telephone was ringing and Tunica hurried to answer it. At the other end, Ranthia's voice sounded urgent. "Tunny, the twister has changed course; it's heading for East Texas again."

Tunica drew a quick breath. "My god. When?"

"I don't know. The radio just said that it had reversed its path almost a hundred degrees. It's swung down into Arkansas now and is heading toward us from the northeast this time."

"Let's start getting the old ones up to the general store," Tunica said. "Also mothers with children under six. We'll see how many we can fit in the cellar of the store. I'll be there in a few minutes."

When she finished talking to Ranthia, Tunica called Sam's office. "When is Mr. Sheridan due back from Los Angeles, Lilly?"

"Why, I just heard from him, Miss Tunica," Sam's secretary said. "He's on his way back now, but there's some kind of problem getting flight clearance. He said he tried to call you but didn't get any answer."

Damn. It had probably been when she walked out to meet

Willow. "You know about the tornado heading our way again, don't you?"

"Lord, yes! Folks are running all over town trying to get ready for it. Some of the store windows are already boarded up. I was just about to leave myself. We've got a storm cellar in our church, if it's not full already."

When Tunica hung up, she got the keys to her station wagon and hurried outside where Willow was playing with Snow. "Come on, baby, we have to go to the village."

"Can Snow come too?"

"I don't think so."

"Please, Mother!"

Tunica paused and looked at the beautiful white dog. She bit her lip. Would there be room anywhere for a dog? "All right." If she had to let Snow out somewhere in the village, she'd just have to do it. "Come on now, hurry."

With the child and her dog in the backseat, Tunica started for Choctaw Village.

Before it left Missouri the twister smashed into the towns of Simcoe, Bethpage, and Lanagan, demolishing at least half of each of them. It had raged in a half-moon pattern in Missouri for slightly more than one hour, on a path that covered approximately one hundred miles. Touching down on seven towns, devastating fifty percent of three of them, it had killed sixty-eight people. Then it swung west into Arkansas.

As the killer funnel swirled into its third state, it drew out of the Arkansas sky a violent hailstorm, freakish for that early in the season. Grape-size balls of perfectly clear ice were thrown along the path of the twister, preceding it by several miles and several minutes at each place it struck. Due south the funnel cloud went now, almost as if angrily taking out on Arkansas what it had failed to do in Missouri: totally destroying towns. It swept along an eighty-mile path, flattening the communities of Decatur, Gentry, Mills, Rudy, and Old Jenny Lind. In each place, it passed in mere minutes but left incredible devastation in its wake. Entire buildings were either totally flattened, exploded to bits, or lifted from their foundations and thrown hundreds of yards. Small tools were whipped up and driven through walls, fenceposts, telephone poles, and people. Men, women, and children were hurled through the air like rag dolls, the breath sucked completely out of their lungs by the powerful vacuum in the vortex of the funnel. Yet, incredibly, some objects were left entirely unharmed. A baby's bottle, still full of milk, was found standing upright in the wreckage of a totally ruined house in which everything else had been destroyed. A full-length mirror remained unbroken in the rubble of a dress shop. A glass-doored cupboard with its china-ware intact was found on a hilltop a quarter mile from the devastated house in which it had stood.

But for the most part it was death and destruction for the small northwest corner of Arkansas. The toll, in one hour, along eighty miles, was five towns hit, five towns wiped out, two hundred sixteen dead.

By the time the Devil Twister was six hours old, it had traveled slightly less than five hundred miles, touched down on a total of twenty-one communities, totally demolished nine of them, and killed four hundred fifty-eight people.

And it still had two states to go.

At the airport in Carlsbad, New Mexico, Sam's pilot shook his head. " 'Fraid we're grounded, Mr. Sheridan. No planes are being allowed in airspace over Texas, Missouri, Kansas, Arkansas, or Oklahoma."

"Oklahoma?" Sam frowned. "I thought the damned thing had already *passed* Oklahoma."

"Operations says it doubled back. There's a radio in the pilots' lounge, if you want me to take you in there."

Sam followed him to a room where half a dozen weary-looking men were sitting around drinking coffee and smoking. A staticy voice coming from a table radio was saying:

"Oklahomans who were so joyous two hours earlier when the Devil Twister bypassed their state, now find themselves suddenly facing the same danger from a different direction. The same tornado, instead of bearing down on them from Kansas, due north, as it appeared it would earlier, is now sweeping in on their flank from Arkansas, to the northeast. With a sheet of hail-mixed rain preceding it, the deadly funnel has already spun across the state line and destroyed Shady Point, Oklahoma. It then blew south and destroyed Wister, Oklahoma. Continuing on a straight course, it has com-pletely wiped out the towns of Octavia, Bethel, Golden, and Garvin,

Oklahoma. In all, the twister spent nearly two hours in Oklahoma, raged along a path one hundred twenty-eight miles long, struck and totally destroyed six towns, and has taken its greatest toll yet in fatalities: three hundred sixty-two known dead.

"The latest report is that after demolishing the small town of Garvin, Oklahoma, it has swept across the Red River into East Texas—"

Feeling sick, Sam drew his pilot aside. "I have *got* to get back there. I'll pay you any amount you want. Name a figure."

The pilot shook his head again. "I'd be willing to fly an outlaw trip without clearance for you, Mr. Sheridan, if we had any clue at all where that son of a bitch was headed next. But it'd be plumb crazy to fly blind toward a devil wind like that. I'm sorry."

Sam made the same offer to the other pilots in the room. They all declined. Defeated, Sam left the room. His own pilot caught up with him outside.

"Am I fired, Mr. Sheridan?"

"No, of course not," Sam told him.

"It's just that I've got a wife and kids—"

"I understand. Stay here and bring the plane back when it's safe."

Sam walked out of the terminal alone and stood for several moments looking up at the sky. So calm here, he marveled. So terrible someplace else. The thought that Tunica and Willow were again in the path of that monster tortured him.

I've got to find a way to get to them.

I've got to.

71

Tunica and Ranthia were getting the old people and the children settled in the cellar of the general store when the telephone began ringing. Ranthia hurried up the cellar stairs to answer it. When he returned several minutes later, his face was tense. He took Tunica by the arm and drew her aside.

"That was Sheriff Masters in Sheridan. He just heard from the sheriff of Cass County by radio. The twister wiped out two towns up there: Blossom and Winfield. It's heading straight for us."

The cold certainty of it made Tunica's eyes widen. "Oh, my God—"

"We've got maybe an hour," Ranthia said. "That's all."

Tunica glanced around at the packed cellar. "There's not much more room here."

"Sheriff Masters said we could bring some of our people into Sheridan. They still have room in several basements."

Tunica put a nervous hand on Ranthia's arm. "You go find some trucks and drivers. Start cruising the village and collect as many people as you can. I'll get some of the young ones to help me move blankets and drinking water down here for these people. When you've picked up as many as you can find, stop back here and get the ones we can't fit into the cellar. Then you can lead a convoy into Sheridan."

"Right." Ranthia touched her hand. "The tribe will pull through. It always has."

Off he hurried then, and Tunica turned back to the dimly lit cellar crowded with nervous old ones and crying little ones. "Lanterns," she said to one of several teenage boys helping her. "Find some lanterns and get more light down here. The rest of you come with me and start filling jugs with drinking water and carrying blankets down here. Hurry, everyone!"

When they got upstairs, they saw through the windows that the sky was darkening and it had begun to drizzle.

One hour, Tunica thought. God.

In Carlsbad Sam had managed to buy a new 1946 Ford by convincing a local banker that he *was* who he said he was: the president of Sheridan Oil. Just to be on the safe side, the banker had Sam sign a chattel mortgage on the company plane that Sam was leaving behind.

During the precious hour that arrangements for the car took, Sam tried placing a dozen long-distance calls to Sheridan, Choctaw Village, Kilgore, Longview, and several other communities in the area. None of his calls could be put through; either the lines were already down or the circuits were being reserved for official emergency calls only. As his frustration increased, Sam became almost frantic with worry. If only he could get *moving*.

Finally, the car was ready. Sam put a box of sandwiches and a jug of water on the seat beside him, and stuck a bottle of bourbon in the door pocket. He started driving. Within an hour he was out of New Mexico.

Then he had nearly the entire state of Texas to cross.

In the Choctaw community the rain was steadily increasing and the air had become very cool; the sky continued darkening by the minute.

At the general store four dozen stragglers huddled in a group just inside the door, Tunica keeping them as calm as possible. Looking out, she saw Ranthia driving up in a flatbed truck. He was returning from leading a convoy of four trucks loaded with people into Sheridan, where Bill Pete Masters had promised to find room for them in reinforced basements of the Sheridan Oil Building, First Bank, and several other of Sheridan's sturdier structures.

"Where are the other trucks?" Tunica asked as Ranthia parked and hurried into the store.

Ranthia stared incredulously at the people around Tunica. "I left them in Sheridan so the drivers could take shelter. I thought we had everybody."

"Load as many of these people on the flatbed as you can," Tunica said. "There's a delivery pickup out back we can use for the others."

Ranthia looked at his pocketwatch. "I don't think we have time for another run, Tunny."

"We've *got* to have time! Get them loaded!"

Tunica ran out the back door and a moment later pulled the delivery pickup around front. The people left over from the full flatbed eagerly climbed aboard.

"Can any of you drive?" Tunica yelled. "Any drivers here?"

Either they could not, or would not admit it. They huddled down on both trucks like terrified children as the rain began to fall more heavily.

Finally Tunica turned to Ranthia and shouted, "Lead the way!"

She got behind the wheel of the pickup to drive it herself. With

Ranthia driving the flatbed, they raced toward the highway. The big drops of rain pelting their windshields suddenly became tiny balls of hail that hit the glass and bounced off. Outside, it was almost like dusk now, the day turning charcoal gray.

Thank God, Tunica thought, she had been able to get Willow to safety. And thank God Sam was away from Sheridan. As difficult as things had been between them the past few years, she did still love Sam and knew she always would. Even if she married Ranthia.

Tunica followed the flatbed as closely as she dared in order to keep it in sight. The rain-hail became so heavy that her windshield wipers were useless; she had to roll down the window and stick her head out into the downpour to see Ranthia's taillights. Then, suddenly, the downpour slackened and in seconds stopped altogether. The sky turned lighter. Drenched, the people riding in the backs of the trucks stared at one another in surprise and felt the stirrings of relief.

Perhaps the devil wind had passed them!

A moment later they knew it was not so. From the north came a low, broken noise like an old man continually clearing his throat. It had a thick, rumbling, guttural sound; a resonance that by its timbre promised to become louder and louder. Tunica, her window still down, heard the noise and was frightened by it. The wind increased and began sweeping up gravel from the road in swirls and pelting the trucks and their passengers on all sides with it.

The paved highway is just ahead, Tunica told herself as her hands began to tremble on the steering wheel. Just ahead. Not even a mile—

Then she saw it. Off slightly to the left. Spinning like a giant top. Whirling directly toward them.

The funnel.

Sam drove up to town just after sunup. It had taken him twelve hours to cross the Panhandle and reach Sheridan. Or what was *left* of Sheridan.

He could not even drive *into* town; massive amounts of debris blocked the street entirely, barely leaving room to walk. Both sides of Pop Joyner Road had been leveled. Staring up one side of the blocked street from the car, Sam tried to remember exactly what had been there. A drugstore, hardware store, bakery, a Nash motor car agency, dry cleaning shop, beauty parlor, the Oil Field Hotel, a barbership, restaurant, another drugstore, a furniture store, and De-witt Tucker's First Bank of Sheridan—now all destroyed. Flattened to the earth as if a giant foot had stepped on them and kept walking. The next block, he could see, was also gone, including the Roxy Theater that Tunica had operated during the war. The two blocks beyond also looked destroyed.

Sam parked the car he had bought in New Mexico and started slowly down the debris-strewn street. Before he had gone twenty feet, a man with a rifle stepped from behind a pile of rubble. Sam halted, startled, until he saw it was one of Bill Pete's deputies.

"Oh, it's you, Mr. Sheridan," the deputy said. "I thought maybe you was a looter."

Sam shook his head, as if dazed. Without speaking, he remained standing there, looking around. Here and there in the ruins he saw an arm or a foot protruding. His face paled and he began to feel ill. He heard the deputy say something and looked over to see him speaking into a walkie-talkie. Several minutes later Bill Pete, his uniform dirty and rumpled, walked up to him.

"Hello, Sam," he said quietly.

"I can't believe this. The whole town—"

"It took a *lot* of towns, Sam," the sheriff replied. "And a lot of people."

Sam returned to his senses. "Is Tunica all right? And Willow?"

"I don't know," Bill Pete said. "Ranthia was here with some village people and said the old folks and kids were in the general store cellar; that's probably where Willow was put. Tunica may be with her or may not."

"I've got to go out there."

As he was walking back to his car, with full daylight breaking, Sam saw people coming onto the street to begin the cleanup, the salvage, the search for bodies. Some of them looked like they were in a stupor. Sam got back in the car and drove off toward Choctaw Village.

When he turned off the main highway, Sam found the narrow gravel road to the village blocked by an overturned flatbed truck. There were bodies strewn everywhere around it. Leaving the car, Sam started walking. He saw Ranthia lying dead nearby. Passing the overturned flatbed, he saw a second truck, a pickup, lying upside down in four feet of water in an irrigation ditch.

Half out the cab window, her face bloated from drowning, was Tunica.

72

Sam went into the water up to his waist, worked Tunica's foot loose from the twisted steering wheel, and pulled her body onto the bank of the irrigation ditch. For an hour he sat on the shoulder of the road, cradling her in his arms, stroking her matted hair, rubbing her graying face as if gentle care and tender love might somehow bring her back to life. Oddly, he did not cry, though his face showed more anguish than he had felt since Ty's death. In a way it seemed to him that he was not holding a woman at all, but a little girl: a strange, mystical little girl who had lived in a nebulous world between the real and the imagined.

"My little Indian princess," Sam whispered to her. "My poor, poor little Indian princess. I'm sorry you died so horribly. I wish it could have been easier for you." After a while, he added, "I'm sorry I didn't make you happier, sweetheart. I'm sorry I wasn't better at that."

The morning sun shone down on them and dried their wet clothing. When Sam felt he had the physical and emotional strength, he lifted Tunica into his arms and walked toward Choctaw Village with her.

"We have to find our little girl," he whispered to her. "We have to find Willow."

He had to stop and rest four times, putting Tunica down each time, but after what seemed like a very long way he finally walked into the village. Some Choctaw men saw him and hurried to help, but Sam would not let go of Tunica, would let no one else carry her; the men then walked beside him protectively in case he faltered or fell. Near the center of the village there was a number of small houses left intact or only partially damaged. Several women came out of one of them, saw Tunica in Sam's arms, and began crying. One of the Choctaw men spoke sharply to them and they became quiet at once. They came over to Sam and guided him into one of the houses, and led him to a bed where he put the dead princess down. He remained for a few minutes as they found clean water and clothes and began washing her. In one corner, watching wide-eyed, was a little Choctaw girl who reminded Sam of Willow.

Sam left the house and walked out to the village center. The old people and the children, according to Bill Pete, were in the cellar of the general store. When Sam got to where it was supposed to be, the store was gone. Only its foundation remained: a square concrete pit completely filled with rubble that rose several feet above the ground. Two pickups were parked nearby and a dozen Choctaw youths were digging in the ruins with a few shovels and their bare hands. Sam went up to the young man nearest him.

"Where are the old ones and the children who took shelter in the cellar?"

"They are still there," the youth answered.

Sam's legs felt like water. "Still *there?* All of them?"

"Yes. No one got out. The devil wind buried them all. That is why we dig: to remove them and bury them properly."

No one got out.

Zombielike, Sam turned and walked away. He went back down the road, out of the village, and returned to his car. Reaching into the door pocket, he got out the bourbon bottle but discovered that it was empty. He started the engine, managed to turn the car around, and headed back to the highway. Driving toward the mansion, he prayed that it would still be standing. Not because he gave a damn about it anymore, but because it was the nearest place he knew to get a drink.

All gone, his mind reeled as he drove. Everyone was all gone. He hunched over the wheel like a man having difficulty seeing the road; the day was clear but his eyes were not.

Turning into the lane that led to the mansion, Sam saw that the veranda was gone, a small part of the roof caved in, and many windows broken, but otherwise the house was still standing. He felt a surge of relief, not just for the liquor inside either; the place *did* have some meaning, whether it seemed important to him at that moment or not.

As he parked in the drive and got out of the car, Sam caught a blur of white off to the side and turned to see Snow bounding around the house toward him. His heart jerked and shuddered. He broke into a run toward the front door.

Before he got there, the door opened and Adelita came out with Willow in her arms.

"The *señorita* Tunica brought the child here before the tornado struck," Adelita told Sam. "She say if anything happen to her, she want the child with you. We take her with us into the storm cellar. All the household help took shelter there, and the oil field workers from the nearby wells, and some of the cowboys from the *señora's* ranch." She was talking about the Spence ranch, which now legally belonged to Sam, but was operated by all the small ranchers and farmers in the area on a co-op basis. "The cellar was full. Many were saved there."

Sam was sitting on the front steps with Willow on his lap, holding her as closely as he had held her dead mother earlier.

"What of—?" Adelita asked, her eyes shifting to the child, then back. Sam shook his head. Adelita's face saddened; she whispered a prayer in Spanish and crossed herself.

A car pulled up and parked next to Sam's. Dewitt Tucker and Tom Prater got out. Both men looked at Willow and frowned, their expressions a silent question. Again Sam shook his head, and his two friends knew that Tunica was gone.

"Owen Milam and his family are gone too," Tom Prater said.

Sam let his shoulders sag for a weary moment and buried his face against Willow's hair. Then he asked, "Who else?"

"There's no telling yet," Dewitt answered. "But lots, Sam. Lots. And the town, well—"

"It's not really a town anymore," Tom began.

"Yes, it is!" Sam snapped. "Yes, by god, it *is* still a town!" He took a breath and his voice calmed. "It's going to be rebuilt! Board by board, brick by brick, store by store. My town will *not* be killed by some goddamned freak wind!" Shifting his eyes to the banker,

Sam challenged, "What about it, Dewitt? Can we do it? Can we build it back?"

Dewitt grinned. "We done it once, didn't we?"

Sam looked at Prater again. Tom's jaw clenched. "Right. It *is* still a town." Then he grinned too. "Just needs a little work, is all."

Sam stood up, Willow still in his arms. "Let's get up there and get started."

Adelita reached for Willow. "I will care for the child."

"Later," Sam said. "When things are normal again. For now, she goes where I go."

Carrying his daughter, Sam Sheridan strode toward his car, Dewitt and Tom right behind him.

They had the funerals first. Many of them. They used undertakers from other communities that the Devil Twister had missed.

Then the massive cleanup began.

A fleet of bulldozers and other heavy equipment, paid for by every member of the community who could afford it, rolled into the ruins of Sheridan and like giant surgical instruments scraped the wounded town clean. Hordes of dump trucks hauled the debris away. While that was going on, an endless line of flatbeds delivered millions of feet of lumber to a growing stockpile outside town. Other trucks brought mountains of concrete, roofing material, nails, electrical wiring, pipes and plumbing fixtures, and insulation material. A huge corrugated shed was constructed and filled with hundreds of tools. An army of carpenters, electricians, plumbers, cement masons, and day laborers was brought in, most of them recently returned veterans who had been unable to find work.

"These are good men," Sam told Dewitt as he watched them working one day. "I hope some of them stay on after the town's rebuilt."

"They will," Dewitt said. "A few fellers have already asked me about loans to build houses."

While they were talking, two men walked up to them, one carrying a large box marked *Photographic*. "We're from *Time* magazine, Mr. Sheridan," one of them said. "We're doing a story about how you're rebuilding the town. All right with you if we take some pictures?"

Sam shrugged his shoulders. "Make it quick. I've got lots to do."

Sam was working from dawn until well after dark every day, organizing, overseeing, assigning, inspecting, approving, staying on top of the massive effort as no one else could have, because it was no one *else*'s town. Everywhere he went, Willow was with him; nearly everything he did, she saw. When she needed rest, she slept on the seat of his pickup, or on a cot in the hastily constructed wooden shack he used for an operations office. Like Sam and everyone else, she lived on pork and beans, Vienna sausages, crackers, cheese, and Coca-Colas. Adelita complained vociferously.

"That child is not *eating* properly, that child is not *resting* properly, she is not *bathing* every day, she is not brushing her *teeth!* You are ruining that child, *Señor!*"

"I am making her *strong,*" Sam argued. "I am making her *smart.* She is learning how things get *done.*" His tone softened. "And it is keeping her from thinking about her mother." He put his arm around the Mexican woman. "There will be time for proper meals and bathing when the work is finished. I'll turn her over to you then, Adelita, I promise."

Adelita refused to wait. Several times she came into town and took a sleeping Willow from Sam's truck or office, rushed back to the mansion to scrub and feed her, then put her to bed and sat guarding her behind a locked bedroom door. Each time it was only a temporary respite; the next day Willow would be up and ready to go with Sam again at daybreak. She *thrived* on going with him. And he delighted in having her go.

We'll do all right, she and I, he told himself—many times. As if trying to believe that it was so.

But deep down inside he was not sure. There was something missing.

73

Georgia was sitting at the kitchen table, doing a crossword puzzle while she waited impatiently for Ella, her black housekeeper, to return from the morning trip to the market.

The crossword puzzle was in a pulp magazine that contained page after page of the checkered puzzles. Georgia had become a crossword addict three years earlier when she quit working. At first it had simply been something to do, a check against boredom, nervousness, the sudden inactivity of nights no longer filled with the muted noise and churning movement of the casino. But an odd thing happened: Georgia began to *like* the puzzles. She realized they were not only fun to solve, but challenging as well. And she discovered, a little to her surprise, that she had a vocabulary far more extensive than she ever used. She had always been a reader, as far back as her early married days with Sam when they lay in bed at night quietly reading aloud to each other. Over the years with Kee, wherever they had gone, by bus, train, car, she always had a novel somewhere at hand that she read in snatches. It was all that reading, she was certain, that had made her so good at crossword puzzles.

When she heard the sound of tires on the gravel drive beside the house, Georgia rose and went to the stove. Striking a stick match, she ignited a burner and set the coffeepot on it. Through the window she saw Ella get out of the car and open the door to get the groceries out of the backseat. Beyond the car, perhaps half a mile away, was the sprawling Hacienda Hotel and Casino, sitting at the edge of the Las Vegas–Los Angeles highway. The hotel was the nearest thing around. Kee had selected this acreage on which to build their home specifically because of its isolation. For a man who had always seemed to want to be in the thick of things, Georgia had gradually come to realize that there was also a quiet, very private side to

Cherokee O'Hara; the Indian side, perhaps: a side that needed isolation and solitude. It was just one of the surprising things she had learned about him.

"Didn't you get the magazine?" Georgia asked, looking in the grocery bag as Ella came through the kitchen door.

"Yassum. I forgot and lef' it on the car seat." She put down the bag and turned toward the door.

"I'll get it," Georgia said. "You put the groceries away."

It was not a crossword puzzle magazine that Georgia retrieved from the car, but the latest issue of *Time*. Back inside, she poured herself a cup of coffee, carried both coffee and magazine into Kee's study, the coolest room in the house, and sat on the end of a big leather sofa. As she sipped her coffee, Georgia thumbed through the magazine looking for the latest news on the Devil Twister. Like most Americans, Georgia had not turned off her radio during the terrible, incredible twelve-hour lifespan of the killer tornado. She had used a roadmap of the United States to follow the funnel's unbelievable one-thousand-six-mile twisting journey, during which it touched down on thirty-six communities, totally destroying nineteen of them. In its wake, the freak wind had left a thousand fifty-three dead, slightly more than one person for every mile it traveled. During its last hours, it had struck seven towns in Texas, including Sheridan, wiped out four of them, including Sheridan, and taken two hundred twelve lives. It had then proceeded *back* into Arkansas, doing minor damage to Fort Lynn, and finally, thankfully, dissipating in Macedonia. It had been one of America's most devastating disasters.

In the days following the tornado, there had been many newspaper, magazine, and radio stories about the recovery and reconstruction efforts under way. *Time* ran a weekly, geographically segmented report on the progress of many communities. Lawrence Spivak, on his new "Meet the Press" radio show, invited the governors of the five stricken states to tell the American public how they were rebuilding. And the genial host of "Arthur Godfrey Time" provided an update on the massive overall effort every morning.

Georgia followed every story, every broadcast, with increasing sadness. She cried when a *Time* article mentioned the deaths of Sheridan Oil Company chief geologist Owen Milam and his entire family; she became nauseated over a photograph of Pop Joyner Road stretching through a long pile of rubble, which included what had been the movie theater originally built by her brother; and she became angry, taking it very personally, when she read about the small farmers in Caddo County, whose homes, crops, livestock, equipment, had all been lost. *Goddamn!* Those were people she had once known, once begun a program to help in her idealistic plan to eliminate poverty from Sheridan and its environs. *Why?* Why in hell did *nature* always have to be against poor people like that? Why did it always seem like God had it in for the hard-knock farmer? Georgia simply could not understand it.

When she found the article in *Time*'s current issue, Georgia saw that it was shorter than usual, almost cursory now that several weeks had passed and there were no new facets of the story to be examined. One community in Kansas was mentioned, another in Arkansas, but the rest might have been written the previous week, even earlier. Everyone was rebuilding: that was that. The story was becoming old news.

Georgia put the magazine aside and finished her coffee. She knew she now had to put the tornado and its aftermath out of her mind before she became depressed about it again. As minor as it might now be considered by *Time,* it was still very major in Georgia's mind, and her disposition was easily affected by it. Leaning back her head, she closed her eyes, and with one hand gently caressed the soft calfskin of the sofa. Kee had ordered that sofa custom made extra long to accommodate his tall frame. A slight smile played on Georgia's lips. He had been like a kid getting a new bike the day that sofa was delivered. Besides her, she had never known him to love anything like he loved that sofa. And, oh Lord, how *many* times they had made love on it.

God, how she missed Cherokee O'Hara.

For many years the angriest day of Georgia's life had been when Sam had whipped Kee and driven them out of Texas. Only one day would ever surpass that: a day in June of 1943, when she became so infuriated with life that had it not been for Ella she surely would have had a nervous breakdown.

It began with Kee ringing the little bell Georgia had put on his nightstand. It was the first and only time he had deigned to use the bell. The idea was that if she was in another room and he needed or wanted something—a glass of water, the fan turned on, a little company—he could ring the bell and it would be heard throughout the house. But he was such a hardhead; even as sick with the cancer as he was, he had only smiled tolerantly at such a flagrant violation of his independence; Georgia had known instinctively that he would not use the bell. The damned thing just set there while Georgia continued to look in on him several times an hour to make sure he was resting comfortably and wanted for nothing.

That morning when he *did* finally ring it, the sound was like a bolt of lightning reverberating through the house. Ella had dropped a breakfast plate she was drying, she and Georgia had looked at each other with stunned expressions, and both had run headlong into the bedroom, bolting through the door like the house was burning. Kee, ninety percent helpless by then, still had enough strength and presence of mind to look at them as if they were crazy before saying what he wanted.

"Move me onto my sofa." His voice was reduced to a whisper.

"Kee, the doctor said you were not to get out of bed—"

A barely raised hand and his direct, unblinking gaze halted her protest before she could finish.

"Move me," he said again.

The women put bed pillows on a kitchen chair, got him out of bed and sat him on it, and by tilting it back slightly and dragging it on two legs, moved him to the study. It was not difficult; he was so pathetically frail by then, weighing barely a hundred pounds. The two chair legs gouged a trail in Georgia's cherished mahogany floor, but she did not give a damn. It bothered Kee, however.

"Sorry about the floor, sugar," he whispered.

"Oh, Kee, stop." She was on the verge of tears, exerting extreme effort to hold them back because she knew he detested crying.

After he was settled on the sofa, Georgia and Ella were going to move his nightstand, lamp, fan, and other things into the study, but Cherokee told them not to bother. It was only then that Georgia realized he had wanted to be moved onto the sofa to die. Somehow, probably in some *Indian* way, she decided later, he had known it was his last day.

For the time he had left, Georgia stayed next to the sofa, holding his hand, stroking his still thick, still jet black hair, softly humming some of the songs they had liked over the years. Her anger must have started during those hours, but she was not aware of it. The deep, consuming sadness of knowing she was losing him, hour by hour, minute by minute, preempted any other feelings.

When Ella heard Georgia scream just at sunset, she knew Mr. Kee, as she called him, was gone, and she hurried to the study at once. She found Georgia with fists clenched at her sides, head thrown back, eyes tightly shut, screaming at the ceiling: terrible, anguished screams, broken only by urgent gasps of breath drawn in noisily as if by a terminal asthmatic.

"Miss Georgia, come sit down," Ella said, taking her by the shoulders, guiding her out of the room. Relieved at how unexpectedly easy it had been getting her away from the body, Ella had tried to lead Georgia to her bedroom to have her lie down. But on the way they passed the door to a screened side porch, and suddenly Georgia, still screaming, pulled away, ran across the porch and out into the desert. She began shrieking at the red-and-yellow-streaked sky, shaking her fists at it, cursing God, the universe, and all in it.

"Goddamn you for killing him like this! Goddamn the doctors for not saving him! Goddamn everybody who ever looked at him like he was a half-breed! Goddamn everybody who ever looked at him like he had no right to have me in his bed! Goddamn Sam Sheridan for whipping his back raw with a belt!"

"Miss Georgia, come back in the house," Ella pleaded, pulling on Georgia's elbow with both hands.

"Yes, goddamn Sam Sheridan! Goddamn him and his *proper perfect* ways! Running us out of Texas like we were trash—"

Ella's eyes scanned nervously. "Miss Georgia, they's scorpions out here."

"Goddamn you, Sam, goddamn you to hell! He was a better man than you!"

The thing that made her most angry that day was that by then she knew it was not true.

Cherokee, Cherokee, she thought as her hand caressed the soft leather that had felt their love so many times. I had to have you. I thought I couldn't live without you. You were the best thing that ever happened to me, and I truly did love you.

Opening her eyes, Georgia's gaze fell on the *Time* magazine. Slowly she shook her head. But you weren't a better man than Sam Sheridan, Kee.

Only now, three years after Kee's death, could she finally admit it. Only now could she see the two men objectively, without hatred for one, anguish for the other. It amazed her that she had ever even compared them. Sam Sheridan had brought oil out of a patch of dry ground where experts said there was no oil. Sam Sheridan had built a *town*—and was now building it *again.* He had raised her son; turned a boy into a man. He stood steadily, without flinching, in the face of any adversity that came his way. He was there when he was needed by people who *depended* on him. He had labored for, fought for, and won the riches of the earth, as a pioneer, a parent, and a *patròn.* There might be other men as good, but Georgia doubted there were any better.

Cherokee O'Hara had been a compelling physical presence, a marvelous lover, and a pretty good card player who eventually owned an interest in a small casino. Slightly insignificant next to Sam Sheridan's accomplishments.

If only, she thought sadly, she could have loved Sam the way she loved Kee.

Georgia wondered in her awful loneliness if she still might.

74

One night when Sam and Willow got home after another long day, they were met at the front door by a disturbed Adelita.

"There is a visitor in your study, *señor,*" she said, and without further explanation scooped the sleepy child into her arms and hurried upstairs. Sam went into the study.

Sitting on his couch, sipping whiskey, looking through a photo album from his bookcase, was Georgia. "Hello, Sam."

Sam could only stand in the doorway staring at her.

"I'm afraid I've upset Adelita."

Sam closed the door and crossed to his bar. "You aren't the first one to upset her lately," he replied, finding his voice. He half expected his hands to shake as he poured himself a drink, but they did not.

"You're not drinking too much again, are you, Sam?" Georgia asked.

"No. I was, for a while. But not now. Too many things to do." Sam brought his glass over to the chair facing her and sat down. He wanted to ask her why she was there, but could not bring himself to.

"I saw that picture of you in *Time,* standing in the rubble with that determined look on your face. It reminded me of how you looked in the old days, drilling for Sheridan number one. I was very moved." She closed the photo album and put it aside. "The article mentioned Choctaw Village too, and said that Tunica had been killed. I'm sorry."

"Thank you. I've never been sure whether you knew about Tunica and me."

"Oh, yes. I know about your little girl, too. Ty wrote me about her before he was killed."

Sam could not believe he had heard right. "*Ty* wrote you about her?"

"Yes. He said he'd only seen her once but that she was a beautiful child. He mentioned that you'd never talked to him about her, but said after the war he was going to be her big brother whether you liked it or not. He said he thought it was going to be fun having a little sister to spoil."

Sam shook his head incredulously. "My god." He took a long sip of whiskey. "We go through life thinking we know everything, and half the time we don't know *anything.*"

"Maybe that's what makes life so interesting. The surprises." Georgia rose and in her stocking feet went to the bar to freshen her drink. "Like my being here tonight." When she returned to the couch, she said, "Aren't you going to ask me *why* I'm here, Sam?"

"All right. Why are you here?"

Georgia had to draw in a breath before she could say it. "I came to see if there was anything I could do to help. I did my share when we built Sheridan the first time; I thought you might be able to use a hand the second time around. Does that sound crazy?"

"Coming from you, I guess not. What does O'Hara think of the idea?"

"Kee is dead, Sam," she told him quietly. "Cancer. He was

bedridden with it when you called about Ty; he died two months later."

The news shocked Sam almost as much as opening the study door and finding Georgia sitting there. He wanted to tell her that he was sorry, *wished* he could tell her; but it would have been an obvious lie. He merely shook his head and said, "That must have been a very difficult time for you."

"Yes. Very."

Sam started to speak again, but hesitated, afraid of the answer to a question that had formed in his mind. But finally he posed it. "Is there—I mean, are you—alone now?"

"Yes, Sam. I'm alone."

Sam leaned forward in the chair, gripped by hope. "Do you think that since we're *both* alone, that, well—"

"Sam, don't," she cautioned urgently. "I know what you're thinking. I'll be honest and tell you that I thought the same thing recently. But I'm not sure it would be right. We don't want to hurt each other again."

"We don't have to hurt each other. We could be good for each other again, Georgia, like we were before—"

Even as he spoke, Georgia was shaking her head. "That was long, long ago, Sam. Those were different people you're talking about. Entirely different."

"We're not all that different."

"Maybe you're not. I am."

"Are you?" Suddenly his voice carried a new tone: a challenge. "Maybe you just *think* you're different, Georgia."

"I *know* I am." Her own tone changed a little also. It hinted of defiance.

"What makes you so sure?" Sam pressed. "Have you got yourself that convinced? Is it that important for you to *think* you're a different Georgia now? Is that the price you're paying yourself for everything you've done?"

"Everything I've *done?*" Her eyes on him were unwavering. "Sam, you couldn't begin to know what I've done."

"I couldn't? *You* see everything so clearly, but everyone else is blind, is that it? I couldn't know, for instance, that you let half the men in Kansas City fuck you while I was away in the army, could I? Only smart clever Georgia knows that. Not poor blind Sam."

Now it was she who stared at him with mouth agape, totally

517

shocked by what he had just said. "How long have you known that?" she asked in a whisper.

"Almost from the beginning."

"How—how did—?"

"Eddie Miller told me. He never knew you were my wife. He told me all about you one day when we were eating lunch on Walgreen's loading dock."

"And you never mentioned it to me." Her words should have been a question, but they were not.

"There was no reason to mention it. You were my wife, Georgia. As long as you were faithful to me *after* we were married, that was all I cared about."

Georgia now shook *her* head incredulously. "I see what you mean about thinking we know everything, and not knowing anything. All those years, you *knew*. And you still loved me?"

"I love you right now," Sam said in the quietest of voices.

She began to cry. "Would you really take me back, Sam? After all that's happened?"

"Come here."

She went to him and curled into a ball on his lap and they kissed a kiss that made them feel very young again. They kissed for a long time, and held each other close for an even longer time, both remembering the feel of the other from times gone by. For a while they cried together; then they laughed at themselves together. But after a while Sam's expression became serious again.

"There's something you have to know. I have my daughter Willow, and I intend to keep her and raise her."

"I wouldn't expect you to do anything else, Sam. May I see her?"

They walked out of the study to find Adelita sitting on a chair in the foyer. "Go home now, Adelita," Sam told her gently. "I'll see you in the morning. Everything is going to be all right."

"*Sí, señor,*" the housekeeper mumbled. A sense of dread had overcome her that she had spent her last day as the female head of the Sheridan household. She started to leave, eyes downcast. Sam nudged Georgia.

"Goodnight, Adelita," Georgia said pleasantly.

Adelita smiled a self-conscious half smile. "*Buenos noches, Señora,*" she said. She was already thinking that *second* to the female head of the mansion would not be all that bad.

518

Sam took Georgia's hand and led her upstairs to a bedroom door.

"This was Ty's room," Georgia said sadly, remembering.

"Yes."

Opening the door, Sam turned on a small lamp. In a child's bed his dark-haired little daughter was sleeping. Georgia looked from Sam to the child and back again.

"Odd, isn't it? It started out being you and me and a child. Then I loved an Indian and you loved an Indian. Now it's come full circle to you and me and a child again. Only this time the child is an Indian."

"When you say it's come full circle, does that mean you're back?" Sam asked in barely a whisper.

"Yes, Sam, it does." Georgia reached down and pushed a lock of hair out of Willow's eyes. Turning, she put her arms around Sam's neck and kissed him warmly on the lips. Then she rested a hand on one hip and walked out of the room.

"Our bedroom still in the same place, Sam?" she asked from the hall.

75

At dawn Georgia was standing on the balcony of the master bedroom, smoking a cigarette, watching a ball of red sun ease up over the Texas horizon. The oil wells and pumps, standing like specters on the prairie, caught its first rays and threw dark shadows. Georgia had one of Sam's robes wrapped snugly around her naked body, its shawl collar turned up and held close at her throat against the early morning chill.

Well, here I am. Back where it all started. Back where I spent some of the worst days of my life. Back in a place I've hated for twenty years.

The flesh over her cheekbones tightened and Georgia realized she was frowning. Had she really hated the place? Or had she merely *told* herself that she hated it; convinced herself that she hated it, in order to give every part of herself, even her mind, to Cherokee O'Hara?

Even now, in the crisp coolness on the balcony, with Sam in bed just inside the French doors, the thought of Kee gave Georgia an inner warmth. It still surprised her sometimes, in retrospect, that she had never regretted the price she paid for him. Name, husband, son, reputation, fortune: he cost her everything. Yet gave her everything. Kee was gone forever now, but she had stored up enough memories of their time together to last as long as *she* lasted.

Yet tonight she had learned something very important about those memories. They did not imprison her. She thought all along that they would; that what Kee had left in her mind and memory would control her body and her emotions permanently. It was not so. Tonight she had made love to and with Sam, and it had been warm and sweet and, surprisingly, satisfying.

You've come a long way from Kansas City, honey, Georgia thought wryly. For a few years back there you fucked every man that had a pulse. Now for more than *twenty-five years,* there had been only two: Sam, and Kee. And now Sam again.

Thinking about Kansas City reminded her of what Sam had told her before they came upstairs: that he had known all along about the men while he was away. *That* had been a shocker. But now that she knew, Georgia realized that it was so *like* Sam. He had carried the burden of that knowledge himself, while lesser men would have made her share it. She had not even told Kee about Kansas City, because he would not have been able to handle it well. Further substantiation of her recent admission that Kee had not been a better man than Sam after all. Georgia wondered if, as the years went by, Kee would diminish in her estimation and her memory. She found herself hoping, for Sam's sake, that he would.

There was one thought nagging at her, one reservation that kept unsettling her newfound peace of mind. It surfaced every time she thought of the little girl in the other bedroom. She had not thought about it since Ty's death. The memory of her abortion.

It's the one lie remaining. If she told Sam about it, her conscience would be clear for the first time in her adult life. God, wouldn't *that* be something! Never again to have to guard her words for fear of exposing something in her past. It would almost be like regaining her virginity.

But what about Sam? Telling him would serve *her* conscience well, but how would it affect *him?* He had so much to do, rebuilding Sheridan; he was probably still not over Tunica's death; there was Willow to think about; a drinking problem that might forever be lurking in the background; and, God knows, like her, Sam wasn't getting any younger. How much damage would it do to the Sam of today to tell him about a tragic mistake made by the Georgia of yesterday?

Too much, she decided. Her conscience would have to bear that burden alone. She was not going to hurt him again.

The sun was almost up now, the shadows of the wells and pumps stretching grotesquely over the prairie. Georgia finished her cigarette and put it out in a brass ashtray on the balcony railing. She drew the robe, which smelled pungently of Sam, more tightly around her. Never had she felt such an inner peace as she did at that moment. It was as if her mind, body, passions, desires, memories, yearnings, joys, sorrows, mistakes, loves, and fulfillments had all miraculously merged and created a balance within her. She felt, at last, that she was a whole, satisfied, and *contented* woman.

"Georgia?" Sam called from inside the bedroom. "Are you out there?"

"Yes, Sam. I'm coming in now, dear."

Georgia went back inside.

Behind her, the great ball of fire in the sky rose fully over Texas.